A
MOUND
OVER HELL

BOOK 1 OF THE DARK DEPTHS SERIES

GARY MORGENSTEIN

INDIGO

Livonia, Michigan

A MOUND OVER HELL

Copyright © 2018 Gary Morgenstein

Published by Indigo
an imprint of BHC Press

Library of Congress Control Number:
2017936818

ISBN: 978-1-946848-01-7

Visit the publisher at:
www.bhcpress.com

Also available in ebook

ALSO BY GARY MORGENSTEIN

Jesse's Girl

Loving Rabbi Thalia Kleinman

Take Me Out to the Ballgame

The Man Who Wanted to Play Center Field for the New York Yankees

•

To my wonderful wife Marcina,
who never stops believing

A
MOUND
OVER HELL

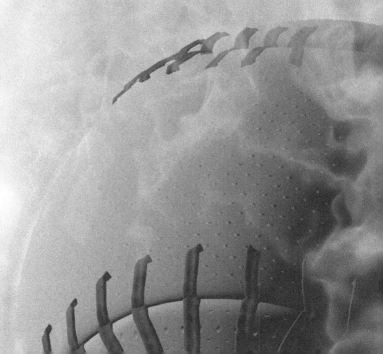

It's the end of the world as we know it and I feel fine.
~ R.E.M. ~

1

On opening day of the last baseball season ever, Puppy Nedick woke up to find a hologram named Greta dancing on his chest. He wasn't happy.

"Good morning, good morning, good morning to you. Did you sleep well?"

The brown wooden shutters automatically slid open, letting darkness spill into the small bedroom. Puppy glared at the ten-inch high alarm clock HG. He so hated Zelda for giving him this birthday present. He stumbled out of bed, landing on all fours.

"Does Puppy need help? Just tell Greta what you want and she will do it."

He crawled under the bed, but couldn't find the plug, though the top of his head found the bedspring, adding a bruised skull to his hangover. Puppy half fell into the bathroom, a step ahead of the pursuing HG.

"I've turned on the coffee. Toast is a 'cooking'…"

He slammed the door and sat on the toilet. This morning I'll find ways to get even with Zelda, Puppy thought. One effective, horrible-I-got-you-since-you-got-me. Greta pealed about the sunlight, as if Grandma wouldn't let the sun come up.

Puppy chose that day's water allotment to shave instead of shower. He lathered up his cocoa-colored face, his watery green eyes, always percolating with surprised disappointment, peered back, boxed by a thick, hooked nose and receding hairline chasing thick black hair.

He slumped at the rickety kitchen table. The vidnews, which went on automatically at sunrise, sang about some skateboarding champions. Apparently they so delighted a visiting Fifth Cousin that the said dignitary decided to skateboard himself. A true man of the people, he went down a hill and hit a rock, crashing head-first into a car. The teenagers whose athletic prowess started all this helped the Cousin, dressed his facial wounds and announced they'd set up a skateboarding tutorial right there in Dayton, Ohio. Everyone was happy. Life was good.

"The true test of Family is adversity." Grandma's Eighteenth Insight skipped across the top of the screen. Puppy swallowed some aspirin.

"I'm very disappointed in you, Puppy." The hologram waited for him in the bedroom when he returned to dress.

"Get at the end of the line."

"Out drinking and in your circumstances."

"Other people paid."

"For how long?" she whined.

"As long as I can persuade other people to pay for my drinks. And hey, I still have a job."

"For five months."

"Instead of tormenting me, help me find my socks."

"Do I look like I have real arms?" Greta shook her head in disgust.

Faint grey skittered across the sky as Puppy shivered and zipped up his black Bronx Hawks hoodie, adjusting the backpack off his aching right shoulder. Commuters pressed past toward the Grand Concourse, edging away from Morris Avenue, which was the tip of the southern Bronx Disappointment Village.

There they went, dashing through the curtain of endless traffic, hurrying against a light; he'd swear on Grandma's bra straps the damn Regs acted as if they could contract failure. That went against everything the Family stood for. As Grandma said in her Third Insight, nothing was permanent if you loved deeply and worked hard. Honesty, ethics, taking care of each other. Everyone believed that. If you failed, it was your fault. That's how you ended up in a DV, like Puppy's parents; he still lived two blocks away, on the Reg side. Close enough to seethe, far enough to remember.

He cut through the DV. The aged buildings' beige and rust brick faces were worn, yet there was always a flower pot in the windowsills. The cars were older models, some even from before the war, bodies scratched, dents hammered out into dimples. Playgrounds, at this hour, were empty. You went to school or worked. You tried to do something, anything, or you stayed out of sight. Otherwise you shamed the whole community.

They said you could eat off the streets of a DV. He had here, many times. Sidewalks were scrubbed. Light poles gleamed. Garbage didn't seem to exist. You filled a trash bag even a quarter of the way and then shoved it down the chute. You took pride in something, even when you had nothing. At least you could be clean. Every one of the eighty-nine Disappointment Villages in what was left of America was the same, an old suit pressed and cleaned over and over until the frayed strands begged for mercy, just waiting for a pretty new tie.

Leaving the DV, as if they ever did, Puppy strolled along the water, pausing near the Drive to watch HG sailboats drift past on the Harlem River, the abandoned buildings of Manhattan's Washington Heights like decayed beggars on the other side. Puppy waved back at the fake boat crew and headed down 161st Street to River Avenue. He paused under the El, the B train rumbling overhead, and waited out the fifteen-minute 8AM shower, squirming into his thin sweatshirt as the temperature dropped eight degrees.

As part of his annual superstition, Puppy stepped on the pile of broken concrete forming a jagged path outside Amazon Stadium and handed his baseball historian's pass to the A30 on the stool by Gate Six. The robot grunted in one bored breath, returning Puppy's card.

"You're new?" Puppy asked.

The robot nodded. "Lucky me."

"We'll go out with a bang."

The A30's eyes swiveled back and forth in faint sarcasm. All 'bots had the same face. Which was no face. Could never tell what the 'bots were thinking, though you were supposed to.

"Nice to meet you." Puppy surprised the A30 by shaking its hand.

"Oh. Okay. Nice to meet you, Mr. Nedick."

"Just Puppy." He paused just inside. "Anyone else here?"

The A30 shrugged. "A few."

Inside, a lone A31 swept the long, filthy pavilion, corralling piles of dirt around a gutted hole five inches deep. There were similar piles of dirt near the other craters; maybe the robot thought the blasted pockmarks of the floor were bins.

Along the interior wall was the famous mural of the legendary Three Amigos, Mooshie Lopez, Easy Sun Yen and Derek Singh, blotched with grime and dotted with bullet holes, the recognizable faces of the New York Yankees greats nearly faded from neglect; indifference is a brutal enemy. The shattered windows of the gift shops had long since collapsed inward onto hazy dark interiors, a few items remaining on the floor: a torn t-shirt, a miniature bat, broken pieces of something stepped on, stomped on, crushed amid the otherwise barren dusty shelves.

A small condiments table blocked an old customer service booth. Puppy examined the soiled packets of mustard and ketchup.

"Excuse me," he called over to the A31 with the broom. "There's no food."

The robot gestured, sending dust onto Puppy's jeans.

"This is not food."

"Yes it is," it answered stubbornly. "Says so on the packets."

"I mean, real food. These go with real food, but you don't just eat them like they're a meal."

The robot waited patiently.

"It's opening day. We always have one stand selling hot dogs."

The 'bot shrugged and wandered off with its broom, shoving dirt into the holes.

Puppy sighed and headed through Section 116. The brown infield and outfield glistened with the morning shower, slowly drying off under the reluctant sun. They'd have rays until 10:40AM; games rarely went more than an hour anyway. A couple of young boys sat expectantly behind the Falcons' visiting dugout on the third base side. Probably cutting school; this was about the safest place in the Bronx, hell, the entire country to hide. An older man slept a few rows up, snoring noisily.

Sitting off to the first base side, the Blue Shirt Officer Brennan tipped his blue cap.

"Top of the morning, Mr. Nedick."

"Happy opening day, Officer."

"Hopefully the crowd will be respectful of the occasion."

Puppy looked around the lower field boxes, seats torn out in chunks, a six-foot mortar wound some twenty rows behind the Hawks home dugout.

On the scoreboard in center field, flanked by the gutted remnants clinging to the main screen, the ancient Grandma, head of The Family which governed America, smiled down. Slightly wrinkled yellow face, slightly smiling, never any disappointment. Do not worry, her expression said, filling the entire screen. I'm always here.

Puppy laid his backpack by his seat behind home plate, a weather-scarred, blackened orange wig rustling feebly beneath the broken adjoining seat, which was forbidden to be moved like everything else in the stadium.

"What're we doing this year?" Puppy tapped the A29's shoulder in the front row. The robot continued studying the squat machine on its lap.

"Same as last year."

"Which was the same as the year before."

"Same as the year you and me started." The A29 frowned at the dials. "Fifteen springs and summers." The robot was pleased by its efforts and, now relaxed, turned toward Puppy. "Folks know what they're getting when they come here." He gestured to the nearly empty ballpark.

"But this is the final season."

"And you thought, let's jazz this up. Me, too."

"Really?" Puppy's spirits lifted.

"They killed it." The A29 jerked its head toward the second level of executive offices behind first base, where the Hawks and Falcons owners hid.

"Why?"

"Why do they do anything? Money."

"Even to do a little something different? Like make the Falcons outfielders triplets…"

"Can't do."

"A pitcher with a personality? One player with personality."

The Falcons lead-off hitter B'run Campanis dozed at the on-deck circle. The A28 umpire headed toward home plate.

The A29 rubbed its metallic fingers together and pressed a button, pointing at the HG players suddenly filling the outfield, stretching their legs. "They wanted to get rid of the them."

"And if a ball was hit into the outfield…"

"They didn't care." The A29 rubbed its nose knowingly at the thought processes of humans. The HG pitcher and catcher materialized on the field, joined by the Hawks infielders, laconically tossing a ball as if slowly thawing out.

"Well, I want to say something before the game," Puppy insisted.

"What about a special graphic on the scoreboard?"

"Can you do that?"

"I wish."

Puppy waited respectfully while Officer Brennan, standing at home plate, led the crowd in Grandma's Blessing, all eyes upraised, chins lifted toward the scoreboard:

"May our love always be for love

May we think of the Family as ourselves

May we work hard and reward effort

May we help those who cannot succeed."

At the robot umpire's call of "play ball," the portly Campanis, buttons undone on his red jersey like he'd dressed in the dugout, waddled to home plate. Puppy gingerly hopped onto the top of the Hawks home dugout and motioned for a couple arriving fans to move closer. The two young women seemed to prefer their privacy and each other's tongues, and took seats down the first base line.

Puppy waved his arms to get the attention of the eight fans. Campanis stepped into the batter's box and scratched his stubble. "B'run, could you wait a second?"

"We got a timetable," the umpire said, irritated.

"Just one second."

The HG pitcher fired a fastball anyway.

"Hello everyone." Puppy silently begged the A29 to freeze the action. "I want to welcome you to the start of the 2098 baseball season."

Beyond the right center field fence, gutted of bleacher seats, a massive crusher truck was parked, two A20s in work clothes, sipping beer, waiting to tear the stadium down.

"I hope you all have a great time this year."

The HG fired another pitch.

"Will you make him stop?" Puppy shouted at the A29, who scowled. Robots were so damn sensitive about being called out for doing anything wrong.

"We've still got lots of tickets for the rest of the season so…" another pitch cut across the plate… "enjoy today's contest between the Bronx Hawks and the Bronx Falcons. Let's give a big cheer for these great players."

An enthusiastic crowd of one, Puppy clapped and shouted before returning to his seat, propping his blue sneakers on the railing and opening his black and white notebook. The only real equipment were the bats, though there were a couple buckets of mottled balls and gloves in the Hawks dugout runway.

The HG pitcher threw an HG ball to the human batter, whose hitting skills, such as they were, was programmed into the system. The play was generated by what the humans "hit," but other than that, everything else danced merrily out of the A29's machine.

Campanis smacked a ground ball toward second, not even waiting for his HG runner to scamper down the line before shuffling like a fat wind-up doll into the dugout. At least button the uniform top, Puppy pleaded silently. Try to look like a damn major league player.

"Game One of the 2098 baseball season, baseball's final year." He wrote in his neat handwriting. There was always hope, even when it was hopeless.

• • • •

ZELDA JONES SHOOK the dice very carefully onto the floor of Puppy's living room, letting out a squeal of joy as she sent her silver car racing around the Monopoly board.

"Your squeaking is really annoying," Puppy grumbled.

"That's why I do it. Keeps you off balance." She grinned triumphantly, clapping her chubby black hands together and scrunching up her slight nose, set like a stranger on her wide face.

"You a dead Allah, dude." Zelda turned to Pablo Diaz, frowning miserably at the little car sitting on the green Pennsylvania Avenue space as if that meant an asteroid would come crashing through the window, ending all life including their weekly Wednesday games night.

"Then buy it." Pablo's frown deepened. "In the long run, it means little."

"Except kicking your butt." Zelda tucked her right leg under her ample rear.

"Perhaps." Diaz watched uneasily as Zelda placed hotels on her latest claim. "Can I go now or do you need a few more minutes to squeak like you've conquered the Caliphate."

Zelda danced with thick gangly arms snaking out in all directions around Pablo. He ignored her with growing difficulty, turning his attention to Puppy.

"How many were out there today?"

"Eight, though two of them spent most of the game making out."

"Is that allowed?"

"Does it matter?"

Pablo rolled the dice and reluctantly held his silver airplane over Pennsylvania Avenue.

"Put it down, big boy," Zelda whispered.

"Tell her to stop," Pablo pleaded.

"Right there. On my lush luxurious property. There you go." Zelda licked Pablo's left ear. He twisted away angrily. Zelda licked his other ear, whispering huskily, "Pay up."

Pablo's long, skilled fingers carefully counted out the money like it was real. To Pablo, everything was real. Games, fun, laughter, all predicates for somber hard work, life lessons, endless practice. He had always been the most driven of them.

Zelda carefully recounted the money.

"That's insulting." Pablo puckered up his long, narrow face.

She acknowledged that with a sweet smile while Puppy dumped another bag of Famous Nebraska chips into a large bowl.

"My assistant's chair is empty, Puppy," Pablo said in that way he had of forgetting to include people in the dialogue bouncing around his head.

"Come on."

"Is there some shame here?" Pablo was mildly indignant. "Pietra did pretty well as my dental hygienist."

"You really think Puppy is right for this, Dr. Diaz?" Zelda held out the neck of the Hartford Heaven beer bottle as a microphone, which Pablo not so politely moved aside.

"Pietra was in the fashion world. All she knew about teeth were her regular cleanings and how they sparkled when she modeled. Now look at her. A year with me and onto dental school."

"Dr. Nedick has a nice ring, Pup." Zelda spooned a chunk of Gussie's Guac onto a chip. "Now that you're entering the mature phase of your life."

"I'm serious," Pablo continued earnestly through their laughter. "You need to find something. This is stable. There's always tooth decay. Accidents. Like chipping a tooth." He indicated the stale chips. "Think about it."

"Puppy's probably annoyed because Greta's been nagging him about finding a new job." Zelda clucked her tongue as Puppy landed on her Park Place hotel. He stared glumly.

"That was a wonderful birthday present, thank you again."

"You're very welcome."

"I could've used socks. Definitely underwear."

"I figured you needed some companionship."

She and Pablo exchanged mischievous looks.

"I do fine," Puppy snapped defensively.

"Oh, tell us."

"Maybe there's nothing to share." Pablo smiled.

"I don't share everything."

"What's her or his name then?" Zelda leaned forward dreamily.

"I'm taking a break."

"The bitch ended six years ago."

"Not long enough from the Gates of Hell. How much fake money do I owe you?" Puppy snapped at Zelda.

"One hundred bucks. Sometime tonight. I need to rest for a field trip tomorrow with the brats."

Puppy very, very slowly counted out the multi-colored bills. "And what about your romances, dearest Zelda?"

Zelda glanced uneasily at Pablo, who unscrewed another beer bottle.

"Nothing," she said quickly.

"You, the queen of the one-night stands?"

"Are you pissed because I gave you an annoying, expensive HG, I'm winning again in Monopoly or because you haven't been laid in a long, long time."

"All three," he conceded sadly.

"We're all pretty celibate," Pablo said a little too emphatically, Puppy thought.

"Not exactly model citizens in Grandma's House," Zelda said. "Late 30s, no marriage, no children." She let out a loud sigh. "If only we were dentists."

"Just wait until you get a toothache," Pablo grumbled.

Zelda clenched her groin in mock anger. Suddenly serious, the mercurial Zelda draped her arm around Puppy's neck. "You have to line something up, Pup. Otherwise they'll just assign you any old job."

"Or consider you don't care," Pablo added. "Baseball historian isn't the most respected job."

"What do you think, they'll send me back to the DV?" Puppy asked. His two oldest friends since he was thirteen frowned. They didn't answer right away.

Zelda and Pablo left around eleven; he waved off their offer to clean up. Tomorrow was an off-day. Three games a week, one hundred and forty game season. Then baseball was done. D-O-N-E. Forever. F-O-R-E-V-E-R. He polished off the last of his Cedar Creek bourbon and worked on the opening game's official report.

"An enthusiastic (the school-cutters boys had cheered) crowd (eight is a crowd, even excepting the two naked women frolicking in the bomb crater) came together as Family for the opening game of the 2098 baseball season. Harry the HG (he made up names for the holograms) pitched a strong game for the hometown Hawks, striking out six Falcons, who were shut down (and half asleep) by Harry's tantalizing curve. Vernon Jackson, the Hawks slugging catcher (and the only one able to touch his toes) led his team's charge with three hits."

Puppy stared sadly at the notebook. He used to write endless pages when he first started. Volumes, epics, describing the weather, clouds, a rare bird sighting, quality of food, conversations of the fans, his own rambling insights, categorizing the HGs, critiquing the batters, comparing everyone to the greats of the past. He gave up when he realized absolutely no one cared anymore. Least of all, him.

Greta danced on his chest.

"Perhaps Puppy would like a girl?"

He peered suspiciously through the top of his bourbon glass. "I thought you just woke me up and ruined my mornings."

Greta laughed. "I have nighttime functions." *Zelda, I really hate you now.* "Asian girl with small breasts?"

"I don't sex watch, thanks."

"Everyone does."

"Only to stimulate reproduction between married couples," he recited mechanically.

Greta laughed dubiously. "Blonde girl, big ass?"

"I'm going to unplug you, Greta," he threatened, standing up with a tipsy wobble.

"Latina? Curvy butt like Annette?"

"That's it." He chased Greta back into the bedroom and slammed the door. "Stay."

"I can go through walls," she replied haughtily.

He half-dozed during Grandma's "Sweet Dreams My Darlings" sign-off at one AM, when the vidnews shut down for the night. Grandma had instituted this on the Day of Surrender when the country collapsed into an hysterical coma after losing World War Three to the Islamic Empire. Yes it's over. Yes we lost thirteen million. Yes we will survive, and yes we will flourish again. Every night for the past twenty-five years, Grandma has ended the day by reading a banal story to a different group of children before tucking them into bed.

Tonight's story was about K'ana the Komb and the importance of grooming your hair. If you don't look good for yourself, My Darlings, how can you expect your fellow siblings to respect you? And if we don't respect each other, how can we have a loving Family? There was also some shit about K'ana taking an unwanted bath in the washing machine and losing a couple teeth which still made her a good Komb because it takes all kinds of Kombs to make a Family.

Fortunately Puppy stumbled into a hole of dreamless sleep. Around six AM, Greta danced onto his chest. Little bitch, he mumbled sleepily, sprawled in his leather recliner.

"Oh my, Puppy is a naughty boy, he has found a new toy."

Puppy punched his fist through her head and staggered toward the bathroom. He tripped over a leg and squinted unsteadily over his left shoulder. A beefy guy around sixty in shabby clothes lay curled up on the floor, clutching an empty beer bottle and snoring like a thunderstorm.

"Isn't he cute?" Greta sang.

Puppy peered at the sleeping man. His broad face must've been handsome before the fleshiness swallowed the cheeks and chin. A snore paused, as if thinking all on its own before rumbling serenely. Something about the man was familiar. Too familiar. Puppy grew angry.

"Hey." He poked the guy's muscular arm. "Mister." The snoring deepened. Puppy pushed harder. "Hey."

The man sat up with a bewildered look which quickly gave way to irritation. "Who the hell are you?"

"The guy whose apartment you're in."

"Huh." The man squinted, trying to focus. Not with those glazed eyes. Reinhardt's Rum, Puppy decided. Greases your liver right out your butt in no time at all.

"Yeah. Huh." Puppy tried tugging the man upright, but he weighed a ton. Puppy slipped to his knee, their faces eye level. Putrid breath raked Puppy's nostrils.

"How'd you get in here?" Maybe he'd forgot to lock the door.

"I don't know." The man's puzzlement seemed genuine. Reinhardt's usually got the brain soon after the liver. "Where's the can?"

"What?"

"The can."

"Of what?"

"Of the can," the man shouted belligerently. "Can. Shit, piss."

He'd just cleaned the toilet. His sparkling tiles were a thing of the past because the old rummy staggered down the hall, lurched into the bathroom and retched all over the toilet. Puppy watched in disgust as the man used a white hand towel to wipe away the vomit.

"Do you mind?"

The guy slammed the door. Tinkle tinkle little pee. Puppy quickly made himself coffee. After more farts, belches and several absolutely inhuman noises Puppy didn't want to begin to understand, the man weaved into the living room, dropping his smelly body onto the couch. He drained the last of the bourbon and made a face.

"Cheap stuff."

"I'm so sorry, I wasn't expecting guests."

The man glanced disdainfully around the messy room and put his feet on the table with a majestic wave of his thick hands. "Got any beer?"

"I think you had enough." Puppy laid a cup of coffee on the table.

"I didn't have anything. They wouldn't let me drink in the hospital."

Finally, some facts. "Which hospital?"

"Dallas Memorial. I had the cancer." The man sipped the coffee and half-spit it back. "What is this?"

Puppy's eyes blazed. "Coffee."

"Sucks."

"Goes along with the cheap bourbon."

"Yup." The man peered. "Where am I?"

"I'm asking the questions."

"Why can only you ask and not me?"

"Because you're in my apartment."

The man considered that reasonable and made another half-hearted attempt to sip the coffee. "Sugar? Oh, wait, am I allowed to ask that?"

Puppy muttered all the way back and forth to the kitchen, slamming a bowl of sugar on the coffee table. The man dumped in about four tablespoons.

"Happy?" Puppy asked.

"I could use some eggs."

"So could I. Where's Dallas Memorial?"

"Texas." The man growled at Puppy's stupidity.

"You came all the way from Texas with cancer?"

"I died there."

Puppy told himself not to laugh. "Then how'd you get here?"

The man shook his head in deep sadness. "Damn do I know. And where am I that I don't know how I got here?"

"New York City."

The man brightened. "I lived there. A hotel on Central Park. The memory ain't terrific. Must be the dying and all."

"You have a name?"

He paused, thinking. "Mickey Mantle."

"Mickey Mantle." Puppy smiled carefully. "Like the old baseball player?'

"I am the old baseball player," Mickey shouted.

"Okay, okay. You are."

"Except I ain't anymore. Except here I am. So I must still be. " Mickey swallowed down the rest of his coffee and polished off Puppy's cup.

"Nice to meet you, Mickey."

"That's better."

"I'm Puppy." Better not to give out last names.

"What kind of retard name is that?"

"Ask my parents. They're both dead."

"Like me." Mickey burped. "I want breakfast."

"How about a shower first?"

Mickey's eyes narrowed. "Why? You a fairy?"

"What's that?"

"Fairy. Fag. Queer."

Grandma's bra straps. "No. I mean, I've..." Puppy thought best not to answer too deeply. "No. Just girls. Take a shower. I'll find food and then we'll figure out where you belong."

"I belong in Heaven," Mickey yelled.

Puppy laid out an old towel and washcloth on the sink, turned on the shower water and tried to find fresh clothes while the old guy scrubbed away, singing some country song Puppy recognized by Merle Haggard, *Okie from Muskogee*.

Mick came out with two towels Puppy would never use again wrapped around his waist. He plopped back onto the couch.

"I left you clean clothes." Puppy put down some bacon and toast.

"They're ugly," Mickey snorted.

"Yours stink."

"So wash them." Mick bit into the bacon and looked up with wondering disgust. "What is this?"

Puppy sighed. "Bacon."

"No, it ain't." Mick tossed it on the plate.

"Because it's not really real. It's AG bacon. Alleged. Or SC. So-called. Most of the foods are synthetic. Because of the radiation. From the war. Any of this ring a bell from your life before you took a bath in rum?"

"I hate rum." Mick took cautious, displeased bites of the toast. "Best you got?"

"It's the best anyone has," Puppy yelled.

The DV Community Center on East 163rd Street was a long, open portable building inside a wire-fenced playground which had been originally built for the Allah Deportations of the late 50s. It took a while to get the stench out and some felt it still smelled of goat, but that made it perfect for the DVs. Nothing had changed since Puppy had shot pool with Zelda or flirted up Noreen Delgado. Same eager kids with suspicious eyes. Same glistening floors and squeaky polished windows. Same long bulletin board with endless index cards advertising work or asking for work, announcements of after school programs, tutors available.

Help me any way I can, said Grandma's Eleventh Insight running along the far wall. Basketball courts echoed with loud grunts. An entire wall of books, about forty feet long and twelve feet high, occupied a wall; kids sat on the floor studying, whispering advice. No one screwed around. If they did, one of the matrons, always fat, always a woman, always ugly, Puppy had no idea why, would bounce their butts onto the street and it would take weeks, sometimes months, sometimes never for the kids to be able to return. There was little room for error in the DV.

Always the kids were here, except for the adults dropping them off with hopeful embarrassment. The parents, who knew painfully they were responsible for this situation, leaving with a quick kiss to hurry back to their shop, store, business, whatever proliferated along the shopping streets like desperate pleas. Give us another chance.

Puppy led Mickey to the front table. The matron raised up her black glasses from the chain around her neck.

"Morning, madam," Puppy said politely. "This is my friend Mickey Mantle."

"Hiya cookie." Mickey winked.

The matron reddened indignantly.

Puppy shrugged helplessly. "That's why I'm here. He wandered off and I'm trying to get him back to where he belongs." Puppy whispered, "I think it's a hospital."

"Hey, I'm dead, not deaf," Mickey barked.

The matron cleared her throat authoritatively. "Can I see your Lifecard, Mr. Mantle?"

Mickey looked at Puppy, who said, "Lifecard. Identification."

Mantle patted his dirty pants. "I ain't got one."

"He doesn't have one," Puppy said.

"I am not deaf, either, sir." The matron smiled. "Where were you living, sir?"

"In Dallas Memorial Hospital. Texas. Where I died."

The matron's smile tightened. "When was that?"

Mantle looked up thoughtfully. "Must've been 1995."

She exchanged a worried glance with Puppy.

"Do you know what year it is, sir?"

"How the hell would I know?"

"He's been dead," Puppy threw that in.

"So he said." The woman frowned. "It's 2098."

"No shit?" Mickey took that pretty calmly. "No wonder I feel so rested."

The matron turned to Puppy. "Where did you meet Mr. Mantle?"

"On his floor," Mick grumbled. "Must be some elevator to Heaven."

Puppy leaned forward. "Him. Where."

The woman blinked at Puppy's shorthand, smiling a different way now. "Home."

"DV."

She nodded. Puppy glanced at Mantle, leering at a busty teenage girl.

"Just sign here, sir."

Puppy hesitated longer than he should've. They sat on a long wooden bench, waiting for the processing and sipping lemonade. A couple of kids skateboarded past.

"They'll take good care of you in the Facility."

Mantle frowned. "I ain't staying with you?"

"I'm not allowed. You don't have any ID."

"Because I'm dead."

"These are the laws."

"If I wasn't supposed to stay with you, then why the hell did I end up on your floor?"

Good question, Puppy didn't ask himself.

2

Busily scribbling on their pads, the six children in neat purple and white uniforms sat in a semi-circle on a tiny patch of brown grass four blocks from the traffic-choked Cross Bronx Expressway. From off to the side, Zelda carefully watched her class.

"Okay stop." She held up her left index finger, agitating the kids of PS 75 into feverish last-minute flourishes with their charcoal pencils.

The kids mumbled nervously, anticipating elaborate praise or deep disappointment. Zelda took Marshall Diem's pad off his lap. He looked up hopefully.

"Is that what you see?" Zelda gestured across the Harlem River at the tall empty buildings.

Marshall nodded uncertainly and pointed at his eyes. The kids giggled; Zelda cut them off with a sharp look.

"Because I don't see that."

"It's there." Marshall reached for his drawing as if it were a life jacket of creativity.

Zelda shook her head. "Show me what you drew but not just on the page. Show me how you thought it."

The baffled Marshall looked at his classmates for help. They were equally puzzled.

Zelda sighed impatiently. "Those buildings are ugly, right?" She held up the drawing, which showed a beautiful home with two parents, a child and trees. "This is not ugly. How did you get from that," she jabbed past the holographic sailboats and seagulls at the squalid remains of Manhattan, still largely uninhabited after the chemical attack, "to this?"

Marshall's eyes watered. Zelda wasn't particularly sympathetic. Maybe if she liked children more. Or at all. Zelda knelt in the circle, the children anxious, their turn at having their art disemboweled by this always stern and slightly scary woman looming any second. Look at Marshall; his cheeks dripped tears.

"There is no right or wrong. But you have to explain what you do and what you feel. You can't just draw shit and say, oh, this is my art." She gave up on Marshall, his shoulders heaving slightly from terrified sobs. "N'ariti."

The girl with thick hair extending past her shoulders sat up straight, considering possible escape across the River. She could just walk across, but no one would tell her that.

"Yes, Ms. Jones."

"What did you draw?"

"I don't know." N'ariti clutched the pad to her chest, the charcoal smearing her uniform blouse.

"What do you think you drew?"

"I don't know." N'ariti suddenly found whatever blind courage exists in a six-year-old. "A window."

Zelda smiled faintly. "Good. Show me."

N'ariti shook her head.

"Show me the window." Zelda waved off N'ariti's offer of the pad. She tapped her own head. "Up here. Show me. Be a window."

Zelda stood very carefully, eyes closed, hands by her sides. "I'm a window," she said out of the corners of her mouth. "I am dirty. Broken. Abandoned. Lonely. Everything is organically emotional. That's what I mean," she suddenly shouted. The children huddled closer together. Zelda went through each of the children, reducing them to tears. It seemed only right that their parents should have the same opportunity with her the next day.

Marshall's mother glowered across the principal's office. Zelda so wanted to slap her silly, thick-headed Reg head.

"My son won't go near windows anymore."

Bennett Chambers, the PS 75 principal, nodded his wooly head in grave under-standing.

"That's good," Zelda protested.

Chambers cleared his throat warningly.

"Well it is," she couldn't resist.

"He was a Muslim Europe orphan," Marshall's Mom said, fluffing her dress. "He still has nightmares."

"Didn't he come here when he was an infant?"

"I can see you're not a mother," Marshall's Mom sneered.

"No, I'm not," Zelda almost added thankfully.

"Then you'd understand the trauma of abuse and terror in an ME orphanage can af-fect even a baby. All those studies show it takes years to shed them of the horrors. Now he has to worry about windows."

"Just keep them open so he won't notice..."

"Zelda," Chambers broke in. "Mrs. Diem, we will make sure that there are no more field trips like this."

The mother rose. "I hope this doesn't sound rude, but I don't want him in this class anymore. Sorry, Ms. Jones."

Zelda shrugged. "He doesn't have much talent anyway."

Chambers took the gasping mother to the door, whispering apologies. He returned behind his desk, coldly staring at Zelda.

"What did that accomplish, Ms. Jones? In your own words."

"Which part?"

"Select one." His teeth gritted.

"I think she's a moron who doesn't understand how to reach her child emotionally other than hiding behind stereotypical fears and blaming everything she does wrong on the kid not getting his butt wiped when he was two months old."

Chambers struggled to conceal his shock. "Is that what you came away with?"

"I didn't know there was a right or wrong answer, Principal Chambers. Which is what I was trying to get out of the class..."

"What you got out of them is hysteria." He held up his pad. "The other parents all have meetings here. Do you think you should attend?"

"I probably don't bring a lot to the table."

Chambers leaned forward on his forearms. "Why couldn't you just let them draw trees?"

"The blackened ones?"

"The holographic ones from Grandma."

"Which aren't real."

"They are if we believe so."

"Which is not a healthy emotion for an artist."

"It is for the teacher."

"I was an artist first."

"And not a successful one, either." He picked up Zelda's file and tossed it back down as if she weren't aware of her life story.

"I had some acclaim. Sold-out shows…"

"And that's why you ended up here." He rolled his eyes. "Ms. Jones. No more field trips. You will stay in the classroom and teach according to the curriculum."

"Which gives a teacher latitude about helping students…"

"Your latitude over the past six months since you've been here demonstrates you take latitude with the latitude."

Even Zelda knew better than to correct him. "Am I on probation, sir?"

• • • •

MRS. GONZALEZ'S EYES burnt skeptically above the brown leather strap stretching across her mouth. Pablo waited another few seconds. The annoyed old woman kicked, making the bicuspid-shaped examining chair swivel slightly. Finding this ploy, Gonzalez kicked a little harder; the chair turned forty-five degrees. Pablo glanced at the ticking machine and then away from the patient, enabling her to kick vigorously with both legs to turn the chair completely around. Her chuckle was muffled.

Pablo untied the strap and rested his right elbow casually on the chair's arm as Gonzalez regained her breathing.

"Steady."

"I know, dear." Gonzalez's eyes locked onto his eyelashes. "And?"

He held out the square half-moon machine in front of him. "Six and a half inches."

"I don't believe it." She suppressed a delighted smile.

"True. I don't lie."

"Machines can. As we know," she said archly.

"I only know the smile-o-meter measured five inches and three quarters two months ago and now it's up to six."

Her eyes narrowed above a smile. "You tricked me, Dr. Diaz."

"You honestly believe that I can trick you, a woman of such experience."

"And age," she snorted. "With a child's toy."

"The entire Family uses this," he said with mock severity.

"Means nothing," she refused to concede.

"Means you're happier lately. The muscles elevate your mood, making you…"

"Are you going to sound like one of those adverts?"

Pablo shrugged another impish grin. Someday there'd be adverts for one of his products. "You're happier."

"I haven't done anything differently."

"That's the beauty of it. You don't have to work at happiness. Most of our siblings still don't get it."

He undid her white apron.

"We're done?" She was disappointed. Eighty-nine-years old and nothing else to do the rest of the day.

"I've got a waiting room full of patients, none of them as beautiful as you."

"Grandma's earrings, I will lose my lunch." She chuckled. "Did you use such charms when you saw my nephew?"

Pablo busied himself finishing up her chart.

"Dr. Diaz, he's a lovely boy."

"I'm really busy, Mrs. Gonzalez. I don't have time."

"For love?"

Pablo eased her gently out of the chair. "To brush my teeth as often as I should." He handed her a green lolly. "Remember to floss."

"If you'll call my nephew." She grunted.

Pablo spritzed disinfectant spray on the chair and replaced the paper cups. He really had to find a dental assistant. The A27 receptionist knocked twice and opened the door. Past its wiggy blond head, Pablo could see the fluorescent yellow waiting room was full. Gentle humming buzzed beneath the seats. Every nine seconds the walls turned into a glistening smile that morphed into rows of perfect white teeth putting the patients inside the mouth, looking out at an HG of Pablo by his office door, warmly welcoming them with a tilt of his tooth-like head. Only the really cynical didn't smile.

"You have two gentlemen to see you, Dr. Diaz."

Pablo glanced at the chart.

"Not patients, sir."

The robot stepped aside to allow two lanky men in casual light suits carrying wide brimmed hats to enter. They had that official look which made his stomach churn.

"May I help you?"

The dark-haired one nodded. "We're from Grandma's House, Dr. Diaz."

Pablo squeezed his lucky aqua marble in his right pocket. "What've I done?"

The men exchanged curious smiles. "What do you think you've done?"

"Nothing at all."

"Neither do we." The sandy-haired man leaned against a shelf, glancing at a photo of Pablo, Puppy and Zelda at the beach in Connecticut, hair flying across their young, laughing faces. Deep tans. Deep joy. They were twenty-one, twenty-two. Why wouldn't they laugh? "Puppy, Zelda, they well?"

Pablo tensed. The dark-haired man shot his colleague a disapproving look. "Excuse him. Sometimes he plays cop. It's inappropriate."

"Yes, it was." The other man wiped dust off the picture frame and carefully placed it back on the shelf. "Then again, you're supposed to handle all situations."

"I'm a good dentist."

"Very good. That's why Grandma is considering asking you to become a Fifth Cousin."

Pablo took a quick sip from a paper cup, swallowed a little and then rinsed and spit the rest. The men grinned.

"Sorry…" He blushed.

"Oh please," the sandy-haired man said. "You should see the range of reactions we get, if we were allowed to say."

"I'm honored…"

"But not too honored." The man eyed him shrewdly.

"No," Pablo said carefully. "Honored enough to both lead and serve."

"Good." The man beamed. "May we take that as an agreement to the next step?"

"Certainly," Pablo said hoarsely.

The men nodded, pleased. The dark-haired man picked up the conversation, "As you know, you can't say anything about this."

"I didn't know."

"Because no one can ever say anything."

"Yes. Of course," he mumbled.

"If your receptionist asks, who are we?" the sandy-haired shot the question.

"Salesmen."

"You put salesmen ahead of patients?"

"A recommendation of a patient. A courtesy. "

The men exchanged pleased smiles. The sandy-haired guy continued, "You do understand this is merely asking if you're interested. That's all. You might never hear back. You might hear back tomorrow. We only do the asking. Others follow up."

Pablo just nodded.

"Nice to meet you, Dr. Diaz." The dark-haired man studied the smile-o-meter. "This really work?"

"Absolutely. Think smiles and you do." Dr. Gerry Rosen had invented the smile-o-meter back in 2081. He'd gotten tired of his grandchildren hiding in closets or under the bed, whimpering, inspired to such behavior by Rosen jumping out from behind doors growling and threatening to eat them. His daughter wouldn't let her children stay with him anymore until he could prove they were happy. So came the smile-o-meter, measuring the width of a smile. Both his granddaughters had permanent marks on their cheeks, but their faces—the Extra Dimple Rosen Girls—became famous when Grandma learned of the invention; she still measured her smile once a week on National Smile Day.

"I'd be happy to strap you in, sir."

The man chuckled. "How much would that cost me?"

"It's part of the regular initial check-up. Nothing free for anyone, of course."

"Of course." The men put on their hats and left.

Pablo slumped into his desk chair, head between his knees to keep it from hurtling off his neck. Cousin.

3

"What about that one?" Zelda pointed at the job posting on the computer, sliding the black reading glasses further down her nose. "Two years copy writing experience."

"About hams."

"It starts in the fall. Perfect timing."

Puppy rapped the screen with the back of his hand. "I don't even eat ham."

"Fake it," she said evenly.

Puppy scrolled down the list. There were entry level positions, continuing the career, changing the career and his favorite category, stepping up. As in you screwed up everything else, what do you plan on doing before it's too late?

"Maybe I can teach." He lingered over a posting for a phys ed teacher at HS 35 in the Morrisania district, convincing himself.

"That's in the DV."

"No, it's not. Jumping jacks, wind sprints. I've seen enough out-of-shape men and women to know…"

"It's 158th Street." Zelda was fixed on the geography. Sometimes he needed a very sturdy crane to move her along.

"Which is going east, putting it beyond that Village."

"I think you're wrong." Zelda searched among the baseball books stacked neatly on his desk. "Don't you have a guide?"

"Somewhere," he said gloomily.

"You have to keep street guides, Puppy. It's the law. 'Know where you are in your heart and your body.' Twelfth Insight."

He stared. "Are you going to quote Madame's thoughts for a long time?"

"No and don't call her Madame. That's disrespectful."

He rolled his eyes. "I think I know the Bronx pretty good. Especially where the DVs begin and end. And the River Avenue DV ends just west of Third Avenue at 160rd."

"I think you're wrong."

"You usually do."

"But it doesn't matter anyway since it would drive you insane to actually teach sports."

"As opposed to writing jingles for Hank's Hams? Bake 'em, broil 'em, flip 'em on the grill. Anyway you do it, you'll get a thrill."

Zelda's dark eyes widened. "That's really good."

"Thank you. It's one of their adverts." Puppy sighed. "I couldn't sleep last night."

She plopped back onto the long pillows on the floor. "Me neither."

He paused on another posting. "Here we go. 'Everyone Needs Shoes.' Smart. Who goes barefoot anymore? Or ever? 'Walton Avenue's largest shoe store, These Boots Are Made for Walking, needs an eager, aggressive individual to make sure every sidewalk in the Bronx looks at our soles.'"

Zelda sneered. "It'd remind you of Annette and her store and your marriage."

Puppy wandered into the kitchen, returning with a couple of beers. Zelda stared dimly at the screen, mechanically opening the bottle.

"I have to do this, too," she said softly.

He took her hand. "Oh shit, what happened?"

"Nothing." Zelda shrugged. "Only teaching brats isn't for me."

"That's very surprising given your love of children."

She snarled mockingly. "I can't just sit in a classroom and make them draw pretty little flowers with cute little birds."

"Didn't you have birds in that showcase you did on Jerome Avenue?" Puppy grinned.

"Real birds. Flying around."

"Wih you squawking and chasing them."

"Flight. Adventure."

"Especially when the birds got into the audience."

"That's art, Puppy." She shook her head in dismay. "I should've stuck with it."

"They wouldn't have let you. The practicality would've worn you down. Chasing birds isn't exactly the route to success in Grandma's House."

"What is?"

"We ain't found it," he stated the obvious.

"Maybe you can get something in the Sport Commission."

"Can you see me setting up the football Augmented Realties? Hut, hut, here I am in the huddle with all these really big guys. Or the NBA. How is the weather up there, Mr. Giant?"

"Fifteen years counts for something, honey." She touched his forehead.

"Commissioner Kenuda hates baseball. Trust me." Puppy aimlessly scrolled along. "Something weird happened this morning."

"I knew it."

"What?"

"Your mood. It's more than just facing a dismal job prospect you will hate and seeing your lifelong dreams die."

Puppy had to chuckle, even if he didn't feel it. He told Zelda about the old guy. She listened intently, interrupting for detail after detail, exhausting him.

"I checked the door three times to make sure it was locked after we left." She assured him. "I even had Pablo rattle the knob. Twice. So how'd he get in?"

"Maybe I sleepwalk and open my own doors."

She didn't like that answer. "Be serious."

"I am. I said it was weird."

Zelda hesitated. "How'd you act with him?"

"The way anyone would act when someone breaks into their house."

"Uh-huh."

"Uh-huh, uh-huh. I told you, I brought him to the community center." Zelda kept staring. "You obviously have some deep and startling insight to bring to this discussion."

"Could've let him stay an extra day or two. You know what The Facility is like."

"I do." His throat closed, making him angry. At her, no, himself. "And that's why, Miss Psychiatrist, I sent him off. Because they're set up to take care of crazy old drunks."

"If that's what you want to think."

"That like any other normal human being I wouldn't want some smelly stranger in my house who could steal my things doesn't cross your mind."

"Steal what?" Zelda gestured around the living room, the sagging brown couch, battered chairs and wobbly coffee table courtesy of a discount store on Fordham Road after he and Annette split. He asked for the worst looking furniture they had. The salesman took pity and only charged for the delivery. If he knew Annette, the salesman probably would've thrown in a dining room set.

Puppy pursed his lips and returned to the postings. Zelda poked him.

"Ow."

"Answer me."

"You didn't ask a question."

"Why didn't you let him stay?"

"Because I have to look for a job, otherwise the Employment Center will just assign me one which I won't like, because I can find something so perfect on my own. Here." He nodded at the screen. "Copywriter. All backgrounds welcome. Basil Hayden Funeral Homes. 'Let Us Do the Dying.' Now let's find yours. Tweet, tweet."

● ● ● ●

A SHAGGY-HEADED MAN with a scrungy beard leaned into a small puddle of beer on the counter.

"It's wet." Zelda pointed at his dripping sleeve.

"You're worth it."

Zelda rolled her eyes. The burly, tight-lipped bartender Jimmy paused in case she needed help. Zelda double-blinked a 'no' and Jimmy went back to drying glasses, keeping an eye on her anyway.

"Well, you don't know me." Zelda took a long swallow on her beer. She was still annoyed with Puppy and, like the mature adults they were, had bickered for half an hour about his poorly suppressed childhood traumas and her unfulfilled artistic aspirations, sending her stomping out of the apartment and down the block into Monroe's.

Shadows danced slowly to Willie Nelson. The silenced vidnews ran in a loop behind the bar; new farms were opening in the Southwest, thanks to radiation minimizing techniques. Would cactus burgers be far behind? Jimmy could serve them on Country Night instead of those stale tortilla chips covered in barbecue sauce squatting on the bar. The guy with the beard wiped the sweet brown sauce off her chin.

"Full service," he said quietly. "I take care of all needs."

Jimmy glared at the man. Maybe because he knew her a long time and thought four straight nights here at the bar letting men wipe her chin was too much. Or maybe it was the guy's beard. Once, a beard or even a moustache got you stomped. Zelda could vaguely remember a hooked nose earning a beating. Now, just a dirty look from a protective bartender.

She double blinked shorthand at Jimmy, who muttered and attended to a customer at the other end.

"And you know what my needs are."

"I can sense them."

Zelda finished her drink and let the guy buy her another. Jimmy poured it slowly, disapprovingly.

"I think you're lonely."

Grandma's clit, give me a break.

"It's been a while since you had someone."

Yeah, nearly twenty-four hours.

"How's my guessing so far?"

"Brilliant. Can you guess my name?"

"Does that matter?"

Zelda smiled playfully. "Are you saying this is just about sex?"

The Beard's smile wavered slightly. "Doesn't have to be."

"I'm single. Obviously. So are you. Hopefully. Did I guess that right?"

He nodded, a little annoyed. "Otherwise..."

"Otherwise you'd get a summons and adultery is ugly. Apartment, job, mark on your name up and down the entire system."

The Beard shifted uneasily.

"Because I'm here looking for love and romance and relationship and sharing and all the things Grandma wants us to have. Otherwise I'm just a slut." Her voice dropped to a husky whisper. "Do you think I'm a slut?"

"No, I..."

"If you do, then I should be reported for wayward pointless sex not designed for reproduction or at least companionship. That's not what you were after, is it?"

The Beard quickly tossed his Lifecard on the bar, agonizing as Jimmy ever so slowly rang up the charges.

"Good luck," he called over his shoulder.

Zelda tapped the bar with her knuckles for a refill. Jimmy slid over a bowl of chips.

"I wasn't letting you leave with that bearded piece of crap," Jimmy growled. He was about six five, two hundred and fifty pounds and could probably stop a crusher truck with a punch.

"I don't need a protector."

"You need to stay out of my bar for a while."

"But I'm a good customer. Without me, the way I draw men into running up big tabs, you'd close. Then I'd be stricken with guilt, unable to work, a drag on Grandma's House. Both of us, Jimmy. Ruination. Shame. "

Jimmy shook his head. "Maybe you should try a girl."

"I have," Zelda sighed. "I screw them up, too."

4

Major Tomas Stilton was still half drenched from the long drive, the tropical rain pouring relentlessly into the open windows. If only he could scratch his face, but he wouldn't give the scum the satisfaction of asking for help. Letting them slip their greasy fingers under the black hood seemed worse than enduring the itching.

Then again, blinded, he didn't have to look at them. Touching was difficult enough. Smelling, sensing. He'd shuddered for an hour; they thought he was just cold, but Tomas was remembering how many Allahs he'd killed. At least fifty. Half during the withdrawal at Sicily. Those seven in the chalet near Nice when his Seals had rescued the last Vice President. Another dozen covering the first convoy of refugee children. A few he killed out of savage vengeance.

Two rough hands yanked him off the hard wooden chair.

One, two, three steps, door creaks open, and one, two over the threshold. Left, one, two, three, steps, feet trailing behind him. Why are you bothering? They'll take you somewhere different next time. If there was a next time.

My beloved, I hope you know what you're doing. Because I sure as hell don't.

He was dropped like a bag of soiled laundry onto a more comfortable chair. Leather, his bulky body squirmed, confirming it. Someone laughed and cut his wrists free of the thick rope. They yanked off his hood. He wouldn't squint in the sudden light. Same principle of not giving them any satisfaction.

Tomas kept his eyes fixed at the bare floor until he grew accustomed to his surroundings. Two young Allahs in flowing white robes flanked him, hands in their laps as if Stilton had stopped by for a beer. Another one, maybe thirty-five or so, sat gracefully on an identical black leather chair. He smiled warmly. This was the guy. Slight, almost frail. Arrogant in that cordial way they had.

"Mr. Stilton, welcome."

Tomas nodded vaguely.

"Are you hungry?"

Tomas waved him off.

"I do not consider it weakness if you need nourishment. It is a long way from the Bronx."

"Yes it is," he finally said. "I'm fine."

The Allah shrugged off Tomas' stubbornness and exchanged amused glances with his colleagues. Tomas wondered if the guns were under their robes or they just had a couple rifles aimed at his head behind the white walls. A generator hummed. They were probably deep underground.

"I am Imam Abboud." He tipped his head slightly.

"Imam?" Tomas held his concern in check. Hood off for thirty seconds and already they'd fucked with him. And you're very and deeply surprised, why? "Where's the Son?"

"The son?" Imam's next look at his colleagues was decidedly less polite.

"Abdullah."

"You will refer to him as His Most Worthy Successor."

The war was so easy to understand sometimes, Tomas thought. He bowed from the shoulders. "I was told I would meet His Most Worthy Successor."

Abboud sneered slightly. "He has ears."

"As I have a tongue."

The Imam acknowledged that with a gracious wave of the hand. "If you speak, I will listen."

Tomas hesitated.

"Did you really think he would come?"

"No, I honestly didn't," Tomas admitted. "But Grandma did." And I should've talked her out of this; no one ever would've known.

"As I said, he has ears." The Imam touched his left ear lobe as if Tomas were very dull-witted. "His Most Worthy Successor is a man of great vision."

"Like the Grand Mufti."

The Allahs mumbled "Allah be praised."

Tomas pressed back the bile. "A man of astonishing vision."

"May His Most Worthy Successor have an ounce of that." The Imam raised his hands skyward, looking shrewdly at Tomas. "He reveres the Grand Mufti."

"As he should. As would any son." Tomas couldn't resist.

Abboud considered Tomas's veiled insolence. "And your grandmother?"

"Grandma is well and sends her blessings to His Most Worthy Successor."

"He is grateful for the thoughts."

Tomas shifted uncomfortably. How long would he have to continue this?

"But…" Abboud abruptly continued. "Such thoughts are natural from everyone to his Most Worthy Successor. He wonders what other thoughts your grandmother…"

"Grandma," Tomas said coldly.

The Allahs in the chairs stirred enough so Tomas could see the outlines of their guns. The Imam calmed them with a wave.

"Grandma." He smiled. "Apologies. That is disrespectful. She has sent you a considerable way without food and drink. Someone very trusted. Her most trusted friend. To here, a place of your enemies. His Most Worthy Successor wonders why."

Tomas placed his elbows on his knees, releasing his lower back with a pleasant twinge. "She would like to discuss the future."

"Why not with the Grand Mufti whose courage created it?"

Tomas took a deep breath. "He lives in the past."

Abboud tossed another wave at the bristling Allahs. "A glorious past."

"Yes." Depending where you sit, you prick. "But Grandma believes it's time to move forward."

The Imam's face curled in curiosity. "Why would His Most Worthy Successor feel that?"

"Because he is a son. And a son must look ahead to his own destiny. Forged by his own greatness. " Tomas smiled quickly. "I could use some water."

The Imam snapped his fingers. Tomas waited until he took a few sips before beginning.

• • • •

SITTING BEFORE THE wide, sooty window, Mickey stared off blankly as fellow patients nudged past his wheelchair like exhausted bumper cars. Mick's mouth chewed as if forming words. Lost words, floating out and away. Puppy thought he could see them like the bubbles he blew out of a bottle as a child. Empty bubbles.

He saw a lot while watching, hands crossed at his waist. No one bothered him, asked for ID, what he was doing there, planning on cutting the throats of any of our patients, sir? If so, take your pick, we don't want them.

Outside the boundaries of the DV, homes like this were called Backyards, places where grandma and grandpa and ol' Uncle Eduardo rocked gently in the hammock. Dozens, hundreds of hammocks, swaying in a soft breeze where sunshine reigned for more than four hours, visitors lined up because it was a great honor to meet people who had contributed so much to their country and the Family.

Here in East Tremont, it was called just The Facility, a place of embarrassment. No hope to advance, even mentor, hand down any important bits of last-minute wisdom. This was the ultimate disappointment, hopefully they'll move on soon, within the hour, counting down one, two, three, and take their fleshy old hairy butts on to wherever you wanted to believe someone went anymore; Heaven and God and religion had been out of fashion for a couple decades.

Puppy clasped Mick's shoulder. The old guy kept staring through the windows, half spears of rusted metal protecting the outside ledge because this would surely be the number one destination for any thieves inclined to scamper up five floors.

"Where the hell you been? Food's worse here than your dump," Mickey growled.

Puppy signed him out, the diffident nurse perking up at all of Mickey's many possibilities for happiness now that he had a home with his nephew. Puppy studied the checklist about health and exercise and mental acuity as they walked back toward his apartment, Mickey sadly shaking his head.

"The whole neighborhood's a dump."

"This is the…" he stopped, too much explanation. "I actually live in the better part of the Bronx."

"The Bronx? I'm in the Bronx?" Mick did a little dance. Puppy pulled him away from a bus bearing down to finish its route no matter how many old men in smelly clothes it had to run down.

"I told you."

"No. You said New York. I got a good memory."

"I'm sure," Puppy said dryly.

"Where's the stadium?"

That made Puppy smile. He pointed west. "Over there."

"Old bitch is still standing. Can't kill either of us," Mickey marveled in relief. "Is it baseball season?"

Puppy nodded.

"We'll go to a game. Sit in the luxury box."

At least he was a fan. Mickey made a sharp turn into Monroe's as Puppy kept walking. He hurried inside where Mantle was already at the bar digging into a bowl of nuts.

"Let me have a breakfast of champions," Mickey said to Jimmy. "Know how to make it?"

"Jimmy, no…" Puppy sat beside Mickey.

"Hell, I'm thirsty. You abandoned me. I deserve this."

Jimmy gave Puppy a searching look. He shrugged wearily.

"Gimme two shots of brandy, Kahlua and cream. And some real nuts, these taste like wood."

The bartender gave Puppy a longer, searching look. "Kahlua?"

"Yeah." Mick spun around on the stool; the place was empty at ten AM.

"They don't have Kahlua, Mickey."

"What the hell kind of bar is this? All right." Mick held up a conciliatory hand. "Somehow the world ain't what it was when I was alive. Gimme a vodka martini. Does the bartender know how to make a martini or do I have to go behind and help out?"

Jimmy's nostrils flared slightly. He noisily mixed the drink.

"Just one." Puppy raised a finger.

"Sure." Mickey smiled impishly.

The bartender poured out the martini. Mickey's eyes lit up and he gulped down half. A Blue Shirt strolled in with a friendly wave of his night stick. Jimmy tensed.

"Morning, Jimmy. Everyone doing well today?"

"Very well, Officer Frick."

"They ain't got Kahlua," Mickey grumbled and finished his martini, holding out the glass for a refill.

"Now that's a real problem." Frick slid onto a stool. "Officer Frick."

"Mickey Mantle." They shook hands.

"He just got out of The Facility," Puppy explained.

"Oh?" Officer Frick wrinkled his nose. "I wondered about the odor."

"I don't smell," Mickey growled.

"I think you do, sir. It's okay. Your friend…"

"Nephew…" Puppy jumped in.

"Nephew," Frick drew out the word dubiously. "He'll take care of you. Eventually." The cop tipped the night stick on the counter and motioned for Puppy to follow, stopping near the men's room. "Nephew?"

"Sort of. I found him wandering in my neighborhood."

"Took pity, very nice." Frick waited for Puppy to hand over his Lifecard, which he scanned on a thin silver device wrapped around his wrist. "Baseball historian?" The Officer chuckled dismissively. Puppy forced a wan smile.

"Should have plenty of time then to take care of the gentleman." Frick examined the discharge forms. "Like I said, you've done a nice thing. But stupidity trumps generosity." Frick gently rapped his night stick on Puppy's forehead. Maybe not so gently. "He left The Facility half an hour ago and you bring him to a bar?"

"He kind of just walked in."

"And forced his way into receiving a drink?" Frick glanced at Mick, toasting. "Two drinks now."

Puppy groaned inwardly.

"Is this the sort of care you're planning on extending?"

"No, sir."

"He's clearly nearing the end and deserves dignity."

"Yes, sir."

"Will I see you in here again?"

"Yes. But not with him."

"Because I will check." Frick scribbled a reminder note with a small pencil in a large purple notebook, then walked back down the bar and warmly shook Mantle's hand. "Pleasure to meet you, sir." He stared at Jimmy. "Mr. Nedick will relay our conversation."

Jimmy glared at Puppy. He really wanted to be on the police radar about smelly old men drinking when they shouldn't and causing problems. Officer Frick made it as far as halfway to the door before Mickey raised his refilled martini glass, calling out, "What's the rush, Officer? Join me for a round."

The Blue Shirt escorted them to The Foyer, the main administrative center for the Bronx, an ugly old building with latticed windows and scorched bricks which sat with a certain haughty air on Sheridan Avenue. After the Allahs nuked Washington, DC, on the heels of the chemical attack on Manhattan, the seat of government had moved to the Bronx.

At the entrance, Frick whispered heatedly to the Blue Shirt on duty, jabbing his stick toward Puppy. The large cop rolled off his stool, annoyed at the inconvenience of having to move, obviously caused by Puppy's negligence and possible degeneracy. The Blue Shirt, identified as Manson Phillips on his NYPD badge, read and re-read the discharge papers, searching for some reason to arrest Puppy or at least take a very active dislike.

Patient: Mickey Mantle. Age: Deceased. Born: Yes. Occupation: Hall of Fame Baseball Player. Relatives: Probably all dead like me. Last Address: Dallas Memorial Hospital and hopefully a cemetery. Health Issues: No sex for a 100 years. Mental State: Maybe.

Officer Phillips returned the papers to Puppy, giving Mickey a bewildered look.

"I'll make sure they get to the right room."

Frick tapped his night stick rhythmically into Puppy's forehead. as he instructed his colleague, "Check the papers when they leave."

Mick dozed on Puppy's shoulder in the simply furnished waiting room. On a long poster by the door, the face of a pleasant faced girl in dreads smiled beneath a sign, "If You Don't Know Who You Are, How Can We?" with stark lettering below, "Take Care of Your Lifecard." Directly above their heads hummed the vidnews, scrolling along pictures of fish hopping happily into nets draped from a long boat somewhere in the Atlantic, a dour captain in a yellow slicker explaining new fishing techniques in a way that made you long for a good greasy cheeseburger; Puppy kind of remembered real meat, dozing into a light sleep where he was a pickle chip fighting off angry cheddar cheese with Mantle's face.

The reedy clerk beckoned them inside. Mick walked unsteadily; he must've thrown down an extra martini when I wasn't looking, Puppy thought as they settled inside the office. Grandma's classic pearl earrings photograph stared down.

"Who's the broad?" Mick drawled.

The clerk stared, horrified.

"He was in The Facility," Puppy explained.

The clerk held the application up to his eyes.

"You got a toilet?" Mick asked.

"Hold it in," Puppy whispered.

"I can't."

The clerk looked up. "Where did you lose it?"

It took Puppy a second. "The Lifecard? He doesn't know."

"I don't even know what the hell it is," Mick yelled.

The clerk disapprovingly fingered the application.

"He had an accident," Puppy said.

"Did you file a police report?" the clerk asked hopefully.

"No."

"I fell on my head," Mick threw in. "I was drunk."

The clerk grunted. "Where?"

"Usually at Toots Shor's joint. Also my own place on Central Park West."

"Manhattan." Puppy raised a knowing eyebrow. "Before."

The clerk narrowed his eyes. "So you lost it outside the Bronx."

"I don't know," Mick snapped. "Might still be in my coffin."

"So the Lifecard could just be misplaced."

"Probably not." Puppy brushed aside any optimism.

"You must look for it."

"How can he look for the Lifecard if he doesn't know where he lost it?"

"Until then, it's merely misplaced. "

"Does that mean he can't get one?"

The clerk frowned. "He can. It's just more work."

Puppy smiled apologetically, which had the effect of hitting a meteor with a stick. The clerk chewed on his lower lip and typed into his computer.

"And the bathroom is where?" Mick whined.

"In a second," Puppy snapped.

The clerk looked up, slightly puzzled. "There is no record of a Lifecard issued to Mickey Mantle."

Mick stood, ready to roll. Puppy tugged him back down.

"Are you sure?"

The clerk's watery eyes glistened with indignation. "Of that name, yes. Perhaps the gentlemen used other names."

Puppy nudged Mick to answer.

"The Mick. The Commerce Comet. I was a jet before I tore up my knee." He rolled up his right pants leg to show a nasty scar on the knee. He rolled the pants back down thoughtfully.

"We do not use nicknames for official documents," the clerk said icily.

"Mick, you have a middle name?"

"Would help," the clerk turned toward his keyboard, eager for this to end.

"Charles. Mickey Charles Mantle," he said proudly.

The clerk's search came up empty. This was especially annoying. Lost or misplaced Lifecards were easy enough because he could send them elsewhere after he stamped a couple documents. Never registered, that was sticky.

"Have you ever had a Lifecard, sir?" the clerk asked.

"Not that I remember," Mickey said. "Now I really gotta pee."

Mantle bolted down the hallway, where he could be heard shouting "where's the fucking bathroom this is a medical emergency."

"It isn't good to never have a Lifecard, is it?" Puppy asked once the commotion outside quieted down. The clerk shook his head. "What does it mean?"

"From my long experience, usually the person or persons…"

"There's only one person involved. I have a Lifecard."

"Person. For now." The clerk raised a warning eyebrow. "It's illegal."

"Illegal."

"Yes," the clerk said meaningfully.

"Well, maybe, but he's off in the head."

"Yet you took him out of The Facility. If you'd kept him there, no one would've cared. Out here, he needs to live."

"Isn't it illegal either way?"

The clerk flushed. "Yes sir, it is illegal. My advice is to return him to The Facility. Sounds a little harsh. I know you people stick together."

Puppy thought about how wonderful it would feel to hit the clerk in the face. "I'm a Reg now," he forced out the words between clenched teeth.

The clerk's eyes fluttered disdainfully. "I'll do you a favor. I'll mark this request pending and we'll schedule another appointment for next week. That'll give you an opportunity to decide what's best for Mr. Mantle and the Family. It could be that he simply shouldn't be out here, roaming around."

"There was no fucking toilet paper." Mick returned, zipping up his fly.

• • • •

ZELDA WALKED AROUND the couch, arms crossed, big brown eyes narrowing and widening as she inspected the sleeping Mick.

"He seems harmless."

"Wait until his bladder wakes up."

She rubbed Puppy's arm. "I'm proud of you for doing something that goes against your grain."

"It's just until he gets on his feet, Zelda. Don't get carried away."

"I'm not." She paused. "Those your old fat clothes?" She gestured at the blue flannel shirt and khaki pants fitting Mick like a blanket on an elephant.

"Better than his undies dipped in raw sewage." Puppy shook his head, sitting on the edge of the chair. "What happens during the day when I have appointments?"

Zelda grinned. "Wall to wall, are we?"

"Yes. I've got the ex-spouse tomorrow."

"Take Mickey. I'd love to see the bitch's response."

Puppy smiled at that. "I can't take him anywhere without a Lifecard in case we get stopped."

"Why would you?"

"Because he's crazy. He went off on the way back when he saw some couples. Let's say he's not enlightened on how people might pair up." Puppy shook his head. "How is someone not in the system?"

"That's not his real name, stupid." Zelda rolled her eyes. "Once he settles in…"

"Only for a few days…"

"Things will come back to him."

Why choose that particular name? Puppy wondered. "So could you watch him tomorrow morning before school?"

"I'm kind of not at the school anymore."

"I thought it was just probation?"

"I pulled out before it went on my record. This way it can be all so positive, Ms. Jones advanced the children's artistic sensibilities and has now moved on to another constructive role in the Family. Fucking entitled Regs and their brats."

"What's the new constructive role?"

Zelda hesitated. "Marketing."

He waited skeptically.

"Selling salmon."

"Grandma's anus, Zelda."

"I'm practical. Saul's Salmon is a great company."

"I think I saw their advert," Puppy said unhappily.

"The guy with the yellow slicker?" she asked. Puppy nodded. "That's Howie Herman's House of Gills. Our guy wears a purple slicker. Shows how important they are by using Grandma's favorite color. Now with the government finally opening up fishing lanes for healthy fish instead of the faux shit we eat, there might be a real future."

"With salmon."

"Can you be a little more supportive since I hate myself for doing this?"

Puppy took her hand. "I don't want you giving up things you love. Like I have to."

"I'll paint pictures of baseball players, how's that?"

Mickey groaned and sat up, peeved at the two intruders. "You a girl?"

Zelda held out her hand. "Zelda Jones."

Mickey held her palm a little too eagerly. "Because girls and boys ain't the same here."

"I'm a total girl. All original parts, Mr. Mantle." Zelda modeled by walking around the couch. Puppy blinked Zelda a warning as Mick rubbed his hands together.

"So I see." Mick smirked. "Your girlfriend's a looker, kid."

"She's not my girlfriend," Puppy said quickly.

"Just friends." Zelda sat beside Mantle. "Childhood friends. See that scar?" She twisted her jaw to the left. "Some assholes threw rocks at me the day I moved into the DV. I was thirteen. My hero Puppy jumped off a wall and knocked two of them out cold and sent the third running and screaming."

"Not before he got this." Puppy pointed to a scar above his left eyebrow.

Mick grunted approval. "What's a DV?"

Puppy and Zelda exchanged baffled looks. He took this one. "Disappointment Village, Mickey. You know, where the…" His voice trailed off, perplexed.

"I don't know."

Zelda squeezed Mick's hand. "DVs are where people who fail have to live until they can get their shit together and find jobs or careers or something to prove they're productive members of society. Sometimes they make it and sometimes they don't. That doesn't mean they're bad people if they don't."

"A slum?" Mickey found a half bottle of beer on the floor and drained it.

"Slums, ghettos, those were places of filth and poverty where everyone gave up, Mickey," Zelda continued in the sing song voice she reserved for when she wanted to be especially annoyingly patronizing. "DVs are places of genuine opportunity. Someday they'll be all gone. Everyone will have a positive place in the Family." She tossed a pained look at Puppy.

Mantle scratched his hand. "Sounds like a lot of crap. Speaking of…" He rumbled into the bathroom.

Zelda stared down the hallway. "Feel. Awful."

Puppy picked up the empty beer bottles. "Good. You can do his dishes."

• • • •

PUPPY HURRIED DOWN Jerome Avenue; either arriving a little late or a little early having the same mixed benefits of pissing off Annette. Ahead, cars crept along Fordham Road as if linked by chains along their axles. The explosion of auto production intended to show the world after the war that America had gone back to its roots as the engine of manufacturing, feel these greasy biceps, we have our own oil so up yours, Allahs, had turned the country into an extended parking lot.

Puppy paused for a black coffee in the lobby of the Family Room, besieged by interminable video loops of happy couples talking about all they've shared, surrounded by growing numbers of children. Like building blocks, Couple A would show off their baby and, on the next screen, Couple B would have a grown child, followed by Couple C with two and Couple D with three until you ventured into grandparent land where they were engulfed by their children and their grandchildren squealing delightedly, all vids ending with Grandma's proud smile and her Third Insight: "There is no Family without a family."

Boisterous happy couples holding hands strolled past to sign up for their marriage licenses on the second floor. Other loving and adoring citizens, eyes brimming with endless wells of endless love, headed to receive extended benefits for upcoming children, either their own or adopted. That was the third floor.

On the fourth floor were the celebrants. One, five, ten, fifteen, twenty years, pick a number, if you made the wedding anniversary, you received some award. Furniture, car, clothes. The lobby echoed with videos of couples talking about their love and offering tips to siblings like Puppy, sipping black coffee and absorbing, well, barraged with wisdom from Alvin Dalton and William Li on their secret to happiness (a joke a day) or Pamela Landers and Patricia Pannarassa (cooking together, just chop chop chop and you'll never mope mope mope) they beamed.

Love joy pleasure family Family children passion commitment.

Then there was the fifth floor for people getting divorced. Grandma's belief was that you were never contaminated, but uplifted. Positive always triumphed even if you were too damn thick to understand. Making the divorcing couples share the same building as all these wonderful men and women immersed in love joy pleasure family Family children passion commitment would inspire reconsideration, a re-memory, a new path, a second chance, a nudge, a shove to where you'd once been and how you might get back there to love joy pleasure family Family children passion commitment.

You never knew what happened on the fifth floor. The first few times Puppy met Annette for their sessions, he was whisked into a room by a couple so delirious they about floated, where they asked him about his feelings of love, insisting he make up a song on the spot.

"I wish I were in love

Then I would feel like a dove

Just give me a cue

And I will love you"

He was able to use these catchy lyrics for further encounters/kidnappings, but Annette screamed rape when she was lured into an emotional intervention. Word got around.
Leave those two alone.

But if you pulled back from the brink, oh boy. Just say you're willing to try again
and you and your potential love mate would be whisked away for a weekend in the
Catskill Mountains to splash about in undulating bathtubs where a saucy HG oozed
out of the faucet cooing about emotional longevity and multiple orgasms. Grandma was
not a prude; sex was important in a marriage. If the massages and fine Wisconsin champagne and all that undulating worked, you might be taken from the monthly pre-di-
vorce meetings and put into a marriage counseling group where you would be revered
for your incredible courage in seeing the light of love joy pleasure family Family children passion commitment.

Suddenly you weren't filing for divorce. You were a success story. You'd be on the
vidnews. In the lobby. The fourth floor. Perhaps lurking in small rooms to persuade bitter
men to compose music. Maybe someday, if you didn't throw yourself under the D train,
you'd make it to fifty years of marriage and have eggs and coffee with Grandma. Real eggs
and coffee.

Then there was Annette and Puppy.

"Where the hell have you been?" Annette Ramos angrily pushed back her curly black
hair, suggesting it was his fault the strands had dropped onto her olive-skinned forehead.

Puppy slid a folding chair by the table and nodded to the wary, silent guard. When
they first started six months ago, enduring the more than five year cooling off period for
time to reconsider their clearly stupid decision to divorce, they'd had an always smiling
facilitator, eager to jump right in and smooth out any disputes. They'd gone through
several facilitators. Now they'd been assigned a guard. Violence was not uncommon in
these situations.

"I have a life." Puppy placed his coffee on the table.

"Like I don't?" Annette took the cup. "Is this mine?"

"No." He sipped quickly so she'd think he spit into the coffee.

"Very unselfish, Puppy." Annette applauded sarcastically. She looked gorgeous, with
her hair sweeping onto her bare shoulders, large breasts struggling to come up for air in
the low cut dress. The better she looked, the more she tormented him.

Their wedding video ran on a small screen on the table. Photos from their marriage were taped to the walls; smiling and happy Puppy and Annette. Several pieces of
jewelry, birthday gifts to her, sat mockingly on a waist-high silver end table from their
original apartment.

"Are you looking at the tape and thinking how much older I am?" Annette asked, worried.

"I wasn't thinking anything." He sighed.

Usually they sat in silence for the first few minutes, glaring, until the guard coughed, signaling they could sit in silence the entire hour but he would report their lack of effort at reconciliation.

"How are you?" Puppy kicked things off.

"Good. Busy." She held up her left shoe, red with gold buckles. "My new line. Business at my store is wonderful."

"Great."

Annette exhaled slow disgust. "You don't care."

"Not really."

"And you?"

"Baseball season started a couple days ago."

Annette rolled her eyes.

"Right." Puppy looked up at the picture of them on their honeymoon in Eastchester, Annette licking a vanilla ice cream cone melting down her chin, while he stuck out his tongue hopefully. She caught the look.

"Are you going to stare at old photos all hour?"

"That's why they're there."

Annette grimaced, clearly sharing the oxygen with him a painful burden. "Well I have news." She played with her gold bracelet. "I met someone."

"Again?"

"Yes, Puppy. Again. I do want to be happy because unlike you, I want a real relationship."

"Who's the lucky guy?"

"Someone very accomplished," she said with a mysterious air. "A name you would know."

"Is it Grandma?"

"Fuck you, Puppy."

"Sorry. I'm very happy for you."

"No, you're not."

"Then I'm not."

"Because I'm very happy." She paused. "Elias and I are in love."

"I hope so." Puppy frowned. "Otherwise it is mere illicit lust." He wagged his finger.

"We want to get engaged."

Puppy felt an unwelcome twinge. "Oh. Great."

"Engaged means marriage is next, Puppy."

That was the final tripwire. You couldn't get remarried until your ex found someone, otherwise the Family had a resentful, angry, embittered sibling running around. It was much better to have two resentful, angry, embittered siblings running around.

"What do you want me to say, Annette? In another six months, we're done with the attempts and free." Even Grandma admitted that it wasn't fair, when all had been exhausted, for bitterness to triumph over love. But it was firmly noted in the permanent files.

"I don't want failure on my record," Annette said. "You're used to that."

Puppy gripped the edge of the table; the guard stirred. He had read the reports on these two.

"I want to do this right. I find someone. You find someone." Annette took off one of her dangling Grandma-like earrings, staring at the purplish stone as if it would somehow undo the huge mistake she'd made marrying him. "Are you at least dating?"

"I don't have time."

"Why, Puppy, why? You don't have a real job. You should have time for countless dates. Every night, someone new."

"Since I don't have a real job, how could I afford such merriment?"

Annette unzipped her purse. The guard rose out of his seat until he was sure she wasn't pulling a weapon. She showed everyone her wallet. "I will pay for your dates. Some of them. Drinks, an occasional meal if it seems promising. Anything. Please, Puppy. I want to be married. Have babies. Lots of babies. And be happy."

The muted wedding video showed them dancing. He could hear the band, a terrible three-piece group with the awful singer who Pablo hired, wailing it out and yet somehow, the worst singer in the West Bronx made their special dance, their song, their wedding song, "The Beatles' *I Want to Hold Your Hand* sound good. Sound right. Sound happy.

He took Annette's money out of spite.

• • • •

AZHAR MUSTAFA COUNTED yet another cloud formation. Eleven puffs. Second highest number of puffs in the past few hours. There were no other clouds drifting past the tiny island. The birds had fled at the sound of the helicopters. He squinted through the ponderous sunshine for some animals to count, observe, play a game in his head to pass the time, but none scampered past.

He checked downstairs in the tiny ship that rocked gently, moored to the makeshift dock. Everything in order. Two rifles mounted on the rack. All the first aid supplies full; even a few syringes of penicillin. Five tins of canned beef and a loaf of bread waited on the table. He hadn't known what else to bring because all he'd been told was to be prepared. For what?

Mustafa sat on the edge of a chair and guiltily ate the leftover lamb his wife Jalak had slipped into his pocket. I can't bring food, he'd insisted. You can't turn on your mobile, how else will I know you're okay? You'll know if I eat? I will feel my lamb melting in your mouth. She'd smiled and he fell in love with her yet again. It often happened several times a week, when she wasn't nagging about something.

Azhar saved a chunk of lamb and returned on deck. A faint noise skipped through the trees. He looked up, expecting more helicopters, but just another white cloud lazily headed his way. The noise deepened into an engine. A gray truck bounced along the poor excuse for a road, stopping abruptly at the gangway.

Two men in plain work clothes dragged a hooded prisoner, hands and feet bound, up the rickety bridge and onto his ship. One sliced the rope around the prisoner's ankles, leaving his wrists still tied. The prisoner stood tall, defiant.

One of the men yanked up the anchor, Mustafa knew better than to protest, and together they tied the prisoner to the outside of the cabin. The hooded figure sat obediently, still with the stiff back; Azhar could see his chin lifted challengingly under the black cloth.

The tall one handed Azhar coordinates and the guards hurried down the gangplank. In a matter of moments, the truck disappeared.

Mustafa stared at the waiting prisoner.

"Are we leaving or not?" the man suddenly barked as if he were in command. Azhar grumbled, fired up the engines and steered northwest, careful eyes on the prisoner.

What have you done, infidel? he wondered. But you do not seem in pain after torture. Mustafa noticed the dark skin on the hands and the legs where the pants pulled up slightly. From the accent, the skin color, an American African Crusader. How did you get here? Thousands of miles past the Surrender Line. Think not such thoughts, Azhar, so you return in one piece to your Jalak and her lamb, however dried out and tasteless. Your pockets will be heavier and you will have done a service for the Imam.

The prisoner's head bobbed slightly. Asleep. Perhaps unconscious. Wonder not. Steer. Abdul's soccer game is tomorrow and he would welcome his father to show up with his head, otherwise you will not know what is going on.

Mustafa grunted at himself, swearing slightly and putting the steering on automatic. He knelt by the prisoner, who tensed, immediately alert.

"What is it?" he asked in perfect Arabic, surprising Azhar. "I asked, what is it?"

"Are you thirsty, defiler of our law?"

The prisoner chuckled. "Yes, thank you. But I'll pass on the water if you're going to say asinine things like that."

Azhar was shamed by the laugh, stillborn in his throat. He slid a straw under the hood, allowing the prisoner to suck the water from the bottle. He did so noisily, finishing in a minute.

"Thank you, Captain."

Mustafa froze, bent over. "How do you know I'm a Captain?"

"It's your ship. I don't hear anyone else. I assume you're in charge."

He nodded, realizing the prisoner couldn't see. "Yes."

"Are we alone?"

"Why?" Mustafa grew suspicious. The Crusaders are all cunning wolves.

"Because I don't want to insult anyone by not including them in the conversation."

"There are two armed guards below deck."

"If they're armed, why keep them there?"

Mustafa bristled. "Because this is my ship and I don't like guns on deck." He moved away, worried. "We are not supposed to talk."

"Because the guards might hear."

"Yes."

"I understand." The prisoner tilted his head. "Do you have any food?"

Azhar swore at himself down and up the steps, returning with two tins dumped into a bowl and a chunk of bread.

"Sure you're not depriving the guards of dinner?" The prisoner's hood pulled in a smile.

"They've eaten enough." Mustafa scooped beef onto a fork and squeezed it under the hood. It fell onto the man's lap. "Sorry."

"Maybe if you lifted the hood to just below my nose." Mustafa hesitated, searching for the trick. "Once I'm done you can slide the hood back into place."

The Captain lifted the hood. Not American African. He looked like one of our Indian brothers. Azhar tossed aside the food from the prisoner's lap and fed him two spoons rapidly, barely giving the man time to chew. "How is it?"

"Terrible," the prisoner replied good-naturedly. "You make this yourself?"

"No," he said, embarrassed. He licked a piece of meat off his pinky and nearly gagged. "Wait here."

"I've got no plans."

Mustafa's curses rose a little as he came back with another bowl, filled with Jalak's lamb. He broke off chunks and speared them into the prisoner's mouth.

"Better?"

The prisoner chewed ferociously. "A little."

"Just a little?" he snapped. "My wife made this."

"Delicious."

Mustafa burst out laughing. "She has other virtues."

"Glad to hear that." The prisoner grinned.

Their laughter was drowned out by helicopters circling overhead, the crescent moon and stars dipping side to side. Mustafa yanked the hood below the prisoner's chin and rushed back into the cabin, flipping off the automatic pilot. Just ahead, he saw a small ship anchored portside. A rowboat splashed into the water and was soon waiting beside them.

Mustafa dragged the prisoner to the side. Hands reached up and pulled the man into the boat, the helicopters continuing to circle like hawks. Azhar picked up the bowls, abruptly tossing them overboard. He wiped the spilled food with the bottom of his shoe, watching the boat hurry away.

What did you come here for, infidel?

5

The morning started off with Mickey chasing Greta with the precious original Mooshie Lopez baseball bat, smashing two lamps and bashing a hole in the living room wall with a fluid swing, righty and lefty. Screaming "the midget will die," Mantle drove the HG into the closet, only for Greta to slip under the door and land on his head.

That's when Puppy found himself with a new and very uneven hole over his desk before diving under the bed and pulling out the plug. Mickey sent the HG machine on a line drive into the bathroom, pulverizing the box so the pieces were embedded into the tiles.

Puppy wasn't all that unhappy about the death of Greta, although the neighbors were, calling the super, Mr. Ivanov, who scolded Puppy for having drunken parties at seven-thirty in the morning and suggesting the need to find non-violent boyfriends or, if that was his longing, finding somewhere else to live. There were also a few threats about calling the Blue Shirts.

Breakfast, three sugar-scalded donuts and black coffee, calmed Mickey down a little. Actually, he was pretty serene, taking in the brief walk by saying little except he wanted a beer or rum and when could he have real coffee and the couch was killing his back and these fat clothes of Puppy's were too big; he recommended a tailor on Madison Avenue.

They waited patiently in the bus queue on West 170th Street. Mick ogled a few girls, who responded with disgust. Somehow, in this mind of his, that constituted a challenge, so he did a little number he later explained as "the walk." Stare, but gently, he cautioned, starting at the woman's brow, ruminating on her eyes, traveling slowly down her face, resting on the mouth, accompanied by his tongue rolling around his lips, before dancing down her throat and resting on her breasts.

This part required subtlety which, to Mickey, meant eyes darting back and forth, back and forth, followed by a big grin suggesting the previous wet tongue and mouth would enjoy themselves greatly if given a few minutes in the cleavage zone. Then the walk stepped down the stomach, pausing on the vagina, Mantle's tongue darting out like a hungry baby snake. The walk took a few steps onto the thighs, and then repeated the process upward.

The first girl, around twenty, not bad looking if you liked flashy red hair and green eyes, stared, astonished, until Mickey finished walking. He winked. She slapped him hard, followed by two women who punched him in the ribs while an elderly woman poked Mickey in the back with her umbrella.

"You can't treat women like that," Puppy scolded. "Ever."

Mickey shrugged. At least they got to the front of the queue.

The bus doors opened. Puppy swiped the Lifecard twice, gesturing at his guest Mickey. The A18 driver nodded diffidently for them to continue down the aisle. Mick stared at the 'bot in horror.

"You coming on or not?" The A18's metal forehead creased.

"There's a fucking monster on the bus. Run for your lives." Mick ran screaming down the steps, knocking over the women who'd slapped/punched/poked him.

Now it was thirty-three years since the final Miners attack and twenty-five since the last Allah alert, just before the Surrender of '73. Still, terror becomes part of a collective DNA and an old man yelling for help set off a mini-panic. A few shopkeepers ran out brandishing bottles, while a shoe repair person sprayed water resistant repellant on anyone nearby and a grocery store owner roamed up and down with an armful of apples. He threw some at the bus, breaking a window. Not to forget a couple of men fainting, a little girl running her bicycle into a light pole and yes, the police he'd narrowly avoided this morning did finally arrive.

And Pablo wondered why they missed their 10 AM appointment.

Pablo let Puppy back into the examining room and touched his right ear with a raised index finger.

"Mick, can you wait outside?" Puppy asked.

Mantle happily slid out of the chair and pocketed a few lollies. "I ain't letting him drill."

"No need, sir. Your teeth are great." Pablo smiled and closed the door. He frowned that familiar somber look and busied himself cleaning the double end probe. Puppy spun around in the bicuspid examining chair, making little whoopy noises.

"Are you going to do that for long?"

"Until you stop me."

Pablo stilled the chair, leaning forward to pick at Puppy's teeth. Puppy pushed him away. "You're overdue for a cleaning. You have food stuck."

Puppy rubbed his finger over his teeth, horrifying Pablo. "There. Clean bill of health. About Mickey."

"His teeth are pretty good for someone who hasn't been living well. There should be more decay. All the teeth are solid. No gum disease."

"Maybe he just has naturally pretty teeth."

"Maybe." Pablo had obviously considered and rejected this line of thinking. "He has all amalgam fillings."

"So?"

"Mercury fillings were banned in 2024. Too dangerous."

"He's old."

Pablo sighed and consulted his notes. "Not that old. He says he's 64. Let's assume he's lying and he's 70. That still means if he had his teeth filled when he was born, the amalgam would've been illegal by four years."

"What if he lived somewhere that disobeyed the law?"

"Renegade dentists using hazardous waste fillings?" Pablo sighed pityingly. "There's something else. He has unusual scar tissue on his gums. At first I thought it might've been self-inflicted from how you've described him. Or from some altercation. But it's a surgical procedure. Pre-laser."

"I guess those same renegade dentists theory is out."

"Yes, Puppy," he said wearily. "His gums were cut, twice actually."

"When did that process stop?"

Pablo exhaled slowly. "Easily seventy years ago."

Puppy cupped his hand under the faucet in the small rinse-and-spit sink.

"Use a cup," Pablo said angrily.

"More fun this way." Puppy licked a green lolly. "He needs a Lifecard."

"Can't they print out his records?"

"He's not in the system."

Pablo shrugged. "Not surprised. He's lived deep in the DV. I saw a lot of this when I worked at the clinic on East 161st. They change names. Forget their names. You know how it is from your Dad." Pablo tenderly clasped his shoulder. "Bring him back to The Facility, Pup."

"I can't. I'm already in pretty deep. Banned from Monroe's and the M43 bus route." Puppy tossed the lolly stick and missed the garbage. "Can you give him a temp medical ID?"

The dentist shook his head adamantly. "I'm not comfortable with that."

"C'mon." Puppy pulled the Lost Lifecard brochure out of his back pocket, unfolding Grandma's chiding expression on the cover. "It says if a doctor examines the applicant and gives him a clean bill of health, he can get a temporary Lifecard."

Pablo hesitated long enough for a deep frown. "I shouldn't, Puppy."

"Is it illegal?"

"It's a question of judgment. To issue a med temp when you have doubt isn't something a wise person does."

"That's why I'm asking you."

Pablo didn't smile. "I'm not in a position to take chances."

"I don't understand…"

"I can't tell you."

"Are you in trouble?"

"No."

"Then why…"

Pablo hesitated with that closed-eye, anguished internal debate expression which he used for everything from bending the law to ordering dessert. He would've made a good martyr. "Because I've been told that I might be asked to be a Cousin."

"Shit. Really? That's wonderful."

"Yes," Pablo said, agitated. "You're not supposed to know this."

"Sure, sure, sure. Amazing news, Pab. Your dream coming true…"

"If it happens. They probably ask a number of siblings, though no one knows how many since you're not supposed to tell." He gave Puppy a warning look. "Now you understand why I can't do anything to jeopardize this. If it happens."

"I think this would only augment your candidacy."

"How?" Pablo's eyes narrowed.

"You're demonstrating compassion and empathy. You're putting the needs of some crazy old guy ahead of your own. Isn't that what being a Cousin is all about?"

Pablo thought on this. "You're playing me, aren't you?"

Puppy spread his thumb and forefinger apart an inch, grinning.

Pablo grunted unhappily. "He has to take the smile-o-meter test first."

"I'm sure he'd love to."

It took two Bobby's Burgers to wash away the supposed agony coursing through Mick's face "like a whore tap dancing on your balls," he'd growled while insisting the meat was human. A slice of Der Vunder German chocolate cake was required when Puppy insisted they return to The Foyer and get the temporary Lifecard validated before Pablo changed his mind.

Mickey wasn't happy about waiting on line again. Two wonderful hours of complaining punctured Puppy's tolerance. Living alone all these years, he'd only had to deal with his problems. He was always there for Zelda and Pablo, but they weren't in his bed or bathroom. Just him with his own guidelines of what was acceptable whining, easily adjusted. Or ignored. Loneliness had its benefits. You alone were the master of your misery.

"Can we take a damn taxi?" Mickey grumbled outside, his shiny new temporary Lifecard safely in Puppy's wallet.

"Monsters also drive taxis." He'd barely talked himself out of a 'bot discrimination ticket for Mick's behavior this morning. Robots were especially sensitive. Perhaps he'd be, too, if there were a law against him having a face.

"Queers and monsters." Mickey shook his head. "I should've stayed dead."

"Still plenty of time." Puppy led them down Sheridan Avenue. "But Grandma gave you a free week's worth of groceries and transportation, so let's hold off a little."

"Can I buy booze?"

They lugged two six-packs of Allentown Ale and half a liter of Vossily's Vodka home. Clouds gathered. Puppy stopped under the awning of a barber shop, the red and white pole circling merrily.

"What's up?" Mick asked.

"Four o'clock rain."

"You got good weathermen," he chuckled.

"Haven't you ever been outside during the day?"

"I was in a fucking coffin," he shouted.

Puppy quieted him. "Pours every day at 4:05PM. Also 10:40 in the morning and then at 11PM. Late night showers are romantic and cozy. Couples huddle. Children snuggle," he dumbly recited the grade school jingle. Rain poured in a slant, thunder and lightning crackling. Some people walked right through, grinning. A few hoisted their umbrellas and skipped along through the growing puddles. Cars slid along, sending up streams onto the sidewalks.

"Everyone looks happy getting soaked," Mantle said wonderingly, the sky lighting up.

Puppy frowned. Guy had to have been in a mental hospital. Yes, that explains a lot, he suddenly decided. "We contend with little challenges like getting wet. Makes you appreciate when it's dry."

Mick shook his head. "Unless you get pneumonia. Or do you appreciate that so you're happier when you get well?"

"Catching on quick."

The sun burst overhead, warming them. Mickey suddenly smiled.

"See?" Puppy couldn't resist a grin.

Mickey sighed. "Queers, monsters and fake rain."

"We don't call each other names in Grandma's Home," Puppy said softly. Unless you're an Allah, he almost added.

They dragged their bags, now including take away from Chester's Fried Chicken, up the steps of the building and into the apartment.

An old tanned man in a straw hat, white linen suit and tie rose politely from the couch. He took off his jacket and easily tossed it onto Puppy's head.

"Get this pressed, boy."

6

It took Zelda only a few minutes to pack up her few personal belongings: pencils, a couple photographs of her and Puppy, and Pablo, scarf and mittens, extra woolen socks and a paint brush. She was careful not to take anything remotely characterized as school property. They could claim the brush belonged to PS 75 since she'd used it in class, but this brush was hers. Bought and paid for. High quality, thin fibers, delicate wooden handle, perfect for quick strokes.

She hid the brush into the bottom of the carton and slipped on her bright red coat, tugging tightly around the waist. You have to lay off the Amblin's Chocolates, girl, she chided herself. Zelda wrapped a blue scarf around her neck.

N'ariti stood in the doorway, smiling shyly. Zelda stared back cautiously. Children were like walking traps. Big sweet smiles and suddenly metal cleaved off your foot.

The girl took a brave breath and marched up to Zelda's desk. "I'm sorry."

Zelda tilted her head carefully. "About?"

N'ariti pointed at the box.

"I have a new job," Zelda explained.

"Another school?" the girl asked sadly.

"No. Something better. Salmon."

"What's that?"

"Fish. You know. Fish." She puffed out her cheeks like gills.

N'ariti took the pad off Zelda's desk and scribbled quickly, using a charcoal pencil jutting out of her back pocket. "Like that?"

Zelda glanced down at the ugliest fish ever seen. Really looked more like a cat. "Sort of."

"I don't think I like fish," N'ariti said.

"Most people don't."

"Then why do they eat it?"

"Because they think it's good for them."

"Is that why you're working there?"

Zelda tore off the drawing from the pad and dropped it into the carton. She paused by the door. "Salmon don't have tails."

N'ariti puffed out her cheeks. "How can you be a window? I didn't understand."

Zelda's hand rested impatiently on the knob. "You really can't. It's about people looking through you."

"Why would you want to do that? They could see your intestines and veins."

"Exactly," Zelda said brusquely. "There's another class coming in. Go back to where you belong before you get your new teacher in trouble."

"What if I see in my brain my salmon with tails? Isn't that what you meant?" N'ariti called out.

Zelda saw tails on everyone all the way home on the Number 6 train, and then back downtown later that day to Saul's Salmons on East 174th Street. Children just didn't know when to shut up; another reason she hated the little brats.

Her new office was tiny and narrow; Zelda could barely take off her coat without elbowing a wall. The chunky department manager Mr. Pietro stopped by, standing behind the glass enclosure rather than the doorway as if afraid she'd touch him.

"Welcome, Ms. Jones."

"Thank you, sir."

"This is a good place to work." He nodded at the Saul's Salmon poster behind him, featuring an ancient, smiling Saul Ribe sitting on a placid fish below the tagline, "Saul Knows Fish."

"I'm anxious to pitch in and make it even better."

Pietro wasn't convinced. "Marketing's important. Creativity is good. You're creative."

"I was a performance artist."

Pietro's eyebrows shot up, lifting his entire face. "I don't want singing salmon. It's not dignified."

"How about dancing?"

"Would you eat a salmon all sweaty from dancing across the stage?"

"No, sir." It was a good point, she had to admit.

"We want salmon serene. You don't want an issue with your food. Take a bite and suddenly they start talking? The food's to eat, not debate. Dignity in your artwork, Ms. Jones. And knowledge." He left behind slightly steamed glass.

Zelda finished putting out her possessions, tossing N'ariti's drawing in a small bin. She wound her way down a couple hallways, nodding at intense and determined colleagues clutching very important folders that would decide the fate of humanity. As close as she'd ever gotten to a business job was selling art supplies; that had lasted all of two months because she kept talking customers out of inferior products.

She passed a conference room; her name was on the list of attendees for a meeting in two minutes called "Is Tuna Salad Doomed? Our Opportunity." Zelda continued to Pietro's office, which was smaller than hers, mirroring the way the Cousins hierarchy was set up. The higher you went, the less perks. Success was not superiority, Grandma's Fifth Insight said. Success was serving.

"Excuse me, sir." She knocked lightly. He pulled his feet off the desk, surprised. "I had a question."

"Usually that's the prelude for scheduling an appointment, Ms. Jones," Pietro said sternly.

She inched around his glass enclosure. "Sorry. First day excitement."

Pietro softened slightly.

"You talked about knowledge," she continued.

"When?"

"When you were in my office a few minutes ago."

"Yes." He grudgingly conceded.

"Since I've never been on a fishing boat," she said and Pietro gasped slightly, "I wondered if I could go out one day to see what it's all about. That would give me a real feel for real fish."

Pietro peered at her. "That's an excellent idea, Ms. Jones. Let me see what I can arrange."

"Thank you, sir."

He quickly frowned. "Aren't you supposed to be in the tuna salad meeting?" He handed her a folder. "Salmon salad. Consider the possibilities."

• • • •

THE NEW OLD guy walked around the living room, sniffing disdainfully at the furniture. Puppy flipped the suit jacket on the chair, which agitated the man.

"I said I want that cleaned." He glared at Mickey, deep in thought. "Sir, would you talk to your boy here?'

"Who the hell are you?" Puppy scowled.

The man clenched his fists. "How dare you take that tone with me, boy."

"Ty?" Mickey stepped between them.

"Yes." The man seemed offended that this was even a question.

"It's Mickey Mantle."

Ty Cobb peered in disbelief. "What happened to you?"

"I got old and died." Mickey tugged on Puppy's sleeve. "It's Ty Cobb."

Puppy just blinked.

"The greatest hitter who ever lived," Cobb said arrogantly. "This your place, Mick?"

"No, his."

Cobb sneered. "You live with a nigra?"

Puppy dragged Mickey into the bedroom and slammed the door. "Okay. Who is he?"

"Ty Cobb. But he ain't the greatest hitter. Pete Rose broke his record. Don't tell him. He got a temper."

Puppy rubbed his forehead. "And you let him in why?"

"How could I let him in? I was with you."

"Yes, you were." Puppy was annoyed over that little fact. "Be honest."

"I am," Mickey snarled.

"You gave him my address."

"No."

"Then spoke to the super and slipped him a few dollars…"

"I spent all my money on booze. Which I could use…"

Puppy held onto Mantle's elbow. "Ty's a friend of yours?"

"We posed for photos once. Hall of Famers and future Hall of Famers. It was for a magazine I can't remember."

"Mickey. Listen to me. I'm happy to help you."

"No, you ain't." He stared hard.

Puppy flushed with shame. "I am. Somewhere inside, very happy. But I can't have your buddies moving in."

"The Sporting News."

"What?"

"For the photos. It was a big baseball magazine. And Cobb can pay his way. The guy's loaded. Made money off General Motors and Coca-Cola." Mickey went back into the living room. Puppy sat on the edge of the bed, listening to them toast, thinking empty, bewildered thoughts. He returned during the second round.

"Ty…"

"Mr. Cobb."

Mickey patted Ty's arm to be nice.

"Ty," he said grudgingly.

"Puppy Nedick." He poured himself a stiff one. "Sorry if I was a little rude." Cobb scowled. "But as Mick has explained, this is my apartment."

Ty raised a disdainful eyebrow.

"You can appreciate, I'm sure, coming home and finding a stranger is a little disturbing."

Mickey nudged Ty, who finally responded. "Your apology is accepted."

"Well thank you kindly, sir." Puppy forced out the sarcasm. "Any friend of Mickey's is welcome."

"I told you he wasn't a bad kid." Mick poured another round, tearing open the bag of Paul's Pretzels and spraying salt over the coffee table.

"We have lots of food for dinner," Puppy said.

"Fried chicken," Mickey added.

"Of course." Ty rolled his eyes.

"So please join us."

"Much better," Ty said, stretching. "I'd like to make some phone calls before supper."

Mick elbowed Ty. "He ain't got a phone. Not exactly a high flier."

"No one has phones." Puppy tried polishing his image.

"Those people usually have some common phone at a barbershop or bar," Ty told Mick.

"No one except the police and the government has phones," Puppy repeated louder.

Cobb grunted dubiously and waited for Puppy to pour him another drink.

Mantle frowned suddenly. "Ain't you dead, Ty?"

"How? I'm here," Ty snapped.

"Me, too. But look." He modeled his torso. "Think."

Cobb pursed his lips. "I have heart problems." He tapped his chest. "Diabetes. Cancer. I had cancer."

"Me, too," Mick said happily. "Liver."

"Prostate." Ty thought for a moment, loosening his tie. "I was in Atlanta. 1961. Then I wasn't."

"And here you are. Like me."

Ty considered Puppy and didn't come away pleased. "In this Negro's house."

"Ain't the Plaza."

"I'll find a phone tomorrow and call my bank. Get us some money."

"At least enough for a cab. We gotta walk everywhere."

"I'll get a car." Cobb paused, studying Puppy. " Can you drive?"

• • • •

FORTUNATELY TY AND Mickey drank themselves into oblivion and passed out early, Ty in the chair, Mick on the couch. Puppy regretted the demise of Greta because it took about half an hour for the boys to stagger awake and another half hour once they sat up, blearily staring off into space. The pseudo-coffee followed by powdered eggs roused Cobb into a state of culinary rage; he wouldn't get ready until Mickey swore to Jesus that their first stop would be a bank.

Puppy was pretty sure the last bank had been closed under the Anti-Parasite Laws of 2068.

Cobb clucked his tongue so much walking down Morris Avenue he sounded like Ringo Starr trapped in a tonsil. He half-shrank into his suit, avoiding contact with siblings hurrying to work, especially since he and Mick were the only Caucs for blocks at a time. He looked like he wanted a very long shower with a pound of soap.

When they got to River Avenue, Mickey let out a happy cry and ran forward. Just before the first pile of rocks, he froze in disbelief.

"What is that?" Cobb asked.

"Amazon Stadium," Puppy said, bewildered. "The baseball stadium. You haven't heard of it?"

"Amawhat?" Mickey shouted, pointing at the ground, the clouds, the El, at a pole, anything for an emotional anchor. "This was Yankee Stadium."

Not since Amazon bought it in 2051. Grandma's thong.

"Let's go inside," Puppy said gently. "There's a game today."

"In that?" Ty sneered.

Puppy tensed as they walked past the A30 at Gate Six. Fortunately Mick was too angry to react to yet another monster while Ty stared dumbfounded at the robot, muttering about the danger of mixing the races.

The old guys looked around the long hallway, wide eyes taking in the decay, unable to talk for a few minutes and embarrassing Puppy as if he had something to do with the broken floors, gouged out walls, shattered glass, and defaced murals.

"I hope Tiger Stadium's in better shape," Cobb grunted.

Puppy couldn't tell him there was no Tiger Stadium, that this was all that was left of the ballparks and it was coming down in five months. He led them through the runway and into the stadium. Mickey and Ty stood in the entrance, horrified.

"My seat's down there."

Mickey and Ty sat carefully, tucking their ankles together, shoulders tight, hands in their laps. They couldn't bear to touch anything.

"Game's about to start," Puppy said cheerfully.

"No one's here," Ty said.

Puppy passed on acknowledging the seven people scattered in the lower field boxes. At least no one was having sex. The men sadly took in the rubble and debris.

"I would not let my chickens piss here," Ty finally said.

Mick wiped away tears and Ty handed him a starched handkerchief. Men didn't cry, but this was an abomination worthy of grief for which he accused Puppy with a vicious glare.

"We just sit in this shithole until one in the afternoon?"

"Game's going to start in a few minutes."

Mick glanced at Puppy's watch. "It ain't even nine o'clock in the morning."

"Yes." Puppy opened his notebook. "Now I'm the baseball historian. I keep a record of every game. This is the second one of the season. The Hawks won opening day, 6-3, a terrific contest. "

The HG Hawks dashed onto the field. Puppy stood and applauded.

"You like that?" The A29 turned. "I figured the fielders could come out together."

"Great work," Puppy shouted back, nodding toward the 'bot. "I've been after him to juice things up."

Mystified, Mickey and Ty leaned forward as the HGs threw the holographic ball around the infield and the outfield. The pitcher warmed up.

"What the hell is all that?" Ty whispered.

"He had one in his house but I killed it," Mickey answered. "I'll take care of them."

Puppy pulled Mantle back into the chair. "These are HGs." He waited, hoping for some response other than puzzled anger. "Holograms." He pointed at the A29 in the front row. "He projects them onto the field."

"Why?" Ty didn't seem to want to really know.

"They're the fielders," Puppy said patiently.

"The midgets play?" Mick asked.

"Sure. It's a lot of fun. Okay, here's the leadoff batter for the Falcons."

Campanis lazily swung a bat, yawning. The A28 umpire yelled "play ball."

"Is he human?" Ty asked.

"Of course. The batters are all people."

Campanis swung and missed at the first pitch.

"Where's the ball?" Ty squinted.

"It was there. Speed gets up to 100, 105 mph."

"But it ain't real," Mickey asked.

"Campanis is real," Puppy said, annoyed. The batter swung and the ball bounced toward the second baseman. The HG runner scampered down the line, easily thrown out.

"What was that?" Mickey pointed somewhere on the field.

"The HG runner," Puppy said.

"The batter doesn't run?"

"No, they just hit."

"But did he hit the ball?" Ty asked shrewdly.

"Sort of. The program's set up for each batter's skills."

"Like a video game?" Mickey frowned. "My kids had one."

"Kind of."

"And this is baseball?" he asked.

Puppy let loose. "It's the best we have. Maybe not perfect, but it's still baseball."

"No, it ain't," Mick growled.

"If you don't like it, don't stay. But be quiet. I have a job to do. Look, you made me miss the next play. I oversee official government records, damnit."

After that first batter, they sat in stoic disgust. By the second inning, they moved back a few rows, whispering; Puppy couldn't concentrate. At the end of the sixth and last inning, he stood and slipped his notebook into his backpack. Ty was asleep on Mantle's shoulder.

"That's it," Puppy said. "If you care, the Hawks won 4-1."

Mantle slid away from Ty, who woke up, irritated. "I want to look around."

"It's dangerous. There are holes everywhere, Mick. Rotting floors. Let's just go home."

Mickey hopped over the fence and onto the field. Ty followed, angrily brushing past Puppy, who doggedly followed.

Mickey walked around reverently, scooping up an occasional rock and putting it in his pocket. Ty knelt, touching home plate. Now Mickey walked quickly down the first base line, breaking into a trot, Ty on his heels. The two heavy-set old men arced around second, gaining speed towards third. He thought they were racing, but if they were, it was not against each other. Shoulder to shoulder, they crossed home plate simultaneously.

They headed into the dugout. Puppy went to stop them, but in a few moments, Mick came back with a battered bat while Ty disgustedly toted a handful of lumpy balls.

Ty took the mound. From the right side, Mickey swung the bat slowly. Ty's first pitch bounced three times before rolling across home. Mick tossed it back. Ty threw another bounder.

"Now I know you're dead." Mickey grinned. Cobb's eyes narrowed. He reached home this time. Mick swung, missing and falling to one knee.

Puppy sighed. But there was some poignant familiarity to the way they tried to throw and hit. As if Mick and Ty were putting on their wedding suits, knowing it didn't fit, but didn't matter because they still thought they were young studs on a happy day.

He did the math. Both mid-60s, so born like 2033. Maybe they played high school ball. Around 2050, 2051. By then, the robot arm pitcher scandals, including the St. Louis Cardinals stripped of their world title, had gutted the major leagues down to twelve teams, six in either league, suffocating under the popularity of the more fast-paced football and basketball. VR and then AR gouged another hole in the sport's heart, putting fans in the huddle or under the basket. Just the diehards, the real fans, wanted the laconic baseball from a distant past, an America which no longer existed, an America few wanted to be reminded of.

Mickey moved into the left-handed batters box, promising to give up the bat soon. Ty threw at his head. Puppy underhanded the loose ball back to Mick, who easily caught it one-handed. His boyish grin would've set new smile-o-meter records.

But how could they not remember what happened next: Miners, rebellion, the Infamous Day of 10/12, ballparks razed to the ground. It didn't explain it even if they'd been in mental hospitals, drunks, good old-fashioned DVs in every possible definition like his father; they had to know something.

Mick lofted the ball into right field. Ty clapped sarcastically and took the bat. Cobb missed the first two pitches, slamming the bat on the ground. On the third toss, he ripped a shot into the right field corner. Puppy sat up. Cobb cracked the next pitch over second base and followed with a rope over the third base line.

Not bad, Puppy thought. Not bad at all. The morning rain splattered his hair. He didn't notice.

"Get the balls, boy." Ty fussily put his suit jacket back on, disdainfully tossing aside the splintered bat. "And take me to my bank."

Mick had wandered into short center field to retrieve a ball.

"There's a fucking skeleton here," he screamed.

7

Light glistened off the tight black curls dampened on his broad head. Sweat clung to the back of his neck and dripped carelessly down his tanned, muscular back. Zelda swallowed and waited another moment as the boy mopped the wood, his triceps popping out. He bent over to dump out the bucket.

"Excuse me," she said.

He glanced up with a polite smile. Zelda stepped around the puddles.

"I'm here for the fishing."

He frowned.

"Fishing. Salmon."

The boy, not a boy, he was mid-twenties with blackish eyes and a strong chin, pointed up and down the dock.

"Right. Lots of boats. I'm looking for *The Intruder*." She waved the authorization from Mr. Pietro. "One of Saul's Salmons boats."

The boy/man wiggled his fingers sadly.

"Does that mean the boat's gone?" She didn't care how hot he was, this was annoying.

He nodded.

"It's supposed to leave at noon. It's only eleven-thirty."

He shrugged that time was of no concern and listlessly moved the mop around, widening the puddles. She didn't understand why a wet dock needed washing.

"But it's no more?" She wiggled her fingers.

He held up three fingers.

"Does that mean it returns at three o'clock?" As he shrugged maddeningly, her voice rose. "Or in three days?" He mopped around her feet, wetting her shoes.

She tried giving him the official letter again, which he ignored and figure-eighted about, mopping. Zelda stumbled a little, off-balance from her aching vagina; the woman last night was voracious. Now she was in pissed off pain.

"One more time. I'm with Saul's Salmon. Your employer. As in, we, pay, you."

"Are you the owner?" he said, grinning.

Zelda was taken aback by his delicate voice. "Well no, I'm not the owner. I work for him."

"Like me."

"Yes," she said, exasperated.

"Only I work for Mr. Lee. He owns *The Intruder*."

His mocking smile irritated her. "You're pretty fucking insolent, aren't you?"

He held up his mop, shrugging sheepishly. "That's why I'm mopping the deck when the ship's not here."

"What'd you do? Be rude to a colleague?"

"I disagreed with Captain Lee. He's the Captain. That's wrong."

Just go back to the office, Zelda, and ponder the virtues of salmon salad and why it has never overtaken tuna salad. Chug, chug, up the hill, taste my gill. No, she frowned.

"You talking to yourself?" he asked, bemused.

"Yes. That's how I think, playing different roles, people attached to my thoughts, ideas, whatever. Are there any flights later today?"

"You mean sailing?" he snickered, but good-humoredly. His eyes made him difficult to dislike.

"Yes. Boats. "

He shook his head. "Tomorrow at eleven."

"Not noon?"

He frowned. "Right. Noon. I think. Captain Lee knows. Why don't you wait for him?"

"I have tons of work."

The guy grinned. "By the time you get back to Kingsbridge it's at least two hours. It'd be almost time to go home."

"How did you know my office was there?"

"We work for the same company." His smile made her swoon. The guy was the bahm diggidy. "I'm Diego."

Zelda sat on a bench across from the dock, sketching several boats, putting happy salmons on deck until she remembered Mr. Pietro's admonition about humanizing fish. Zelda humanized or life-sized, life-sensed everything. She preferred brushes to people; one had promise, the other only dabbled. When she was six years old, she'd disrupted her class, imagining her charcoal pencils talking and singing. The children and teacher and school thought she was disturbed, but her parents fought for her artistic expression.

Until her father's tie business faltered and they were moved into the DV. Then her parents had no time to worry if their daughter talked to trees or made games with shoes or gave forks names, first and last, occasionally a middle initial. The DV school didn't care; they focused on specific, practical routes to success since you were already crouching in the shit if you were there. Staging shows on the sidewalk produced by/directed by/starring the Incomparable Zelda Jones and expecting someone to cough up coins to hear you prattle on about the souls of birds only deepened the poop puddle.

Except she had a teacher named Mr. Willis, hunched and gray, whose eyes watered when she performed in the hallways or classroom, who showed her how to draw and where to kick someone when they bothered her. Right below the knee, then the groin, he said with that quiet dignity. He sponsored her application to the Regulars School and, when she appeared before the invitation committee, they treated her like an undiscovered genius. She hadn't known Mr. Willis was a famous performance artist whose wife and kids were killed in the chemical attack. He'd refused pitying honors, moving from Manhattan to the Bronx and settling into a DV building, insisting he was one. He hadn't protected his family. What more could stamp someone as a disappointment?

She caught up to Captain Lee as he slung his backpack over a shoulder, heading toward the end of the dock.

"Captain, I'm Zelda Jones from…"

"He told me," Lee grunted, never breaking stride. "Noon tomorrow, stay out of the way."

"Thanks," she called after him.

Diego joined her, buttoning his denim jacket. "Told you it wouldn't be a problem."

"I could've gone back to work if you'd known the schedule."

Diego slipped out the drawings from her black bag. "Not bad."

"Gee thanks."

She reached for them, but he turned away, studying one in particular. "This me with the devil wings?"

Zelda flushed. "I was just fooling around."

"I like it. We all had wings at one time," he said. "Can I have it?"

"No, these are my sketches. For my job." She shoved the drawings into her bag and looked around.

"Bus is that way," Diego pointed to the left. "Unless you'd like to have a drink."

• • • •

THE PUMPKIN'S CAVE burrowed in the shadow of the 145th Street Bridge. Children still risked their lives on a dare to scamper onto the crumpled iron remnants twisting like broken arms to futilely reach across the East River. Every year some stupid kid fell, thinking they could jump, slipping beneath the sewage and setting off another round of nightly Parenting Skills on the vidnews for mothers and fathers all over America whose lack of diligence let a precious commodity die, whether in the garbage of New York, a river in Idaho, or a forest in Tennessee.

Your children are my children and my children are our children, Grandma's stern face would flash, seeking out that parent sipping a cold beer on the porch, indifferent to their kid discovering matches in the basement. We lost thirteen million people. We can't lose any more.

Puppy lowered his head down the narrow old bomb shelter passageway, led by a tatted TG with a long green ponytail whose sharp fingernails gestured at a chair. He cradled the package under his arm, still standing. Ponytail gestured again, puzzled why Puppy hadn't sat. Her fingernails clawed and he got the message.

After a few minutes alone in the dank room, bare bulbs embedded in the wall and smoke whistling from the floor like 'bacco geysers, Pumpkin barreled out of a wall, a driverless truck on an icy road, falling heavily on his long, blue bean bag which raised him back up. Not that someone six-seven and three hundred pounds needed a lift, but Pumpkin was all about the presentation.

"Puppy Nedick," he tried to smile, but his orangish face held to a sneer.

"Pumpkin Meadows."

The large man slowly rolled up his sleeves over his albino arms, staring at Puppy with some surprise, as if anyone got inside without an appointment.

"Still with the baseballs."

"One last season."

"Must break your heart."

"It does, Pumpkin. It does."

Pumpkin giggled happily at Puppy's discomfort. "And what will they do with all that land beneath your stadium?"

"I don't know, but I bet you do."

"I might. Care to hear?"

"No."

"Yes, you do."

"I really don't."

"Because it would hurt too much?"

"Because it'd bore me."

Pumpkin laughed. "Always such a poor liar."

"As we were taught in the DV. Honesty, integrity."

"They will raze the park to the ground and build a factory complex. As if it never existed. No plaques, monuments, just dust. Finally."

Puppy flinched.

The large man grinned and gestured around the room like it was a cathedral of his most devout greed. "Here I am. There you are. It must be a special favor since you've never asked me for anything. That hurts. An old friend, eager to help another old friend in any way I can."

Puppy was glad his sneakers had thick soles so Pumpkin's verbal shit didn't soil his socks.

"I need a temp Lifecard."

"Oh?" Pumpkin's eyebrow lifted in mock interest. "For a boyfriend?"

"No."

"Girlfriend?"

"Just a friend."

"Must be a good friend to break the law."

"It's just until we find him in the system." He didn't think Ty had a record any more than Mickey and he wasn't about to chance going back to the clerk's office.

"I didn't think you consorted with criminals, Puppy. Such a paragon of ethics. The golden boy of baseball. Once," he sneered.

"You're the only criminal I associate with, Pumpkin," he snapped.

Pumpkin held his gasp for a long time, releasing into a loud echoing chuckle. "Shame. We're more interesting people." Pumpkin lit a 'bacco. "And why should I help you of all people, Puppy Nedick?"

"Because it makes you happy to see me squirm."

Pumpkin's laugh loosened some dirt on the ceiling. He clapped, rolling around on his pelvis. "Absolutely right. Even for that joy, which is priceless, I need to conduct this in an appropriate business manner."

Puppy unwrapped the red seat cushion and laid it in front of Pumpkin. "From the bleachers of Fenway Park."

The orange face settled into cold scrutiny, turning the cushion around. "How do I know that's true?"

"Because you know what a seat from Fenway looks like. You're an expert."

Pumpkin grunted. "Where'd you get this? It was a forbidden stadium."

"They all were and it's not illegal to have baseball memorabilia."

"Yes it is. The law's just not enforced. No one cares about this stupid game."

"Some people still do or else you wouldn't be interested."

Pumpkin smelled the cushion, smiling at a scent. "The other week a person offered a chair from the Cleveland ballpark. There was little interest."

"This is Fenway Park, Pumpkin. Not Cleveland. Not Detroit. Fenway fucking Park."

Pumpkin smirked. "What must it be like to think as you do with all those romantic notions?"

"I don't think about how I think."

"Never did," Pumpkin said dismissively, handing the seat to Ponytail, who wrapped it in thick plastic in a matter of moments before disappearing down a hallway. "I will confirm in my way."

"When?"

"In a rush, aren't we?"

Puppy nodded warily. "I guess I'll leave it."

"Don't you trust me?"

"No."

Pumpkin couldn't manage genuine hurt. "What else do you have?"

"It's all I got."

"This isn't enough, Fenway fucking Park or not."

"Pumpkin. I ain't got anything else."

"You? The famous Puppy Nedick? You must have a closetful of former illegal baseball stuff. Or something of actual value. Bibles are always sellers. Especially the Hebrew one. Extinction does breed curiosity. There's a wonderful market for Judaica, especially anything ME or CE. Their religious paraphernalia, skull caps, the prayer shawls…"

"No Bibles, shawls…"

"Shame." Pumpkin was briefly disappointed. "What about one of these?" He snapped his fingers and Ponytail returned with gray headphones. "Ever seen one?" Puppy shook his head, fortifying Pumpkin's faith in Puppy's ignorance. "Anti-Narcissim Act of 2068…"

"I went to school, remember?"

"Always the star student, I recall," Pumpkin's voice dripped disdain. "Outlawed for the obvious reasons along with all social media, cell phones and the like, but in 2077, headphones were restored for private use only, you probably didn't know that. It actually has a practical use. Screw neighbors complaining about loud music. Get me a Bose and I'm yours."

"I wish."

"But no cellulars. Amazing how many people didn't turn them in, hoping Grandma would actually restore the satellite links. Dreamers." Pumpkin frowned. "How about bank statements? Collectors love those. Or canned foods from Christian Europe?" Pumpkin excited himself. "Some of those disgusting Brit foods like canned beans? Or German beer. Oh, if you only had a six-pack…"

"Nothing, Pumpkin. That's the truth."

"And the great Puppy Nedick doesn't lie." Pumpkin tilted his head side to side.

"I'm jammed."

"Yes you are." Pumpkin chuckled gleefully. "And I'm thoroughly enjoying it."

Puppy closed his eyes a moment. "Please, you fat sack of shit."

Pumpkin clapped. "That's much better."

• • • •

DAVID FISHER'S OFFICE had all the charm of a maximum security prison. He didn't want to be there, so he did everything he could to discourage visitors. A thin, angry balding man in his thirties with a dull look, he'd inherited the Hawks from his mother, which made him angrier, because a dead parent's wishes were revered. If your mother or father left you a rabid animal who bit off your left arm, you learned to eat with your right.

"I'm pretty busy, Puppy." Fisher gestured around the metallic office with its uncomfortable silver chairs. The window onto the stadium was corked off with aluminum shades so he didn't have to be reminded that he was the owner of a baseball team.

"Your time is precious to me, Mr. Fisher."

Fisher grunted dubiously and tried out a new pen on a notebook, grumbling when the ink didn't flow.

"Good start to the season, don't you think?"

Fisher peered at the tip of the pen.

"Very spirited games. And that touch with the HGs running onto the field together really excited people."

"I don't give a shit, Nedick."

Fisher flung the pen into the garbage and squinted suspiciously at Puppy, who always wanted something. Last season it was buy more potato chips. This season, change the HGs.

"I know, sir. But I need your permission for the Hawks to sign two new players. You're down a couple."

"Did someone die?"

Puppy shook his head. "Remember last year we finished the season with just seven players each? The Falcons added two more."

"If that pile of pizza dough Boccicelli wants to waste his money, let him."

"You really want Boccicelli having an advantage?"

Fisher darkened. He hated Boccicelli. "Same price?"

"Absolutely."

"Don't try to squeeze in anything extra on me like toilet paper for the clubhouse. They don't have to shit there. That's why they have homes."

"I'll let them know. Thanks, Mr. Fisher."

"Bring them in."

"Pardon?"

"I have to meet them." Fisher glanced at the ceiling-to-floor oil painting of his heavy-set mother, whose scowl suggested terminal indigestion.

Puppy reluctantly opened the door and beckoned to Mick and Ty, mouthing "behave" as they followed him back in.

"David Fisher, owner of the Bronx Hawks, this is Ty Cobb and Mickey Mantle."

Cautious handshakes all around.

"I hear you're joining our little team," Fisher said without making eye contact.

Ty shrugged and peered distastefully at the oil painting. "Who's the broad?"

"My mother Anna, who owned the team," Fisher said proudly. "Twenty-three years. She was a strong believer in strong character."

"That's us," Mick said. "You got any scotch?"

"I don't believe in drinking, Mr. Mantle."

"It's for me, not you."

Puppy stepped in. "Again, they're delighted to be Hawks."

"Let's see when we get the contracts," Ty said.

"What contract?" Fisher snapped.

"The moral contracts," Puppy said quickly. "To play hard and play to win."

"That was my mother's motto. She felt that since she won the team in a fair game of chance, the games the team play should also be honorable." Fisher circled Mick and Ty in bland curiosity. "How old are you gentlemen?"

"What year is this again?" Ty asked.

"They're experienced." Puppy quickly opened the door to send everyone merrily on their way.

"I know that, Nedick, but this is part of the welcoming ceremony which Mother did with every new player. Where'd you play?"

"You don't know where I played?" Cobb roared.

Fisher flinched. He should've just given them their two bars of soap allotment and let it go but no, he had to show respect to that old witch's memory. He checked her urn every morning to make sure the ashes hadn't escaped.

"I'm Ty Cobb, asshole. This is Mickey Mantle. Play? Where'd we play?"

Puppy nervously pulled on Cobb.

"Right here under your fat ass. You own a baseball team and you don't know who we are? What the hell kind of candy ass shit organization is this?"

Puppy dragged the two old men into the hallway before Fisher's lower jaw hit the floor. He popped his head back in.

"They're honored to play for the Hawks, sir."

"Depends how much we get," Cobb shouted.

• • • •

GRANDMA LAID THE silver tray on the gleaming wood-and-glass table, spooning out two sugars into Tomas' purple cup. He knew better than to wave off her homemade chocolate chip cookies; somehow he'd have to find the strength to chew.

"You look tired," she said, settling into the high-backed chair in the small, comfy sitting room in her House. There was a master bedroom to the left and a guest room to the right; a study directly ahead where Tomas, alone, would come and go through a fake door behind the desk. Otherwise the large, two-story building tucked inside a maze of carefully guarded HG forest in Van Cortlandt Park was a long playground for visitors wandering around and giving Tomas endless indigestion as head of her security.

Children, as if a Noah's Ark of America, stared down from the great vid mural over the purple couch. They sang softly, swaying side to side, arms around each other's waists.

"There's nothing you can do that can't be done,

Nothing you can sing that can't be sung."

"I'm fine," the Major said. Three neutral ships, Chinese, Brazilian and Sengalese, were needed to make it back more than three thousand miles to the narrow neutral zone, then a fat double payment for a small twenty-footer at the edge of their territorial waters of ten miles. Good thing the Allah Navy was a joke. He'd leave out the two dead Aussies who had rented him their boat; Grandma wouldn't approve.

"What about you?" He didn't like her pale color. "Have you been bathing in the bio-regens?"

She breezily waved her hands, free of jewelry, wearing only dangling earrings and a simple heart-shaped necklace. Her doll-like body tucked in a simple purple dress, Grandma always looked as if she were about to go out or retire for the evening. She lazily kicked off her shoes.

"Is that an answer?" he persisted.

"As good as you'll get, Major." Grandma studied him, her probes knocking about his mind. She frowned. "Did you have that snarly attitude across the sea?"

"I kept off my knees," he said sourly. "I didn't want to tempt a beheading."

"Tomas," she said sternly.

"I behaved and said little. And they listened."

"And?"

"You know what they're like."

"I do."

"I don't trust them."

"Nor do I." She frowned.

Twenty-eight years of devout service since Grandma found him semi-conscious in the hospital along with the remains of the 230th Battalion, the rest of the men and women floating off the beaches of Sicily. She'd stared into their eyes, held their hands, fed them, sang to them, reassured them, revitalized them. Promised them all this would not be in vain.

He would kill his own mother to protect Grandma.

"I trust us. Who we are. What we have to offer." Grandma's urgency softened into a smile. "You don't even trust that much." He shrugged and bit into another cookie. "You're not exactly a walking advert for the Family sometimes."

"I trust you. The only one."

"Inside of half a cup of tea, you've blown up everything we stand for," she said with mock disapproval. At least he hoped it was mock disapproval. "How did they leave it?"

"The Imam will talk to His Most Worthy Successor."

"Good." Grandma thoughtfully stirred her tea. "Two of the Collectors insist he'll respond."

"If they're still the Collectors and not feeding us disinformation." When Grandma continued stirring, he persisted, "Which is a possibility."

"The Son hates his father," Grandma said firmly. "We know of the fights."

"If this isn't a trap. For them to suddenly reach out…"

"Not so suddenly, Tomas," she said vaguely, raising an eyebrow so he wouldn't pursue.

"For how long?" he asked anyway.

Grandma rummaged about his mind. "Long enough."

"I only know about that Saudi prince and the Pakistani merchant…"

"And a dozen more," she scolded. "This one's different. This time they can't ignore their hunger."

He wasn't sure if she meant the reported food riots in the Caliphates of France and Germany or another sort of stirring. "They're still Allahs."

"And we're still Americans." Grandma sighed and squeezed his Gelinium leg. "I should've sued for peace in '65 instead of letting more of you die uselessly for pride."

"You saved us, Grandma. The Allahs only understand one thing." He made two thick fists which Grandma slowly uncurled, one finger at a time.

"Not all of them. I have to believe that. Otherwise I lied to all of you when I said there would be another future."

A mop-headed little girl poked her head in.

"What is it, honey?" Grandma asked.

"I left my ball."

The child crawled under the couch and retrieved her basketball.

"How's your passing?" Grandma held up her hands. The girl glanced anxiously at Tomas, who nodded; she gently tossed the ball. Grandma caught it in one hand, twirling the ball on her left forefinger before whipping it back across the room. The child gasped as the ball knocked into her chest.

"That's how you pass. Again."

The girl's eyes narrowed and she fired the ball at Grandma's head. Tomas tensed; eight-year-old girl kills Grandma with basketball was not a vidnews headline he wanted.

Grandma smiled, pleased. "Were you afraid to throw it too hard because of who I am?" The girl nodded carefully. "Aren't you taught that we are all equal and deserve the same treatment?"

The girl hesitated. "Your Ninth Insight is revere the old."

Grandma cleared her throat and underhanded the ball back. The girl bowed from the shoulders and dribbled her way out the door.

"Do I look that old?" Grandma spooned more sugar into her tea.

"Not a day over ninety-two, Lenora."

She grunted dismissively and stared off for a moment. "You're sure no one saw you?"

He flushed; her stare hardened.

"That's not an insult, Tomas."

"Yes it is," he said stiffly.

"This cannot get out. We're still not quite ready."

8

Jalak Mustafa wiped her hands on a dishtowel and watched Azhar snore on the couch. She angrily switched off the football game. He woke up with a bleary smile.

"Hello, my she-cat."

"It's two o'clock."

"I must've dozed."

"For three hours it is sleep, not a nap."

Mustafa knew the best response was a sweet smile conceding her righteous anger.

"What are your plans?"

He wondered who won the football contest. She snapped the towel at his head.

"Your friend the Imam has no more exciting adventures?"

"I'm sure I'll hear soon."

"I can't wait for another prayer mat. I can cook the next one since we don't have dinner tonight."

"What happened to the fish?"

"Your sons ate it. They are growing boys. They expect their father to bring home food every night."

Omar paused at the front door in his black Holy Guardians Disciple robe. The gangly fifteen-year-old, six feet of adolescent sullenness, grudgingly said, "I'm going to the mosque."

"Study and learn and be one with Allah." Jalak smiled.

"Yes, of course," Mustafa added cheerfully.

Omar shook his head and left. Jalak smacked the towel into Azhar's head again.

"You forgot to pray with him this morning."

Mustafa sighed. "Shit."

"Yes. Shit. And you have such a pretty new prayer mat."

He also knew it was best to let her bang dishes and pots in the kitchen and swear his name several dozen times. As it was best to slip out the door before she found some horrible chore for him around their modest home, a couple kilometers from Sitges Beach outside Barcelona in the Caliphate of North Africa.

A bouncing soccer ball rolled around the side of the house away from the kitchen; his ten-year-old son Abdul also knew it was best not to be in his mother's vision when she had her moods.

"Papa," Abdul called out happily. He adored his father.

Azhar placed his finger over his lips. Abdul, short and round like his mother with his father's easy nature, dribbled the ball knee to knee like he was marching in the band. When they were safely down the sandy road, they exploded in a wild game, chasing each other through sad-looking grass.

"Wait." Azhar caught his breath.

"Papa, are you going to die?" Abdul asked, frightened.

"Only from your mother's cooking." He straightened up as the gas mercifully departed. "But not to worry. She said there is no food tonight."

"We're having chicken."

"Are we now?" One day I will smack your behind with a towel, Jalak, he smiled at the prospect. "It's not stolen?"

Abdul thought a moment. "That would be wrong. Mama's hand would be chopped off."

"And we don't want that."

"No," Abdul agreed. "Omar thinks a thief should lose two hands. One is not sufficient punishment."

"What if the thief seeks Allah's mercy and decides he will never steal again?"

Abdul frowned. "Then he would have no hands to change his mind."

Azhar rubbed his son's neck. "We must always be able to change." He grinned. "Except beating your father in football."

Mustafa dribbled down the side of the road, Abdul futilely trying to steal the ball. A black jeep filled with three black-robed Guardians with machine guns cut them off with screeching tires.

"Assalamu alyakkum wa rahmathullaahi wa barakato," Azhar said softly.

"Wa alaykum assalam," said the stern passenger in the front seat, slipping menacingly out of the jeep.

Mustafa put his arm around Abdul's trembling shoulder.

The Guardian's face curled harshly. "Football in the afternoon."

"The boy has finished his studies."

"One never finishes their studying while there are infidels. While you frolic, devils walk among us." He poked Abdul in the shoulder with his gun. Mustafa's fists clenched. Safeties went off.

"My brother is praying now against our enemies," Abdul said, chin lifted.

"Your brother?"

"My son Omar Mustafa. He is a scholar honored by the Imam." Azhar said this carefully to avoid any sense of challenge.

The Guardian sneered. "Imam Abboud?"

"He is a friend of my Papa."

Mustafa tried quieting the boy.

"He gave him a prayer mat. Did he ever give you one?"

Mustafa's eyes closed and he held Abdul's hand, waiting for death. Five seconds went by and they were still alive.

"And for what would the Imam give a prayer mat to one who plays football in the afternoon?"

"It's a secret," Abdul said.

"My son talks."

"Yes, he does. But I ask the father."

Mustafa swallowed. "It is a secret."

"Is the prayer mat a secret, too?"

Jalak nearly dropped the chicken when Mustafa and Abdul walked into her kitchen trailed by the three scowling Guardians.

"Is Omar okay?" Her eyes glistened.

"Yes, yes, my darling. I wanted to show our friends the Imam's prayer rug."

He led the black-robed men into a square room with white curtains. Abdul pointed to the khaki and brown prayer rug featuring the Masjid an-Nabawi's Prophet's mosque in Madina.

"See?" Abdul said a little too robustly. Mustafa shook him.

"I do." The Guardian knelt and touched the soft velvet. "I have seen this gift to others. Only a few." He rose, eyes narrowing. "And you use it?"

"Every day, True Believer," Mustafa said with deep piety.

"I hope so."

The Guardians looked around, poking at furniture with their guns, disappointed at not finding some reason to burn down the house as a Gateway to Hell. They nodded brusquely and left.

Jalak came into the room, eyes wide with terror, rubbing her hands over and over into the checked dish towel.

"What was that about?" she asked hoarsely.

"They thought we were infidels," Abdul said.

Jalak dropped her towel.

• • • •

TY STEPPED GINGERLY over the broken stool as if it came from one of the radioactive areas of Los Angeles. At the other end of the clubhouse, Mickey banged open lockers, clanging louder and louder until the last one came off the hinges. He kicked it across the room, the saucer-like metal jarring the pudgy catcher Vernon Jackson awake, who hurried to join the rest of his teammates cowering in the corner.

"Are you kidding me?" Mantle picked up one of the three bats lying outside the smelly bathroom, deciding which wall to smash.

The two old men exchanged wordless contempt.

"This shithole makes your apartment look nice," Ty grumbled.

"The good thing is you don't have to sleep here." Puppy forced a smile. "If I can show you the uniforms...."

"I'm not wearing that crap." Ty pointed at the team in their forlorn white t-shirts and blue pants.

"That's kind of the official uniform." Puppy opened a locker. A mouse scurried out. "He's not on the team."

No one dared to laugh.

As the team shuffled onto the field with the enthusiasm of gargling with poison, the A29 stood up in the front row, calling out, "Over here."

Mickey turned pale. "I ain't talking to a monster."

"Don't call them monsters. That's against the law. It's a robot."

"It ain't human."

"They're very nice. It just wants to discuss your programs."

Ty squinted shrewdly. "What's that?"

"It'll create an HG program which reflects your skills."

"So the midgets can run and catch the ball like us?" Mickey asked.

"Simply, yes."

They exchanged more silent contempt.

"Look, it's a job."

"How much we getting paid?" Ty finally asked.

"I made a hundred grand my last years," Mickey said, staring uneasily at the A29. "I'm not playing for less."

"I got twenty-five grand, which was best back in 1921 until that fat half-coon Ruth got eighty grand or something," Cobb growled. "Since this is, what year again?"

"2098," Puppy said wearily.

"We oughta get about fifty million each."

"Sounds right," Mick agreed.

Puppy took deep breaths. "Probably not to start. You'll get paid into your Lifecards every week."

"What's that?"

"The card in your pocket that I gave up one of my prize possessions to get," he snapped back. "You can use it for everything."

"Like American Express?" Mick asked.

"What's that?"

"My money goes into my bank where I can see it," Ty said stubbornly.

"As I told you, the banks are all gone."

"You telling me there's no Yids walking around paying interest?"

Puppy was momentarily speechless. How could they have not heard of the First Anti-Parasite Laws which got rid of banks and the entertainment industry? "The vermin banks stole people's money. Grandma stopped letting them get away with it. Now everything goes directly into this." He held up his Lifecard. "One stop shopping."

Ty snorted. "Where do you earn interest?"

"Interest isn't earned through work so why would you get it?'

"What if you need a loan?"

"For what?"

"A car. A house."

"You buy it."

"And if you ain't got the money?" Mick joined in.

"Then you don't get it. You only buy what you can afford." Puppy shook his head. They must've been in the home for a long time. "Any other financial questions I can answer?"

They rolled their eyes and tentatively followed him to the robot, who eagerly shook their hands. Ty and Mick carefully checked their fingers.

"You're the new guys, right?"

They nodded cautiously.

"Don't worry, this won't hurt."

"Better not," Mick warned.

The A29 stepped around, assessing them and making notes onto its machine. "I'm figuring speed isn't your forte."

"I had eight hundred and ninety-two stolen bases, asshole." Cobb scowled.

"Doesn't look like you can move like that anymore." The A29 tapped Cobb's butt, turning to Mickey. "You another speed demon?"

"I was until I hurt my knee."

"I wouldn't know." The A29 smirked.

Puppy gestured for it to speed things up before Mick and Ty turned him into a talking garbage can.

"But I bet you're a powerful one." The robot squeezed Mick's biceps.

"Five hundred and thirty-six homers," he said proudly.

"Almost as many as Mooshie Lopez," the robot added. "And you, charm boy?"

Cobb shrugged modestly. "I went for hits where you had to run and not trot."

Mickey playfully shoved him.

"Positions?"

"Center field," Mick said.

"Right field," Cobb said.

It took a couple minutes for Puppy to persuade the old guys to allow a DNA scan of their fingers. The A29 finished with a mechanical flourish. "All set, boys."

"Can we see?" Mickey looked over its shoulder. The robot hesitated, but Puppy nodded.

A Mickey HG suddenly appeared at home plate, younger and sleeker by more than thirty years.

"Holy shit," Mickey muttered, astonished.

"Now here you go running around the bases at the crack of the bat."

The HG raced down the first base line and tore into second with a head-first slide.

"Holy shit," Mantle muttered again.

Puppy leaned forward, staring at the HG dusting himself off at second with a sheepish grin.

"Now you, charm boy."

The Cobb HG, also younger and sleeker, made a diving catch in right-center field. Ty whooped a little before catching himself.

"I was better than that."

"I can ratchet it up."

Puppy scrutinized the Cobb HG throwing the ball into the infield.

"Do me catching the ball," Mick said. "By the center field monuments."

"Monuments?" the A29 frowned, glancing at Puppy.

Puppy wandered up the first base line, passing the Cobb HG trotting back toward the dugout with a sour, arrogant expression. The Mickey HG made a running one-handed catch and he, too, returned to the infield, grinning boyishly. He waved at Puppy, who waved back dully.

Fuck me sideways, Puppy thought suddenly. Can't be.

• • • •

THE DOE-EYED SALESPERSON in the men's department at Chase's tilted his head quizzically as Pablo hefted the gray socks for a third time in each hand.

"Need help, sir?"

"No, as I said twice before," he grumbled.

The salesperson worked on commission and held his ground. "Brown goes with your eyes."

"You think someone will look from my ankles to my eyes?"

"The first thing someone looks at is your hat and your shoes. If they're looking at your feet, socks are just around the corner."

The salesperson waited for Pablo to acknowledge his brilliance with some faint trace of civility. But Pablo always wore gray socks and if he changed now, was that the wrong change? And was he supposed to change or proceed as always? Wasn't staying the course arrogant? If he changed, would that seem opportunistic?

Pablo bought both pairs, mumbling a grudging apology to the salesperson, and continued onto busy Fordham Road, compacted stores jostling for customers with blaring promises of astonishing savings so that you could stumble through one shop and out another and, inside of fifteen minutes, change your wardrobe, buy living room furniture and book a vacation on the Connecticut beaches.

Two pairs of socks were enough for today. Pablo paused for a taco on the corner, pointing out to the owner of the stand that he was being particularly chintzy with the hot sauce. He wandered away, munching with no appetite, looking for a routine gone awry.

An odd feeling since routines were his life. Linear, straightforward. Two hours of study every night, no matter what time he got home. Work six days a week. Date twice a month, whether he wanted to or not. Seven patients a day, whether in person or just reviewing their files. Aqua marble in right hand pocket, which he had found when he was thirteen, the day he first met Zelda and Puppy.

And gray socks every morning since he graduated dental school fourteen years ago. Now one day a week, they'd be brown. Pablo shuddered slightly, stopping by a shop window to make sure he didn't have hot sauce on his face.

He should just relax. He'd gotten this far by doing what he did. Never around but through. They'd noticed him. Where? How did it work? Did they cull through lists of dentists to find one or three or ten a year? A quota. Not for dentists but for former DVs, he was certain. If there weren't enough of them then the whole system didn't work, it'd be elitist and Grandma's dream of an America without Disappointment Villages would die. Back to slums, ghettos, barrios, hopelessness. They had to prove the whole damn concept worked, acknowledge the failure and fix it through yourself, not fix the failure by blaming someone else.

Pablo never blamed anyone else. After suffering bankruptcy, his father had re-opened his bakery in the DV and, exhausted from twenty-hour days, fell asleep smoking, burning down the whole building on Gerard Street. Pablo blamed himself for not working late that night with him. His now widowed mother washed clothes and developed skin cancer from the chemicals. Pablo blamed himself for not supporting her sooner. The whole world just waited for Pablo to take responsibility for something. Allahs, the destruction of Washington, D.C., tacos with insufficient hot sauce.

He sat on a bench overlooking Eastchester Bay. An HG sailboat passed with the waving passengers. Pablo refused to wave back.

He should go to the mixer in his apartment building tonight. Maybe he'd meet someone. Or would they say he was trying too hard to find a partner to beef up his chances at Fifth Cousin.

Who'd put up with him anyway?

An elderly man shuffled past, his white hat stained, shoes worn, bare ankles crusted with eczema. Pablo smiled, giving the grateful man the brown socks and returning to the office three minutes early.

• • • •

"YOU'RE BURNT," PUPPY pointed to Zelda's forehead.

"I worked outside today."

"I thought you were a slave to the business world of windowless offices."

"Salmon is a different world."

The waitress slid through the crowded dance floor at Monroe's, jiggling to Van Halen's *Jump,* and laid the large platter of fries on the table.

"We need an extra plate," Zelda complained.

"She doesn't want my food touching hers," Puppy explained.

"That's not it."

The waitress only cared about the consequences to her tip and pushed back toward the bar.

"Why do you tell people that?" Zelda sipped her beer.

"It annoys you. Back to your hard day at work."

"I had a research field trip. And you, First Cousin Puppy? Tell me what you did to advance America today."

He brought her up on the meeting with Fisher and his new players; Zelda salivated as he ever so slowly ate fries. Finally the waitress delivered her from torture and set down two plates. Zelda scooped up the potatoes and drowned them in ketchup.

"Those old boys really are nuts," she said.

Puppy shrugged dismissively. "I just wonder if they're crazy."

Zelda sighed. "I knew you shouldn't have let the second one stay with you."

"His name's Ty Cobb."

"Sorry. When he told me how intelligent I seemed for a Negro, I shut down."

Puppy took a long swallow of the Gilligan's Ale, laid his backpack on the table and slid the Baseball Hall of Fame book onto his lap, nervously looking around.

"I don't think you have to worry, Pup. Been a long time since someone with a Yankee cap was arrested."

Puppy still had her walk around and read over his shoulder. "This is what the real Mickey Mantle looked like."

Zelda squinted in the half-light at the black and white photos. "Okay."

"That's what the HG today looked like. And here." He turned the thick book to a marked page. "This is what Ty Cobb looked like as a player and this is exactly, I mean, exactly what the HG captured."

"But that's the point of HGs, to make the players look young."

"Creating an exact double of the person they say they are? Don't you think that's a little odd?"

"Maybe they're related. Great-great-great-great grandchildren."

"I think that's too many greats."

Zelda returned to her fries, chewing. "That would account for their athletic abilities. In the genes. And the resemblance. In the genes."

"And them knowing their statistics, home runs, stolen bases?"

"They could look it up."

"Access to baseball stats is restricted to historians." Puppy pressed forward. "Ty rattled off his numbers for every year of his career. Every year, Zelda. Twenty-four seasons."

"He's sharp for a bigot."

"Mickey doesn't remember much."

"Then he's stupid."

"You're missing the point." Puppy ordered another round.

"I can't imagine another point." She gave him a curious stare. "Unless you think they're really Mickey Mantle and Ty Cobb."

"Of course not." He shrugged weakly, only strengthening her smile.

"Grandma's bra straps, you do. Are they ghosts? Oooooh." She swayed in her chair and shoveled down more fries.

"Maybe you should slow down on the potatoes."

Zelda's nostrils flared. "You're mocking my weight because I don't agree?"

"No, I think you're getting fat even if you weren't being obnoxious."

The waitress put down their drinks. Zelda ordered onion rings.

"Mickey got into your apartment somehow…"

"How?" he demanded.

"He picked the lock. You remember what guys that age in the DV can do. Then he let his buddy Ty in. I'm not saying they're bad guys. Since this is the last season, it somehow makes sense they would show up…"

"Exactly." Puppy smacked the table, making the fries jump. "The last baseball season. And here they are."

Her eyelids fluttered mockingly. "Puppy."

"You have a better explanation?"

"No. You're probably right. The theory makes perfect sense the more I ponder."

He frowned suspiciously. "It does?"

"Yeah. They've returned to help you. Guardian angels from the great baseball stadium in the sky. Watching over you…"

"Screw you, Zelda…"

"They might be here now. Oh look." Zelda picked up a fry between her thumb and forefinger, making the potato dance. "It's the baseball ghosts…"

Puppy angrily dumped all her fries onto his plate; Zelda shook her head pityingly.

"Do you see how stupid you sound?" She waved down the waitress for another order.

"Not really."

"Until you do, get Ty a Lifecard. You don't need any trouble."

"Already done. I saw The Pumpkin."

"Why'd you go to that pig?"

"I couldn't ask Pablo again."

"Why not?"

He hesitated. Zelda twisted his forefinger until he cried out.

"You can't say you know. Because I'm not supposed to know."

"He met someone?"

"Sooooo far off." Zelda went for his pinky. "He's under consideration to be a Fifth Cousin."

"Hell no."

"They just gave him a heads up, nothing official. But if they ever found out he told someone…"

"I won't say anything." She stared moodily into her drink. "Why didn't he tell me?"

"I knew you'd go there. He only said something because I asked for the med info for Mickey's Lifecard."

"Okay." Zelda only half-believed him. They drank in silence for a while. "Pablo a Cousin."

"I know, right? He'll never smile again."

They clinked glasses; Diego paused by their table, holding the hand of a sweet-faced girl.

"Hi." Zelda's face fell.

"Hi," Diego answered. "You come here?"

"Looks like it."

"Me too." Puppy couldn't resist adding to the awkwardness.

"This is Puppy," Zelda said.

"This is Caily."

"Hi," Caily smiled at everyone.

Zelda wondered what to say that wouldn't sound totally stupid. Limited options. "You live around here?"

"162nd Street. You?"

"North."

"Near our offices," Diego said. Zelda blushed and didn't know why. "Well. Enjoy the night. See you tomorrow."

"Bye." Caily followed Diego to the bar, holding both his hands so they swayed behind his back.

Puppy grinned. Zelda flushed.

"He's a sailor. It's work."

Puppy hummed *Anchors Aweigh*. Zelda twisted his pinky until he yelled.

9

As always, John Hazel stepped out of the car by twisting to the left and placing his right leg firmly on the ground. The Gelinium microprocessor never buckled, though he half-expected it to finally give out. Or maybe hoped it would, so he could apply for a special synthetic, realistic-looking leg and have some fun. You had to show decay, chronic pain, emotional turmoil at walking around with metal for toes; the checklist was bewildering. His buddy Chuck from the 238th Division had applied and they just flat-out discouraged him with all manner of questions except how'd you lose your leg below the knee?

Chuck, being the Sgt. Chuck Daniels who swam back and forth to the smoking transport ships to rescue the rest of the company off Calais in '69, had finally, as he'd told the story, overturned the desk, knocking the fucking A18 or whatever number it was clear into a wall, where he threatened to make it an artificial limbs donor.

They denied Chuck his request. They were going to deny him anyway since he was a vet. Like A1s with faces, they didn't want ex-soldiers blending in. They just used the drunk and disorderly charge as an excuse.

Hazel sidestepped a rusted-out lawn mower holding court with assorted other machines past their prime, and walked into the worn-looking country store.

A bell tinkled, which the red-bearded older man with eyes like the muzzle of a .38 ignored, continuing to ponder the crossword puzzle behind the counter.

"Morning." Hazel nodded affably.

The man ignored this, too. Hazel glanced at the shelves of canned food, feeling eyes darting from his back to his Ford sedan, alone in the parking area. Hazel laid three cans of Fenster's YumGood Baked Beans on the counter.

"Good thing I'm driving alone."

The man scribbled out a new word.

"I'll take some bread."

The man jerked his head, inviting Hazel to come around and help himself. John deliberated a moment on the row of crisp, fresh breads.

"What do you suggest?"

The man grunted.

"Yup, all look good."

He laid a loaf of black bread alongside the cans. "How's the licorice?"

The man again silently suggested Hazel should decide. John measured out a mixture of red and black, weighed them and laid the bag on the counter.

"Think that'll do it."

The man put aside the crossword puzzle and started tallying the goods.

"I also need a map."

Cold eyes indicated a rack behind him. Hazel found the state of Massachusetts and tossed it down.

"Heading to Overton."

The man's eyes narrowed ever so slightly.

"Am I going in the right direction?"

"That's what a map's for." The man's voice was surprisingly gentle. He held out his hand for Hazel's Lifecard.

"Be surprised how the quality of maps differs." Hazel slid over the Lifecard. "I do a lot of traveling."

The man finished ringing up and showed John the sum, glowing in the center of the Lifecard, to make sure he was comfortable with the charges. So old school, Hazel nearly smiled. He nodded and took his package, then suddenly tossed an orange wig from his pocket onto the counter. The man's eyes narrowed again, ever ever so slightly.

"Appreciate the conversation," John said, glancing at the blue baseball cap with the criss-crossed "NY" hanging in the corner. "Let's go Yankees."

The tires of the Ford sedan crushed pebbles, kicking them sideways as it eased out of the tiny lot. The engine faded away.

Derek Singh, former Yankee great, original member of the famed Three Amigos, stared at the orange wig for a few long minutes, resting his Gelinium microprocessor left leg on a stool. He limped slightly into the back office, effortlessly shoving aside the heavy desk with his broad back. Singh pulled up a long rectangular piece of wood and looked down at the Vendt sub-machine gun, an orange wig wrapped around the barrel. He picked up the baseball, wedged patiently in the corner.

Why now? Derek chewed on a stick, his trademark during the seventeen-year career that ended on 10/12 beneath the rocket fusillade at Amazon Stadium that ended so much. Singh looked at the orange Miners wig again, the strands knotted all around in a circle. Easy to duplicate. He sniffed. Grandma's clit. Can't easily duplicate the smell of death.

But why now?

• • • •

BY THE THIRD at-bat, Mickey wasn't even trying. Just to confuse the A29, he bounded back and forth between the lefty and right-handed batter's boxes, giggling. The three breakfast of champions he'd slugged down didn't help.

He dribbled a roller to short. Mickey shook his head, skipping back to the dugout.

"I'd never miss a fastball that badly."

Ty gave him a dirty look and headed toward home. At least Cobb was sober. And he certainly wasn't goofing around. Puppy's teeth gritted as Mickey loudly sang *Okie from Muskogee* sprawled on the floor of the dugout.

But Ty was as taken with his youthful persona as Mantle, like two savages seeing their reflections in the water for the first time. He'd spent the first three innings shouting himself hoarse to correct some of the HG Ty's fielding mistakes, such as throwing off the front foot or failing to observe angles heading to the ball. And he charged onto the field when he was called out at second stretching a single into a double, yelling he wouldn't slide like he was pouring himself a fancy glass of champagne; Ty Cobb goes into the base with spikes flashing. Sharpened spikes.

Cobb bounced a grounder to third and chased his HG down the line, screaming for it to speed up and beat the throw. Ty puffed back, leaning over the railing.

"Did you give me the slowest HG you got?" he snarled at the A29.

The robot looked helplessly at Puppy.

"It's the program, Ty," Puppy explained.

"I would've beaten that out. I beat out shit grounders like that my whole career." He reached for the A29, who dashed up two rows, terrified. "Fix the midget to make it realistic or I'll turn you into a goddamn coffee pot."

Cobb stomped into the dugout. A few balls bounced onto the field, then a glove sailed toward first base, followed by a bat broken into three pieces.

Their spirits improved by the end of the game. They celebrated in the clubhouse, Cobb with a three-for-four and Mickey going two-for-three and a walk in their nearly 22nd Century debuts.

"That was a helluva catch I made." Mickey congratulated himself, sitting on a stool naked, sipping a beer.

"You didn't have any wind," Cobb said dismissively. "I had to deal with a gust."

"I had fucking gusts, too. At the last minute."

"Both of you played great," Puppy said, pulling up a stool near their lockers.

"I always played great," Cobb said, ignoring his teammates silently filing out, puzzled by all the excitement.

"Hurry up, the stadium is closing." Puppy gestured about the empty clubhouse.

"I ain't finished my beer," Mickey protested.

"They'll lock us in. The rules."

"Ain't for cleaning up, is it?" Ty sneered.

"Nothing can be moved, remember that," he whispered even though they were alone. "Skeletons, skulls, bullets, whatever is out there has to be kept exactly where it was."

"Why?" Ty asked.

They really don't know. Ty Cobb and Mickey Mantle wouldn't, Puppy reminded himself. He didn't know quite how much to tell them since he wasn't sure why they were here. Maybe he'd give them the topline schoolchild version of Bad People Do Bad Things to Good People. He reflexively touched the thick scar at the base of his neck where his father, flying high in the atmosphere on Virginia Lemon Rum, had mashed his skull with a boot after Puppy returned home from third grade chanting:

"Hate kills

We are more

Feel the love

Come through the door."

They'd taken his father away for a few days until his mother pleaded that he be given another chance as a parent. One child abuse outburst was all you were allowed; not a capital crime like pedophilia, but you lost all rights to your kid which pretty much meant all rights within The Family. Whatever they'd done in The Study, tucked near the Van Cortlandt Park skating rink, worked, because Alvin Nedick never went near him again, always standing back in the shadows of dim resentment.

Puppy waited until Mantle returned after splashing water under his arms from the chipped sink.

"There was a terrorist attack here in 2065 to protest the war. Amazon...Yankee Stadium has been kept open as a memorial to treason and you can go to jail for moving anything out of place." Puppy tapped his watch, suddenly feeling shame. "We gotta go."

"That it?" Ty snarled.

"No. But it's enough for now."

They walked in moody silence along River Avenue.

"Is that robot fixing my program?" Ty abruptly asked.

"I'll talk to him," Puppy said amiably, eager to talk about anything else but World War Three. "Mick, any tweaks to your program?"

Mantle thought a moment as they passed under the El. "I could be a little faster, too."

"Running the bases, fielding?"

"Everything." Mickey warmed to the idea. "Like before I hurt my knees."

"The Commerce Comet," Puppy said in mock awe. "That's the wonder of the HGs. Makes you anything you want."

Ty sized him up warily. "Not what we want, what we were."

"Back in the last century. When was your last game again, Ty?"

"September 11, 1928," he answered slowly.

"And you, Mick?"

He closed his eyes to think. "September 28, 1968, Fenway Park. Popped out. That was it." He looked in pain at the abruptness of it all. Too slow on a fastball and it's over.

"Long time ago. You guys need these HGs to look good, so I'll make sure..."

"Look good?" Cobb scowled.

"Well yeah. I mean, you're like well over a hundred years old."

"Are you saying we can't play anymore?" Cobb thundered.

"Guys. Be realistic." Puppy spread his hands pleadingly. "You really want to take a chance on your legacy being tarnished by reality?"

"We don't need that HG crap," Ty ranted.

"But you're..." Puppy gestured at their old, chubby bodies.

"What?" Cobb's eyes bulged in fury.

"Nothing. The HGs are just so fast," he replied angelically.

"So are we," Ty shouted. "Mick and I are still Mickey Mantle and Ty Cobb."

"That's right," Mickey echoed. "I'm the fucking Commerce Comet. That's how I died and that's how I came back."

Cobb's nose nearly brushed Puppy's chin. He calmed down just slightly. "But we're going to need to practice a little."

• • • •

ZELDA'S MIND GLAZED quickly over the monofilament lines. Or leaders. Why she should've been surprised that her stomach was visiting somewhere near her eardrum, well, surprised her. She'd never been on a boat before. She didn't even swim. Floating on your belly on the East River sewage discouraged most youngsters, though Pablo and Puppy had dived underwater once; they were in the hospital for two days.

But she put on a brave front even when she ran out of Elmer's Ding-Dongs. They sailed straight into the Atlantic Ocean, unfamiliar sea smells filling her nostrils. So much on shore was augmented, sometimes she wondered if she were real. Weather, sunshine, clouds. That was the sun. Those were clouds. This was an ocean. There was hope. Maybe they'd all have to be fish again. Her pretended gill face turned to the sky, drawing an irritated look from Captain Lee, rushing past. He'd been pretty clear about her staying out of the way. Diego had been even clearer about doing whatever Captain Lee said; mopping the ocean might be next.

She found a comfortable chair on the left side, port, she had to remember such things, portside of the fifty-foot ship, tucking her sketch pad under her knees and reclining for a few minutes.

"Threadbin herrings." Diego showed her a bucket of squirming little fish.

"That lunch?" She deeply regretted not bringing a sandwich.

"For the salmon. Bait. You need something to catch something. Or someone. All kinds of bait." He winked broadly, as if worried she or the swooping seagulls might miss it.

Lee cleared his throat disapprovingly and Diego hurried to the right side. Starboard.

"We got drinks if you're thirsty," the Captain said.

"I'm fine. This is really helpful, sir."

Lee grunted and disappeared below, giving Zelda a clear view of Diego's tight butt in even tighter jeans. Oh don't do that, child, she tingled as he tossed his tank top onto the deck, adjusting the nets.

He passed by again, sweaty and chiseled and very smelly.

"The Atlantic Bonito are still around. The Croakers, too. They finally opened up passages. Now with the Alaskan salmon hurrying east. North, then southeast," he corrected himself. "No one's sure what we'll really one hundred per cent find. Might not even be real salmon yet."

Zelda leaned forward. "Are you saying we'll be selling some other fish as salmon?"

"Already do." He looked at her as if she was very stupid.

"I know that, the artificial processing. But we're going to market making a big deal about real salmon."

Diego shrugged carelessly. "Hopefully it's the real salmon. I don't make them. God does."

God. Not a word she often heard. God was discredited. God was Islam and the power of fanaticism, of belief gone wrong, gone deadly, gone genocidal. Religion had a bad name and it was called jihad. Sharia. If the Judeo-Christian God had been such a big bad ass, then why'd we lose? Bet on something else.

She gave Diego a closer look. A closet religo, she decided from the way he held himself with that certain surrender of faith. Fall into the net and God will rescue you from the smelly fish. He seemed happy, singing, tying and untying ropes. Sure. God will make sure you're not some salmon's appetizer tonight, she grinned. Me, they fight over who gets a chubby leg.

He caught her look and smiled back. Zelda flushed and returned to her sketches.

They finally anchored after an hour, where she dozed, hopefully not with her mouth open and drooling. Diego sat cross-legged, watching her. She touched her blouse to make sure all the buttons were in place.

"You snore," he called across the deck. "But not too loudly."

"That's a relief. I wouldn't want to scare the salmon away."

"No worries. They ain't here."

Lee popped his head up the steps. "Tracking says there's a storm due east."

"Shit." Diego frowned and began pulling on the lever to pull up the anchor.

"A real storm?" Zelda asked.

Lee sighed. "Yes, ma'am. We'll be fine."

Other than annoyed winds racing across the bow, the return was smooth. They pulled in just after the 4:05 rains. Half drenched, Zelda waited for Lee and Diego to finish securing the boat for the night.

"Thank you again, Captain Lee."

"You never asked a question." He sounded disappointed.

"Your crew took care of all my needs."

Embarrassed, Lee raised an eyebrow and hurried past.

"I meant these." She waved her sketches at his fading back.

"Can I see?" Diego asked.

"No. They're just creative thought starters. Jumping points to go boom and bang. Raw mental sewage needing to be filtered."

Diego burst out laughing. "That is a lot of shit for pictures of a ship and the ocean."

She smiled sheepishly. "I guess."

"Do you need to get home to cook your sketches in the oven or do you have time for a drink?" he repeated his invitation, once rejected.

Zelda shifted her weight. "How old are you, kid?"

"Old enough," he grinned.

She regarded him through splayed fingers, shaking her head. "Did you really just say that?"

"Yes." He had such a wonderful smile.

10

The Metro North train rambled past the cars creeping along the Major Deegan Expressway, headlights oozing envy. Puppy looked out the grimy window at the line of stalled autos. A favorite game of DV kids was hood jumping. You gained traction on the rear bumper, then leaped spread-eagled onto the roof, clutching the sides. Sometimes the driver would notice half a body blotting out his back window and attack with a hammer; stuck in traffic, they needed a diversion.

Now you jutted your legs back, as if diving, rising up on stiff elbows and hurtling your pelvis forward into a squat on the hood, moving your feet so they weren't squashed by a large tool, etc. You rapped your knuckles triumphantly, once if it was the first car of the day, twice if the second, on and on. Denting or doing any damage was discouraged. Occasionally a windshield wiper made the ultimate sacrifice.

Skilled hood-jumpers could mark seven cars before they had to kick a driver in the forehead. Drivers also had a sub-genre for how many hood-jumpers they could knock off their car.

Puppy had jumped six; that's where he first hurt his right shoulder. Smart move, two days before he was pitching in the borough-wide college championship game at Amazon Stadium.

He glanced back down at the brochure.

"At Basil Hayden's, you put your life in our hands. Our trained staff will make sure you die without any concerns. We make death relaxing, stress-free, just another experience. Let us take you where you're going anyway. Why travel alone?"

The train rocked violently and screeched dead on the tracks. Passengers held onto their seats. An A10 conductor roamed up and down the aisles.

"No worries, everyone. A deer sat on the tracks and now he's no more. We have the finest trains in the world. No worries."

Puppy leaned over, blocking the A10. "How long will this be?"

"Until they remove the head from the front of the train. I'm not an animal expert. But we have the finest trains in the world. No worries."

"I need to get to Brewster by twelve-thirty."

The conductor popped open its old-fashioned watch. "That might be a problem. But we have the finest trains in the world, so no worries, we'll get you there eventually."

"I can't be late."

The conductor didn't need to be told twice. "Job interview's at precisely twelve-thirty?" Puppy nodded. The conductor pursed its lips, annoyed at this inconvenience but eager to show its resourcefulness.

Puppy followed the A10 outside.

"102," the robot called. Another A10 walked forward; the next train station, Bay-view, was a quarter-mile away.

"This one has a job interview," the conductor said.

"That isn't good timing."

"Whether it is or it isn't, it is now."

102 studied Puppy for clues. "Where?"

"Basil Hayden Funeral Home in Brewster. Twelve-thirty."

102 glanced at its black leather watch. "Cutting it close."

"Then why are you standing here?" the conductor shouted, returning to the train as its colleague hustled Puppy into a Metro North transport van.

Job interviews were sacrosanct. A headless deer disemboweled on a Metro North train was no excuse for being late. Other than an immediate family member dying or in critical condition, the applicant dying or in critical condition, or the birth/adoption of a child, there were no excuses. If you couldn't demonstrate sufficient respect to meet a potential employer on time, how could they trust you?

This was only the second job interview of his life. When he'd graduated from Bronx College, the baseball historian job just opened up. The previous occupant died. No one else had applied. Puppy was bright and had been a ballplayer and didn't say anything offensive during the interview with the diffident A26; the job hadn't been worthy of a human selection process.

He made it to the funeral home with seven minutes to spare. Adona Hayden stared grimly at Puppy's application, tapping her thin yellow fingers and finally, wearily, leaning back in the large leather chair in her office. Miniature coffins hung gaily from the walls.

"Here you are, Mr. Nedick. Alive and well."

Puppy nodded gratitude for not being in one of the miniature coffins.

"But why are you here?" Hayden continued. "You're alive. You could be anywhere. Yet you're here."

He ran through a whole list of possible reasons why he was in Basil Hayden's Funeral Home in Brewster, New York, while still breathing.

"I'm losing my job in five months. My friend insisted I had to apply and show perseverance."

Adona smiled. "Were there other openings?"

"None of them sounded interesting."

"Working with dead people does?"

"My friend, Zelda, can be annoying. I thought if I applied for the job that was furthest from my background, it would annoy her."

"Yet I asked to see you."

"I'm a little surprised, too."

Hayden sat on the front edge of the desk, her feet dangling by his knees. "I don't want someone who enjoys death. What kind of crazy person is that? Oh let me fondle a corpse. Because that's probably what you think we do here."

"I, I really don't think you do that."

"What do you think we do, Mr. Nedick?"

"Bury people."

"Just throw them in the ground?"

Puppy took a breath. "There's a process."

"Which only involves the corpse? Because at the end of the day, it's dead flesh. Rotting away. Soon gone, leaving only bones, Mr. Nedick."

He was afraid to ask for something to drink.

"This is about living, Mr. Nedick. The living. Those who lived. This is a new world." Hayden's foot banged into his knee. "We're no longer forced to cremate. The war's long over. We have room for bodies. Grandma spoke at our national Death Care convention last year, it was so inspiring, that one of the most difficult decisions she ever made was outlawing traditional funerals. The mass produced cremations broke her heart."

Puppy wished she'd stop kicking his knees.

"We're back. You could die this very moment. Keel over, Mr. Nedick." Adona squeezed his shoulder encouragingly. "And your family would see you all dressed up. A nice suit, not that rag you have on. Good shoes. Big smile. Not some ashes. A new era of death."

Adona's toe found his shin as she reached around for his application. "I think you could work, Mr. Nedick. Let's go downstairs and see how you do around dead people."

• • • •

WEEDS AND ROCKS streamed over the broken concrete on the playground off Clay Avenue and East 163rd Street. At one end, a bent basketball rim pulled the neglected backboard forward as if trying to leave. Puppy stepped through the mangled wire entrance.

Ty stopped cold. "This is a park?"

"Best we got." Puppy led them in.

"There's gotta be a real field," Mickey said, nearly falling over some blocks. "I don't know why we couldn't use the stadium."

"I told you. It's illegal to practice on off-days."

"That don't make any sense," Mantle persisted.

"Does it make sense to have holograms?"

That quieted them down for a moment.

Cobb doubtfully took in the length of the playground, about a hundred feet. "Who's shagging flies? I can check a swing and send it out of here."

Puppy tossed them each a glove. "Let's play catch first."

"What's this made out of?" Cobb sniffed disdainfully at the pocket.

"I don't know."

"It ain't leather. I only use the finest material."

"This is all I could find." Four weathered, dried-up gloves.

"Well, we ain't using them in a game."

Mickey weaved unsteadily on a vodka cloud. He flipped the ball to Cobb. The two men played catch, slowly lengthening out the distance to about twenty feet, complaining about tight muscles as if greeting an unwelcome friend. Sitting near the entrance, Puppy marveled at the way they threw, even old, even fat. With Mickey, even tipsy.

The fence rattled.

"Afternoon, sir." The Blue Shirt on the other side tipped his hat.

"Afternoon, Officer." Puppy quickly stood.

"What do we have here?" The cop pointed the nightstick at Mickey, chasing down a missed throw.

"New players for the Hawks. They're just getting their arms in shape."

"Here?"

"Nothing wrong with that, is there, sir?"

The Blue Shirt thought a moment and couldn't come up with any infraction over two old panting men dripping sweat, soft-tossing a baseball.

"I thought they used HGs." The Officer brightened at finally finding something odd.

"They do. But there are still humans who bat."

"Then why are they throwing?"

"Warming up muscles. So they can bat."

The Officer frowned. "Is that safe? What if a ball comes out of the playground and hits a pedestrian? Or damages a car?" His mind raced with a lengthy list of disasters.

"We'll be careful. We're just throwing and taking some soft BP."

The Officer frowned again. He didn't like unfamiliar acronyms. "BP?"

"Batting practice. Underscore practice. Seriously, sir, look at them. Do you think they can drive the ball over the fence?"

The cop watched Ty bend over, gasping. "Are you sure it's safe for them?"

"I'm supervising, Officer."

The cop nodded doubtfully. "I'm in the neighborhood if you suddenly need help."

Ty and Mickey stood with hands holding up hips, grimaces too pronounced to conceal.

"How you guys doing?" Puppy asked.

They grunted, offended at his audacity.

He grinned. "Up for a little hitting?"

Mickey examined the chipped bat, knowing it would fail him. Ty waited thirty feet away. The back end of the playground, nestled against an abandoned building, served as the outfield wall.

Mantle motioned Puppy closer. "You're the catcher. Then catch." He tapped the scuffed bat on the invisible catcher's box.

"He's afraid," Ty called out, smiling maliciously.

Puppy did a little grumbling of his own and moved up, anxiously watching Mickey's practice swing arc near his head.

"Give me a damn target," Ty yelled.

Puppy sank. Mickey swung and missed. So did Puppy. He corralled the ball at the other end of the playground. Another pitch. Another swing. Another jaunt down to the 163rd Street end.

"I'm going to be three hundred years old by the time you hit one damn ball," Cobb complained at Mick.

"Because you're throwing crap."

"How can I have a rhythm when I'm waiting an hour for the ball to be found?" Cobb walked over and flipped Puppy the ball. "Pitch."

He swallowed. "I'm good just catching."

Ty shoved Puppy aside and gingerly squatted. "Come on, fool, before my knees lock. I had arthritis."

Out of the corner of his eye, Puppy saw the left side of the fence fill up silently, then the right. More were crossing the street.

Puppy stopped about twenty-five feet away. Mickey waved him further back. Puppy put up his hands at forty feet. Or four hundred feet. Four thousand. Didn't matter.

Eighteen years.

He squirmed, nervously touching his right shoulder to make sure it was there. He went into his tight, economical wind-up. The pitch died half-way, rolling past Mick. Cobb stepped aside. Once the ball stopped, Ty tossed it back with a dainty, underhanded gesture.

"Don't hurt your hand, Gertrude."

His next pitch flared on three bounces behind Mick, who didn't flinch. The ball nestled along the fence.

By now, all three fences were filled by hundreds of silent DV teens in white shirts, the better to show cleanliness, along with crisp blue jeans, black socks and black sneakers. Like a black-and-white shawl, the kids blotted out the surrounding streets. The toes of their sneakers were wedged into the fences, backs straight, eyes expressionless. Straight across. Up and down. A checkerboard of wariness.

"Who's that?" Ty asked.

Puppy smiled faintly. "The neighborhood."

The playground was at the vortex of two high schools: HS 22, where trades were taught so skills like masonry and boot making could eventually be built into businesses to thrive outside the DV, and HS 44, where academically inclined kids, from prospective architects to food engineers, studied and prepared for Reg exams; Puppy's alma mater.

At four-thirty, after school and before part-time jobs, DV kids would patiently roam, searching for curiosities to augment their learning. Look at the bum, imagine how his life could've been different. Why would anyone have kitchen curtains that color? Is that shop window really going to get people to eat dumplings?

Ty shook the fence. "This ain't a public exhibition, punks."

Their perfect balance kept them erect. A freckled-faced Asian kid looked quizzically at Puppy as if he was responsible for this bad behavior.

Puppy grabbed Ty's wrist. "That's considered rude. Not that you care."

"I don't want someone watching me practice."

"People watched you practice your whole career. Let me handle this." He half-shoved Ty back toward Mick and approached the teens. "Sorry. Old. Grump."

They ignored the shorthand.

"Baseball."

Half the fences peeled off; they'd seen enough. Back flipping in The Arc, or landing straight up using The Pole, they steadily wandered away.

Puppy focused on the frecklie kid, who had a look of leading himself. No one led others in Grandma's House; it was all by informed consensus.

"Baseball?" Frecklie frowned. It'd be rude to comment on Ty and Mick groaning slightly as they played catch. The last thing a DV ever did was show disdain for someone's efforts, no matter how pathetic.

Puppy used some shorthand for the catching, throwing and hitting gestures, all tightly contained in miniature moves. Frecklie had no idea what he was talking about. More kids left.

Frecklie stuck out his palm questioningly.

Puppy gave him the ball, which Frecklie flipped, losing control. He reddened, muttering. Puppy firmly placed the ball back into the teen's palm.

"Baseball."

The kid tugged down his right eyelid. Puppy acknowledged the sadness gesture of baseball's demise and pointed at the kid's chest. Frecklie scowled defensively and ran his eyes back and forth like a 'bot reading. Puppy arched his eyebrow and indicated the playground with a questioning shrug.

Frecklie angrily flashed ten fingers ten times to indicate a recent test score. Puppy jutted up his thumb at the academic prowess, wiggling his forefinger like a crawling snail in the air. And tomorrow?

The boy hopped straight down and walked away to join his friends.

"Fun," Puppy called after him.

"Fun always costs," the teen said over his shoulder.

"But a job pays."

Frecklie narrowed his dark eyes and raised an empty right palm. Some more kids also turned, raising up their palms. Puppy grinned.

Some shit never changes.

• • • •

ZELDA YAWNED UNDER her desk. Diego hadn't left until three in the morning and then she couldn't fall asleep. He'd brought quasi-illicit coffee from Mexico; she was still flying on caffeine. Why didn't the planet conquer the Universe when we had real caffeine for fuel, she wondered, her musings about the failures of the human race cut short by Mr. Pietro's legs passing by. She unraveled and followed him down the hall.

"Mr. Pietro, sir. Can I walk with you?"

"Only as far as my office." He reluctantly considered her. "How was your field trip?"

"Very enlightening."

"I can imagine an afternoon at the ocean would be," he said sourly, hoping to lose her by abruptly veering down a corridor.

She kept pace. "I have great ideas for the new campaign. Don't worry. No singing or talking salmon."

He walked a little faster.

"Our New Home Will Come to Your New Home."

Pietro slowed down with puzzled deliberation. "What does that mean?"

"The new home of salmon. The migration from Alaska to the Atlantic."

"Migration?"

"Of the fish. You know how the war threw off the eco-systems?"

"Did it?" he asked sarcastically.

"One of the consequences was salmon relocating."

"Like the refugees from Los Angeles?"

Something about his tone troubled Zelda. But if she worried about annoying people she worked with and knew and socialized, she'd be a mute.

"Without the radioactive quality."

Pietro led them into a conference room, closing the door.

"Why did you ask to go on the boat?"

Zelda hesitated. "So I could do my job better, sir."

"Which is drawing, Ms. Jones. That's your job. To help lead the charge so salmon salad can overtake tuna salad after centuries of second-class citizenship."

"What if the salmon don't show up?"

"Where?" He was flustered.

"In their new home. My slogan is catchy, needs work, but it means nothing if the salmon doesn't come this way. The boat didn't catch anything. Since all the Scottish salmon stays with Muslim Europe, what happens if the Alaskan salmon got lost? A continent is huge and I mean, salmon is tasty, but how good a sense of direction could they have?"

Zelda pressed his hand so he couldn't open the door. Pietro's look wasn't friendly.

"It's important to understand all aspects of our jobs, Mr. Pietro. As you must know, one of Grandma's favorite songs is Pink Floyd's *Another Brick in the Wall*. We can't ever be bricks in the wall, not questioning and challenging and growing."

Pietro wasn't happy about her referencing Grandma. He was even less happy when Zelda began singing *Another Brick in the Wall* complete with brisk dance steps. A curious crowd gathered in the hallway. When Zelda finished, her new colleagues applauded lustily. Pietro's glare sent them scurrying back to their desks, returning to Zelda.

"I don't have any answers to your questions, Ms. Jones. Except there is one answer to mine. According to your employment history, this is the fourth job you've had in three years. If you lose this, you would be officially labelled questionably employable. Do you understand it's in your own best interest, whether it makes salmon happy or not, for you to keep this job?"

Zelda remained alone for a few minutes. A gray-haired woman popped her head inside the conference room.

"I love that song, Zelda." She winked. "We have karaoke outings once a month. Maybe you could be on my team."

"Not if you want to win," Zelda said glumly.

• • • •

LIGHT GLINTED BRIEFLY in the clouds. Sometimes Tomas thought he was the only one who could see the trace of her 'copter. But he knew he wasn't. That's why three stealth 'copters followed her. That's why ten armed men, two with bazookas along with a SAM team, fanned out around the landing field, with five more snipers on rooftops flanking the entrance to Van Cortlandt Park.

Except there were only four snipers today. Running across West 239th Street, Tomas reviewed the orders, his orders, changing every three hours, ten hours, occasionally not at all, predictability was an enemy. Five.

He messaged Artito. *Northeast rooftop now. Serve tea elsewhere.* Tomas slowed, avoiding attention, then limped around the corner, the Gelinium throbbing.

On way, Artito messaged back.

Tomas kicked in the door of the apartment building, scattering glass and horrifying a family of residents. He hit the elevator button and bounded up the old staircase.

Seven flights. His knee throbbed, his breaths came shorter; he pulled his gun. The door to the rooftop was open a few inches. Tomas crouched and burst in, firing off a few rounds.

"It's me, Major," Artito yelled, hiding behind a chimney.

Tomas stayed low. "Did I prefer blondes or brunettes in London?"

"You screwed everyone, Tomas. There's no one up here."

The Major rose carefully to hip height and waited for Artito to come around the corner. The Lieutenant held his gun up, irritated.

"You going to examine my cock next? Sir."

Tomas scowled. "Where's Dano?"

Artito's dark face creased.

"He's supposed to be here." Tomas moved around the rooftop. "Did you check to see if he's dead?"

Artito's eyes lowered briefly. "He's off, sir."

"What do you mean he's off?"

"Orders had only four rooftops covered." He hesitated. "Yesterday was five. Today's Tuesday."

"I know what fucking day it is." Tomas continued searching the rooftop, ashamed a small part of him hoped to find a piece of Dano lying butchered. "He's not here."

"Yes, sir."

"I screwed up."

"Happens, sir."

Not to me. It can't ever happen to me. Yet it just did.

Artito smiled reassuringly. "Your message was encrypted, sir. No one will know."

"Loyalty and all that."

"Only a few of us left, sir."

"And that excuses you not correcting me when a decision is made based on erroneous information?"

"No, sir." Artito stiffened. "That was wrong of me."

"Damn straight. There's a broken lobby door downstairs."

"I'll handle it, sir," Artito saluted somberly.

When Tomas returned to the original landing site, a small two-door car waited, exhaust fumes seemingly generated as much by the anger of the elderly man behind the wheel as from the Chevy engine.

Off a sigh, Tomas walked around to the driver's side. Albert Cheng slowly rolled down the window.

"Morning, First Cousin Cheng." Tomas tipped his head forward slightly.

"Good morning to you, too, Major Stilton." Cheng's wrinkled face twisted scornfully. "Where is she?"

"We investigated a security breach and altered plans."

"Was there one?"

Tomas hesitated. "The information was investigated and rejected."

"Meaning you forced me to reschedule my meeting for no good reason."

"Dismissing a security concern regarding Grandma is always a good reason," he replied coldly.

Cheng didn't care for that answer. "Where is she landing?"

"I can't say," Tomas answered, happy to respond like that. "I'd suggest you reschedule or wait. First Cousin."

Cheng scowled, looking like a doll left in the dryer. He abruptly drove forward, running over the tip of Tomas' left boot.

That's the Gelinium leg, General Cheng. Not that you knew anything about that from behind your desk, Tomas nearly mockingly saluted.

• • • •

ZELDA SLID INTO the seat at the rear table of the brick-walled restaurant. Pablo had been waiting for half an hour. He stared sullenly into his tomato juice.

She kissed him apologetically on the cheek. "Sorry, gorgeous."

Pablo pursed his lips peevishly.

"If this had been in the ancient days, I could've just called you on my portable phone."

"Cellular."

"Or sent a message by the world wide web."

"No one longs for narcissism. Much better this way."

"Like having you in a stinky mood, throwing down tomato juices, pigging out on breadsticks, instead of saying, hello, darling."

He sucked on a tomato-drenched lemon wedge as if he needed to sour up more.

"Do this with your upper lip and see how it feels." Zelda lifted up her mouth in a hideous smile.

He wasn't amused. "You're forty minutes late, Zelda."

"I was getting lashed by my new boss." She made whipping noises, cringing in mock agony.

"Already?"

"I have been there almost a week. My inquisitive mind takes getting used to." Zelda worked on the new breadbasket. "How's the master of the dental world?"

"He's fine." Pablo paused, waiting for the waitress to leave with Zelda's vodka order. "I know Puppy told you."

"What?' Her eyes widened innocently.

"Please. He can't keep a secret."

"We're not supposed to keep secrets from each other, Pab."

"Except this one." Pablo glanced around uneasily.

"Course. So what's the next step?"

"Forget you knowing about it."

"Okay. Okay." Zelda munched on a breadstick. "Anything else we should forget?"

Pablo broke off a piece of bread, pulling out the inside dough. "You're the one who left in the middle of the night."

"I like my own bed."

He sighed slowly. "We just skip over it then?"

"You're like my brother."

Pablo cringed in horror. "Which is expressly forbidden. Incest is a capital offense…"

Zelda squeezed his wrist. "I had a weak moment."

"Thanks. I'm like a comfy pillow?"

"Yeah." She squeezed tighter. "I felt bad about myself, honey. My fat butt. My life."

"So screw around with Pablo and get through the night."

"Yes. That so wrong?"

The waitress brought Zelda's vodka, which Pablo sipped.

"Pab?" She nudged him.

"How I felt clearly doesn't matter."

"I'm here to listen…"

"Let's just forget about it."

"Sure. Emotional suppression is much healthier."

"It's not like it hasn't happened before."

Zelda held up three fingers; he yanked down her hand.

"I can't do things like that anymore, Zelda," he said. "All my emotions need to be focused if, you know, it happens."

"The thing I don't know."

"Yes. If we were exploring a union, that's different. But a one-night stand." He shook his head, slightly horrified.

Zelda blushed. "That'll teach you to get aboard the Zelda Jones slut-a-rama. Sorry I seduced you."

Her voice carried to another table. Zelda stuck out her tongue at the customers.

Pablo took her hand. "You're not a slut. Passion thinks, sometimes wrongly," he quoted Grandma's Twelfth Insight.

"Where would we be without Grandma in awkward moments like this?"

Pablo paused. "We can't ever do this again, Zel. It's too much for me."

"Same here."

"Really?"

"Yes, really, Pablo. I have feelings…"

"I didn't say you didn't."

Zelda looked off. "We did something dumb, we won't do it again and we're sorry. How does that sound?"

"Perfect. And I did enjoy myself."

"I'm a good lay. All the boys and girls say so."

"Yes you are." He frowned. "And I'm not?"

"That's a very egocentric thing for a Cousin Candidate to worry about." Zelda opened a menu. "You're paying, right? Because I'm really really hungry."

Pablo ordered a Bloody Mary.

• • • •

UNLIKE BOCCICELLI, AT least Fisher would let Puppy sit in his office, where he had the option of bruising his lower back and thighs in the medieval furniture. Boccicelli made no pretense at any hospitality. He'd nodded reluctantly when Fisher had sat carefully on the edge of the thick, black leather couch. But the Hawks owner was in a meticulous suit. He looked washed and cleaned.

The Falcons owner was less overjoyed when Puppy planted the butt of his faded jeans on that expensive leather chair and leaned back, wrinkled shirt and all, with a soulful, pleased expression.

"I don't have much time." Boccicelli looked like a mad baker had glued together different doughs. Even his eyes were pasty.

"Neither do I," Fisher chimed in.

"Good thing I talk fast."

They didn't respond to his charming smile.

"I have a great idea to make this last baseball season memorable."

"Who cares?" Boccicelli asked.

"Who cares is right," Fisher added.

Puppy paused to allow his deep concern for their welfare to blanket his face. ""I'm just trying to keep you from qualifying for special assistance from the Sports Commission."

Fisher's eyes glazed in alarm. "What're you talking about?"

"If attendance continues under ten people a game, the business will be considered a failure."

Boccicelli glared. "I never heard of that."

"When's the last time you read the major league baseball by-laws as amended by the Closure and Demolition Act of 2065?"

Boccicelli dreary eyes said never, but he stiffened gamely. "Not for a while. And you have?"

He tapped his chest. "Baseball historian."

"He is," Fisher agreed.

"Despite the destruction of all the major league ballparks, Amazon Stadium will continue to be run as a business as well as a shrine to remember treason," Puppy carelessly tossed out the pertinent clause.

"The Cousins know this is a failure. That's why we're shutting down." Boccicelli was proud of his mental acuity.

"Yes," murmured Fisher like a drum keeping tempo.

"Failure doesn't mean giving up. If you make an effort, that'd be noticed. Failure opens up many doors. I was a DV."

Boccicelli paled. "This isn't a DV scenario. That much I know."

"Are you sure?" Fisher whispered. Boccicelli slapped his clammy hand away.

"Who knows?" Puppy shrugged at the many enigmas of Grandma's House. "The laws can be vague. Maybe I'm over-reacting."

"I think so," snickered Boccicelli.

"Could just be a matter of them freezing any property settlements until it's decided."

"Freezing?"

"But we've paid a lot of money in rent," whined Fisher. "Tell him, Boccicelli."

"Does Grandma reward failure?" Puppy said. "I'm sure your mother taught you that, Mr. Fisher."

Fisher thought about the childhood spankings for mispronouncing a word.

"You were put in this situation by your mother." Puppy waited for Fisher to lift his head from his lap. "And Mr. Boccicelli, didn't you inherit the Falcons from your grandfather? Good, decent, law-abiding heirs…"

"Yes we are," Boccicelli insisted.

"Which will be taken into account. But failing to uphold the value of an inherited business is…"Puppy's voice faded away.

"What?" Fisher grasped his elbow. Puppy's sad eyes painted a dire picture that might include more spankings.

Boccicelli nervously ate a bar of Effie's Chocolate without offering any. Fisher went straight for Simpy's South Dakota Single Malt Scotch. They munched and gulped for a few minutes before Boccicelli wiped his smeared face clean like a boxer returning for a painful last round.

"You mentioned an idea, Nedick," Boccicelli asked haughtily.

11

Every so often, one of the orphans would try crawling under or over the chain-link fence, searching for some way out. The silent sensors went off a good twenty feet before they even approached. A smiling, slightly scolding Parent would wait on the other side, arms crossed, shaking their head. They'd sit the child down on a tree stump suddenly growing out of the ground, subduing the youngster with the magic, and wipe away the tears of a loved friend leaving, the fear they'd never be taken themselves.

That never happened. All the children from Muslim Europe were wanted eventually.

Even though Grandma hadn't arrived, Tomas wolfishly watched the cluster of Cousins gathering on stage for the ceremony. This was the safest place in the country. Twenty stealth 'copters flew in vectors while creaky old M-3 tanks watched on the adjoining hills. HG flower gardens swept up and over in bucolic duplicity.

There was no set timing for a Cousins Adoption. When the children were old enough to learn never to discuss their experiences, they were placed on the Loving List. There was no reward system. There were no good children and bad children, just children who were sometimes good and sometimes bad.

Tomas never quite got the way a Cousin was selected as a new parent; Grandma had once tried explaining over numerous pots of tea, but the metrics, the emotional/intellectual tests just danced over his bald head. Trust always ruled. That much he got, Tomas thought, rechecking the position of his first platoon as Cheng neared in his small purple car.

Trust and love.

Eventually, a Cousin had to have a family, whether their biological own or from someone else. And while a Cousin needed greater skills to lead, they couldn't lead and not be as one with anyone else. The grand dichotomy ruling all of Grandma's Family as her Second Insight: How to show and yet be shown.

As wonderfully as the children were treated in The Camp, they were still children saved from the Allahs. Most of them came from ME orphanages, traded for food. All of them had scars. How long would it take for the scars to show? The trauma of losing parents could be felt in a newborn, much less a two-year-old who watched their father beheaded or their mother raped. Or their father raped and their mother beheaded. Combinations of cruelty tested finity.

Confidence in the ability of a Reg to handle such a situation could be risky. Even training by the Parents didn't guarantee success. Nor did being a Cousin. But they were a Cousin for a reason. So the childless couples bonded with the kids in The Camp.

When the first wave of orphans were rescued just after The Surrender in 2073, some simply didn't adjust. There were stories of children turning on their new parents, friends, teachers. Acts of violence like the twelve-year-old who chopped up his parents and two sisters while screaming Allahu Akbar wasn't isolated, if rarely reported, but the whispers spread. Kindness and generosity and loving fell before the fear of a knife in the chest in the middle of the night.

Some around Grandma even feared the children were plants, brainwashed in the orphanages and sent like ticking time bombs to begin the final Islamic assault by once again poisoning America from within. Remember Los Angeles. Washington. Manhattan.

Grandma would have none of that. Tomas remembered the angry meeting where she nearly twisted off the head of a Second Cousin who suggested, no, insisted the shipment of orphans must stop. Keep them in The Camp, but forever. A compromise was reached. Orphans would continue, but their existence wouldn't be publicized. Private routes would be found. Children would be saved, but secretly. Cousins as parents made perfect sense.

The decoy 'copter hovered directly over the stage. The several hundred children sitting patiently in their white shirts and purple pants gasped excitedly; some applauded as if at the start of a show. Tomas slid into position as the second decoy prepared to land behind the audience. The children stirred, calling out for Grandma, the adults on the stage grinning knowingly.

Tomas checked the security positions. All was quiet. These orphans were especially well-behaved. Surviving terror at a young age was a strong teacher. A third 'copter fluttered along the stage, dipping over the children, who stood and waved happily with more shouts of "we love you, Grandma."

He always hated this part. Alone, Grandma bounded out of her tiny car and sat beside a little boy in the back row. She joined in the applause, waving as a fourth 'copter dashed back and forth. The children slowly recognized her, whispering and nudging while Grandma handed out sweets up and down the aisle like she'd just wandered in, waiting for one of them to tell her what to do.

Today it would be a dark-haired kid around ten.

"Grandma's here!" he sang out.

"Are we covered?" Tomas voice rose over the din. All points quickly reported. A squirrel would've been arrested thirty miles away.

Grandma lifted the boy into her arms. She was so damn strong, Tomas marveled. Grandma's face brightened; her smile was a ray of sun captured in a cup, someone once wrote. The children stood as one, as did the adults.

"Don't I get a kiss hello?" she asked. The little boy peppered her smooth, light yellow face with wet smooches as the rest of the children surrounded her.

"Do we have eyes on her?" Tomas barked. North, south, east and west all answered affirmatively. He still pressed forward nervously until he was by her side; Grandma held two new children while at least five others held onto her flowing purple dress. With a cluck of her tongue, she scolded Stilton for intruding.

Too bad, he thought.

Grandma climbed easily onto the stage, watched by fifty snipers. As the children returned to their seats, Grandma held up a little girl around four, who squealed in sudden delight. Second Cousin Dana Torryes and her wife Cleo jumped out of their seats; Grandma stepped back, beaming, to allow the new family to get acquainted with hugs and kisses before sitting on a simple wooden stool. She waited until all the chocolate had been distributed to the children.

"Dome," Tomas whispered into his comm device.

The invisible protective cone slid down, the stealth helicopter holding a position directly over Grandma. Only she heard the faint hissing as the dome clicked into place. She hated the Dome. She fired a brief glare his way before concentrating on the children; better a scowl than a missile, Tomas thought grimly.

"Are we happy for Freja and her new parents Dana and Cleo?"

The children cheered through their envy. Grandma gently waved them back down with her girlish laugh.

"Families make us happy. There is nothing more important than love," she recited her First Insight. "Nothing gives us greater joy. You might think that chocolate is pretty tasty," this generated some hesitant smiles, "but to feel a mommy and daddy around you, that is what we live for. That is the hardest thing of all."

Grandma cleared her throat. Damn, Tomas realized. I forgot the lime water. Damnit, man.

"All of you are lucky to have escaped to America. All of us are lucky to have you. You have all been through a great deal. I know that. You can cry. Go on. Cry if you want."

She waited for the sniffling to stop before continuing in that gentle voice like fluid in the womb. "You are strong. The stronger you are, the stronger will be the Family. But you must leave behind something. For all that you endured in Muslim Europe…"Grandma sat erect until the collective shivers faded. "For all that you endured, for all that they did to you, remember what you cannot keep here. You brought it, as much as if it were an extra finger." She chuckled at some of the children examining their hands for the additional pinky or thumb.

"It is hate. Hate is natural for our enemies. They worship hatred. But the strong overcome that. The strong know that hate is like a," she paused, searching for the simplistic metaphor. "Like a bad cold. Everyone gets infected. No one can say to you, what's wrong, why don't you hate? Because you will say. I have hated. And now I am above that."

The children squirmed, confused. Grandma smiled. The words were for the Cousins behind her. She felt their unease. So did Tomas, who wasn't even aware of his hand resting on his .38. His eyes landed on Cheng's blank face. Too blank, trying to conceal his reaction. Tomas frowned.

"You're the vanguard of a new Family, my darlings. Does anyone know what vanguard means?"

After a puzzled moment, a blond boy raised his hand. "It means in the front of something."

"Good, darling. What's your name?"

"Dietrich Mueller."

"Lovely name, Dietrich. Where are you from?"

"Berlin." He paused, grimacing. "It used to be in Germany."

Grandma stood.

"Dome up, up, up," Tomas hissed. He didn't want Grandma walking into the wall of the damn cone.

She stopped at the edge of the stage. Tomas breathed a little easier. "It is still Germany, Dietrich. It will always be Germany. And Denmark." She nodded at Freja. "Or Paris. London. Madrid." Grandma's voice thundered and, as always, Tomas half-expected lightning to strike.

"Someday, you will return. As part of this vanguard of ideas. A vanguard that will conquer the world like no other weapon."

Grandma's blazing eyes connected with Tomas's. His head ached.

• • • •

ALL THEY NEEDED were streamers, Cheng grumbled silently, watching the children waving candles at Grandma's departing 'copter. Next time fireworks. Oh no, too much old America. Dare not do that. Someone might wave the flag.

The First Cousin was in a foul mood and Hazel being late only aggravated it. Just being here aggravated him. Needless nonsense, wasteful showmanship. If you had nothing to do all day since someone else was running the damn country, then maybe this was a useful allocation of energy, followed by soaking down in a bio-regen bath and letting your toady shampoo your hair.

And how the hell did Lenora have her own hair at her age? Cheng angrily ran his fingers over his thinning scalp, finding another reason to be irritated.

Hazel passed through three checkpoints, posted every five feet outside the sitting 'copter. His press pass, a large square dangling around his neck, stamped him sufficiently; even in a closed ceremony, reporters couldn't roam about without identification as if they were ordinary people. No one trusted them.

The First Anti-Parasite Laws originally outlawed all media, but Cheng made a persuasive case that they could be useful, if watched. Grandma, ever eager for openness, agreed. If they didn't question, they were no better than the Allahs. But how to maintain honesty in a job that begged for duplicity? No one wanted a repeat of their dangerous unchecked power; all journalists were interrogated on a monthly basis for signs of personal bias seeping into their reports. Not quite on the level of the police monitoring potential pedophiles, but not far, either. They are what they are because of what they do.

"Apologies, First Cousin." John bowed insincerely and half-hopped onto the opposite seat in the 'copter cabin. "The adoption scene always touches me."

Cheng rolled his eyes, but Hazel continued as if he were alone.

"I didn't have any sweets and hugging arms when I got to America. Just rolled down the gangplank in a wooden cart and got dumped in front of a Purple Gown. 'Member them?"

"Yes." Albert was already bored.

"They all had moles on their cheeks. Ugly mothers. Not like the ones today. Took us away like we were yesterday's garbage. In a way, we were, reminders of what was coming from the Allahs. Cleaned out France of too many Christians. Already made the Jews disappear."

"How can you remember? You were only two years old," Cheng snapped.

"Beaten by my older adoptive brothers, the kids in the 'hood in Boston. Called a retard, spy, Camel. Me." He tugged on his blond hair.

"The fondness of childhood memories." Albert sneered. "Yet look how wonderfully you turned out. A respected vidsports personality."

Hazel stretched his Gelinium leg so it lightly brushed Cheng's shin; he grinned inwardly at the First Cousin's discomfort. The Fake General's discomfort, he thought acidly. "With a few bumps along the way."

Cheng leaned back with a deadly stare. "It would give me great joy to hear your life story, Hazel."

"But you're busy."

"No, I don't care. Anything?"

"Tomas Stilton never left the country."

Cheng's eyes fluttered closed. "He did. You just lost him."

"I have someone in his security guard…"

"He left." Cheng's rheumy brown eyes drilled into Hazel.

"How do you know?"

Cheng couldn't very well explain Tomas had activated his A3 double to cover himself. "Did Derek Singh respond?"

"He will eventually. And then I'll be invited to talk…"

"And will say what I tell you. Hopefully we can catch this now, before Grandma goes too far." Hazel waited patiently. "She's altering the school curriculum."

"Again?"

"This time it's significant."

John automatically tapped the vidrecorder lashed onto his left shoulder. A journalist would vidrecord his own funeral, Cheng thought wryly.

"That crap she threw out today will be in there," the First Cousin said.

"Grandma's always talked about overcoming hate."

"This is different."

Hazel's eyes narrowed. "How?"

"I've given you enough."

"You've given me nothing, First Cousin. I've given you everything. Trust and love."

The First Cousin frowned and tapped on the cockpit door and the 'copter slowly rose; he grinned at Hazel's uneasiness. "I'll drop you off, don't worry."

Hazel glanced down at the fading treeline.

Cheng handed the reporter a slim sheet of paper filled with Grandma's tight neat scrawl.

VANGUARD FOR INTRODUCTION TO SCHOOLS:

- Teach origins of anti-Muslim legislation of 2030s and impact on society
- Teach origins of anti-Muslim immigration laws of 2040s and impact on society
- Teach origins of Muslim deportations of 2050s and impact on society
- Teach restrictive immigration laws of 2060s including impact on society
- Teach Arab history
- Introduction to the Quran

It took Hazel a few moments to be able to physically hand back the paper. He was pale.

"You can't let this happen, Cheng," Hazel shouted.

Two Black Tops stood in the doorway of the cockpit with Pflia machine guns; Cheng brusquely waved them back inside.

"She's letting in some of the Camel refugees, isn't she? Bullshit dissenters, we all know the stories, poor fucking things who don't want to squat to Mecca and bugger little boys and only want freedom. That's what she's up to, isn't she?"

Cheng wished it were only that.

12

"Touch my ass again and you'll be pissing out of your ear." The full-figured woman wearing Puppy's black bathrobe waved a frying pan like a tennis racket.

Puppy dropped both bags of groceries onto his living room floor and froze.

Ty helped up Mick, angrily wiping the blood from his mouth.

"Bitch," Cobb growled.

"You want a piece of me, too, Grandpa?" She clenched her groin.

No, Puppy thought. No. This was not possible.

The woman suddenly sneered at Puppy. "Think you can explain how to turn on the shower?"

How could this be?

She rapped the frying pan against Puppy's head, and not gently, either. "Shit for brains, you mute?"

"Mooshie."

"The lips work. Excellent. Maybe the hands and feet are next. Shower, bubblehead. I smell like old farts. And clean clothes would be nice. Something not so shabby." She plucked at the frayed sleeves.

"Mooshie Lopez," he said dully.

"I bet you're the smart one of the group."

"Watch her," Ty warned. "I'd hit the chiquita but I don't hit women."

"Don't let that stop you." Mooshie loosened the belt loop.

Ty considered the swelling around Mick's mouth and backed off slightly. Lopez grunted and threw the pan into the sink.

"I don't do powdered eggs, either."

She headed into the bathroom, Mick and Ty warily giving way. Stunned, Puppy followed and leaned against the sink, staring. Mooshie waited impatiently.

"You want a peek?" She tugged at the bathrobe.

"Please. No."

"Don't think I'm good looking?" Lopez self-consciously brushed back her thick black hair.

"Of course I do, I mean, you're…right?"

Lopez laughed that baritone of joy, the Mooshie roar, the happiness that could knock down a lamp post, the laugh of love that Grandma had recorded as the sign-off to the vidnews every night. Sleep well my darlings and don't forget to laugh.

Soon Mooshie's laugh had become a signature. A new line of shoes. You want them to make you happy, don't ya? Cue Mooshie laugh. That artificially processed cheeseburger hit the spot? Cue Mooshie laugh. Wouldn't it be nice to get away for a weekend in Albany at Hudson Inns? Cue Mooshie laugh.

Puppy smiled weakly. Mooshie cupped his chin.

"I don't understand it, either, handsome. But here I am and I smell like dirt." She tugged aside the shower curtain.

Puppy headed directly into the bedroom, ransacking the drawers. Mick and Ty watched from the doorway.

"Who's the chiquita?" Cobb flicked a cautious eye toward the loud singing. Mooshie was all over *Street Fighting Man*.

"Mooshie Lopez." He was annoyed by their puzzled looks. "Mooshie Lopez. The greatest baseball player of all time. Who you had to hear of."

Unless you really were dead. Because Mooshie played from 2041 to 2065.

"She slapped me," Mick complained as if Puppy were a Blue Shirt and would produce a pair of handcuffs.

"No doubt well deserved."

Puppy left a blousy blue Donuts Rule t-shirt, black boxer shorts and a pair of jeans by the door.

"There are clean clothes outside here, Ms. Lopez."

"Thanks, gorgeous," she called back. "More soap would be nice."

He dropped a fresh bar on the clothes, added bottles of shampoo and conditioner, and rushed into the kitchen, making a fresh pot of coffee. Lopez returned, struggling with the jeans zipper.

"A little tight. Got anything else?"

"Give her your fat clothes," Mick snarled.

She tossed her hair defiantly. The Mooshie flip. Runners in scoring position, key moment in the game, cap comes off, crowd sizzles, screaming with anticipation, toss the hair side to side, crowd is about apoplectic, back and front, curls circling her head like a spider's web, stadium's wobbling from the din, opposing team's frantic, panicked, *she's flipping the hair*, cap back on and with a whoosh the ball's rocketing into the right field bleachers.

Mick and Ty backed away as she sat down with a derisive snort.

Puppy fried up some crumpled Edison's Crackers in oil and placed the plate down, carefully setting out the knife and fork. Mooshie grinned her famous gums-and-all grin.

"They still make this?"

"It's not easy to get. There's a place on College Avenue. I think the guy stockpiled a cache during the war."

Mooshie speared a bite and lolled her eyes happily. She peered at Mick and Ty as if just seeing them. "Who are these old farts?"

Remember there's a logical explanation for why you're introducing them. "Mooshie Lopez, this is Ty Cobb, and the man with the roaming hands is Mickey Mantle."

Mooshie chewed. "Hall of Famers."

"That's right," Cobb snarled. "I was voted in the first class of eligibility."

"As you should've been."

Cobb brightened. "Finally, some who knows who I am."

"Great great hitter. I know. I broke your old record for hits. Oh wait. Pete Rose had did that already. Ah, well, I broke that sucker's, too."

Cobb's face fell.

"And I also stomped the shit of your lifetime batting average. .370." She proudly tapped her chest. "And you, farm boy." Licking the last of the crackers off the back of her hand, Mooshie turned to Mantle. "I broke your record for most home runs by a switch hitter. Oh yes. I also set the record for most home runs by any player ever. 810 homers."

Mickey gulped.

"Along with winning 283 games." Mooshie held out her cup. "More coffee, handsome." She grinned. "I forgot your name."

"Puppy Nedick," he said hoarsely.

"Puppy. I get the bedroom, of course."

"She's staying here?" yelled Ty.

Mooshie reared back her fist and the two old white guys fled into the bathroom.

• • • •

PUPPY BUZZED FEROCIOUSLY on Zelda's outside bell. She finally answered.

"Yeah?"

"It's me."

"What do you want?" she asked anxiously.

"I have to come in."

"Now?"

"Yes. Now. Zelda. Now."

Zelda paused inside the intercom. "Can it wait half an hour?"

Puppy shivered in the cool air. He'd left his warmest jacket for Mooshie.

"No. It's important. Huge."

Zelda swore softly.

He waited outside. Zelda lived in the Highbridge district, populated by quiet little apartment buildings where everyone exchanged big neighborly smiles and then hid inside their homes. As he stood there, seven people passed with kindly comments about the abrupt April chill. After ten minutes, he was about to buzz more angrily when that sailor kid from the bar came out, smiling sheepishly.

"Hi, Puppy." Diego shook his hand warmly. "Sorry for the delay. You can go up now."

"I don't know why you couldn't wait." Zelda padded into the living room in an oversized sweatshirt designed with birds. She grudgingly dropped a bag of Krusty Pretzels on the coffee table.

"Now I understand." Puppy smirked.

"We were just talking."

"Whatever you say." He held up the empty bottle of South Carolina cabernet.

Zelda threw a couch pillow at him. "I say the truth."

"I can't talk when you're stinky."

She padded off into the kitchen and returned with a bag of Oregon Sallie's oatmeal cookies, which she cradled, eating slowly.

"Fine, be however you want to be, whatever." He took a deep breath. "Mooshie Lopez is in my apartment."

"Oh." Zelda started on cookie number three.

"Did you hear what I just said?"

"Yes. You interrupted a date with a sweet guy for another hallucination."

"Are Ty and Mickey hallucinations?"

"You're right. They're real and now they let in another DV."

Puppy leaned forward angrily. "It's Mooshie. I'm telling you. It's fucking Mooshie. I know it. I mean, the gestures, the phrasing, everything."

"Because no one knows how Mooshie Lopez talked." Zelda clenched her groin in classic Mooshie-style disdain. "All you had to do was watch one of the zillion vidclips."

"No one could be this good."

Zelda opened her mouth in mock rapture.

"Ty and Mick and Mooshie have come back. Stop laughing, Zelda. For some reason, I know not why, they have returned. Stop the ghost moaning. I want you to come over and meet her. Interrogate all you want. You'll see. You know her in and out as well as I do. Probably more because I didn't dress like Mooshie as a teen."

"You did once." Zelda laughed.

"And I was lovely. Will you come over?"

"Not now."

He clasped his hands. "Please."

"Don't you see I'm upset?"

"Yes. Do you see I'm upset that you won't believe me?"

Zelda sighed. "Tomorrow. Maybe."

"Not maybe…"

"Fucking tomorrow." She smoldered with two cookies in her mouth, looking like a petulant squirrel.

"Want to talk for a few minutes why you're upset?"

Zelda shook her head, her eyes glistening. Puppy reached for her hand. She threw a cookie at him.

Diego was sitting cross-legged outside the building on the stoop, waiting. He bounded up respectfully.

Puppy scowled. "What'd you do to her?'

"Nothing." Diego stiffened.

"You obviously have a guilty conscience to be waiting here."

"Stand down, man."

Puppy exhaled as much to calm himself as offer up a silent apology. "How about a walk?"

They turned up Ogden Avenue, passing a few late-night delis closing to make the midnight curfew and join the other shuttered stores.

"So she's okay?" Diego finally asked.

"Actually she's pretty upset."

"You shouldn't have insisted on coming up," Diego said. "We were in the middle of something."

"Maybe I had a good reason. Look, kid."

"Diego."

"Diego. I'm not answering any deep, personal questions about Zelda. And I'm not getting involved in her relationships."

"Who asked you to?"

"You did."

Diego shrugged sheepishly as if he'd forgotten. "I like her. Just so you know. I like her."

Puppy relaxed slightly. "Me, too."

"She says you're like brother and sister."

"Better because we chose each other," he contradicted Grandma's Twenty First Insight about blood ties.

"I'm trying to understand her." Diego floundered a little. Puppy felt bad for him. He'd spent more than twenty-five years understanding Zelda with very mixed results. "I'm not after sex."

"See, I don't want to have this conversation…"

"I like her." Diego tapped his chest, then his temple. Puppy repeated the shorthand. Diego smiled, relieved.

"I told her that and she threw a shoe," the young man said wonderingly.

Puppy laughed. "She likes throwing things."

"It's very appealing."

"As long as you duck." Puppy hesitated. "I'd do anything for Zelda. Anything. But as I learned years ago, she's going to do what she does and it's more often I'm there with the proverbial shovel cleaning up, instead of helping at the start."

"Do you think I'm stupid to chase after her?"

"You could make a good case for the idiocy of both relationships and loneliness."

Diego paused. "Does she have anyone else in her life?"

Puppy shook his head. The kid's sweet. And a DV. Since Zelda's batting average in lovers was about .100, maybe he could help. It's probably a big mistake.

"You and I didn't talk," Puppy cautioned.

"Oh no," Diego said eagerly, tapping his lips. Puppy touched his ear doubtfully. Diego squeezed his tongue. There were few stronger DV assurances.

"Show Zelda how you feel, but be prepared for her to push back. Knowing," he wagged his finger, "that she wants space, at the same time also wants you to show how much you want her."

Diego's eyes crossed. "That's not easy."

He chuckled. "Buckle up, young man."

Did he just call someone a young man?

• • • •

CLARY SANTIAGO SQUEEZED into the small passageway, rusting nails scratching her forehead. Rotting wood drifted down like foul-smelling snow. Her back bumped against the back wall; she had nowhere to go. As the door handle slowly turned, Clary chambered her right knee into her chest; if only she'd been able to do that when they'd torn off her clothes. The first time.

Her bare heel slammed into the Allah's forehead. He grunted in pained surprise. Clary re-loaded her foot, squinting through the pale shadows for his nose, mouth. Any target to cause him pain.

"Stop that," Azhar hissed.

Clary kicked with both feet, baring her teeth.

"Stop. It is Azhar."

Clary panted, creating icy puffs in the cold Spanish night. She went to kick again, but less certainly.

"Azhar, see?" He lifted himself higher on the ladder and stuck his angular, bearded face into the hiding place.

She frowned. He was the kind one. But the others were kind at first. They smiled and gave her chocolate. Then they held her down.

Allahu Akbar, they kept saying.

Azhar left for a moment, returning with food sloppily piled on a metal tray. He poked the fork to re-arrange the eggs and bread into something appetizing, then placed a glass of milk by her right leg. Clary tensed. She had a clear shot. She could break his nose. But she didn't want to die hungry.

"I won't tell anyone where you are." Azhar tenderly reached for her ankle, stopping as Clary recoiled like a frightened animal. Which she was. You poor child, he thought. Allah, cover your eyes. I can only do what I can do.

He offered the fork. Instead of driving the utensil into his forehead, the eleven-year-old grabbed the plate and devoured the food with her fingers, glaring as if Azhar were poisoning her. Clary held out the plate. "Mas."

"Later." He smiled gently.

"Mas," she repeated as if he were the one cowering in the attic.

"Later, child."

Clary snarled. Azhar fumbled in his pockets until he found a couple sticks of gum, which she chomped into nothing.

He returned to the main dining room in the El Ciudad Orphanage just outside Barcelona. Two bearded, black-robed Guardians looked up from the card game with angry disappointment.

"Where's the girl?" growled the pock-marked Ali.

"Sick."

"So? Hamza likes them sick." Ali grinned lecherously at a portly man with bad teeth, who acknowledged his taste with a crooked, hungry grin.

Azhar wanted to rip the hair from their faces, one strand at a time. He managed a comradely laugh.

"Not like this one."

Ali shrugged. "Get the new German. Her mouth is perfect."

That set off another avalanche of vile laughter. Azhar slammed down the coffee cup, turning their laughter into menacing silence.

"Is that a yes, my Guardian, I will do what Allah wants?"

Allah does not want this, Azhar's eyes fluttered closed. He cannot want this.

"Captain Mustafa?"

But the girl is an infidel. She will be gone soon like the others and all you will remember is she kicked you in the forehead and would've cut out your heart if you hadn't fed her. Still would. She hates you. All the children hate you. As you should hate them since they are your enemies and would gladly kill you and your sons and your wife.

Azhar found enough strength to meet Ali's suspicious stare.

"My volunteer shift is over, Guardian. I must return to my boat to make money for my family and our people, praise Allah."

Ali frowned in half-drunken thought, then abruptly abruptly clasped Azhar's shoulder as if they were old friends. "Go then. Hamza will fetch the German."

Hamza rose with an eager grin. Mustafa turned away in shame.

13

Anyone could wander into the spacious Cousins Living Room. It was encouraged to the point of being mandated. At least three times during their school careers, children went on field trips to a Living Room, prodded if necessary to ask questions and voice opinions. Coming home and telling your parents you forgot to introduce yourself to a Cousin was the only "unofficial" excuse a parent ever had for smacking their child's bottom.

The Lobby was open every day from 6AM-1AM; blankets were left in a large container outside for anyone showing up too early or too late, though Blue Shirts often patrolled the area, providing refreshments and pillows or just a friendly nice-to-finally-meet-someone-from-fill in the city chat. Inside, a liberal amount of free food and drinks were stacked against a wall, purple lounge chairs scattered neglectfully in the laconically casual manner of a hastily arranged, endless town hall meeting.

Some couples had their wedding receptions there, strident arguments about trusting Canada blending into a wedding dance; many an innocent sibling has caught the bouquet. There could be a funeral service tucked behind a demonstration of the latest SC broccoli casserole stil steaming from Schenectady, an impromptu speech about the need for legislation to govern sidewalk repair or even the occasional fist fight, almost always an attack on a Cousin, at which point visitors would step aside to give them room.

When the Living Rooms first opened in 2066, siblings started taking Cousins directly into their homes to discuss the conduct of the war, the propriety of different haircuts (multi-colored dreads and bleached crew-cuts were hot then), recliner chairs versus love seats, pretty much everything and anything. Helpless about denying someone time, Cousins found themselves eating eight, nine, ten meals a day, wandering around in mismatched clothing gifts, a scarf over a t-shirt, three pairs of socks, sleeping very little.

Grandma put a stop to that during a *Sleep Well My Darlings* talk. Using dolls (actors were forbidden for anything that might confuse reality with fiction), Grandma patiently explained that everyone had a role in The Family, but your job couldn't prevent someone from doing theirs. In what became the famous "If Grandpa snores, how can I think?" vidcast, Grandma demonstrated that even though Grandpa was noisy, that was no excuse for Jeddidiah not to study. She had to learn. Grandpa needed his rest. If Jeddidiah woke Grandpa, then he wouldn't be able to think because he was too tired. Yes, an extra bedroom for Grandpa would be wonderful, but the only way to get a larger apartment would be through better jobs and better jobs only came through hard work and if you were too tired to work...

That saved Cousins from obesity and finding forty hours in a day to do their jobs, but nothing about the crowds; Puppy waited nearly twenty minutes to get past the siblings who'd surrounded a lanky Third Cousin admitting there was consideration to adding another rain shower in the middle of the night pending research on the effects of disrupting children's sleep. The issue of better railways came from a couple who said they'd spent two days traveling from Ohio for a glimpse of Grandma and well, the facilities weren't up to their barn. Third Cousin Bunyasarna found that unacceptable without blaming anyone for the inconvenience, except referencing the Allahs, as if they still lurked by train tracks, planting C-4 explosives.

Finally Puppy squeezed up the steps to the Third Cousins rooms, dropping in on a few more conversations between Cousins and siblings on the lack of good painting supplies in Wisconsin, a suspected illegal rodeo in Wichita and an elderly woman who insisted she had proof that Allahs were really Martians; a Cousin patiently read her fifty-three page report with considerable gravity.

Puppy shyly entered the ten-by-twelve foot office dominated by a basketball backboard. A miniaturized football field ran wall to wall lengthwise; footballs and helmets sprouted like cacti on the modest purple rug.

Sport Commissioner Elias Kenuda, well over six foot, broad with a massive head, fired a jump shot into the basket. Hazel sat on the sole chair, legs crossed at the ankles, shaking his head.

"Never touched net," Kenuda insisted, his long dark hand swallowing up the ball.

"I heard some."

"You heard voices. Not net." Kenuda frowned at Puppy. "Did you hear the ball graze the net?"

"I can't say, Third Cousin."

Kenuda sighed and concentrated on dribbling behind his back. Hazel watched Puppy with a curious smile.

"I think he's your next appointment." Hazel winked at Puppy, as if a Cousin would dare schedule a real appointment with a sibling.

Elias loosened his tie with his left hand and hooked a clean shot with his right. "Grandma's earrings, that was silent. I don't want to hear disagreement from either of you."

Puppy joined Hazel in an enthusiastic nod.

"Good." Kenuda sat on the edge of the desk, smothered with sports equipment. He fiddled with a football. "What can I do for you?"

Puppy shifted nervously.

"Relax. He's not nearly as imposing as he wants you to think," Hazel said.

Kenuda glared in mock severity. "Actually, I'm worse."

"I'm Puppy Nedick, the baseball historian."

Kenuda frowned very deeply.

"He works for you, Elias," Hazel helped out.

"Many people do. I try to know everyone. When have we met?"

"Never, sir."

Kenuda took this as Puppy's fault. "Why?"

He shrugged, looking at Hazel for help.

"Because he's the baseball historian." Hazel laughed. "Why would you need to meet him?"

Kenuda nodded gratefully. "But now you're here, Mr. Nedick."

Hazel gestured for Puppy to talk or be gone.

"I'd like authorization to use real people in this baseball season."

Elias frowned and looked at Hazel. "What does he mean, John?"

"I think, and correct me if I'm wrong, Puppy, but you want to have more people as players."

Puppy hesitated to correct his new ally. "Close, Mr. Hazel."

John beamed at being recognized without an introduction.

"I want to use all human baseball players. No HGs. The players hit, run and catch."

Kenuda burst out laughing; Hazel eyed Puppy carefully.

"Like real athletes?" the Commissioner asked.

"They are."

Kenuda's smile faded. "You're comparing a baseball player to a football player? Basketball player? Boxer…"

"What he's saying..." Hazel jumped in.

"Let him say what he's saying. If he can."

Puppy glanced at the football helmets stacked on a shelf like beheaded 'bots. "They're not even close to those athletes. They can just do what they can do. Which probably isn't much. But it's the final season. I thought it'd be fitting."

"It'd be fitting to have them mowed down at the last game." Kenuda scowled, reining himself in off a look from Hazel. "What would this consist of?"

"Not much difference. I mean, financially. There are enough players. We'd need more gloves. More bats. A few extra balls."

"It's already adding up."

"I'm sure there's some equipment lying around somewhere," Hazel said. "So much was seized for evidence. It's gotta be in a warehouse somewhere."

Kenuda twirled the football and peered at Puppy. "Why the request?"

Puppy looked at the mute, mocking helmets again. "It's not a real memory shrine unless it provokes real memories. HGs don't do that."

Kenuda glanced at Hazel, who shrugged agreement on Puppy's point.

"I think there's more."

He met the Commissioner's accusing eyes. "I love baseball. I played, but hurt my shoulder so I couldn't continue. I guess it's all wrapped up, somehow."

"Things usually are, somehow, whether they should be or not," Kenuda conceded. "Even in this instance. But you don't have any legal right to ask this. The owners should be coming forward." He looked at Hazel.

"Fisher and Boccicelli," John said distastefully.

"Yes." Kenuda rolled his eyes. "I understand why you came instead of those worms." He frowned. "I'll let you know."

Puppy inhaled. "When, Third Cousin? The season's already underway." He felt Hazel's approving grin.

Elias slowly smiled. "Soon, Mr. Nedick." He flicked another shot cleanly through the net.

• • • •

TY LAID HOTELS on his yellow properties with an imperial flair, sneering around the table. "You're getting squeezed, senorita."

"You wish I'll squeeze you, Gramps." Mooshie rattled the dice and ignored Zelda's pointed stare, as she had for the past hour since Zelda had first come in, gasped slightly and sat on the couch, eating through a bag of Popping Popcorn.

Blushing, Ty angrily turned to Zelda. "I'm sorry, but I would not."

"What?" Zelda kept staring at Mooshie.

"Mix the races."

Puppy warned Zelda to stay put, and tapped Mooshie's arm. "It's your turn, Ms. Lopez. I don't mean to rush you."

"You rushed us," Mick complained.

"Because we ain't famous," Ty snarled.

"You are. Just not as famous as me."

Mooshie rolled a six, slowing her silver plane down as if about to crash into a bridge. Ty's smile went around to the back of his head.

"Now look at this." Ty chortled. "Look where the great Moosie…"

"Mooshie," Puppy icily corrected him.

"Mooshie has landed. On Park Place. On a hotel. Owned by whom?"

"It's yours, Ty," Mantle said helpfully, who had only an empty six-pack and twenty bucks.

"Mine. Mine. Mine." He waved a fistful of dollars. "Pay up, senorita."

Lopez grudgingly counted out the multi-colored dollars; Ty licked the tip of his fingers greedily.

Mooshie finally returned Zelda's stare. "It's me, honey."

Zelda tilted her head, mutely studying Mooshie for the fiftieth time. Lopez angrily gestured Zelda and Puppy into the bedroom, slamming the door.

She grabbed her groin. "She going to do this all night because otherwise I'm leaving."

"Zelda's a little…"

"Zelda has a voice," Jones said evenly. "Zelda's just a little curious, because Zelda is not quite the hopelessly romantic gullible…"she couldn't think of another adjective…"person like Puppy."

Mooshie sprawled onto the bed, leaning on her right side. "What do you need to know?"

"Who you are."

"Here I thought you were a big fan."

"Do your Mooshie for her, Zel," Puppy encouraged.

Lopez grinned. "Go ahead, chickie. Do me."

Zelda gave Puppy a dirty look. "And then I return to my questions."

"Sure, sure." Mooshie showed more gum.

Zelda hesitated, then squirmed her shoulders side to side. She leaned forward, right hand on right knee, foot pawing the pitching rubber. A sneer curled her face like a fist; Mooshie chuckled. Then Zelda scooped up imaginary sweat from her chest, licking it off droplet by droplet before kicking her leg up and firing a fastball, howling and clenching her groin in the trademark gesture of Mooshie triumph. Or disdain.

Puppy applauded lustily.

"Not bad." Mooshie smiled. "Your girlfriend is kind of cute."

"I'm not his girlfriend."

"Still cute."

"He had nothing to do with it."

Lopez roared. Zelda's resolve weakened slightly before the incomparable, distinctive laugh.

"You're a good actress," Zelda persisted.

"Thanks. I got nice notices in those two flicks. Need the names or you'll say anyone could look them up?"

"*Hills over Hell* and *Mr. Patricio Gets His*," Puppy referenced the two starring vid-movie roles at the height of Mooshie's career, quoting the dramatic last line of *Hills*. "I'm going down that hill and killing me some Allahs. Who wants to join me?"

"They were good." Mooshie rolled easily off the bed. "But nothing I say is going to mean anything to Zelda."

"Because you're dead. One million people attended your funeral."

"That's all?"

Barricades were trampled. Blue Shirts retreated in fear. A simple casket triggered riots across America with curfews in just about every city.

Zelda scanned Mooshie again, finally turning to Puppy. "It could be wonderful facial reconstruct."

Mooshie suddenly poked Zelda in the chest. "I'm losing my patience."

"Truth isn't easy."

"What do you know about truth?"

"That when you're dead you're dead."

"Except I'm not. And don't ask how because I don't know."

Their heated faces were inches away.

"Turn around, Puppy," Mooshie said firmly.

He shook his head, worried. Both the women's fists were cocked. Zelda might be carrying her blade.

"I said turn around," Lopez hissed.

Puppy obeyed.

Mooshie slowly unbuttoned her blouse. "If you're such an expert on Mooshie Lopez, then you probably saw all my vidmovies. I mean all of them."

Lopez's blouse landed by Puppy's feet.

Oh shit.

"Like the ones I did underground near the end. What were they, Puppy?" Mooshie's hand reached behind for her bra clasp.

"*Passion Play* and *Dark Depths*," Zelda said, stopping Lopez from undoing her bra. "I don't want to see your tits. Maybe just a little. Let me hear you sing first. Not the theme songs. The one where you're putting your clothes back on in *Passion*. Mooshie Lopez never missed an opportunity to entertain an audience."

Puppy risked a beating and turned, convinced someone landed a gut punch. Mooshie's hands came to her heart, palms rubbing. Her dark eyes fluttered half-shut.

"When they say they want you

"They really want this."

Her voice lashed out in pain. She tossed aside her bra and grabbed her large breasts, legs spread defiantly, hair flipping side to side, back and forth.

"Because I will never let them have this

That is mine."

Mooshie's hands fell to her side and she waited. Zelda's mouth trembled. That was the voice, the anguish. She'd played that song over and over, falling asleep to it, waking up to it. An anthem of adolescent agony. If Mooshie could have her heart broken, maybe she could survive, too.

"I sound like shit," Mooshie rasped.

"Well, you've been dead for thirty-two years," Zelda said softly, slowly clapping.

Puppy stood by his dresser, hands clasped, trying not to stare at Mooshie's incredible breasts. He'd also had his own anthem of adolescent needs.

14

Mooshie wrapped Puppy's bulky jacket tighter around her waist, trying to stop the shivering as she hurried past the unfamiliar buildings she should recognize along the desolate Grand Concourse.

165th Street. 166th Street.

She looked around cautiously before approaching the 167th Street subway entrance. Rotting wooden boards covered the staircase. Lopez slid sideways around and underneath; her legs gave out and she stumbled down the last few steps, landing hard on her wrists and knees. She vibrated, standing slowly.

You've been dead for a while. Take it easy.

The dark couldn't conceal the stink. Lopez lifted her slim, muscular legs over discarded bottles and down another flight of steps. She stopped, peering at the platform.

Nothing. Just the cold.

Mooshie tripped on the cracked floor, wincing. Pain feels good, she smiled shakily. She stood there waiting for a memory, finding nothing but a wary passing rat; they'd clearly sent out the word to avoid the crazy human.

Even in the inky stillness, she could see the edge of the platform ten feet away. Mooshie walked gingerly and stopped, waiting again. For what? There'd been a sensation. A knee? The back of a chair, a thick cushion, a shoulder, some touch.

Nothing disembodied drifted towards her. Ghoulish curled fingers, upraised palms. Maybe it had been an accident. A bump, jostle, crowded subway platform, commuters eager to get home. She probably had been drinking.

All pure guesses except the sensation and the long dark and here she was again. She waited a foot from the edge, looking around. Panic started. Clammy hands and a skipping heart. Steady, she told herself. Mooshie leaned over, peering down at the tracks. Her shoulders arched together, trying to feel something. She'd been twenty-five pounds heavier over the thick muscles. One nudge wouldn't have worked.

She could easily imagine the rest. If it had happened like that. What if the sensation in the small of the back had been from landing on the tracks? Maybe those black metal lines were the memory. Maybe she'd stumbled backwards, tripped. Maybe she had been drinking really heavily. Mooshie had done a lot of that. Maybe she toppled and the train roared over her. Pureed Lopez.

Mooshie fitfully clutched her groin at the platform. Empty, filthy, smelly rat home. Think this was a meeting place for anything other than memories you can't remember? She kicked some bottles onto the tracks, wildly dumping over a garbage can and shoving all the refuse onto the rail. Cans, bottles, chicken wings.

A fat appreciative rat trotted over to check out the panting intruder in the oversized jacket who was feeding the brothers and sisters on the tracks. Mooshie knelt, beckoning with a finger.

Did you see anything?

The rodent suddenly squeaked an unpleasant sound of dread, jumping over the platform and disappearing onto the tracks.

I hear you, she muttered. I hear you.

• • • •

VERNON JACKSON'S UPPER lip disappeared somewhere into his hairline.

"Run?"

Standing between home and the dugout, the other seven members of the Hawks murmured uneasily.

Puppy silently warned Ty and Mick to shut up, which only deepened the rest of the team's anxiety. Something wasn't right. Called in an off-day. Told the HGs were gone. Now there was that weird leathery glove on the really old guy's hand while the second really old guy swung the bat as if measuring their foreheads.

"Yes. Run, Vern." Puppy hopped in place like he was stamping out a fire. "You hit the ball…"

Neal Shen, whose HG had played first, raised his hand. "A real ball?"

Ty yanked the baseball out of his dried-out glove and threw it at Shen, who barely ducked. "Yeah, that. And stop your belly aching. In the old days I would've hit you in the nose."

The team tightened their ranks, butt to butt.

"Run. Hit." Puppy paused. "Catch. Throw. Like real baseball players."

Dimitri Izansky nervously raised his hand halfway, figuring that'd only get him hit in the leg and then he wouldn't have to run. "Why?"

"Excellent question, Dmitri." Puppy clapped enthusiastically as if Izansky had discovered a way to make real cream-filled donuts. "Because we're turning back the clocks."

Everyone looked at Ty and Mickey.

"We want, in this good-bye, lights out and sleep well my darlings, to play the game the way it was once played."

Ty spit on the ground.

"Commissioner Kenuda thinks it's a great idea. We got permission to practice here because I know you're not used to running. Or throwing. Catching. Hitting a real ball."

"Which is the hardest thing in sports," Mickey added.

That set off another round of anxious mutters.

"But you can do it. Yes, Shannon?"

The gangly bald woman retreated behind Shen, who panicked, thinking he was a target again. He ran into the dugout, falling down the steps.

Puppy waved aside their concerns about the loud crying in the runway. "Shannon, you played real baseball, didn't you?"

"High school in Dallas, Texas."

"I died there," Mick called out happily. "You know where I'm buried?"

Shannon stepped behind Vernon. Actually all the remaining players hid behind the wide catcher.

"You're a pro, then." Puppy craned his head to find Shannon, who was kneeling. "All of you are. You know the game. You're committed. You've done this for years, watching the HGs. They were you. Their talents came from your talents. You were their inspirations. And look, the Falcons will go through the same thing."

"They'll be real, too?" Jackson asked.

"Of course. You're playing each other."

That relaxed them a little and justified their wisdom in cowering behind Jackson.

"But I play differently," Cobb warned.

Ty wisely interpreted Puppy's blazing eyes and stepped back.

"We're getting real equipment. Not this crap." Puppy took Mickey's bat and tapped it on the ground. It cracked. He held it up as evidence. "Good stuff. Major league. Any more questions?"

Vern's followers nudged him. "What about the pay?"

"You're still getting paid."

"For only hitting. And not a real ball. We should get more."

Puppy sighed. "You know you can't change an employment agreement, Vern."

"We can if the employer agrees," Jackson said stubbornly.

Puppy's voice hardened. "I had to go to bat, so to speak, to get Fisher and Boccicelli to agree and then, then, I met with Third Cousin Kenuda."

They whispered in the huddle. Mickey and Ty each picked up part of the splintered bat.

"We need more money," Jackson insisted.

Ty and Mickey flanked the group, tapping the bats on their open palms. The huddle got a lot tighter. Puppy just watched.

"You got paid for doing this for how long?" Mickey asked.

Vernon lifted his chin in fake defiance. "Nine years."

"Nine years?" Ty clucked his tongue. "Nine years pretending to be a baseball player."

Bat slap, bat slap, bat slap.

"You stole money," Mick accused.

"I never stole anything." Jackson trembled.

Cobb edged closer. "You made fun of our game with your pathetic farce."

Bat slap, bat slap, bat slap.

"Now we're giving you a last chance and you want to steal more money?" Mickey yelled. "I'm gonna give you a whupping you never knew could be."

Mantle chased Vernon around the infield landing blows until the chubby catcher collapsed between third and home. Puppy interceded before there was much more blood. Jackson moaned.

"What's it going to be, Vern? You're the team leader." He gestured at the five remaining players holding hands and chanting Grandma's Blessing:

"May our love always be for love

May we think of the Family as ourselves

May we work hard and reward effort

May we help those who cannot succeed."

"We're afraid of looking like shit," Jackson whispered.

"So am I." Puppy squeezed the catcher's bruised arm; Vern groaned. "But I won't let that happen."

Jackson was doubtful. "And we won't pay for our own toilet paper anymore."

They shook hands on the deal; there had to be a lot of old napkins in the concession storage closet. Mickey and Ty began organizing fielding practice; they'd have to take turns sharing the glove.

Puppy saw a silver head glisten by the entrance to Section 116. Damn, he berated himself, catching up with the A29 just outside the stadium.

"Hey." Puppy touched the robot's shoulder. It turned with sullen metallic eyes. "I'm sorry. I should've given you a head's up, but Fisher and Boccicelli got the letter of approval just late yesterday."

"Fifteen years," the A29 said. "We started the same time. You didn't know anything. I showed you around. Pointed out where to go in the stadium. What to avoid. How not to fall in the rocket holes. Kept you from making mistakes."

"Yes, you did," he replied softly.

"Yes I did," the A29's voice rattled. "Was there ever a complaint about my work?"

"It's not about that."

"Oh, I know. I was being dry. This is because you need humans."

Puppy pursed his lips. "It's our last season."

"And I can't appreciate that? Who came up with the HGs running on the field together? All those acrobatic catches? Home runs bouncing off the brocades?"

"They were great."

"But not human."

"No." Puppy shook his head. "They're just representative of humans."

The robot's eyes glittered angrily as it waved at the broken ballpark. "It's the humans' fault this happened, not ours."

"Believe me, I know. Can I help somehow? What if we reassigned you to another job?"

"Take someone else's position? Let's collude and stab someone else in the back." The A29 shook its head in disgust. "We don't do that in the Little Extended Family. I thought you humans didn't do that anymore. Oh wait, you just don't do that to each other."

Three 'bots—ticket taker, concessionaire and janitor—stepped out from behind a beam, standing so closely they seemed one.

Puppy tried again. "If you ever need anything."

"Anything what?"

He frowned. "I don't understand..."

The robot tilted its head. "You don't even know my name. You don't even know I have one. It's Harold. That's my name. Harold."

Harold joined its friends for a last collective glare before they remembered their place with rounded shoulders and lowered eyes, and shuffled up the subway steps.

● ● ● ●

OUTSIDE THE ORPHANAGE, two Holy Warriors smoked cigarettes, leaning in casual menace against the silver van, machine guns slung over their shoulders. Azhar hurried past with a murmured greeting.

Hussein resentfully tossed silverware into the large plastic container, clearing the communal dining room.

"Why are the sex traders here?" Azhar jerked his hand at the window.

"Selection time." Hussein leered.

"That was just last month."

"Appetites, appetites." Hussein plucked an uneaten fig from a plate.

"They took eight last time."

"Now they take more." Hussein's lecherous smile grew. "Is there one they should put aside for you?"

Azhar raced up the stairs to the top floor, where he tapped on the square in the ceiling leading to the attic.

"Clary?"

Please be there. He rapped harder; voices passed in the hallway, heavy boots, dark laughs.

"Sweetheart, are you there?"

He forced open the door, blood dribbling under his gouged fingernails. A lonely doll with one eye stared back in the hiding place.

Azhar ran down the steps and tore open the first door on the left.

The barrel of a machine gun pressed against his temple.

A Holy Warrior stepped in front, the gun never leaving Azhar's head. Two girls around twelve were tied naked to their cots as a doctor in a white robe examined them. Neither girl was Clary. Thank you, Allah. For what? For giving away two other children? Shame flooded his face.

The Warrior shoved Azhar into the hallway. He passed another Warrior with another pious greeting and tried the other bedroom. It was locked. Someone cried from within. A girl. A boy. He couldn't tell. Azhar ran down to the first floor and tried two more doors. Both were locked.

From outside came terrified cries. Azhar knelt by the window on the staircase, peering over the ledge.

A boy, chained in the middle of a group of five naked youngsters wearing red lipstick, was kicked viciously in the side, dragging his manacled colleagues to the ground in a terrified tangle. A Warrior roughly lifted the boy up and set him back on his feet, straightening the line as they were tossed into the back of the van.

"Careful. No bruising," admonished the physician. "That is for the clients to do."

He laughed at his joke.

Five girls in white dresses and painted faces, also chained together, were dragged across the driveway. Azhar leaned forward trying to recognize Clary beneath the lipstick; the girls all wore blonde wigs.

"Have you lost someone?" Hazma asked.

Azhar muttered, rising.

"The kitchen needs mopping."

"Then why are you standing here?" Mustafa snapped.

"Because that is your job. Not peeking at little girls." Hazma tilted his head shrewdly. "Ah. It is the angry Spanish girl. With the big brown eyes."

If he called her name and she wasn't there, she would be unsafe. They would take her out of spite. And if it were Clary down there, chained like a dog, what could he do? Tuck her under his arm from the mouth of the Mufti?

"There are others." Hazma clasped Mustafa's shoulder. "She had no ass."

Azhar hit Hazma in the stomach just hard enough so he bent over, gasping.

The sex trader's van roared away, trailed by two Ford jeeps of Warriors, triumphantly firing their guns.

15

A very fat woman peered suspiciously at Puppy. There had always been fat women manning the DV community center info desk. As a kid, he used to think it was the same one, year after year, built downstairs in the back like a banned humanoid 'bot.

He held out his Lifecard again. "Work."

She rubbed her ear, considering him carefully, as did everyone in the center, quietly shooting pool, playing darts. She snapped her fingers, gaining full attention, and held up Puppy's childish drawing. The sketch was passed around. She returned to her paperwork with a careless shrug.

A tall teen with long earrings and black leggings wandered over. He looked Puppy up and down with wary distaste. He made the sign of a D and V with his fingers. Puppy tugged down his lower lip in acknowledgement.

The kid narrowed his eyes, not entirely convinced but, of course, Puppy would be easy to find if he was lying, and pulled a pen out of Puppy's pocket, scribbling down an address. He turned his palms up. The fat woman gloated as she ran Puppy's Lifecard through the deduction machine to pay for a round of Aubrey's Strawberry-Coated Choco Treats.

The row of tiny brick houses snuggled protectively along East 155th Street as if too small to make it on their own. He knocked just once on a bland rust-colored house. There were no doorbells in DV homes; that was rude and noisy. If someone wanted you, they would wait for you to respond. If they wanted the visitor, they'd hear.

About five minutes passed before Frecklie opened the door. His left eyebrow raised slightly, discharging caution down his face.

The immaculate house gleamed from years of scrubbing and vacuuming, showing in the faint pine-scented antiseptic odor, scuffed dining room table and chairs, and thin brown rug curling up four square against the walls; a neat garden flowered above the window ledge. Frecklie waited until Puppy ate a piece of AG apple pie from the deep white porcelain dish on the kitchen counter, searching for signs of displeasure. He beamed when Puppy held out his plate for another piece. Guest satisfied. Until that happened, there could be no conversation. Puppy would have to plow his way through the entire fridge.

Puppy accepted a cup of coffee and tapped his watch. Tomorrow. Puppy accentuated that with the forefinger snail gesture.

Frecklie nodded, but didn't answer. Maybe he'd been wrong about this kid. Puppy tapped his lips and touched his ear. Never heard from you.

Frecklie turned up his palms and touched the top of his head. Waiting.

Puppy shrugged. For?

A very pretty slim Asian woman in her mid-thirties with thin black hair tied in a bun stood in the door with an unpleasant stare that seemed perfectly at home on her lean face. She put down the grocery bags and walked past Puppy as if he didn't exist, jerking her thumb questioningly; Frecklie nodded, wincing. The teen opened his mouth and the woman cut him short with eyes so narrow an ant would've choked on the lashes.

No introductions until she was certain she wanted to meet him. She turned her back, fumbling with the buttons on her blue cloth overcoat.

"Reg okay?" Puppy asked, his shorthand a little rusty; this one would chew his elbow off if he inflected wrong.

The woman nodded grudgingly.

"I have three jobs open at the stadium," Puppy explained. "I figure taking tickets would be best."

Why. The woman half-raised her hands; the delicate fingers were spotted with cuts.

"Because it's handling money. You need to be smart."

Frecklie's pleased smile at the trust quickly faded under his mother's hard look. She wiggled a forefinger on both her hands.

"The other jobs are cleaning up and running the concession stand. There's no real food and there's no way the stadium will ever look nice, so handling tickets at the door is the winner."

Beth waved good-bye.

"Yes. It quit."

The woman lifted her left shoulder in a mockery of the ancient 'bot tilt, fixed decades ago in the final models; prejudice had a long memory.

"Yes, a 'bot job."

Beth half squatted as if pooping.

"It's not a crap job." Puppy grew annoyed. "What else does he have going?"

Her veined hands tensed, pointing at her son.

"Everyone in the DV's a brain." He smacked his temple; Frecklie repeated the gesture and the woman rose up slightly on her toes, bouncing like a boxer. "He needs more for the University application. Otherwise he'll end up at Bronx College like I did. He's too bright for that."

Puppy politely looked away so she and her son could exchange comments. Frecklie pleaded silently. She sighed softly and rubbed her finger and thumb together.

"Minimum wage," Puppy answered.

Frecklie shook his head. "Ten percent above what the robot got."

Puppy helplessly flung his hands in the air; Frecklie laughed. The merriment didn't last as the woman slowly turned toward Puppy, a faint ridge of impish freckles sliding off her nose, though that didn't thaw the cold blue eyes.

"Contract?" she asked.

"Of course."

"Guaranteed for the whole season."

"Sure."

"With pay raises every ten games."

"I can't do that."

Beth folded her arms, glaring.

"I can't. It's the law." Everyone was expected to do a good job so extra rewards like bonuses and anything other than an annual raise were forbidden. Hard work was a given, not a goal.

Her mouth twisted disdainfully. "If other jobs open, then Ruben has the option."

"Depending if he's qualified."

"My son can do anything."

"Anything he's qualified for, Ruben gets first shot."

"In the contract."

"Can't. The law." No favoritism, side deals, nepotism. Nothing smelling of getting ahead on anything but the merits. Family businesses were especially monitored. Corruption, bribery, laziness, all the same sins.

Beth conceded with a grunt and stuck out her hand. "Beth Rivera."

"Puppy Nedick." He fired his most winning smile. "Pleasure to meet you."

Beth sneered as if meeting him were a step above an appendectomy without anesthesia and slammed the bedroom door behind her. Frecklie made amends by offering another piece of pie.

"Is she always this charming?" Puppy asked.

Frecklie nodded wearily.

• • • •

PABLO'S EYES WANTED to dribble out of their sockets; that seat in the corner of the B22 bus looked so nice. But he'd never taken a work seat, reserved for people exhausted from their jobs. You could be on crutches and blind, and if someone were half asleep from a long day, you gave them your seat. The only way you could keep your butt planted was if you were also pregnant.

This morning Pablo had examined the entire second grade class of PS 88, finishing up with a smile-o-meter flair by playing the Rosen Girls' *I Got Smiles* vidmusical of dancing lips and whistling cheeks. The kids wouldn't leave, sending his schedule into the toilet.

Two emergencies, an unexpected wisdom tooth and an infected root canal, turned the waiting room into the 6 train at rush hour. It wasn't until eight o'clock that the last patient left, mumbling thanks through the novocaine. Then all the paperwork, documenting the procedures, follow-ups, a great deal of potential fraud in cheaters wanting to have holes drilled in their teeth, he thought testily.

The bus rolled unsteadily up the hill. A young red-haired woman tugged on Pablo's sleeve, waking him.

"Sir, please sit."

"No," he mumbled sleepily, forehead leaden against the pole.

"You've worked hard."

"Everyone does."

The woman frowned. "Do you think Grandma's Tenth Insight is wrong?"

The bus quieted so deeply he could hear the stop light change colors.

"Course not." Pablo pushed up from his heels, reciting, "But we must believe that our fellows work harder than us. Otherwise, it becomes selfish resentment."

She smiled faintly. "Especially for someone exhausted."

The passengers stepped aside so he could slump into the corner seat. Pablo was asleep in a few moments. When the bus stopped, the redhead handed him a thin envelope.

"Get some sleep, Dr. Diaz."

She stepped casually out the back door. It took him a weary few beats to react to the envelope on his lap. *How'd she know who I was?* He tapped his name plate on the white coat. *Never even undressed,* he shrugged sheepishly, pocketing the envelope. *Worse ways to meet someone than on a bus.*

Pablo picked up some vegetables and rice at the corner market and collapsed on his long black couch. Crosby, Stills, Nash and Young played on the stereo. He sipped a glass of Huntsville pink wine, forgetting about his dinner, eyes hypnotized by the circling album.

He propped himself up and forced down a bite of the rice. Outside, the pugs began barking.

Pablo munched on a stalk of broccoli by the window. Twenty across and thirty rows deep, the fawn and black-furred pugs marched resolutely. Children, spilling out of bed near midnight once a month for this occasion, gathered noisily along Bruckner Boulevard, waving to the well-trained real animals, who kept pace, though a few skittered in anticipation.

The leader, a tall kindly man wearing a black top hat, blew sharply on a whistle and the pugs skipped and hopped and ran toward the crowd. Children fell to their knees, hugging the dogs, feeding them, playing fetch. Soon the children and the dogs were one mass and you couldn't really tell who was fetching for whom. The late night snacks of hamburgers, pizzas, rolls, bones, and bowls of pasta littered the street.

In an hour, the leader blew the whistle and the dogs reluctantly reformed their lines, wagging their curly tails, looking forlornly at the waving children. Another blast of the whistle and off they marched to a new neighborhood.

There weren't enough animals to meet the needs. Robot pets had failed; enough stories of children mutilated by a malfunctioning orange cat had shuttered the industry. In the Bronx, pugs were favored; this was Grandma's home, pugs were her favorites and she was allowed one indulgence. Across America, different breeds found different cities.

Boxers in Chicago. Jack Terriers in North Carolina. German Shepherds in Oklahoma. Share and share. Grandma wouldn't allow one child to be jealous because they didn't have a pet.

Try sharing this food, Pablo thought and tossed the veggies into the garbage. He sliced some cheese, pouring more wine than he needed. He was exhausted beyond sleep. He sat on the chair, dully watching Grandma's *Sleep Well My Darlings* on the vidnews rolling across the wall behind the couch. She tucked in triplets. He hadn't seen that before. When's the last time you watched?

Three boys, all curly-haired, darkish faced, probably Southeast Asian, lifted up their faces. Grandma kissed one on the forehead, another on the nose and the last on the chin. She sang *Sleep Well* in her light, slightly discordant voice, playfully making fun of her singing and encouraging the children to join in.

After a last chorus of "we watch each other all night", they hugged. The children contentedly closed their eyes. Grandma turned off the light, her round almond-shaped eyes shining alone on the screen, watching her Family go to sleep.

Pablo yawned, dribbling wine down his chin. The forgotten envelope hung out of his white coat, tossed on a chair. She wasn't bad looking, he smiled, tearing it open in between sips. Maybe she'll be Mrs. Dr. Pablo.

He stared at the note. Simple. Clear.

Pablo poured more wine.

• • • •

THE WHITE LETTERING of the Salvatore's Furniture sign faded down the side of the old five-story brick warehouse on the deserted end of the Grand Concourse at East 204th Street. Hazel parked behind a line of rusting cars languishing in front of boarded-up storefronts.

The Black Top lifted his reflector face-mask just inside the bland metal door, which took a few minutes to find along the featureless building designed to be ignored. Expressionless except for bored suspicion, the BT studied the pass for a long time. He looked Hazel up and down.

Hazel tapped the signature again. "Order of Sport Commissioner Kenuda. It's all there."

The Black Top folded his arms, black armored elbows grazing the two guns on his hips. His job was not to be rushed.

"Temporary loan of equipment," Puppy explained.

Now the BT noticed Puppy; he wasn't pleased. He ran Puppy's Lifecard through a small security device outside the front door, disappointed when no notification of Puppy Nedick, notorious criminal, came back demanding his capture.

The BT disappeared inside. They waited silently in the faint moonlight. The door slid open. Another BT escorted them down a crusty hallway, up a flight and into a storage area, slipping out silently.

"Fucking Black Tops," Hazel growled.

Three shelves loomed over them. Hazel propped a ladder against the wall and half-hopped up the steps. Puppy noticed the Gelinium.

"Sicily," Hazel explained over his shoulder.

"First or second battle or would you prefer I don't ask?"

"Appreciate that much courtesy."

"There were a lot of veterans in my DV when I was a kid. We learned the rules. Especially showing respect."

"DV was the only place where we got that. Go outside and people would spit at you. But as a soldier, you dared not respond. You had to take it. Ever hear of the tomato medal?"

Puppy shook his head.

"How many times you stood there as someone threw shit at you, blaming you for losing the war. Rotten tomatoes at a bad stage performance…"

"I get it."

"I knew a guy, claimed to be eligible for twenty-seven tomato medals. Tony Teller. I heard he blew his brains out. He left a note: 'This makes tomato medal number twenty-eight'. I figure it's probably a true story. If it's not, it's still a good one." Hazel stared off. "Though sometimes we didn't take it. I broke the skull of a sucker in Jersey once. He asked me if I faked the injury. I dumped his body in a trash can. Maybe he was even dead." Hazel shrugged and steadied the rickety ladder. "Anyway. I was at Second Sicily, though I was on ship for the first invasion. Never made it that far ashore. I lost the leg trying to recapture that boot. Shit like that never works. There's a reason why something's gone. Jobs, love, wars."

Puppy allowed Hazel his moment before changing the subject. "What else is in this building?"

"Just junk, I think. Supposedly there's a room full of cellular phones, Allah robes, even cans of bad foods passed off as technological breakthroughs. The food scandals of the '70s. Grandma's a pack rat."

Hazel's rummaging sent dust onto Puppy. He finally tossed down a large burlap sack. "Nothing's marked. Though you don't need to label these."

He gingerly stepped back down and flipped out a blade lightly taped to his ankle, traditional DV style, slicing the burlap and then the plastic covering six bats.

"Damn." Puppy slid out a sleek, black bat. He sniffed. "Real wood."

"Yup." Hazel's eyes gleamed as he swung a white ash bat. "Isn't this an Albert Cheng model?"

"Hell yeah." Puppy scampered quickly up the ladder and threw down another bag. It bounced a little. Hazel was already stacking gloves carefully.

"I thought they'd burned a lot of these after the trials." Puppy slipped on a fielder's glove. Cracked, dried out, yet it still felt wonderful. He found another bag with ancient jockstraps, which he quickly closed.

"Who knows what they really burnt," Hazel said. "When I first started in sports, I found this amazing piece someone had done, documenting all the baseball burnings."

"That the Anglia documentary?"

"No, no." Hazel crouched, holding out a catcher's mitt. "That one was approved. This was rogue."

Angry citizens tearing down baseball fields, confiscating equipment from neighbors, and axing/hammering/smashing to smithereened shit the remaining nine ballparks that had comprised the rest of the major league homes: Wrigley Field, Fenway Park, Braves Field, Forbes Stadium, Phillies Field, Houston Aerodome, Cleveland Civic Center, St. Louis' Golden Arches, and Minneapolis-St. Paul Baseball Fields.

In each city center, the rubble was dragged away on robot-driven trucks with waving schoolchildren hanging onto the side. Huge smelt-like holes swallowed up the steel and concrete, while smaller surrounding fires devoured the equipment, magazines, books, trading cards, photographs, banners, anything resembling memorabilia.

"This woman filmmaker caught the attacks on the manufacturers."

"Wasn't that approved?"

"Not on the workers," Hazel said quietly. "Must be thousands of people from Rawlings, Louisville Slugger, Wilson, on and on, buried beneath the razed buildings."

"They say there are bodies under Fenway and Wrigley," Puppy added.

John flipped the mitt back into the bag and slipped on a catcher's mask. "They say a lot of things." He went back up the ladder and opened another bag, whistling softly as he unfurled an American flag draping nearly to the floor.

"Ever see one?" Hazel's voice was gentle.

"In school. I was five, six."

"Before they burnt 'em all away after 10/12?"

Puppy nodded, tenderly touching the edge of the flag. "Every morning, singing the song."

"The song being *The Star Spangled Banner*," Hazel said tartly. "Remember any of the words?"

"Pretty much. Almost got it perfectly, but I screwed up a few and my father threatened to throw me off the roof if I ever got it wrong again. I figured it wasn't worth it."

"It's always worth it," Hazel said coldly. "After 10/12 they took the flag from us, too. Here we were getting mowed down by Allahs using American weapons from NATO since the damn Allahs had been voted, fucking voted, as head of NATO countries and you couldn't even have a flag on your sleeve. In your pocket. You're an American soldier and… that's how the term red stripes started."

"Tearing the stripes and putting them into your boots." Puppy said, surprising Hazel. "Like I said, there were a lot of vets in my DV."

"We sang it anyway," Hazel lowered his voice; the death penalty for flying the flag was still on the books, though not prosecuted since the late '80s. "Backwards. Like the Chinese or the Jews." Hazel gently rolled the flag back into the bag and shoved it deep onto the shelf.

They silently sorted through a few more bags of equipment, Hazel peering sadly at a stiffened batting glove. Puppy gave him a careful look.

"I didn't figure you for a lover of baseball."

"I'm not." He laughed disdainfully. "I'm just a reporter. Not allowed to have strong opinions anymore. Actually any opinions. Otherwise how could you trust what I report?"

"Then why'd you suggest we come here?"

"Because it's a great story."

Puppy leaned on a bat. "I don't want you making fun of us on the news."

"Freedom of the press, Mr. Nedick," Hazel said, his face tightening.

"Not freedom to mock. Not freedom to twist. Freedom to tell," Puppy quoted Grandma's Twenty Second Insight.

Hazel sneered. "You going to quote her all the way back in the car?"

"Nah. I'm taking the subway."

• • • •

THE THREE BOYS stood patiently outside Gate Six in their ill-fitting dark suits and ties, stiff like scarecrows. They would've waited for hours, soaked, frozen. Nothing was supposed to dissuade you. Puppy had waited for three hours, also in his father's suit, for his first job at fifteen, digging up dead trees. Never once had he loosened the tie or even wiped dirt from the crisp white shirt. Head drenched in sweat, he'd shoveled for nine hours, never looking up. His hands bled for two days and he had to wash the shirt three times to get it back into some form of usable wear; he also wore that same shirt and tie the day he left the DV for Bronx College. His father had already sold the suit for booze.

Puppy glanced questioningly at Frecklie's pals.

"Jobs. Now three." Frecklie shrugged at the simple math and introduced Paquette and Ariel, twins.

"Nice to meet you."

Ty pushed past them dragging the unsteady Mickey, who wore the dim and delighted smile of a man still drunk after six hours of sleep. The teens frowned. Such behavior got you into the DV, not out.

"That's two of the players, one of them ovbiously ill," Puppy explained, leading them into the stadium.

Frecklie compressed his widened eyes into a casual glance around the empty pavillion. He was disappointed, annoying Puppy. What did you expect?

Puppy gave Frecklie the ticket box with the Lifecard swiper; the boy waved off the stool with a roll of his eyes. Paquette got the broom and Ariel was shown the concession stand.

"Chips." Puppy held up two bags of Jordan's Chimp Chips.

Ariel held his thumb and forefinger apart. Puppy grinned and told him to borrow Frecklie's swiper if he had a customer. The kid's face could've lit up the sunrise.

An unmarked truck idled along River Avenue. The A22 driver honked the horn. Puppy, trailed by Frecklie, came back outside and walked up to the driver's window.

"Delivery." The driver said, a second 'bot staring with that shrewd aimless quality.

"Great. Just pull up."

The A22s exchanged smirks. "Far as we go."

"You can just drive up…"

"Far as we go."

Puppy caught the driver sneering at Frecklie. Okay, that's what this is about, he nodded to himself. "Need me to sign something?"

"Long as you got lots of proof."

It took about twenty minutes for Puppy's Lifecard to process; the security machine kept jamming for some odd reason. The A22s slowly, very slowly, opened the back door.

"You got five minutes to unload, otherwise we take it with us to the next stop." The A22 leaned against the subway pillar, setting the alarm on its watch.

Frecklie fetched his friends and the three teens helped Puppy lug the equipment to the gate. An alarm buzzed and the truck door closed.

"Hey." Puppy pounded on the driver's door. "There's still a couple bags."

"You see any?" the driver asked its colleague in the front seat, who shook its head with grave certainty.

"Open the back door."

"I got stops and a schedule."

The truck edged away.

Puppy grabbed the robot's head. It howled and the vehicle lurched to a stop. "This is borrowed from a Black Top security center. You want to explain to them at the end of the season why all the equipment hasn't been returned?"

The A22's eyes rolled around nervously. Its colleague nodded quickly. Puppy walked, slowly, very slowly, to the back of the truck and pulled out the last of the bags. The automatic door closed and the truck backed up, stopping a couple inches from Puppy, before rumbling away.

Inside of fifteen minutes, the equipment was stacked by home plate. The Hawks and Falcons players milled around as if expecting the bats, balls and gloves to start dancing. Ty examined a bat, shaking his head.

"What's this made of?"

"Wood," Puppy said.

Ty flipped it aside. "This the good stuff?"

"Best we got."

Cobb held a glove away with his fingertips. "Supposed to be real leather?"

"It was once." Puppy sighed. "There are no more baseball equipment companies, Ty. They were outlawed. This is it." He grew frustrated. Holding the gloves and bats in the warehouse was magic. Now he was ashamed. Memories have no shelf life when you re-live them. "This is from the World Series. The last World Series in 2065."

Cobb spit on the ground. He grabbed a bat and swung it in a menacing arc. The players backed away, murmuring like natives witnessing a god walking into the jungle.

"You slobs, take a bat and a glove," he snarled. They didn't move.

"Ty, I think we should just hand them out," Puppy suggested.

"How are they gonna know which feels right?"

"I don't think we're quite there yet."

Ty glared at the players, who inched away again. He suddenly grinned. "That means our team gets the best. Mick."

Mantle woke up, propped against the fence. He waved merrily and then went back to sleep. Cobb sighed unhappily. "Hawks slobs. Line up."

Puppy encouraged the Hawks to obey. They formed a line. He clustered the Falcons team in its own line. He and Ty handed out the gloves and bats. The players walked away, wonderingly swinging the bats and shoving their fingers inside the gloves. Ty peered into the opposing dugout.

"Who's the Falcons manager so we can exchange lineup cards?"

"Manager?"

"Yeah. The guy in charge."

"I know what a manager is, Ty."

"I keep forgetting. You're a baseball historian. So who's in charge?"

Puppy really didn't want to answer. "No one."

Cobb squeezed the bat handle. "No manager. No coaches, either?'

"We're lucky to get soap for the shower."

Ty stomped around angrily. "I'll be my own coach."

"And manager?"

Cobb slapped him on the cheek. "Bright boy."

"Isn't that too much work? I think it's more important to focus on playing."

"You saying I can't do it?" Ty scowled. "I was player-manager for six years with the Detroit Tigers and would've won a few pennants if I had anyone as good as me. Now get those assholes off the field so my team can practice. What the hell are they called again?"

Ty clapped his hands to gather the Bronx Hawks for the first batting practice in America in thirty-three years. The players shuffled forward tentatively.

"Jackson," Cobb barked. Vern stepped out from the semi-circle. "You're the catcher." Jackson nodded unsurely.

"That a goddamn yes or a no?"

"Goddamn yes."

"Godamn yes, skipper. That's what you all call me. Skipper. I'm the manager. The boss. You don't listen, you get fined. After I've reamed your asses. Jackson," he snapped as Vernon tried rejoining the team, thinking this was a brief interrogation. "You understand the importance of a catcher?"

Jackson shook his head.

"You're like the field leader," Puppy said.

Cobb flared scarlet and beckoned Puppy over with a gnarly middle finger. He wrapped his arm around Puppy's neck like a comfy noose. "Never say anything when I'm addressing my team. I don't care if the stadium's on fire. I don't care if three whores with big tits are lying on second base, calling my name. Never open your mouth again."

"Yes, skipper." Puppy smiled and Cobb slapped his cheek again, this time with some authority. Puppy rubbed his jaw and sat by Mick, who managed to stumble sitting down.

"Can you play?" Puppy whispered.

"Course." Mickey belched. "Ain't the first time I was a little relaxed before a game." He squinted around the empty stadium. "There is a game, right?"

Puppy patted his shoulder. Mickey tipped over. Puppy straightened him up before going into the Falcons clubhouse.

Boccicelli paced angrily, wheeling on Puppy. "What is all this?"

For a moment Puppy wasn't sure if he meant the equipment or the sullen Falcons players. "The team."

"I know it's the team. I've lost enough money." He glowered at the players so there'd be no doubt who was responsible. "The gloves and things. I'm not paying for them."

Wiping his suit of any airborne germs especially transmitted by baseball, the owner rolled out of the clubhouse which, Puppy figured, might've been his first visit in years. Maybe ever.

"Mr. Boccicelli," Puppy said as they walked down the dusty hallway. "All this is free."

Boccicelli hadn't expected that. He removed the handkerchief from his mouth. "How?"

"Commissioner Kenuda is loaning us the equipment used in 10/12."

Boccicelli went white. "The very same equipment?"

"Yes, yes. Game Seven and everything."

Boccicelli shuddered. "I'm not sure I like that, Nedick."

"Why not? It's free," he repeated slowly.

Boccicelli pressed the elevator button. "What happens if the equipment is damaged?"

Puppy thought a second. "Like how?"

"A broken bat. That occurred a few years ago, remember? Or if one of the balls goes missing."

Puppy tried imagining someone hitting the ball into the bleachers. "I don't think that'll happen."

"Get it in writing. We are not responsible for breakage." Boccicelli stepped into the elevator. "You made this arrangement. You're responsible. You've already gotten us in trouble with the Little Extended Family. I had three 'bots in my office yesterday complaining about you, Nedick."

• • • •

TWO BICYCLES THUMPED down the chipped front steps in a race they were both destined to lose. The red bike flipped over, sending the little girl smashing against the metal fence, while the blue bike overturned and pinned the little boy. Lots of howling and screaming.

Maybe next time don't ride down concrete steps, Zelda thought, watching the parents tend to their brats, wiping blood, scolding over torn clothes and dented equipment. The rest of their brood played their own stupid games. Seven of them, Zelda counted distastefully, finally able to get into the building sometime before her sixtieth birthday.

DVs were like incubators, parents scrambling to produce as many children as possible before their organs gave out. Anything to increase the odds. The more kids, the better chance some will make it out. And the more kids, the more the population was replenished. They cannot defeat our will to live on. Love, love, Grandma had urged. About four million children had died in the Allah War. That required a lot of love.

The apartment was up five flights at the end of a narrow staircase. Food smells changed on each floor, as if entering a different restaurant zone.

Zelda slowed down, wheezing on the fourth floor landing.

"Hi," Diego called down from the top floor. "Need help?"

Zelda waved the bottle of wine with a brave smile.

His apartment was tiny, especially by the standards of these old buildings, which dated back to the mid-twentieth century. Anthemic rock posters, Van Halen, Rolling Stones, U2, circled the rectangular living room, also doubling as a bedroom; a sheet peeked out of the pull-out couch.

But the floors gleamed and the windows sparkled onto the courtyard.

"That's about it." Diego grinned as she soaked in the room. "Unless you need to inspect the bathroom."

"Maybe later." She smiled back. They stood awkwardly for a moment. Diego ushered her toward the couch. She swallowed a deep mouthful of wine.

"Yes, cheers." He clinked his glass.

"Sorry. Thirsty."

"Steps are a bitch. But you're getting better. A couple days ago you only made it to the fourth floor."

Zelda flushed.

"My neighbor Mr. Genado saw you. Strangers stand out in the DV."

"I remember."

"That why you never came up?"

Direct, blunt. Zelda filled her mouth with cheese and crackers, buying time. His steady look gave her no room for calm.

"I grew up in a place like this."

"You said."

"Just like this. I wouldn't be surprised if this was the same couch. My parents lived in a large closet off that way." She gestured vaguely toward the hallway. "I mean, really a large closet, but they rented it as a one bedroom."

Diego absently rubbed the stem of the wine glass. "Pleasant memories."

"Not here." Zelda took a quick sip; she didn't want to get loaded. "Memories with friends. Funny how for all the emphasis on the family, the DV is the worst place for that. All that stress and pressure and fear. Who can ever relax when you look at your parents and hate them for putting you there, and they look at you, wondering if you're just the same. How about you?"

He shrugged. "Four sisters."

"Regs now?"

Diego held up a couple fingers. "One fell off a bridge. The other under a truck."

"Shit…"

He waved her off. "Didn't make it."

"You will." She squeezed his wrist.

Diego leaned away, surprising her. "No guarantees. I could flunk the Navy test."

"You're going into the Navy?"

"Just covering myself in case the private boats don't work. I'm studying for the ocean fishing license now."

She crossed her knees. "I just don't see you as a sailor."

"How do you see me?"

Zelda didn't answer quickly enough and he darkened.

"As just a DV?"

"No guarantees. As you just said." Zelda took a longer sip. "You invited me here."

"If you didn't want to be here, then you shouldn't have come."

"I'm not sure I want to be here. Big difference."

Diego's eyes narrowed. "I want you here."

"I'm glad."

"But not if you don't want to." He hoped that was the balance Puppy had mentioned.

"I just said I don't know. You live here, I don't. You might get out. What if you don't?"

"The Navy's a lock. They'll take almost anyone."

"And what does the Navy do anymore?"

"Patrol."

"What? Connecticut?"

"I don't know. I haven't taken the test yet."

They sipped their wine, exchanging sour glances.

"I'm making spaghetti," he finally said.

"I'm not hungry."

"We can eat out."

"If I'm not hungry for spaghetti here, why would I be hungry for spaghetti outside?"

"Because it's not a fucking DV apartment," he exploded.

Zelda stood up, stopping by the door. "You're a nice kid, Diego. Stay with someone your own age. Similar life cycle, both starting out. I'm past all that. Thirty-seven isn't young."

"That's not old."

"It can be." Zelda smiled shakily.

She took a 'bot cab to Daffy's up on 210th Street; she was too embarrassed to go to Monroe's after she'd told Jimmy the bartender she finally met someone.

16

Clary hobbled forward, landing hard on her knee. Pain ran from toe to hip, distracting her from the perro from the orphanage chasing her.

"Puta, puta, puta." The vile stinking breath wafted forward. The perro laughed. "Puta, puta, puta."

She shimmied up the tree, tearing her black lingerie. A thin strand hooked onto the branch. She slid up a little higher. Now her thighs were bleeding.

"Madre de dios," she whispered, crossing herself. "Save me."

The Allah stood beneath the tree, sniffing like the perro he was. He had tried her before. Three times.

"Come, puta," Hazma cupped his hands on the sides of his matted beard and called out in Spanish in all directions. "No one will hurt you."

They'd chased her for miles. She didn't know where she was. North, south, east, west. Her home was in the east. Tierre del Bueno. She'd had a nice home with lots of dolls and a good father and a good mother. Then a bridge was blown up outside town, killing many Allah soldiers. They blamed the Crusaders. The Allahs came and made her watch as her parents were beheaded. All the children had watched, sitting in the stands at the gymnasium, the mats laid out along the wood floor. Mats where she had practiced. Where she had won awards for gymnastics.

She was glad her father was blindfolded so she didn't have to see his eyes. She had seen her mother's before they dragged her away. Shaking her bruised cheeks, lips swollen, Clary's mother lifted her neck up almost out of her body, pleading with her daughter.

Pleading what? Live. That was Clary's belief.

"Come on, puta. Little Clary." Hazma looked up, but it was too dark. He wandered away.

Go. Go. Please, go.

He sniffed and suddenly stopped, turning back to the tree. Even in the blackness, she could see the yellow rotting teeth flash in a smile. Clary held her breath.

"Little Clary," he said, holding up his hands. "Come down, little darling. Otherwise I will burn the tree. And then that pretty little skin will be all blistered and scarred. Even the slavers won't want you. Maybe just the wolves."

She held still. He flicked his lighter and a flame danced on a branch. He suddenly shoved the smoking ember into the bottom of her bare foot. She screamed.

"Yes, little Clary. Think how much it will hurt all over your body." His voice hardened. "Now get your puta ass down. I am fucking tired. Doin't worry. I'm not too tired."

Her vision was good from hiding so often in the attic. She saw him spreading out a blanket of grass.

"Na'am," she said softly.

Licking his lips, Hazma reached up to help her down. Clary pulled her knees into her chest and jumped. Her heels drove into his nose, breaking bone and spraying blood. He fell back, groaning. Clary somersaulted over his head, landing and running through the dark forest, panting like a perro for hours until she limped along the beach road. The ocean air salted her drooping eyes.

The sun reared its dim light threateningly. She had to hide. She wanted to dig a hole in the sand, dig a deep deep hole and maybe she could turn it into a tunnel which would take her where? Nowhere. She had nowhere to go except back to the orphanage and she would rather die but she remembered her mother's stare.

She wished she remembered how to cry.

Clary dragged her bleeding feet across the road, kneeling by the grey van in the driveway. She fainted for a moment and then crawled into the back seat, pulling a thin blanket over her head.

• • • •

PUPPY CARRIED THREE beers to the rear table. They had to celebrate something. Maybe just surviving was enough.

They'd only made it to the third inning when the alarm went off in the dugouts, signaling that it was time to haul butt off the field after the allotted hour of play. By then, the Hawks had rolled to a 10-1 lead.

How runs were scored, who scored, who hit, who even threw the ball was a blur and Puppy would be up half the night trying to sort it all out for his report. He wasn't entirely sure if the Hawks Dante Tifaldo or Vernon Jackson had collapsed at second base.

"Wasn't bad for the first game with real balls, right?" Puppy asked hesitantly.

"Except for the skulls," Mick muttered.

"I'd take skeletons over what we got," Ty snarled. "Embarrassing. Worse than I could imagine."

Behind the bar, Jimmy suspiciously monitored their table. Puppy hoisted the glass reassuringly.

"You have to lower expectations a little."

"A little?" Ty snapped. "They didn't even know where their positions were."

"Now they do," Puppy said. "Shortstop isn't really self-defining. It's short compared to what and how is it stopping anything? And left field, is that left field from the perspective of home plate or left field from the perspective of the outfielder? Like stage right, stage left…"

Cobb shook his head. "We got reputations."

"What does that mean?"

"We're used to playing at a certain level of competition," Mick said.

"You were drunk today. You struck out four times."

Mantle reddened. "I always get off to slow starts."

Puppy calmed himself. "If we're patient with you, then you have to be patient with them."

"And I had to pitch," Ty jumped in. "I ain't a pitcher. Least when the alarm clock went off we could all go home."

Puppy angrily pushed through the dancing crowd to the bar. He picked up a bowl of nuts.

Jimmy wiped the counter. "You watching them? I don't want Blue Shirts here."

"You know, this is supposed to be a happy day. An historic day."

"It was. You made the sportsvid."

Puppy paused. "We did? What'd they say?" The bartender wiped a glass like he was about to serve Grandma. "Just tell me, Jimmy."

"It was on the funny spot in sports."

"Where they show clips of people running their skis into trees?"

Jimmy attended to a couple of customers. "Guess it's the same thing."

As if cued, the vidnews rolled into the sportsvid. The charming presenter with the dimples introduced a repeat of the "Funny Side of Sports." Jimmy yanked the music plug out of the wall, generating disappointed protests. He turned up the sound of the vidnews.

"Shut up," he yelled. "One of our own is on."

That quieted the bar.

"John Hazel has a charming report about a sport that's about to finally die. John."

Hazel stood in front of Amazon Stadium at night. Asshole must've gone there right from the warehouse, Puppy thought.

"Thanks, Chip. Some of you probably think baseball's already gone. Don't worry. The cesspool of treachery has about five months to go. But a baseball historian, Puppy Nedick…"

Puppy in his Bronx College uniform flashed onto the screen, throwing a pitch.

"…a former ballplayer himself, petitioned Third Cousin Kenuda, our Sport Commissioner, with an idea to highlight the game so no one would ever forget. Ready for this? Use real players."

Quick shots of lumbering, fat players over the years accompanied by HGs flashed across the screen.

Kenuda stood in front of his desk, twirling a football. "Mr. Nedick asked if we would allow humans instead of HGs to finish up. We thought it would be amusing. That is mockery turned inside out."

A few clips flashed of Vernon crawling towards home plate and Neal getting hit in the head with a throw.

Prick. You snuck in and filmed the game.

Hazel returned. "So if you want a good laugh and have an hour to kill with nothing better to do, check out this historical monstrosity from a time of hatred and false pride in being an American."

The sportscaster stepped aside for the iconic shot of part of the Amazon Stadium scoreboard collapsing on 10/12, which silenced the bar.

Jimmy plugged the music back in and the dancing slowly resumed, the report lingering in the air. The bartender gave Puppy a searching look filled with disappointment.

"You really making fun of baseball?"

"No, just the opposite," Puppy tried explaining, but Jimmy walked away. A few patrons passed with curious stares, not quite knowing what to make of Puppy, but leaning toward disdain.

He slammed the nuts bowl onto their table. Cobb looked up, fuming.

"How come they didn't interview us? We're the stars."

"You know what, fuck you, too."

Puppy stormed out of the bar and back home. Mooshie was in the bathroom, singing. That lightened him up quickly. Mooshie Lopez, urinating on the same toilet. He sat on the couch, propping the computer on his lap, and started his report.

"Game Three. April 25, 2098. This was historic and astonishing. For the first time in thirty-three years, men and women ran the bases of Amazon Stadium. They hit the ball. They threw. They pitched. They caught. They slid. Not an HG in sight."

Okay, he murmured, a little too celebratory, especially since the Little Extended Family is coming down on them for anti-robot bias.

"…They caught. They slid. They demonstrated some of the finest excitement of HG-inspired baseball."

"And where the hell did the HGs get their shit from?" Mooshie rested her chin on her hands, looking over his shoulder. The white towel covered her head.

"I have to be polite."

"Lucky we didn't turn them all into can openers after the shit they pulled. Posing as humans. Made in whose image?" Her full lips curled. "Enough of that. What do you think of me?"

Mooshie grandly tugged off the towel. Gone were the thick, luscious black curls. Now chopped blonde hair hugged her scalp just above the small ears.

"You don't look like yourself," he stammered.

"Not a bad thing since I'm dead."

"But you looked good."

Her long grin made him blush. "Would you tell me if I didn't?"

"Sure." He knotted his forefinger and index finger toward his eyes, DV for always true. She patted her heart. "Bet you had the picture."

His blush deepened toward crimson.

"Come on, gorgeous." Mooshie pouted huskily, draping her legs, bare to the knees, across his ankles. He nearly fainted. "Admit it."

The Picture. Mooshie diving head-first into home, her powerful ass muscles reared up as if about to launch a missile strike into Allah Land. For most adolescent boys and girls in America, it was the original entry point into sexual fantasies. Estimates were about ninety-five percent of siblings under eighteen had that picture of Mooshie's sacred naked ass, sans Yankees uniform. Maybe fifty percent over eighteen. For a while, rumors smoked that every third potential divorce mentioned the photo. A few captured Allahs had her rear in their backpacks. Few? Thousands. Hundreds of thousands. Don't kneel to Mecca, but toward Mooshie's butt crack. Send Mooshie's ass to the Grand Mufti and end the war, was a favorite bar slogan.

No one ever knew if it was a doctored photo or if Mooshie had snuck into the stadium and had a picture taken of her patented head-first slide with her uniform bottom around her knees.

"Yes, you did." She tickled his chin.

"I didn't," he shouted as if fourteen. "I considered that sacrilege. Zelda had one."

Mooshie raised an eyebrow. "Did she show it to you?"

"I wouldn't look. Pablo did."

"But not innocent little Puppy?"

"No," he said adamantly, cheeks burning. "You're having fun, aren't you?"

"A ball." She dumped crackers onto the coffee table. "How'd the old coots do?'

"Good."

She tilted her head doubtfully and knotted her fingers by her eyes. Puppy described the worst-played baseball game in human history. At least no one got seriously hurt.

She sipped a beer. "What're you going to do?"

"More practice. Lots more practice."

"What if it doesn't work? Your best players are about two hundred years old."

He hesitated. "Not all of them."

Off his long, pleading stare, Mooshie sighed deeply. "I can't, hon."

"Just play every few games. We need a pitcher."

She moved into a chair. "Look at me. Even with this disgusting hair style, put me in a baseball uniform and I'm recognized."

"That would cause some questions," he conceded.

"Especially since they killed me, handsome."

His mouth dropped. "I thought you..."

"Killed myself? Toppled over drunk? Nope. Figure as long as I'm back, I'll find out who. But it was probably Grandma."

"Grandma wouldn't do that."

Mooshie squeezed his wrist a little too hard. "A believer. Touching. I was a nuisance. Much better to discredit me and the Miners. No, kid. I don't even want to see what Yankee, sorry, Amazon Stadium looks like. I pitched my last game that day. Dodging the bullets. The bodies. The screams." Mooshie leaned forward, elbows on knees, seeming smaller in memory. She returned with a distant smile. "What other crap do you have to write tonight?"

"The kind that smells good."

"My specialty." Mooshie deleted "astonishing" from his report, then erased the entire paragraph. "How many errors today?"

He glanced at his notes. "Twelve."

"Not bad for both teams."

"That's just the Falcons."

She rolled her eyes and nudged him aside. Mooshie Lopez was writing his game report. He couldn't believe it. He watched her beautifully molded face with those high cheekbones and thin lips work thoughtfully, laughing to herself, mouthing the words, frowning with mental edits as she two-fingered on the keyboard. At midnight, he cooked up a platter of Edison's Crumpled Crackers.

Mooshie handed back the laptop.

"Game Three. April 25, 2098. We had real people today. Not greats like Mooshie Lopez, the best player in history, but solid local talent who tried their best to play the game like it hasn't been played in a long time. They did their best. One of the better ones was Vernon Jackson the catcher who had two hits. The oldest guys..."

Mooshie, he murmured scoldingly. She shrugged, grinning.

"...were Ty Cobb and Mickey Mantle whose ancestors once played well and whose talents maybe they haven't entirely inherited. Mantle never hit the ball and Cobb got only one hit. He also pitched which he did okay considering the Falcons couldn't hit the side of Grandma's ass with a building..."

Mooshie! He shook his head, laughing.

"...but the game was sloppy overall and one-sided, not perfect like HGs. That's what you get with humans. Maybe they'll get better."

He cleared his throat. "I'll make a few edits."

"Leave it," Mooshie said sternly. "I don't do tweaks."

"Referring to Grandma's butt..."

"You think she'll read this?"

"Someone might."

In all the fifteen years, no one had ever responded to any of his entries. More than two thousand and not even a complaint about a comma.

As he shut down the laptop, Mooshie yawned and kissed him on top of the head.

"Mooshie likes to sleep late so make sure the Two White Grampas don't wake me up with their belching and farting."

Shit. The two Grampas. Where were they?

"Nighty-poo, little boo." Mooshie shuffled down the hallway with a tiny wave.

"Please lock the door if you go out again," said Puppy.

She peered back around the corner, eyes narrow. "You spying on me?"

"You don't have a Lifecard, Ms. Lopez."

Mooshie's expression eased. "Good point. But don't spy on me. Ever."

Puppy put on his socks and went back to Monroe's.

17

Second Cousins Patel and Cruz peeled off outside the conference room with dismayed looks; Cheng nodded reassuringly and caught up with Grandma as she returned to her living quarters. He waved off an offer of fresh coffee and stood silently by her desk.

Grandma glanced up as if surprised to still see him there. "I upset Fran and Carlos, didn't I?"

"You were rather distant."

"I was very heartened by the West Coast clean-up but I still want settlements, at least around San Diego, by the end of the year."

"As soon as it's safe."

"No, Albert. As soon as the scientists find the means, which has lagged greatly. I want the radiation levels down to zero by the end of the year. And I want Americans living in Southern California by early next year." She waved off his protests. "Minimal American populations is an open window for the Chinese to meddle and I won't have it."

"They probably funded the damn terrorists."

Grandma glared. "That's a lie and you know it."

"Makes perfect sense. The great world power gone…"

"And they lose the buffer against the Caliphate. Next year in San Diego. The year after in LA."

"We can celebrate the 22nd Century there." He tipped his shoulders forward slightly and she reddened.

"Your sarcasm isn't appreciated. Now if you'll excuse me, I must prepare for those wonderful physicians. Children living outside the womb at three months."

"I know. I put that on your calendar since health is one of my areas. Along with education."

She shot him a sour look and made coffee by the walnut side table, lingering over each scoop. "What's the progress of importing real coffee?"

"You're changing the subject."

"There are reports of black market caffeine. The neutrals down there in Brazil will work with us. I want that done. The Family should have real coffee in the morning. That's a true family breakfast. If only we could manage bacon."

"I'll handle creating pigs along with undoing the effects of the Allah nuclear terrorist attack on Los Angeles."

Grandma dropped a coffee cup and stared with heavy eyes, probing. He let her in just slightly, the years giving him new insights into protecting his thoughts. Or, he sometimes wondered, were her powers waning? Along with her judgment.

"I won't be deterred."

"You can't release those curriculum guidelines, Lenora."

"Can't as in shouldn't? Or can't as in I won't be allowed?"

Cheng stiffened. "Ultimately, it is your decision."

"Yes, it is."

"But we need to discuss this further."

"Everything's quiet. Have there been any flare-ups?"

"There are occasional Kill Allahs signs…"

"By whom? Children."

"Children are taught," he said coldly.

"Yes, they are. And we're not living in our bubble forever, Albert."

He swallowed slowly. "Meaning?"

"I want to teach everything that happened. Whether we fare well or not."

"There is only Allah treachery."

"Please don't insult me, Albert. We wrote the history to satisfy our losses." She waved her arm. "And don't lecture about LA and Washington and Manhattan. We need to understand why it happened. We can't wallow in resentment and hatred."

"So you want to re-write the truth?"

"Truth, my darling, is perhaps the most subjective fact of all. I think we've reached a stage where we can discuss the events leading up to the Allah War."

"Such as?"

She flushed at his quiet insolence. "Like the deportations. Did we over-react? Did we banish loyal Americans?"

"Who believed in sharia, world conquest, hiding behind terror cells in mosques."

"They could just as easily have abandoned that religious nonsense like the Christians and Jews."

"There were no nuns or rabbis strapping bombs around their waists, blowing up school buses in our cities."

"I'm not defending that." His silence infuriated her. "They were largely disloyal, no protests against the terrorists, little support for America. I lived that, too, Albert. But perhaps we should've let the Muslims who wanted to follow their religion do so, as we allowed the others. Quietly, until they came to their senses about God and miracles instead of rounding them all up and out the door. You can do the right thing and still get some of it wrong." She pursed her lips stubbornly, the traditional sign that debate was over. "I'm going through with this, Albert."

"Changing the educational curriculums still requires passage by First Cousins."

Grandma smiled wintrily. "Not if it's a Grandma Story."

Cheng barely kept his anger checked. "That is very unwise, Lenora. Everyone will hear it."

"That's the point."

"Including the damn Allahs."

Grandma put on her reading glasses. "Your disapproval has been noted, First Cousin. Now if you'll please excuse me."

He didn't move. "I want to see the script beforehand."

"Of course, Albert," she said without looking up. "You are my loyal First Cousin, after all."

Her gloating sarcasm followed him down the hall. Not this time, Grandma.

• • • •

FRECKLIE SQUATTED BY the entrance to the DV community center, eyes lowered in embarrassment. Puppy stood over him for a moment, slowly unfolding the tiny white square of paper that Frecklie had stuck inside his door frame.

Only families were allowed to communicate beyond these casual notes and regular mail, easily the finest postal system in the world with four deliveries a day, and that, only in an emergency.

All siblings registered key members of their families for interconnect between the vid news, specially coded for your residence only. Emergency meant emergency. No "how was school" or "what's for dinner." It had to be something like "leg mangled, in Lebanon Hospital." Implicit in any family communication was the question of why? If you were in a family, you'd know what was happening, you'd see them, share, spend time together. No mysteries, no sudden, "what do you mean Uncle Matsori's socks store is closing?" You'd have suffered with Uncle Matsori, listened to his complaints, problems, helped him sort it all out over endless piles of Darnell's Cream Donuts. That's what a family does. Anyone who needed to message more than "fell down elevator shaft" wasn't doing their job.

Friends, well, there was no communication that constituted an emergency with friends. Someone's gone missing. They have no family, poor bastard, something had to be done, even grudgingly. If you wanted to talk, you had to go through the Main News Link, using the password and code of the friend to demonstrate you really knew them, which would be projected on the continuous crawl of the vidnews in one of the four corners, representing geographic points of the country. The last four digits of your Lifecard would sync up with the last four digits of the supposed missing person. The searcher would flash in orange, the searchee in red, pulsing on the screen for five hours.

"Gordon. Are you okay? Juan."

Puppy had never used this feature. He didn't know anyone who ever had. Friendship was somewhat suspicious in Grandma's House. If it was a prelude to forming a partnership and raising children, then official engagements was the way. But people who remained friends for too long suggested they really didn't want familial relationships. They were taking the easy way out, abdicating their duties as members of a Family. There were no honorary "aunts" and "uncles." Godparents had been banned for more than thirty years as undermining the family structure since too many of these unofficial relatives were just that, good friends. Where was the incentive to connect? Friendship wasted emotions. Friends couldn't really love; pointless, circuitous relationships delaying the necessary.

They'd all believed in friends equaling brothers and sisters, once. Those flaming war posters of broad-shouldered men and women clutching rifles beneath the slogan Defend The Family, a hook-nosed bearded Allah feasting on the naked flesh of a child. But they weren't really brothers and sisters, or even cousins. They'd just washed ashore off the beaches of Morocco, Spain, Britain, Italy. Bloated swollen bodies unrecognizable except for the stench of defeat. With the shame came the stigma. Maybe real brothers and sisters would've fought harder.

They'd actually learned something from the Allahs and their seemingly infinite tribes. Only blood mattered. Under Grandma, America became the bloodstream. All of them, the red and white blood cells. Family, real family. Everyone was a mother and a father. Breed like rabbits and, if you couldn't, adopt the ME orphans.

Can't, Frecklie had written.

"Why?"

Frecklie's embarrassment deepened. Puppy lifted his chin.

"Why?" he repeated.

The kid hesitated, then choked his throat with both hands.

"Your Mom?"

Frecklie choked again. Puppy pulled his hands away before he blacked out. Damn DV parents.

"Why?" Puppy asked.

The teen hesitated a little longer, then reluctantly ran his finger across his throat and pointed at Puppy.

He almost asked why again. "I only met her for like four minutes. What could I possibly have done to make her hate me?"

Frecklie tapped his temple and rolled his eyes about the mysteries of mothers.

Puppy stretched out his tight legs across the sidewalk, thinking. "You like the job?"

The kid nodded.

"Want to keep doing it?"

He nodded more emphatically.

"What about your friends?"

Frecklie tapped his chest and then walked his fingers along the ground. They are with me.

Puppy eased himself up. "Where's your Mom work?"

Frecklie waved his arms in alarm.

• • • •

PUPPY WALKED DOWN the two steps and was buzzed into the basement of the red brick building on East 164th Street, centered amid the rows of traditional artisan workshops. Clothes, shoes, hats, socks, underwear, scarves, all handmade.

Humming sewing machines sang behind a wide oak door at Ruby's Dresses. An old woman with gray hair squinted up from the folding table, which served as the front desk.

"Are you picking something up?"

She gestured at the neatly packed brown packages of clothes wrapped with string, sitting five feet high in the corner next to rolls of cloth covered in transparent plastic.

"No, ma'am. I'd like to talk to Mrs. Rivera."

"About?" The old eyes shaded slightly.

"Her son."

A few moments later, Beth leaned against the back door in the alley, giving him nowhere else to stand except by the black garbage cans, a suggestion that was where he belonged. She rubbed her thin neck slowly.

"What did you do to Ruben?"

"Nothing."

"Because I'll kill you if you hurt him."

He held up his hands. "I want to talk about the job."

Beth sneered slightly. "There's nothing to discuss, Mr. Nedick."

"Puppy."

"Mr. Nedick." Her hands were dotted with scabs. She blushed and shoved them into her jeans, angry he'd noticed. "My son had the one experience. I thank you. That'll be enough."

"You signed the contract."

"A mother can always renege for the protection of her son."

"How the hell am I hurting him?"

"I don't know yet."

Beth turned to go back inside. Puppy touched her elbow. Beth's look could've melted him down to the bone.

"He likes the job."

"He's sixteen. He likes many things, not all of them good."

"What's wrong with taking tickets at a baseball game?"

"It was a robot job." Her brown eyes darkened. "There could be trouble."

"No, it's all worked out. Third Cousin approval."

"Oh, a Third Cousin approved?" she said sarcastically. "That makes everything okay."

"Just this." He tapped his heart and waved his hands outward. I was a DV, too. That agitated Beth even more.

"Means nothing," her voice was low.

"Meant enough that I hired him. And more DVs."

The woman paused a moment and he pressed on.

"I don't even know if Frecklie will work out."

That got Beth defensive. "Why not?"

"I said I'd give him ten games as a trial. There's more than just taking tickets. It could be a bigger job. We'll see."

"You're saying my son can't do a job at a baseball place? Where no one goes?"

"We had our biggest crowd yesterday," he shot back, touting the first double-digit attendance in a year.

Beth's nostrils flared suspiciously. "You hired him because he was a poor little DV?"

"No. Because I was desperate. Robots quit. I needed people. Who the hell wants to work at a baseball place?"

His honesty held her a moment. Beth's eyes narrowed. "You won't take advantage of him."

"He's already acting like he's the boss."

She fought away the creeping smile. "Five games. Then I'll decide."

"Ten games. Then we'll decide together."

She glared. "Five. Or get yourself a 'bot."

He searched for some heroic stance; there was none. He nodded. "What's with this attitude?"

Rivera sneered as if he were a moron for not deciphering her contempt. She went inside and locked the door. Damn, she was pretty, Puppy grinned.

• • • •

STEAM FOGGED THE tiny window, obscuring the rooftops below the six-story building. Pablo tried adjusting the shower, but the pipes had only hot on their mind. The water cascaded in a wide spray, enveloping the glass-enclosed stall.

He sat back down on the tiny wooden stool, his bony knees up to his chin. In the fifteen minutes since he'd found the note, *Shower*, attached to the bland front door, he'd only taken off his pants, which he'd folded and used as a cushion to keep them pressed. Obey directions and not look wrinkled. All six feet of Pablo curled up, heels of the black socks skimming his thighs.

Do it. Just a damn shower. Obviously the thirty-minute one you took this morning, swallowing up the weekly water allotment, didn't cut it.

Pablo scanned the ceiling and corners for the cameras, hoping no one noticed, before slipping off his socks and neatly folding them on top of his gray suit pants. He slid off the red tie, jacket and white shirt, tucking the cuff links into the pocket, one in each. He squished down the pile one last time.

He looked around again but the steam had crawled out of the stall, surrounding him like a tent. This all couldn't be from the shower, he was convinced. There wasn't that much hot water in the Bronx. He rubbed his bare feet along the slippery tiles, searching for an underground spring, which made no sense since they were on the top floor of an old building off Moshulu Parkway. If there had been an underground spring, it would've scalded the residents on the floor below.

What residents?

He placed his boxer shorts on the pile and stepped gingerly into the shower and then right back out, swearing at the heat. No wonder no one talked about becoming a Cousin. Pablo fortified himself and eased inside. Water pelted his face. He grew accustomed to the slight pain and reached for soap or shampoo, but found nothing.

Okay, he steadied himself. I'll wash with plain water if that's what you want. He turned three hundred and sixty degrees several times, discarding songs to sing because he didn't know how happy he should be.

He was not happy at all, just puzzled. How long do I stay in? Until the water goes off, he decided grimly. If you want to wither my skin into wrinkled red puffs, then go ahead.

The door opened and an absolutely beautiful woman with red-hued skin and straight black hair falling to her navel slipped inside as if he'd been expecting her.

"Good morning, Dr. Diaz." She kissed his cheek.

"Morning."

"The water's very hot." Her black eyes twinkled. "Does that bother you?"

"I thought it's supposed to be this hot."

"Why?" she asked in genuine curiosity.

"Because it's a test."

She laughed merrily and he chanced a look at her full breasts and flat, muscled stomach. "To see if you can suffer third degree burns?" The woman adjusted the knob and the temperature decreased slightly from the inside of a volcano. "Better?"

"Yes. Thank you."

Her firm arm groped past his shoulder. "No soap?"

He shrugged sheepishly.

"You were going to suffer third degree burns and not even get clean for your efforts?"

"I didn't know where they kept the soap."

She smiled skeptically. "Will you wash my chest?"

"Why can't you do it?"

"It'd be more fun if you did."

"There's no soap."

"Your wet hands will do."

He pressed back against the tiled wall. "I prefer to focus on just washing myself, thank you."

"You're so polite."

"Thank you."

The woman grinned. "I guess there's no shampoo, either?"

"Probably in some cabinet," he answered.

"Which you didn't ask about."

"Ask who?"

"There's always someone to ask, Dr. Diaz."

"So I screwed that up?"

"You mean by not washing your hair?"

He bristled. "I washed it already. Twice. Probably dried out the scalp for a month along with wilting in this steam."

She glanced down. "Not entirely wilted."

Pablo covered his erection. "Sorry."

"I'm flattered." The woman raised her face to the spray. "Should we have sex?"

Pablo tensed, quickly juggling a variety of answers which all included a direct quote or partial quote from one of Grandma's Insights about random promiscuity, though nothing about showers with naked gorgeous women came to mind. "Probably not."

"That's fairly non-committal."

"Under the circumstances."

"Which are?"

"My first meeting. Not you. Here. This interview."

"With who? I'm the only one here."

"Test." He said, frustrated she didn't get it. "This is part of the test."

"Everything is part of a test, Dr. Diaz. Pass one and on to the next."

"Did I pass this?"

She frowned. "What was it?"

"I don't know," he snapped. "Getting a hard-on. Losing it." His hands fell away. "Showering for ten minutes with a beautiful naked woman without using soap. And you're probably not even real."

"Do you think I'm real?"

His jaw jutted out. "Does it goddamn matter?"

She turned off the water. "Does losing your temper?"

Pablo sighed. "Yes."

"Which you think was wrong." The woman opened the glass door. "Do you think it was wrong, Dr. Diaz?" She bent over and handed him a bar of soap and a bottle of shampoo left outside.

"Thank you," he whispered. "What do I do now?"

"What do you think you should do, Dr. Diaz? I have plans. Not everyone can spend all day washing their hair."

The woman slipped into a purple bathrobe, leaving his robe hanging on a hook. He slowly dressed. His black socks were wet.

Pablo hurried out of the silent building and actually walked two blocks toward the subway before admitting that he didn't want to rush back to work. He didn't know if that was a good thing or a bad thing, but he was hungry and his skin tingled as if he was a second course at a barbecue, and he was perplexed. Besides, he didn't want to imagine the woman's breasts dancing among molars.

Usually when he was this bewildered, he would hide. Not physically, but crawl into the Pablo part of himself that disconnected into a calm parallel universe, which he'd first discovered, powered by that most universal of inter-galactic emotional fuel, misery. Parents forever arguing because they had to blame someone for their failures and it would get out if they were heard blaming their children. His only sister was dead. During a school trip to the nation's capital, she'd been incinerated in the dirty nuke bomb that took out DC. She was eight years old.

His father and mother stopped arguing after that, though when Pablo was accepted to Bronx University with a pre-dental major, a pretty damn impressive leap from the DV with both undergraduate and graduate school guaranteed, his dear old Dad had insisted the only reason Pablo made it was because his sister's name was on the wall of victims at the black-marbled memorial at 1600 Pennsylvania Avenue.

Otherwise you'd be shit like me, his dear old Dad had said, the same dear old Dad who burnt down his own bakery a few months later.

Pablo, deep in thought by a traffic light, aimlessly turned down a clammy street scabbed with old buildings and into Needleman's Coffee Shop. Proudly Serving Since 2036.

Three greasy men with spines bowed by irritation picked at the remains of breakfast at a front table. Scuffed, grimy tiles continued up the walls, giving the long, rectangular restaurant a cylindrical, tunnel-like feeling.

Pablo sat in a booth across from the empty counter at the rear. Two glass cases held piles of pastries and cakes. A blackboard told everyone that today's special was split pea soup. Yum-delicious.

An old guy with a tuft of hair like a solitary wing handed Pablo a menu.

"What'll it be?" he asked gruffly.

"I haven't looked yet, sir."

"Then look already," the waiter said peevishly, retreating behind the counter. He folded his arms impatiently.

Pablo sniffed at the discolored fork and wiped it clean with his handkerchief. "Coffee and a cup of the split pea soup."

"That it?" The waiter was stunned. "We got fine Reuben sandwiches. Fries that'll make you piss down both legs. And you only want the goddamn soup?"

Pablo tried placing the waiter's accent a moment, and smiled. "Bring me the soup, then the sandwich and fries."

"It's on marble rye. But save room for dessert. Black-and-white cookies come in fresh daily."

"I can't wait."

The waiter shuffled off, pleased. European, Pablo finally placed the phrasing. Probably one of the Last Exodus, the few Jews who had made it out of ME, where they'd been slaughtered on the spot, and the final bits of CE territory, where they returned to ghettos and suffered blame for the war; Israel was the first victim of the Islamic Empire.

Pablo munched on the best pickle he ever had as the waiter beamed and refilled his cup.

"I've never been here," Pablo said, curious about the way the waiter's shoulders raised up slightly to the left as he laid the soup down.

"Now you are." The waiter was offended "Eat." A bell rang and an A18 in a tall cook's hat dropped the sandwich onto the counter, making the fries dance. The waiter scowled and the A18 ducked back by his stove. The waiter trudged over apologetically.

"Goddamn robots. I say, two courses. Soup, then sandwich. Not soup-sandwich. You want me to keep it warm."

"No, looks good." Pablo took a bite and his eyes lolled dreamily.

The waiter brightened, proudly pointing around the restaurant. "Since 2036. Ten years of making people happy."

Pablo didn't correct the man's mistake. He was quite old; the Alzheimer's cure didn't work on everyone. And Pablo was enjoying disappearing into the Reuben sandwich.

"What kind of meat is this, sir?"

"Corned beef. What else do you make a Reuben out of?" the waiter barked, muttering about the ignorance of the young.

Pablo placed his thin spiral notebook on the table, munching on another sour tomato which was becoming addictive. Disappearing into himself meant finding order to face chaos. He understood it was always temporary, but structure reassured him.

What happened? He wrote across the top of the page.

Testing resolve.

Testing ethics.

Testing reactions.

What else? He added below.

Sex drive. He quickly crossed that out, then scribbled it back in. Cousins should have children, he thought.

What about the soap and shampoo? How does he handle irritation? Water too hot? A metaphor? What if the water was just too damn hot? An old building, seemingly abandoned.

Cousins face problems of all kinds, he circled this phrase, pleased; he rewarded himself with another sour tomato, prompting the waiter to happily refill the bowl and remind Pablo about dessert.

How did you do, Pablo? He wrote this out carefully as if inscribing a holy tablet.

Lost temper.

Bickered with girl.

Never asked her name.

Got hard-on.

Looked stupid looking for cameras and source of steam.

Looked like fool sitting in socks.

Had no answers for anything.

Pablo leaned back wearily and bit into the cookie, half chocolate, half vanilla icing. One of the best things ever. If this cookie had been in the shower, his entire mood would've been different.

He grinned and wrote, How to act like someone eating a black-and-white cookie when you're not?

● ● ● ●

AZHAR RAMMED THE car backwards into the crowded garage, flattening Omar's bicycle. Clary bolted up as if electrocuted, hands out like talons, teeth bared.

"It's okay." He closed the garage door, not moving until they were concealed in darkness. "It's Azhar." Clary's lower lips trembled in relief. Mustafa wrapped the blanket around the girl's shivering body and carried her through the kitchen and up the steps.

Jalak stared, stunned, the vacuum still hoovering away on the landing.

"Get the first aid," he shouted, laying Clary gently on their bed. It took a few seconds to persuade her to let go of the blanket. He brushed at her hair, but she snapped her jaws. "I would never hurt you. Let go, little one."

Her eyes brimmed warily: the beard, the nose, the scent of a man like the scent of all those men. But this was the nice one. He had fed her. He had sung her songs. He had smiled; not just afterwards.

Clary's bleeding fingers fell away. Azhar opened the blanket.

"What is this?" Jalak hovered, almost as terrified as Clary.

Mustafa grabbed the first aid kit and clumsily poured rubbing alcohol on a bandage, spilling much of it.

"Who is she?" Jalak demanded.

"Just help me, woman."

Jalak and Clary exchanged suspicious stares. Jalak grumbled and tugged off the remains of Clary's ripped clothes, wiping away the blood and applying antibiotic ointment. The little girl watched carefully as Jalak finished bandaging her torso and cleaning the scrapes on her thighs, cheeks and forehead.

"Give her some aspirin," Mustafa ordered.

"Is she in pain?"

"What do you think? Look at her."

Jalak didn't move, wishing away Clary from her home. Azhar angrily fetched the pills from the medicine cabinet, cradling Clary's neck as she sipped the water.

"Let her sleep," he said.

`"Here?" Jalak shrieked.

Clary recoiled like a cornered animal.

"Yes. Here." Azhar finally persuaded Clary to slide under the sheets, sending Jalak raging out the door.

"Sleep." Azhar smiled. "You are safe."

Clary didn't believe him, but she was so tired.

Mustafa hurried past Omar, dressed for the morning prayers.

"What's going on, Father?"

"Go back to bed." Azhar followed his wife down the steps.

Jalak kicked the basement door closed, shaking with fading self-control. "Who is this girl?"

Azhar deliberated how much to lie. Be with those who are true in word and deed, says the Quran. How could that apply to a wife?

"I found her in the car."

"She was stealing it?"

"Does the child look like she can drive? The poor thing was sleeping in the back seat."

"Why?"

"Why, why, why? So many questions. Do I know? Allah knows. Ask him."

Jalak fluttered her lips angrily. "Don't hide behind Allah. She has run away."

"The girl is here. That is enough. She'll sleep and get well."

"What do you mean get well? She cannot stay. Call the Warriors."

"No." Azhar grabbed her wrist. "No."

Jalak stared suspiciously. "You know who she is."

Mustafa sighed. Jalak would wear him down eventually. "She is the girl I told you about from the orphanage. The sweet Spanish one."

"An infidel lies in my bed?"

"Oh shut up. Do you think Allah cares about your linens?"

Jalak went white. "They will look for her."

"They might. Or not. There are many children there. The sex traders came last night, Jalak. They would've taken her."

"That is not my concern."

"It's mine," he said defiantly, almost proudly. "I don't want her violated by those pigs." He shuddered. "She'll be sold in the market as a whore."

"So? That is what she is," Jalak said obstinately.

"No. She is eleven years old. And scared." Jalak pulled away. "Would you want a Crusader to send back Omar or Abdul if they'd escaped?"

Jalak spat contemptuously on his bare feet. "Never compare my children to one of them."

"All children get frightened, damn you."

Jalak ran up the basement steps. The front door was ajar. Omar was hurrying along the street, glancing guiltily over his shoulder at his father in the doorway.

No, Omar. No.

"What happened to my bicycle?" Abdul yelled from the garage.

18

Derek Singh held up his hand until the skittering feet on the roof of his country store passed.

"That a squirrel?" asked his former teammate Easy Sun Yen, squirming uneasily; he'd never taken to the woods. Sunken tubs filled with gin and brunettes, always on the hefty side, that was his idea of fun. Sometimes Derek had joined him. Once, so did Mooshie. The Three Amigos singing and splashing each other.

2062, Singh smiled nostalgically. An August road trip to the Midwest. Damn hotel in Cincinnati banned them. All the damn hotels in Cincinnati banned them. Hell with them. They rented an old mansion and partied 24/7. They were the Yankees. They could do whatever the hell they wanted.

"Nah," Derek said playfully. "Spaceships. They land every day around this time. Little green men."

Sun Yen frowned. Somewhere he'd lost his humor. Age'll do that, Derek thought, rocking in the chair and sipping the brandy. They sat in silence as two old men do, remembering what they couldn't have anymore.

"And this guy Hazel said nothing?" Sun Yen was a little disappointed, having traveled from Boston, where he still could find an occasional hefty brunette to share a bathtub, to this forest of squeaking animals and smelly trees.

"Acted as if I should know."

"Maybe you forgot."

"Forgot what?"

"What you were supposed to know."

Derek scowled. He only forgot the small things nowadays though sometimes the big things drifted away, too, like the battleships who abandoned them on the beach.

"He gave me the damn Miners wig around a lot of crap and that's it."

"Well no one knows who he is."

"How many you ask?"

"Many as still have a pulse. Tekkie Donaldson recalls someone named John in North Africa."

Singh sighed wearily. "He's too young to have served with us."

"Oh." Sun Yen frowned again.

"I figure he signed up early 70s in the last wave. I wasn't going to ask too much so he didn't think I cared." Derek stretched out his good leg. Sometimes he couldn't tell the difference. After sixty all the aches hurt the same, mechanical and otherwise. "Probably not."

"Probably not what?"

"Probably no one would know him no matter," Singh said.

"Then why'd we ask and take chances?"

"With who? No one cares about us anymore."

"They're caring about something," Easy said. "Else why did this Hazel come out of nowhere?"

"That's what we're trying to figure," Derek said impatiently. "Made a point of his knee."

"How so?"

"Gelinium."

Sun Yen arched an eyebrow. "On the beaches of Sicily?"

"Don't add up. Our asses were flying across the Channel to England by then."

The last desperate attempt to stop the Caliphate ended on the British beaches in 2072. There was no Dunkirk this time because there was no one to rescue them; the American Navy was nearly gone. The entire 7th Army surrendered, hundreds of thousands of soldiers kneeling for days in the sand, watching the feet of the Allahs march past, England invaded for the first time since William the Conqueror in 1066. Once fully ashore, the Grand Mufti's armies, the Second and Twelfth Arab Legions, confiscated every boat that could float and sailed them down the Thames, their ships blackening the water like bugs, each sail fluttering with the crescent moon and star.

"Maybe he served and got it elsewhere." Sun Yen thought a moment. "Only other way is if he were in the riots. Handed them out there like a whore's tit."

In the late 70s, nearly twenty thousand veterans across the country had been killed, protesting for respect. Not food, not money, not socks. Respect. Remember us with a stamp. A day. An hour once a year on the vidnews. But America couldn't show respect to someone it was ashamed of. Much easier to shunt them aside. Or find a pretext to slaughter them. To finish the job the Allahs started. The job the soldiers were supposed to finish. Around and around the circle went.

"They only gave the Geliniums to soldiers."

Sun Yen's eyes narrowed. "And Black Tops."

• • • •

ZELDA PROPPED HER eyelids open with her thumb and forefinger. Actually she thought of propping open her eyes with the blades she and every former DV kept taped to their ankles. Her fourth meeting of the day. All about salmon salads. How was that remotely possible? She glanced at the thick twenty-six-page marketing deck emblazoned with striking yellow letters intended to shock the room into ecstasies of creative fervor, lips drooling ideas, blood-stained imaginations streaming out of their ears, hearts throbbing and pulsing with memorable moments in marketing history.

The woman in a long-sleeved black dress stared around the table. If Zelda recalled the stupid thing called the org chart, which she had first thought was a joke with its arrows pointing up and down and sideways like a bad drawing, this lady with the face of a boar was her direct supervisor, not Pietro, who was manager of the entire Bronx office.

Boar Face didn't like Zelda. Perhaps, like all wild creatures, she had that cunning sense of enemies in the jungle. Or woods, wherever boars roamed. Boar Face instinctively felt Zelda's diffidence, her inner laughter, how she took none of this corporate shit at all seriously. What was a thought-starter, Zelda had almost asked an hour ago before her brain oozed into a peanut butter-crusted glaze. Upselling propositions, positioning and then branding. Boar Face dribbled on about branding, branding, branding; if Zelda shoved her fingers down her throat, maybe she would knock down the woman with a heave and end all their misery. Only she seemed the only one miserable.

Grandma, you banned all languages other than English, how about banning marketing lingo?

"Jones was on a boat." Boar Face pointed. "Would you like to share those insights?"

Zelda faded back into the room from the little sweet alcove starring Diego's smile. "No."

"Excuse me?"

The conference room of twenty-one people simultaneously looked into their laps. One of those cartoon balloons on the animatevid would read "uh-oh."

"I mean that I just found out there may or may not be salmon in the Atlantic yet," Zelda said quickly. "But it was very valuable. We go to greater lengths for our fish."

Everyone's heads perked up slightly to see if Boar Face would lash Zelda with the long wooden stick she carried around like a riding crop. Boar Face frowned.

"What lengths?"

"Pardon?"

"Lengths. You said a word. A word can be dynamic. It can change perceptions. That doesn't mean it's the right word. We have to determine that. Lengths. What do you mean?"

"I'm not sure."

Boar Face twirled the pearl necklace around her fleshy neck and turned to the other side of the conference table.

"But you're right about the words," Zelda plunged ahead. "I, um, kinda think we haven't listened carefully enough to you."

The twenty-one people in the room poured silent venom. Oh too bad, you wish you were getting out of trouble this easily. She flashed a quick sneer around the table.

"Obviously." Boar Face rapped her stick. "Go on, Jones."

"I don't know the word. But maybe we should come up with a few words rather than all the art and videos and tag lines. Something that says salmon salad. But that also says be."

"Be?" Boar Face frowned.

"The salmon."

Zelda ducked past colleagues, alternatively snickering and looking for places on her skin to pinch. When she got back to her office, the memo was already flashing on the tiny digital directive boxes on their desks, which comprised the sole electronic means of communication.

"Each of you will submit one word per my suggestion at this morning's meeting. Deadline is eighteen minutes." A clock started ticking down like a bomb.

Zelda had a lot of words. The memo said one word. Would she be better off if she did only the one word and demonstrated she could pay attention and follow orders like the other headless imbeciles, or should she be bold and submit several words, showing how creative she was. Business environments were just so dumb that she had to waste her time considering these alternatives when she should be expending her limited attention span/interest on answering the question. Meetings, offices, memos, all this make-work so someone will eat salmon salad.

And keep this job, stupid girl, she scolded herself.

Boar Face twirled her necklace, feet on her desk. Zelda had sat for about three minutes since being summoned, taking in all the self-proclaimed award-winning marketing campaigns plaques that proclaimed her boss as a "champion of creativity," according to an award from the Marketing Alliance of The Northeast.

Boar Face twisted her pasty face. "Eight words."

"Yes."

"Better. Tasty. Luscious. Classy. Prime. Delicious. Powerful. Fin-tastic." Boar Face paused. "Is that a real word?"

Zelda shook her head. "I made it up."

"But not the others?"

"I think those are established and acceptable English words."

"I know. I went to the University of Pennsylvania," she said haughtily.

"I went to Bronx Arts School. I think we used the same English."

Boar Face looked as if she'd found a scabrous insect in her tea. "I shouldn't have to do your work for you. Pick a word. Stand behind it. Fight for it."

Zelda peered at the woman's silvery sheened shoes. The damn shoes just pissed her off. People shouldn't wear silver sheened shoes with silver buckles. It was dumb. Insulting in some way to people who would never wear shoes like that and yet had to sit here in an office, on the subway, street, anywhere, and be reminded of how stupid those shoes were and what kind of world they lived in where people like Puppy's ex-wife Annette sold shoes like that and people like Boar Face wore shoes like that.

Zelda vowed to stay late one night and carve up all the shoes she could find in Boar Face's office.

"They are pretty crappy words," she said.

"You admit that?" Boar Face pawed the ground, already tasting Zelda's flesh.

"Well sure. Those idiots around here have never done anything creative. The whole campaign is off."

Boar Face lowered her ridiculous shoes and walked around the front of the desk, fussing with her short blonde hair. "My campaign?"

She'd be cleaning fish by the end of the day. "It should be more personal. I wanted to give the salmon personality."

"Personality? Like a person?"

"Except like a fish. But Mr. Pietro said no."

"Pietro," Boar Face nearly spat the name. Pietro, the boss. Pietro, a simpleton. Pietro, who made four times her salary when she went to the University of Pennsylvania. "What did he say, exactly?"

"I don't know, exactly."

"You don't remember what your bosses say?"

"I don't pay that close attention."

Boar Face snorted. "Try to remember."

"I had sketches of salmon as kind of people, so we could show an organic community. Mr. Pietro didn't want happy salmon in evening clothes dancing. Something like that."

Boar Face perked up. "Do you still have those sketches?"

"I save everything."

"But you don't pay attention to your bosses."

"Well no." Zelda frowned, puzzled by the repeated question. "I would if they said something interesting."

• • • •

MOOSHIE POPPED SOME nuts onto her curled tongue, avoiding her reflection in the glistening mirror behind the bar. Her purple eyeliner was set off by rouge cheekbones and bold red lipstick suggesting her mouth would leap off at any minute. The official honeymoon night kits still used the whore makeup, she thought, rolling her eyes. All girls at fifteen got one; boys at the same age, along with shaving and grooming needs. Nice of Zelda to lend me hers along with the cheap-ass jewelry and sweater three sizes too big. Maybe two, Mooshie grunted unhappily. Gotta find some real clothes. I am Mooshie Lopez.

"What can I get you, ma'am?" Jimmy leaned on his elbows.

"Schaeffer Ale."

Monroe frowned. "Ma'am?"

"You don't serve that anymore?"

"For like thirty years."

Next time just order what's on tap. Mooshie selected an IPA from Jersey City. Jimmy poured and wandered away down the bar.

"Excuse me, bartender."

Monroe came back, wiping the counter, which couldn't gleam any brighter.

"You still got live entertainment?"

He gestured at the large black speakers hanging from the four corners of the ceiling. "Just the tapes and if there's ever something on the musicvid. With the new crap they play, mainly the tapes. Can't beat real rock and roll." Jimmy thoughtfully wiped away the circle near her glass. "But you're right. They used to, long before I bought the place."

"When was that?"

His eyes retreated suspiciously.

"I'm not a cop." Mooshie tapped her eyes and pointed at his. Monroe kept his cold stare. "I'm a singer prowling the neighborhood to see who might want a hot crooner. You interested?"

"No thanks."

"Brings in business."

"I make enough." Jimmy caught her glance around the nearly empty bar. "It's early." Grumbling, Jimmy left to serve a forlorn old man. Mooshie slid onto the adjoining stool.

"How are you, sir?" she asked the wizened old guy, who muttered into his shot glass. "Bet you remember when Monroe's had live music?"

"Don't remember nothing." He downed the drink, smacking his lips. Mooshie gestured for Jimmy to refill; the man smiled gratefully.

"My mother told me there was a small stage over there." She pointed near the foosball table. "They had great acts, top names would pop in suddenly and gig it up. Nellie Charles, Monte D'Ang, Big Bob Button, John Griebel, The Seafarers."

The old-timer took his whiskey to a table.

Jimmy smirked. "That one of your fans?"

"I'm more charming with a microphone."

Jimmy yanked the plug on the music, muted the vidnews about the upcoming National Spelling Bee in Des Moines and reached behind the cash register, handing her the microphone. "Charm me."

"Any requests?" she asked.

Jimmy folded his arms skeptically.

Mooshie balanced on her left hand and hopped easily onto the bar. Jimmy stepped back, surprised by her agility.

"Thank you everyone." Mooshie reclined on one hip, draping her legs over the bar. "Good to be back at Monroe's. This hunky behind the bar asked me to sing a song for the late morning crowd. Here's one from that great singer, Mooshie Lopez. One of her best. *Love Her or Love Me.*"

She took a deep breath and sang softly:

"When the heart goes still
All's I have is my will
Don't give me your shit, man
Love her or love me."

The old man's eyes lit up, slowly standing as if strings were attached to his ears.

Mooshie picked up the tempo:

"You went down on your knees
And bled your palms into peas
Don't give me your shit, man
Love her or love me."

The old man started tapping his feet and clapping his hands. Mooshie hopped off the bar, blasting it out.

"You lied and you lied
For the love you revived
Don't give me your shit, man
Love her or love me."

Mooshie ran her hand along the old-timer's bald head, her voice dipping seductively.

"Cause I can love for a day
Or a lifetime, just say okay
Just don't give me your shit, man
Love her or love me."

The old man applauded wildly, whistling so hard he nearly shot his teeth across the bar. Mooshie returned the microphone. "I'll work for vodka until you're sure."

Jimmy searched her. "Law says I gotta give you something."

"If you insist. One more thing. You let my friends Ty and Mick back in."

The bartender's wisps of hair swayed. "Damn bums nearly wrecked the joint fighting."

"Because they were bored by the music, hot buns." Mooshie smiled. "I promise they'll be chaperoned."

Jimmy reluctantly nodded. Mooshie glanced out the window.

"Last request. Got any idea where I can get a Lifecard? I lost mine."

• • • •

DIEGO ACTED VERY professionally as he helped Zelda up the gangway onto the boat, stopping just short of saluting.

"Ms. Jones. Welcome aboard."

"Thank you, Diego." She blushed. "Am I on time?"

"Five minutes to spare. Would you like to sit below deck?"

Zelda followed him down the four short steps. She settled onto the battered cloth chair.

"I appreciate you doing this on such short notice."

"We catch fish. That's really short notice." Diego grinned. "Be underway soon, Ms. Jones."

Zelda hated his smug smile as if she'd crawled along the dock moaning "Diego, Diego, take me back." Her letter, squared neatly and tucked in his doorframe, explained she needed to do more research and hoped their past relationship wouldn't impact their business dealings.

Boar Face wanted to go along, but Zelda finally persuaded her that it was a small boat. Zelda was now the most extraordinary employee ever at Saul's Salmon, her supervisor had bleated. Or some such insincere nonsense, Boar Face mooing that she adored Zelda personally and professionally, and that she brought the sort of creativity she, Boar Face (real name Katrina Munson), had long wanted but had been denied by Mr. Pietro, a nice man but, between us, an egg shell on the floor.

Zelda wasn't sure about the intellectual properties of egg shells, but assumed they weren't high. Her mission was to focus on "being a salmon or whatever fish they called salmon" and come up with all the sketches and ideas she wanted. Then Boar Face (Katrina) would whip them into proper and masterful marketing and, if Mr. Egg Shell (Pietro) failed to see how this would break out of market, she, Boar Face (Katrina) would go to Mr. Saul Ribe (The Boss) himself. Yes, that Saul, whose kindly, myopic face stared back from the package of every Saul's Salmon as if he were the father of all fish.

Zelda balanced her sketchbook, plugging mentally into the boat's engines. Even the loud humming couldn't conceal the Captain's angry shouts. Lee stomped downstairs, apologetic and irritated.

"Ms. Jones. You're not supposed to be on this ship."

She reached for her authorization. "Diego said…"

"Yes, he did." The Captain reddened. "But this is my ship."

"Sorry. I'm doing a marketing campaign."

"Blast the salmon. Stay out of the way and never come on my ship again unless I personally greet you. Saul can shove his business."

Zelda slumped in the chair, too angry to sketch. After a few more minutes of one-sided yelling, Diego dropped down, flashing his winning smile. "Seems I messed up a little."

Typical DV shit. Show how smart you are because it's assumed you're not. She'd done that her whole life. Abandon ship, girl.

"You couldn't just tell the guy?"

"I was afraid if the Captain said no, you'd think it was me talking."

Zelda leaned against the wall. "You're an idiot."

"Sometimes." Diego abruptly kissed her on the lips, hard and just once. She reluctantly shoved him away.

"Idiot. Are you in trouble?'

"A little." He grinned. "A lot. You're worth it."

"No I'm not, moron. You can't lose jobs at your age. I lost three by the time I was twenty-five."

"I'm twenty-four."

Too young, Zelda. Too naïve. Too cocky.

"They see a pattern. Less is expected. Soon nothing will be offered."

"That how you ended up here?"

She shoved him into the wall and he laughed, uncertain if she were playing or insane.

"I'm glad you're here," he said softly. "I better get back on deck."

She wasn't sure if she were allowed to join him, but chanced it anyway. Standing by the center console, the Captain gruffly ignored her, while Diego winked a few times, attending to straightening the inside of the hatch. Suddenly the young man let out a loud yelp, windmilling his arms. Behind the wheel, Lee nodded calmly.

Zelda joined Diego at the prow. A thirty-foot boat drifted aimlessly, chasing its own tail. As the ship neared, a greasy-faced man waved from its deck.

"What's the problem?" the Captain asked over the loudspeaker, slowing down his vessel.

"Engine trouble," the man blandly replied.

"Want a tow?"

"Already called the Coast Guard." He gestured at a medium built man in a bulky overcoat and gray hat, clearly dressed for different weather. "He needs a lift."

"To where?" Lee frowned.

"Where you're going."

Diego flashed a wary look at the Captain, who leaned over the railing, hands clasped, motioning for Zelda to step away.

"How do you know where we're going?" he asked.

The other captain pointed at the registry on the port side: Bronx, New York.

"What're you doing so far out?" Lee asked firmly.

"Going there. Engine gone. If you don't want to, don't."

Lee thought a moment. The man in the bulky overcoat waited patiently as if at a watery bus stop.

Strange, Diego shorthanded.

Very, Lee shorthanded back.

"Okay. We'll call the Coast Guard, too. They're awfully slow."

Diego flung over a rope and secured the boat, then balanced a wooden gangway between the two ships. The man half-stumbled onto the salmon boat. He doffed his hat with a slightly bewildered look.

Diego brought the new passenger below deck where he settled into a chair, knees stiff, coat still buttoned, hat resting on his lap, as if he wanted to be prepared the moment the journey ended. Diego mumbled about Lee cracking the whip and hurried up the creaky steps.

Zelda introduced herself, but the guest merely smiled dimly. She even chattered on about salmon, but he maintained that distant expression, examining the nautical decorations. Finally, he managed to ask "Where is the bathroom" in a heavy accent, "w's" morphing into "v's".

Once the ship docked, the Parisian Collector casually doffed his hat, mumbling thank you with each tip of the hat and disappearing down the dock into a crowd of partygoers.

Zelda slung her bag over her shoulder. She'd sketched nothing useful except Diego without his shirt. She tossed the crumpled paper overboard.

The Captain stopped her by the gangway. "Sorry I blew my top."

"I understand. He can be infuriating." She shook her head at Diego, double-checking the knots in the ropes.

"I'm not supposed to pick up passengers." The Captain hesitated. "I should've turned around when I saw you, but I didn't want to screw up the schedule. And that would've got bird brain in trouble. As for our guest…"

Zelda squeezed his hand. "I never saw anyone on board except us. And you authorized my passage."

The Captain sighed at Diego's forged signature. "You really like that kid."

She sighed. "Yeah. A lot."

Lee tipped his cap, about to leave, then stopped. "The Coast Guard never got a report from that ship."

Strange, she shorthanded.

19

Two DV teens in baggy suits and glistening shoes falling off at the heels waited patiently by Gate Six. With a knowing paternal air, Frecklie introduced Aito and Estes to Puppy, the famous baseball historian. Frecklie shorthanded so quickly that Puppy missed a couple words, though he was pretty sure he was referenced as a genius at handling mothers.

That greatly relieved Aito and Estes, who evidently also had mothers ruining their lives. The kids eagerly rushed inside the stadium, eyes popping wonderingly. Frecklie assumed the role of tour guide, *this mural was hit by machine gun fire and over there was a store selling souvenirs, camel brain they're items you buy to remember the game, and over there was a restaurant named Planet Hollywood specializing in real meat hamburgers.*

Who are they? Puppy pulled Frecklie aside.

Hard workers.

For what?

With a big wave, Frecklie happily embraced the entire crumbling ballpark. Everywhere.

The boy found a broom for Aito, who danced along the floor merrily attacking dirt as if it were the 22nd Arab Legion outside Prague. The other new janitor Paquette approached from the north and together they surrounded piles of dirt in a masterful flanking maneuver. If only the Allahs had been so cooperative. The helpless Arial stood with head bowed before his dusty barren stand, glumly rolling a bag of chips back and forth, fearing he'd been fired before he started. To the rescue came Mrs. Balinksi, the other big surprise of the morning.

Lugging a rickety shopping cart bulging with trays and pots, Balinski stopped tentatively, making sure she was in the right place because there were oh so many baseball stadiums clustered along River Avenue.

Once she saw the famous baseball historian, Balinski rushed over, the shopping cart tipping dangerously, and babbled on about her food stall and how wonderful Puppy was to give her this opportunity. Determined to find his place alongside these titans of sports culinary wizardry, Estes offered his services with a polite bow, his skills at cleaning forks seconded by Frecklie, and soon an ancient folding table was dug up, literally, under part of a wall.

Balinski and Paquette scrubbed the table while Aito swept away the excess soap; it looked like they were trying to row a boat. When the pierogis and kielbasis came steaming out of the containers, Puppy felt it was safe to hurry off to the Hawks clubhouse.

A very quiet clubhouse. Except for Mick's snores.

Eyes collectively downcast, the team followed Ty's clomping spikes around the bare concrete floor. If you watched just the feet, you could see Ty's foot grinding down threateningly micro-inches from toes and heels.

"I ain't never seen such crap in my life." Ty circled warily, the players pressing into their lockers. "You are the worst pieces of dog shit players ever. Ever."

Puppy cleared his throat. The team looked up gratefully as if his harrumph were the sound of a hammer being laid down near their half-finished gallows.

"We have kielbasa for sale today."

The players jumped up, believing breakfast was on the way. Cobb threw a ball against a locker and it ricocheted crazily around the room, settling in the corner, split open.

"No one moves. No one eats. We got a goddamn game today at this goddamn ungodly hour." His scowl heaped blame on Puppy for disrupting his sleep patterns. "But you ain't going anywhere until I see some sense of understanding how badly you sucked."

The team lowered their collective eyes, eyelashes grazing the floor. Of course they sucked.

Cobb slammed a bat by Jackson's foot. The catcher jumped a few inches. "Have you ever caught a goddamn game?"

Vernon shook his head.

"So I got a catcher who can't catch. Fielders who don't know how to put their gloves on and throw like this." Ty made mincing steps. "What are you pieces of shit going to do about it?"

Shannon raised her hand. "Practice more."

Ty raised his hands skyward. "Finally. Of all of you, the colored girl's the only one with sense."

Shannon smiled, unsure how complimented she should be.

"Yes. Practice. Practice until your goddamn feet swell like balloons in the desert." Ty stepped on Dmitri's foot and he howled. "Practice until you got calluses ten inches thick. Bleeding, infected, disgusting calluses." Ty held out his hands for a glimpse of their future. "Practice until you don't think and then practice some more until you can. Do all of you get me?"

Mick snored louder. Ty kicked the stool from under him and he landed, awake and retching, on the floor.

"These are wonderful words, don't you think?" Puppy asked the clubhouse. Ty's furious glare sent him back a foot. Puppy cowered next to Vernon. His presence gave Jackson courage. The catcher raised his hand.

"But we won."

Vernon had said something so profound that Ty was speechless. He leaned over, his nose rubbing between Vernon's eyes.

"Say that again, fatso," he said hoarsely.

The team averted Jackson's helpless stare. "We won. Isn't that good?"

Ty's nose pressed deeper into Vernon's face. "Is that what you think?"

Vern wasn't sure what he thought. He wasn't sure of his name.

"Is that what you all think, you sniveling, whining useless lumps of crap?" Ty swung the bat and they ducked. "You won because the other team sucks worse than you. Not because you're good. You're not even good enough to be shit. You're beneath shit. I wouldn't feed you to a hog."

Ty considered making Vernon an exception. The catcher gulped.

"Now we're going out there today and you're going to hustle. You're not going to run across the mound on your way to third base. You're going to touch second base first. You're gonna learn left and right field. Which are on the sides of center field." Ty kicked Mick in the ribs, waking him again. "You're gonna look like goddamn major leaguers. Now kneel."

Cobb took the right knee to the ground and clasped his hands. "Are you all Hebes? Get down on your goddamn knees."

Puppy gestured for the team to kneel and clasp their hands. Everyone was fairly confident that Ty was going to behead them with their bats.

"Lord Jesus Christ. I hope you ain't given up on us yet."

The players' eyes widened in alarm at the illegal praying. They started standing; Puppy emphatically waved everyone to remain kneeling.

"These godless heathens ain't worthy of you. But I know your heart is large and I'm hoping you'll find room for them. They're stupid and they're useless and they will be a real test for you, Lord. So whatever you can do, send it along because this goddamn country is going to hell."

Ty did something weird with his hands, waving left to right across his torso as if chasing a fly, then touching his forehead and chest.

"Amen." Mickey belched.

The manager waited for Puppy by the entrance to the dugout, blocking the door with his arm, smiling shrewdly.

"You're pitching BP."

"Excuse me?"

Cobb pressed the ball into his hand.

"Ty, I can't..."

"I can't, I can't." Ty danced daintily on his toes around Puppy. "Get your worthless ass out there, Mabel. I can't pitch BP too."

Cobb shoved Puppy up the steps. He stumbled onto the field. A glove landed just over his head, followed by a fluttering Hawks cap.

"I don't have a uniform." He tried one last act of defiance.

"Fatso." Ty called over to Vern, busy examining the bats. "Give Mary Jane your t-shirt so she feels like she belongs."

Self-consciously covering up his belly rolls, Jackson flipped his shirt to Puppy.

"Any other excuses 'cept you're a gutless coward?" Cobb sneered, hands on hips.

That'll do.

Puppy walked toward the mound. The players quieted down, watching. At least there weren't a lot of fans. He counted four so far. Five stadium staff. Perfect. He pawed at the pitching rubber, looking around the wrecked stadium. It hadn't looked quite so shabby when he stood here in 2081 for the city-wide championships. Basically the Bronx and the north end of Queens were represented, Staten Island still underwater, Brooklyn finally drying out, Manhattan containing pockets of civilization.

His Bronx College played against the traditional Reg-infested Bronx University. Here. Right here, except there were about 10,000 fans, the contents of both campuses and families, friends, swarming behind both baselines. Annette had sat off to the left of the home dugout. Row 12, Seats 2,3,4, only her hotshot lawyer parents Cara and Nadi never showed; Annette was a Reg from Philly and for all the admonitions, insights, endless lectures, a DV however dipped in bright paint would eventually rust. All those people cared about were climbing up and out of their holes like rats with a new hairdo. Course he'd want to marry our daughter.

But Annette had believed in him back then. Hell, he believed in himself. Cocky bastard. He'd gone 14-2 with a 2.45 ERA, striking out about ten a game. And hitting around .250, too. The things you think you can do when you're twenty-one.

Like tear down records in your senior year of college. He just didn't want to win the championship, he wanted to be the best ever. Mooshie's record of 14Ks in a single game held for decades; he was going to rip it down.

First inning, struck out the side. Second inning, someone managed a squib to second, next two batters swished and missed. Third inning, struck out the side; Annette's boobs nearly bounced out of her blouse. Grandma's clit, he loved her so much then. Fourth inning, two more strikeouts.

His fiancé found a piece of blank cardboard and a magic marker and held up the sign. Puppy 10, Mooshie 14, brandishing it high over her head and parading up and down the aisles so everyone could see.

The buzz intensified. Bronx College led 7-0, if anyone was paying attention to that.

Fifth inning, first batter popped out. Second batter grounded out, 6-3. Puppy sweated, doing the math. On a 1-2 pitch, he broke off a slider and felt something pull in his right shoulder. Not just pull. A little person was holding onto his muscle like a bell, ringing pain.

He sat alone at the end of the dugout, towel over his head; his teammates and manager figured he was superstitious. He didn't want anyone seeing him chomping on the cotton fabric as a pacifier.

In the sixth inning, the leadoff hitter smacked the ball into the gaping artillery hole in the left field stands. Next one lashes the ball into the right field corner. Single scores him, triple scores that runner. Suddenly it's 7-3.

Puppy persuaded the manager that he was fine. He bore down and got the next batter on strikes, a grounder scoring the run, and the third out retired on a lazy fly to center.

Puppy 11, Mooshie 14, Annette carried the crossed-out updated numbers through the stands.

Top of the seventh, a leadoff double followed by two groundouts cut the lead to a couple runs. Annette climbed on top of the home dugout, leading the crowd in barking.

"Oof, oof, Puppy. Oof, oof, Puppy."

He nailed the third out on a sinking fastball, nearly going to his knees in agony.

Puppy 12, Mooshie 14.

Bottom of the seventh, his teammates gave him a little cushion, taking a four-run lead into the top of the eighth. The leadoff batter homered into a mortar chasm in right-center, but the next two hitters singled. First and second. Puppy waved back the manager into the dugout. Only way he was giving up the ball was if his shoulder sailed across home plate.

A bouncer to short set up first and third, two outs. Annette's boobs danced on top of the dugout. Fans of both teams were rooting for him, clapping and barking rhythmically.

Puppy 13, Mooshie 14.

He went into the clubhouse during the bottom of the eighth, heaving in the toilet and swallowing down four aspirin. The manager asked how he was and Puppy dry heaved again. Just nerves.

The little guy ringing the bell now had friends. By the top of the ninth, Puppy could barely see through the pain. Wavy blurs, dry heaves, knees wobbly. His ears hurt and he didn't know why. He snapped one off at the knees on a 3-2 count.

Barking shook the Stadium.

Puppy 14, Mooshie 14.

The second batter lofted an infield pop. The second baseman squeezed the ball, earning hate from his teammates for denying Puppy another chance at a strikeout. He gallantly waved his gloved hand for everyone to relax. He didn't know how much longer he could raise his right arm.

Two outs. The BU cleanup hitter swung the bat slowly, waiting.

A curve caught the outside corner. Strike one.

"Oof, Puppy, oof."

A fastball dipped at the knees. Strike two.

"Oof, Puppy, oof."

He walked behind the mound, rubbing the ball. His teammates were silent, afraid a word would break the spell. He wound up and the ball floated slowly toward home, catching the hitter off-balance with a feeble swing.

Strike three.

Annette flung her signs into the air and ran onto the field. Puppy fell to hands and knees, surrounded by teammates who lifted him up, then lifted up Annette. He clenched his groin to the sky a la Mooshie, laughing hysterically. He threw up on a teammate. The players carried the lovers together in the air and they kissed, big happy smiles because they owned the world.

"Come on, man. I'm getting cold," Vern complained, waiting to hit.

Puppy rubbed the ball. The oh so charming Frecklie's Mom sat about eighteen rows behind the visitor's dugout trying to be as inconspicuous as you could when players out-numbered fans. He tipped his cap and, sneering, she moved back a few more rows.

Puppy stared into the rickety waist-high screen behind home. His pitch made it on two bounces. Vern swung anyway, corkscrewing into the left-handed batters box. Some hoots echoed out of the Falcons dugout.

Ty clapped encouragingly. "Way to keep the ball down."

Puppy waited for the shoulder to hurt. Nothing. A slight twinge from disuse. He threw another pitch that landed in front of home. Vern missed that one, too.

"Nice," Cobb shouted approvingly.

"Why don't you roll the ball?" yelled a wise guy in the Falcons' dugout.

"That is rude." Shannon stepped toward them.

The Falcons kept up the mocking calls. Vernon skip-stepped away from the next pitch, which still caught his shin.

"Just throw the damn ball," Ty yelled. "Throw, it, hard."

"Bring back the HGs," another Falcons wag said, producing laughter.

A blur shot behind home and into the Falcons dugout. When Ty was finally dragged away, two Falcons were unconscious and a third was spitting out teeth.

● ● ● ●

THE NARROW RED micro-fibric seat wobbled beneath Tomas' bulk, his hands il-luminated by the dreary black-and-white images flickering on the Tremont Avenue mov-ie screen. The droning melodrama was a whisper in the deserted theater. Grandma had been overly sensitive to accusations of propagandizing all entertainment. Too sensitive, he thought. Get it done like she got everything else done from wiping out social media to the Miners.

But Grandma insisted the heaving bosom cinema recalled her childhood. Where ex-actly that childhood was, she never said, smiling enigmatically. Beijing, Manila, Ho Chi Minh City, Pyongyang, Mombai. He suspected Paris since most of the approved movies were old French New Wave, peppered with saucy Italian and absolutely dim-witted Brit-ish comedies.

Music was fine, let it roll and rock in all directions. Vidnews and vidshows were largely ignored; dutiful white noise. Live theater had been hooted away for its banality long ago, shorn of subversion. Movies, old tear-jerking movies, a couple cinemas in each major city presenting Sunday matinees of ancient Disney animated films, was about all that was left. Safe. Her head of security preferred safe.

Tomas sensed that all he knew about being safe was slipping away.

The round-faced man in the bulky overcoat two seats away dove into the popcorn with hungry relish. Tomas faked attention to the screen, where a reedy-looking young man dangled a 'bacco from the corner of his mouth, seducing a pretty girl with his eyes and motorcycle.

"I have waited two days." The Paris Collector leaned over casually.

"Not enough food?"

He grunted and resumed devouring the popcorn.

"How is Paris?"

"We survive as always."

The world's oldest profession as perfected by the French had found a permanent home, Tomas thought sourly. "Is the interest from the Son genuine?"

The Collector nodded.

"Are you sure?"

"We cannot be sure of anything with those people."

"That's not good enough," Tomas whispered harshly. "I worry about a trap."

The man chuckled, spraying popcorn on the seat in front. "Why risk that? An assassination Of would unleash nuclear retaliation. Even the Council of Muftis is beyond that. They are too fat in their wealth."

"But the Son isn't."

"He is restless and young. Very smart."

"Is it just him?"

The Collector sighed. "He wouldn't do this alone. He wants to succeed."

Tomas pressed into the seat, the images sitting on his lap. "Grandma needs more than that."

The man dug out a stray kernel from his back tooth. "The Son can only go so far on faith."

"So can she."

The man turned, offering the popcorn. "Who would question Grandma?"

He had some nagging ideas. Tomas scooped a handful of popcorn into his mouth.

"You do not like any of this," the man asked as a statement.

"That's not for me to say. She thinks this is a last chance for real peace. Her legacy."

"Writing history while you still live it can be dangerous," the Collector said.

"We have to make sure that doesn't happen." Tomas grabbed the raised overcoat, pinning the muscles onto the side of the man's neck. "This is not good enough."

"You want guarantees?" The man jerked away with surprising strength. "Peace is more dangerous than war. Most of the world is used to this arrangement. You live well enough. So do they. Yes, the goats blow each other up from time to time over some argument, but they're Allahs. To them it is like pissing. But one powerful person now wants to change. Ask yourself why, Tomas. Twenty-five years since the Surrender. A Surrender she pushed for."

"We had no choice. They could've taken America proper. Grandma wouldn't have really launched the nukes." The Major briefly imagined the empty movie theater filled with Allahs and shuddered.

The Collector sipped noisily on his cola. "They're not the same as before."

Tomas craned his neck slightly.

"They don't maintain weapons or discipline," the Collector continued. "That iron core of purpose is gone, except for the religious fanatics."

"They're all fanatics," Stilton muttered.

"No," he shook his head emphatically. "I live among them. I know. Some are willing to die, where others won't. They have the Empire they always felt was promised."

"All the more reason to defend it."

The Collector paused. "They could be taken."

"Militarily?" Tomas asked. The Collector nodded.

By who? Our will to fight, except for the Miners, had been broken. This was not virtual reality on some mobile device shared with people who weren't your friends, emotional silos of fake communities. This was real and we hadn't been ready to fight because we forgot what we were fighting for. We were tired of losing, blaming ourselves for mistreating Islam because somehow it had to be our fault for them starting the whole damn thing. Allies, friends? European whores waving the white flags and giving away the countries they stopped loving long ago under the banner of human rights. Only the Russians had really fought hard. And the Jews in that last battle of genocidal martyrdom in Jerusalem. He rubbed the Gelinium as if it stored all the dead. There would've been nothing left if Grandma hadn't said enough. Time to rebuild, my darlings.

Now time to build something new. We don't have the soldiers, planes, ships, hell, guts for anything else except peace with an enemy who wanted us dead. The realization made him sadder than he wanted to admit.

Tomas slowly returned the bag of popcorn. "Grandma wants to meet the Son."

"I will set it up." The man shook out the last of the snack into his palm, greedily licking the salt.

"Not yet. I want to meet him first."

"The Son will not prefer that."

"Grandma won't like it, either. We'll just have to lie to both of them."

• • • •

FISHER PACED BACK and forth in front of his desk and then around the furniture; all that was missing were a stop light and a few street signs. He finally leaned against the wall, hoping it would collapse and take him away from all this aggravation.

"Nedick, this is not acceptable behavior. We never had an HG act like this."

"Because they're not real."

"My players suffered injuries," Boccacelli said with grave concern as if he cared. "This man must be disciplined."

"Yes, Nedick. He must be disciplined," Fisher added.

"I already spoke to Ty. He lost his temper. It won't happen again."

"Baseball players are violent." Boccacceli straightened his tie. "There's a reason why we have the HGs. You people are prone to this. Look at what you did the last time."

"I didn't do anything, sir," Puppy said coldly.

"Your DV friends did. The Miners were mostly DVs."

"They're all gone. Look at the bones in the outfield."

Boccacelli flushed. "Cobb's your responsibility."

"Yes sir, he is."

The Falcons owner scowled.

"And we're already out of toilet paper," Fisher whined.

Mrs. Balinksi's kielbasa hadn't agreed with everyone. "I'll tell them three sheets per poop, no more."

The owners frowned skeptically.

"And then there's these added labor costs." Boccacelli sneered. "I see two more on the payroll. I imagine both are DVs."

"Excellent guess, sir. They work hard and they also work cheap," he said tightly.

"With good reason. Doing what exactly?"

"Maintenance and concessions."

"Maintaining what?"

"The ambience so people are motivated to eat. If they eat, they pay. If they pay, you get a cut."

Fisher moved away from the wall. "Cut like money?"

"Yes, Mr. Fisher. Fifty percent."

The owners tried containing their greedy smiles.

"What're they eating?" Fisher asked.

"Pierogi and kielbasa."

Fisher tried silently mouthing the words.

"From the Polish region," Puppy said.

"That's Muslim Europe food," the Hawks owner gasped.

"It was a CE Polish country which served kielbasa and pierogi long before the Allahs took over."

"We'll have to check," Boccacelli warned. There were instances of vague trouble for people serving cuisine of enslaved nations. "How many of these polishey things were eaten today?"

"Thirty kielbasa. Twelve pierogi."

The owner's eyes widened.

"Fifty percent," Puppy continued. "We get more food stands, you get more money."

Fisher brightened. "Who'll eat this foreign food?"

Puppy flashed five fingers on each hand five times to indicate the attendance. "We're well over the cutoff." He paused. "And if you petition Commissioner Kenuda to have the games restored to the full nine innings, think of how many more kielbasa and pierogi you can sell."

The owners' eyes gleamed.

20

Puppy motioned for Frecklie to stop twenty feet away. Far enough. The sun began descending somewhere over Manhattan, signaling maybe another half an hour of light. Even now, the tangled weeds along the back wall of the playground on Clay Avenue formed a canopy of shadows.

Ready? Frecklie gave the sign of impatience, up on the toes, protectively holding the side of Puppy's old weathered Derek Singh glove as if afraid it'd get hit by a ball. Puppy used a Santo Danero model, the Cubs left fielder from the '65 team; he'd searched his bedroom, but the Mooshie Lopez glove had fled. Hopefully Mick hadn't sold the mitt for booze.

Puppy looked around again, expecting millions to descend from the sky in Grandma's stealth 'copters, brandishing cameras to project the moment into the holographic sky. Overreaching Is Not Ambition, Grow Within Yourself. A giant Grandma holding a tiny Puppy by the neck, carefully rotating his shoulder. See Grandma, he'd look up into those comforting brown eyes the size of clouds. Not a twinge. Not an ache. Nothing yet to suggest surgically repaired muscles would launch a vicious protest campaign against this lunacy. Even fools can be right. Sorry, Grandma. You never struck out fourteen batters.

He had to try. If the shoulder hurt, close the door on the past. And the future. This room is your room forever. Ty could taunt all he wanted and give him a pink gown for his next birthday, but sometimes blind emotionally-laden stubbornness, I'm doing it so get out of the way, is the best damn guidance because it leaves so little room to realize what an idiot you are. Baseball was ending and somehow he had to slip in that last layer of his dream.

First Puppy had to strike himself out.

He lobbed the ball, which bounced off the tip of Frecklie's glove. The teen underhanded the ball back with an air of vague disgust. He knew enough to know that wasn't a pitch.

Puppy waited another few moments for the sun to scamper west. He went into the tight wind-up and fired. The pitch went right through Frecklie, who chased it down.

No pain, Puppy half-smiled. Yeah, a regular stud from twenty feet. Frecklie tossed the ball back wildly, elbows and legs in opposite directions. Imagine what Ty would say about that throw, Puppy's smile broadened. He stepped back to thirty feet.

Frecklie sat cross-legged, holding the glove up and away with a prayerful gesture. To his surprise, the next pitch wedged into the pocket of the glove, knocking him backwards. He bounced up on his shins, delighted, and flipped the ball back.

Frecklie patted his heart. Good.

Good. What was good, what do you know about good? I was once great. Puppy fought the anger chasing the doubt and threw again. Frecklie chased after the pitch which would've broken at the waist. A softball fastball, but a strike.

He rotated the shoulder. Frecklie anxiously walked the ball back.

Hurt? Frecklie tapped his own arm. Puppy impatiently shook his head, turning rudely and retreating until he was about fifty feet away, then a little more until he was under the weed canopy, gray shadows creeping around Frecklie. He wished the dusk would swallow up the kid and he could do this alone.

From just over sixty feet, Puppy took a long breath and threw hard, hip rotating. The ball ran steadily at Frecklie, hitting him in the chest and knocking him down. The boy gasped and rubbed his breastbone. Puppy waited. One, two, three, four, five.

Grandma's bra straps, he grinned.

No pain.

Frecklie crawled to his knees, still dazed. Off to the left, the wire fence sang out like rusty birds. Along the top, seven DV teens wedged their shoes into the squares, standing erect, expressionless. Off to the right, another eight kids took up similar positions. No pleading urchins with soiled faces, they wore clean white shirts and perfectly patched jeans.

Puppy walked halfway toward Frecklie as a few more kids found wedges just below the top of the fence.

"You told them?" Puppy asked angrily. "This was private."

Frecklie shook his head and touched his ear. They heard.

The fence cooed again and soon about fifty kids filled the fence top to bottom in staggered rows. Almost as one, they raised up on their toes, then down again, then up and down one last time.

Puppy tugged on his ear. Heard what.

Frecklie's eyebrows raised in deep surprise. He pointed. About you.

• • • •

THE THREE A14S in gray suits squished together on Kenuda's cramped couch, finding pleasant expressions which didn't match the wary glitter of their rotating eyes. The stares suddenly locked into place, covering Kenuda like a scanning device. Vile little ashcans, he smiled back politely. The middle one inched forward. They'd been silent for about five minutes.

"Again, we stress how unfortunate it is that we've had to bother you, Third Cousin." The robot motioned about the office at the balls and helmets and nets; Kenuda frowned at the subtle irony. "We've always enjoyed the fondest relationship."

Kenuda nodded agreeably. "Any problem in my department is my problem, Steward."

"I'm the Steward," the robot on the left complained.

"Sorry…"

"I'm the Executive Director," continued the middle one. He tapped the colleague to his right. "Our Coordinator. I appreciate we do look alike."

"Not at all." Kenuda's cheeks ached from smiling out of that trap. "How can I help you?"

"It's your baseball, sir."

"What baseball?"

The robots exchanged mystified looks. "At Amazon Stadium."

"Yes, yes, yes," he snapped. "What about it?"

"Members of the Little Extended Family were replaced, Third Cousin."

Kenuda tried to remember. "Was some hate law broken?"

"Not yet."

"Not yet means it might be." Elias hoped a glance at this watch would hurry them along. Nothing hurried along a 'bot unless it was a bulldozer. Circuitous, maddening things that acted as if they could take a lifetime doing a small deed. Well, they could.

"When the humans replaced the HGs," the middle one began as if Kenuda were one of his leathered basketballs, "we lost three jobs."

"As I recall, you officially lost only that one position." Kenuda twirled a football for effect. "Your colleagues then quit."

"They would've been next."

"Had you been threatened?"

"We saw what happened," the Steward blurted angrily. The Executive Director patted his arm.

"Let's say that the 'bots who'd worked so long were aggrieved and reacted emotionally." The metallic face indented at the cheeks. "But their fears were warranted. Seven new jobs have been added to the stadium staff. Jobs which are supposed to be earmarked for robots."

Elias twirled and stalled. No paperwork or requests came to mind. "What're the jobs again? Baseball's not exactly at the top of my list."

"The things we do best," the Steward rasped.

Kenuda's smile frosted. "You do so much well."

The three robots bowed.

"There were three maintenance positions, three at the food stands and someone is doing something with the grass. All positions guaranteed under the equal opportunity laws."

"Not exactly guaranteed. Robots are to be considered."

"They've gone to DVs. Thanks to that baseball historian."

Kenuda raised an eyebrow. The Executive Director regarded him with a shrewd smile.

"You're aware of this, aren't you, Third Cousin?"

"Yes, Executive Director. I'm aware of everything that happens in my area."

"And you approved…"

"I approve everything, as I just said. Baseball's given a little latitude considering it's the final season."

"We don't see how that matters," the Executive Director said firmly. "We hold 82.4 percent of the stadium staffing positions at NFL games and 77.3 percent at NBA arenas. At the least, we expect that percentage to hold for any baseball jobs, whether it's for one game or the whole season."

The robots simultaneously nudged back together, crossing their arms and staring at Kenuda with their damn insufferable rotating eyes. He couldn't make his eyes go 360 degrees, but he could twirl a football pretty quickly. Eyes and football spun around for a few tense moments. Suddenly Kenuda fired the ball over the mini-goal post, where the tip stuck in the wall. Red lights flashed and a symphonic voice chanted "Touchdown."

"And as Sports Commissioner, I determine the percentages."

"What numbers are you suggesting?" the Executive Director asked.

Kenuda wiped the couch clean with a fresh cloth after the robots left and then sat behind his desk, flipping the basketball from palm to palm. This started his morning wrong, but unless he made a hook shot from the doorway, it would constitute the most excitement of the day.

Other than their clattering obsequious duplicity, that's what really angered Elias Kenuda about this visit. Percentages of robots at football and basketball games had been fixed for years. He'd changed it once, by .04 percent after taking over five years ago, just to demonstrate some leadership. Besides that, what had he done? The sports already reigned supreme. Every game was a sell-out. Players were near perfect beyond getting an occasional speeding ticket. He could boast, as he did at Third Cousin meetings, that his players produced among the highest number of children of any profession. His P&L was priceless.

Wind it up and watch it run. Elias Kenuda wanted more than making a basket with his eyes closed from fifteen feet. He'd been one of the youngest Third Cousins ever. He should've been First by now; at least Second. Now his temples grayed and occasionally his fingers ached. Probably from all the damn twirling; he angrily bounced a ball on two hops across the room into the net.

Blue lights buzzed and a voice shrieked "Swish."

Kenuda smiled. It didn't suit his face.

• • • •

FRIDAY WAS DATE night everywhere in America. Blue Shirts didn't roam bars or restaurants or movie theaters, dragging away the solitary and lonely and pathetic. Nor would ruffians turn over your table or servers spit in your food. But if you were out, it was best to at least go through the pretense of acting as if you had someone in your life, fast tracking your way to an engagement and marriage and children and the rightful place in the Family.

Pablo squeezed Puppy's wrist again and made gentle clucking noises, batting his eyebrows.

"Just once is enough," Puppy said, moving Pablo's strong fingers, but Zelda pressed both their hands back into the table cloth.

"We don't want anyone thinking you boys are having a spat and won't produce cute little African-American/Latino/Caucasian children. Now Puppy, flutter those pretty green eyes longingly."

Puppy fluttered. The waitress laid down their Danielle's Veg-Burg Delights with an approving smile.

"So how many?" Zelda asked softly.

Guessing who was like them trying to survive being single, and who really meant to squeeze and flutter was a long-time game.

"Forty-seven people here," Pablo said.

"How can you count so fast?" Puppy asked.

"Because I went to class in school. Twenty-three groups. Forty-seven, us being the odd number."

"I've been called worse." Zelda grinned, sucking the juice off her pickle.

"Along that far wall, we have, I'd estimate, nine couples, five of whom are smiling, three eating, one staring off. That makes five on dates."

"Do explain, Great One." Zelda snatched Puppy's pickle.

"The staring is genuine, as would be the eating, but let's leave something for problematic rotation and say three are comfortable eating and the fourth isn't. Four are smiling because they genuinely mean it, one is putting on."

"Or just friends which mean they mean it more," Zelda said.

"Don't confuse him with your cynicism," Puppy scolded.

"I've already factored that in," the dentist said airily. "On that wall," they swiveled like 'bots toward the tables beneath the large vidmural of children picking vegetables, "we have ten more couples. In the past couple minutes, three clinked glasses, a sure sign of a date."

Zelda clinked their glasses. Pablo scowled.

"Two are holding hands with twisting fingers."

"Ah, the dead giveaway." Zelda seductively ran her index finger up and down Pablo's hand.

"Stop. You're our matron of honor." Puppy laughed.

Pablo continued as if they weren't there. "And look at tables one and five."

"You numbered them?"

"How else? Their looks of interest are genuine. Look at number four over there by the kitchen. One's already snapped angrily, so that's a date, probably the last, and I'll say odds favor two of the remaining three also on dates. I haven't gathered enough information. Wait." He held up his hands. "Table two is sharing the menu instead of 'I don't care, order what you want.' True love."

Puppy drumrolled with his palms. "And the number is?"

"Twelve."

He looked for confirmation from Zelda, who shrugged and ordered another bottle of Indiana pinot noir.

"I'm right," Pablo insisted.

"Who are we to question a Fifth Cousin?" Zelda laughed and Pablo nearly slid under the table. They ate quietly for a few minutes.

"Now who's this singer you insisted we had to see at Monroe's?" Pablo sipped the wine.

Zelda stuffed her face with fries so she wouldn't smile. "Dara Dinton. She's making her professional debut."

"An absolutely amazing voice," Puppy added.

Pablo's eyes flitted between their grins. They always left him out of secrets because he could never quite get the joke. "I know there's more."

Zelda dipped her fries in Pablo's mustard, which she knew annoyed him. He slapped her hand away again.

"It's really Mooshie."

Pablo frowned deeper. "Who?"

Puppy lowered his voice. "Mooshie Lopez."

"Mooshie Lopez?"

"Yes," Zelda and Puppy said together.

"The Mooshie Lopez?"

"Yes," they chorused again.

"Singing?"

Another joint nod. The good doctor leaned back in his chair. "Uh-huh."

Puppy took this forward. "Remember the old guy with the strange teeth who you examined in your office…"

"Keep it down…"

"He's not some wasted ass DV. They're really Mickey Mantle and Ty Cobb. Now Mooshie's come back, too."

"With bad teeth?"

Zelda jumped in. "It's really her, Pabby Boy. Wait until you hear."

Pablo waited a moment for the punchline. "You understand that's not possible."

"Absolutely."

"Totally," Puppy agreed.

"Then why do you persist in insisting it's real?"

Puppy sighed. "Because it is."

"Do you have proof?"

"Once you meet her…"

"I mean real, tangible proof which could be presented."

"Whoa, presented where?" Puppy asked.

"Before the Science Commission."

"You're reporting this?"

Pablo laughed humorlessly. "Life beyond death would be something of a scientific breakthrough and might change a few ways we view the world."

"And help you."

Diaz leaned forward angrily. "You think I'd use this for myself?"

"It would kind of clinch becoming a Fifth Cousin."

"How dare you."

"How dare you even suggest revealing something we told you in confidence."

Pablo struggled momentarily with that. "You're right."

"Damn straight."

"Lower your voices," Zelda warned as a few diners turned.

"Although I think this is absurd and impossible, I'm willing, as part of our friendship, to approach this scientifically."

"Thank you, my precious."

"I will conduct tests."

"You're not going anywhere near Mooshie with one of your tongue depressors."

Pablo reddened. "I have a responsibility on several levels and yes, a candidate for Cousin is one of them, along with being a health officer. If this is nonsense, we'll act as if it never happened."

"No." Puppy shook his head back and forth.

"Zel," Pablo said wearily. "Make him listen."

She pushed away her plate. "I'm with him, honey."

Pablo rose sadly. "Okay. I'll do you a favor and act like we didn't talk."

"Good. How about acting like we don't know each other."

"Puppy!" Zelda scolded.

"I can do that, too." Pablo stormed away.

They finished their beers in silence. A young woman leaned over from the adjoining table.

"We guessed you guys were just friends. Sorry we had you wrong."

By the time they got to Monroe's, Puppy's mood had shifted from rage to anxiety. Fridays at Monroe's catered to the young, who had the energy to go out after a long work week, and the old, who weren't bound by any niceties about dating, just getting out of the way. He'd told Mooshie that Friday was the wrong night. Mondays or Tuesdays were best with smaller, more attentive crowds; she'd slammed the door in his face and told him to get screwed under a goat.

Behind the bar, Jimmy jerked his head angrily toward the line waiting to use one of the bathrooms.

"She's been in there thirty minutes," he snarled.

While Zelda secured a table, Puppy apologetically pushed to the front of the queue and rapped on the bathroom door.

"It's Puppy."

"Suck me."

He smiled sheepishly to the dozen or so irritated people with fading bladder control. "Let me in, Dara dear."

Mooshie yanked him inside by his belt buckle. She wore a beautiful tight black dress above knee-high black boots. He recognized them from Zelda's pre-fat closet. Mooshie looked terrified. That terrified him, but now wasn't the time for a contest.

"You okay?" He sat on the toilet.

"If you give me a pep talk about how it's like the bottom of the ninth with the score tied I will cut your throat."

He mimed tearing up paper. She clenched her groin.

"You still have the same amazing voice, Mooshie."

"Except it's been dead and call me Dara, dimwit." She searched for herself in the mirror, sighing at the cropped bleached hair and overdone eyes and lips.

"You can cancel, Ms. Dinton."

Her dark eyes blazed. "That'd break your heart. This breaks your heart. Mooshie Lopez scared. I ain't never been scared. Of anything." She poked at the lipstick with her finger. "Too red, right?"

"It's perfect."

"Would you say if it wasn't?"

He shook and nodded his head simultaneously.

"Get Zelda," Mooshie shouted.

"Why?" he asked, hurt.

"Because she won't bullshit me."

As Mooshie shoved Puppy out the door, Jimmy turned up his hands questioningly.

"Next time get her a dressing room. She's a star."

He slid next to Zelda and told her Mooshie's request. With a squeal bordering on orgasmic, Zelda bounded like a pug toward the bathroom. Ty took the vacated chair; Mickey fell onto a spare seat, spilling their drinks.

"Where's the senorita?" Ty smirked.

"Getting ready."

"Oh my, cue the music."

"Damn right. And her name's Dara Dinton." He glared at Mantle. "You drunk already?"

"I don't know. What's it your business?"

"Because I don't want you falling on your ass tomorrow when I'm pitching. Aren't you the manager? Do something." He downed half of Ty's beer.

The bar rocked with Mooshie's nervous laugh as she headed toward the microphone in the corner.

"Sing something in English," Ty pleaded.

"I'll try, White Grampa."

Zelda grabbed a chair from another table and slipped back next to Puppy.

"What'd you say?" he asked. She smiled meaningfully, suggesting he had a better chance of sleeping on Pluto tonight than understanding.

More couples and would-be couples straggled in, panicking Puppy. Conversation centered on love and romance and sex, not Mooshie, talking over her shoulder to the piano player.

"Will you make an announcement?" Puppy returned to the bar, where he wasn't greeted with joy.

"Why? They'll hear." Jimmy poured a beer.

"And kill the vidnews sound," Puppy yelled. He waved his arms for attention; getting little. "Evening, everyone. On behalf of Monroe's, we want to welcome you to a special night of music from an amazing singer."

"Cut the crap, handsome," Mooshie shouted into the microphone. "And let the people decide if I'm any good."

That earned the first applause of the evening. Mooshie nodded to the pianist, who played softly. Puppy shot her an encouraging smile. She sneered.

"I'd like to start off with an oldie which my mother loved." Her eyes twinkled impishly. "I bet you haven't heard this one for a long while."

Mooshie jumped up and kicked the stool away.

"Let the lovin' in, baby.

Let the lovin' in."

Shit, she's singing *Lovin' It*, her number one hit from the first album, *Lovin' It All*. Puppy and Zelda exchanged astonished looks.

"If you got my beat,

Then you're getting a treat.

'Cause you gotta let my lovin' in."

Mooshie wailed a wild animalistic cry, delighting the crowd. She spun around, flinging out her arms and flipping her head from side to side. Unbound. Unleashed.

Screw you and your tongue depressors, Pablo.

"Because it's date night, bitches." Mooshie leaped out of the song with a wiggle of her butt. "Time for some baking and shaking in Grandma's oven."

He and Zelda's grins circled their heads at the line from Mooshie's song *Baking Babies*.

"You ain't gonna add to the family like this. I want some kissing. I want some loving." Mooshie hopped on a table as if levitated. "I said kissing, bitches."

The two girls shyly kissed.

"I said kissing, not wiping away lipstick."

The girls opened their mouths and the crowd whooped.

"That's right. You. You and you and all of you. I want to see some tongue."

Around the bar, couples kissed. Mooshie stared expectantly at Puppy and Zelda, who kissed lightly and broke away, embarrassed.

"You too, White Grampas." Mooshie singled out Mickey and Ty, running away to hide in the back amid good-natured laughter. "You ain't never too old for a new kind of loving. Ever, darlings."

The piano cued her back into the song.

"There's no excuse to be sad,

If you gotta heart, then baby baby baby."

She pouted, hips rocking back and forth, milking the beat.

"Give it a launching pad,

And let that goddamn lovin' in."

The bar roared. Zelda and Puppy brushed away tears.

Mooshie played two long sets. In between there was a lot of alcohol. When Puppy woke up on the kitchen floor the next morning, Zelda was crawling out the door holding her shoes and dry heaving. Ty and Mick were sprawled on opposite ends of the couch, legs crisscrossed. Puppy shook them awake and stumbled into the shower as they fell back asleep, snoring. Soap, water, shampoo, nothing helped once his mind remembered and sent his body into mild hysteria.

Seven thirty AM. He pitched in ninety minutes.

He staggered past his bedroom, drawn back by Mooshie's empty bed. Worry about pitching hungover or worry about where you lost Mooshie. Good choices. Mick and Ty stumbled into the bathroom making all sorts of unnatural body sounds.

"Where's Mooshie?"

Mick squatted on the toilet, yawning; Ty carefully shaved.

"Who?" Mantle asked.

Lopez stood in the doorway, the black dress a little looser, as if it'd been peeled off a few times without regard for zippers. Hand on her right hip, she shook her head at the two old naked men. "That is some awfully ugly white shit."

Ty threw a towel. "Feast."

Mooshie gagged and strolled into the kitchen, Puppy trailing.

"Where've you been?"

"What?" she glared.

"It's seven-forty." He pointed at the clock, yelling into the bathroom. "We gotta game, hurry up. I was worried."

"Don't be. I make friends." Mooshie shook the empty Edison's Crackers box. "We're out already? Least we got coffee." She kept twisting the stove knobs. "You forget to pay the gas?"

Chimes tingled throughout the apartment.

It took Puppy a few moments to recognize the cue. Oh no. Not today.

The vidnews wobbled slightly from the effort of the first Grandma Story since 2085. Puppy and Annette had just finished sex for the second time that morning when Grandma's kind, warming expression had circled the room. Annette had burrowed under the bed in case Grandma figured out she'd faked an orgasm.

On that day, Grandma had told the Story of food, its nutrients and the effect of radiation from the Allah attacks, reminding everyone just how much worse it would've been if America had retaliated with nuclear weapons. Instead, she could tell the Story of new farms opening in the Middle West, wheat and corn crops flourishing. Not just nature, not just the regeneration of the soil, but the advances in food engineering.

The days of the SC and AG foods had begun, a quiet mocking of a hungry, grateful nation who, watching while sitting stuck in trains and buses with engines shut down, one long red light for traffic stretching just west of the Las Vegas radiation belt, had probably skipped over Grandma's vow that someday America would once again feed the world. Their bellies were the priority.

Now another Story would freeze the nation. Mooshie wasn't the only one who couldn't cook breakfast. Ovens and stoves went cold. All mass transit stopped. No cars could move. All meetings in businesses halted. Elevators stalled. Factories, cash registers, stacking canned goods on the shelf, morning exercise, showers, flushing toilets, anything that anyone could possibly do to distract them from watching was forbidden. Even breeding was against the law; no fiery orgasms when Grandma settled in next to vidnews host Etsy Valdez on the daily morning show *Wake Up My Darlings*.

Even after the trees died and the sun's rays weakened through the war-scarred atmosphere, Grandma still refused to move her My Darlings talks inside. Stubbornness or hopefulness were two sides of a confident mind. Massive planting in the 70s and into the 80s, along with the diffusion of the tainted clouds, brought back some green; the scientists insisted that was all to be expected, considering.

In this reality she permitted, hunks of dead trees comprised America's forests. So came the HGs: birds, animals, bright trees flourished. The foods they mocked as So-Called and AlleGedly fed her children. Rain was on schedule and every so often real downpours drenched an area. Snow was coming back to the mountains. Those indomitable fish survived; she thought the likes of Saul Ribe and Pops Tai were supernatural, summoning versions of salmon and tuna from the oceans.

Slowly the world would return and then the HGs would disappear along with Disappointment Villages. No more entrance exams from DV children saddled by the failures of a generation which had committed the worst failure of all: fear.

Once the fake, and Grandma shuddered at that word but it was true and truth couldn't be denied even by the single-minded, but once the fake and the false were gone, they had to deal with reality again. No magic other than their minds and their courage. They'd survived their own stupidity and that's what the war was, as most if not all wars were, anger unleashed until pride took over, permitting no turning back.

Except there was nothing behind the pride except bravado. The men and women maimed and killed so a flag could be waved sickened her. A flag representing what? What was the vision except causing death in the name of an idea?

"If you could move over just slightly, please." The frazzled cameraperson apologetically motioned Grandma to the right.

"Of course, Patty. You're making us all look good."

All of us together. For nearly thirty years it'd worked. Grumblings and bickering were to be expected from a Family. Defined a Family, didn't it?

Tomas had darkened at the notion, roiling up slowly that we weren't ready, the country wouldn't accept this Story. The country or him? Lenora sighed wearily. And Albert, dear dear Albert, her comrade, former lover, trusted right and left hand, he didn't believe in this either. She attuned to doubts all around, even from the crew, edgy at setting up a visit inside the House. A vase had already been broken, Lenora gluing back the pieces so the shaken grip didn't faint. Coffee spilled and cookies dropped, ground into the purple rug.

Grandma's Bedroom was a terrifying place. She fluffed up a pillow.

"Grandmother, please." The diminutive director Ian Schrage darted forward, hands prayerfully at his chest. "Don't move. The light was so perfect."

"I don't want perfect, Ian." She smiled.

"But I do."

"And your wishes overrule mine?"

The room went very quiet. Ian hopped onto the bed, his bare feet gripping the purple quilt.

"Yes," he said defiantly.

"Then I must defer to your superior wisdom."

"That would be nice." He managed a wry smile and hopped back behind the camera, the crew glancing at him with anxious admiration.

This was the America she wanted. Grandma muffled a grin so Ian wouldn't get completely carried away, although with his ego, how could anyone tell the difference. This is what she had to get across tonight. How they've come of age. How they're ready.

"Everyone quiet please." Ian squirmed in his chair and cleared his throat. "Three, two, and one."

Lenora sat up ramrod straight, eyes clear, shining, feeling like seventy again.

"Good morning, Grandma." The stunningly beautiful Etsy flashed her dazzling white teeth. "A big day, today."

"For everyone." Grandma beckoned two children to sit beside her on the long purple couch. "I don't do this very often."

"It's only the third time." Valdez held up three fingers.

"Yes, the Food Story was the last one. Very important, right, R'hin?" Grandma snuggled a chubby little girl who looked like a Zelda clone, if clones hadn't been outlawed as a capital offense.

"Yes," the girl said shyly.

"And, of course, the Surrender Story," Etsy said solemnly.

"The sad and the happy," Grandma said quickly. "We can laugh and cry in the same day, don't we, Gil?" She tousled the thick hair of a thin boy with oversized black glasses. "Today, I want to tell everyone about something that happened long before the Surrender. Before the War. R'hin, do you know what happened before the War?"

The little girl blinked. Half an hour ago she was on a school bus heading to third grade on East 181st Street before a smiling Blue Shirt took her in a car to this big studio.

"I didn't do my homework." Her lower lip trembled.

Grandma hugged her. "That's okay, sweetheart. We're not perfect."

"People are like countries, right?" Valdez asked her one pre-arranged question.

"Yes." Grandma pursed her lips. "Sometimes we make mistakes. The Allahs who wanted to kill us were bad. But not all the Allahs were bad. We know how religion and God makes people hate."

You couldn't wait until tomorrow, Puppy sighed, listening in the clogged streets to the audio from huge speakers mounted overnight on the side of buildings.

"But we were very angry at the Allahs. Innocent people got hurt." Grandma sat the children on each knee. In the control booth, Cheng glared openly with no respect. She took a deep breath.

"We sent all the Allahs away because we couldn't trust them. They didn't behave like real Americans. We protected their mosques, places of worship like churches, and made sure no one hurt them as they went onto the boats back to Arabia. There were a few injuries, but, of course, nothing compared to what they did to us."

Cheng shook his head minutely, opening his thoughts, begging Lenora to stop.

"As we didn't trust the Allahs, they didn't trust us. So they sent a lot of Europeans to us. One hundred and eighteen boats. More than a hundred thousand from France and Germany, remember now, the Allahs were elected in those two countries. A number of countries in Europe actually. They didn't just invade everyone. Anyway, lots of boats. Lots of people. Lots of children. Lots."

Grandma stared at Cheng, his eyes watering.

"We didn't let them in. We worried it was a trick. This was just after the Allahs attacked Manhattan and the Grand Mufti, he is their leader," she addressed R'hin and Gil, squirming in boredom, "insisted those were terrorists and he had nothing to do with it and honestly, why would we believe him? Look what terrorists did to Los Angeles. Terrorists and their government had the same goals. Surely among more than a hundred thousand people there would be Europeans who were secretly Allahs. That had happened before. I couldn't risk that, losing another city, more of my Family."

The First Cousin slipped out of the control booth, Grandma's voice echoing down the hall.

"We made the ships stay at sea. We airlifted food and water and medicine until we could figure out how to make sure everyone who came in was one of us. Then the storm hit. It was a very bad storm. Worse than a hurricane, it came out of nowhere and sank all the boats. All the children." She paused. "We couldn't do anything and, after that, the Allahs destroyed Washington and the war was truly on."

Grandma took a long sip of tea.

"We told everyone the Allahs had sunk the ships, but they didn't. It was a lie. We didn't think the Family was ready for the truth. I think you are, now."

Grandma folded her hands. Etsy looked frantically at the director.

"Thank her and you're done," Ian hissed into her earpiece.

"Really?" Valdez blurted.

"Yes." Lenora patted her arm. "That's the end of this Story. Soon they'll be a new one."

21

For several minutes, no one moved, finally milling about like spilled sand; they didn't know what to make of Grandma's Story. Puppy had hoped the speech, which he didn't understand, in part because he hadn't paid complete attention, throwing up twice from nerves, would trigger a national emergency. BT 'copters would plunge out of the sky, armored vehicles would race down the Grand Concourse, the sun would really disappear and torrential rain would wash everyone down East 161st Street.

But the game wasn't cancelled.

Frecklie gave him a big smile and thumbs up as he rushed through Gate Six and down Section 116, hopping over the fence and through the dugout into the clubhouse, pausing to dry heave into a dissipated wall.

The team slumped lazily before their lockers. When Puppy came in, the whole clubhouse went mute. He wandered down each row until he came to his locker, flagged with a lopsided sign: PUPPY, each letter in a different handwriting. The team watched him lovingly open the door. A big pile of shit, clearly contributed by each member of the Bronx Hawks, sat in a bag. Everyone broke up.

"Welcome." Mickey rubbed his hair. "Now don't make me chase any balls near those skulls."

Once Puppy finished dressing in the too small white t-shirt and too large blue uniform pants, Ty beckoned him into the office.

"How you feeling?"

"Great."

"So glad to hear that. Think getting polluted the night before a game was smart?" Puppy's head ached from the reminder; he slowly shook his head. "Mantle can drink and play. You can't. You ain't gifted. You gonna emulate anyone, it's me."

That scared Puppy a little, but not enough to shut up. "Why didn't you stop me?"

Ty turned scarlet. "You think I'm your fucking mother." He shouted into the clubhouse. "Do I look like anyone's mother?"

The players gratefully shook their heads. The manager nearly sat on Puppy's head.

"If I ever find out you were drinking the night before you pitch, I'm gonna knock out all your teeth."

Puppy wouldn't care what Cobb did as long as he said it a little quieter. He started toward the door when Ty grabbed his left elbow.

"If the shoulder hurts, you tell me. Or I'll slide into your ears."

As Puppy stumbled onto the field during the Falcons infield practice, Frecklie hopped onto the top of the dugout and very noisily windmilled his arms.

"What's wrong?" Puppy whispered.

"There's a big line."

"Of what?"

"Fans. There, there, there." Frecklie pointed.

"Okay, okay, okay. Calm down."

Irritatated, Freckle smacked his chest. Am calm. He made little people with his fingers. Puppy shrugged. "Get."

Frecklie ran his finger over his throat, pointing at the executive suite on the second level.

"I don't have time to argue with them. You have to handle this, kid."

Frecklie went so white his freckles looked like HGs. He coldly shoved a paper and a pen at Puppy, who skimmed it as Ty bounded onto the field, glaring at his starting pitcher.

"I can't sign any authorizations."

"As the baseball historian, you're an employee of the Sport Commission. I looked it up when I started."

"Pretty smart..."

"Just sign," Frecklie yelled and raced back up the aisle with the approved work order. Puppy followed Vernon between the first base line and the stands, where about a hundred or so fans were scattered.

Shit, he blinked.

Ty spit 'bacco on their shoes. "Where's the tea, girls? I could bake some crumpets if you like."

"We're gonna warm up now, skip," Jackson explained, pounding his glove.

"Oh my." Cobb delicately put his fingers on his lips. "I didn't realize this was the bullpen."

Jackson swallowed. "You want us going out there?"

"No, up your ass, you dumb black bastard." Cobb sputtered. "Get out there. Now."

Puppy briefly turned back near second base. Frantic DVs were directing siblings in all directions behind home plate. Officer Brennan was running back and forth, tipping his head in greeting so quickly sparks seemed to flash around his receding hairline. Puppy couldn't see the crowds swarming the concession stands inside, overwhelming Mr. Ruiz's taco supply and Mrs. Balinski's pierogi stash. Forget the congestion by the one entrance, Gate Six, from Aito steadfastly triple-checking each ticket price, while Frecklie and five new DVs ran past the patient, troubled fans who decided against work today, looking for a diversion from Grandma's Story as they ambled in a messy line back under the El.

Hundreds and hundreds of fans.

Puppy crunched over a carpet of shattered glass which stretched before the bullpen in right center field like a glittering moat, guiding Jackson by the hand through the doorless frame. The catcher moaned. Both pitchers' rubbers were buried beneath piles of rusted debris wrapped in tangled wires fallen from the scoreboard. Their spikes woke rows of rifle shells, which rolled toward a dirt-encrusted home plate.

Vern pointed to skeletons leaning against the back wall, guns by their feet as if waiting to resume the fight. Puppy carefully toed some mottled orange wigs.

"Leave them be," the catcher warned, not moving.

Imagining, Puppy looked up at the remains of the scoreboard, frozen with Grandma's smile. "I guess Black Tops were positioned up there. Or maybe these guys were fighting 'copters. Or just fell."

"All that matters is they lost. That's why they're bones and we're not."

Puppy grunted and walked back. "Ever seen pictures of the stadium before October 12?"

Jackson shook his head.

"The scoreboard went from right to left field. They posted lineups, statistics. Had games, vids, photos, music. Attention, ladies and gentlemen. Now batting. Players had numbers." Puppy leaned against the wall, disturbing a rat which scurried in search of quieter digs. Jackson almost fainted. "This used to be called Yankee Stadium, before baseball started skidding into the toilet and needed businesses to pay. The whole place was beautiful. All the ballparks were. They had personalities like people."

Jackson jerked his head toward the fleeing rat. "That's what was lurking. Tick-tock."

Puppy frowned. "You believe that?"

"Don't you?" Vern asked warily.

"It's hard to believe something so beautiful could represent something so wrong."

"Sometimes that's the easiest way for wrong to get inside your shirt." The catcher kicked the ground nervously. "What pitches you got?"

"Fastball, curve, changeup."

"Sinker, splitter?"

"Fastball naturally tails away from righties, into lefties," Puppy said proudly.

"Let's do it, historian, 'cause the less time I spend with these ghosts the happier I'll be."

Puppy threw up on Vern's shoes.

• • • •

BOAR FACE SMILED so broadly she could've swallowed a squirrel.

"Mr. Saul is very happy." She leaned against the glass wall to block out any intruders, though much of the staff still hadn't made it in by noon after the Story. With her big-shouldered black dress and jacket, she pretty much eclipsed all the light from the hallway.

"What did Mr. Pietro say?"

Katrina pawed carefully at Zelda's drawings. "We know where he stands."

"But you have to show him first," Zelda persisted.

Boar Face's smile froze a little. "And why is that?"

"Collegiality."

"Of course," Boar Face said with mock gratitude. "Once I have his job I'll be very collegial."

Zelda knew she was roaming a little far out of her comfort zone, which is why she'd avoided the work world. Succeed and do well, but not at another's expense. That wasn't success, but corruption and elitism. A Family helps each other, Zelda silently recited Grandma's Seventh Insight.

"I kind of wish you would show him."

Boar Face's shadow blotted out the chair.

"Since I'm part of this," Zelda went on.

"Your insights and my guidance," Katrina apprehended each syllable. "Partners."

"I'm glad my drawings inspired that…"

"Inspired by my guidance," she repeated wintrily. "As I'm inspiring your rise." She sat on the arm of the chair; Zelda hoped she wasn't propelled through the glass wall like a see-saw. "With me in charge, there's an opening for you."

Zelda stared dimly. No one had ever offered her a promotion before. Other than art and dance and acting classes, she'd never even received a grade above a C. Boar Face sensed that and charged through the swamp.

"I appreciate all this is new for you. Which is why your perspective is so wonderful. Fresh, like the sea air." Katrina dragged Zelda and the chair closer to the desk. "Mr. Saul is a legend. But old. The organization needs new ideas. That's what struck me about your sketches. Your salmon boy with the curly-haired fins and tail is priceless. My knowledge and your etchings make a powerful combo, Zelda."

Zelda smiled politely. "But Mr. Pietro…"

"Pietro would nail you sitting down and then nail me standing on my head without wiping off his pecker," Katrina growled, quickly resuming that sweet smile. Chomp on bones, swallow tendons. "Zelda, stick with me. I'll teach what you need to know."

• • • •

PUPPY BARELY MADE it to the Couples Room ahead of Annette. On his way, he'd been frozen outside a discount clothing store on East 175th where that piece of crap Hazel smirked through the window as if knowing Puppy was standing there, watching the vidnews.

"Bring back the HGs. Local pitching legend Puppy Nedick, who doubles as the game's historian, tried his hand at the AlleGed sport this morning."

Three clips of baseballs ricocheting off the left, center and right field walls.

"Ouch. Oh not to be a baseball. But the good thing about the AG sport is pretty much anyone can try. No skills required. Check it out for yourself. Least they have some good food."

Hazel bit into a hot dog and barked, ending his two PM vidsports report with a smirk.

Annette swept into the Couples Room as if riding a white cloud of happy. She startled the guard with a peck on his cap and gave Puppy a big smooch on the nose.

"Hello, dear Puppy." She frowned. "Why the sad face. Did you not get a doggie biscuit today?"

"Screw you, Annette. I'm not in the mood."

"Be cheerful. It's a beautiful day." She rolled up the white shutters before the guard could stop her; they were a line of defense against an ex being tossed out the window. "Almost sunny. We're young and alive."

"More or less."

Annette scooted her chair closer. Puppy tensed.

"Am I too close?"

"Depends what you're planning."

She flapped her lips, making a popping noise. "You look well. Lost weight?"

"A little. I've been vomiting more than usual."

"The less fat opens up your eyes. And me?"

"Gorgeous as ever."

Annette waited for the guard to agree, spinning her red curls around. "What about the color?"

"Astonishing." Either she was on medication or plotting something. Sometimes she'd get this way after a shopping spree.

"My potential fiancé agrees. He likes you, by the way."

Puppy slid his chair back a few inches. "I don't know him."

"Oh yes you do."

"No."

"Oh yes you do." Annette deliberated if it'd be fun to repeat the exchange one last time. "Elias."

He thought for a second. "Elias? Doesn't go ding dong."

"Try Elias Kenuda." Annette grinned as Puppy fell down the dark hole and out the other end.

"Kenuda's your fiancé?" he said dully.

"Not officially. Remember Grandma's wishes. That's why we're here."

"And stop talking in that sing-song voice," he snapped.

"Sorry. Love has buoyed me into the sky." Annette shook the gold bracelet on her left wrist. "From guess who?"

"Elias Kenuda."

"Oh, Puppy. Puppy, Puppy, Puppy. Elias and I agree you have such a way about you."

"You and Kenuda talk about me?"

"Oh yes."

"Stop saying oh yes."

"He likes you. And?"

"What?" His lips didn't move.

"Do you like him?"

"Oh yes. Maybe we can have a play date."

"That'd be lovely because he knows."

"Knows what?"

"That we were, you know."

"You can say married, Annette. It's why we're here."

They smiled at the relieved guard, who saw the day coming when these wretched people would be gone.

"I didn't go into details, Puppy. Oh, before he officially met you, I did complain a little about our, you know."

"Marriage," he prompted.

"Saying that perhaps you weren't the best husband for a number of reasons."

"Which were?"

Annette frowned. "I didn't say. So many choices. Oh, maybe I mentioned you always had a lot of potential, all unrealized, of course."

He didn't argue.

"Certainly I wouldn't go into, you know."

"I don't know."

"Neither does anyone else. Like Kenuda." Her eyes narrowed. "I'll make sure he only hears good things so he supports your moronic baseball."

"He's supporting baseball?"

"If I stop saying oh yes will you stop repeating back my words? Good. Oh yes, he thinks, what does your Zelda say, it's the bahm diggity." She cackled. "Bahm diggity baseball."

"Get to the point."

"That is the point. Elias Kenuda will do whatever he can to help."

They stared with frozen smiles like a couple of gunslingers itching to draw.

"If?" Puppy asked softly.

"If?" Annette's voice rose two octaves. "If you find someone."

He exhaled very slowly. "And should I not discover the love of my life?"

"It doesn't have to be the love of your life. Look at us."

His eyes watered from an equal brew of anger and hurt. Annette's lower lip quivered; she knew she'd gone too far, making her rage defensively.

"Anyone. Him." She pointed at the guard, who recoiled. "One week, Puppy. Or else I will tell Kenuda every dirty filthy little thing you ever thought and did and they'll bulldoze your beloved stadium right now. Understand?"

"I hate you so much." Puppy kicked the chair across the room.

"And I hate you, too," hissed Annette, crouching on the table.

The guard called for back-up.

• • • •

AZHAR STAYED AWAY from the orphanage for three days. He spent most of the time on his boat, washing the deck and gaining strange satisfaction out of dumping suds into the ocean. He couldn't look at Omar, the sullen smirks of the teen pushing his father away from the table, so Mustafa ate in the basement until Jalak's loud and constant marches to the washing machine drove him outside.

Last night he ate the kabsa laham under a tree. Jalak blandly took away his plate and fork as if this dining area were natural, leaving a bowl of pistachios and a clean napkin, then marching into the house and turning out the back light. When he woke the pistachios were gone; a breakfast roll with butter and figs had taken their place.

Finally he returned to the orphanage, switching to the midnight to six shift. He sat downstairs in the main waiting area, aimlessly polishing the wood. Around two, Clary came out of the kitchen holding a tray of fruit and tea. Her eyes were half shut, swollen from the purple bruises on her forehead and cheekbone. She dropped the tray, widening eyes stretching the puffy tissue like clay.

The bandage on her right cheek didn't move.

"I must explain," he said quickly.

Clary gave no sign she heard. He risked a step forward.

"It wasn't me. My son Omar, he is with the Holy Warriors. He did this. Allah forgive me for such a child that I brought into this world, it was him."

Her crooked smile scared him.

"I will do whatever I can to help. I swear by God."

Azhar knelt and took her hands. Cold hands, drained of warmth, of life. He frowned at the bandage taped tightly to her cheek. He didn't want to see anything that would deepen his shame.

"What did they do to you, child?" he whispered, gently pulling off one side of the tape. She stared with lifeless hate as he lifted the bandage.

A cross had been burnt into her skin. He wanted to cry.

"They will pay who did this."

No child should ever smile like Clary. She moistened her lips, her voice a razor. "Mentiroso! ¡Me ha engañado desde el principio! Ahora voy a vengarme a todos. Un día, un día pronto voy a aparecer en el orfanato como un soldado desde infierno y matar a to-dos para todas que nos infligieron a mi y mi familia. Tu familia."

She knelt very daintily, as if training to be a proper young girl in a proper home, and picked up the fruit, wiping up the tea and resetting the cup and plate onto the tray. Clary smiled once more, bowing slightly, and walked up the steps to serve one of the filthy na-ked mullahs who had already raped her twice that night with more promised.

Azhar left before the end of his shift. When he got home around four in the morn-ing, the house lights blazed. Two glaring Warriors loitering by the hood of a black Lincoln in the narrow driveway.

Jalak greeted him in the hallway, nervously wiping her hands on her burqua. Omar stood by the steps like a guard, Abdul at the top of the staircase, staring down, the only one honest enough to wear fear.

"The Imam waits for you," Jalak said.

"Here?" he asked stupidly.

She nodded at the closed study door.

Imam Abboud sat patiently in Azhar's favorite worn corduroy chair, flipping through a football book. "Your son likes the game."

"He's just a boy," Azhar apologized.

"Is he good?" The Imam closed the book.

Azhar shrugged. "Not enough to succeed. But it gives him joy."

"And you?"

"Yes. We play together."

"Then it is a success." The Imam gestured Azhar into another chair. "You are a good man, Azhar. Returning the Crusader child wasn't easy. I hear you took a liking to her. That's understandable. You are a parent. That's why Omar said you wanted him to get the credit for capturing her."

His mind spun like a carousel.

"Allah tests us in many ways. Especially when dealing with the Devil. I am pleased."

Azhar mumbled thanks.

"Speaking of Satan, what did you think of the Crusader woman's words?"

It took him a moment. "The Grandma? Oh, I'm not for politics, Imam."

"Still, you must have an opinion."

"I would revere in yours."

Abboud frowned. "They are weak. To apologize as if it would matter anymore. Still, the Messenger of Allah was asked, "Can the believer be a coward?" To which he said, "Yes." He was then asked, "Can the believer be a miser?' To which he replied, "Yes." And finally he was asked, "Can the believer be a liar?'

Abboud waited, but Azhar thought better of answering.

"No," the Imam snapped. "Truth, Azhar. Truth must be paramount." He played with the edge of his white robe before looking up intently. "Do you know the Grand Mufti's son Abdullah?"

Mustafa was thrown by the abrupt question. "Not personally."

The Iman smiled. "Now you will."

"But why?" Azhar blurted.

"For truth." The Iman stood. "Enjoy your sons. Omar is a fine boy. Pious. Abdul plays football well. I also have children. Three girls. Yes, Allah tests us all." He sighed wearily. "Thank you for the hospitality at this hour. Oh, and there is no need for you to volunteer at the orphanage anymore."

Azhar knew he should not ask why. Still in their places as if by order of God Himself, his family waited anxiously once the Imam left. Azhar stared at Omar, who barely blinked in response as he turned up the steps.

"So?" Jalak nudged Azhar.

"I'm hungry. Get food on the table, woman."

"I want to know…"

Mustafa rolled a football along the floor and kicked a perfect shot into Omar's head, knocking him to one knee. Azhar's fingers dug into the boy's arm.

"Never lie again."

Omar shook himself free. "Do not worry, Father. I did just this one time, out of respect for what you might have been."

"Might've been?" Azhar thundered. "You don't know what might've been means. What we sacrificed to give you a world where it is all right to betray a poor child. Where a father hates his own blood…" Over Jalak's gasp, Azhar shouted, "Never talk to me that way again. Ever. Do you hear?"

"It is not your world anymore, Father. It is mine." Omar calmly stared at his father's raised fist and laughed. "I must pray."

Once his brother left, Abdul slid his arm around Azhar's waist. "Are we in trouble, Father?"

Mustafa closed his eyes and asked Allah for forgiveness. "No." He smiled bravely. "Come and practice before your mother poisons us with breakfast."

22

Kenuda sneered disdainfully at the Three Amigos mural.
"Those were the traitors, right?"

Puppy stiffened. "No. Mooshie died under mysterious circumstances and Easy Sun Yen and Derek Singh served with distinction in the Marines."

"No one served with distinction." Elias shook his head at the failure of the American military. He touched the mural as Boccicelli and Fisher held their breath.

"It was a famous artist." Puppy wanted to slap his hand away. "Latsha Di. Perhaps you heard of her?" Kenuda sniffed. "She also painted the Children's Main Mural in Grandma's House, the Catastrophe of Los Angeles and the Midtown Pile, if you've ever seen that."

"I have, Mr. Historian." Kenuda said dismissively of the famous mural on the side of the abandoned Chrysler Building in Manhattan, depicting the carnage of the Allah chemical attack. "Well, shall we continue?"

Exchanging rolls of their eyes, Kenuda and Hazel walked past the DV teens lined up along the pavilion with brooms in hands, floor swept clean, heads slightly bowed like a custodial army.

"Careful, sir." Frecklie pointed at a gaping hole, disappointing Puppy, who would've enjoyed watching Kenuda crack open his skull.

"What is this?" Kenuda asked everyone.

"One of the mortar craters, Third Cousin," Puppy answered with excessive pleasantness. "The Miners were arrayed there." He gestured toward the outside wall; Kenuda and Hazel moved away. "The BTs shelled them from up there." He nodded at the shattered escalators at the end of the huge hall. "There was a vicious crossfire from the souvenir shop." He took them past the broken glass and around a few more holes.

Kenuda shook his head, not for the victims. "It's a mess."

"It's supposed to be that way."

"Yes, I know." Elias nearly tripped into another hole, grumbling. A DV handed him a plate of tacos and pierogi; the Third Cousin recoiled.

"Tacos," Puppy said helpfully, resisting the urge to take a bite and make yummy sounds. "Pierogi."

"We are allowed to have food from enslaved nations," Fisher piped up.

"Mexico is not part of the Caliphate," Kenuda said with disgust. He smelled a taco and found the courage to nibble. He grunted in surprise and finished off the snacks as Puppy led them into the ballpark.

Kenuda's large frame froze in the entrance. Maybe Puppy was being excessively hopeful, but for a moment, he thought he glimpsed genuine dismay.

"Why is the field so brown?"

"We can't water it, sir," Frecklie said defensively. "But we do trim the grass, sir."

"Which is allowed," Boccicelli said.

"Not really," Frecklie said.

Kenuda patted his arm. "It's all right, son."

The Third Cousin walked to the edge of the field, pausing to frown at bullet shells, tattered orange Miners wigs and an occasional bone.

"This is the shittiest athletic stadium I've ever seen," he said quietly. "An absolute disgrace. It shames the very notion of athletics and excellence and men and women striving for their best."

Fisher and Boccicelli bowed their heads, pleased by the praise. Kenuda's eyes nearly jumped out of his head.

"How can I possibly lend the office of American sports to this?" he asked Hazel.

"Like Puppy said, it's supposed to be this way…"

"I know, damnit. But you can't let people walk around. Is that a rat? A rat in one of my athletic forums?"

"There are lots more in the bullpen," Puppy said.

Kenuda folded his arms moodily. "It's far far worse than I thought."

"You could rope it off, Third Cousin, and add explanations," Frecklie said quietly.

"What?" Kenuda turned.

Puppy nodded for Frecklie to continue; the kid was going to anyway.

"Like a museum."

Elias moved closer to Frecklie who kept his steady stare. "Explain."

"We keep all the craters, but rope off the areas and put up signs saying what happened. We could do the same all over the ballpark, pointing out the various treacheries."

Kenuda smiled faintly.

"But we'd need to spruce it up a little. Like the field."

"That's against the law," muttered Fisher.

"Shut up, you idiot," Kenuda growled. "It is against the law, son."

Frecklie shook his head stubbornly. "According to the Treason Act of 2066, Amazon Stadium was to be maintained as it was on 10/12." The teen summoned his last bit of courage. "The field was not brown that day."

Elias thought about this. "The Little Extended Family could probably handle all this."

Puppy gestured at Frecklie to keep quiet.

"Bots, sir?"

"Well yes. Oh, of course, we'll keep on some of the DVs."

"No, it's got to be all DVs," Puppy insisted.

Kenuda scowled. "If I'm making this baseball restoration official, then I've got to maintain the same percentage between robots and human workers as there are in football and basketball."

"Why?"

Kenuda stammered and looked at Hazel for guidance; the journalist looked away. Elias continued, "Because it's the law."

"No it's not, sir," Frecklie chimed in.

"Are you telling me how to conduct business of the Sport Commission?"

Puppy stepped between them; Frecklie was young and stupid enough to throw a punch.

"If you want the stadium to really resonate as a museum to treason, what better way than to use all DVs since so many of the Miners were?"

Kenuda liked and disliked that argument.

"Besides, this gives them training. Remember Grandma's Twenty-Second Insight?"

Elias looked at Hazel again, who shrugged. "Not at the tip of my fingers."

"The goal is to have no disappointments in the Family," Puppy said with an even smile. "Having the DV kids take this on will help them get into Reg schools and out of the Village. It'll make them learn more of their history and become better siblings. It's a win up and down the line."

"They cost more," Boccicelli blurted, thinking of all that toilet paper.

Kenuda didn't even look at him. "That's your profit, not mine." He stared at Puppy. "No 'bots?"

Puppy made a zero with his thumb and forefinger. The owners nearly fainted.

"That would cause a great deal of problems with the Little Extended Family," Elias said very softly.

Puppy grinned. "Probably would, sir."

Kenuda slowly smiled, thinking sweet vindictive thoughts.

• • • •

PUPPY WAITED ON a concrete bench outside Zelda's office building. He handed her a sandwich. She sniffed, surprised.

"This smells almost edible." Zelda shook the sandwich suspiciously, catching a tomato before it hit the ground. "What'd you do to get this?"

"It's from Mooshie. I woke up this morning and found real coffee, too.

Zelda laughed. "That sounds like song lyrics."

"Could be. She's always singing, writing." Puppy nervously played with the crust of his sandwich.

Zelda grunted vaguely, wallowing in the glory of the lunch. She finished with a dreamy smile, peering at him.

"What's up, Pup? Usually you'd have scarfed down your sandwich and been halfway through mine by now. Wait, that's me."

He shrugged uneasily. "I have a small favor to ask."

"There are no small favors between friends, just large expectations."

Puppy sighed. "I saw Annette the other day."

"How's the Queen of Bitches?"

"Lovely as always."

"Castrated and insulted you?"

"What else is new?"

Zelda had almost stopped their wedding, knowing in her heart that it would be wrong, that Puppy deserved better. Annette was a cold, haughty asshole masquerading as a human being long enough to corral Puppy, never appreciating him, trying to remake him, clenching her groin at her superior Reg parents by marrying a DV. All of this Zelda had seen, dropping subtle hints like "she really doesn't love you, she's mean, you'll regret marrying her, do you really want her to breed," and other light-hearted remarks.

By the wedding, when it was real, when Puppy stood in the Family Entrance room before the large mural of Grandma, Zelda about blew. Pablo had dragged her away, pouring champagne funnel-like down her throat until she could reluctantly fulfill her role as best person, quietly and respectfully and dead drunk at Puppy's side.

"I only have a forty-five minute lunch hour." Zelda wiped the mustard onto her sleeve. "Someone came up with the idea of chopping celery into salmon salad. Folks are dancing in the hallways."

"Annette's about to be engaged to Elias Kenuda, the Sport Commissioner…"

"I know who he is, Pup. You don't have to say more." Zelda frowned. "She's using that against you somehow."

He nodded glumly.

"Let me guess. She'll say shitty things about you to Kenuda."

"She already has a little. Nothing too untrue."

"Like what?" Zelda grew angry. "You were the perfect husband."

"Not really, Zel."

"You were always loving. You didn't drink, hit her, cheat, be an asshole."

Puppy accepted the compliments. "Obviously that wasn't enough and let's please please not relive my marriage. This is now. She's threatened to sabotage baseball unless I get engaged super quick."

"What's super quick?"

Puppy held up a finger. "As in a week."

"Bitch bitch bitch." She finished Puppy's sandwich.

"So I thought, temporarily, maybe, you know."

She stared into Puppy's eyes and felt sick. "You and me?"

"Yes," he said enthusiastically. "Just so she can get officially engaged and off my back. Soon as they're married, boom, we're history. I'll take the blame, incontinence, impotence, it'll go on my record. I don't care."

"We have to show a line of courtship or they'll think we're faking to break the rules."

"Lifelong friends turn into lovers."

"Great story."

"I know, right? Who wouldn't believe that?"

"We'd fool Grandma herself."

"Exactly." He clasped her shoulder.

"Exactly," she repeated dully. "And what do I tell Diego?"

"The boy?"

Her voice hardened. "Yeah, the boy, Puppy."

"I thought that was just another ride."

"On Zelda's slut-a-rama?" She shoved him.

"No. But he's a…" Puppy ran a steady hand past his chin. Only so high.

Zelda inhaled so deeply her mouth went dry. "He's no Puppy Nedick."

"All right, that sucked, I'm sorry…"

"Just go away, Puppy."

He frowned. "You really like that kid?"

"Go away."

He smiled. "Shit. Shit. You're in love."

Zelda pushed him off the bench. "Maybe I am."

"That's great."

"Who knows, Puppy? Probably end up like you, divorced, breaking the law, alone, bitter."

"Forget I asked about…"

"Pathetic, sad…"

"Okay, Zelda."

"I probably should accept your generous offer because no relationship I've ever had worked anyway so why should this."

"I really think we need to talk."

"Get the hell out of here or I'll kick your ass and you know I can."

He tried one more time. "Zel."

Zelda pointed a trembling finger at the subway entrance.

"Will you at least accept my apology?"

"No." She brushed away tears. "And leave the fucking potato chips."

• • • •

BETH GOT LOST the first time she'd visited, wandering along Bruckner Boulevard, her heart pounding as if she'd lost him; the priest had died years ago and there couldn't be any records. She hadn't paid attention to the original drive in the dark, the many turns north and south, east and west, in case someone were following the Chevy with her dead husband in the trunk. Finally after running up and down the streets for two hours, sheer hysteria waxed a little memory and she found the courtyard of the broken building on East 156nd Street.

She brushed aside the weeds, kneeling before the slight bump of dirt. Light rain splattered, but she stubbornly wouldn't pull up her scarf. She didn't need to measure off steps anymore. The first few times, she had counted carefully, foot in front of foot, tipping unsteadily through eighteen steps until she landed at the proper grave. It was possible she was off and praying to someone else beneath her knees.

Father DiNado had rushed through the original ceremony, but Beth insisted he go through the rites again.

My husband deserves this, she'd hissed.

DiNado had been apologetic, mumbling about the danger. Best to pray quickly and quietly. God will hear anyway.

Even the prayers of cowards? she'd sneered.

Beth smoothed out the grave. No headstone. No marking of any kind, rocks, pebbles. Flowers? A joke. She'd left roses at the original Sacred Mary Church graveyard. They'd been burned. Graves had been trampled, dug up, surrounded by vicious signs: Look What God Did to America. To avoid such desecrations, all religious burial grounds had been moved to anonymous locations. Cremation was encouraged. Do what you need in the privacy of your own home. Nothing officially stopped anyone from praying, but the churches were finally torn down by mobs. See? Religion breeds anger.

Some brave folks said let us have our churches out of sight; we won't bother anyone. Unfortunately, the new rural locations bred cults. Old ideas and beliefs flourished. Black Tops razed the grounds of at least a dozen religious retreats, thousands dying. Public practice of religion was officially outlawed under the Anti-God Act of 2080.

Perhaps God really did only listen to Allahs.

Beth kissed her husband's grave and drew the sign of the cross in the dirt, then made it a little bigger. She crossed herself and laid down a single rose. Eduardo had brought her one rose every Tuesday even when they had no money; he'd never disappoint her. At the end, despite his pretty brown eyes sunken with diseased despair, his breaths short and labored, the single red rose would still appear in the narrow blue vase on the kitchen windowsill overlooking their garden.

Close your eyes, Eduardo would say. Turn around because I know you cheat. Here. Red rose. You can't even tell it's dyed.

I thought it was real. Beth would giggle playfully, sniffing the flower.

Beth finished praying and headed home along the desolate streets, remembering so intently she didn't notice the Brown Hat until he was by her side.

"Evening, ma'am. Need help?"

Beth lowered her eyes and kept walking. "No, thank you, Detective."

Detective Buca kept pace. "You're out late."

"Exercise."

"Where do you live?"

It was safer to hand over her Lifecard, which he studied on his connector device. He flipped open a notebook from the pocket of his bulky brown overcoat and made a couple notes.

"May I go now? My son will be home and I have to make sure he's done his homework."

"Is that what you were praying for?"

Beth stared hard and said nothing.

"Must be forty, fifty graves."

Beth trembled from rage.

"Husband? Wife? I had one, too." Buca returned the Lifecard with a final nod. "Vets camp, huh? You must've been an athletic teenager."

"Nothing illegal about that, either."

"Actually, Mrs. Rivera, crossing yourself in public is illegal. But it's dark and I doubt any judge would believe I saw it. I'm not entirely sure I saw anything. Did I?"

"No, Detective."

In one motion, he flipped the notebook closed and back into his pocket. "The last subway leaves in less than fifteen minutes."

"Then you shouldn't detain me any longer."

Buca stepped aside. "I was just out walking, like you. Have a good evening."

Instead of being angry Ruben was still at his girlfriend Dale's, Beth was relieved. She poured a tiny shot of Vermont Vodka, scooped out the rest of the peach pie down to the crumbs and went into his room.

The blue bed skirt was slightly awry, which meant he was hiding something under the mattress. Fortunately Ruben was a plodding idiot when he tried deceiving her. She easily lifted the bed and pulled out a wide book wrapped in brown paper.

Beth sat on the floor and opened *Great Baseball Stadiums* across her muscular thighs. Three or so pages were devoted to each of the old ballparks. She sighed. Just like him to plunge into this totally. Take tickets but you have to learn everything. Good trait for persistence, bad to allow emotions to consume you. Another dreamer.

Beth absently flipped another few pages before finding a couple folded sheets of paper tucked inside. There were sketches of a ballpark, notes dotting three levels, and circled numbers up to twenty pinpointing the field. In his tight, neat handwriting, Ruben had scribbled: "Here is where the first Miners treasonous assault began."

Beth's hands trembled.

"…more than seven thousand siblings were slaughtered…attempted assassination of Grandma…almost plunging the world into nuclear holocaust…"

She was still on the floor, book back under the mattress, when he came in. Frecklie warily looked around.

"Homework done?" she asked dully.

He nodded with scholarly assurance, slowly grinning under her doubtful stare. "Dale helped."

"Good." Beth brushed past. "It helps to have a smart girlfriend."

He soon heard her chopping vegetables as if cutting down a tree. She exhaled loudly between chops. It was a scary sound, even for his insane mother. Frecklie locked the door and taped Puppy's baseball book to the back of his dresser, just in case.

• • • •

FRECKLIE RAISED A questioning eyebrow down the line of the fifteen well-dressed DV teens until one flat-faced girl in a jacket and tie touched her temple.

"She says…"

"I understand." Puppy smiled. He motioned the girl over. "How long to clean up the Three Amigos mural?"

She glanced at Frecklie for guidance, who was irritated by her hesitation. She quickly gestured a hammer hitting the nail, the universal DV sign for work, then flashed three fingers. She hesitated again and wiped a forefinger on her palm. Costs.

Puppy waved that off and climbed up the five-foot high ladder. The DVs closed ranks, almost protectively. He started explaining, then stopped; the kids grew concerned.

"My shorthand's rusty."

An acne-faced boy called out, "We speak Reg, too." But not happily, their tight smiles said.

Puppy nodded gratefully. "We need the pavilion cleaned up, but without fixing it. Does that make sense?"

No more explanation was needed; they all knew their history.

"But some of this is simple wear and tear and neglect, and some inflicted by 10/12. We have to be really careful to walk that line. Like here."

He tapped a necklace-like string of bullet holes just over Singh's left shoulder. "We can't fill that in."

"But we can paint around?" Pigtails asked.

"Yes."

The color was navy blue. Set us off like Gods, back when you could be, Mooshie had explained at breakfast as he gathered the ex-players' ideas. The white was important. Stark. Make it sing, she insisted.

"Just there?' Acne asked.

Puppy hopped off the ladder and walked the group to the Gate Six entrance. "From here to there," he pointed halfway down the long hallway, leading them to the shuttered Gate Five.

"There?" A pale girl with deep blue eyes gestured across to the broken store.

"Not yet. Just the walls and wash the floors." They all looked sadly at the cracked concrete.

"My father and I make plaques," piped up a chubby boy in a flowered dress.

"I got the ropes," added a girl with squinting, suspicious eyes.

"Great," Puppy said.

"Food." Frecklie flicked his hand at the three small silver carts near the entrance to the Amazon Clubhouse store. "The eating stations aren't appetizing here in the hallway."

"We can't open up the stands inside. That's too much," Puppy said. "One area at a time."

"No," the boy shook his head stubbornly. "We'll build something new."

"I'm not sure we can."

"Grandma said it's about maintaining what happened. Adding on is fine as long as we don't change anything."

Everyone waited. Finally Puppy nodded, breaking out their smiles. He wagged a warning finger. Careful.

Puppy led them inside, trailed by uneasy murmurs. Some of the kids peered under the seats, while a few wandered down the rows. Frecklie clapped his hands once and the DVs snapped back obediently. He nodded for Puppy to continue.

He lifted up a seat, which twisted half off with a rickety groan. Three hands shot up confidently.

Just fix behind home. A better background helps us pick up the balls, Mickey had said, forcing down the black coffee with a longing look for one shot of anything with proof on the bottle. If they were restoring his Yankee Stadium, he'd go on the wagon.

"Navy blue," Puppy repeated, taking them down to the railing. Frecklie readily hopped over; the rest of the kids held back, shrinking a little. As children, they'd been terrorized by parents and teachers that the demons and ghosts living in Amazon Stadium would get them if they didn't study hard. Maybe some of them hadn't studied hard.

Embarrassed, Frecklie angrily pulled the gate open for the faint-hearted. He waited impatiently as the DVs warily shuffled forward, clustering by the fence in case one of those eight-foot, fire-breathing demons swooped down.

Puppy knelt and pulled up the brown weeds. "This too."

More murmurs.

"I want it green. But we can't remove anything down there."

To reassure the uneasy kids, Frecklie rummaged in the grass and pulled up a bullet.

"Old. Useless. Can't hurt you." He went around shoving the bullet under each of their noses; a few sniffed.

Puppy flipped a bone from hand to hand. Eyes nearly popped out of heads. "Leave these alone, too." He didn't need to repeat that. "Who knows about gardening?"

All fifteen kids raised their hands. Puppy and Frecklie exchanged proud smiles.

• • • •

PABLO RE-CLIPPED THE dental bib around Ja'mal's neck with an apologetic shake of his head.

"Sorry, Mrs. D'Hedri," he said to the twelve-year-old's stout, stern mother standing in the corner of the office. "I can't find a good dental hygienist. I've gone through three of them."

"Wouldn't seem to be hard. It's a good job." She indicated the problem clearly began with Pablo.

"If you know anyone…"

"I've got enough on my mind with this boy." Mrs. D'Hedri had the warmth of Pablo's drill. "Chewing all night. Headaches. Grades have dropped."

Ja'mal considered whether he could escape down the spit sink.

"Let's see…"

"Seeing isn't enough." She joined Pablo in studying her son's open mouth. "Finding out's what I need."

Pablo cleared his throat. "Mrs. D'Hedri, I believe there's only room for one of us in Ja'mal's mouth."

"Why? It's big enough for him to talk back."

Ja'mal silently pleaded with Pablo to save him.

"I think it's best if I examine Ja'mal alone."

"You're not going to plot anything like he does with his father?" She poked Ja'mal in the ear.

"I'll report any subversive conversations."

Pablo kept a straight face and escorted the scowling mother out of the door; she promised to take a seat nearby. Ja'mal smiled gratefully.

"Okay, man. You were a champion smile-o-meter on your last visit." Pablo studied this morning's results with grave disappointment. "What's up?"

Ja'mal sighed. "Too much external pressure."

Pablo was slightly taken aback by Ja'mal's mature response. "In what way?"

"The Academy tests are coming up."

"Why didn't your Mom mention that? Those are brutal."

"You've taken them?"

Pablo shook his head. "I didn't grow up a Reg."

Ja'mal turned curiously in his chair, big liquidy eyes undulating. "DV, huh?"

He cleared his throat. "Let's stay on you. When's the tests?"

"There are always tests."

"Ja'mal, tests are specifically structured…."

"Not for the Academy." The boy's voice broke over referencing the main Reg test to determine career strengths and possibilities. And limitations. "It never stops. Prepare, study. I want to be a doctor. Not a dentist, but a real doctor who saves lives."

"I do my part," Pablo snapped.

"I didn't mean to offend you, Dr. Diaz."

"Of course you didn't."

"But I'm scared."

Pablo patted the boy's shoulder. "Everyone's scared. Your whole life's ahead and you're worried one test could determine success or failure."

"That's supposed to make me feel better?" Ja'mal started climbing out of the chair.

"No. It's supposed to help you deal."

"How can I deal if I'm too scared? If I don't pass, my parents will blame me."

"They always do," he said. "You have to tell your Mom you're worried."

"You think she's the type you can talk to?"

Pablo nodded sympathetically. "Would you like me to?"

"But this is all confidential," Ja'mal panicked.

"I won't…"

"If you say something, don't you have to say it all?"

"I can shade things."

"I thought DVs didn't lie," the boy said coldly.

Those eyes, Pablo wondered. Like he borrowed them. Not the ones I've been staring into for five years.

"Isn't it about balancing confidentiality with truth? Have you any experience with that, Dr. Diaz?" Ja'mal shifted; clearly he was conducting the interview. "Duty versus compassion. Where's the balance? Would you betray a patient to help them? Or a friend to do what's expected? Is betrayal expected? Is that what you think?"

Pablo rammed a tiny light into Ja'mal's mouth; the boy gagged. Same teeth. Same slightly crooked molar upper right, number thirty.

Mrs. D'Hendri burst into the room. "What's taking so long?"

Ja'mal's eyes lolled. Terrified, he slid onto the floor, ripping off the bib and crying hysterically. Pablo held the boy. glaring at his mother.

"Ja'mal's grinding his teeth at night. Hence the headaches. He's clearly enduring a lot of external anxiety."

Mrs. D'Hendri opened her mouth to protest.

"Let's try reducing that, ma'am. Help Ja'mal find ways to reduce stress."

The boy's sobs subsided and he looked hopefully at his mother, who nodded grudgingly. Pablo shoved a green lolly into Ja'mal's mouth.

● ● ● ●

ZELDA TOOK THE steps two at a time; at least to the first landing, then one step for the next three flights. Blaring quick-paced music with lots of urgent horns forced her to ring twice. Waiting, she nervously shifted the bottle of wine and packaged dessert between her sweating hands.

"Hello?" A dark-haired female copy of Diego smiled from the open door.

"Hi." Zelda peered over the woman's shoulder. Diego slowly entered the field of vision.

"Hey," he said simply.

The woman stepped aside and touched her mouth toward Diego.

"My sister," Diego awkwardly introduced them.

"Capri," she filled in the name.

"Zelda. His girl friend."

"I was just leaving," Capri announced, grabbing her plate of food off the table.

"Please, don't leave…."

"Oh, I just dropped by." She tossed a fork, knife and a piece of bread on the dish, gulped down half a glass of red wine and rushed past. "Nice to meet you." She blew a kiss at her brother and closed the door. Diego shrugged sheepishly and turned down the music.

"My sister has funny eating habits." He nodded at the table, laden with steaming food. "Hungry?"

They ate Sherman's Chocolate Cake in bed, polishing off the Austin pinot noir in between sex. Diego brought some brandy out after midnight.

"This is the real stuff. Captain Lee got a few bottles somehow."

Zelda squinted to read the label without her glasses. Diego took loving pity.

"From France." He read the incredibly small print and poured them each three fingers; they sipped, murmuring approvingly.

"Did you mean it about being my girlfriend."

Zelda nodded slowly. "Yes."

"What changed from thinking I'm a dumb DV sailor boy?"

"You still are." She playfully pushed him. "Maybe I need one."

He grew serious. "Some brief rummaging in the mud fling?"

"No," she said at his doubtful look. "No. I really like you, remembering my record of only lousy relationships."

"And jobs?"

"Yes, thanks. Jobs, too. Pretty much everything except my friendships with Puppy and Pablo."

He took a cautious sip. "Ever do it with them?"

She firmly shook her head to strengthen the lie. "Just best friends."

"That's important." Diego thought a while. "Love's love."

"Not according to Grandma."

"I think loving a friend helps you love a lover. You see what you can't get away with and then you don't try that with someone you love romantically."

She turned on her side, impressed. "Insightful. But shouldn't you be able to do anything with someone you love romantically?"

"I never have."

"Me neither." Zelda flipped on her stomach and squeezed his hand.

"I got a job coming up," he said carefully.

"Great, where you going?"

He poured more brandy. "Captain Lee said we can't discuss it. Like really can't discuss."

"I can't stowaway?" she grinned impishly.

"Seriously, Zelda," he said with alarm. "I might be gone a while and didn't want you to worry."

"Or think you went off with some other girl?"

"Yes," he continued gravely. "Especially since you're like my girlfriend now."

"Not just like. Am. You are the bahm diggity." She rolled onto him, spilling his brandy.

23

Mrs. Hayden twitched as if just informed there was a vaccine for immortality. She tiptoed back behind home plate and waited for Puppy to guide her toward the stands. She shuddered, but the dugout wasn't any more enticing.

"I cannot allow the Hayden brand to go here. I'm surprised at you, Puppy. You seemed to have more sense than that."

"That's the beauty of the idea, Ms. Hayden."

"Your lack of any fundamental notion about business?"

Hold your ground, soldier. He dug his worn black shoes into the slightly yellowish-green infield grass. "Of course, Amazon Stadium is weathered."

What would she have thought before they painted the seats in a semi-circle from third to first. Which cost money. Which cut into Fisher and Boccicelli's bottom lines. Which meant Puppy had to find alternative resources.

"Weathered isn't the word I'd use. Try gloom. Despair." This from a woman who had dead people living in her basement.

"Yes." He raised his finger. "That's my point. Gloom. Despair. That's what your, our," he risked using the pronoun, "clients feel."

Mrs. Hayden considered using Puppy's skull as a salad bowl. "I bring them light and joy."

"In the beginning they don't know that." He steered Hayden's arm back toward the field, hoping the rest of her body would follow. "Amazon. Ancient. Old. Like death. That's what people see. But you don't."

She narrowed her eyes impatiently. "I don't?"

"Only Basil Hayden Funeral Homes sees through the gloom and brings happiness and relief to such a sad, mournful place of such sad, mournful memories."

"There's no other advertisers." Her serpentine tongue lashed at the faded façade of the second levels. "What went there?"

"Verizon Wireless."

"Cell phones." She laughed coldly. "When's the last time there were any advertisers?"

"October 12, 2065." She reached for her coat. "You're the trail blazer, the person who looks into the future. Doesn't it bother you that you can't get into NFL or NBA games?"

"I've tried. But they're always sold-out."

Puppy leaned with intimate urgency against the railing. "Are they really? Or don't they want you, Ms. Hayden? Oh, we're too happy to have funeral homes. We bounce and kick a big fat ball you can't miss."

"Maybe," she conceded. "But I don't want this. It's beneath death."

"You don't want to reach your fastest growing customer?" That got her attention. "Who comes to baseball games?"

"No one."

He risked a digit by wagging his finger. "DVs. Baseball's fan base was always more DVs."

"Miners," she sneered.

"DVs, ma'am. Poor health. Stress. You know they die in greater numbers than the rest of the population. Haggard DVs shuffling to their seats, coughing, bones brittle, vitamin deficiencies, alcoholism, mental instability, sexual deviation, moral predators deservedly toppling on the edge of death. Hordes of shapeless, overweight, thrombotic, diabetic fans barely able to stay alive through the end of the game, wondering what happens if they don't make it, who will make sure they're not wrapped up in a big garbage bag, who will comfort their emaciated loved ones who will also probably die pretty damn soon."

She stared, turning the hairs on his neck into needles. "Talk more."

"I have the person who can answer all your questions." He turned toward the Hawks dugout, repeating loudly, "I have the person who can answer all your questions."

Ty popped onto the field dressed in a smart new suit and tie. Puppy dragged Hayden over.

"Ty Cobb, meet Adona Hayden, owner of Basil Hayden's Funeral Homes. Ms. Hayden, Ty is player-manager of the Hawks. "

"And a Hall of Famer in the first eligible class," he added, leering slightly.

Hayden sniffed at Ty, frowning. "That smell." She frowned again. "It's formaldehyde."

"No, Jen and James Cleaning Fluids." Puppy laughed several octaves higher than normal. "We keep everything very sterile around here, including the players."

"I think I know formaldehyde," Hayden insisted.

Ty grunted. "Enough chit-chat. We here to do business or are we gonna stroke long ones all day?"

Hayden actually laughed like a human being. "Wouldn't that be nice? My marketing guy here has been selling me the beans."

"As they do." Ty winked. "Them's who can, don't."

She nodded uncertainly. "What would be the costs?"

Ty pulled her aside with a disdainful look at Puppy. "Look around. It's a barn."

"That's what I think."

"Like finding an unkempt piece of land in the swamp. A piece of land that might be valuable. Dirt cheap. Buy before it's popular. That's how I made a mint with Coca-Cola."

Her tongue darted greedily. "How much is a mint?"

"Millions." He poked her ribs and she giggled, light-headed from counting that many numbers. "They're desperate. They figure a heavyweight like you buys in, everyone else'll be interested. Hayden leads, the world follows."

"Yes, of course. But will anyone really see the ad here?"

"Attendance is up 650 percent this week. This week alone. And you wouldn't shoot only for this dump. Television, radio." Ty spit 'bacco juice over her head.

"Do you mean vidnews and vidrad?"

"Yeah, sure."

Adona stared. "I'd get good terms?"

"Best possible. Full creative control. Plus two spokespersons for the price of one."

"Oh really." She paused playfully. "Who would that be?"

"I'm one of them." Ty beamed. "Long as you use those fluffy velvet pillows, honey. I don't want neck pain from eternal sleep."

• • • •

MOOSHIE DRAPED THE straight black hair wig over the foam mannequin's head, unnerving Puppy slightly. She adjusted a thick red curly wig, resettling onto the stool in Jimmy's office, now her dressing room. Three shows per week. Last night, standing room only.

"I don't feel comfortable interfering, handsome."

He peered into the end of her red lipstick. "It's important."

"And Zelda's personal life isn't? You want her to give up a guy she loves so your crazy ex-wife is happy?"

"It's larger than that."

212 | GARY MORGENSTEIN

Mooshie laughed so hard she had to re-apply her lipstick. "I ain't asking her. I like Zelda."

"And I love Zelda."

"Maybe she loves you, too, moron. Ever think that?"

"What do you mean?"

"Loves you. Like she wished you really meant to marry her."

Puppy dropped onto the desk. "She said that?"

Mooshie shook her head. "Just a feeling from the way she looks at you."

He studied her. "What, you've got some ghostly insights?"

"Damned if I know what I got," she said into the mirror. "Memories all fused to-gether. I think I know something and then suddenly I don't. Pisses me off."

"So you won't talk to Zelda?"

She smacked his forehead with the heel of her palm. "No. You should be able to find someone. You're not bad looking, although a romantic charmer you ain't."

"Well I can't, okay? I need someone I trust. Someone who'll really go along with this. In three days."

"Isn't this against the rules?"

"Like stealing someone's prized autographed baseball glove to buy an illegal ID from the Pumpkin?"

"How do you know?"

"Pumpkin left me a squared note. 'Puppy Lies.'"

Mooshie sighed tiredly. "Sorry. I should've asked. Figured I could always replace it easily enough."

"It was the most important thing in the world to me," he said softly.

"Now it's gone." She snapped her fingers. "Lesson learned. Nothing should be the most important thing in the world."

"It wasn't about a thing, Mooshie. It was about you."

"You got me in person, sweet cheeks." She playfully slapped his face and glanced at her reflection. Puppy gloomily drew a sad face on his hand with the mascara.

"What would the engagement mean?" Mooshie asked carefully, discarding the red curls for her own cropped hair. She fuzzed it out like a porcupine.

"Nothing. I'd just say I'm officially engaged, now Annette can be."

"How carefully do they check? Used to be a team of Brown Hats would grill you to make sure you weren't faking for money, favors."

Puppy shook his head. "The government's so happy people are breeding to catch up to the Allahs, they kind of look the other way, I hear."

Mooshie spiked her hair more, pleased. "Kenuda's a Cousin, right?"

"He's a Third Cousin. Commissioner of Sport."

"They still have the cap on the number of Cousins?"

"There were problems with elitism so they opened it up. No one knows for sure how many. Pablo's going for Fifth Cousin, but that's a secret."

"I'll probably forget in five minutes, anyway." Mooshie made a sour face. "There were five Firsts, six Seconds, seven Thirds, eight Fourths and nine Fifths, in the beginning."

"How do you know?"

Mooshie shrugged, memories like a faucet turned on and off by someone else.

Jimmy rapped on the door. "Five minutes, Dara."

"Thanks, hon." She tugged on her needle-like hair. "Okay, I'll do it."

"What?"

"Get engaged to you."

His mouth dropped in shock. "You?"

"Yeah me." Mooshie shook her fist. "But don't even think of touching Mooshie's Golden Forest."

• • • •

THE EARLY MAY night was chilly and the Riverdale streets were deserted. It was a nice neighborhood with well-kept buildings, some dating back to the end of the last century, some built after the first brief clash with Iran in 2033.

They'd moved into one of the newer ones, courtesy of Annette's parents. He was never sure if they gave them the glorious, already furnished two-bedroom apartment with a river view because they loved their daughter or simply wanted to show up Puppy like hey, you'll never afford anything like this.

They were right, he had to admit. That's why he'd decorated the fire escape. Take that, Despicable Ma and Pa Reg. Laid down a thick rug, put out a battery-powered lamp and mini-fridge and cooked SC eggs and cheese on the tiny portable stove. White wine, Van Morrison overseeing the entertainment. They'd fall asleep some nights, even when chilly like now, huddled under the blankets in their spare room, as she called it. Maybe Annette loved it because she wanted to be hopeful, as if the fire escape would breed and take over the rest of the apartment, devouring the stuffy, expensive dark wood furniture and showing her parents how wrong they were.

See how his little stove turned into a real one? How about that two-by-three shag rug growing into wall-to-wall? Munch munch eat that big ol' eighty inch TV. Back when Annette believed in him. Back when Puppy still wanted to prove her wrong.

Maybe he still did and when would that stop?

At a light, he watched A20s scrub red graffiti off the side of a building. They paused to inspect their work.

"You can still read it," Puppy said.

The three 'bots turned sullenly. One of them grumbled and fetched a bucket of brown paint off their truck. It wouldn't match the building, but it would blot out the

KILL ALLAHS message. Third one he'd seen in the past couple days, Puppy wondered, buzzing Annette's intercom.

"Who is it?" Annette rasped.

"Me."

There was a long pause as she selected various disastrous scenarios. "What'd you do?"

"I have news. Will you let me in?"

Annette greeted him in a shapeless robe and big tortoise shell glasses, yawning. He had to gesture for her to step aside and let him in.

"It's nearly midnight," she complained, indicating boxes of neatly stacked shoes. "I've got a presentation in the morning."

"And I'm pitching." This time he wanted to make it out of the fourth inning.

"Oh. Well. Pardon. Want something to drink?" she asked mechanically.

He shook his head.

"I could find some food if you're really famished."

"I'm fine."

Same apartment. Same furniture, paintings, knick-knacks. He'd have thought she would've burnt everything and started over.

Annette waited. "I'm not giving you anything."

"You think I came here at midnight to ask for a painting?"

"Then why are you here?"

"Can I sit down?"

"If you have to." She yawned again and caught him glancing at her breasts. She flushed and tightened the robe. "I'm tired, Puppy."

He figured it'd be easy. That's the point, isn't it, he asked the painting of Grandma beaming majestically over the Bronx. Very smart to make divorce so difficult.

"I found someone."

"Someone?" Annette squinted suspiciously. "A partner?"

"Yes. We're very happy and we're going to be engaged."

She scrunched up her face, taking this in warily. "Who is it?"

"Dara Dinton."

"I never heard of her."

"And that means she's not real?"

Annette shrugged. "Where'd you meet?"

"The bar where she sings. What's it matter?"

"Just curious." Annette tilted her head. "How old?"

"I don't know…"

Annette's eyes brimmed with doubt. "You don't know."

"She's a little older." If you count the time in Heaven, around seventy-five. "Honestly, I don't care."

"Uh-huh." Annette frowned. "And you're really engaged."

"You think I'm lying."

Annette pursed her lips. "A singer."

Puppy tossed off a few chords from *Sgt. Pepper's Lonely Hearts Club Band.*"

"Is it a boy or a girl?"

"A girl. I just said that."

"Because The Beatles were all boys."

Puppy flushed. "Are you trying to trick me, Annette?"

"I'm just trying to make sure this is true. A girl. Dara…"

"Dinton," he helped. "Very nice."

"Uh-huh." Annette twisted her fingers nervously. "For real, Puppy?"

"For real, Annette," he said softly. "You and Kenuda can get married."

"You're happy?"

Puppy really didn't know how to answer that. "Sure."

"That's not like really enthusiastic."

"You want me to jump up and down?"

"I want to make sure this will last."

He bit the inside of his cheek. "I won't change my mind, if that's what you're worried about."

"Or she might," Annette snapped back. "There is the ninety-day exploratory period."

"I was married before, I know."

"I'm just reminding you. I don't want to be embarrassed."

"Again. That's what you mean. Puppy screws up getting engaged. Like Puppy screws up everything else."

Annette's shrug infuriated him.

"I love Dara and she loves me. Passionately."

"Well good because I love Elias wildly and he loves me wildly."

"I'm glad we're both madly in love."

"Isn't it beautiful." Annette glared. "When are you filing the papers?"

"Tomorrow after the game."

"Good." She yanked open the door. "Make sure they send me a copy."

"I think that's the law."

"Thank Grandma's kneecaps. Good night."

"Screw you, too, Annette."

She perched herself on the windowsill and watched him leave the building and head down Riverdale Avenue, then crawled onto the fire escape with a bottle of wine, huddling beneath an old wool blanket. It was too late to tell Elias the good news.

• • • •

ABDULLAH BIN-NASR THOUGHT very highly of himself, which left no room to think highly of anyone else. Even faking obeisance or respect was difficult and often accompanied by a sneer which, when that angered his father, he explained away as a unique link between his mind and his mouth which few if anyone, except perhaps the Prophet Mohammad, could experience.

His father thought it was much shit as he thought much of what his eldest son suggested was much shit. Abdullah thought his father was much shit. He thought he was old and tired and dangerous because the world was forever young, forever birthing. Someone needed to oversee the new. That would be him.

Only one could lead. As had the Prophet.

"Give me your name again." He crossed his small ankles; Abdullah was barely five-three.

"Azhar Mustafa."

"A fine man," the Imam said.

"As you mentioned." Abdullah gestured for Azhar to stand; Mustaka thanked Allah silently for steadying his creaky knees. "That was a strong story of courage with that Crusader girl, Azhar."

He forced out the words. "I did what needed to be done."

"Which unfortunately, many don't. They can only do what they're told. Can you do what you're told, Azhar?"

He nodded.

"What if you're not told why you're doing something?"

"I assume my lord knows better."

Abdullah frowned. "You know I am superior."

"Yes."

"But why?"

Azhar peeked over to the Imam for guidance, who waved his hand in vague encouragement.

"You are a great man."

"Am I?" Abdullah smiled. "Well, yes. But why?"

Mustafa grimaced. "Your charities resonate throughout the Caliphate."

"That is governed by the teachings of the Quran. Have I anything to do with that?"

"The Word must be put into practice, my lord."

Abdullah shifted in his wide chair, intrigued. "And you think some don't?"

He looked again for guidance from the Imam, who shook his head.

"I think some don't. Following Allah is difficult."

"Some fail?"

"Yes."

"Like who?"

Azhar looked directly at Abdullah, alarming the Imam. "Only Allah knows."

"Yes, he does," Abdullah was amused. "Clearly so do you."

"I didn't mean…"

"You're allowed to mean, Azhar. You're allowed to have thoughts. Because understanding Allah is, as you say, difficult. Many believe they talk directly. Do they talk to Allah or do they hear themselves thinking they are talking to Allah to justify what they believe and how they behave?"

Azhar's mind scrambled to follow.

"Who is to know that?" Abdullah shrugged. "God must speak to many. Do you think he speaks to Crusaders?"

Mustafa vigorously shook his head.

"But what if a Crusader wants to know Allah?"

"They must study and accept Him in their heart."

"What if they share the ideas of Allah but in their own way?"

"I don't think that is possible."

"But we share our holy books with the Crusaders and the Jews. Moses. Jesus. People of the Book. Why can we not share our minds and remain true? If our beliefs are so strong, our Prophet so strong, what should we fear by the thoughts of others?"

Azhar wanted to dig an escape hatch. "I don't know the answer."

The Son squeezed both of Mustafa's wrists. "No one does. Except me."

"Blessed be," the Imam murmured, eyes glistening.

"With help." Abdullah smiled. "I'm told you're a good sailor."

He nodded. "The best, my lord."

The Mufti's son laughed. "We will get along well, Captain."

24

Hazel waited at the corner of Decater and Bedford Park, the glittering colors of the HG Bronx Botanical Gardens an Earth-bound rainbow a couple blocks away. Hazel smiled at the families strolling past in the mild May evening, jolting a few memories of being ten, an older orphan struggling to lose his French accent, and his parents Greta and Gail, long dead, taking him for hours and hours through the Gardens. He never realized the flowers weren't real.

Hazel felt a slight pinch in his neck. When he woke, the black hood was still around his head, hands tied in the familiar Navy Seal clove hitch knot. His legs were free, allowing him to stretch the Gelinium.

Derek Singh pulled off the hood and Hazel blinked rapidly, a little angry.

"Was that necessary?"

Singh grunted. Easy Sun Yen reclined in a thick easy chair as if waiting for a vid-movie to come on. Three old, muscular men stood with arms folded, yawning; they were beyond menacing stares.

"I come to your planet in peace," John quipped. Singh nodded and someone yanked off the knot. Hazel rubbed his wrists. "Any poisoned drinks or you're saving that for the ride home?"

Derek used his heavy boot to slide a tottering chair by Hazel. They were in the back room of a store, probably Singh's. John waited with a faint smile.

"What do you want?" Singh finally asked, straddling the chair.

"Same thing as you. To finally finish the job."

Singh shot a quick glance around the room. "It's a little late for that. War's over. We have peace and prosperity."

"Not unless you live under Allah rule, which is pretty much the whole world except for North America and the neutral zones in the Caribbean."

"And China."

"Xinjiang and Gansu are long gone to the Allahs. They're still fighting in Yunnan and Henan."

Yen shrugged from deep within his chair. "Their problems, not ours."

"We're just retired siblings," Singh said.

"Dabbling in commerce," Yen added. "Me with my haberdashery. Derek the country grocer."

Hazel turned, waiting for the others to chime in, but they just stared. "Sicily?"

The one on the left with the crooked scar on his forehead nodded.

"Me, too. 238th."

They didn't do more than peer. Hazel sighed inwardly. "You heard Grandma's Story."

"Yup," Singh replied simply.

"The Story's the first step to redoing the curriculum. She backdoored this apology instead of letting it get debated in the Cousins Council. Children will learn lies."

"Like they haven't all this time?" Yen snapped; Singh shot him a warning look.

"Why do you think she's doing this?" Hazel looked around.

"Clearly you got the answers."

"I think she's paving the way for a rapprochement."

"That an English word?" The ex-Marine with the crooked scar drawled.

"No. French. Like me. They rescued my ass." Les enfants de transport aerien, back in 2063. Tens of thousands, shivering on the beaches at Dunkirk, waiting for the planes. The Allahs had finally developed a sense of history not about themselves.

Singh leaned forward on the back of the chair, staring at Hazel. "We all know the history. We were there."

"So was I," Hazel tapped his Gelinium.

"238th. Sicily."

"That's right. May 2069."

"Bloody awful."

"Damn straight."

"Your rank?"

"I'm sure you already looked me up."

"My memory's fading."

"Lance corporal."

"Medals?"

"A few. I tossed 'em at the White House during the memorial ceremony." Millions of vets from all over American came that day, asking one more time for respect.

"Medals to the rubble. One pile of shame," Yen recited their chants that day before the Black Tops crushed them. Literally crushing bodies, vets hobbling away on one leg, falling onto one arm, flattened beneath the huge blood-splattered wheels of the armored vehicles.

"That's right."

"But you got away," Singh said.

Hazel unbuttoned his shirt. "Not without leaving with this."

Singh stared expressionlessly at the three inch scar just above Hazel's heart. "Knife?"

"BT hook blade."

"Nasty shit."

"Yes it was."

"Could also be a razor twist." Yen stood and rocked his left wrist side to side.

"I wasn't a DV."

"No, you were adopted by Fifth Cousins."

"And happy about it."

"They brought your ass over in the de transport aerien," Singh's voice dripped venomously, "and then let you enlist?"

"Some Cousins still believed in fighting."

"Not many."

"Mine, did."

"Dead now."

"That's right. Sorry you can't interrogate them."

Derek pressed his nose inches from Hazel's face. "What do you want?"

"Remove those in the way. Same as 10/12. Except this time, do it right before Grandma turns America into a mosque."

Singh nodded and two of the former Seals flung Hazel onto a cot, where he was quickly strapped down. The one with the scar pulled out a long, glowing prong while Yen tied down Hazel's right leg.

"What the fuck are you doing?" Hazel shouted before they stuffed a tissue in his mouth.

"Vets got the Geliniums. So did the BTs. Theirs have trackers."

Hazel felt another pinch in the neck and stumbled into the darkness.

• • • •

THE LAST WHINING and annoying patient didn't leave until after seven; Pablo controlled his compulsiveness so he only finished half the paperwork, glancing as much at the clock as the retina-numbing forms. He wrapped Puppy and Dara's engagement present twice because the bow was uneven, then shaved again.

Moisturizer time, he sighed sadly at the creases around the somber eyes. Pablo debated over three ties and hurried into the waiting room. The dark-haired and sandy-haired men slouched comfortably as if Pablo's office were their living room, watching a tennis match from Louisville and exchanging biting comments about the players' styles.

The dark-haired man opened a brown leather notebook.

"Must be tired, Dr. Diaz."

Pablo suddenly understood. He shrugged, careful not to admit to fatigue.

"You're not tired after working fourteen hours?" the sandy-haired man groaned at a poor serve. "Because you're superhuman or aren't challenged enough by the job?"

"I suspect there's a right and wrong answer to that," Pablo replied carefully. "As always."

Pablo jiggled the marble in his right pocket. The dark-haired man muted the vidnews.

"How's it going?"

"Shouldn't you tell me how the Cousins review is going?" Pablo squeezed his hands, then stopped, afraid they'd take that as nerves.

The dark-haired man motioned for his colleague to answer. "It's not a review. You've already been reviewed."

"Then the process," Pablo said in exasperation.

"Do you find it difficult?" the dark-haired man leaned forward.

"Kind of maddening, the obscurity of it all."

"As a man of science, you prefer clarity."

"Instead of riddles, yes. Naked woman in the shower, a boy turned into a talking puppet."

The dark-haired man smiled. "Neat tricks. Wish we'd thought of them."

"You had nothing to do with it?"

The sandy-haired man fiddled with the cuff of his trousers. "If you can't handle this, then how can you handle the rigors of being a Cousin?"

Pablo smiled. "Good point. But I can't answer that if I don't know what they are."

The sandy-haired man grunted. "Then how do you know you're capable?"

He hesitated. "Perhaps I'm not."

The men exchanged curious glances.

"Honesty." The dark-haired man smiled. "Honesty about yourself is a key. Knowing what you don't know so you can discover it without preconceptions of your ego. Dispassionate passion."

"My specialty."

The men laughed.

"I'm serious."

"You are a serious man, Dr. Diaz," the sandy-haired man admitted. "For someone who's personal life is in turmoil."

Pablo laughed bitterly. "I have no personal life."

"What about your friends?"

"Which ones?"

"You only have two. Zelda and Puppy. Nice of them to still invite you to the engagement party after the fight."

He put down the gift-wrapped bottle of Arkansas champagne. "Sometimes friends argue."

"About?"

Pablo deliberated. "It was a misunderstanding."

"Over?" the dark-haired man said skeptically.

"His fiancé. I don't think she's the person she makes herself out to be."

"Oh." They raised their eyebrows. "What does she make herself out to be?"

He weighed the words around his back molars. "A real human being."

That satisfied them a moment. Pablo smiled at the small victory.

The dark-haired man continued, "And how about Zelda?"

"What about her?"

"Isn't it a little awkward, the two of you."

Pablo's eyes narrowed. "Not at all."

"Even after you slept together?"

"We didn't."

"Ah," the dark-haired man smiled humorlessly. "Deceit is the shawl of honor."

Pablo's lips twisted. "Grandma never said that."

"I just did."

"It's a crappy line." Pablo squared his hips. "What do you want?"

"What do you want?"

"If I say I want to be a Cousin, that suggests ambition. If I seem blasé, that suggests indifference. What if I just want to do some good? That satisfy you?"

"If that's what you think."

"But not what I'm supposed to think."

The men exchanged sad looks.

"The damn riddles are getting tiring," Pablo snapped.

"Riddles are tiring for people who don't understand," the dark-haired man said. "Or for people who spend their lives observing."

Pablo flinched. "Add that to your damn report."

The dark-haired man held up the blank pages. "That's up to you."

• • • •

WAVING OFF JIMMY'S offer to do the honors, Zelda poured the champagne into their four glasses; Mick sadly held up a bottle of soda.

"We're proud of you." Puppy nudged Mick, who growled from his bowels. Mantle was marking a week on the wagon and his batting average was up to .255; he finally clocked his first homer, an inside-the-park job when the Falcons centerfielder collapsed on the warning track.

"Okay, gang." Zelda raised her glass, waiting until Puppy angrily shoved the empty extra chair by another table. She sighed. Friendship was faith. Pablo would be here. "Two White Grampas, thanks for coming to the engagement party."

"Ain't no food," Ty muttered.

Zelda snatched a bowl of pretzels from an adjoining table. "Fully catered. I might have some SC chocolate in my purse if I get a smile out of you."

Zelda clearly had had a few before coming, plus the drink alone where Puppy profusely apologized for his insensitivity. Zelda tickled Ty's chin and his lips parted grudgingly.

"See how we Negroes always makes the white folks happy? Now on to the new couple."

Tradition insisted the prospective best person throw the engaged couple a formal toast within twenty-four hours, so they got used to the notion straight away, like breaking in a pair of shoes.

An older couple paused by the table to shake Mooshie's hand; autographs and photographs had been long banned as part of the Anti-Narcissism Act.

"To my new friend Dara." Zelda and Mooshie clinked glasses. "And my old friend Puppy." They clinked glasses; Mooshie carefully watched Zelda's cloudy expression. "And to our new friends who are like old friends, Mick and Ty."

A few tables listened in.

"Let their love transcend," Zelda said, her hand shaking slightly as she recited Grandma's Love Pledge. "Let their love be as one. Let their love light themselves and let their love light all of us." She stood. "To Dara and Puppy."

"To Dara and Puppy," the bar shouted, applauding.

Zelda poked the blank Puppy. "Your turn."

He couldn't remember the words. He knew he'd said them to Annette, otherwise they wouldn't have had all those wondrous years together.

Mooshie held up her glass and he joined her, wobbling to his feet. This is Mooshie Lopez I'm engaged to. Fake or not. Dead or alive.

"Let me help my fiancé. His mouth is frozen with love." She said to the packed room. "I was married once before." Actually three times. Paula the gymnast with a short leg. Jen the writer, who wrote poetic crap. And after she'd retired, briefly to Jeff, the burly restaurant owner. Puppy despised those names.

"To my beloved. Who I love and know loves me." Mooshie waited; Puppy just stared stupidly. "Repeat, my shy guy."

The bar cracked up.

"To my beloved. Who I love and know loves me," he repeated.

"We stand together, to serve each other and The Family."

"We stand together, to serve each other and The Family."

"May our fortune be our love."

"May our fortune be our love." Puppy grinned stupidly.

His fiancé kissed him tenderly on the lips. He nearly fainted.

The patrons shouted, "May their fortune be our love."

Mooshie winked, grinning. "And to show my love to my love, I want to sing a song that from way before any of us were born, from a group called The Four Seasons."

In the corner, the pianist tinkled the keys and the drummer picked up the slow beat. Jimmy grinned and tossed her the mike. Mooshie sang *My Eyes Adored You*. The music stopped and Mooshie nestled on his lap, in his arms, kissing him fervently; his knees buckled, sitting down. The bar went nuts.

• • • •

THE BEEPING IN the medicine cabinet startled Zelda; she nearly swallowed her toothbrush. Damn, she muttered. The beeping continued, not growing louder, just with that same disappointed haughtiness that she needed a reminder at all.

Zelda peered at the date. Okay, she said to the little red box with the smiling beeping light which all women in America had. I forgot by two weeks, she held up a couple fingers, dropping her sticky toothbrush back into the Frida Fried Dumplings oral hygiene cup Puppy bought her to celebrate Grandma's birthday last year. Zelda rummaged under the sink for the monthly pregnancy test kit, squatted on the toilet and peed into the cup.

She laid the purple receptacle on the sink and returned to the kitchen, pouring coffee and finishing off a raspberry donut while she drone-dazed into the vidnews. Two stinky looking teenagers in North Carolina talked about their scientific breakthrough in purifying water.

So nice we have geniuses to make up for the rest of us, Zelda thought, tugging the bakery box out of the fridge and pondering which of the three remaining powdered donuts had the cream filling. She bit into the middle one and apple spurted onto her chin.

Sorry, little guy, it's your turn. But don't think you other two are off the hook. I said I wanted cream filled and that is what Zelda will have.

Oh no, fat girl with the double chin, save us, pleaded the chunky donut to the left.

Don't listen to him, beautiful girl, beseeched the donut guy hugging the right side of the box. He's tricking you. Eat him and save me so we can live in eternal togetherness like Puppy and Mooshie.

Zelda dropped the box onto her lap, frowning at the other voice in the apartment not coming from her head.

"Congratulations. You're going to be a mother."

Accusing the vidnews, Zelda hoped it was an advert for baby powder or baby food or some gross product. Nope, just Grandma and some kids singing the stupid locomotion song.

"Congratulations. You're going to be a mother."

Zelda dropped the donuts and hurried into the bathroom. The cup was jiggling side to side joyfully.

"Congratulations. You're going to be a mother."

She tried choking the cup, but it kept congratulating her. Zelda shoved it under the sink and hid behind the shower curtain until the damn thing shut up. She brought the cup into the living room and took a deep breath. The brief message danced gaily around the inside of the cup.

"Bring this cup into a Parents Benefits Center to register. We're so happy."

Zelda finished the last donut and stared dully at the vidnews. Grandma's sweet voice joined her on the couch.

"Aren't they precious?" Grandma hugged the three children squirming like puppies. "They're the Machado triplets: Joyce, Marlene and Rita. Don't you just love them?"

She looked directly at Zelda. "Who wouldn't love them? Who wouldn't want triplets?"

"Shut up," Zelda said.

"The joys of parenting enrich everyone. Especially you." Grandma's eyes grew larger.

"Shut up." Zelda pounded on the vidnews, but the protective glass bruised her hands.

"If you're not a parent yet, don't panic. Go to any Benefits Center for your tests. And if that fails, don't worry, darlings."

Zelda smashed a dining room chair against the screen.

"We have babies for you."

She pounded again and again until the screen cracked and Grandma's huge eyes disappeared with a sad sizzling sigh.

25

Grandma finally snapped at him to stop by the one hundredth and eighty-fourth slide. Cheng let the screen flash a few more photos of KILL ALLAHS scribbled on the side of apartment houses, schools, government offices and simple bodegas before switching off the projector and turning on the lights in her small study.

"Was anything coordinated?"

"There's no evidence to suggest that. Not even a mottled orange wig."

Grandma stared off. "Any assaults?"

Cheng nodded. "There's footage."

"Oh, I'm sure," she said coldly, offering him an Austin cognac, which he gratefully accepted. It'd been a long night of poring over follow-up reports to her Story.

"Serious injuries?"

"Some broken bones. Mainly Mediterranean and Hispanic ancestry, the complexion and all."

"Let's renew the ban on facial hair and women's scarves."

"Will that really help?"

Grandma took a long sip, longer than usual, the skin on her chin drooping. "It'll remind people."

"We should start arrests."

She slammed down the glass, spilling cognac on her skirt. "That'll show concern."

"And you're not?" Cheng sipped slowly.

"There'll always be angry people. I understand that. I'm not comfortable with the assaults, but let's find out who had a mustache or beard that might've precipitated it."

"And scarves. It'll only get worse."

Grandma gave him a nasty stare. "I want schools adopting this curriculum immediately. And I don't want a debate, Albert. We've got to start somewhere. One hundred and eighty-four incidents isn't bad. I expected worse."

"Give it time."

"It's the price we'll pay for real peace. Real love, Albert."

"Perhaps you should start by showing me some."

"What're you talking about?

He waited a moment before answering. "Why won't you trust me, Lenora?"

Grandma smiled as if surprised he took this long to ask. "Because you'll be unhappy."

"I'm unhappier being left out. You're doing something significant without involving me. Which by law…"

"Are you going to recite the Family Vows…"

"Just the one pertaining to you consulting the First Cousin before launching a major new policy."

"I haven't launched it yet."

"But you hope to."

She poured them another drink.

"Is that why Major Stilton activated his A3?"

Her jaw tightened in grudging respect. "Very good, First Cousin. Do you also track when I use my A1 cover?"

"Yes," Cheng said steadily. "It's my job to run the damn country, Lenora." And you get all the credit. Me, the grief. He'd founded the Cousins, the whole concept. Structure, giving the people something different. Not just a new government but a new idea. Sure, she was the driving public force; he wasn't exactly warm. But someone had to be a shit so she could be the doting grandmother, rising above the petty bureaucratic struggles and difficult, ugly decisions.

"I need to know what's going on," he continued. "So where is your head of security going?"

Lenora sighed.

"I'll find out eventually."

She flinched. "That almost sounds like a threat."

Cheng smiled. "Never, Lenora. I'll support everything you do, as I always have." His voice hardened. "But I need to be in the loop."

Grandma sighed again and made them a fresh pot of coffee.

• • • •

ALL 104 POUNDS of Ian Schrage, most seemingly contained in the tall plant-like red hair, hopped off the top of the Hawks dugout and, with a dignified air reserved for conquering generals and creative types, marched up to Ty and Mick.

They stepped back with meek wariness.

"You look like undertakers." He jammed his palms into their kneecaps.

"I'm the undertaker," sniffed Ms. Hayden.

"Yes, obviously. They're not." He sneered. "They are baseball players. Look up in the sky, dearie. What do you see? Yes, you see it is a baseball stadium."

Schrage bounced like a ball not fully inflated toward home plate. "This being a base. That a field. This a dugout. Keeping up, now? Who may I ask sanctioned said wardrobe, when according to the terms of my employment it said, as I need to repeat to all: The director shall have complete creative control."

Puppy raised his hand slowly. "I did."

"Ah, the historian. Of course, you have a great knowledge of fashion." Ian fingered Puppy's droopy black hoodie.

"We told him to check with you," Fisher said over Boccaccelli's shoulder from the comparative safety of the fourth row.

Ian shut his eyes as if not wanting an answer. "You are again?"

"Owners of the teams."

"Well, well, well. And you have directed how many adverts? Supervised how many advert campaigns? What was that? I can't hear." Cupping both ears, Ian hopped back onto the top of the dugout. The owners gasped and moved up a few rows. "Stay there. You. Bad hair girl."

Hayden maintained her resolve as they met by the on-deck circle, snapping, "I want them to look dignified. I was promised creative control, too."

"Well that person lied." He whistled at Mick and Ty. "Now get out of those disgusting suits and into your uniforms before I charge overtime."

Fisher and Boccacelli nearly keeled over. Ty and Mick disappeared into the dugout. Hayden motioned Puppy over and together they followed Ian to the two coffins between home and the mound.

"Can I see the revised script?" Ms. Hayden asked.

"Revised assumes it was a script at all." Ian scowled at the cameraperson. "Did you see there is dust on the hood? Wipe it." He flung a handkerchief. "Yessss?" he snapped at Hayden, wondering why she was still standing there.

"I want to know what they're saying, Mr. Schrage."

"You will when I figure it out. Ah, there they are, the handsome gentlemen." Ian grabbed the uniformed Mick and Ty by their hands as if greeting long-lost uncles. "Look at you." He took them on a little circle around the coffins. "How do you feel?"

Mick peered into the coffin. "Like we been at this rodeo before."

"Where's the velvet pillows?" Ty roared.

"Yes, where are they?" Ian clapped his hands and two assistants raced over with pillows. "These, sir?"

Ty and Mickey pressed their faces against the pillows and grunted, satisfied.

"Excellent." Ian placed the pillows gently down. "Get in. Feel the sense of the product."

"How do you think we got here?" Cobb muttered.

"He's thinking of the limo service we use," Puppy interrupted. He had to nod three times before the reluctant White Grampas climbed into the coffins.

"Be careful with them, they're top of the line," Ms. Hayden shouted.

Ian's leathery face squished together as he bounced in front of Hayden. "Go sit there."

"I'm the client. I'm paying a great deal of money."

"I'm the client. I have money. I can't match my colors," Ian mocked savagely. "In the seats. Now. Or I walk and then you've wasted my upfront fee."

She glared.

"Is that a yes or a no?"

Adona gave Puppy a dirty look for hiring such a person at such a cost and joined Boccaccelli and Fisher.

228 | GARY MORGENSTEIN

"Thank you." Ian bowed and leaned into the coffins, whispering. "How's it feel?"

"I think I dozed," Ty admitted.

"It's a lovely product."

"I wish my family woulda used this the first time around," Mick said.

"These men are naturals." Ian proclaimed happily. "Let's get this voyage underway."

Boccaccelli stepped shyly onto the field, coughing in different octaves until Ian raised an eyebrow.

"You are who again?"

"Boccaccelli, owner…"

"I know who you are," Ian rasped, squirming into his director's chair by the first base line. "Unlike thou, I'm not a moron. What do you want?"

He gestured into the Falcons' dugout, where the team sat, stone-faced. "If the Hawks players are being used, so should my team."

Puppy hurried over. "That's because Ty and Mick are stars."

"Because they play my team."

"Because they're my stars." Fisher jumped onto the field.

"I'm not paying for more actors." Hayden rushed into the fray.

They yelled at each other for another few minutes while Ian checked camera angles and Ty and Mick dozed in the coffins.

"Is everyone done?" Schrage screamed. They quieted. "Pardon, I must consult with the historian." Ian beckoned Puppy near first base. "This seems a very sensitive issue."

"Technically the two teams share everything."

"Except me."

"Yes. Sorry."

"I am not changing my vision for your stupidity."

"I wouldn't ask you to." Puppy smiled. "Just work them in somehow. No one's smart enough to figure this out except you."

"Cut the crap, girl." Ian's lower lip puffed up as he studied the expression-less Falcons. "Perhaps there's a way. As long as you do not talk to me again. Ever."

"Gladly."

• • • •

MOOSHIE SWIVELED AROUND in the narrow dressing room, inspecting the tight red dress in the trio of mirrors. She patted her butt. "This look good?"

Zelda faked sudden attention. "Yes. Hot."

"Want to generate a little more oomph on the hot?"

"Sensational."

"But not fat? I was a size four once. Eight for a while after they retired me." She popped her head out the door. "Darling, could I get the black and mauve in this cut, size six?"

"I was never a four." Zelda clenched her fingers, wondering if they were swollen.

Beth entered with a grim air, the two dresses folded over her arm as if she were selling discount cancer treatments.

Mooshie glanced at the tag and darkened. "Honey, these are eights."

"Yes, ma'am."

She took her scowl in Zelda's direction. "I said six, didn't I?"

Zelda shrugged, staying out of the way. No wonder Puppy recommended this dressmaker. Just his type. A pretty bitch.

"Eight's best." Beth didn't smile nor engage in any basic retail procedures like pleasantries or deference or acting as if she cared about customers, other than a quick searching glance at Zelda's butt.

Lopez put her foot onto the stool and tilted her head quizzically. She didn't smile either. "Are you saying I'm an eight when I know I'm a six?"

"I can measure with my eyes."

Zelda muffled a grin.

"How about just giving me what I want?" Mooshie snapped.

The woman shook her head. "I won't sell wrong sizes. It's my job to know what fits, not yours."

Grandma's Capitalism Reform Act of 2076 enshrining honesty in business was about ten years after Mooshie's death, explaining her bewildered anger. "What if I go elsewhere?"

"You came here because of our reputation for quality. If you want to go elsewhere out of vanity, that's your choice. Please let me know if I can serve you any other way."

Mooshie stared at the closed door for a few moments. "That's one nasty DDV."

"DDV?"

"Deeply disappointed villager." She smirked. "Ones who won't budge from their sour position, who piss on the whole system. Used to be the whole damn DV. They had riots back in the early 60s at the start of the war. You know that?"

Zelda squeezed her swelling ankles and imagined blowing up and never fitting into anything. Oh, sorry ma'am, we just sold the last size fifty-six, but we have some tents out in the storage shed. She'll be like a balloon that can't fly. They'll tie a rope around her neck and roll her up and down the hills. What happens the first time her belly falls over her belt at work? Good thing she's already fat. No one notices fat girls having babies.

"Later they blamed the Miners and the revolt and the security needs. But it was the government who first herded people inside the DV communities, then threw tests down their throats. You get out if you score this highly on this test. Math, science, all psych-balanced, all rigged to keep a steady supply of cannon fodder against the Camels. Same old story about war, the rich decide, the poor die. Bat-shit crazy Grandma and her cronies wrapped all the crap in a bow and said it was Christmas. When there was one. You had to prove you belonged in the Family. Worthy, deserving." Mooshie sneered. "All about blaming someone for the war going to hell when the people in the DVs, they just wanted to fight. They did fight. It was the Regs who screwed up. Who ran. Americans running. On the battlefield and in the war rooms."

Mooshie paused for a breath. "That girl reminds me of my first wife Jen. Same insolent suck my butt look. I miss Jen. I think I loved her most of all. Plus she always told me if I looked fat even though I was a size four."

Mooshie bought three size eights, double checking on the return policy with the smug Beth, and led them to a bench by the water, where Zelda ate the last of the Irene's Iced Cakes, licking the chocolate crumbs off her fingertips and then turning on the gold wrapping.

Mooshie wiped Zelda's hands and whispered, "What's up, sweet cakes? You haven't stared at my tits all morning."

Zelda shrugged, her lower lip quivering.

Mooshie nodded severely. "Are you sure?"

"About what?"

Lopez hugged her. "It's all over your face, brown eyes. Surprised Pup's friend didn't suggest you buy baby clothes. When'd you find out?"

"The happy cup sang this morning. Don't tell Puppy."

"I won't."

"I'm serious. He and Pablo can't know. No one can. I'm finally doing well at a job…" Zelda recited her list of things that-had-been-going-well-for-once-in-her-life-and-which-were-now-in-a-big-stinky-dumpster.

"Then get rid of it."

Zelda gasped. "What?"

"Have an abortion." Mooshie shrugged. "Quick, easy. I had two."

Zelda gasped again. "Mooshie, that's illegal."

"Oh shit, what else did the bitch do while I was dead?"

"No more abortions. That's a capital offense."

Mooshie tossed the rest of her ham and cheese hero into the garbage before Zelda could stop her. "As if Grandma needs a reason for insanity, but why?"

"We lost thirteen million in the war, Moosh. We're surrounded by Allahs, who breed like animals. We need the babies, the children. That makes sense to me."

Lopez gave her a pitying look. "So you execute someone for getting rid of an unwanted baby."

"Look, I don't want to debate the politics, okay?"

"Okay, okay." Mooshie said soothingly. "Know whose kid it is?"

Zelda sighed.

"Terrific. Can you narrow it down?"

"I had an upsetting month."

"And needed to feel you had something going for you."

Zelda nodded glumly. Six guys. No. Seven. Six on the bed, one of the floor.

"Been there. Most of my life," Lopez said softly. "Did you consider condoms?"

Zelda laughed. "What're those?"

"Those latex baggies that slip over the guy's pecker?"

"They've been outlawed since the Next Generations Act of 2078. Condoms, any birth control devices or pills. That's also a capital offense for women, men, doctors, anyone."

Mooshie shook her head disgustedly. "What happens next?"

"The results have gone into the Central Information Department. The cycle cup is hooked up. And no, I don't know how. They give you a month to come forward. If you're married, great. Or even if you're engaged. Accidents happen so they overlook the slight illegality. If you're single, I'm not so sure. I've never known anyone who got pregnant outside marriage or impending marriage or if they did, admitted it."

Zelda laid her head on Mooshie's shoulder and cried for a few minutes.

"Do you want the kid, chubby cheeks?"

She looked up, puzzled. "Not at all, but that doesn't matter. I can't keep it, Moosh."

• • • •

JALAK CAREFULLY LAID down another three pairs of socks, stopping Azhar from zipping up the suitcase.

"I only have two feet," he protested gently.

"You'll get wet. You don't look where you're going." She averted his eyes. "Did you count your shirts?"

"Twelve should be enough."

"For each day?"

Mustafa tugged her down to the bed. "Don't try to guess how long I'll be away."

"It would help so I know if something's wrong." Her eyes watered.

"Nothing will be wrong. It's a simple fishing trip."

Jalak's lips pressed together. "We have been married eighteen years. Now you decide to lie?"

Azhar grabbed the suitcase. "And after eighteen years, could you finally stop doubting me? Or do you think I will be swimming around with young girls?"

"I don't worry about the girls, Azhar," she said fearfully.

He paused reluctantly at the front door, hoping a text or email or call would arrive on the wings of an angel and rescue him. He checked his cell with the screen saver photo of his family. Nothing. Abdul hugged him tightly, too tightly. He was also scared.

"When will you be back, Poppa?"

"Soon. It's just a fishing trip."

"Do not ask questions of your father." Jalak smacked his shoulder. "He will be back when he is back."

Mustafa kissed Abdul and gave Jalak a strong smile. "Practice cooking when I'm gone." She didn't laugh.

Azhar tossed his suitcase into the back of the car. Omar passed in his long black robe, eyes lowered, sullen, withdrawn.

"See you soon." Azhar extended his hand. The boy clutched the Qaran to his chest and hopped onto his bicycle, pedaling away furiously as if his father were a Catholic priest. At least he wasn't scared. Just angry.

What have you given me, Allah? Mustafa wondered as he drove to the main Barcelona train station, parking in the long-term lot. He'd been instructed by the Imam to behave at all times as if he were simply a traveler with no special privileges. While a line of Crusaders buying rail tickets stretched across the shabby station, Azhar only had to wait a few minutes on the Believers queue.

He boarded the express train, flinging his bag into the overhead bin with a spasm of resentment and quickly falling asleep to Ali Khan's enchanting ballads on his phone. He dreamed of opening the suitcase where Jalak popped out, naked except for his socks, holding a plate of dried out lamb.

Azhar woke, quickly looking around in case someone on the train had the power to listen to his dreams. Only Allah, he reminded himself. You should be honored for whatever you are about to do. It is important. The Mufti's son. The Son. Then why did the Imam seem uneasy? He sighed deeply and cautioned himself to save some oxygen.

He dozed again, exhausted by the internal anxiety. Once they crossed the border at Andorra, the train sat for about an hour. Azhar ate the kabsa laham, watching through the window as the engineers were joined by two other workers sadly shaking their heads.

Breakdowns were common on the rails. If there ever were an explanation, it was that the Crusaders had sabotaged the railway system as their godless souls were driven away from holy lands. That was nearly thirty years ago. Azhar risked some analysis to get his mind off the lamb. Surely the problems should've been fixed by now. The buses in the city also crept along like old women, smoking disrepair. Only the autobahns seemed clear, cars whizzing past the clogged Crusader car lanes.

Or perhaps they still sabotaged. He'd seen the crucifixions, Infidels signs draped around the Crusader necks, planted every so often along the roads, usually to celebrate a holy day. How many of them were mechanics? Perhaps one of them pulled out a plug here and there. But if the Crusaders sabotaged trains and buses, why not the autos? He suddenly saw in the shadows of approaching dusk, Clary kneeling with a blowtorch, cutting wires, laughing. He shuddered.

Little was ever fully told because only Allah ultimately understood. Mustafa wished he understood something of what Allah understood, as heretical as that was. How else can we obey? The Mufti's son, he understood what Allah understood. He also understood what man didn't understand, like straddling the two worlds.

Stop thinking and pray there is food at the other end of the trip.

The train groaned forward, as if it could hear his thoughts. Allah on wheels, he smiled. The workers waved happily to all the peering passengers by the windows and the express gathered steam, heading non-stop to Le Cirque, about forty miles west of the Bay of Biscay. Azhar was the only person to get off, earning curious stares as he, too, waved at the train, continuing north to the Caliphate of Paris.

He carried the suitcase into the tiny station.

"As-salam alaykum," said the bored clerk behind the window.

Azhar nodded a reply. "I am a simple traveler and would appreciate, Allah willing, knowledge on getting to Dambier."

The clerk wordlessly slid a map through the grill, pointing.

"Thank you. How does one get there?"

"There are no trains."

"Which is why I'm here enjoying your hospitality."

The men exchanged respectful nods. The clerk slid a bus schedule on top of the map.

The ancient bus waddled arthritically, stopping only once when a cage rattled open and chickens flew out of the back window. After the chickens were quickly rounded up by the passengers and driver, the relieved owner running up and down the aisle twice to express his deepest thanks, the vehicle, generously named, coughed into Dambier a mere thirty minutes late; in the Caliphate, that was considered early.

Azhar hurried down several cobblestoned hills and over a small bridge that was annoyed by his weight. He made a wrong turn in the dark and panicked slightly. He'd been told nine-thirty, the latest. By ten he finally found the small harbor, more a wooden dock with several sleeping ships rocking.

A single light on board guided him to a sixty-foot boat. A man nearly as wide as the dock stood with hands clasped, his expression assuring one and all that he could stand here in silent patience until Mohammad came down for a visit.

Azhar nodded. The man waited.

What am I to say? he thought frantically. He was only given directions.

He bowed. "Azhar Mustafa."

The man raised an eyebrow. Mustafa was so poor at the bullying art of his people.

"I am the Captain of this vessel. Are you the crew?"

The man studied Mustafa carefully and stepped aside.

"Is that a yes or a no?"

The man turned his back and resumed his statue-like waiting. Maybe Mohammad was visiting. Azhar carefully descended the metal steps below deck. A twin of the man stood before a door.

234 | GARY MORGENSTEIN

Abdullah walked out, re-arranging his gold robe. "Captain. Welcome aboard."

• • • •

THE HUGE VIDSCREEN filled with the charred upper deck of Amazon Stadium, gloomy morning rain clouds approaching carelessly. Sweeping down over the battered and blackened scoreboard, the camera paused in deep center field, waiting patiently.

Suddenly they panned over the new outfield grass as if a throw were heading toward home, flying over second base and past the mound until the camera rested on the two mahogany coffins surrounded by the mute, expressionless starting lineup of the Falcons. They tapped their bats once. Twice.

The coffins squeaked open very slowly. Ty and Mickey sat up. They put on their baseball caps and turned toward the cameras. Baroque piano music kicked in.

"I'm Ty Cobb."

"And I'm Mickey Mantle."

Together, "We're the stars of the Bronx Hawks."

"Our job is to score runs," said Ty.

"Hit homers," added Mick.

Collectively, "And win games."

Ty said, "But sometimes, life strikes you out."

Sad music.

The stone-faced Falcons parted to allow Ty and Mick to climb out, casually slinging their bats over their shoulders as if they always dressed in a coffin.

Watching in his living room, Kenuda chuckled at the vid while Puppy nervously sipped expensive Tennessee Tom bourbon.

"When that happens," Mick said, "you need a cleanup hitter."

"Someone who knows what it's like to score the winning run."

Close-up on the coffins. Ty and Mick's bats tap the Basil Hayden's Funeral Home logo.

"You need a slugger like Adona Hayden..."

Quick cut of the calm and reassuring Ms. Hayden leaning near the Hawks dugout, waiting for someone to die so she could leap into action.

"Ms. Hayden and her team will do all the hitting for you," Ty and Mick said.

In the background, Frecklie and two other DVs in black suits ran in a jagged line around the bases.

"Top notch coffins." Mick touched the wood.

"And the velvet pillows are first class," Ty added.

"Taking the eternal journey in style."

"From the service to the flowers."

One of the Falcons handed Ty a bouquet of roses.

Kenuda roared and slapped his chair, nearly knocking Annette off the arm.

"Hayden does the dying for you," Ty said.

Frecklie and the boys slid across home and lay there, unmoving.

"We know how important that is." Mick winked.

He and Ty climbed back into the coffins.

More swelling baroque music and then the voiceover, "Basil Hayden's Funeral Homes. Give us the ball. We'll take care of Death."

The lights went on in the huge sunken room with high ceilings reaching just shy of Jupiter. Mooshie looked sick and angry; she gulped down her drink.

"Was I right about Ian Schrage?" Kenuda bounded onto the thick, plush carpet. "Is he a genius or isn't he?"

"Amazing, Elias." Annette repositioned her spread of appetizers on the gleaming black coffee table. "The salmon is real and fresh. It's Saul's."

"There's time for fish and there's time for business. And the business of the people comes first. Dara, what did you think?"

Mooshie smiled bravely. "I'm still putting it together, Cousin."

Elias sat between them on the couch, which was more comfortable than any bed Puppy had ever slept on. Kenuda took their hands; Annette watched enviously.

"No Cousins here. Except for Puppy, who is an employee. It's Elias."

Annette's strands stuck out a little.

"Elias." Mooshe gazed deeply into his eyes. "I think it's inspired."

"And she's the creative one here," Kenuda said, gazing back.

"I design shoes…" Annette tried.

"Yes, shoes." Kenuda rolled his eyes. "I like the gloomy appeal of death visiting death, with Hayden as a tour guide."

"Makes you unafraid," Mooshie chimed in.

"Courage. We need courage in these times. Boldness. I approve. It'll go out tomorrow morning on *Wake Up My Darlings*."

"Can we start the dinner party now, honey?" Annette asked.

"Damn straight. Keep the food warm. Time for the tour." He squeezed Mooshie's hand so together they gestured around the living room. "The living room."

"Magnificent," she oohed and aahed syllable by syllable.

He stood by the fireplace, ready for a portrait. "This is real wood."

"Smells it."

"That was my idea," Annette said. "The wood."

Puppy helped himself to more bourbon.

"The llama rug, leather furniture. All hand-crafted." He leaned over to Mooshie, making this more a private discussion. "Not what you get in the stores."

Mooshie murmured delightedly.

"Both of you. Into the study."

"Elias," Annette protested. "Can't we wait until after dinner? We already had the funeral."

"Nonsense," he thundered and marched down the hallway decorated with sports memorabilia, ducking beneath balls into a large wood-paneled study with an oaky smell. "Are either of you squeamish?"

"I sat in one of the coffins," Puppy said.

"I've done that, too," Mooshie added.

Puppy poked her in the butt.

"Look down." Kenuda pointed at the wide brown and gold rug. "What is it?"

"Hand-crafted?" Mooshie asked breathlessly.

Puppy poked her again.

"Elias, please don't make them guess," Annette said wearily from the doorway.

He waited for two seconds. "The prayer rug of Imam Khali, the Butcher of Stockholm. This is where his filthy camel body touched. Look." They all bent. "A trace of blood. Supposedly where a brave American finished him off while he was praying to his Godless God…"

"The battle of Stockholm, 2064?" Mooshie asked.

"Yes." Kenuda was surprised. "A student of history as well as talented and beautiful?"

"It's not fair, I know."

"Then you're going to appreciate this."

"I'm not watching, Elias." Annette squirmed.

Kenuda pressed a button over the fireplace. A door slid open to the left, lit by soft purple light. Two crossed scimitars dominated the huge closet. A tattered crescent moon and star flag hung off a hook. Elias brought out a black crystal jug on a silver plate.

"Sure you're not squeamish?" Kenuda pulled out a shrunken head. Annette groaned and hurried down the hall. Puppy's stomach churned, but his fiancé calmly examined the head.

"Who was it?"

Kenuda touched her shoulder a little too warmly. "They say Elijah bin-Qatar. Ever hear of him?"

"Yeah. He kicked our ass in Sicily."

Elias frowned. "I wouldn't say kicked our ass."

"He drove us the hell out of southern Europe. We lost 125,000 soldiers on the boot. What would you call that?" She returned the head, a little more shrunken in Elias's eyes. "I thought he escaped."

"Very dead." Kenuda shook the head.

"What he wanted us to think. We were down to assassination squads after that because our soldiers were overrun everywhere. They stood and fought and got slaughtered and we did nothing," Mooshie said harshly, catching herself before the men's curious stares. She switched on a smile. "I read he faked death to avoid being on the list. Typical Allah cowardice."

"Typical." Elias nodded. "There's more. I have..."

"Elias!" Annette yelled.

"After dinner. How about seeing the view?"

"Sounds lovely. Puppy, why don't you help your lovely ex?" Mooshie slid her arm through Kenuda's and strolled off toward the balcony.

Annette was swigging red wine out of the bottle when Puppy wandered back into the kitchen.

"Can I help?"

"Boy, she's got you well trained already. You never helped me."

"You never cooked." He scooped up an oversized chunk of salsa with a chip while Annette checked the chicken roasting in the oven.

"Dara's very nice, Puppy."

"She says with an air of slight surprise that Puppy could find someone so nice."

"Kinda." Annette grinned. "And pretty for a woman of her age."

"Astonishingly."

"How old is she again?"

"I already said I don't know." He couldn't figure it out so quickly. Mooshie was 46 when she died. Or was it 45...? "It's not important, Annette."

"Just that you're in love?"

"Yes."

Annette basted the chicken. "And she loves you."

"Is that a question or statement."

"She seems a little, you know, standoffish."

"She's shy. Entertainers usually are off stage."

That bought a brief delay in the interrogation. "You met in a bar."

"Where she sings."

"Was Dara married before?"

"I think so."

"You don't know that, either?"

"What's it matter?"

"Because there are special papers for divorced couples. You have to make sure everything is legal and correct, Puppy."

"They are legal, Annette. Did you invite us over to make sure our engagement is on the level?"

"No. I wanted to be nice." She slammed the oven door. "I really do want you to be happy, Puppy. I realize how hard that is to believe. Because you hate my guts and think I suck and you're probably amazed I could get a Third Cousin. So we're even."

He kissed her on the cheek. "I want you to be happy, too, Annette. And I'm not surprised at all you could get someone like Kenuda."

"Really?"

"Maybe a little. And I don't hate your guts."

"Really?"

"Usually."

"Screw you, Puppy," she said with a pleased smile. "Remember to cut your food properly. I don't want to be embarrassed." Annette took another long sip and yelled, "Dinner's ready."

• • • •

MOOSHIE CRAWLED BACK into bed carrying a bottle of white Arkansas Chablis. She poured herself a drink and rubbed cream into her hands. This was the first time he shared a bed with the woman he used to fantasize about oh, only three, four times a day as a kid. And well into his marriage. He blushed just remembering and edged away.

Mooshie laid two pillows between them.

"I'm sure we could find barbed wire cheap." He reached for the wine. She slapped away his hand.

"You got a game tomorrow. You got enough to do working off that gut."

Puppy self-consciously edged further away. "What'd you think of tonight?"

"Is this the part where couples lay in bed and gossip about the evening?"

"Yeah. It's called communicating."

She made a face. "I never was good at that."

Somehow he wasn't surprised. "Annette's not terrible, right?"

Mooshie shrugged and dabbed cream on her face.

"I mean, not to spend much time with because then she's overbearing. But she deserves to be happy…" Mooshie cut him off with a loud and sarcastic yawn. "Sorry. What were you and Kenuda talking about?"

"He showed me his spectacular view. I didn't have the heart to tell him I lived in that neighborhood with a place twice the size where you could almost touch Manhattan, just before."

"He seems to like you."

"Oh yeah." Mooshie mischievously tossed her hair, absently undoing the top button on her blue pajamas.

Puppy stared at her breasts and nearly slipped off the bed; Mooshie grabbed his collar.

"You're gonna sleep on the floor if you don't watch those eyes."

"Actually that's illegal now that we're engaged. We must sleep in the same bed."

"What about sex?"

He paled. "What about it?"

"Ain't happening."

"Fine," he said, relieved.

"You gonna report me since that's also illegal?"

"I'll just smile in the morning and everyone will assume."

"Happy ain't the emotion I leave my lovers with."

He didn't want to imagine. Below, the pugs marched past for their midnight walk. Studies had shown the sound of their barking and padding feet quieted people even during sleep. And those still awake, troubled, tired after a long job shift, plain bored, unwilling to brave the chilly late night air for a furry hug, would often stand by the window, smiling, soothed.

"I never had a dog. You?" Mooshie let the curtains fall, settling into the single rickety chair.

"This your way of changing the subject, dear? So much to learn about each other."

Her sudden glare iced his grin. "Why'd you do that commercial, Puppy?"

He sighed. Somehow he knew this was coming. "It makes money. Fisher and Boccaccelli whine constantly about expenses. I had to grovel to paint the seats behind the dugouts because everything goes on their bottom line. The Commissioner authorizes, but the teams pay. I mean, shit, Moosh. I got Kenuda's attention."

"By using a funeral home?" she snarled. "Have you no respect? I can't believe the White Grampas did it."

"Maybe they understand the importance of promotion."

"They weren't there on 10/12. You don't mock that."

"I'm not mocking anything. Where'd you see 10/12 mentioned in the advert?"

"You showed the whole goddamn stadium. What they did."

"Because it's the law, Moosh." He lowered his voice. "Baseball isn't exactly a hot ticket item for advertisers, bones and bullets and all. Besides, I'm working for Hayden after the season."

"Embalming?" she sneered.

"My baseball historian job goes away, so welcome to the world of the living dead."

"You sold out."

"Like hell. I'm going to be forty years old and I don't have a goddamn career. You know how that reads, Moosh."

"You're dabbling." The fiery Lopez temper exploded; wine dripped down the wall. "Mick says it's a wake during the games."

"It's hard to generate exuberance when almost all the fans are DVs."

"Sitting there on their hands, mouths sealed. I know how we are. Never draw attention. Never act improperly because Grandma's clit, we're always judged."

He smirked. "We?"

"Always we." Her voice was ugly. "Do you really think of yourself as a Reg? Ever? Or always the DV, hoping no one realizes it, no one sends you back. Hey, how'd this guy get through? Guess what, asshole. The people who cared about this country were always DVs. Miners, baseball, almost all of them were DVs, asshole."

"Could you please stop calling me an asshole? I feel like I'm back with Annette."

Mooshie turned off the light on her night table, closing her eyes. He kept staring until she opened them again.

"Yes, darling Puppy?"

"Will you help?"

"It won't stop you from asking anyway."

"You can say anything to those you love. Grandma's Sixth Insight." Mooshie groaned. "My arm's holding up." He twisted his shoulder in a little show and tell. "But my mechanics are off. I need help. Mick and Ty aren't pitchers…"

She turned on her side, staring leadenly. "No."

"Why not?" Puppy asked angrily.

Her face softened beneath the cream. She looked like a sad ghost. "I don't know. I just know you have to do it alone. Otherwise it's too easy. Idol comes back from the dead and shows adoring, simple-minded former stud muffin how to properly throw a curve."

"I wouldn't tell anyone."

Mooshie draped her legs over his knees and cupped his chin. "Hot buns, just pitch. Throw. You have talent."

"How do you know if you've never seen me play?"

"I'm here. Ty's here. Mick's here. Why else?" She smacked his eyebrow. "Hate the batter. Hate the other team. Hate like you hate, all stored inside."

"I don't hate like you do, Mooshie."

"Yes, you do. Everyone does. You just gotta find it." Mooshie kissed him on the forehead. "Now get some rest. And stay on your side of the bed."

26

Zelda wanted to summon a thunderstorm of barf hail on all these happy couples. Two thin men who looked like they shared the same toothbrush bowed their heads together. A stout woman and a stout man, definitely a king-sized bed pair, clenched fingers, staring straight ahead as if already imagining high school graduation for the kid. And two especially pretty women, slick black hair around their shoulders, tongued away the wait.

And Zelda. She surreptitiously popped a buttered roll into her mouth, piece by piece. Butter always helps, she decided. Chocolate's such a cliché. A woman with a flat face smiled across the exquisitely furnished room, thick leather chairs swallowing up the biggest asses. No comfort was too much for Grandma's Mommies. Zelda didn't make that up. There was a poster of Grandma flanked by several deliriously happy pregnant women, Grandma saying, Nothing is too much for my Mommies.

She craned her neck trying to read all the posters, searching for one which said, Single Mommies Rock, Too.

The flat-faced woman hovered. "Hi. I see you're alone."

"No."

"You're not?" The woman double-checked the empty chairs on either side in case she made a mistake.

"He's coming."

"Oh. Well until he does…"

"He's sitting there." Zelda laid her palm on the chair before the woman could sit. Clearly deprived of oxygen at birth, the woman tried sitting on the other side. Zelda laid her hand down there. "He's not real decisive."

"You don't want to be disturbed. I understand."

"Good." Zelda pushed her eyebrows into her hair line, finally sending the visitor away. I should've brought the chocolate.

"Ms. Jones?" A voice from above guided her toward a sliding door with etchings of dancing children. She followed the HG children singing on both sides of the hall into a lovely office with more cushy furniture. Zelda thought about stealing one of the oak and leather chairs and fleeing, but the door quickly slid open to the sounds of more squealing brats.

"Hello, Zelda." Paula Stobbs, a sturdy woman with kind eyes and a faint moustache, took the chair next to her. "How are you?"

"Great."

"Excellent. Very happy you came right down. Exciting, huh?"

"Yes." More children laughed from somewhere. Zelda wished she had one of Puppy's baseball bats. "They're not real, are they?"

"Sounds it, don't they? Well, if you can just hop up on the table. This'll only take a second." She slipped on clear examining gloves.

"For what?"

"To examine you."

"Why?"

Paula's bright smile faded a little. "We have to make sure the test was correct. It is ninety-nine percent accurate, but as Grandma says, mistakes are a part of life."

Zelda cautioned herself against too much hope. Reprieves didn't happen to her. Only really happy and hopeful people are rewarded with miracles. She was right; Paula nearly stuck her chubby hand so far up Zelda could lick her fingertips, pulling out with a merry laugh.

"Confirmed."

"Yay."

Paula tossed the gloves and patted Zelda on the knee. "Is your partner joining us?"

Zelda cleared her throat. "I don't have one."

"Oh." Paula seemed genuinely disappointed. "So you're not married?"

"No."

"Engaged?"

Zelda shook her head.

"Oh. Well. Single." It was like someone invisible twisted off Paula's head and replaced it with a different colder person. "Planning on bonding with the child's father?"

"Um, no."

Stobbs darkened. "Know who he is?"

"I could guess, but that wouldn't be right."

"No. It would be illegal." Paula sadly sat behind her desk. "Do you understand your responsibilities, Ms. Jones?"

From Zelda to Ms. Jones. Soon it'll be Naughty Single Slut. "Not totally."

"Your baby now belongs to someone else." Paula forced a smile to reduce the sting. "It's still possible you can keep the child if, of course, you find someone suitable to marry. That happens, this is life, and a father will initially balk or the mother can't consider marrying them until they finally come to their senses. That's also strictly monitored. We don't tolerate just any parents, even the biological ones. Either they truly want the baby or someone who does will adopt the child. That's your situation at the moment. If a partner comes forth and we can sort out if that's the right one, we'd confirm that with a DNA test."

Zelda's mind wandered; this was too surreal, there had to be a safer place where brats didn't grow inside you.

Paula sensed her drifting. "Honestly, Ms. Jones, do you envision someone coming forward who would make a good partner? Or finding someone else who you would genuinely love and who would genuinely make a good parent?"

A real relationship. That doesn't happen to people like her, either. She shook her head.

"That answer is not really official, by the way." Paula scribbled something in Zelda's chart, forcing out another smile. "Things change."

"I don't like children," Zelda suddenly said.

"What?" Paula nearly leaped out of her seat.

"I was a teacher. I liked teaching them, but I think they're really annoying. I would've hated me as a kid. Course I'll do whatever for the law. I'm here, right? Tested two days ago, made my appointment. But I never wanted to be a mother."

Paula wrote for a few minutes, ignoring Zelda's sobs. "You have to begin Parent Training within two weeks. Normally it's a month, but in your case..." She didn't need to say more. "Your employer will be notified in the next two weeks, which gives you the option of telling them first. I recommend that. It's more personal and defuses the shock. I know this sucks, Zelda. The next eight months will be painful. But you've added a soldier in the fight against the Allahs. That counts for something."

Zelda hated everyone on Earth.

• • • •

FRECKLIE HAD FALLEN asleep again by home plate, curled up in two frayed towels tied together. The smell of the freshly trimmed grass tickled his nostrils; the sun danced overhead. He rose onto his hands and knees; his crazy mother would be sticking squared notes all over Dale's house any second to check up on him.

To regain as much clarity as he could on a couple hours sleep, Frecklie walked to the mound. Now pitching, Ruben Rivera, he bowed. The smell of new paint blotted out the smell of grass. From foul pole to foul pole, the shining blue seats said good morning.

About eight of his staff were asleep in the aisles, careful not to smear their jobs. Another few slept on the dugout floor. Frecklie clapped his hands, the echo jolting them up; they rubbed their eyes childishly. He trotted past second, slowing down. Even after skull-picking, he was still squeamish. He carefully monitored the level of the grass, which in the short outfield was about two inches, rising up to his ankles as he neared the track warning, no, the warning track, get the names right, he scolded himself, making a note in his pad; he already had twenty or so confusing shorthands like bullpen to around the horn; he never heard any music.

Frecklie frowned at the uncut grass. How much clearer could he have been? Bo-Dan, burly with long dreads, explained the problem, holding out a sad looking lawnmower. Bo-Dan pressed the button and the engine coughed and died. He turned up his palms. Frecklie turned up his.

Fix?

Bo-Dan sadly shook his head. This was his father's lawn mower that'd broken. He'd have to work off the expense; one less crew grounder, no, ground crew, Frecklie made another note as Bo-Dan waited. Frecklie gestured with both forefingers and Bo-Dan hurried off to find or borrow another machine.

Hopefully no one would hit long drives today. Frecklie smiled, proud of himself. He was learning.

T'Dina met him by home plate. She looked frustrated. He raised his shoulders questioningly. The lanky girl took his hand and led him back inside the stadium to the murmur of breaths beyond the shuttered Gate Six. For a second, Frecklie thought a dragon had decided to attend today's game.

T'Dina spread her arms so wide her shoulder blades nearly touched.

Frecklie unlocked the gate. As the metal rolled up, thousands of silent eyes stared back. Fans snaked back past River Avenue, under the El and up the 161st Street hill.

T'Dina and the rest of the staff gathered in a semi-circle. How many were out there, Frecklie asked.

T'Dina cleared her throat and held up five fingers, then three fingers, made a zero and a one. Her forefinger slashed the air. I counted, she said proudly.

They're here to see the museum, Frecklie realized. Where were Sh'anda and Aito? He hurried past the purple roped squares and circles and took the broken escalator two steps at a time. Tucked in a corner were the sleeping Aito and Sh'anda, arms around each other. Frecklie kicked the wall over their heads and they shot up, wiping dust out of their long hair.

They switched on Dale's system; somber music and grim-faced HGs rose around the roped areas, beginning their lectures about 10/12. Frecklie ran from exhibit to exhibit, making sure everything was working; Dale would kill him if she knew he doubted her brilliance even for a moment.

Frecklie ordered Gates Five and Four opened. Bo-Dan and three burly friends struggled with the rusted locks, considering the piles of rubble on the ground. If no one missed skulls, they wouldn't miss rocks. Frecklie encouraged them to have fun and they happily bashed the gates open.

T'Dina dashed out and began guiding fans to the different gates. The DVs politely reformed lines; Bo-Dan, Tyrius and Angel handled ticket-taking.

Bo-Dan tapped his watch and raised an eyebrow. Six-thirty. Too early.

We're not keeping them standing outside, Frecklie snapped.

The fans started filing in. The three concession owners stiffened as if Allahs were right around the corner.

"We'll need more food," Frecklie told Mrs. Bilinski.

"I cooked up my whole fridge." She gestured helplessly at the suddenly meager steaming trays of stuffed cabbage.

"Me, too," said Sam the Hot Dog Man.

"They're not sitting here hungry," Frecklie said as the fans quietly passed, milling about since there was no one to direct them to the right sections. His head nearly exploded until a couple of the sleepy workers stumbled down the steps.

Calm down. You're acting like your mother.

The grim little girl behind the taco stand raised her hand politely. "I have lots of cousins."

Frecklie finally got the HG system all set up. He hit the button.

"Mooshie Lopez, Derek Singh and Easy Sun Yen were three of baseball's greatest players," said the pert HG, walking around the wide-eyed fans clustered beneath the Three Amigos mural. "Right where you're standing, treasonous Miners shot at this beautiful mural, which Grandma had personally commissioned from the famous artist Latsha Di. Black Tops gunned them down all over the hall."

The HG somberly gestured toward the bold purple Grandma lettering: "Remember those who died on October 12, 2065 because the Miners wanted war, not peace, and baseball let that be."

On the walls, meticulously spaced every ten feet were photographs of victims of 10/12, smiling back sadly. D'Neese Sh'Piro, eleven, died behind home plate. Alex Manci, forty-three, died outside Gate Five.

Surrounding each of the gaping holes were thick purple ropes, twisted like pretzels. Photographs of children at the game dangled over the craters: "Miners set explosives… Miners launched mortars into the left field grandstand…Black Tops protected civilians, but Miners fired into the crowds…"

Siblings murmured wonderingly as the HG pointed out bullet shells along the path to the first of twelve roped areas, where it told them about the more than four hundred children taken hostage by the Miners and used as human shields, plaques at each stop reiterating the message, while the Taco Girl's cousins unloaded four trucks brimming with Pan Asian-Latino delicacies, joined by another relative, a fat woman with a blue-tressed wig who rolled in a handcart of boiling pastries.

Between the history and the new food, the pavilion was clogged with fans eating quietly, peering at the HG bodies of the victims silently floating overhead, falling to the ground in mute spasms of death and rising up again to form a mass of sad faces outlined against the huge copper plaque above the entrance to the former Amazon Clubhouse, where the names of all the murdered were listed.

HGs trailed with polite somberness throughout the crowd, answering questions:

How many people died on 10/12? —Seven thousand, six hundred and forty-two dead and ten thousand, two hundred and two injured.

How many were children? —Three thousand and three children died and six thousand and forty-two were injured.

Is that the worst terrorist attack in American history? —No, but it is the worst attack ever committed by Americans on Americans.

What happened to the criminals? —All eight hundred and fifteen of the captured Miners were executed by lethal injection.

What about the Allahs attacks? —The Allahs killed two million, five hundred and ten thousand siblings in the Los Angeles nuclear terrorist attack; one million, eight hundred thousand and eleven siblings in the Manhattan poison gas terrorist attack, and four hundred and thirty-nine thousand in the Washington, DC nuclear attack.

The crew finally guided the crowd into the ballpark, which caused another human traffic jam because everyone stopped in wonderment at the shiny seats and the neatly trimmed grass as if, by sheer positive blinders, they could block out the rest of the shabby stadium.

Where the fans eventually sat, hands folded, faces smeared with various delicacies.

Dale touched Frecklie's back and he nearly rolled down the steps. The pretty fifteen-year-old boy in the sparkling red dress with the biggest blue eyes in the world kissed him gently. You okay?

He had five thousand, three hundred and one, nope, Dale made five thousand, three hundred and two siblings inside a stadium with nothing to do.

Terrific.

Now what? Dale asked. This was her first baseball game.

Wait, he gestured a batter.

She yawned; Dale was easily bored.

BP wasn't for another hour. He ran into the Hawks clubhouse, empty except for Ty grumbling over the lineup card in the manager's office.

Cobb scowled. "Are you on my team?"

Frecklie shook his head.

"Can you read?"

He hesitated warily.

"'Cause if you can, the sign on the clubhouse door says players only. Now get your scrawny chink ass out of here."

Frecklie raised his chin. "I need your help, Mr. Cobb. Your fans are here waiting to meet you."

Ty quickly shaved.

At home plate, Cobb tipped his cap back off his forehead, squinting at the crowd as if he'd found them in his bathtub. "Are these the mute retards?"

The boy wasn't sure what retards meant, only that it was similar to chink and spic and nigra and queer and all those other words Ty was fond of.

"Yes, sir. They'd like a real Hall of Famer to tell them about baseball."

Ty smiled approvingly and cupped his hands on either side of his mouth. "Listen up, everyone." Frecklie handed him a microphone. Cobb grunted. "Thank you for coming out so early. We'll start making the signs bigger about when the game officially starts for any of you who can read English."

Frecklie moved a couple steps behind and gestured, He means well.

"Now how many of you know anything about baseball?"

No hands rose. As Cobb growled, Frecklie gestured, Please someone.

Dale stood up and Frecklie fell in love with her even more. "How do you hit the ball, sir?"

"Well that's a goddamn smart question, little girl. Hitting a baseball's the hardest thing in all sports."

Frecklie tossed him a bat.

"You got a little white sphere coming at you like ninety plus miles per hour..."

Frecklie gestured, Sometimes one hundred plus. The crowd oohed slightly. Ty grinned.

"Damn straight. It's curving, dropping, rising, falling and you got less than a second to react. That's right, less than a second. You got to decide to swing and then where you want to place the ball. Any of you want to take a shot?"

When Dale leaped over the fence, Frecklie decided he'd propose the moment he graduated high school next year. She curtsied.

Ty looked past her pleadingly. "Any boys?"

Some of the DVs chuckled knowingly.

"Just me," Dale said sweetly.

"Figures. What's your name, honey?"

"Dale."

"Like Dale Evans, the singing cowgirl."

"Yes," she curtsied again.

"You're even prettier." Ty winked. "Ever swung a bat?"

"No, sir." Dale smiled.

From behind, Ty wrapped his arms around Dale and adjusted her grip.

"That's good for a lady."

"I try to do what a girl can do."

"Ain't much."

"You'd be surprised, sir. Girls will be girls and boys will be boys and sometimes they get all mixed together." Dale wiggled her butt into Ty's groin and the crowd burst into applause.

They never stopped applauding. Sometimes they got it a little wrong, like when a foul ball bounced into the stands and back onto the field. But there was noise. Not just clapping. Dale, unleashed, started barking after Puppy struck out the first two batters and the crowd shyly, then exuberantly, picked up on the sound. No matter what Puppy did after that, good or bad, they barked. He surrendered a long home run in the second and they barked. He caught a swift one-hopper back to the mound and they barked. He struck out so pathetically he nearly toppled over and they barked.

And when Ty took Puppy out after five innings with a 5-2 lead and eight Ks, Frecklie loved how that abbreviation rolled off the tongue, Dale, never to be outdone, began howling. Soon the lower field boxes were a forest of wolfish dogs.

After the game, Frecklie flapped his legs over the gaping hole and balanced the sketch pad on his lap, sitting high up in the far upper deck under the white wooden trim in left field, the "brocade." He loved the word brocade. K brocades. Brocade Ks. Around the horn with brocades and Ks.

He turned the page of Puppy's *Great Baseball Stadiums* book to Fenway Park. That was a ballpark, he marveled, sketching more ideas on his pad. That wall. The Green Monster. His stadium would have a monster. Somehow, a dragon. He loved dragons. Maybe fire could come out of the scoreboard. Yes, he enthusiastically scribbled quicker, nearly losing his balance for a moment.

Frecklie wished his mother could see him near the top of the deserted stadium, afternoon rain coming, no rows below him, just a huge gaping hole where a rocket or missile or something had hit. She'd flip out.

He rocked a little and laughed.

• • • •

MOOSHIE SWUNG BY his table twice during *Be My Baby*. The first time, Kenuda hoisted up his glass; the second, he leaped to his feet and toward the stage, cheering and nearly drowning out the bridge until she quieted him down.

After the first set, she glad-handed through the crowd, cheeks peppered with well-wishing kisses, while Jimmy laid out a tray of food by Kenuda's table. With mocking flair, Jimmy unfurled a white table cloth and laid down two candles. Elias waved him off as if he were a fly and pulled out her chair.

"I've done the best I can under the circumstances," he apologized, glaring at the bottle of South Texas champagne. She boomed out a laugh when the cork popped without any spritzing foam. Kenuda smiled sheepishly.

"To astonishing music," he toasted.

"Thank you, Third Cousin."

"Elias. Please. Elias." He took a small bite of the cheese and nearly gagged. "How did you get this assignment?"

"I came here a long time ago. I knew the previous owner."

"You don't look that old."

But your lines sure are. "It was a good crowd tonight."

Kenuda took in the youngish patrons, heartily and noisily drinking. "Must be the neighborhood."

"I take it you don't get down here often. I'm flattered."

"After we met, I had to make sure you were who I thought you were."

Mooshie tensed. "Who's that?"

"An enchanting talent. What were those songs?"

"Middish 20th Century African American music. Motown."

"Ah, yes," he said enthusiastically.

"Never heard of it?"

"No idea what you're talking about." Kenuda smiled. "I prefer smarter music. Bach, Beethoven, Mozart. When the world had civilization."

"I prefer fun."

"Delighted to hear that." Elias pushed aside the suspicious looking SC cold cuts. "You must do better than this, Dara."

"They're good people," she said evenly.

"I've no doubt. There's a wondrous energy afoot. But you are the performer, not them. You lead, not them."

"Cousin talk?"

"Common sense. Loyalty is a building block, not a door. This owner…"

"Jimmy Monroe. The guy who found you a candleholder and a tablecloth."

"Because I'm a Cousin."

"But you're not supposed to be shown favoritism."

"Exactly. Still happens. Human nature." Kenuda paused. "You need to play at better places for the sake of your career."

"Enter Elias."

He shrugged modestly. "It's my job, Dara. Sports only goes so far. But entertainment has enormous possibilities. They've been, I feel," he lowered his voice, "somewhat neglected. Understandable. All too often, art's a stalking horse for propaganda and a free society needs to trust what they see. Grandma correctly wiped away all the entertainment parasites, the ones the Allahs didn't nuke in LA. But it's time to rethink its role. We need more opportunities for song, dance, movies. Athletics isn't just hulking men and women. They're balletic and the people love it. Why can't they love real ballet?"

"What's to ensure we don't go back to those wild days when artists spoke and manipulated political ideas through their art?"

"The time of social media?"

Mooshie nodded. Maybe he could also think with his brain.

"We're past that. Now the art, the accomplishments, even this wretched champagne and rancid cheese, speak for themselves. Not amplified into a million distortions of influencing, persuading, lobotomizing our free will into part of the smart set. I love your music because I do, not because someone said I'm a fool if I don't. People have learned they can find truth on their own. Football players call their own plays. No one asks for my permission."

"Baseball players call their own pitches."

"Yes, sorry." He sighed. "Puppy's very enthusiastic and hopefully this last fling will be good for him. I'll help him once the season's over. But first you." He stared. "Let me make some calls. No pressure."

"You're a Third Cousin."

"Perhaps a little pressure."

Mooshie smiled. "What do you get?"

"More time with you, Dara."

"Who is engaged."

"As am I."

"To my fiance's ex."

"A nice girl. Loves her shoes." Mooshe nearly poured her drink over his smirk. "I'm here simply as an admirer." He waited anxiously until she clinked his offered glass. "Now promise after you're done tonight, you'll let me take you to this little place on Tremont which serves real Argentinian wine. Please. Or I'll be forced to drink this urine and it will be on your conscience."

• • • •

PABLO BRUSHED PAST without so much as a good morning or apology for waking Zelda at five-thirty.

"Don't you answer your bell? I nearly froze on the damn bench."

"You know I sleep soundly."

They both blushed. He grudgingly dropped a bodega bag on the kitchen table. Zelda yawned and set out the coffee and donuts.

"I'm trying to lose weight." She pleaded with the donuts to dance off the table, but they sat there smiling jelly smiles.

"Good idea." He grunted at her belly flopping out of the robe. She angrily pulled it tighter and spitefully didn't offer him any napkins or plate or utensils. He spilled coffee on the table and looked like he'd lap it up. Zelda grew more worried than annoyed.

"Is something wrong?"

"Because I woke you before the sunrise?"

"That's one clue."

He looked terrible. Handsome face unshaven, big eyes bleary. Worse, the way he grimaced as if in the middle of one hellacious inner argument which he kept losing.

She ate the donut, but slowly, in case someone talked her out of it. "So?"

Pablo stared hard. "I need your honesty."

"Always."

"Do you think I'm a passive observer of the world around me? That I live watching others live and feel my daily comments, inwardly and outwardly, on their lives really suffice for mine?"

Zelda took a long sip of the coffee to sort through Pablo Speak. "I think so."

Pablo rubbed his stubble sadly.

"But you always have. At least after college."

"When I changed?"

"When you thought you had to change. No more DV shit. Like you showered your soul or something."

Pablo quietly repeated her words as if Grandma had added a new Insight.

"What's happened, honey?"

"I can't say."

Zelda leaned her chin on her fist, staring. He sighed.

"It's a Cousins issue. This is all internal. So that you can embrace externally."

"Figuring out who the hell you are, simply."

He cleared his throat. "I guess."

"Are they dumping you?"

"No." He frowned, suddenly alarmed. "I don't think so. No one knows how it starts so how can you know if it ends. I imagine they'd stop coming."

"People visit?"

Pablo hesitated, then nodded. "Or someone behaves oddly. I can't say more."

Zelda squeezed his hand. "This is what you wanted your whole life, Pab. You can do it. Whatever that is."

"I'm not so sure, Zel."

Last time she'd seen Pablo tear up was when they were fifteen and he knocked three Regs unconscious for calling them DV dogs because they'd wandered north of 167th Street. He kept kicking the kids, sobbing, until Puppy and Zelda dragged him away, where he trashed an alley full of garbage cans.

"You're ashamed of what you were, baby. At some point you have to realize that's who you still are."

Pablo clamped his teeth together to keep from answering. "Does that work for you and Puppy?"

"No. Our failures are good road maps."

"I didn't mean…"

"It's okay. It's true. But you're smarter and more ambitious."

"So we always thought."

"Maybe not that much smarter." Zelda grinned. "But don't quit, jerk. You have no other friends but us, you strike out in love and you're pushing forty. What else you got going?"

"What if I fail?" he whispered.

"You won't."

"You're so sure?"

"Yes." She nodded emphatically. "One of us has to do something. You have to succeed for all of us."

Pablo cried silently for a moment. Finally, he asked, "And how have you been?"

That was always the mystery of friendship. You wanted to share something with someone you loved, but if they were going through shit, was it fair to dump on them? Sometimes you had to take turns, especially when they might be the father of your child.

"Terrific. Can I have the rest of your donut?"

He made pig noises and she kissed him on the forehead, leaving jelly on his eyebrows.

• • • •

PABLO WIPED MUSTARD off his chin as the Needleman's waiter beamed expectantly.

"I've never had a kasha knish."

"Like something an angel would make, right?" The waiter persisted until Pablo acknowledged the pagan concept of angels serving deli food after death, indicating he needed more time to decide the next course. The waiter's opinion of Pablo's decisiveness as a customer dropped as he shuffled behind the counter.

Too defensive, Pablo scribbled in his notebook.

Dentist isn't enough.

Teeth are taken for granted.

What isn't?

Bold bold bold

Be what you are but different, he murmured Grandma's Eighth Insight.

Diaz waved over the waiter, ignoring the beeping watch for the second reminder of his nine AM patient.

"Pastrami or corned beef?"

"I'm not sure yet," Pablo said pleasantly. "Just give me a second. Those gentlemen near the door, how often do they come here?"

"Every day."

"Every single day?"

The waiter was offended. "Why wouldn't they? Best pastrami and corned beef in the country. Not that you'd know…"

"Give me pastrami on white with mayo."

The waiter shuddered. "That would not be possible. You will have it on rye with mustard or you must leave."

"Fine," Pablo muttered, staring at the laughing men. He crunched on a pickle, imagining winged cherubs in a huge bowl of mustard, and wandered over to their table.

"Good evening."

The men grew silent.

"I'm at the other table. I've been here before." Pablo slid over a chair. "I like the food, too. Dr. Pablo Diaz. I'm a dentist."

Their suspicious eyes were cold, "go away" blinking over their heads. Pablo's social skills were never great and it took him a minute to figure out what to say.

"I'm getting the pastrami." He scanned their table, settling on a bulky sandwich. "What's that?"

"Brisket," muttered the thin man with wispy hair.

Pablo sniffed. "Real beef?"

"Why wouldn't it be?"

"Not much cattle left after the war."

"What war?" grumbled the chubby man with blotchy skin.

It took Pablo a moment to process that; Puppy's old DV baseball players popped into his head.

"The war with the Allahs."

"Finally we kicked their asses," the man said, earning pleased nods from his friends.

Pablo frowned and gestured at a plate of brown kernels and bow-shaped noodles. "And that?'

"Kasha varnishkes." The third man sighed.

"Where do you get it?"

"Russia's best."

Russia? The Caliphate of Russia?

"Mine's from Warsaw," the wispy haired man disagreed.

In the Caliphate of Bulanda.

"Nah, the best comes from Brooklyn. They get it from Jerusalem." The chubby man's blotches flared.

Jerusalem was ashes.

"What do you think you're doing?" The waiter stormed over. "Back to your table. These are regular customers since we opened in 2036 and they don't get bothered."

As the waiter prodded Pablo to the rear with the tray, the pastrami sandwich slid off. The old man's hands blurred as he caught the food, tucking the meat between the bread with two lightning fingers and slamming the plate down in one motion.

"Rye bread. Mustard. The way it was meant to be," he said gruffly.

Pablo peered at the neat sandwich, astonished. Everyone waited. He slowly chewed through his unease.

"Best in America," Pablo said, very carefully. He waited until the waiter shuffled back behind the counter, then he threw a pickle toward the other table, which the blotchy-faced man snatched without even looking. Pablo fired a sour tomato; the wispy-haired gent plucked it out of the air. With a pitch that would've made Puppy proud, Pablo fired a pickle down the heart of their table; the three men simultaneously pulled apart the briny cucumber in equal thirds, munching away.

"No food throwing," yelled the waiter.

Pablo smiled grimly. He would order dessert.

• • • •

PUPPY WAS LYING on his back in center field as large shuffling skeletons danced in a circle and chanted baseball songs. He didn't recognize the lyrics or the language or the music. But they were definitely baseball songs since they wore baseball caps, which they waved triumphantly as, in turn, they stomped on his shoulder. This hurt intensely and he swam up through the overgrown grass, gagging as it filled his nostrils and mouth and ears; since when did he breathe through his ears? Was that why his head was floating off his body?

254 | GARY MORGENSTEIN

From the ceiling, Puppy looked down at the bed. He had a skull for a head. Mooshie grinned a skeletal smile, laughing insanely and reaching for his penis.

The pain remained past waking. Brushing his teeth hurt. Showering hurt. Lacing his sneakers hurt. Anything where he used his right shoulder hurt.

Ty had called an off-day practice, furious about yesterday's 8-1 loss. It was all their fault. Playing with just six fielders versus the usual nine for the Falcons might've had something to do with it.

In the fourth inning, Cobb had gone into second with spikes high, gashing the Falcons shortstop, who took umbrage at having his thigh sliced like an AG steak, especially when the play wasn't even close; Ty was out by five feet on the attempted steal. But he was angry he got a bad jump; the Falcons shortstop's thigh seemed as good a scapegoat as any.

The shortstop shoved Ty, who decked him with one punch, then kicked the second baseman in the chest. The Hawks rushed out to help. Mick flattened the first baseman and Vernon completed the destruction of the opposing infield as the fans stood and barked and applauded happily at the newest wrinkle to this fascinating game everyone had always said was boring.

By the time the calmer folks, led by the umpires, impressed order, the three Hawks were tossed for starting and continuing the fight. Puppy wanted to think that his aching shoulder was because he'd wrenched the Falcons' catcher off Mickey's back, but he knew otherwise.

He was the first person in the clubhouse today because he wanted to hit the aspirin supply; Ty grumbled past.

"Where the hell are your friends?" Ty yelled.

"It's only eight."

"What does that matter?" Cobb overturned stools. "Will you be there?"

"Here I am, skip. I'm not the ghost."

"At this goddamn meeting." He flung a crumpled piece of paper at Puppy.

Puppy read, frowning. "They can't suspend you."

"Good. Take care of it."

Ty slammed the office door in Puppy's face. Mickey helped straighten up the clubhouse; Puppy dropped the stools a few times. Mick gave Puppy a shrewd look as he buttoned his jersey with his left hand.

"Mornings are the worse."

"For what?"

"The pains." He tapped the scars on his knees.

"It's just a little stiffness. Mooshie takes up a lot of room and we only have a small bed."

Mick grunted. "That must be it."

Puppy carefully tied his spikes. "She's pretty selfish. Lucky I don't fall on the floor."

"Think how much the shoulder would hurt then?"

"The shoulder's fine, Mick."

"Drinking never helped. I thought it dulled the pain, but not really."

"I have no pain and I don't drink much."

"I figure they have better medicine now for sports injuries."

"I wouldn't know."

"We ain't got a team doctor?"

Puppy shook his head. "No one had ever been hurt before yesterday."

Along with the police and teachers, doctors were the Three Amigos of The Family. Trust, faith. Only the best, like Cousins without the mystery. If you couldn't trust a doctor, a teacher, a cop, how could you trust anyone? They were the bedrocks of daily life.

If a physician made a diagnosis and the patient refused, it was put before a medical board. So if the board agreed his shoulder needed surgery, and Puppy had never heard of a board overturning a doctor's diagnosis, then he would have the surgery. Another simplistic way Grandma protected her more stubborn children. And Puppy was not having surgery. At least not until the season was over.

Puppy tossed the burlap sack into the locker, grimacing.

"What's that?" Mick asked.

"My fan mail," he said shyly.

Mantle chuckled. "You?"

"Yeah. Me." Puppy reluctantly fished out several letters.

"Dear Mr. Puppy, I saw you pitch on the vid screen. You were very funny and I'd like to pitch when I grow up."

"Dear Puppy, I haven't watched baseball since I was a little boy. I think you're terrific and you remind me of the days my grandfather talked about rooting for the Philadelphia Phillies."

"Dear Puppy, You stink. I prefer the HGs. They don't give up as many home runs."

Mick chuckled his way through a few more letters.

"None for me?" he finally asked, half-serious.

"Nothing I've seen. I'm the local kid so it makes sense I'd get…"

Mantle cut him off with a shrug of his thick shoulders. "I don't care, Pup. You deserve it."

Puppy blushed and mumbled sheepish thanks; Mick gently smacked his cheek. "It's kind of nice just playing for once and not worrying about all that other crap. I had enough attention in my life which did me no good except lots of fun, but him." Mantle peered at Ty's closed door. "The guy thinks people should applaud when he farts. He didn't get even one letter?"

"Nada."

They both grinned devilishly.

• • • •

BOCCICELLI AND FISHER stood in the far corner of the office as far from the fuming Cobb as they could get without levitating outside the window.

"De la Puente is very upset, very upset." Boccicelli glanced down at his notes. "He required five stitches. And Larsen might have a head wound."

"If he ain't dead, he's all right," growled Ty. Puppy shot him the fifteenth warning look since they rode up in the elevator.

"Ty is accustomed to an aggressive sort of play," he explained again.

"There was blood," Boccicelli snapped.

"Only five stitches," murmured Fisher.

"Would you like five stitches in the leg?"

"No." Fisher edged away, unsure who was the greater enemy at the moment.

Ty gave Boccicelli the finger. The owner thrust out his chest like a fat rooster. "You're the smart guy, aren't you?"

"Ain't difficult in this room."

"Well, you'll have more time to study because you're suspended three games without pay."

Cobb fired murderous stares. Boccicelli moved a little further away.

"No one's getting suspended." Puppy smiled reasssuringly.

"Yes he is. This is the second fighting offense."

"Ty will apologize…"

"Like hell I will…"

"And we'll chalk this up to enthusiasm. The fans loved it."

Fisher and Boccicelli exchanged uneasy glances. The Falcons owner said, "Yes they did. A little too much. We don't want the DVs all riled up."

Puppy frowned. "It's a baseball game."

"We know that. But all the barking. And the applause. Who knows where such behavior will lead."

"To a real game," Puppy said slowly.

"Or more violence. Riots. Worse. Remember 10/12." Boccicelli's mind nearly exploded at the thought of bloodshed and mayhem because of this vicious old man. He calmed down with difficulty. "Your DVs can howl. Seems suitable in a way." He sneered. "We understand it'll never be like football or basketball, where the fans innately understand what is proper."

"Backgrounds matter," Puppy's mouth barely moved.

"Precisely." Boccicelli clasped his right shoulder; the pain didn't register through the anger. "So then, we're all agreed Ty Cobb is suspended three games…"

Puppy nudged the cursing Ty away.

"If he's suspended, I won't play. Neither will the rest of the team."

Boccicelli blanched. "Are you threatening us, Nedick?"

"No. I'm just stating a fact."

"Then we'll get other players. That shouldn't be hard." Boccicelli looked at Fisher for support, but the Hawks' owner wasn't so sure.

"I bet the fans will love that. You might have to cancel games until you replace us. We have a great advance sale for my next start. That means where they buy tickets ahead of time. We're talking maybe ten, fifteen thousand fans."

Fisher tugged hysterically on Boccicelli's sleeve, but the Falcons owner waved him off. "I won't be intimidated by a, a…"

"Baseball player?" Puppy helped.

"Daring to strike. Which is illegal no matter who they are."

"Who's striking?" Puppy coughed. "A bad cold is sweeping the clubhouse. Wouldn't surprise me if the Falcons catch it, too."

Fisher covered his mouth with his handkerchief.

"I'll bring back HGs," Boccicelli shouted.

"I'm sure Third Cousin Kenuda would love that after he approved the museum." Puppy paused to let Fisher cower behind a chair. "Unless you'd like to hear a solution."

"Yes, yes." Fisher pleaded.

"We're a society of laws. In your mind, Ty broke a law. He should be punished."

"Hell I will…"

Puppy waved Ty back into the chair. "Since he hates the Falcons so much, why not have Ty instruct them in some of the finer points of baseball? Might make the games a little more competitive."

"You want me to teach those clowns?" Ty roared.

Boccicelli's peevish glare cut short Fisher's laugh. The Falcons owner puffed up and, with an imperial flourish, said, "Since it upsets him so much, that seems fitting punishment."

"Yes, agreed," Fisher said.

"I ain't doing it," Ty shouted.

Puppy dragged him from the office and into the hallway. "Listen. You're going to teach them your finer points of baseball."

"Fuck I am."

"The Ty Cobb way."

Ty's eyes widened appreciatively. "Everything?"

"Everything. Then who'll be left to complain?"

Cobb grinned. "You got brains for a colored boy."

Puppy rolled his eyes. "It must be from my alcoholic white father."

• • • •

AZHAR WATCHED A fourth naked girl wander down the hallway. This one walked funny, rubbing her thighs without any self-consciousness. He lowered his eyes onto his shoes, tucked beneath the metal chair.

"Got a smoke, luv?" She was about fifteen and blonde, lipstick smeared on a surprisingly delicate mouth.

He shook his head without looking up, which still gave him a view of her slim legs. Moans dribbled out from behind the door. How long can this go on?

The prostitute lifted his chin. He hadn't seen another woman's breasts in eighteen years. In the past half hour, he'd seen eight. All the more magnificent than his wife's, which were slightly droopy, the left a little larger. This girl's nipples were perfect. All their nipples were perfect. Their stomachs. Thighs. Asses. Feet. Crusader witches.

Azhar pretended to fuss with his shoes. The girl knelt and re-tied his laces.

"Who you with?"

"A businessman," he said simply. Abdullah traveled as a Saudi mining expert, Azhar, his assistant. Allah protect them if either were asked a question about a cave.

She finished and tapped his shoes as if he weren't paying attention to the curve of her white back. "Tell your boss if he still has pop, number ten is special."

"I will tell, certainly."

The girl laughed, deeply amused, scratching her vagina and returning to her room. They are all so wanton, he thought. He couldn't imagine Jalak here, he shuddered. Ever, despite any privations. Or her sisters, ugly as they are. But Jalak's world was not wiped clean. Then embrace a new one, he grew angry at the Crusader prostitute's stubbornness. Learn a new way, find Allah. Or fight back. Instead, they spread their legs.

Azhar yawned, eyes down as a chubby naked man strolled past with the happiness of a well-done blowjob. Abdullah had warned against any eye contact.

Then why are we here? His anger returned. This is the great mission? A cesspool, this city. Perhaps the Son required fortification, but must they be so young? Worry yourself not. The Crusaders, they deserve this. No they don't, he suddenly thought, ashamed. Clary could just as easily be in one of these rooms.

Azhar fingered the silver crucifix, deep and safe in his pocket. While waiting for the Son to finish meetings, as he had waited all day since docking last night, he'd wandered down Great Jones Street in the Crusader shopping district. Infidels edged aside on the street; he'd done his best to seem haughty and privileged, only he was embarrassed. He'd hurried into the nearest shop, a small jewelry and antique shop called The Dead Past, glass cases filled with silver artifacts.

The elderly owner moved silently by his elbow.

"Just looking," Azhar said gruffly.

The man disappeared without vanishing. Azhar peered at a row of crucifixes. Same size as Clary's scar. Should he call it a scar? Mark. Savage, bestial mark. Azhar squirmed inside his own thoughts, glancing at the owner to make sure his anger was private.

"A cross, sir?"

Azhar snorted disdainfully. "How can you sell these?"

The man pointed to the sign on a wall: The Collectors. "Throughout Europe, we're allowed to sell remnants of the disgraced Judeo-Christian world to remind everyone how well our lives have improved under sharia."

Azhar returned the bow; neither was sincere. He pointed to a small cross in the top row. The owner slowly removed the necklace, as if to give Azhar time to reconsider. Mustafa snapped his fingers impatiently.

Same size. It could fit exactly into the mark. You'll never see her again, why are you doing this? Azhar had paid the owner and quickly left, continuing to sightsee, though without any enthusiasm.

The whorehouse door finally opened. Abdullah nodded briskly as if he'd done nothing more the past two hours than linger over a meal. On the staircase, the Son adjusted his tie, using the wall for a mirror. He is a Mufti's son. Naturally he can see himself in brick, Azhar thought sourly.

"Are you sure you don't need anyone?"

Mustafa thought of the blonde girl in number ten, careful not to answer in any way that might suggest disapproval. They went into the alley and Azhar drove the small Italian car through the dark streets of the Caliphate of London.

Muslims in traditional garb wandered along the well-lit streets of Islamic shops. Side streets, the Crusader shops, were dark; the curfew had started three hours ago. Infidels were shot without warning or question. Mustafa steered around a figure lying in the road, hopefully sleeping.

"Shall we go back to the hotel?" Azhar glanced into the rear view mirror. Abdullah sat in stony silence.

Azhar eased through London, past the shattered half of Big Ben and the shell of their Parliament, the crescent moon and star waving over the aged buildings which looked like decrepit, once proud old women. Animals grazed on the lawn of Buckingham Palace. Just like the pictures, Azhar thought wonderingly. Jalak and the boys would love a souvenir. He sighed and drove along the Thames, London Bridge brimming with tourists snapping photos.

The Son shoved a flask over Azhar's shoulder.

"No thank you, my lord."

Abdullah grunted and noisily swigged. "Is vodka not to your liking?"

"I'm driving, sire. I wouldn't want to get into an accident."

A displeased grunt was followed by another noisy sip. "You've never been to London?"

"I've never been outside the Caliphate of North Africa until now, other than on water."

"Haven't you been curious?"

"No, my lord. My family provides enough wonders for me."

Abdullah laughed heartily. "What are your impressions so far of the great world beyond your dining room table?"

Azhar hesitated. "A triumph."

Abdullah's drunken breath laced his ear. "Of what?"

Allah, please find me in this wretched place. "God's will."

"All Allah's doing."

"As is everything."

"Which you believe?"

Azhar nervously gripped the wheel. "Yes."

"All this," the Son banged on the window, "is because we are devoted to Allah?"

"Yes." He prayed at a red light.

"If the Crusaders believe in God, and many of them were fervent, then why did we win?"

He should've listened more to Omar's bleating at dinner. "Our faith is stronger. Our religion stronger."

"Our God stronger. Only there is just one God. Unless you believe in polytheism?"

Azhar wasn't quite sure what that meant.

"Many Gods," Abdullah helped. "It was the Jews who first said, one God. To which we agreed."

"Yes," he mumbled uneasily.

"Then the Jews had something to offer? If they did, why did we eliminate them? Oh, don't worry." He clasped Azhar's shoulder, "I won't ask for any explanation."

"Thank you."

The Son smiled. "Life is much simpler when we don't think, isn't it?"

"Yes."

"When we accept. Stop."

Abdullah staggered out while the car was still slowing. He weaved toward the gleaming mosque as Azhar sloppily parked at an angle and followed.

"Do you know what that was?" Abdullah pointed to the tall building. "St. Paul's Cathedral. More than four hundred years old. Holiest of holy, Azhar. Their great Crusaders are buried there. Were buried. We dug them up and dumped them in the river. The Thames. Come Azhar." Abdullah dragged him by the wrist, but he stiffened, afraid.

"Come Azhar," the Son hissed. "Come see what we did. What we extinguished. What we remade according to our law for there is only one law and it is Allah's. That is what I believe. That is what you believe. But if we believe that, then what does Allah say to Jesus? Isn't he in Heaven? No, course not."

The Son smashed the flask on the floor. "Only true believers. I'm a true believer. You're a true believer. Believe in what we believe, Azhar. This is what we believe."

Azhar gasped, aware of the heresy, the sacrilege, puzzled by the riddles. Allah would strike them down. He closed his eyes, waited to be extinguished, briefly regretting not touching the young blonde's breasts before he died. Abdullah burst out laughing at this sorry statue of fear.

"Nothing happened," the Son said softly.

Allah is wise. He will wait for the best time when my guard is down.

"Nothing will happen." Abdullah took Azhar's sweating hand. "Come inside and see. Take a picture to someday show your family. For someday we will return this church to its rightful owners."

Azhar knew whatever he did would be wrong.

• • • •

ZELDA FINALLY RAN out of conference rooms to hide in. She had started in 102A, which smelled a little stinky from all the fish samples curling up on a plate from the night before. The eight-thirty meeting almost left as soon as they arrived, thinking she'd booked the space, but Zelda made a big pretense of acting distracted, up late working, must be the wrong room, don't we have someone to clean up?

That worked for a while in 106B, where she dully studied a power point on sales plans for the Southern region. Knoxville seemed an especially big market along with Little Rock. On page five of the plan, she noticed one of her salmon characters, Diego.

"Catch me if you can." One of his big brown eyes winked and her heart sank before off she went, apologizing to another group.

In 110C, she forced down some almost tasty SC fruit, pocketing half a blueberry muffin as she nodded knowingly to the nine-thirty meeting colleagues carrying their power points and pads and pens and gossiping about where they went last night and all the fun they had.

She threw up around nine forty-five, an excuse to hang out in the coffee alcove, waiting for the earlier meetings to bring their leftover food to share. Two sesame bagels later, she summoned the courage or, really, just ran out of hiding places, and headed toward Katrina's office.

Get it over with, Zelda told herself. She tugged down her white blouse and rounded the corner.

"Here she is." Boar Face snatched Zelda by the elbow and into the office. "You must've heard us talking. Thinking about you. That's the way a business runs. Zelda Jones, please meet Saul."

Wizened Saul Ribe politely tipped his white-haired head. "A pleasure, young lady. There's nice things being said in your direction."

"Thank you." Zelda flashed a grateful smile at Boar Face.

"She was the key in the lock, Saul," Katrina explained.

"Salmon could be a mystery to some. The whole concept of fish. Who are they? What do they want? What do we want from them?"

"To eat 'em," Zelda cracked.

Saul roared. "But to do it in a nice way so the salmon aren't upset."

"Nor the customers," she added. "Eating living things is disgusting but we do it, so we might as well do it with humor."

"Isn't she wonderful?" Boar Face beamed.

Saul leaned against the door, absorbing Zelda's extraordinary insights into the world beneath the sea and how it relates to the world on land and how that generates money.

"Katrina said she found you in the education world."

Zelda glanced curiously at Boar Face, snorting slowly. "I was an art teacher, but I didn't get along with the school authorities."

Katrina hugged her. "They didn't understand her mind as I do."

"Understanding's important," Saul agreed.

"The parents and kids also didn't..."

"But I saw enormous potential," Boar Face continued.

"Finding good workers is so difficult," Saul said.

"I actually started with Mr. Pietro." Zelda smiled sweetly.

"Ah," Saul said sadly.

"Yes," Boar Face agreed solemnly.

Zelda tensed. "Is he dead?"

"Moved on," Saul explained as Katrina's eyes twinkled triumphantly around Mr. Pietro's corporate carcass. "Fortunately we have Katrina and her remarkable gift for discovering talent."

"I only had to give Zelda direction, show her my vision and then harvest." Katrina reached up to an imaginary fruit tree.

Saul studied Zelda as if she were an apple. "What were some of Katrina's best ideas?"

"Giving personality to the salmon, right, Zelda? You loved that one." Katrina pawed the ground with her high heels.

Zelda squirmed in the tight skirt. Deep breath, balloon girl. You don't want to find out what happens to unemployed single pregnant women.

"Actually I think..." They waited. "The dancing came first. Singing and dancing salmon gave birth to the personalities. Diego was your best character."

"Yes, Diego."

"You came up with him on the bus, right?"

"Oh yes. The uh…"

"The bus driver was the model. And then she turned to me. I'm good at executing other people's ideas."

Boar Face smiled like she'd just gobbled down a monkey.

"Keep it going. I won't rest until tuna salad is an afterthought." Saul shuffled down the hall as if suddenly very bored.

"Wonderful man. Genius, actually." Katrina picked up a thick folder. "Good, Zelda. Knowing how to talk to the boss is very important."

"Especially knowing what to say." She smiled coldly.

"That's my job," Katrina returned the frosty look, hued with warning. "Stick with me. You might actually learn something."

I don't have a choice, Zelda realized sadly. All her life, failure had given her real options.

27

Derek motioned Yen down so they could catch their breaths. Neither would admit that sixty-five-year old men playing soldier in the middle of the night needed naps.

Yen grunted gratefully and lay on his stomach, hoping the forty armed men who had crept along the desolate country road were all in place. They had no communications devices that wouldn't be detected.

Singh glanced at his watch and signaled two minutes. Yen rolled over on his back, staring upside down through the electrified fence. At thirty seconds, sparks flashed one, two, three, done. The men exchanged pleased nods and Yen rolled back onto his elbows, cradling the Bannister C20 rifle.

Singh finished slicing the wire and slid forward, rising to hands and knees and then a bent back trot. On all four sides, khaki-uniformed men and women hurried forward. Yen peeled off slightly to the left, waiting around the side of one of the long horseshoe shaped cottages until a Black Top guard strolled past on his two-fifteen patrol. Yen cut his throat and motioned for Singh to follow.

Using a twister blade, Derek popped open the lock. The room was dark, not even a night light. Twenty beds, ten on either side. Yen jostled the first orphan, who bolted up, gasping. He placed his hand on his lips; the men edged down the rows, waking the children.

"Where?" asked a girl in a heavy Eastern European accent.

"Safe," Singh answered.

"Safe here." She shook her head and the other children stopped putting on their shoes and jackets.

264 | GARY MORGENSTEIN

They'd expected this; Singh was half-surprised at how obedient they were. Do what you're told in the orphanage. Do what you're told in this bullshit camp where you're kept out of sight. Like we are. Shove all of Grandma's mistakes under a rug in the woods.

Derek sat on the bed as Yen anxiously tapped his watch and held up two fingers. At least there was no gunfire yet.

"What's your name?"

"Patricia."

Singh managed a smile; children made him uncomfortable since he lost both of his during 10/12. "This is not safe anymore, Patricia."

"Grandma says…"

"Grandma lies," blurted a fat little boy in a thick wool hat and shorts.

"Yes, she does," Singh said, standing. "If anyone wants to stay, that's fine. Just keep quiet until we're gone so the Black Tops don't kill your friends."

That set off a little murmuring. Patricia stubbornly folded her arms. At the far bed on the right side, a teenage girl reached under the mattress and pulled out a snot-nosed Kenyon rifle.

"Put your guns down." The girl leaned toward a small communicator on her wrist. "This is Bedroom Five…"

Yen shot the BT plant through the forehead; hopefully there'd be equally good shots at all the cottages. , Singh and Yen exchanged worried glances. We overlooked that.

"Her accent always sucked," said the boy by the adjoining bed, ignoring the BT's blood splattered on his arm.

Yen quickly bound and gagged the suddenly docile Patricia as the orphans watched almost listlessly; they'd seen worse. As he left, Yen tossed an orange wig on Patricia's chest.

They hurried back through the split fence, lines of orphans flanking them.

A shot rang out. Then a volley, followed by screams. Singh and Yen kept a steady pace as 'copters whirred into the night. By the tree line, two Miners fired a mini-SAM, blowing up a ship. The blazing debris and seared limbs rained around them, along with gunfire from two more 'copters.

They crossed the road, stopping by the convoy of trucks. Behind, missiles and 'copters traded fire. Six separate groups waited. Singh and Yen ran along the vehicles, signaling by pounding on doors. The convoy roared ahead as the Miners led more than two hundred Muslim Europe orphans deep into the other side of the forest.

They ran for half a mile away from the 'copters pursing the empty trucks before turning left at a cluster of broken trees. The air parted and, with a slight collective intake of surprise, they disappeared inside the vast cave.

● ● ● ●

BETH'S HANDS WERE caked with flour and eggs, joining the chocolate which stained the patched red apron; she had no sense of embarrassment before Puppy.

"My son's not here."

"Know when he'll be back?"

"He's with his girlfriend." Beth started closing the front door.

"Can I wait?"

The thought of Puppy in her home was much like finding piles of rotting rats on the couch.

Beth grudgingly stepped aside, leading him through the house and out the kitchen door into the tiny neat yard. He wondered if she'd scour the floor where he stepped or just tear up the tiles. Beth half-heartedly straightened the wobbly metal table; Puppy squeezed uncomfortably into the small chair, which gave her pleasure.

"I don't know how long he'll be."

"I haven't any plans."

"I do, Mr. Nedick."

"Don't let me stop you. Smells good." He awkwardly buttoned up his jacket with his left hand. "Nice night."

Beth disappeared for about ten minutes while he ignored the all too familiar view of the backs of the weathered apartment buildings, clothes fluttering off the fire escapes and draping the flower and vegetable gardens like diffident canopies.

From inside the house, pots slammed, a dish broke and Beth cursed very precisely so he would hear every word and know who was to blame for the cooking accident.

She returned, spreading out a napkin and laying down a thin cheese sandwich.

"Thank you." He smiled gratefully. "I haven't eaten since breakfast."

Beth waited to make sure she had properly served her guest. Unless it was rancid, the proper response was a polite murmuring of approval while you ate silently. Dropping a slice of cheese because you weren't used to eating with your left hand was wrong.

Offended, Beth picked up the cheese and took away the sandwich. More banging in the kitchen. In about fifteen minutes a sizzling AG hamburger on a burnt bun dropped before him like a grudging sacrifice.

"Thank you." He smiled again. "I haven't eaten since breakfast."

He grimaced and held the burger with both hands, chewing out those appropriate gentle murmurs. Beth yanked away the burger.

"What the hell's wrong with you?" Puppy wiped ketchup off his chin.

Beth gestured at her pained mouth and sneered.

"I'm not lying," he insisted.

She winced and grimaced and made all sorts of faces he suspected had little to do with his opinion of the hamburger.

"The food is good."

Beth didn't buy that. He'd insulted her hospitality and made it seem as if she couldn't cook. What faults would be next?

"It's not your damn food." He shouldn't tell her. Or anyone. "It's my arm. It's a little sore from pitching and hurts to hold the burger. That's why I made a face." He simulated her wide range of expressions.

She softened slightly. "How bad is your arm?"

"It'll pass. I hurt it nearly twenty years ago."

"Then why would you pitch again?" Beth seemed genuinely baffled by his stupidity.

"Because it's a dream. Another last chance."

"So you hurt yourself so badly you can't hold a hamburger for a dream?"

"Yeah. Maybe if you'd ever had one, you'd understand."

Beth slammed the sandwich onto the table and turned out the back light when she went inside. It was even colder in the dark. He stormed in, finishing the burger.

"What is your problem, lady?"

"Don't you lady me." Beth poked her finger into his throat.

"You hate me."

"Yes." She nodded matter of factly, returning to her pie.

"But why?"

She squished the dough in the pan as if it were his head. "You're a bad influence on my son."

"Really? By giving him a good job, promoting him…"

"He got promoted?"

"Yeah. Twice."

Beth slammed the pie into the oven. "Parroting the propaganda."

"What're you talking about?"

"The museum ll about 10/12."

"That was his idea."

Beth went white with rage. "That's not possible. He doesn't think like that. Never thought like that. Until you."

"I don't think like that, either."

"You don't think at all, do you, Mr. Nedick?"

"Not as much as other people and I'll probably live longer. I care about baseball. And I care about your son."

"He's not your child."

"I wish he were," Puppy said quietly. "I wish I'd had a kid like that."

"So you could ruin his life?"

"How am I doing that?"

"You're filling his head with nonsense." Beth rushed into Frecklie's bedroom, the mattress creaking up and down, returning with the sketch pad which she shoved at Puppy.

"He's drawing stadiums. Stop smiling." She yanked the pad back. "There are no stadiums. There will be no stadiums. He's dreaming like his father did, which killed him. I won't let my son be killed by dreams. Look what it's done to you."

He took a breath and grabbed her wrist with his right hand. "It's given me a reason to wake up. It's made me think that my life wasn't a complete waste, no career, bad marriage, no children, looking forward to writing copy for a funeral home in a few months because that's all there's left. So let the boy draw his pictures. Let him dream. Otherwise what the hell do we have other than baking pies at midnight?"

"Get out, Mr. Nedick," she said very quietly.

Beth seethed for half an hour after Puppy left. That put her way behind on sewing. But she couldn't concentrate. She tried working on the Gutierrez wedding dress only to rip apart the stitching; by one AM, she gave up.

When Frecklie finally came home exhausted after humping the sex she-devil Dale all night, Beth was in the dark backyard, kneeling and praying. He hated when his mother prayed because it usually had to do with him.

• • • •

KENUDA SLIPPED ON his new checked overcoat, squirming around pleasurably at the wonderful real cotton material. His A12 waited in the doorway with that insufferable way the garbage cans had of silently entering rooms or knowing what you wanted. Damn, for just a human secretary. But we took away their faces, meh, meh, he muttered darkly, so must be nice to them.

"Yes?"

"You have one more visitor, Third Cousin."

He sensed it would sneer if it could.

"I have evening plans."

"At six-thirty. It is five, which leaves sufficient time."

"Not if we reschedule."

"He's sent by the Family House."

The A12 returned with a tall, stiff-looking guy who couldn't figure out what to do with his hands.

"This is Dr. Pablo Diaz." The A12 handed Kenuda a file, cheerfully closing the door. Kenuda sullenly pointed Pablo onto the couch.

"Did I get you leaving, Third Cousin?"

"Yes," he grumbled, stopping on the first page. "You've not even been accepted yet?"

Pablo shrugged. "I was told you'd be my mentor."

He tossed aside the file. "I haven't received any word. You're supposed to wait."

"I'm sorry. Maybe I jumped the gun."

Kenuda raised an eyebrow.

"I know I'll be accepted. If I could get a little help. A glimpse ahead."

"By breaking the rules?"

"By starting my training on stronger footing. Is that breaking the rules? Otherwise why would I be given your name?"

Kenuda almost smiled. "You're an arrogant little shit, aren't you?"

"Yes. I'll have to shed the ego to be successful."

"So you think. Save The Family through better dental hygiene."

"Will this be more half-answers, sir? That's all I've gotten so far."

"You think there's something wrong with the process?"

"I think simple and direct is better, Third Cousin."

"Because serving as a Cousin is simple and direct?" Kenuda clucked his tongue. "It's all about half-answers, Diaz. Be bold but not too bold. Without ego, but confident you know what you're doing. Move up because it helps The Family, but not yourself. But if you don't help yourself, how can you help The Family."

"That seems to be my brief experience, sir."

Kenuda grinned. "Where are you screwing up the most?"

"I tend to observe."

"Observing isn't a good trait."

Pablo nodded unhappily. "I like to know the facts."

"Assuming there are facts."

"There are always facts."

"Not necessarily the right ones. Sometimes the wrong ones are more important." Kenuda glanced at his watch and poured a couple large Montana brandies. "You do know all this is confidential."

"Of course."

Kenuda weighed the somber, earnest face and decided Diaz wouldn't give up the nuclear codes under torture. "I played basketball."

"Yes, at Temple."

Elias raised the glass in grudging respect. "I was good, but my fatal flaw was trusting teammates. I was a point guard and they couldn't handle my passes. Bullets, right through their hands. I led them perfectly and the pass still went out of bounds. I looked like shit. I don't like looking like shit, Diaz. I talked to them, practiced endlessly, but they sucked. What would you do?"

"I'm not a sports fan."

"I'll let you get away with that for now. I kept passing. I could've taken the shots, but how would that've helped?"

"What if you made the shots, sir?"

"What if I did? Then it would've been Kenuda the star, instead of Temple University the team." He shrugged. "We still finished 6-15 in my senior year, but that was the right thing. Helping. So here I come to Fifth Cousin, years later. I realized I was wrong. Leading means rising above. They won't tell you that because you'll hear all of Grandma's warnings about elitism. She's right. Unless you lead for a reason, Diaz. If you know you're good, lean into it, because that's where you'll make a difference. Just don't let anyone know how good you are."

"Are you, sir?"

Kenuda snorted. "During the first session with my mentor, First Cousin Albert Cheng, I explained my dilemma from college. They love moral quandaries and seeing how we'd get to the other side. He said Grandma doesn't want us to do what she says. That's where everyone gets tangled up. Like you. Do what's right. Show them you have the balls to set the agenda. Take risks."

"Like breaking the rules by meeting my mentor?"

Kenuda smiled. Brash, pretentious and somewhat annoying. Familiar, Elias? "You like pop music?"

"I prefer Bach, sir."

"So do I. But Dara Dinton has presence."

Pablo grinned. "I'd be honored."

• • • •

HAZEL SNEERED AT Frecklie's hand outstretched over the gaping crater which was framed by jagged rocks, ending somewhere down there in the darkness.

"It's dangerous," Frecklie insisted again.

Hazel patted his right leg. "Works fine."

The reporter had nearly fallen into the hole by Section 120. Show off, the teen sighed. He wouldn't care if the guy fell into the hole. He didn't like him. Something about the way he shorthanded, but not meaning it. Big smile, way too cheerful. Frecklie didn't trust especially happy people; his mother said they were usually covering up.

But Puppy insisted he show the guy around. More repairs were required now. About fifteen thousand fans came to the last game. They needed usable seats.

Hazel balanced pigeon-toed around the crater. He wavered a moment, but never panicked or showed any fear, concern, nothing. He kind of enjoyed the wobbling. Was he doing that because he enjoyed it or is he giving me the finger, Frecklie wondered. Hazel smiled triumphantly and hop-skipped to the other side.

"Where's this lead?" Hazel asked.

"Below."

"I know. Where below?"

"I've never been."

"Can we go there?"

"Why? There are no seats, just the hallways to the clubhouse."

"So you have been?"

"Only at the clubhouse. Not everywhere under the stadium. It's dangerous."

Hazel peered into the hole and followed Frecklie past the shuttered concession stands.

"There was quite an assortment of foods here once," Hazel commented on the worn signs for barbecued chicken, sushi and pizza.

"We have new ones now, too," Frecklie snapped.

"Hey, I was just saying." Hazel smiled disarmingly. "Can those booths be re-opened? Might be nice. Retro."

"Let's worry about the hallways."

"You're the boss."

Frecklie choked back an answer and navigated around a four-foot high pile of concrete. Hazel paused by Section 220 and watched a few minutes of the Falcons batting practice.

"Are they bunting?" he grinned.

Frecklie wasn't sure what that meant.

"Bunting." Hazel mimed hands apart on a bat.

"I know, I know."

"Are you something of a baseball expert now?"

"Something," Frecklie said, struggling to show respect. "How much of the stadium are they fixing?"

Hazel looked around sadly. "Up to these second levels. Though who knows. Wouldn't it be something to do it all?"

Frecklie perked up. "Think they will?"

Hazel shrugged and jotted into a notebook. "Let's go below."

"I told you, fans don't go there."

"And I'm telling you, I have to check out the whole ballpark for my report for Commissioner Kenuda. Unless you want the damn fans sitting on laps." He gestured angrily at the blue seats flanked by faded rust.

Frecklie edged around the debris in the basement, glancing uneasily at the holes in the ceiling spitting grainy half-light. Hazel moved quickly until they were in gray darkness, doors on both sides.

"The clubhouses are back there," Frecklie said, irritated.

"What's in there?" Hazel pointed.

Frecklie shrugged.

"Probably electricity rooms," John mused aloud, running his hand on the walls as if reading. He tried a door, but it wouldn't budge.

"I don't have the keys," Frecklie said defensively.

Hazel grunted, muttering.

"We should go back."

John yanked on a door; it gave slightly. He pulled a screwdriver out of his inside pocket and twisted between the door and the frame. The knob shattered onto the floor.

Frecklie liked none of this, but couldn't help following into the room. Hazy dust twisted into thick clouds.

Hazel cursed and fell to his bad knee. He held up a skull, then a bone. He got on all fours and scurried forward, moaning as he stepped between the skeletons. Frecklie lit a match. The weak flame flickered over rows of skeletons in army fatigues holding rifles, orange wigs glittering on their skulls. It was a circle, Frecklie realized. Huddled together against some enemy.

"See any shells?"

Frecklie shook his head and dropped the spent match, which Hazel quickly pocketed.

"Show some fucking respect. Know who they are?"

Frecklie hesitated. "Miners?"

"Miners," Hazel rasped. "Know why they were called that?"

Hazel viciously mocked Frecklie's shrug.

"Because Grandma thought they belonged in a cave. Cavemen. Primitive views. Miners, in a cave, get it?"

Frecklie knelt by a skull. "DVs, right?"

"Yeah, kid. All the Miners were DVs."

"Weren't they also…"

Hazel's forearm pressed against his throat. "What?"

He barely swallowed. "Traitors."

Hazel sighed. "No. The traitors were in the government. Still are." Hazel shone the light onto the air vents just below the ceiling. "They must've gassed them. The freedom fighters retreated here, a last ditch stand, hiding with the kids." The flashlight darted onto the small skeletons. "Helping them."

"Or using them as hostages."

"What?"

"They took hostages. That's what the plaques and the HGs say. I looked it up in the library."

Hazel was disgusted. "Then the Black Tops killed the children instead of rescuing them."

Frecklie couldn't answer. He tripped over a rifle, earning a string of curses to be careful. He held the weapon, imagining. Miners had hidden all over Amazon Stadium that day. Under the stands, behind the bullpen, in the bathrooms. Posing as groundskeepers and concession stands workers, selling food at the seats. They'd taken over the scoreboard, public address system and much of the security guards. How could they have done that without the players knowing? When Mooshie Lopez, the most famous athlete in America, had shown some sympathies afterwards, saying she couldn't tell who was innocent any-more, that only fueled the connection between baseball and the Miners.

That's what he'd been told his whole life. What they'd all been told.

Frecklie pointed the gun at the air vent and blithely pulled the trigger. The gunshot startled them and the skeletons shook. Once Hazel stopped shouting and his own heart-beat slowed, Frecklie returned the rifle to its unseeing owner, patting the orange wig.

"Make sure no one sees this."

"I should tell Puppy."

"No one." Hazel jabbed his chest. "Otherwise they'll turn this into another exhibit. Do you really want that?"

His mother was angry enough at what he was doing, calling him a brain-washed boob and throwing the Stadiums book at him. At least she hadn't spoken to him for more than a day. Frecklie shook his head.

Hazel grunted, satisfied. "Let's see what other wonders Grandma left her children."

The starless night managed a few dribbles of light onto the deck. Grandma's candles, Tomas thought, sitting beside the nice looking kid with the terrified eyes drooping over the side of the boat.

"Sorry, sir," Diego leaped up.

"Relax." Tomas shook out a 'bacco. The boy declined with excessive gratitude. "I de-veloped the taste in Italy. Figured, how much worse could things be?" He tapped his knee. "What're you most worried over?"

Diego's throat bobbed nervously. "Nothing, really."

"Maybe being hauled out in the middle of the Atlantic by some strange guy."

"I trust Captain Lee." Diego nodded at the Captain behind the wheel, gaze locked ahead as if a long chain held his eyelids.

Tomas smiled faintly. "Why?"

The kid frowned for just a second, probably to make sure he had all the grammar right. Tomas tapped his throat. Just speak. Diego grinned and tapped his temples. Think-ing. Tomas gave him a moment, looking starboard into the darkness.

"He's my friend," Diego suddenly said.

It took Tomas a second to come back to the conversation; his mind was on the ship out there, waiting.

"Friends are good, Diego. I've lost some." He pushed the anger aside, glancing over his shoulder as if Grandma were hovering. She's here, somehow. "You have a more seri-ous friend?"

Diego blushed. "Think so. She's worried I'll never be anything because I'm a DV. But she was and she's something, so why the worry?"

The boy waited for some brilliant response. Stilton couldn't afford to waste anything too wise on the perpetually erect pecker of this horny sailor.

"She'll come around." He patted Diego's shoulder. "Either they do or they don't."

"Thank you, sir," Diego said, a little disappointed.

"Thirty-five degrees," Captain Lee said softly; the lapping waves quieted from the intensity of his voice.

Tomas peered. *Damn eyes are going now, too,* he scowled at the ocean until he saw a light twinkling. He nodded; Lee returned the signal and they picked up steam. Diego occupied himself by fussing with the ropes.

Even half a klick away, the ship dwarfed theirs. Two more blinks and Diego helped Tomas into the small rubber dinghy. The boy's eyes shone with fear. Tomas gave him a confident smile he didn't feel and paddled to the unmarked vessel, where he awkwardly climbed up the rope ladder and onto the deck. He grinned.

"At least the lamb will be good."

"This way, sir," Mustafa hid a smile as he led Tomas past two hulking men who frisked him, and down three metal steps into the stateroom.

"Major Stilton." The Allah warmly shook his hand. "Thank you for coming."

"Thank you for having me." Tomas glanced longingly at the rich buffet on the table.

"Hunger and thirst is understandable." Abdullah guided Tomas over the fruits and vegetables, cheeses, lamb and chicken dishes. Tomas politely filled his plate and waved off the wine, sipping water in silence as the two men assessed each other.

Younger than I thought, Tomas picked at the hummus. *Confident and arrogant, but they all are.*

"Thirty-four."

"Pardon?" Tomas asked.

"I'm thirty-four. If you didn't already have that information."

"I did," he lied.

"You're sixty?"

"Fifty-six next month," Tomas answered sourly.

"Happy birthday. How is Grandma?"

"She sends her respect to you and your family."

"And mine to yours. My family, well. They would not be so gracious."

"Which is why we are here."

Abdullah played with his robes. *Prick is nervous.* Tomas caught the way he rubbed the thumb and forefinger together. *Does he do that while thinking or lying?*

"Our world is at peace, Major. No wars since the Surrender..."

"Truce."

Abdullah smirked and bowed slightly.

"You've had your troubles," Tomas continued. "Still some unhappy Sunnis in the Peninsula."

"A family argues. Sometimes there is blood. Overall, sharia has brought prosperity. Happiness." He raised a finger. "To those who accept."

Tomas ate a fig and waited.

"And to those who don't…" his voice trailed off sadly. "We can go on like this for a long time. We have the lands, you have the nukes. Fortunately those of my people who equate suicide with victory can amuse themselves other ways."

Like raping nuns, Tomas ate another fig.

"But in the long term, it will rot us away. We are conquerors. You are builders. Once we built. A thousand years ago, a glorious time of science and medicine…"

"Please," Tomas said quietly. "How about no speeches? Unless you want me reciting the Declaration of Independence and all that stuff about freedom."

Abdullah's mouth tightened. "You do not like me, Major?"

"I'm not sure yet. At least not going in."

"I like you," Abdullah said as if granting Tomas a royal favor. "You're brave. I could take you for ransom and what would your country do? Launch a nuclear missile? But you're here because you believe there could be more to this world."

"I'm here because Grandma does. She respects your beliefs and welcomes a dialogue. But the leader of the world's greatest democracy…."

"The only democracy." Abdullah sneered.

"Making it even more important." Tomas sneered right back. "She, too, can talk about her sadness at a world where tyranny is supreme."

"I'm not here to dismantle sharia. Or betray my people."

"Then why are we here, Abdullah? Are you playing the spoiled older son who worries his father might live a long time?"

The Arab sadly shook his head at Tomas' ignorance and poured more wine. This time, Tomas accepted a glass.

"As I started to say before you invoked your American patriotism, my people once saw no conflict between faith and freedom. Science and Allah. Physicists, chemists, philosophers, doctors. Muslims, Christians, Jews, we all lived together in peace. I want to return Islam to those glory days."

"That was more than a thousand years ago."

"History is patient."

Tomas ignored Abdullah's raised glass and took a long thoughtful swallow. "But those Allahs, sorry, Muslims, had armies. I count your navy consists of three men including yourself."

Abdullah laughed. "There are more. But would I give you names? How do I know you wouldn't tell my father? A conquered nation always looks for a way to supplicate."

"Not America."

"Once that was true," Abdullah stared coldly. "I have allies. I have armies. I have merchants, eager to trade. Clerics eager to preach the true Allah of peace and brotherhood. Hands, reaching out. But they see no sign of friendship other than an emissary who clearly will recommend against this."

"I will give Grandma the facts."

"The facts are, Major, that we do have Sunni problems in the Peninsula. The damn Afghans never give up. Chinese Muslims are making demands. So are the blasted Muslim Russians. They're still Russians, no matter. The Crusaders, sorry, Christians, make for poor second class citizens. Productivity is not great. A resistance of sorts. Pathetic, but annoying. Nothing would unite Islam more than, as your Miners once said, finishing the job."

"That would be very stupid."

"And war is smart?" Abdullah pointed his glass at Tomas' leg. "But if there's to be another way, my friends and I need a partner. We need Grandma."

• • • •

TY WRAPPED HIS arms around the frame of the bullpen door and stared suspiciously at Puppy warming up.

"What's he got?" he asked Jackson.

The catcher peered through his mask at Puppy. "He got good stuff."

"He looks labored."

"I'm taking it easy..." Puppy tried.

"I ain't talking to you." The manager squatted by Jackson. "A catcher has to tell the truth. You ain't stupid enough to lie to me, are you?"

Jackson played nervously with his mask. "I'd tell you if he was shit, skip."

Cobb grunted doubtfully and glowered at Puppy. "I want a complete game." He kicked dirt at Jackson and headed back toward the dugout. Puppy mouthed thank you.

"You can't go nine, Pup," Vern said.

"And disappoint my fans?" he grinned bravely.

Fans spilled out beyond both foul lines, stirring eagerly as the Hawks took the field. After the recitation of Grandma's Blessing, Puppy waved his glove at Frecklie standing behind home. The kid clapped his hands and, for a moment, the stadium was still.

Dale cartwheeled out in a bright yellow dress, followed by three friends also wearing yellow outfits. They catapulted around home plate and formed a square about the peevish robot umpire, not programmed for such nonsense.

"Go Hawks," they chanted, leaping.

The crowd applauded cautiously.

"Go Hawks," the cheerleaders repeated.

More polite applause. Dismayed, Dale bounced onto the shoulders of Sallie Ann, a gorgeous red-head, and they trotted from foul line to foul line shouting "Go Hawks" until the crowd responded merrily.

As the Falcons leadoff batter stepped into the batter's box, Dale jumped like a cat onto the top of the Hawks dugout.

"Booooo." She cupped her hands. The crowd was uneasy. Shouting only positives was rooted in their core.

"Pussies." Dale wiggled her butt. "Boo Falcons. Boo Falcons."

Puppy wasn't sure which was funnier, Frecklie covering his reddened face or Dale wiggling her rear up and down the top of the dugout.

Finally the uncertain boos started, gathering wary momentum as if the neighbor in the adjoining seat jumped in, giving permission. The catcalls streamed louder and louder. It was fun.

"Play ball," the A28 shouted again.

Dale cartwheeled onto the field and started barking. The crowd joined in. The umpire was maybe not so happy because it ordered Dale to leave. She barked and cartwheeled and defiantly wiggled her butt in its face. The crowd liked this even more. The 'bot chased her down third base and across the infield, Dale cartwheeling and the umpire yelling play ball. Dale stopped near first, a little dizzy, and the umpire jerked its thumb.

"Out."

"What?" Dale blinked, baffled.

"I'm throwing you out, Miss."

"I don't play," she snapped as Frecklie ran onto the field.

"If you're in my stadium you listen to me. Now get your ass out of here."

Dale definitely threw the first punch; Puppy heard the crunching of her hand on the 'bot's head ten feet away. Her three dancers cartwheeled around the fallen umpire, but Frecklie slipped under their kicking thighs and smacked the A28 in the chest.

It took about fifteen minutes for the dancers, Dale and Frecklie to be dragged away by players from both teams. Pausing on the top step of the dugout, Dale shook her penis at the 'bot, earning the loudest cheer of the 2098 season and sending Ty into a stunned heap.

Fortunately for Puppy, the umpire was a little dazed and provided a very generous strike zone. Puppy didn't have much, but he set the tone from the first pitch when, under strict orders from Ty, he threw at the leadoff batter's head. As expected, the Falcons starter responding by throwing at Puppy when he came up in the third inning. Both benches cleared and the confused umpire searched for Dale, assuming she was behind everything wrong with its Universe.

It was that kind of an ugly game, especially his pitching line: seven innings, four runs, eight hits, three strikeouts and three walks. Ty, still sifting the notion of dry-humping someone with a penis, showed mercy and pitched the last two frames.

Puppy took the last of the Ibuprofen and hurried out of the clubhouse, carefully unfolding the tight square note as he headed along Jerome Avenue, glancing at addresses. Beth waited inside the alcove of the shabby burnt orange and beige bricked building. Without any greeting other than disdain, she shoved the square note into her purse, snapping the latch shut with some regret it wasn't one of Puppy's fingers.

Beth buzzed once and they were let through a bruised, unmarked red door. A faint smell of pained sweat hung over the tiny waiting room of bamboo chairs and a tattered green couch. From behind a beaded entrance, a thin old Chinese woman waddled out and gave Beth an affectionate hug.

The older woman and Beth spoke quickly in Chinese; Puppy flinched at hearing anything beside English; all other languages were banned. The elderly woman circled Puppy warily and sighed. Beth's voice took on a pleading quality. They disappeared through the beads, speaking in incomprehensible whispers.

Beth returned alone. "She doesn't trust you."

"Why?"

"Because it's illegal. She saw you on the vidnews and fears you'll tell since you're so important."

He wanted to rip off his burning shoulder. "I thought it was all set."

"What can I say? My grandmother doesn't like your face."

"I'm so sorry. Cosmetic surgery is also illegal so here we are."

Beth turned toward the door. He was desperate.

"Please. If I can't pitch, I'm afraid the whole damn baseball season will somehow go down the toilet. Please."

Beth grumbled about the hand her brain dead son had dealt her and pushed back through the beads. The women's voices screeched in more Asian jibberish. Popping her head out, Beth coldly beckoned him inside and turned out the lights in the examining room.

A tiny candle flickered. Puppy shyly removed his shirt and lay on his stomach. Beth closed the door as her grandmother fussed with the acupuncture needles. He wasn't fond of needles.

"You're staying?" he asked.

"She doesn't trust you."

"But I'm supposed to trust her?"

Beth made walking gestures with her fingers. The grandmother chattered and he rolled onto his back. Beth's eyes widened at the scar on the front of his shoulder.

"Thought I was lying?" he asked.

She looked away, guilty.

The fun and games with needles on both sides of his shoulder lasted about half an hour. He fell asleep; Beth shook his arm.

"It's over."

He dressed silently, looking around for the old woman, but she'd vanished. He and Beth waited at the traffic light down the block from the office.

"How's it feel?" she asked quietly.

"Good. Thank you."

"My grandmother knows what she's doing."

"I'm not surprised. I have faith in your whole family," he said with a big smile. "Can I buy you a meal or a drink to thank you…"

Beth combined anger and embarrassment into one deadly stare and hurried through the intersection.

"What's with you, lady?" he yelled at Beth, who disappeared down the subway steps. "Fine. Bye bye sweetness."

Puppy flapped his right arm in a seal-like wave. There was no pain in his shoulder. No. Pain.

$$\bullet \ \bullet \ \bullet \ \bullet$$

"YOU OKAY?" MOOSHIE zipped up Zelda's sweater jacket.

Zelda stared emptily out the cab window, counting blocks. "How was the gig?"

"Too many Regs." Mooshie met the A21's curious metallic gaze in the rear view mirror. "But oh the sound system." She sighed dreamily. "Like a recording studio. They loved me, of course."

"Of course."

"Elias brought some strange good looking guy who didn't say a word all night except stared at me like our fucking cab driver. Hello." She banged on the glass window. "You got a problem?"

"Sorry ma'am. I seen you on the vidnews."

Mooshie relaxed. What a ham, Zelda smiled.

"You remember my name?"

"Dara Dinton." The 'bot turned away bashfully. "I got one of your tunes on the rad. Copied it this morning. The Beach Boys cover."

"Cover?" Mooshie said in mock indignation. "You saying my version of *I Get Around* is some shit imitation?"

"No, no, no." It took both hands off the wheel; they nearly grazed a bus. "You're much better."

"Damn straight." Mooshie slid away the glass and stuck her head onto the robot's shoulder. "If you got it, play it."

They listened to Mooshie's version four times, the last with her singing along, before pulling up before the two-story house with the wide front yard in Pelham Parkway. The 'bot's black eyebrows raised knowingly as he looked between the women, trying to figure out which one was pregnant. Lopez slipped two tickets into its pocket.

"This is for Thursday's show. Bring a friend."

The A21 tapped the tickets as if they were a real face. "Thank you, Miss Dinton. I'd be honored."

"Just applaud, scream and act delirious."

"How can I not?"

She kissed it on the forehead; the A21 pulsed a blush.

Mooshie led Zelda past the discarded red bicycles on the front walkway, ducking under Happy Birthday Danielle balloons hanging from the porch, and into the narrow hallway. A gray-haired woman greeted them with a friendly smile, wiping her hands on the checkered apron.

"I've been baking cookies. Chocolate chip, which I hope you like. One of Grandma's recipes. Forgive the mess." She shrugged helplessly at the toys and balls and plates all over the living room. She motioned them onto the comfortable plaid couch where they waited quietly. Children squealed somewhere in the back.

"It's play time. I give them an hour to run wild." The woman suddenly noticed Mooshie, asking pleasantly, "Who are you?"

"Dara Dinton. Her friend."

"Friends are good, too."

Zelda wondered how the woman could talk and never stop smiling. She hated her.

"And will you be accompanying Zelda every week?"

Mooshie nodded slowly.

"Well then, we can all have a most pleasant relationship. Zelda, how do you feel?"

"Scared."

"Parenthood is daunting. The most important job we will ever have. For no matter how long."

"Seven and a half months," Zelda said.

"But you're still a mother and always will be. Have you told your employer?"

Zelda shook her head. "Not yet. It's a busy time of year."

"You're afraid?"

"I just got the job and I'm doing well…"

The woman's smile deepened, somehow. "They can't take that from you. If they discriminate in any way, any way, Zelda, their business will close and they will go elsewhere."

Elsewhere hung ominously.

"They're there to support you. Nurture you, along with your friends. As we will."

"So what happens here?" Mooshie jumped in impatiently.

"Zelda learns to be a mother and how to love her baby."

"The baby you're taking."

"Moosh…"

"You think your friend is being punished." The woman had heard this one many times. "You, Zelda, feel like a bad girl."

"The worst."

"You made a mistake. Everyone makes mistakes. But you can't allow that to seep into your child and have it come out angry. Is it a boy or a girl?"

Zelda shrugged and the woman's smile faded slightly.

"You didn't ask?"

"I don't want to know," Zelda shouted. "I just want this to be over."

The woman sat on the coffee table, tucking a couch cushion under her rear. "This is all natural, sweetheart. The anger, pain. Self-loathing. Why didn't I tell him to withdraw before climaxing? Why am I a slut? Where is my sense of responsibility?"

"Which this'll change?" Mooshie asked sullenly.

"Always," the woman said with arch confidence. "As you will learn over the next seven months and sixteen days, every single American child is precious because this is what we face."

The room went dark and a screen as wide as the wall edged out. Endless streams of half-naked dirty Allah children kicked soccer balls back and forth until the balls became rifles, firing as the crescent moon and star fluttered over Moscow and Berlin and Paris and London and Rome.

Zelda stared at the children, smiling, laughing, playing. She hated them, too.

The lights came back on and the screen retreated into the wall.

"It didn't have to be that way," Mooshie said stonily.

"Pardon?" The woman finally lost her smile.

Louder, "They could've been beaten."

The woman was flustered. "That isn't the point."

Zelda didn't like the way the woman studied Mooshie. Two brats with pigtails burst into the room and froze, clutching their dolls safely away from Zelda, who was obviously planning on burning all their toys.

"Darlings, meet Zelda Jones," the woman said, relieved not to deal with Mooshie. "She's going to be your Mommy." The woman considered Zelda with a resigned sigh. "First, we'll start with your diet. You have a puffy face, obviously too much sugar. That's now banned from your Lifecard."

"You're not taking away my donuts," Zelda snarled, scowling at the girls as if they'd be a grudging second choice dessert; the children hid behind a chair.

The woman laughed. "I love your sense of humor."

Mooshie poked the matron in the thigh. "She ain't kidding, honey."

• • • •

ANNETTE'S POUT COULD ruin a sunrise, Puppy thought as she stomped into their last ever Couples meeting. Except today, the best game he'd pitched since he was twenty-one. Seven innings, only one run, Ty gambling on a diving catch which skipped past to the wall, four hits, two walks and eight strikeouts. Curve, slider, fastball, change, everything clicked. Fans barked themselves hoarse. Eighteen thousand and thirty-two of them, Frecklie had announced proudly.

Even the Merry Owners were happy, airily dismissing the plumbing bills to re-open bathrooms as part of doing business, though they still didn't see why there had to be toilet paper in every stall.

Eighteen thousand and thirty two. And they all came to see him pitch. The hell that it sounded arrogant, selfish, egomaniacal, un-Family like, counter to Grandma's teachings; who cared?

He was a star. Fans barked out a bus window on his way over here. Hazel had spent half an hour interviewing him for the Late Sports Show. He just got two sacks of mail from as far away as northern California. Forty-three women mailed in proposals. Another ninety-six just offered sex.

And there was still no pain. He asked Frecklie why his mother had suddenly acted so kind when she obviously preferred he get hit in the head with a line drive. At first the kid hesitated and Puppy's mind jumped to a trap where the grandmother, if she really were a grandmother, would stab him in the eyes with her needles next time. My shoulder's fine, but I can't see home plate. But Frecklie assured him that his grandmother was very nice, he didn't understand how his mother turned out this way, and he could only guess that Jesus had something to do with this.

That was a secret, he insisted, red-faced. So your mother prayed for me? Frecklie had mumbled it didn't work that way even though he wasn't sure how it worked since you didn't see Jesus and nothing ever happened that she asked for anyway. Except it had worked for the Allahs, Puppy added, two men of the world discussing God behind home plate in a deserted stadium.

That'd freaked out Frecklie a little, mixing Jesus and God and baseball with Allahs. The kid had hesitated again, wanting to say something important, but Dale danced up the steps and into his lap. Puppy went into the clubhouse to give them time to make out. He would definitely make out in his stadium if he weren't engaged to a ghost.

What if he slept with just one of his fans? he suddenly thought. That'd only break like three or four adultery laws. It'd been a long time between triples.

Annette angrily slid into the chair. "Talk to me, Puppy."

The guard stirred uneasily. These crazy people were supposed to be done.

"About what?" Puppy ignored her edge. "My sensational pitching?"

"Your fiancé and Elias." Annette tossed her hair in rhythm to her drumming, impatient fingers.

"What about them?"

"What about them?" she mocked. "Elias saw her two nights this week." Annette threw down the hair brush. The guard moved closer.

"I think, lunatic lady, that Elias saw Dara sing."

"Uh-huh. He got home at two this morning." Annette's lower lip quivered.

Puppy finally realized her point. "Honey, they're not having an affair. Dara's just a wonderful singer. You should come hear her."

"I have my instincts." Annette windmilled her arms like she was a burning tree with very expensive jewelry.

"You're wrong."

"Uh-huh."

"Stop it, Annette. Elias loves you."

"Why wouldn't he?"

Don't tempt me. "Dara loves me. You love Elias. I love Dara. It's like an isosceles triangle."

"That's three sides, idiot. This is four. Add Elias loves me. A square. Or rectangle…"

"No one cares because nothing's going on."

"Because it would just figure, wouldn't it?"

"What?" he said between clenched teeth.

"That you'd pick a fiancé who'd want mine."

Puppy bent her brush handle. "Are you suggesting that in my twisted, devious criminal mind, I found someone solely to screw up your relationship?"

"Sure seems that way."

"You're more insane than I thought."

"I love him, Puppy." She broke down. "I love him."

The guard hovered by the table with a box of tissues, unsure if this was a clever prelude to violence.

He sighed. "I know. I'll talk to Dara."

"You will?" She brightened.

"Of course. It's nothing, but appearances can be appearances. Or something."

"So you don't think I'm crazy?"

"I do think you're crazy, but I don't want you upset."

"Thank you." Annette pricked his thumb with a barrette.

28

E very so often, Tomas would omit an unpleasantry from his daily security report: a small protest over the quality of SC foods, an altercation between 'bots and siblings at a bus stop, or a song whose lyrics were a mite mocking about the HG parks. He couldn't stand not seeing Grandma smiling, optimistic. This morning reminded him why he did it.

"So no children were injured?" Grandma asked dully, her makeup not quite so careful.

Cheng shrugged. "Unless we consider the five BT plants."

"They were orphans once, too."

"Yes, they were. Then five deaths. The sixth…" his voice trailed off.

"Is where?" she demanded.

"We have extensive medical facilities on site."

"I want him brought to Lebanon Hospital immediately."

"It's a her, originally from Norway, and that isn't wise."

Grandma ignored Cheng and turned to Tomas. "Do it."

Cheng shook his head imperceptibly. "Grandma, it'd get out. The weapon was very much a Miners specialty. Someone will talk."

"We can cover," Tomas said.

"I don't want any lies," Grandma snapped.

"Then you want the truth?" Cheng exchanged an uneasy look with Stilton.

"I want nothing said. This, this," she sputtered, squinting at the report on her lap, "Ase Pedersen had an accident during firearms training. Do it. Now."

Grandma waited until Tomas arranged for a medcopter to bring the teenager to Lebanon Hospital; given the girl's extensive head wounds, he doubted she'd survive. Lenora nodded grimly when Stilton finished.

"What do the prisoners say?" she asked hoarsely.

Cheng sighed. "The BTs didn't take any survivors."

"Why not?"

"There was a fight, ma'am. The traitors were firing SAMs."

Her voice grew small. "The BTs made no attempt to rescue the children?"

Albert squirmed, giving Tomas pleasure. "Apparently that wasn't an option. Policy was followed."

Grandma turned to Tomas. "Is that so?"

Cheng reddened at the insult, but kept quiet. Stilton nodded. "Since there was no indication that the orphans were taken against their will, there was the assumption that they cooperated."

Grandma stared so hard Tomas felt his brain dance. "The children wanted to leave?"

He hated lying to her. "Of course not. Obviously they were coerced. But the BTs, in the heat of a firefight, weren't sure."

"And the search for the children?"

Tomas gestured at the folder. "It's in the…"

"I know it's in the goddamn report, Major," Grandma shouted. Both men flinched at the unusual rage.

"I'm sure there'll be some ransom demands," Cheng jumped in soothingly; Tomas tossed him a grateful look. "Let's wait."

"Let's wait means you have no idea where they went."

Cheng stiffened. "No, Lenora. We have no idea other than this was a sleeper Miners cell."

"Because of the orange wigs they left?"

"And the rifles…"

"Which they've just been hiding for thirty years?"

"It's possible."

"Waiting for?"

Cheng stared. "Your Story must have triggered this."

"Miners don't march peacefully, Grandma," Tomas said.

"But you're not sure it was the traitors. Or even who they are."

Albert shifted slightly. "Who else would they be?"

Grandma exhaled slowly to indicate this subject was concluded. "Let's discuss the Son."

Tomas glanced up, surprised.

"Of course I know," Cheng snapped. "Since your first contact with the Paris Collector a year ago. It's my job. As it was your job to keep it secret."

Tomas tipped his head respectfully.

"And I still think it's madness."

"Don't mince words, Albert." Grandma scowled.

"Do I ever? He's a charlatan. A bored pervert. I can show you photos. He's no different than any of them."

Grandma shook her head wearily. "Since he met the Son, let's ask Tomas what he thinks."

They waited for Tomas to form a suitable answer; there was none other than blunt honesty. "I don't trust him, either, ma'am."

"As you've said over and over." Lenora pursed her lips. "It must start somewhere."

"They don't want real peace. This is a ruse to get us to lower our guard."

"No. An opportunity to talk."

"And you think his father and all the Allah scum will allow this?" Cheng persisted.

"I don't know, Albert. I'm hoping that the only disloyalty I need worry about is from the Camels."

Cheng flinched visibly. "You know I'll support whatever you decide. We both will." He took in Stilton. "But let's first rebuild our defenses just in case."

"With what?" Grandma's eyes blazed. "To what end? To losing another thirteen million? No. The world is out there and we need to rejoin it. Someday we will be the world power again. But not blind and stupid like before. And not through dead soldiers. Our hearts and minds will prevail. Our wisdom. Our love."

She was crazy, Albert decided sadly. Old and crazy. The HG sunrises, temperature manipulations, fake trees, happy children, peppy police. She bought all her own fantasies. He had tried. He could always remind himself of that. He had tried.

"What're the next steps?" Cheng asked.

She nodded gratefully. "I will meet Abdullah."

"We can probably hook up an HG to about a thousand kilometers," Tomas said.

"Who said anything about HGs?"

Stilton smiled shakily. "How else, ma'am?"

"In person." Grandma folded her hands in her lap as if deciding on reupholstering the purple couch.

Tomas and Cheng abandoned any pretense at politeness.

"That can't be done," Stilton said, alarmed.

"And we can't possibly protect you," Albert added quickly.

"Oh, I'm sure you can."

"No." Stilton angrily swung his head back and forth. "I insist we use holographic contact. This could be a trap."

Grandma laughed. "Unlikely. If they hurt me, Albert would launch every nuke we have. Let's reconvene tomorrow morning with some options. If you'll both excuse me, I've got to go sit through two hours of badly done Mozart."

Tomas and Cheng walked silently past the skipping and singing children of the vid-murals, stopping by the entrance to the underground conveyor where the First Cousin's car was parked. Albert indicated Tomas should follow, and they went down the heavily guarded elevator and into the front seat of the tiny car.

Tomas stretched out his leg, nearly knocking a hole in the glove compartment.

"Sorry, I prefer a small car." Albert seemed genuinely apologetic, turning on the rad. Mooshie's *Dark Depths* haunted the soft leather interior.

"Quiet and deep

My heart is gonna creep

Into your dark depths

Take me with you

But be prepared

I'm blacker than coal

And I ain't got no soul."

Cheng frowned. "Familiar, right?"

"From the 60s, I think."

286 | GARY MORGENSTEIN

"Originally by Mooshie Lopez." Albert listened a moment longer, his face softening in a pleasant memory. "What are we going to do, Major Stilton?"

Tomas has readied himself for this and decided to say very little. "Do as she says."

"Of course we will. But how do we do as she says without incurring risks?"

"I don't see how that's avoided."

Cheng leaned against the driver's door to give the Major a little more leg room. "The Collector's report says Abdullah has support. Your thoughts?"

"As I told Grandma, I largely dismiss that intelligence. They've been embedded so long and the Allahs have given them so much leeway, it's hard to believe anything they say."

"You think the Collectors have turned?"

Tomas shrugged. He wasn't sure what to think at the moment. "They insist Abdullah has the support of at least four major army groups in Europe and North Africa. All cousins." He smiled faintly. "How real those armies are, I don't know."

"How real are any of them?" Cheng asked quietly.

"There are still a billion Camels with guns. That's real enough."

"Unless they're fraying and feuding, as they usually do, and their strength is a mirage."

Stilton stared through the faint light of the underground, tanks at either end flanked by motionless BTs. "Then Grandma's right. They want and need peace."

"Or they're not prepared for war."

Stilton considered whether to mention the Paris Collector's similar thoughts. His mistrust of Cheng won. "I don't have that intelligence."

"I do, Tomas," Cheng said. "Their tanks are rusty, their ships are listing, there've been mutinies and desertions across the Islamic Empire. The European Caliphates haven't as much as pretended to conduct any military games in four years."

There was similar so-called intelligence before the war. Allahs won't fight. They're cowards, perverts, blind fanatics. Yet they kicked our asses. Allahu Akbar.

"I'm sure Grandma's taken that all into account," Tomas said slowly.

"Are you certain she wants to?"

Stilton stared coldly. "She misses nothing."

"Oh, I know." Cheng laughed bitterly. "But she's ninety-two, Tomas."

"And healthy. She'll live another ninety-two years."

"We can only hope. But at that age, this age," Cheng indicated his own wrinkled body, "you're not so sure. You think time will never run out. She's worried that she's left the job half-finished, Tomas. That we rebuilt, brilliantly under her leadership, but it's not quite enough. We're still surrounded, still no trade, knowing all it takes is one Camel fanatic to assume power and attack us again. As you said, a billion of them. So it's understandable she'd want a real peace. A world where those fears are gone. But after meeting Abdullah, do you really think he can be trusted?"

"What are you suggesting, First Cousin?" Tomas snapped, feeling queasy.

"That we must do everything we can to protect Grandma and the Family."

"They're one and the same."

Cheng didn't answer.

• • • •

DIEGO DRAPED HIS arm around Zelda's waist and she spooned a little deeper. He groaned slightly.

"Easy. Little Diego's kind of sore."

She kissed his hand. They'd screwed for three straight hours. He couldn't talk about his trip and she couldn't talk about the baby. That pretty much left sex and Indiana gin. He felt so good and she missed him so much. Just say it, girlfriend, she heard Mooshie and chuckled.

"What?" Diego tried resting on his back, but she tugged his arm back.

"I'm just thinking of a friend."

"What kind of friend?"

Zelda reassuringly sucked his thumb. "Dara. She's a singer."

"Should we see her one night?"

"If we ever get out of bed."

Diego murmured approval into her neck. "I missed you, Zelda."

She tensed. "I bet."

Diego propped himself onto an elbow. "What does I bet mean?"

What're you waiting for, she asked herself. Not waiting for anything, just trying to enjoy love for the first time when I know it'll end. Honey, are you really that fat? Yes darling, I swallowed a fetus. Dipped the brat in chocolate. Went down in one gulp.

"Means I missed you, too. Can't you tell?"

Diego shook his head sadly.

"Really?" Zelda sat up, annoyed. "I made you dinner and we got naked…"

"Like you had to."

"I don't have to do anything," she snapped. "How can we fight the first night you get back?"

Diego sat up a little taller. It became a ridiculous contest until they both rested on their heels, holding pillows.

"I love you," he said abruptly.

"Shit." Zelda stumbled out of bed; he pursued her into the living room.

"See?" Diego said, wounded. "That upsets you."

"It does."

"Because I'm a stupid DV…"

"No, dickhead."

"Then why?"

Zelda sighed. "Because I'm pregnant." Diego grinned. "It's not yours."

He frowned. "Whose is it?"

"I don't know. It might be yours. Or not."

"How many choices are there?"

"What's it matter?" she yelled. "More than thirty three per cent." He calculated on his face, which only pissed her off. "That's why I can't say I love you."

Diego blinked, puzzled. "Then you do love me."

"Didn't I just say I can't say?"

He grabbed away the bottle of gin, warning her about pregnancy and alcohol. "But if you could say, you would." Diego cut her off from the wine cabinet. "But you can't say because you're pregnant and you don't know who the father of the child is and what if it's not mine but you're in love with me."

Zelda threw up her hands. "Bingo baby."

"Then get a DNA test."

"No no no. Because that'll identify the father and what if it's someone I barely know and he has to come forward and take responsibility over a stupid one night stand."

"How many one night stands?"

"Seven," she said weakly. He started calculating odds in his head. "Fourteen percent."

"Not bad odds for someone you love."

So young, so stupid, Zelda sighed. "You want to be with a pregnant woman who might be carrying another guy's baby?"

Diego considered this a little too long. Zelda searched for chocolate in the kitchen.

"Did you sleep with anyone after me?" He stopped her from dumping all the silverware on the floor for the sake of a Kleindorff Caramel Chew.

"No."

"Why not?" Diego squeezed her wrists, hard. "Why didn't you sleep with anyone after me?"

"Because I liked you."

"Now you love me."

"I'm such a hot mess."

"That's why you need Diego."

She finally just rested her head on his shoulder. "I'm a lot older than you."

"Thirteen years. Just over thirty three per cent difference."

Zelda kissed him like she'd never kissed a man or woman before.

• • • •

MOOSHIE WHISTLED TO let him know she'd finished dressing. She was propped up in bed, watching the ancient *Make Room for Daddy* vidshow.

"This is such shit." She laughed. "Don't you think Grandma would've come up with better after all these years?"

Puppy slipped into bed and pulled up the covers. "It's safe. Simple problems. Wise parents. Obedient children, after they realized their mistakes. Family love ultimately conquers all. Why change?"

Mooshie switched back to the vidnews. A pumpkin factory was opening in Oklahoma, celebrated by dancing cowboys and cowgirls.

"We should get a bigger bed." Mooshie tried humming the Okie theme song but gave up after a few bars.

"Why, nothing happens."

"Is my baby horny?"

"I embrace celibacy," he snorted. "Besides, we can't afford a new bed."

"I can. I got a record deal."

He turned, careful not to cross the imaginary line in the middle of the mattress. "Kenuda set it up?"

"No, Dinton's voice."

"The reason we need a bigger bed is for your ego."

"Yours ain't so small, either, hot buns."

"Fair enough," he conceded. He'd made her watch the lengthy Hazel interview twice. The Bad Ass Historian. "Apart from your musical genius, how did Commissioner Kenuda get the deal?"

"He brought people down to the club from Parkway Records. They were blown away." Mooshie rubbed cream into her arms.

"This from one of the late nights you spent with him recently?"

Mooshie grinned. "Jealous, big boy?"

"No. But Annette is."

She seemed genuinely surprised. "Are you kidding?"

"I wish. She can be a little paranoid."

"She'll get over it." Mooshie muted the vidnews forty minutes before it mercifully went off the air for the night and flicked off her light, slipping on black eye pads. It was like sleeping with a pirate with D cups.

"Once Annette convinces herself about something, she can't go back. Otherwise it's admitting a mistake. She's incapable of that. How do you think we stayed together for so long?"

"Clearly it wasn't the sex." Mooshie turned away.

"Moosh, you have to scale back seeing Kenuda."

She flipped back onto her back with a growl. "I'm not doing anything with him. I have some morals, big surprise."

"I'm not accusing you," he insisted. Mooshie briefly lifted up the right eye pad for half a glare. "Just let them get married. It's only another five months."

Mooshie blindly lit a 'bacco. "Who knows how long I have."

"What makes you say that?" he asked nervously. "Did you get some message?"

"From who?"

"The beyond."

She laughed out the smoke, slowly growing serious. "I need Kenuda, Pup. I need to find out who killed me. Kenuda can open doors." She ditched the 'bacco and rolled over again.

"That the real reason?"

Mooshie slowly pulled the eye pad up over her glare. "Meaning."

"Maybe you like the attention. Being famous again. Adoring fans moaning your name. Giving everyone the clench," he grabbed his groin, "by singing all your old hits."

Lopez stared coldly. "They took it from me. They needed a goat and put me in a pen. I could've kept playing. I had another five years easy. And I could still be singing, damnit. I was the best with everything I ever did and they stole it. Ain't no way, hot buns," the heel of her hand smacked into his forehead, "anyone's doing that again. No one. Including you."

He blinked back tears. Maybe her coming back had nothing to do with him. Maybe Mick came back just so he could sober up. Ty, so he could be nice to Negroes.

"You gotta cry over everything?"

"Just you." Puppy smiled weakly.

Mooshie blushed and slid the eye pad back on. "Your ex will have to deal."

Puppy crossed into her half of the bed. "Annette dealing with dealing with unpleasantries isn't a pretty thought."

Mooshie patted his knee. "The Bad Ass Historian will think of something."

• • • •

AZHAR SMILED POLITELY as Jalak shoveled a pile of grilled lamb over the rice. She never served him, Omar never made small talk and Abdul never turned down an opportunity to play soccer. He was home yet he wasn't.

Since returning last night, he felt odd around them, too. He'd unpacked carefully, slipping the silver cross in his pants pocket; Jalak did a laundry right then, as if afraid he'd brought home some infection other than awkwardness.

Azhar pushed away from the kitchen table, patting his stomach. "Your best kabsa laham yet, Jalak. Don't we think so?"

His sons stared incredulously.

"Well I do." Mustafa slipped on his jacket. "I'm off for a drive."

Jalak followed Azhar to the door, whispering loudly, "Where are you going at this hour?"

"It's only eight 'o clock."

"Decent people are home."

"If I drive for fifteen minutes, I'm not worthy of meeting Allah?"

Jalak squinted warily. "Why don't you walk?"

"Because my legs have been at sea and I'm getting old."

He had to detour about five miles. According to a fellow driver who pulled alongside in a battered van, the Al Karama Road was closed for some queer cleanup; the Warriors had tossed a couple metnaks from a hill. Why still do such perversions? Mustafa shook his head. If you must, find a website. The Warriors could only monitor so much. But to troll in bushes, as he heard they often did; so many Crusader perversions still to cleanse.

The orphanage parking lot was fairly empty. He strolled inside without anyone noticing; money clanged onto a table from the card game down the hall. The Imam had said he couldn't work there anymore, but nothing about visiting.

Azhar hurried up the steps and slipped inside the cramped alcove, closing the door. Breathing overhead stopped.

"Little one, it is Azhar."

A soft animalistic growl seeped out.

"I have not been around because my job here was taken. They did not like how nice I was to you and the other children. Perhaps you don't think I was nice. I believe you hate me and wish me ill."

Sharp raps of a small knuckle agreed.

"Someday you'll believe me. I have a present. I'd like to see you, but understand you would rather not."

Harder raps, more like a fist.

"I understand. I ask Allah and your Jesus to bless you. I'm leaving the present on the floor. It isn't a trick. When you hear the door close, I'm gone." He waited a moment, hoping, then sighed and laid down the gift.

Plastic knife clenched between her teeth, Clary jumped effortlessly onto the ground and grabbed the package, then leaped back up into the hiding spot in about five seconds. She tore open the wrapping, feeling in the dark until she traced the outline of the cross. Clary stifled a sob and pressed the necklace to her chest.

Like Papa gave me when I was eight.

Kneeling outside the door, Azhar could hear Clary crying.

• • • •

ZELDA FINALLY THREW Diego out of bed after two happy days that left them both waddling; she'd called in sick, not exactly a lie. When she got to the office, stacks of folders had moved onto her desk like an annoying roommate. Atop the yellow, blue, orange and red piles so neat they appeared made out of stone was a note from Boar Face.

'See me.'

Zelda didn't get a chance to sit before Katrina angrily waved the latest sketch of the advert spot.

"What is this?"

"Salmons on an outing."

"Yes, which I got from the title. Salmons on an Outing." Boar Face noisily dropped her black high heels on the desk, nearly knocking over her University of Pennsylvania diploma. "There are grandparents in this picture."

"It's a family. I'm leaning into our family."

"Grandma's Family?"

"Right. Capital 'f'."

"With two old utterly sickly looking grandparents hobbling on canes." Boar Face's snout wrinkled.

"I'm showing the supremacy of salmon over tuna."

"That's not clear. The fish look unappealing."

"Exactly." Zelda's jazz hands swayed as her voice rasped, "We've been here before tuna. We'll be here after tuna. Salmon. The eternal fish."

Boar Face glanced at the copy and smiled that insincere smile. "No one wants to eat old fish, Zelda."

Zelda leaned onto the back of the chair. "The point isn't eating, Katrina. Otherwise we'd make people feel bad about scarfing down friends. I'm getting across the wisdom of salmon and how there's a reason why they've been around longer than tuna."

"Is that true?"

"I don't know. It's a zillion years ago. Who'd prove us wrong?"

Chewing her lower lip, Katrina pondered the various tuna sympathizers who could wreck her career; red lipstick smeared her teeth. "There are serious laws against misleading advertising, Zelda. Very serious laws."

"I bet we could find a scientist."

"Where?"

"Bronx College."

Boar Face grunted disdainfully. "Use Bronx University, where intelligent people teach. Call the science department and see who'll back us up."

Zelda figured she might as well finally share her joyous news, two days before the deadline. She closed the door just to annoy Boar Face.

"I need to tell you something."

"I need to be in conference room 102 now."

"This is important, official. Legal."

"I've done nothing wrong."

"It's me."

Boar Face waited for Zelda to admit to a series of vicious murders.

"I'm pregnant," she said quickly as Katrina narrowed her eyes. "Don't worry, I'll do my job, be at my desk every day."

"You're married?" Katrina asked softly.

Zelda shook her head. "Not engaged, either. So this is only…"

"For the term of carrying. You at three months?"

She reddened. "Almost eight weeks. I'm also fat."

Katrina kept staring. "You'll get fatter, too. I blew up by twenty pounds in the first four months."

"I didn't know you had a child, Katrina."

"I don't." Katrina's eyes watered. "I lost the baby."

"I'm sorry."

"I was better off. Carrying for four months was painful enough, knowing…" She caught herself at Zelda's teary face. "If you ever need to talk."

"Thanks. I will."

"And if anyone here ever gives you any crap, I mean one wrong blink, you come right to me." Boar Face licked her lips.

• • • •

KENUDA WANDERED AROUND Cheng's office, but there was little to look at, the tiny room nearly barren except for basics, as if showing anything personal might reveal a weakness. The First Cousin grunted again over Kenuda's plan. Little shit always grunted at me. I could pull his pecker and he'd complain he hadn't come long enough. Kenuda was crabby and tired. Annette had given him crap until three in the morning about Dara.

"I'm branching out," he'd insisted. "Entertainment plus sports. It's a niche begging for someone."

"Why can't you find someone else to fill it with?" Annette had whined.

Because Dara was the most exciting woman he'd ever met. Annette's jealousy was tiring. He hadn't thought the relationship would go this far. That he was forty-four and still only a Third Cousin after all these years suggested loser. Higher end women wanted someone on the rise; sports were smelly, no, just not serious. Annette was eager to harvest her eggs; a child would help him along with a wife. He'd heard the gossip. Kenuda got his nuts broken by a football. Kenuda prefers screwing a basketball. Or teams. At least the starting units. Kenuda's skating by.

Marriage would give him stability. But there was a reason he hadn't ever married; that very stability frightened him. With stability came sameness.

Look at that one, Kenuda risked a sneer toward Cheng. Licking Grandma's butt for nearly forty years. He'd been her boyfriend during the last part of his baseball career; a drunk and needy journalist had spilled dirt one night after Super Bowl CXXIV. Albert and Lenora, the Untold Romance. Whisking him into the House at all hours. Security guards had said they were noisy, too. The greatest shortstop of his day, who Lenora came to see October 12, 2065 for her first and last baseball game; apparently she hated the sport. But the seventh game of the World Series was great cover to root for her lover and relieve the stress of the failing war, the awful losses and then, ironically, she nearly gets her head blown off.

Cheng, this dreary old reporter rasped, had stayed by her side, Cubs uniform bloody. She'd been hurt far worse than known; perhaps even life and death for a while, nothing was ever certain. Other than Cheng was suddenly named a General.

Kenuda scowled at the shriveled asshole. A General who led the retreat. He wanted to nuke the Allahs, insisted this drunk, but couldn't go against Grandma's wishes. Wouldn't dare go against his meal ticket, now that baseball was banished. Sold out his beliefs to become the first First Cousin.

"He was an asshole as a player, too," the reporter said, finishing the expensive brandy. "Everyone on the Cubs hated him. But for pure hate, rivalry, oh, he and Mooshie despised each other. She never missed a chance to hit him in the head with a pitch. They dueled with bats once." The reporter cackled so loudly his teeth nearly flew out. "The Moosh had knocked him down, he charged the mound and Derek Singh, he was injured that day, threw a bat like a javelin to Easy Sun Yen at third who speared it to Mooshie and her and Cheng banged bats until they were down to handles, then they wrestled. Look it up."

Cheng tossed aside Kenuda's report and rubbed his eyes, nodding for him to sit.

"Do you believe in a soul, Kenuda?"

"No, sir. That's a religious concept."

"No, it's not," Albert said disgustedly. "Soul is in your thoughts, an essence of passion and life. It's why dying people survive and how great art is made." He stared at Kenuda and shook his head. "You don't get it. That's clear from the plan."

Cheng brushed the folder aside disdainfully. "Why are we doing this?"

"So that everyone can come to Amazon Stadium and remember what happened."

Albert winced. "Where's that? Putting ropes around holes so folks don't fall in? Painting more seats? Selling more food? How does eating a hot dog help people remember treason? What lessons are learned?"

"These exhibits…"

"Everyone has heard the same shit over and over. So what?"

Kenuda was furious at himself. He should've asked Hazel for help. Or Nedick. Your ego always gets in the way.

"What would you suggest, First Cousin?" he asked meekly.

"I'm not the Commissioner, am I? But it's a good thing I know a little about baseball." Cheng tossed the report into the garbage. "It can't be just about making money. Though your mind can't grasp anything else. Like leadership." Albert sneered. "Perhaps it's time for a new assignment of responsibilities, Third Cousin."

Elias stiffened. "I've already taken care of that."

"Pardon?"

"Third Cousin Turashami died two months ago. I've been overseeing entertainment, beginning with overhauling the antiquated music area."

"Why don't I recall approving that?'

"Because you've been too busy leading, First Cousin. As have I."

Cheng leaned back, reconsidering Kenuda. "So you have. Music." Albert's eyes narrowed. "I heard a Mooshie Lopez tune from the 60s on the vidrad the other day."

Elias smiled smugly. "My idea."

"Music from the war years is a perilous path to walk." Cheng caught Kenuda's alarm. "I actually prefer it, but there's a reason why it's rarely played anymore."

"I thought…"

"Clearly not thoroughly, but you're a young man. You don't remember how such music became anthemic to the rebels. Especially Lopez's songs."

"Not everything is remembered," Elias said smugly.

"No," Cheng conceded. "Not everything. Mooshie was a wretched person, but an amazing voice." He began singing softly, "'Be brave with your heart, love ain't never smart, let God sleep in the bed with us.' It's called *Drapes*. All right. Be careful. But nostalgia music might work. Just might," he mused. "In its day, the sound was wonderful, a musical renaissance until it got twisted like everything else back then." He paused, dancing with one leg on a memory. "You've already implemented a waiver, correct?"

"For what?"

Cheng's disdain returned. "Mooshie's songs are still outlawed."

• • • •

ZELDA TIGHTENED THE knot on Diego's new tie. "The flowers weren't necessary."

"I thought I'd make a good impression and let them see I'm responsible." He nodded toward the Parents' house.

"If they can't see that, then fuck 'em."

"And you better not swear."

"Oh?" She grinned. "Any other tips on my crappy shitty behavior you'd like to make?"

He glanced at his watch. "We don't have time."

The woman tossed Diego a surprised, but approving glance as she placed the roses in a glass vase.

"Thank you, these are beautiful. I don't remember the last time someone brought flowers."

"I thought, given the occasion. You know, the uh, occasion, it would be nice." His stammering increased as the little demons in pigtails skipped into the room. They looked at Diego, sorting out what someone with such a nice smile was doing with the she-pig in the dreads.

"Girls, this is Diego. He's Zelda's friend."

"What happened to the other one?" They turned accusingly toward Zelda.

"She couldn't make it anymore," the woman explained.

Zelda had received a curt official letter that Mooshie's negativity and suspicions were not welcome in a setting of warmth and love, asking if she needed a temporary "friend" assigned during the pregnancy, implying Zelda's taste in companions matched her choice in sex partners.

"But Diego's much nicer, isn't he?" the woman asked.

The girls took Diego by the hands and led him toward the couch; Zelda wondered if there was an oven behind.

"So do we play games?" he asked.

They simultaneously said "oh yes, lots."

"Not lots," the woman said with a scolding smile. "Today we get acquainted. Would you like some brownies, Diego?"

"I'd love some."

If he didn't stop smiling Zelda would smack him.

"We made them," the girls chorused, offering the plate to Zelda, who waved them off; the children frowned, plotting other ways to poison her.

"I'm having another brownie," Diego announced and the girls applauded.

Zelda had enough. "Now what?"

The woman frowned. "We're a family. We do what families do."

"Being together," Diego said.

The woman and girls leaned forward as if Diego were the most fascinating person who ever lived.

"You can do pretty much anything as long as you love each other," he said, shooting Zelda an encouraging look. She plopped besides him, determined not to smile.

"Isn't that always the case? Finding the way together. And what memories do you have of your family, Zelda?" the woman asked.

"Very happy ones. Always a lot of love."

"Your mother died young, didn't she?"

Zelda reddened. "Sort of. I was twelve."

"Suicide's a painful thing for a young girl."

The children were horrified, certain Zelda had a role in her mother's death.

"I didn't know that," Diego said.

Zelda shrugged. "That was a long time ago."

"Were you close to her?" asked one of the girls, startling Zelda.

While she'd helped her bewildered father with the arrangements and set up the house for visiting mourners, she hadn't gone to the funeral, which brought Zelda before the DV Community Board for questioning. If you couldn't love and respect your dead mother, how could you possibly love and respect The Family as a whole; if you ever made it out. What if she hadn't loved and respected her mother, Zelda told the committee, which sort of gasped since Zelda's failure was theirs. My mother was an asshole, she beat me, she beat my father, I'm not sorry she jumped off the roof, only that she didn't do it sooner.

Zelda had been put on probation for two years and monitored monthly through a bored general practitioner, psychiatry had been outlawed a few years earlier under the Anti-Parasite Act, who asked if she had any bad dreams. Just life, she'd told him once. Zelda liked making adults gasp. She still did.

"Um, not really. She was kind of..." her voice trailed off as everyone waited. "Troubled. I don't like troubled people. I like happy people."

"You don't seem happy," the other child said.

"Maybe not at this moment." Zelda glared at the girls. "Usually I'm very happy." She poked Diego for backup.

"Zelda's always happy and singing."

"Sing," the children said.

"Yes," the woman clapped. "We'd love a song."

Zelda looked helplessly at Diego, who thought for a moment and sang *On the Road Again*. *He has to pick the song he played over and over when they fucked?* The children clapped rhythmically. Zelda reluctantly joined in. The girls held hands and danced in a circle.

"That is family." The woman spread her arms to absorb all the joys of the world streaming through the purple curtains. "Warmth and joy and love. Discovering talents."

The girls took Diego into their circle and danced. He made them laugh. He made the woman laugh. *He makes everyone laugh. He'd be a good father. Shit, don't think like that, Zelda. You're not keeping this baby.*

Diego gestured to his lips and heart. Finally, she gestured back her love. Diego beamed and spun the girls around a little quicker.

"Join us, Zelda," he called out.

• • • •

DIEGO HAD LEFT Zelda a squared note on her pillow just after midnight. The subway took about forty minutes and then the walk along the dark streets another half an hour. Captain Lee stood outside Basil Hayden's Funeral Home, impatiently smoking a 'bacco.

He shook his wristwatch at Diego, who shrugged apologetically.

"Trains."

Lee sniffed. "Yeah, they're dousing 'em in lilac shampoo lately."

Diego blushed. "Strawberry. Sir."

Lee shook his head at the many mysteries of Diego. His blue van was parked at the rear of the warehouse. The captain rattled the fence and a light flickered on. An A24 came halfway toward them, stopping with a peevish air.

"Neither of you look dead."

"For which we're grateful," Lee snapped back. "We're here for the Thomas order."

The A24 hunched over suspiciously. "You got proof of that?"

The Captain held up a fistful of greasy bills. The A24 smiled greedily.

Diego stepped warily around the twenty small coffins on the long wooden dolly just inside the right of the large warehouse. Rows of finished and unfinished coffins covered the musty floor. A few A24s busied themselves unpacking plastic wrapping while another on a lift shouted warnings about scuff marks.

"Are these ours?" Diego whispered to Lee.

"Well they ain't mine," their robot grumbled from ten feet away; some said they could hear a fart in Nevada. They just creeped Diego out and he stepped away. "Where you going? We ain't loading them."

Lee gave the A24 a dirty look and they wheeled the dolly to the van. It took about fifteen minutes of silent sweat. Diego waited in the front seat, looking in the rear as if expecting someone to sit up in the coffins, until Lee paid and they drove toward Eastchester.

The Captain finally broke the silence. "No one's in there."

Diego looked again. "I know. "They're just so small."

"Don't question…"

"I'm not. I was just with some kids."

Lee gave him a meaningful look. "Whose?"

Diego hesitated. "I shouldn't say."

"But you're busting to."

He smiled sheepishly. The Captain was his friend. Zelda's baby wasn't a total secret, though he wouldn't think his sisters would be happy. Or Mama. Can't you find a girl like you, they'd ask, as if he hadn't asked himself that. Older, sometimes not so nice, not exactly the slimmest body and now she got a child that might not be his. Fourteen percent not his. Well he'd made bizarre decisions before and his life wasn't so bad.

Like riding in a van with little coffins at five in the morning.

"It's not something I'd talk about with just anyone."

"We trust Grandma. The rest of the world, it's up to us," Lee said.

Diego detected a slight hurt in his voice. The Captain's been the best boss he ever had. Didn't know shit about boats and he trained him, believed in him despite his many fuck-ups. Lee was mature, had to be way over forty. Near Zelda's age. Wonder if she really was thirty-seven or maybe older. Her breasts sure seem young.

"Either tell me or don't light up with grins like that."

"Sorry." Diego wiped his mouth to force away the memory of Zelda's nipples. "I got a girlfriend."

"So I guessed. The one from Saul's Salmon?"

Diego nodded. "She's a little older."

"You wouldn't open a bottle of Rhode Island red wine unless it's been aged."

The Captain's wisdom amazed him sometimes. "I love her."

"Does she love you?"

"Yes, sir."

"Then that's all that counts. Was it her kids?"

"Oh no." Diego paused. "She's kind of pregnant."

Lee gave him another long look. "Yours?"

"Not sure."

The Captain shook his head. "I don't like the sound of that."

"I wasn't too happy, either. My odds are…" he hesitated. "Either me or two other guys."

"She's been sleeping with two others?" Lee exploded.

Good thing he hadn't mentioned the fourteen percent. "But I love her."

Lee sighed wearily. "And you went to the Parents House with her."

"Yes, sir." Diego fished the small box out of his pants.

"That a ring, son?"

Diego nodded. "With a diamond."

Lee shook his head at the faith of the young and stupid. Where would the human race be without them?

• • • •

PUPPY NEARLY CLOSED the door on Kenuda, figuring he was only bringing awful news this early: the stadium burnt down, baseball was banned again, Annette wants him back. He stepped aside with a bleary wave and Elias entered in time to see Ty and Mickey's naked bodies exchanging places in the bathroom.

Puppy hurried into the kitchen, kicking empty beer bottles under the sink and making coffee. The Commissioner forced down a couple sips, studying Ty and Mick wrapping towels around their tubby butts as if the Bronx Zoo had been moved into Puppy's apartment. The players disappeared into the bedroom; Puppy held his breath, hoping Mooshie really had left already.

He waited a couple beats for screams about naked ghost bits. "Dara's at the recording studio."

Kenuda's eyes gleamed, making Puppy uncomfortable. "*Dara's Dreams*. Love the title of her new album. Gems, pure gems, like her. You're very lucky."

"So are you."

"For?"

"Annette."

"Yes, yes." Kenuda decided against any more coffee. Puppy brought him the last of
the Callison's Original Peppermint Cookies, which he inspected carefully before attempt-
ing a small bite. He shuddered. "You're wondering what brings me here."

"I'm figuring something terrible."

"You have a gloomy mindset, Nedick."

"Based purely on experience."

"You can look at life either way. I prefer the optimistic. Rest assured, all goes well.
Attendance is booming, not what we get for real sports, but not bad considering."

Mick and Ty passed by on their way back into the bathroom.

"How do they hit with those guts?" Elias asked.

"A famous player, Babe Ruth, once explained that he didn't hit home runs with
his stomach."

Elias spent a moment pondering the physiques of baseball players. He shuddered
again. "I'm very pleased. First Cousin Cheng is very pleased. He was a well-known player himself."

"I know, sir."

"The exhibits your young DV friend suggested are very popular. But are they achieving the objective?"

"Which is?"

"Getting siblings to understand what happened."

"I think it's pretty clear. If kind of grim. Attendance has dropped since the exhibits
were installed, except for when I pitch," he paused to make sure that sank in. "Chanting
the names of the 10/12 dead by the hot dog concession puts a damper on things."

"We still need that, otherwise there's no point."

Puppy frowned. "I feel like we're walking in a circle, Third Cousin."

Kenuda coughed slightly. "There's been some disquiet in the country since the Story."

"How so?"

He hesitated. "There've been demonstrations, minor, peaceful, but a few arrests.
Some actually not so peaceful. Orange wigs have been left at baseball stadiums."

"There are no ballparks left."

"At the rubble. Fenway Park, Wrigley Field." Elias consulted a list. "Braves Field,
Forbes Stadium, Phillies Field."

"The Miners are still around?"

"No, they're long gone. But Grandma's Story opened up the wounds again. Lots of Kill Allahs signs. Even a few murders of Arabic-complexioned siblings."

Puppy stiffened. "Why would baseball be blamed again?"

"Stop it," he said harshly. "Wigs have been left by government buildings, schools, everywhere. It's not about baseball. "

"But it could be."

"You're not even mentioned in Grandma's Daily Greetings to the Cousins." As Puppy frowned, Kenuda explained, "That's the progress on the top priorities of the day. How to feed more people. Lowering the percentage of HG nature. More schools. On and on. Never a word about baseball."

"It's good to be invisible, I guess," he said with relief.

"I wouldn't know." Kenuda sighed. "This is about me, Puppy. First Cousin Cheng doesn't like me very much."

"That's hard to understand."

"Not really," Kenuda admitted wryly. "He won't authorize any further work until I come up with something with soul. Whatever that means."

"It's where you get tears in your eyes out of nowhere."

"I was never a DV. I wouldn't know."

"Your loss."

"Perhaps." Kenuda smiled faintly. "We're in this together, Nedick. If the season fails, I'll probably be reassigned duties."

"I'm toast either way."

"Maybe not." Elias paused. "Family revenues are tight. The lack of trade hurts. You didn't hear that from me. I could see that if attendance holds up, perhaps there'd be another season. Calm down. But I can't recommend anything if I'm not Commissioner."

Puppy went into the kitchen, taking a very long time to return with a cup of coffee.

"We need to tie everything together," he announced.

"Meaning?" Kenuda gestured impatiently.

"We have to make baseball more fun. Like it used to be. Really like it used to be. That'll bring fans in. Lots of them. Trust me."

"That's a line Cheng will never cross."

"He will if Grandma approves."

Kenuda swallowed. "The woman was nearly killed on 10/12."

"Right. Time for forgiveness."

• • • •

ANOTHER COMMUNITY CENTER Sour Fat Lady watched Puppy lay his pencils on the table as if that were a diversion so he and Frecklie could steal the folding chairs and table which dated back nearly forty years to the time of the last American president.

"Thanks for letting us use the space."

The woman made a mental note of the various Grandma Work Ethic posters, a calendar from 2083 and sketchy looking coffee cups in the cramped, little used basement, should it be necessary to file a Blue Shirts report.

Frecklie curled his lips and angrily gestured at her disrespect. She mimed a baseball being farted out of her wide butt.

"I'll have to try that pitch." Puppy grinned, sending the woman stomping up the steps like a hippo. Without asking if they were ready, she opened the door and the men and women shyly came down the steps, half-expecting really anything. There'd been no public announcements, of course, just Frecklie and his staff of forty-eight whispering around the DV.

A lithe man around fifty in a thin gray jacket bowed respectfully a few feet from the table and handed over his Lifecard.

"I saw you pitch, sir."

"Thanks and please don't call me, sir."

"You were in high school."

This was going to be so difficult, he knew. But options were limited. Kenuda had insisted he couldn't allocate any more upgrades; he'd already danced across a line by approving the exhibits, reseeding the field and painting everything along the lower levels. When Puppy approached Fisher and Boccicelli about reinvesting some profits into higher quality maintenance to spike the ticket sales and concession revenues, they'd twitched and moaned about their bottom lines. He'd mentioned the profit law requiring ninety-six percent to be plowed back into every business. Fisher had fired back that since baseball had been officially announced as dead, any profits went into escrow.

Get it from the bookkeeper, he'd smirked.

"You struck out twelve and pitched a complete game shutout," the man said proudly as if Puppy were his son. Yeah, my father never saw me pitch. He wouldn't go near the stadium.

"I'm too old to go nine innings anymore."

Frecklie tapped the paper for him to move off memory lane.

"Anyway, sir," Puppy said. "We need electricians, welders, those sort of workers."

The man waited.

"Money's small. It's not a secret we're doing this, communities coming together show how we love each other," he quoted Grandma's Twentieth Insight and the man made a face. "It's for Amazon Stadium."

The man brightened. "My kids can do that."

Puppy and Frecklie exchanged quick looks. "This isn't about the kids, Mr. Amelio. Unlike the other repairs, this is more complicated. The teens did a wonderful job." Puppy tossed Frecklie a nod; he'd sulked for a day. "But we need the grownups."

The line moved down until they filled the basement, staring open-mouthed.

"But, sir, we only work in the DV," Mr. Amelio said quietly in case BTs leaped out of the peeling walls.

"That's right. And the stadium's located in the DV."

The adults murmured, all of them thirty, forty, fifty, sixty years old, some even older. They'd spent much of their adult life apologizing since their only worth was their children. Except for a few remarkably resilient adults, honored on the vidnews for climbing back out of the DV, they'd long given up.

A slender youngish woman half raised her hand. "I wouldn't take the money."

That set off more murmurs of approval.

"Ma'am, we have to pay you…"

"No. Love can't be bought," she quoted Grandma's Thirteenth Insight. "Where are you getting the money for materials?"

Frecklie patted Puppy's right shoulder.

All the adults turned and tapped their neighbor's shoulders. Puppy had never seen this before. Once everyone was certain they'd tapped all the arms, they reformed a line and waited patiently to tap Frecklie's shoulder, then, almost with a religious air, tapped Puppy's right arm.

For that fifteen minutes, the ache in his shoulder vanished.

• • • •

DALE SHOOK HER blonde curls, making a tiny windstorm. "Will you stop looking over my shoulder?'

"You said you knew what to do." Puppy leaned his chin on a rusted rifle.

"I do, but this is really old shit."

The scoreboard console still had bullet holes on both sides but, miraculously, none of the fusillade had damaged the equipment. The five skeletons in orange wigs lying on their sides against the back wall had obviously taken much of the barrage.

Frecklie poked his head inside. "How's it going?"

"Get the hell out of here," Dale screamed and Frecklie obediently disappeared; he'd seen Dale's frustrated temper tantrums before.

An old man with a grease smeared face and dust balls in his hair crawled out from behind the console with a wrench. He nodded hopefully.

Dale gestured. Sure?

His next nod was a little less confident.

She made disgusted sounds and yelled, "Come back in." Frecklie popped back warily. "Tell them to turn on the breaker now."

Puppy looked out the window at the three distant figures hanging onto the front of the scoreboard in left center field. They'd spent the last ten minutes playfully swinging like monkeys from one end to the other; the other adults hammering away with their power drills on the upper decks waved back playfully.

"Do it, I said. The garage area breaker's working."

Frecklie went outside, hopping up and down with a series of loud whistles. The scoreboard shivered and Grandma smiled.

"It's still just Grandma," Puppy snapped.

"I can see that." Dale gestured moron-fool-twaddle brain. EDIT MAIN SCREEN flickered on her panel. SPORT danced onto the screen.

"Select baseball," Puppy said helpfully.

"Oh, really?"

Dale's deft fingers selected the sport, then adjusted the clock. 8:05 flashed on the scoreboard. The DV grown-ups on the scoreboard whooped it up. Ball, strike and outs features flashed, followed by the innings. The most beautiful zeroes Puppy had ever seen. He patted her shoulder.

"Don't touch me. I'm promised."

"Sorry." He counted his fingers. "Will we also have music?"

"If the file isn't corrupted. It's been ten years, yes?"

He cleared his throat. "Thirty-three."

That made Dale angrier. Honey, you better be real good in bed or the smartest person in the world because charm you ain't got.

"What's that?" Puppy pointed at a button marked video.

"Video."

"Yes, I can read. Can we see if it works?"

"It might not be online and that could take down the whole system," she said, protective of three hours of work, not including using blow torches to break through the rusted doors.

They had no time. Kenuda hadn't exactly said yes.

Puppy pressed the button.

The scoreboard trembled. Rasping music blared with an underwater muffled sound. One of the frightened adults jumped into the bullpen. As if disgorging something in its throat, the scoreboard gagged and red, white and blue lights streamed over the outfield. The last two DVs leaped.

A wild-eyed Mooshie HG in Yankee pinstripes rushed out waving a bat. "Come and get it, Cubbies." She clenched her groin and whirled toward a Cubs HG, brandishing a bat.

It's Albert Cheng, Puppy marveled. This must be from the 2065 World Series.

"You're getting yours, Lopez," the Cheng HG growled.

"By who?" Mooshie taunted.

"Me and my little friend."

The two HGs battled loudly, flying over the outfield, joined by more Yankees and Cubs bat-wielding HGs clashing to the garbled music. Now the HGs fought all over the stadium with bats the size of trees until only Mooshie remained, floating on a cloud-like mound, while Albert waved his bat back and forth, two Gods. Mooshie threw a ball which exploded into a monstrous white cloud.

"Welcome to the 20…"

Everything disappeared except the red, white and blue lights, which slowly faded.

"What happened?" Puppy cried.

Dale shooed him away. "It's old like you."

"But the scoreboard's working."

"For now."

"So that might blow?"

"She got it turned on," Frecklie said from the doorway.

"I know. But we need the HGs." He was greedy.

"Maybe it was just that corrupted program," Dale muttered.

"Can you create a different one?"

Maybe, she gestured.

Yes or no, he gestured back.

"Next time don't touch anything." Dale pointed a long red fingernail inches from his left eye.

"Next time make sure the work is done right."

Frecklie pulled away the flailing Dale. "She can do it."

"Good. DVs don't quit."

Dale swung the wrench at Puppy's head.

"Tell your sweetgums girlfriend we also need the music fixed. And the public address system." Puppy propped the skeletons in chairs, carefully arranging their wigs. "One last thing. We're not called the Hawks and Falcons anymore."

• • • •

MUSTAFA SQUINTED AT the silhouettes by their bed and grabbed a heavy metal ashtray from the nightstand; Jalak screamed. A Holy Warrior disarmed him while another turned on a light. They waited.

Azhar swallowed his heart, quickly dressing and assuring his wife hiding beneath the blanket that nothing was wrong. He followed the Warriors down the steps, nodding confidently to his sons on the top of the landing; Omar sneered as if this had always been a matter of time.

Azhar was still tying his shoes in the back seat because he would not allow himself to be beheaded barefoot when the black car pulled over to the side of the Maktoum Road.

He was steered by the elbows into the rear of a small truck where the Imam sat alone like a special delivery package. The Warriors closed the door.

"Azhar, my friend, good to see you." He indicated a folding chair. Mustafa shook his head, preferring to stand. He would not die on his knees, no matter what he had done. Abdul would be proud of him.

The Imam laughed. "Why the long face?"

"I have served the Caliphate and the Mufti and Allah to my fullest heart," he said.

"Yes, you have. Why else would you be here?"

Azhar glanced at the stone-faced guards. The Imam angrily motioned them out of the van. Once the door slid closed, he waited until Azhar wobbled into the seat. "An apology. This is all last minute, but the Son requires your help."

Mustafa hastily composed himself so he wouldn't look like a sniveling coward or a dim-witted fool, finally managing a brief bow. "Anything."

"Good." The Imam handed him a folder and knocked on the door, which quickly opened. The Guards helped him down. "The keys are in the ignition. Everything else is clear. You must leave now."

Azhar sat behind the wheel, reading until he heard the Imam's car pull away. He scanned the list of names once more, frowning.

Mustafa ignored all speed limits and safety considerations, getting to the orphanage in less than fifteen minutes. The children were gathered in the lobby, manacled together, eyes lowered, flanked by smirking workers.

"Finally, we can breathe without inhaling their filth," Ahmed said, nudging one of the boys with a stick.

Mustafa grabbed the stick and flung it away. "Is this all of them?"

Ahmed scowled and showed Azhar the matching list. Mustafa bounded up the steps and into the alcove. He knocked on the ceiling.

"Clary, come, we must leave." He repeated this twice, banging on the ceiling before risking a foot in his face and slipping aside the little door. He panicked and raced down the hall, opening doors, asking the remaining fearful children where Clary was.

He looked at his watch. Twenty-five minutes before the ship had to leave. He hurried down the staircase on the other side of the building, pausing at the sounds from the basement. Singing.

She was scooping up garbage with her bare hands, the rotten apple dropping from her mouth like a surprised dog.

"We must go," he said.

Clary backed away. He grabbed her arm and she kicked his shin. Azhar caught her taloned hand inches from his cheek. "You are going to America."

Her eyes widened suspiciously, searching for the trick. Finally she nodded warily. Mustafa tucked Clary under his arm and up the steps, dumping her in the lobby like a sack.

"This one, too," he gestured for Clary to be manacled.

Ahmed stepped forward. "The whore isn't on the list."

Mustafa twisted her scarred cheek from side to side. "Is she worth anything? Who would touch her? Ugly. And nasty." He poked Clary with the stick; her glare turned feral. "I will take her off your hands and, if there is a problem at the other end." He shrugged, allowing them to consider how he'd dispose of the body. "Now give me the keys in case I must unshackle the infidels for a beating."

Ahmed and his friends smiled, pleased. They helped Mustafa chain the kids inside the truck and he drove off on two tires, squealing onto the road. Children started crying in a symphony of fear.

"No tengas miedo, chiquitos," Clary said softly. "Vamos a America."

Slowly they quieted. Someone laughed cautiously, the whole truck, including Azhar, joining in. He suddenly stopped the van, their dread returning, but when Mustafa unlocked the chains, they burst back into happy chatter, rubbing their wrists and hugging each other.

Azhar flung the manacles into the bushes on the side of the road. The children cheered.

• • • •

MOOSHIE COULDN'T WATCH Kenuda's dreamy stare through the glass anymore without losing her place and forgetting the lyrics. She asked for ten and the musicians stretched, laying down their guitars and sax.

Kenuda shouted "Bravo" as she came out of the recording booth. "Sensational. I heard it all, thanks to this gracious young man." He acknowledged the sleepy-eyed sound engineer.

"Just laying down tracks." Mooshie sipped green tea and honey, sprawled on the couch in her dressing room.

Elias pulled up a chair and whispered, "Are the musicians to your approval?"

"Absolutely first-rate. Thank you again."

He clutched his heart as if it would break. "The *Dara Dreams* album will be a huge hit."

"It's called *Hills Over Hell* now. Thanks again, Elias. For someone like me starting out to get this kind of break…"

Kenuda pressed his finger to her lips; she flinched. "I believe in you, Dara. Those covers are brilliant," he referred to the Barton 3 *Wallow with Me*, Dylan's *Just Like a Woman,* John Griebel's *Father Time* and the Sunshine Cloud's *I Love You Immensely* cuts.

"Dara doesn't do covers. Dara brings her own unique quality." She paused shrewdly. "What'd you think of the Mooshie Lopez songs?"

308 | GARY MORGENSTEIN

He frowned. "Let's only use a couple until you've established yourself. It's an image issue."

Mooshie shook her head. "I got to take chances and stand out."

"Aren't there any other singers from that era?"

"None." She bristled. "Let's put those four songs on the back end, but push out *Bursting at the Seams* as a single. Then offer up Barton 3, Dylan, Griebel, Sunshine Cloud and Mooshie as a package to the radsynds."

Kenuda hesitated. "How about we use the song but list no credit?"

Mooshie darkened. "Out of shame?"

"She was a traitor, Dara. Her songs were banned."

Lopez spit into the cup, surprised but not. "Banned?"

"I took care of restoring them because I know how important that music is to you. I honestly don't understand why credits should be an issue…"

"Because artists shouldn't be screwed. She wrote the fucking songs, she deserves the credit. Look, if there's going to be a debate every time I want to record a song…"

"I never said that. I'm probably over-thinking." Kenuda's mind whirred so quickly his hair fluttered, resentment at Cheng's patronizing threats buried beneath Dara's beautiful eyes.

"Please." She pouted; he finally relented with a weary sigh. "Thank you."

"I'm very fond of you, Dara." The Commissioner squeezed her shoulder.

"How can you not be?" Mooshie carefully shook loose as the engineer announced the break was over. "Let's get back to work. guys. We're adding another Mooshie Lopez song."

Kenuda winced slightly. "Try to keep them at a minimum Friday night. You're singing at the Stanton."

"Where's that?"

His eyebrows knitted. "You haven't heard of the Stanton? It's on the Grand Concourse. It's a fabulous new club."

"Prestigious?"

"Very. The usual open doors, which means Grandma might show."

"Grandma."

Elias cupped her trembling chin. "If you're not ready for that, we can reschedule."

"Oh no. I'm ready for her."

• • • •

THE DISTASTE OF the scowling large men for the orphans could fill a mosque during Ramallah. Azhar kept them by the bow, put the pilot on automatic and handed the food out to the children. They lined up patiently, holding out their plastic bowls, then sat quietly at the rear of the large, sturdy ship, afraid to talk, make eye contact, or comment even silently on the vegetables swimming in a greasy red sauce that had long ago overwhelmed the rice.

Except for Clary, who tapped Azhar on the shoulder and pointed at the open, un-ending sea.

"Three hours, maybe." He held up three fingers and she smiled. Azhar made room on the seat, but she shook her head. No, my little one, I would not touch you, he wanted to cry at her fear. Crusaders were known for cunning sexual practices. Harlot nuns, rapacious priests. Grandma had many lovers, including women. Homosexual perversions were common. How would this child, these children survive?

Better than in the Caliphate, his thoughts shamed him. No. Not shame. Anger. He glared at the three mute men holding rifles.

Touch one of them and I will kill you.

Three hours turned into just over four, five, the seas swirling, the children asleep, crawled into little balls, hands around each other. Only Clary stayed awake, her head drooping, worried the ship would turn into a prison and the guards would rip off her clothes. Finally she slumped, exhausted with hope, in the corner.

A light flickered in the distance, once, twice. Azhar rapped sharply on the center console, alerting the men. They re-checked the rubber dinghys attached starboard and port. Azhar signaled back to the other ship three times. He turned off the engine.

The orphans woke with a collective uneasiness, tightening their circle, fearful little animals. Clary whispered gently, rubbing a few heads and handing out water, which they greedily gulped. The large boat, probably a sixty-five footer, ambled forward, stopping a quarter klick away.

Say nothing, he'd been told, orders he didn't care for. What did these people look like? The ship was not the American Navy. No markings, not even a name, number. Nothing to identify them. Neither was his ship, he shuddered, unease deepening. Azhar glanced back at the orphans, standing and holding hands, Clary in front, hands on hips, waiting. His children who he'd never see again.

Perhaps this wasn't a good idea. Americans are pigs. You should've let me hide Clary, Azhar thought sadly in the direction of home. We always wanted a daughter. Fool, he grew angry. Too much sentimentality, these bastards are just Crusaders, infidels, the Caliphate is better without them, The Son is wise to send them off. Let their weak souls and perverted genes infect America. Our enemy. These children are our enemies, enemies of Allah, your wife, your sons.

The boat blinked twice. The large men dropped the dinghys into the water and lowered the children. Clary helped guide her friends down. She was the last to leave.

The folder with all the orphans' files tucked under her arm, Clary wiggled her fingers good-bye. Azhar sunk to his knees and held out his hands. Clary's face twisted in violent debate, eyes watering. Finally, she just nodded, wiggling her fingers for a last time and climbing over the side.

"Gracias, senor," she said, disappearing into the dinghy.

Diego's mouth dropped as the little boats pulled alongside.

"They're children," he said to Lee as if discovering fire.

"What'd you think they were?" The Captain jerked his head toward the coffins lined up in the rear of the boat.

"We're killing them?" Diego asked, his horror increasing.

Lee disgustedly shook his head at the boundless stupidity of his first mate and leaned over to help the children onto the boat. As they boarded, the youngsters' eyes locked onto the coffins. They were terrified.

Clary scampered up last, growling at Diego's outstretched hand. She swung her legs onto the deck in a slight crouch, looking between her orphans and the coffins.

"Que es esso?"

"Para esconderse de Allahs," Lee surprised Diego with the foreign response, directing the words to the group. The frightened children waited for Clary to answer. She nodded brusquely and opened one of the boxes, pulling out a tiny blue pillow which she shook mockingly; the orphans laughed nervously.

"Tienes hambre?" Lee gestured at sandwiches on a small table.

Clary cracked the air with her fist, stopping the children from chowing down. "Esperamos hasta llegar a Estados Unidos." She peered at Lee. "Sera abuela estar alli?"

"Finalmente."

The children murmured excitedly about meeting Grandma. Clary clapped her hands for quiet. The captain hesitated and gestured to the coffins. "Por favor, usted sera mas seguro."

Clary lifted each of the coffins and made a gesture of breathing deeply; Lee showed the air holes on the sides.

Diego finished counting heads and nudged Lee. "There are twenty-one of them, Captain."

The orphans tensed at the low suspicious whispering.

Lee bowed politely at Clary and pointed at the coffins. "Veinte." He waved at the orphans. "Veintiuno."

"Si." Clary pondered this and pointed toward the heavy tarpaulin in the corner.

"Excelente," Lee said, grinning.

Clary motioned for him to be patient as she guided each of the children inside the coffins, whispering gently as she closed the lids. She burrowed under the tarpaulin with a loud, contented sigh.

"That girl's gonna break a lot of balls and clits when she gets older." Lee laughed, poking Diego to get underway.

The Allah ship still watched them. Lee waved and received a wave back. Their engines eased into low gear and turned steadily north by northwest. He heard the Allah boat move in the opposite direction.

Lee passed Diego, still shaking his head.

"Where'd you learn Spanish?"

"Who was talking Spanish?" he raised his eyebrows in shock. "That's illegal, ain't it? Now get us rolling, we have to deliver the coffins back to Hayden's before sunset."

The Captain was deliberating over an AG chicken sandwich when the whirring of blades exploded overhead. Bullets riddled the deck, soaking the food with Lee's blood. Diego steered wildly away from the trio of black 'copters, but more bullets lacerated the ship, ricocheting into his side. He screamed at the children to stay in their coffins, but they popped up like dolls in an amusement park shooting gallery, falling in rows, draped over their wooden boxes.

"No!" Mustafa screamed at the flashing tracers and turned the boat around.

"What're you doing?" One of the large men grabbed the wheel.

Azhar whacked him in the forehead with a crowbar and headed directly toward the smoking Crusader ship. Hovering impatiently, the 'copters poured a last round into the slowly sinking vessel.

"Tarak hadhih almintaqat ealaa alfawr," bellowed a voice over the loudspeaker.

Azhar froze for a moment before his rage melted all reason. He continued forward at top speed. The 'copters fired five feet in front of the bow. Azhar veered to the right and both large men flung him across the ship.

"Assalamu alaykum, assalamu alaykum," the men cried, waving their arms pleadingly. The 'copters deliberated before firing a few rounds well off starboard and merging back into the clouds, leaving only the sound of their fleeing ship's engines, Azhar's sobs and something that could've been the wail of a dying child.

29

On August 5, 2073, the day World War Three ended, Grandma met the Grand Mufti at the Louvre to sign the Truce, insisting on a private ceremony to preserve some dignity. The Mufti had insisted on the site of the Martyrs Slaughter on the Rue de Rivoli, where National Front partisans had executed and burned more than two thousand Allah children.

They compromised on a quiet spot in the Tivoli Gardens. Just the Mufti, his mob of smiling black-robed murderers, herself, Cheng and Tomas. The terms were harsh: America and the protectorates of Canada and Mexico isolated on all sides, no foreign trade, no remilitarization, the United States could keep its nuclear stockpile, the little left after the unilateral disarmaments of the 2030s and 2040s.

The round table was populated by a tea pot and a few cups. Cheng and Tomas stood off, flanked by the Holy Warriors. Grandma moved slowly, as if hoping somehow the Atlantic and Mediterranean and Pacific Fleets would rise from the depths, captained by a zombie Navy, the sky would blacken with the Air Force and the beaches would part and Tomas' many friends would climb out of their graves and this unthinkable loss would turn into a mere nightmare.

All she had left was the pen to sign The Truce. The Surrender. Cheng looked sick, Tomas stoic.

"Let us hope our peoples can live in peace now, Allah willing." The fat Mufti, who looked like a rotting Jack-o-Lantern, had smiled through his blackish teeth.

Grandma scribbled her name. Her face hardened and she flung the pen aside, grinding it beneath her sturdy shoe. Tomas figured he could take out about five Warriors and hoped Cheng could handle the other two. Grandma could easily disembowel the Mufti if it came to that. A last temporary victory.

But the Mufti merely sneered with the graciousness of the victor and handed the broken bits of pen to Grandma with a chivalrous air. "Your souvenir, Grandma."

Not since that day had Tomas seen the hatred return. He was relieved. Maybe some sense was right behind.

"Should I continue?" Tomas held up the report.

Grandma nodded sadly and curled up a little tighter on the couch in her private study, tiny with bright purple rugs and cheerful paintings of children and families.

"The Coast Guard encountered the first debris at approximately 2200 hours…"

"How long after?"

"The rendezvous with the Allahs was scheduled for 1400 hours."

"Could there have been survivors if they'd received help immediately?"

"We couldn't chance any official presence," he stiffened.

Leonora pursed her wrinkled lips. "We should've had some ships in the area as backup."

"That wasn't the deal." The twenty orphans had been released by Abdullah as a sign of good faith in the peace process.

"And this was?" she rasped.

Tomas held his breath. When you deal with the Devil, he thought carefully. She nodded for him to continue.

"The bodies of the twenty orphans were all recovered."

She stared hard. "Were they abused?"

He shook his head. "Just murdered."

Grandma's eyes fluttered. "What were the ages?"

"Is that really necessary?"

Grandma's stare cut across the top of his head, making him queasy.

"Eleven girls, nine boys," Even though he'd memorized the report, he faked reading just to avoid her stare. "Ages six to twelve from various parts of southern ME."

"Give me some histories," she whispered.

He didn't have to read these. "Deloras Villafane, seven years old. Her parents were part of the Resistance. She was given a hysterectomy to ensure she didn't breed." His voice broke. "All the girls were given hysterectomies."

Tears slid down Grandma's cheeks. "What where their names?"

"Lenora…"

"I want their names," she said harshly.

Tomas flung aside the folder. "Read them yourself. I won't torture you. That you can do."

Grandma read aloud all twenty names, stumbling over pronunciations, then tossed the file into the fireplace and watched it quickly burn.

"What about the crew?" she asked over her shoulder.

"They retrieved the Captain's body." He paused. "But not the first mate."

Grandma whirled. "Where is he?"

"I'm sure he'll be found…" He paused. "Unless the Allahs took him prisoner."

"Why would they do that?"

"Because they're animals."

"That doesn't explain everything, Tomas. Though I wish it did. Make sure Admiral Tiridad clamps down on the Coast Guard. We can't afford any leaks."

"I already did." Tomas hesitated. "Captain Lee has no family I'm aware of, but Diego Vasquez, the missing sailor, had left a contact in case of emergency."

"No one's to know, Tomas," she said sternly.

"His family will worry…"

"I said no and that's a damn order. Get word to Abdullah."

He smiled malevolently. "How about something very simple like go fuck yourself, you filthy Camel."

"This tragedy doesn't change our plans. He wouldn't have done this. There was no reason. He had nothing to gain. Nothing," she said as if trying to convince herself. "These were rogues, people from his end who want the negotiations sabotaged."

His mouth dropped. "What the hell are you talking about?"

Grandma slapped him hard on both cheeks. "Never forget yourself, Major. And never forget I decide the future of this nation. Take a couple days off. You're worn out and no good to me."

• • • •

314 | GARY MORGENSTEIN

HER APOLOGY FLASHED on his beeper during the second round when he changed from beer to whiskey: "I'm so sorry. You know I can't do without you. Sleep well, my darling."

Tomas had this theory about apologies. That it's all well and good for someone to say they're sorry, but the apology doesn't wipe out the original blast. It wasn't like some demon had taken hold of you. Whatever you said was inside. Maybe you regretted it. Maybe because it was wrong or because it hurt someone's feelings or hurt you, in some way. But you said it. You meant it at that time and that time is what we are, strung together. Reflection's a waste of a breath, left in the past, lost.

He paid for the drinks and hailed a cab outside Monroe's; the place hadn't changed in thirty years. The ride uptown dragged on through the endless traffic and he jumped out at Ogden Avenue, closing the distance quickly on foot.

The woman answered sleepily on the second buzz, coming alive when he said Diego sent him.

"Can I get you something?" the chubby black girl asked.

"I'm fine, Ms. Jones." He took in the messy, well-thought-out apartment filled with colorful art hanging on walls, sketches taped to mirrors, all different styles; the girl changed her mind a lot.

She smiled as he scanned the living room. "You like art?"

"Don't understand it, ma'am."

"Zelda."

"Zelda. I still don't understand it."

"That's the great secret behind art." She playfully pressed her lips. "No one does. No one ever did. All this great parade of endless bullshit when all the artist cares about is displacing some pain."

He shrugged politely.

"So Diego sent you with some message?" Zelda offered him cookies. When he declined, she nervously stuffed one into her mouth.

"I don't even know him."

Zelda laid down the plate and pulled a razor from her slipper. "Who are you?"

He squeezed her wrist and kicked the falling blade across the room. "I had to get inside. Sorry. I'm afraid there's been an accident."

"With Diego?"

Tomas hadn't played out the story. Too damn angry. Or drunk. "There was an event at sea. The ship sunk and Diego's dead," he said flatly. Show emotion and it only deepens their hurt.

"Dead." The word tasted horribly. "Are you sure?"

Tomas nodded. Either he's stuck at the bottom of the ocean or camel appetizers by now.

Her fingers dug into his forearm. "Sunk how? What about his body? What was he doing?"

"I've nothing more to say. Again, I'm sorry for your loss."

She yanked his arm as Tomas turned to leave. "Or you can't say? That's it. Diego was doing something secret."

"He told you?"

"He's the father of my fucking baby. Are you with the government? The Black Tops?" Zelda sniffed to find his identity.

"Listen to me." Tomas held Zelda's face very tightly. "Diego listed you as his next of kin. Obviously you meant something. I did you a favor by letting you know. Now forget this visit for your sake and the sake of your child."

"He has a mother, sisters..."

Tomas tugged his right earlobe and shook her roughly. You deaf?

Zelda stumbled on numb feet into the cold night without a jacket, just a thin red scarf she'd been using as a cleaning rag. She munched on the last of the Della's Super Crunchy Chocolate Chip Cookies, pieces toppling out of her pocket like a trail leading down Jerome Avenue. She frowned at the midnight crowd, noisy, clamoring siblings hopping up and down as if the ground were too hot to stand on.

Zelda clung to the rear of the crowd as the barking neared. Confident pugs marched across the wide avenue, their perked ears waving back, flared snouts sniffing happily. At the midnight whistle, children ran forward, hugging pugs, rolling on the ground, feeding them treats, throwing balls; who was happier was hard to tell.

A fawn pug raced in circles near Zelda. She scooped up the squirming dog, kissing its cool fur. A couple children flanked her, gesturing to let the pug down so they could play. Ugly children, Zelda thought. Sneering ugly children tugging on her jeans. Zelda tightened her arms around the pug and the children complained to their parents. Sneering ugly stupid parents all happy with ugly children outside at midnight trying to steal one more thing from her.

She ran through the crowd with the pug, who settled down, enjoying the ride and the air fluttering on its face. People shouted and pointed. Zelda made it as far as one block, telling the pug not to worry, she knew shortcuts, this was her neighborhood, she grew up there, Puppy grew up there, Pablo grew up there, Mooshie grew up there, her dead boyfriend grew up there.

The Blue Shirt gently held her arm; this was not the first time someone tried running off with a pug.

"C'mon, ma'am, give me the doggie."

She kicked his shin and managed another half a block before she was surrounded by three stern Blue Shirts. Zelda flailed helplessly at the air, leaping from one foot to the next as the pug climbed onto her shoulder, barking. "He's mine. Please, he's mine."

The Blue Shirts carefully took the pug. Zelda held onto the old black metal light pole, beyond crying, just needing something to hug. She abruptly grabbed one of the Blue Shirts, who kindly patted her back. She never knew loneliness could hurt so much. Maybe because she'd gotten so used to it.

• • • •

THE NAMES OF each of the players were written neatly on the top of the boxes stacked in the center of the clubhouse; Frecklie had checked four times to make sure they had the right names with the right sizes.

Mick was the first to snatch a box, a wide grin traveling in a semi-circle around his head.

"They moved Christmas to the summer, too?"

"You could say that."

Mantle grunted and sat in front of his locker. Slowly the rest of the team searched for their names, quietly unwrapping. Vern was the first to cry out.

"Look at this." He danced around the clubhouse with the pinstripe top. "Number eight?"

Puppy smiled. "Also worn by Yogi Berra and Bill Dickey, two of the greatest Yankee catchers of them all."

Players shouted out their numbers as if they'd won a contest: 1, 2, 3, 4, 5, 6, 9, 10.

The owner of number 7 was very quiet, turning the uniform over and over again.

"What do you think, Mick?" Puppy sat beside him.

Mantle shook his head back and forth in disbelief. "Never thought I'd wear it again."

"Life's amazing, especially when you throw in death."

Mick smiled that illuminating boyish smile. "I got another chance."

"You ain't screwed it up yet."

"Leading the fucking team in homers," he grumbled.

"And RBIs." Puppy clasped his shoulder. "Go on, see if it fits."

"Why wouldn't it?" Mickey spent a few minutes sucking in his stomach to loop the black belt.

Ty stomped out of his locker in his Yankee pinstripes, dampening the enthusiasm of the room. "Whose goddamn idea was this? Oh wait, I hear a voice. Could it have been my star pitcher who thinks his crap melts in your mouth because he struck out ten worthless pieces of shit last time?"

"Yes, skip."

Cobb pressed his nose into Puppy's throat. "You gave me a Yankee uniform?"

"Yes, skip. 'Cause we are the Yankees again."

Mickey pounded his bat against the locker and the team whooped it up. Ty cut out their tongues with a glare, returning to Puppy.

"I hated the fucking Yankees."

"I know. Success breeds envy."

Mickey snickered.

"I don't want to be a Yankee. I want to be a Tiger. That was my team."

Puppy leaned forward. "Maybe someday they'll come back."

"Yeah, along with banks and white people." Ty scowled around the clubhouse. "And what about this number?"

"Thirty-seven. Casey Stengel. Great Yankee manager."

"I know who he was and that clown couldn't hold a candle to Joe McCarthy." Ty fingered the sleeve. "Is this real cotton?"

"As close as we'll get."

Cobb grunted at the silent, anxious team. "Are you all happy with your little stripes and numbers like you're in a fucking prison?"

They all nodded happily about their little stripes and numbers.

"Then say some thanks, you goddamn heathens. Down."

Ty knelt and the team eagerly followed, clasping their hands and closing their eyes. Puppy suddenly realized they'd been praying regularly.

"Lord Jesus, thank you for these uniforms even if Puppy Nedick thinks he did it. We appreciate what you've done working with what you got, which ain't much. We ask you to help us out and make us," Ty paused, pained by his own prayers, "make us worthy to wear these uniforms of real major leaguers. Amen."

The team mumbled amens.

"All right, assholes." Cobb kicked over a stool. "Show me what you got."

As the players headed toward the dugout, they mouthed thanks to Puppy.

Batting practice wasn't much since the two teams spent most of the time examining each other's uniforms, the Cubs *nee* Falcons proudly showing off their navy blue colors. Ty angrily separated the teams, though every time he turned away, he smiled like a four-year-old swimming in a bowl of chocolate pudding.

Since Lydia was pitching today, Puppy wandered down to the bullpen to loosen up his stiff arm. Frecklie waited with a catcher's mitt by the back row of skeletons.

"Can't we ever move them?"

"Not yet." Puppy said, soft tossing. He jerked his head toward the stands. "How's Miss Cuddly?"

Frecklie sighed. "She told me she'd slice off my testicles if I bothered her."

"I love the tender mating rituals of young lovers."

"She's really sweet, Puppy. Except when stressed."

"I have faith in your judgment, kid."

The boy blushed. "Thank you. That means a lot."

Puppy twirled around to show off Mooshie's number 88 on his back. "Thanks for getting Beth to do this."

"She wants me to be happy, sometimes."

"Your Mom's talented."

The boy frowned again, figuring out the notion of being proud of his mother. Frecklie squatted behind home plate and Puppy threw ten pitches, none of them close to the strike zone, all of them producing a wince.

Puppy slipped off his glove. "Maybe that's it for now."

Frecklie walked back. "How much does it hurt?"

"I just pitched a couple days ago. Probably should've rested…"

"Muscles should be stretched," Frecklie interrupted. "Not be in pain."

"You're a doctor now?"

"No, but my great-grandma is." He paused. "Didn't she help?"

Puppy's eyes narrowed. "You're not supposed to know about that. It's dangerous."

"So's everything we seem to do."

Puppy couldn't argue that. He stared at the new second level, adverts for Hal's Healthy Hot Dogs and Munchkin's Golden Ale flanking the Basil Hayden's Funeral Home sign on the first base side. Work continued on the upper level, jackhammers singing. Just a few more days.

"When are you going back to my great-grandma?" Frecklie persisted.

"It was only a one-time visit."

"You can't do acupuncture that way."

"You can if you'll go to jail."

Frecklie's anger grew. "Who said just once?"

"I did."

Frecklie threw down the catcher's mitt. Puppy sighed. "Your Mom. I appreciated even that much."

"She did it for me."

"I figured. Be thankful you have someone who loves you that much."

Frecklie's eyes suggested he could do very well without such love. "You're going back to my great-grandma until your arm's better."

Puppy traced circles in the dirt; he didn't know why, maybe it was the simple closure of it all. "And lie to your mother?"

He snorted. "I do it all the time."

An HG demon soared overhead, severing Puppy's pulse for a moment. The demon swirled, firing exploding baseballs in all directions as the early arriving crowd, around twenty thousand, cheered wildly.

Puppy and Frecklie gingerly stepped into the outfield for a better look.

Hissing on its hooved hind legs, the demon cackled; Frecklie smiled, recognizing one of Dale's crazy late night voices. A dog in a Yankee uniform trotted over and sniffed disdainfully, growling; the howling demon fired more fiery baseballs.

The Yankee dog ducked and grew bigger and bigger, barking loudly, deafeningly, joined by the fans. The demon covered its ears. The Yankee dog threw its own baseball which smashed into the demon; the incinerated remains flew all over the field.

The dog puffed its chest and became Puppy with canine features.

"Do I look like that?" Puppy cringed.

Frecklie nodded.

WELCOME TO OUR HOUSE dangled in the air. The crowd roared as the show ended. In the control room on the second deck, Dale took bows, blonde curls flapping in all directions.

"You're going to marry her, aren't you?" Puppy asked.

"Sure." Frecklie's eyes glistened.

He gave the boy a long look. Hey, friends tried talking you out of Annette, too. But none are so blind as those who get sex regularly.

• • • •

THE IMPERIOUS A8 librarian bulged its round metal eyes and returned Pablo's Lifecard. "This does not say you are a Cousin in training."

"It says I'm being considered."

The 'bot shook its head. "Considered, is not is."

"I already have a mentor."

"In waiting."

"Do I look like the type of person who fails?"

The robot wanted to answer all humans are failures, but carefully shrugged. "I can only give you access to which you're entitled."

Pablo followed the A8 down a long silver corridor into a small airless room, where he was set up on a laptop. The robot signed him in and stepped back.

"You're limited to dentistry through the ages and attendant themes such as health and nutrition." The sneer was difficult to miss as the 'bot waved the synced pass card for Pablo's clearance and quietly closed the door.

Pablo set out his notebook with two pens and three pencils, wondering where the cameras were as he slipped off his jacket and rolled up his sleeves. He ignored the beeping patient calendar reminding him that Maxine Duong was scheduled for an eleven AM check-up and put the lucky marble near the pens, searching the year by year list of new restaurants in the Bronx since 2030, finally locating Needleman's; there'd been no new restaurants since 2085. Wanting to protect the existing restaurants, overwhelmingly family-run, Grandma made opening new ones especially difficult.

Clicking on the link took him to a dully colored page, Needleman's. Food You Know. Established 2036. The waiter was right about that. Pablo scrolled through the familiar menu. Hot and cold sandwiches. Soups of the day. Desserts. Black and white cookies, of course.

None of this food, in its original form, was available anymore, Pablo thought, looking at a handful of pictures from the gallery. With rare exceptions, farming had turned to genetically engineered foods. How did you make genetically engineered pastrami, he wondered. He shrugged, figuring you could if you could, but something didn't sit quite right.

The bakery, for instance, where they got the "mouth-watering" rugelach, whatever that was, was in Manhattan. Maybe bakeries had returned to downtown New York. He cross-checked and didn't find any new bakeries in Manhattan since just before the attack in 2072. Maybe this bakery had somehow survived. By transporting mouth-watering rugelach every day through Manhattan to the Bronx when few people ever crossed the border?

Frowning, Pablo rolled the marble around his palm. And the knishes. Also from Manhattan. He checked Yonah Shimmel. Closed. He grunted. Hard to get the best knishes in the world from a place which didn't exist anymore.

He leaned back, thinking, then clicked on Who Are We. Needleman's Inc., 2034, but there wasn't a link. Pablo finished making notes and waited for the A8 to return.

"Find what you wanted?" The A8 leaned over to sign him out.

"Almost." Pablo could feel the robot shuddering at the rare touch of a human hand on its body. Not quite forbidden, but there better be a damn good excuse for a human manhandling a robot. Pablo slowly withdrew his fingers from the 'bot's wrist. "I need to look up a business."

"If it's within your clearance."

"It's a restaurant, nutrition for The Family."

Pablo turned up his hands innocently and gave the robot the name. He stood in the corner while the A8 checked. The 'bot returned, disappointed; it preferred to be helpful. Unlike humans, it needed a purpose.

"That's coded."

"Sorry?"

"The original business license is security coded."

"But it's just a deli."

"Since it's security-coded, I can't explain that."

Pablo smiled disarmingly. "You're so knowledgeable. There must be only finite reasons for a restaurant being coded."

The A8's eyes revolved; the human was in need of assistance. "Theoretically, either the contents or the personnel would require security clearance."

"In your estimation," Pablo bowed respectfully, "would deli food fall under that category?"

"Unlikely since this was before the extensive crop damage beginning in 2061."

"So it'd be the personnel. Were any of the workers Jew refugees requiring special attention?"

"The workers are all native born."

Pablo frowned. "Your thoughts and insights then? Purely theoretically, of course."

The 'bot's eyes settled squarely on Pablo. "Theoretically, the workers might not be human."

"What would they be?"

If the 'bot were allowed to have a face, it would be sketched with pity at this inferior lifeform. "They could be part of the early A1 class. Theoretically, of course."

• • • •

AZHAR PRODDED THE burning sock with a stick. Each night since coming home, he'd torched another piece of clothing from the bag hidden behind the washer in the basement, innocently adding them to the trash fire in the backyard. The black socks were the last; he was so intent watching the smoke curl around the dancing embers that he didn't hear the shouts from the house.

Still holding the blackened stick, Azhar rushed in through the kitchen as Omar shoved past the white-faced Jalak up the staircase.

"You can't leave," she yelled.

They glared at Azhar, approaching in bewilderment.

"What's going on?" he asked hoarsely

Omar fled into his room while Jalak slammed their bedroom door in Mustafa's face.

"What's going on?" His loud knocks were answered by crashing glass and Jalak's wailing moans and prayers.

His sons' room was filled ceiling to floor with religious artifacts, quotations from the Quran, three crescent moon and star flags and the ubiquitous five-foot high Fazat Allah victory poster of the Grand Mufti, crushing the map of Europe beneath his foot. In the corner, Abdul huddled on his bed as if an overnight guest, a few color photos of Club Madrid football star Said Abdella taped over his pillow.

From his bed, Omar stared at Mustafa with pure hatred; he thought of Clary, as if he ever stopped.

"Talk," Azhar said sternly.

Omar turned away in disgust. Azhar gestured for Abdul to wait outside. The boy shook his head, glaring at his brother.

Finally Azhar stepped toward Omar. "I said talk."

The boy clenched his arms around his knees, scowling. "It is the Holy Warriors."

"Isn't it always?"

He sneered. "I have been ordered to live at the Martyrs Home."

322 | GARY MORGENSTEIN

"Why?"

The sneer twisted deeper. "Why else? To continue my education."

"Is that common?"

"No," Abdul called out. Azhar silenced him with a look.

"Is that true?" Mustafa turned back to the eldest boy.

"In certain cases," Omar said slowly, carefully gathering his words as if reading off a prepared page. "In certain cases, where the student's home is not suitable."

Azhar blanched. "Are those bastards saying your parents…"

"Parent." Omar stood. "Mother is a faithful woman. You are not suitable, Father. I will be infected with your weakness and heresy. I cannot open my heart and mind to Allah while living here. Your sins are many."

"Sins? I've always obeyed Allah."

The boy's face curled in disdain. "I leave in the morning."

"The hell you do. I don't permit it. Do you hear me?" he thundered.

Omar frowned, genuinely puzzled. "That is not your decision anymore."

Azhar shook him roughly, hoping the madness would fly out of Omar's ears, lips, head, ass, crawl out from beneath his toenails. But the boy kept shaking his head with smug pity.

"I'm still your father." Azhar eventually released him and the boy toppled onto the bed.

"I obey Allah. He loves me."

"You stupid little shit. How do you think he dispenses His love?"

Omar flinched.

Following Azhar out the door, Abdul scowled disgustedly at his brother and grabbed his pillow, draping the blanket over his shoulder and walking silently down the steps into the living room. He bundled himself on the couch, snacking on pistachio ice cream with his father before collapsing with surprisingly loud snores.

Azhar fell asleep in the armchair, leg draped over the arm, toes brushing his son's curly hair, wondering what he believed in.

30

Clary managed a few last drops of spit which she rubbed on the man's caked, white lips. That was it, she was out of saliva. Two days on the dinghy and she had no water left in her body. Even her eyeballs were dry; she shielded herself from the faint late sun.

The man moaned. At least he wasn't dead yet. How was she not dead? The bullets had torn into the tarpaulin, missing her on all sides. When they were done shooting, she'd waited a long time before crawling out onto the deck of the sinking ship. She kicked a few of the bodies to see if anyone was alive, but if they were, it was just barely and what could she do for them anyway.

She had to get off the ship and somehow, in the way she was somehow alive, one of the rubber boats was still floating. She hopped over the bodies and started down the side when the man moaned again in English.

What could she do for him? Except he was a sailor and maybe he'd know how to get the boat somewhere. Clary had dragged the man, bleeding from his stomach, along the deck, stopping to clear a path by shoving aside the dead orphans. The man helped a little, pushing along on a knee and an elbow, but it was really all her.

Getting into the rubber boat was something else. She wrapped her arm around his waist and tried lowering them together, but her hand slipped and they fell into the boat, where she lost her right shoe.

He'd nearly rolled into the ocean and she thought about letting him sink; she could probably figure out which way to go. But he had such a sad look. As they floated away from the disappearing ship, Clary pulled out an oar, stuck to a dead boy's leg, and began paddling.

The man shook his head and pointed toward the setting sun, giving a direction. West. He had a nice smile, kind of like her cousin Pedro. Whatever happened to him, she wondered. Maybe Pedro was also wondering whatever happened to her. What really ever happened to anyone she knew.

When Clary got tired of paddling, they drifted. The sailor tried helping but he was pretty bad. They went in a circle once and they both laughed. That's when she worried she would die because you shouldn't laugh at a time like that. Maybe because they had no water or food and her mind was grubby and her clothes were ripped and wet and stained with his blood and she couldn't stop shivering. That's when he gave her his thin jacket.

She tried fixing his wound, thinking about what the Allah nurse did at the orphanage, but she had no medicine and knew better than to use sea water and besides, every time she touched his stomach he groaned, which scared her. Better just let him go quietly to Jesus. She didn't know if she could eat him. Maybe if she had a fire but they were in the boat and how would she cut off his flesh anyway. Maybe if she somehow sharpened the oar, but she needed it to row.

She kept paddling until her shoulders screamed, trying to remember a song to sing but she couldn't; they landed at this beach. She'd dragged him to the tree line and then passed out. It was getting dark and the man gurgled and moaned, frightening her. She wanted to run but where and it didn't seem really right to leave before he died.

He tugged on her arm.

"Please," he whispered.

"Si." She had to say something.

He reached into his pocket and handed her a small black box. Her mother had lots of these with beautiful rings and necklaces and bracelets. She was supposed to get them when she was confirmed. But Jesus had gone somewhere else.

Clary took the box and smiled. The sailor found a pencil and a damp piece of paper. He scribbled an address, shoving that at her.

Address, box. "Si."

The sailor used his right hand as a mountain to show a big belly. She frowned. He pretended he was rocking a baby and she nodded.

He smiled weakly, gurgled, this time with blood dripping out of his mouth. He coughed and closed his eyes.

Clary sat with him for a few minutes until his soul went to Heaven. She kicked away her left shoe, pulled off the man's shirt and ripped long shreds. She yanked off his shoes, shoved the fabric inside and laced up his sneakers. They almost fit, she thought proudly. She should've taken one of the dead orphans' shoes, but she could only do so much.

She rolled him on his back and folded his arms; she'd seen her uncle in a coffin. Clary made sure the man's eyes were closed. She ran down to the beach, testing the sneakers, and returned with a handful of water; she wiped away some of the caked white from his lips. Clary said a prayer, crossed herself and hurried toward the trees.

She walked for a long time in the dark next to the tall trees. No cars or people passed. She almost fell asleep but it was cold and she made herself keep walking, otherwise she'd die. Clary remembered a song from the orphanage, "Grandma morte, estamos felices," and when her mouth hurt from thirst, she just hummed but had to stop because her throat hurt.

Near a clearing, a house blinked Burt's Motel in red lights. She squealed softly at recognizing el motel; she didn't care if none of the other words she'd seen along the road were familiar, because none of the signs were in Arabic. That's all that mattered.

A big man with a moustache stared from the open door.

"Yes?"

She hadn't figured out what she'd say. If all the signs were in English then they probably didn't speak Spanish. And how would she explain herself. With all the bullets and dead people, it was probably better not to tell the truth. Always was. Clary leaned weakly against the doorframe. She was so tired and thirsty and hungry.

The man kneeled and a woman with gray hair looked over his shoulder. She gasped.

When Clary woke, she was lying on a cot with a washcloth on her forehead. She fell onto the floor and crawled into the corner, alert and scared.

"Well what are you doing?" The woman laid a tray of soup and bread on the coffee table. "Come on, honey, don't be frightened. You been sleeping a while and it's time to eat. What's that, a growl? Come on."

Clary didn't trust the smile. She really didn't trust any smiles. She backed away, remembering how she got here. Stupido. Run.

She staggered and fell to her knees. The woman helped her back on the couch, rubbing her forehead.

"Where do you think you're going?" The woman sat her down firmly as if there was no way Clary was getting up without permission. "Now you eat."

She sniffed at the food and the woman clucked her tongue. Finally Clary took a bite. She had two bowls, all the bread and was working on some cookies when the man with the moustache came into the room.

"How is she?" he asked gruffly.

"Hungry." The woman rolled her eyes. "Thirsty, too. I'll get you more, honey."

While the woman went into the kitchen, Clary glared at the man in case he had any ideas about touching her. It hadn't worked in the orphanage, but maybe America was different.

"What's your name, girl?" the man asked.

Clary gripped the soup spoon and decided if he came near, she'd jam the handle into his eye.

"Don't you talk?" he frowned.

"Not if you ask like that, Burt." The woman returned with some cheese, which Clary quickly finished. Clary blushed, puzzled by the woman staring at her cheek. America was a Crusader nation. Why did she look so upset by the cross?

The man leaned against the wall, staring suspiciously, while the woman touched Clary's face.

"How'd you get the scar, honey?" she asked.

"Must be a believer," Burt said. "Jesus Christey?"

The woman shushed him, embarrassed. "Where do you live?"

She had to say something, but knew speaking Spanish would be stupid.

"Think she's from the fool school?"

"I don't know. They treat them well, but…" She fussed with Clary's tangled hair, sighing at her clothes, bruises.

"I don't want to get mixed up in this, Grace." He pointed at Clary's scar.

"Should we send her out in the middle of the night?"

"Let the police handle this."

Clary understood police. She pointed to her throat, waving her hands sadly.

"She can't talk," Grace said.

"I got it," Burt answered. "But she still comes from somewhere they do things like that."

Grace patted Clary's arm. "Let her sleep here tonight and we'll figure it all out in the morning."

Clary nervously shoved her hands into her pockets.

Burt suddenly leaned over. "What are you hiding, little girl?"

She bared her teeth, hissing softly.

"Lemme see."

She bit his forearm. He finally shook free with a pained howl and raised his fist. Grace pulled him away.

"Let her be," she snapped. "Poor thing's all messed up."

"That's why she shouldn't be here." Burt wiped away a trickle of blood.

"She's staying the night, Burt."

"Not until I see what she's hiding," he whined. "Could be a goddamn knife or religious spell or something."

Grace stared questioningly at Clary. "Show me what you got, honey. I'll give it back."

Sighing, Clary started putting the sneakers back on.

"And those ain't a child's shoes," Burt added menacingly.

"Girl, I'm talking to you." The woman wasn't so nice anymore. "You're not going anywhere until you show us what you got or we're calling the police."

She couldn't have police. She didn't like this ugly woman and this mean man who wanted to touch her. She handed over the jewelry box. The people's eyes went wide when they saw the diamond ring.

"Did I tell you?" Burt triumphantly held up the ring toward Grace. "Where'd you steal this?"

Her heart pounded. Americans were bad, too. The ring wasn't theirs. Wasn't hers either, but the sailor had given her the address of the fat lady and a baby.

"Mama," she shouted. "Mi Mama, mi mama."

She cried hysterically and the woman hugged her.

"Damn you, Burt Winston, it's the child's mother's ring."

"For Grandma's sakes, she's a thief."

"Does she look like a thief?"

Clary lowered her eyes, sobbing silently. Grace gave her back the ring while Burt watched skeptically.

"It's okay, honey. Put your mother's ring away." The woman led her into a small office and made up the cot with clean sheets and a blanket, then turned out the lights.

"Sleep well. No one's going to bother you."

The door locked. Clary slid into the bed, trying to remember the last time she slept on anything clean. She stunk and apologized to the sheets.

When Grace opened the office at eight the next morning, the window was open and the little girl was gone, along with the cigar box of petty cash from the pried-open top drawer.

"Burt!" she screamed.

• • • •

KATRINA STIRRED HER coffee around and around, sitting across from Zelda at the rear of the empty veggie burger cafe a few blocks from their office. "What're you going to do?"

"I asked myself that a million times in the past couple days. Like I have lots of choices?"

Katrina leaned forward. "You do."

"Wish I saw them. Put up with the Parents. Let them take it. Find my life again."

"You won't. You're never the same." She waited until the waitress refilled their coffee before continuing, "You think it's over but it's not. The baby's always inside. You're always reminded. You see families with children and you remember. All the bullshit they teach, finding your inner mother, it doesn't last. I hated the girls they gave me as pretend children."

"I wonder if we had the same ones? Pigtails."

Katrina laughed. "They all have pigtails. No. You're forever changed, Zelda. That's why I'm a bitch."

Zelda figured a little job security demanded she protest, even half-assed. "Who isn't?"

Katrina shifted her chair closer. "I took that other choice."

She felt a little queasy, which kept her big mouth shut for once.

"I never carried to term, Zelda. I would've killed myself. I was all alone, no family, the guy went screaming when I told him. I'd just started out my career and you know, for all the talk about no discrimination against unwed mothers, it's there. The looks, shame, what's wrong with you, can't you do your part, don't you know we're surrounded." Katrina shook her head. "A friend of mine knew a doctor who knew a doctor. I went in the afternoon, called in sick the next day, and was fine."

Zelda really wished she had some pie. Any flavor. "They just…"

"Yes. As easy as getting pregnant without the fun."

She'd only had fun with half of them. Three actually. What percentage was three sevenths? She thought of Diego, blinking back tears. "How'd you explain?"

Katrina pursed her lips. "An accident. It's easier than you think. They really don't want to prosecute women. It's a big bluff."

Zelda thought of all the street posters of pregnant women surrounded by adoring men and women. "But it's murder. Treason."

"And making you carry a baby which they're taking away is cruelty, torture. If Grandma loves us, why make us suffer? It's not like we used birth control. That would be treason. But we got pregnant. We let that happen and then they take away our child because we don't have a partner. There are no words for that."

Katrina edged closer; they could've been two lovers stealing a moment. "You say you fell. Then they file a report. You're watched for a while, for what, I don't know. Maybe that you're going to convince other women maybe."

"Aren't you doing that now?" Zelda asked quietly.

"No," Katrina touched her hand. "I'm helping a friend."

• • • •

MAISE CHU KEPT sighing as she stuck needles into his shoulder and back. Puppy tried relaxing, but he was scared and couldn't stop tapping his toes and drumming his fingers; finally she squished the back of his neck into the examining table. He lay still for a moment, concentrating on the flickering candles, but he got a headache. He tried calling out to Frecklie in the waiting room, but great-grandma's wrinkled steel fingers crushed his lips together. Silence was an enemy because it allowed him to think.

The numbness in his right fingers provided brief elation from the pricking pricking pricking until he realized he hadn't experienced numbness before and this time it wasn't going away.

He wiggled his fingers, swimming away from the panic. "I can't feel. Numb."

Maise smiled the blissfulness of someone who knows better.

"Frecklie," he shouted and the boy popped his head in the doorway, alarmed. "I can't feel my fingers."

Frecklie pointed to Puppy's fingers and his great-grandmother shrugged and jabbed another needle into his lower back, chattering away with a wistful air.

"What'd she say?"

"I don't speak Chinese."

"Does she gesture?"

The teen sighed helplessly. "She's really old. I think before there was gesturing and shorthand. Or maybe language."

Puppy laid his forehead on the examining table. Now his entire right arm went numb, which he explained to Frecklie in a calmly hysterical tone, which the boy related to Maise by dropping his arm lifelessly.

The old woman nodded sagely and left the room.

Frecklie held his hand until she returned and pulled out the needles. Feeling returned to his arm, buoying his spirits. Puppy spun his right arm in an arc; no pain. Wondrous wide movement. Curveball, sliders, sinking fast ball, bring it on.

"Thank you, Great-Grandma." Frecklie picked up on his relief. Puppy also bowed.

Great-Grandma made a sad face and shook her head.

"What's wrong with her?" Puppy asked him.

"I don't know." Frecklie held his palms up questioningly.

Great-Grandma stuck her thumb down.

"Is this some Chinese shorthand?" Puppy asked.

"I told you I don't speak Chinese."

"She's not talking, Frecklie."

Puppy took Maise's gnarled hands. "Ma'am, is my shoulder okay?"

Maise touched his shoulder and stuck her thumb down again, pursing her lips sadly.

"I think that's a no," Frecklie said.

"Oh, I didn't pick up on that."

Puppy mimed throwing, still no pain, and gave a thumb's up, grinning as if his sheer hopeful joy would make everything better. Maise twisted his thumb downward, eyes glistening. She kept shaking her head over and over.

Just to make sure they understood, Maise also twisted Frecklie's thumb downward.

• • • •

DALE NUDGED HIM with her yellow painted big toe.

"Are you going to read all night?"

"Just until we have sex again." Frecklie turned the page of the Hall of Fame book.

"So you're just screwing me in between reading the baseball book?"

Frecklie nodded, violating rule number one of Loving Dale: Never Ignore Her. Dale jabbed her sharp elbow into his rib. Sometimes she did this with real intent. Tonight he wasn't sure and he didn't have the patience. Puppy had been so upset he couldn't talk. Or wouldn't talk. Maybe he just needed to talk to someone his own age. Someone he thought could really help.

He jabbed the edge of the book into Dale's thigh and they wrestled a moment, finally kissing and screwing really quickly, which usually calmed her down for a few minutes. He went back to the Hall of Fame book, searching for an answer among the great pitchers while she pissed.

Returning, Dale dropped by his side, shaking the narrow bed in her narrow room, decorated like the set of an old-time Western with a saddle hanging on the wall and a row of black cowboy hats hooked over the bed. Dale put on a hat and pretended to shoot him.

"Will you stop? This is important." He held up the book.

"How?" Dale crossed her legs.

"I'm helping Puppy."

"What if he can't be helped?"

"He can," he said angrily. "Don't you have studying?"

"I know everything." Dale dismissed the first phase of her Reg exams next week, which would determine whether she could apply for computer engineering school.

"Everything?"

"In the whole world. I fixed the scoreboard, didn't I? And that was rusted shit stuff. I had to hack out three viruses." Dale played with her blonde curls. "Should I be a redhead?"

"No."

"You think I'd look ugly?"

"Yes."

She slapped him playfully. "What if I don't go to Bronx University?"

"Then don't. They have computer engineering courses at Bronx College."

Dale rolled onto her back. "What if I don't do either one?"

He tossed the book aside. "And do what?"

"I like what I'm doing at the stadium. I want to do more."

"What about next year? This is the last season."

"You said there'd be more."

"I hope there is," Frecklie said.

"You're going to be a baseball architect."

"If there's another season."

"Then I'll design the scoreboard show if there's another season," she said.

"What if there's not?"

"Then what'll you do?"

If Puppy couldn't pitch anymore, then there surely wouldn't be any more baseball.

"I want to get married, 'seminate and make demons fly, Rubie," Dale said softly. "I don't want to be with the damn Regs at school. I heard some of them talking at the game today…"

"There's Regs coming?"

She made a disgusted sound at his surprise. "Lots. They sat in the second level. They laughed at the game and said the players are fat and old."

Frecklie's jaw tensed. "You sound like my mother."

Dale tenderly kissed his shoulder. "She's not always wrong."

"You say that because she likes you."

Dale nodded.

He took a breath for courage. "You're taking the Reg test."

Dale sat up, glaring. "Are you giving me orders?"

"Yes because you're smarter than me and if anyone should go to college it should be you."

"I am smarter than you and are you saying you're not taking the exams?"

"Only if you will."

"Fine."

They shook hands. Dale played with his fingers, peering at the page. "He's ugly."

"Amos J'anos was a great pitcher for Cincinnati."

"Why?"

"Because he fooled batters."

"How?"

He sighed, annoyed because he didn't remember much of J'anos. "Read yourself since you're smarter than me."

Dale propped the book on her wonderful white thighs and he started getting hard again. "He was a failure in the beginning."

"Not if he was in the Hall of Fame." He went to take the book, but she crawled to the other side of the bed.

"His career sucked in the beginning because he couldn't throw hard."

Frecklie slid over, curious.

"He hurt his arm and they sent him to play with the rebels."

"What?"

"Miners."

"Must be the minors. They used to have them. Minor leagues for younger players to learn the game." He nearly fell reaching for the book as she danced away, laughing and reading.

"With the minors," she drew the word out into three syllables, "he learned to throw a knuckleball. Do you know what that is?"

He shrugged.

"Some baseball expert." Dale smirked. "It doesn't hurt the arm and he pitched until he was 56. How old is Puppy?"

"Close to that." He smiled. "Can I have the book back?"

"What do I get for it?" Dale rolled onto her stomach.

• • • •

TWENTY BODIES. TWENTY-ONE pairs of shoes. Cheng locked the small, stiffened black shoe in the lower drawer. Who are you, child, and where are you hiding?

This was overlooked, Admiral Tiridad had apologized. We miscounted in the rush to destroy the boat and the bodies.

What about the bodies of the sailors who found them?

Everything has been cleaned, First Cousin.

Except you, little one, he thought, hurrying to the underground security tram three levels below. Two Black Tops flanked him, Rochester machine guns casually draped across their thick pants. Eventually they surfaced beneath a clump of trees nestled in the northern sector of Van Cortlandt Park.

He chased the HG squirrels around the trees before another team of Black Tops arrived in an armored truck; they drove into a tunnel concealed beyond some stumps, running beneath the House.

More Black Tops left him inside Grandma's living room. He hadn't ordered this level of security since the war ended.

Grandma looked worn as she sat down with a distracted smile.

"Have you been taking the bio-vits?" he gently scolded.

"I must've forgot."

"Lenora...."

"Don't worry." Her smile faded. "I'll live to see a world where Muslim and American children play together."

His face tightened in disgust.

"Despite your qualms," she said.

332 | GARY MORGENSTEIN

"I've moved past that, Grandma. I only insist one last time that this meeting with the Son be HG."

She shook her head violently. "No. I can still feel the filth of his father's fingers on my palm. That has to be washed away, Albert. If I can't touch his skin, feel the warmth and the comfort of true partnership, a new real beginning, then…"

He imagined her in the same room with this Camel, shaking hands and giving away their country. Albert sighed. He glanced around for the cookies and tea. He couldn't remember the last time she'd forgotten to serve.

"Any ideas for where?" Grandma asked after a few more minutes of silence.

"I like meeting in Cuba." With a raised eyebrow, she indicated for him to continue. "Cuba's sort of forgotten after the Allahs violated the Truce and we drove them back, so in their arrogant minds, it doesn't exist. Their nearest base is Caracas, but intel says it's in bad shape. Rotting fleet, undertrained Marines. The whole Camel Latin American occupation is flimsy. Their forces can't try anything."

Grandma smiled. "We can actually defend ourselves somewhere? I thought it was all cardboard ships."

His mouth tightened. "You can be protected and rescued if need be given the nearness to Florida." And we have stashed some nukes in Miami you don't know about. But I prefer to save them.

She nodded, staring off. He cleared his throat to regain her attention.

"I know Tomas has handled this from the beginning," Cheng said.

"And he'll continue," Grandma said sharply.

"Of course. But given the need for cooperation with the military, it's imperative I participate fully."

Grandma's weariness deepened. "You want to contact Abdullah directly?"

"I need to be a part, is all I'm saying."

"Bringing you in could scare the Son off, especially after his people attacked our children."

"If it scares him off, how committed is he?"

She considered that, finally nodding. Grandma watched him fidget. "Is my First Cousin suddenly shy?"

"Never. Just careful." He took a deep breath. "I'm worried what'll happen here when you announce a real door has opened to Islam."

"People will be upset."

Upset. He stared, more worried than angry. She hasn't thought this through. Just show up on the vidnews and say all is forgotten, and Americans will rejoice. Forget the sullen parades, the cremated bodies, crippled men and women, childless families. Forget the smoke of Los Angeles and the ruins of Washington, the skeleton of Manhattan. Forget the shame. The thirteen million. Let's dance with the murderers.

Peace is not a real concept without victory.

Albert squeezed her thin wrist. "Lenora, they'll be more than upset."

"I've prepared them with the Story," she answered indignantly.

"But you need more."

She fluttered searchingly inside his mind. "Baseball?"

"Indeed."

Grandma walked away. She never did that. "Baseball, Albert?"

"They're up to twenty thousand a game, perhaps more."

Her eyes widened. "You told me there was just a few hundred fans…"

He shrugged, also a ltitle baffled. "It's hit a chord. The last season and all. Like a big party. They've even opened up the scoreboard. That witless Kenuda has managed to do something good for once."

"I'm glad you kept me informed," she said coldly.

"Because I knew your reaction."

Grandma conceded that with a nod.

"There's an opportunity for a theme."

"Baseball and revolution. Where've I heard that before?"

"No. Baseball and forgiveness."

Grandma stared into her hands, the sounds of 10/12 thundering in her mind. "You want me to publicly endorse treason?"

Some would call what you're doing treason.

"Forgiveness. We must move forward. Isn't that what this summit is about? Enemies can be friends. Why not our own people?" Grandma flinched. "Ironic how we're switching sides…"

"Yes, isn't it?" She frowned.

"I'm expanding on your vision, Lenora. You want me to support you, then let's really do this right. We can talk about this being baseball's last season and honor the memory of those who died and those who played…"

"Traitors."

"I was on that goddamn Cubs team that day, Grandma. My uniform was splattered with your blood. Don't insult me and the men and women who were true Americans."

Sighing, Grandma nodded slowly. "Go on."

"We've already restored some of Amazon Stadium with plaques and tributes…"

"Have you?"

"You've been busy. And I knew you wouldn't like this." You're not the only one who can keep things, he thought sullenly, easily brushing aside her mental probes.

"Can't you think of something else?"

"There is nothing else, Lenora. The incidents are rising. Abandoned churches were burnt down in Cincinnati and Atlanta, criminals shouting they were mosques. There were protests in Kansas City, San Francisco and Minneapolis against the Story. Parents have pulled children out of the school districts where you introduced the new curriculum. They're calling you a liar."

"Once the education plans fully phase in…"

"Hate always trumps education, Lenora."

"That goes against everything I believe…"

"Which doesn't change the facts, damnit. We can't make this reality into a pretty little hologram. Over a thousand people have been murdered since the Story because they looked like Allahs."

Grandma was horrified, slumping into her thick chair. "Why do they always…"

"You really ask why?"

"I must try." Grandma activated a small vidmural of children splashing in a pool, silently watching. "Do you really think baseball could work?"

"Baseball fans were the cesspool of resistance, the sewer of nostalgia for the days of the American Empire. Embrace that base with your public approval and we're building the foundation for peace."

"You sound like you suddenly believe in this summit." Grandma patted his cheek, while quietly searching his thoughts.

"If you believe in something, then I do."

"You've always been there for me, Albert."

His eyes watered. "Yes I have, Lenora."

They kissed tenderly on the lips.

"I assume you have a plan as always?" she asked.

"You might not like everything." She grunted. "But we have the perfect role model. Actually, two perfect role models."

31

In the corner of the empty shadowed playground on Clay Avenue, Frecklie peered over Puppy's shoulder at the open Hall of Fame book. Puppy tapped the side of his head with the ball to teach his brain to grasp the concept, flipping the pages over and over; Frecklie squatted, catcher's glove sadly perched on his head.

Five knuckleball pitchers in the Hall of Fame and not a single word of advice. Dancing faintly in his memory was the notion that a knuckleball was not thrown with the knuckles. Frecklie had strongly disagreed, being sixteen and still believing in such ideas as words meaning what they said.

Puppy'd tried pressing the ball against his knuckles while his right thumb provided a foundation, but the pitches just flipped up apologetically or darted left and right; if baseball were redesigned with a moving batter's box, maybe it'd work.

There had to be a simple answer somewhere. That was why people once had the world wide web, he realized, if only it hadn't offered tips such as how to make enough chemicals to destroy Manhattan.

Frecklie pointed again at the photo of J'anos' winding up. "Fingers into ball."

Hoyt Wilhelm and Phil Niekro and Tim Wakefield and Kendall Atkins and Amos J'anos and now Puppy Nedick. And your other option is what, exactly?

Frecklie trotted a few feet away, pounding the glove.

Puppy waved briskly. Too far.

The boy fluttered his fingers on his chest. Too much pressure?

Puppy angrily motioned him further back and dug at the concrete, emulating a mound. Using two fingers digging into the ball, he threw ten feet over Frecklie's head. A slender little old man seemingly came out of the ground to grab the ball.

"What're you trying to do?" the man asked.

Even thirty feet away, the gruff voice was unmistakable. Puppy tipped forward in a neck bow, nudging the baffled Frecklie to follow. Cheng walked over, flipping the ball with a loving smile. Frecklie kicked the book under his coat.

"Is this ball regulation size?"

"Yes, First Cousin Cheng," Puppy said. "We used the supplies in the Dead Past Warehouse on Bruckner."

Cheng chuckled. "I think I hit this one in the '62 Series."

"First or fourth game, sir?"

"Right. You're also the historian." He looked at the trembling Frecklie. "I'm only a First Cousin, son. No need to be rattled. Now be impressed by this guy, he's averaging ten strikeouts a game."

Puppy tipped forward again at the compliment, his mind racing about what a First Cousin was doing in a deserted DV playground at dusk.

"So why are you learning a knuckler? I'm figuring that's what you're trying unless it's some secret new pitch."

"I'm improving my repertoire, First Cousin."

Chang sniffed. "Are you planning on throwing it properly?"

"We don't know how," Frecklie admitted gravely.

Albert laughed. "So I saw. This way, Puppy. Use the four knuckle grip." Cheng gripped the ball with four fingers pressed downward into the middle of the seam. He gestured for Frecklie to back up, letting the boy stop about fifty feet away. His pitch danced merrily halfway before tiring and rolling to Frecklie's feet. The teen was afraid to pick it up and acknowledge Cheng's failure.

Cheng did a little jig. "Pretty damn good for an eighty-three-year old shortstop who hasn't thrown anything for more than thirty years." He slipped on Puppy's glove. "J'anos taught me the knuckler. We were in Chicago on the Hyde Hotel rooftop. And soused on rum, back when I could drink." Another nostalgic sigh. "We kept throwing and hitting balls onto the street until the Blue Shirts stopped us. Took five of them," he recalled proudly. "Those days they didn't arrest celebrities. It's much better now, equality before the law."

Cheng reluctantly returned Puppy's glove, staring carefully. "You have some time to talk, son?"

They hadn't even settled into a rear table at Needleman's before the waiter hurried over, smiling a row of perfect white teeth.

"Albert Cheng, good to see you again."

The First Cousin squinted. "Who are you?"

"Ruffian Slatz, of course. The usual?"

The First Cousin turned up his palms at Puppy. "For both of us."

"Who's he?"

"Puppy Nedick."

The waiter grunted at his outstretched hand. "Never heard of you. But this man. The grace, the skill. The greatest player of them all."

Cheng beamed. "We know that. Bring some knishes, too."

The waiter shuffled away with an extra bounce in his step.

"I used to come here a lot, a great little after hours place for some real food. Bring the dates over and ply them with pastrami and give them a bit of the old Bronx." Cheng frowned. "The waiter was old then, if I recall."

Puppy took in the faded décor. "Nice."

Ruffian returned, standing patiently until Albert nodded approval of the coffee. "Two sugars as always."

"Yes, right." Cheng smiled thinly. "If you'll give us some privacy, please."

"Still a prick, I love it." The waiter chuckled.

Albert stirred his coffee. "You don't trust me, do you? Why should you?" He paused. "But do you trust Grandma?"

"Of course," he said hoarsely.

Cheng inched forward, twirling a pickle. "Why?"

There could not be a good answer to this question, he thought, buying time with another sour tomato.

"Can't answer it, can you?" Albert snorted. "Don't worry, most folks can't. They trust her, love her, the eyes, the smile, the voice. Everyone has the one passion for Grandma. Me, it's the way she loves children. They're our lifeblood, Puppy. Grandma knows we make the future every moment. Pure faith and love, Puppy. In ourselves. In our destiny."

Cheng smiled; Puppy would've needed a microscope to find the warmth. "You're engaged to some singer, right?"

"Dara Dinton. She's very talented."

Cheng waved him off. "So Commissioner Kenuda says. He has great plans for Dara. You jealous of her success?"

"Not at all."

"Because you love her?"

Puppy smiled as vaguely as he could muster.

Cheng patted his hand and, with a sigh, took a bite of the corned beef sandwich, grunting approval and sending the waiter away. He nudged aside the plate, gesturing for Puppy to eat his hot dog before it got cold.

"If I tell you Grandma needs your help, can you do it on pure faith and love?"

Puppy chewed very carefully and nodded.

"Are you sure?"

He swallowed. "Can I ask what it is?"

Cheng laughed loudly, this time for real.

• • • •

ZELDA KILLED MORE time. She did a lot of that lately. Stopping for coffee, stopping to pee, stopping to eat, stopping to poop. It was like her body was in feces-urine overdrive disposal to give her mind a chance to think without any distractions.

Katrina had been wonderful, insisting she come in late, leave early, stare off into space in the office. Don't worry about work. I know what you can do. Mr. Saul knows what you can do. Everyone is supportive. We love you, Zelda.

FORGIVENESS.

She stared without blinking at Grandma's huge smiling face looking down from the billboard on Webster Avenue.

FORGIVENESS.

Purple letters against a white background. No children. Just her, one on one. Code for serious; everyone understood that.

FORGIVENESS.

For what? Would you forgive me for murder, Grandma? Killing a future scientist or doctor or dancer or who knows, soldier someday? Little Diego or Little Pablo or Little A'ndy or Little Bari or Little Canseeka or Little Dru or Little I Don't Remember Your Name, heck, Grandma, I would've liked to have ridden a bike but my mother the slut was a murderer. If only she had courage I could've grown up in a real house with real parents and real love.

Zelda clenched her groin at Grandma, eventually finding the rows of two-story houses off 164th Street. The door of Ruby's was slightly ajar. Zelda admired a few dresses hanging on hooks in the waiting area. Size eight. Size ten. No size twelves anymore, she panicked.

"Yes?" Beth stepped out, quickly losing her cold stare.

"Hi. I'm Zelda. Puppy's friend."

"I know. You were here with that entertainer." She made a face and bent over a pile of receipts on the desk. "What's your last name?"

"Jones. But the order's for Lopez…I mean, Dinton."

Beth waited until Zelda was sure.

"Dara Dinton."

Beth returned with a large box, which she started opening.

"I trust you."

"Don't." She held up each of the four low-cut shimmering dresses in gold, black, blue and gold.

"They're the bahm diggity," Zelda said, carefully stroking the soft black material. "You do nice work."

Beth blushed and nodded.

"Wish I could wear these," Zelda said.

"Why not? You'd look great."

Zelda rolled her eyes.

"I have your size in the gold and black."

"No, you don't, I looked."

Beth scowled at the treacherous dress rack. "I can find something similar. I've got a gorgeous purple…"

"Hey, you already made the sale." More embarrassed than she understood, Zelda tucked the box under her arm and hurried out, going a block before Beth grabbed her at the corner.

"You forgot your receipt." She shoved the slip into Zelda's coat pocket and stormed away.

"Sorry. Come on, I said I'm sorry," she said to the retreating Beth. Zelda pursued and caught up a block away, tugging on Beth's sleeve.

She whirled. "That was a shitty thing to say."

"You're right."

"I don't give a crap if you buy clothes from me. If anyone buys clothes from me. I'll wear them all myself. But it's outrageous to accuse me of only caring about money as a businessperson. I won't be insulted like that."

Zelda grinned. "Guess I'm not the only one having a bad month."

Beth softened. "Guess not."

"Do I need to apologize again?"

"Not this time." Beth gave her a long look. "Which direction are you going?"

Zelda frowned. "None really."

They walked in silence along 164th Street past Diego's apartment, her fourth time on this block in the past few days. Diego's sister had left her squared notes asking if she'd heard from him, which Zelda ignored, figuring it was better for his family to think she's a jerk then have to lie in person.

At least tonight Zelda didn't go inside the building and sit by his door eating a sandwich and finishing off a bottle of wine, hoping that asshole Black Top agent was wrong.

Zelda barely kept up with Beth's quick pace and sudden stops, as if the dressmaker were unsure whether she wanted to ditch her or not. They waited for a light as another billboard drifted down from a stealth 'copter and secured itself on an enormous stand across the street. FORGIVENESS wrapped itself around Grandma's head like an obedient snake; even after thirty-plus years, people still murmured wonderingly at such tricks.

Except for Beth, who sneered and darted forward through the bumper to bumper traffic. She jumped onto a couple hoods, ignoring the drivers' shouts while waiting for Zelda to clumsily cross.

"Pretty good," Zelda said between labored breaths.

Beth shrugged. "I don't get much exercise all day."

"I used to be three hoods."

The woman smiled faintly. "My best was five."

"Puppy once did six."

"Figures," Beth said dryly. The women smiled tentatively. "I go home for lunch sometimes."

Zelda studied the greenish cake sitting perfectly centered in the chipped blue and white plate. Beth's kitchen was just like her parents, warm with cooking smells, redolent with cleaning fluids. Except this one had love.

"You know what that is?" Beth laid down a small fork.

Zelda didn't want to guess.

"Crushed parsley and honey. It's good for the baby's digestion."

She didn't bother asking how Beth knew; women just did. Zelda took a bite, managing a weak smile. "Wonderful."

"No, it tastes awful. The honey gets worse every year. And the parsley was pathetic. But it's healthy for my son and especially good for a pregnancy. How far along are you?"

"Eight weeks."

Beth glanced at her left hand, but Zelda shook her head.

"And please, Puppy doesn't know."

"He's the father?" Beth's eyes bulged.

Zelda hadn't laughed that loud since her last night with Diego. "No, just a friend. Who I still haven't told."

"I worried about telling my husband. So many fears about the future."

"Oh yeah."

Beth smiled sympathetically and held up an empty palm. Alone?

Zelda nodded.

340 | GARY MORGENSTEIN

Beth gestured at her head and heart, raising her shoulders.

What can I do? Zelda fought tears, shrugging. "What'd you do about your fears?"

"What makes you think they're gone?" Beth dumped the disgusting parsley cake in the trash and served a thick piece of SC apple pie.

"Then what'd you do?" Zelda asked between grateful bites.

Beth hesitated, slowly crossing herself.

Zelda pulled apart her lips. Helps?

The woman nodded cautiously, touching her mouth and pressing her fingertips against Zelda's chest. Join me.

Zelda jumped up, red-faced. "I should be going."

Beth frowned. "Don't do it."

Zelda trembled. "What?"

"What you're thinking of."

"I'm thinking of more pie." She laughed limply. "Maybe some ice cream. Bottle of wine. Thanks for your hospitality."

Beth grabbed her arm with strong supple fingers. "The hell what Grandma thinks. Care what He who created her thinks."

"If the He who created her cared, this wouldn't have happened. Or are you going to give me a lot of crap about free choice? I'm a painter. I read a lot about old artists, struggling with their humanity and your God."

"Your God, too." Beth tightened her grip. "Your baby's God."

She wrenched free. "It's not my baby. It's Grandma's baby."

Zelda ran down the steps and into the cold night.

• • • •

CLARY SETTLED ONTO a stool at the far end of the counter, longingly peering at the sweet foods beneath the plastic covers as if she could eat them just by imagining. She could probably steal some. All the Americans were looking at the face on the television.

The famous Grandma. Two days in America and she meets Grandma. She was very old. And not a Crusader. Yellow. An Asian. She didn't look so mean, someone who would burn children in ovens and make stew of their hearts. Like a switch turned on her brain, Clary hummed the song all the children in Allah Land were taught, *Abuela esta Muerta*. It reassured her in a strange way.

Nothing else did.

The trees were very sad, along with the animals. Strange animals who she sometimes saw through. Ghost animals. And the towns. There weren't many. America was supposed to be full of big cities where the Devil had parties, but she'd only seen little places. Now she hadn't looked too carefully, being afraid. Maybe the big cities were hidden. They had lost the war. Maybe they had moved the cities further away from the Allahs. Sad wilted trees and ghost animals and sometimes a car. The people well, they seemed stupido. She could steal anything easily. She stole some socks and an extra t-shirt from a clothes line. The candy and band aids, of course. The money from the motel and the woman's shoes and sweater and scarf. Like it was okay for children to steal.

The Americans were very surprised by what Grandma was saying. They stared like they thought their eyes and ears were lying, and then suddenly they started cheering. A few men slapped each other and Clary grabbed a fork in case there was a fight, but they just hugged and kissed. Maricon, she sneered in disgust. Another man waved his red cap with a B on the front and danced with a woman whose underwear showed. Clary needed underwear but didn't know how she could steal that woman's.

As Grandma kept talking in this very soft kind way, the Americans got quieter. They didn't seem so happy anymore, like someone was telling them it was time for bed. Clary understood a couple words. Islam. Muslims. They gasped and made upset faces, like the Allahs did if the food was cold or you didn't swallow the mucus from their penises. Maybe this wasn't a safe place. She hadn't found a safe place yet. She'd slept in the sad forest last night and today kept hidden in the woods along the road.

She'd seen a sign, New York, 100 miles. The address in her pocket said New York, Bronx, but she figured that was pretty close.

She was so hungry. Clary pocketed a donut from the plastic dome and finished the glass of water in one gulp when Grandma's face disappeared. People mumbled, unsure how to act. Grandma had only talked for about five minutes but she seemed to say a lot.

A waitress tossed a menu down. "You eating?"

Her tone wasn't mean, just curious; Clary could be anyone except who she was. She had tried talking yesterday at that tiny store. Simple Spanish even the idiota Allahs understood. I am hungry, how much. But the man behind the counter made a nasty face like the Spanish hurt his ears and asked, "You an American?" Well no, idiota, if I'm American I would speak English. She tried again and he came around and kept saying "American, American?" She got so mad she pulled down the scarf and he saw the scar and turned away. Since she was too horrible to look at, she was able to steal candy and skipped out the door making up a song about ugly men with little penises.

This waitress peered at the bandage on her cheek, but only cared whether Clary was eating.

Act like you belong, Clary decided, scrambling back onto the stool and confidently studying the foreign menu. A lot of the pictures looked good. She pointed at a hamburger and the waitress asked something. Clary nodded slowly. She'd taken a lot of money from el motel.

Two of the American men sat down to her left, talking about Grandma and Allahs. They were confused. They seemed half happy and half mad.

"What do you think?" The fat one suddenly asked her. "Is forgiveness the way?"

She shrugged. Shrugging worked with people. Usually they only wanted to be the ones talking.

"Kid's probably as confused as us," his fatter friend said. "Baseball good, Camels bad."

"Not anymore," his amigo said.

The waitress put down the biggest hamburger she'd ever seen along with potatoes and a soda. Clary waited politely until the men started their sandwiches.

"Manners, nice," the fat man said. "Bon appetite." He held up his plate. "Eat while we can."

The tall man craned his neck at Clary, who'd already eaten half her burger and was considering ordering another.

"Where you from, girl?"

She poured more ketchup on the potatoes. Acting deaf also worked.

"Let her be."

"Just asking."

She ate quicker.

A man in a blue uniform put both his hands on their shoulders. "I thought you boys were on diets?"

They all laughed about that. Clary felt the policeman staring. She turned with very calm eyes and smiled.

"Hello," she said her only English word.

"Hello," he answered pleasantly, watching her eat. "Bundled up nicely." He motioned to Clary's many layers of clothes.

Clary barely chewed the last of the burger, wiped her mouth and grabbed the check.

"Where's your parents?"

She shrugged and the policeman lost his smile.

"Parents? Mommy and Daddy?"

She looked into his cow face and smiled. "Muerte."

Clary hurried to the cashier by the door, feeling the policeman staring.

"Be sixteen fifty, honey."

Clary looked helpless.

"Sixteen fifty."

Clary flung a twenty dollar bill on the counter, not waiting for the woman to tell her it was right. She ran back into the woods, making sure she was going in the direction of New York, Bronx.

The Blue Shirt finished thumbing through his notebook. "Was the bandage on that girl's right cheek?"

His friends nodded and the cop raced out the door.

• • • •

JALAK ANGRILY SPILLED the bag of pistachios onto the counter and began counting. Blasted thief in the souq had his hand on the scale. Can't trust anyone in this filthy place. She let her anger intensify and spill into an assault on the fatty lamb. We should've stayed in Cairo. They would've rebuilt eventually; at least that was home. Not this shithole. Resettlement, no money down, come and reclaim our ancestral lands stolen by the Crusaders.

The house was probably built by our ancestors in the fifteenth century, she grunted, flinging a grizzled piece of lamb into the sink. If her husband would only fix things but where is he? Disappears every day and leaves me to face the shame. That's what happened, Jalak suddenly decided. The pistachio thief salesman knew who she was. The butcher knew who she was, a family, a whose son lived in the Martyrs Home because of an unsuitable parent.

They were fortunate not to be beheaded like the perverts and tossed into the sea, Jalak trembled.

"Are you home?" Jalak shouted at Abdul, walking up the staircase.

"No, I'm a ghost."

Big mouth. No respect, like his father.

"And do your homework."

The soccer ball bounced up the steps.

"Without the ball." She stood at the bottom waiting, arms folded. Abdul kicked the ball over her head, running into his room and locking the door before she could catch him. "Stay there and do your homework," Jalak yelled into the keyhole before returning to the kitchen to exact revenge on the washed potatoes in the sink.

A bearded man in a frayed black hood peered through the window. Jalak gasped and pointed the long knife.

"Get out of here," she shouted.

"Apologies…"

"I said get out…"

"What're you doing, woman?" Mustafa rushed in, smelling of fish from a short trip with tourists. He bowed over the sink. "Allah have my head for my wife."

Abdullah chuckled. "I have two wives. I understand. May I?"

Mustafa shoved Jalak aside and frantically opened the back door.

"You're not letting a bum into my house…"

As Mustafa started explaining, Abdullah tossed him a warning glance.

"I wouldn't dream of it, my woman. My feet are too dirty for your floors and my breath is filled with a stench that would mar that wondrous meal you're cooking."

Jalak wasn't sure what to say, so she allowed anger to talk. "That's right." To Azhar, she said contemptuously, "Go talk to your beggar friend on the street."

344 | GARY MORGENSTEIN

As they walked down the driveway, Azhar tried apologizing profusely, but Abdullah would have none of it.

"She's a perceptive woman. Would you want her letting in someone dressed like this?"

"Your wisdom." Azhar respectfully lowered his head.

"Common sense in a marriage is difficult." The Son led Azhar a few blocks away. Mustafa was surprised that they didn't get into a car, but instead sat on a bench near the sea. Azhar shifted slightly away, reddening.

"My odors," he apologized.

"You're a fishing captain. You must make money. It mustn't be easy after what I did to you."

"You? I made my own shame."

"By trying to save the orphans?"

"I jeopardized security and the lives of your men."

"Those al'abalahs," Abdullah snorted. "That's why I do what I do. And why you rescued that little girl from the orphanage."

"I lied."

"Yes, you did." Abdullah smiled thinly. "But it was to return her to the infidels, with whom she belonged. Then they kill her. We have a long road ahead."

Azhar shrugged limply.

The Son squeezed Mustafa's arm. "Do you worry about your son?"

"Omar has a strong heart..."

"He's lost to them. At that age, there's no turning back."

"He is but sixteen..."

"Lost," Abdullah said firmly. "Accept that. Accept that he is our enemy."

He shuddered at the image of his son in a black robe holding a scimitar. "I can't."

"Abdul is our future. Perhaps it will be soccer. Think of Abdul scoring goals against the Crusaders, a stadium full of Muslims and... " he caught himself. "...non-Muslims.

We'll need to find a different word for them. Perhaps even for us."

They watched sleepy sailboats pass.

"I'm sorry your life is upside down, Azhar," Abdullah finally said. "But it was necessary."

"Allah needs me to be suspected of heresy?"

"No, but I do." The Mufti's son leaned forward. "I imagine your wife won't care if I take you off on another trip."

"I believe she'd thank you."

They grinned together for a moment.

"May I ask where we're going?"

Abdullah leaned back with a mischievous smile. "No. But pack warm clothes."

He didn't think it'd be wise to ask Jalak to knit him a scarf.

• • • •

ZELDA SLOWLY WALKED up the wide chipped steps into the abandoned building. The nearest light was on the next floor. She used both hands on the railing, smiling wryly that falling might do the trick except for the broken bones.

Two more flights up, where she paused to catch her breath, glancing through the soiled square window at desolate East 166th Street, then down a corridor lit by a simple exposed bulb. There were no sounds other than her rasping.

One last brave sigh. The door opened on the fourth knock. A narrow bed with a fresh sheet greeted her, come lay with me, my mattress is firm and you shouldn't be here long. This was the only furniture, except for a wobbly floor lamp, light spilling apologetically onto a dour woman silently washing her hands at the sink. Least she used soap, Zelda thought.

A friendly man in a white surgical gown and a reassuring smile came out of another room.

"Dr. Watt." He iclasped her hand. "Good to know you, Zelda."

"Same here. I wish the circumstances were different."

He looked around as if they were at Lebanon Hospital and it was her fault she couldn't see the nurses and doctors running around saving lives.

"Next time. There's no reason why you can't have many children."

"I had two after." The dour women held up a pair of fingers.

Zelda thought Dr. Watt was going to applaud and vidup photos of the dour children on the peeling wall. Instead he nodded grimly and told Zelda to sit while the woman laid gleaming hot, really very sharp instruments on a towel on the kitchen counter.

Her thighs pressed together.

"Can I give you a head's up how today will go?" Watt didn't wait for her to answer. "Before abortion was outlawed, doctors used mifepristone, a pill to eliminate the pregnancy. That was in '69…"

"'68," the woman said without looking up. "Right after we lost France."

The doctor's glare indicated he preferred no further interruptions. "Then in 2076, all of these horrific surgical abortions were banned."

"Four million," the woman muttered the mantra.

"Yes." Dr. Watt grimaced as if he personally knew each of the chlldren who died in the war.

"May I ask a question?" Zelda asked hoarsely.

"Anything."

The woman turned around in case her knowledge was needed.

"You said it's horrific."

Dr. Watt held up his hands. "Not what we're doing to you, Zelda. This is a simple procedure. We can give you general anesthesia, where you're asleep, conscious sedation, where you're awake but sleepy, or local, where the area's numb. No pain. I prefer the suction aspiration. Something soothing about the sound."

He smiled as if *Suck Out My Fetus* were a #1 hit on the vidrad.

"I mean…" Zelda, just close your eyes and don't interrogate the man. "Why are you doing this if you think it's so horrible to kill a baby?"

Dr. Watt rested his strong hands on his lap; clearly he'd answered this before. "I would never do this if a woman were married or engaged. But why should a single woman be punished? With no contraception, mistakes are guaranteed. Look what happened to you after an innocent night of drinking with an attractive man."

Or seven, she smiled nervously.

"Why should you suffer because monsters slaughtered our people?"

"They're not monsters anymore," the woman said.

"I forgot," he sneered. "No nasty words anymore. Forgiveness."

"Four million," the woman mumbled.

"That's why I don't accept payment. That'd violate Grandma's Twenty-First Insight, money corrupts good." The doctor impatiently glanced at his watch. "We should get going, Zelda. The surroundings aren't the best, but we must be careful. Any more questions?"

Zelda slowly undressed, the clothes glued together to her sweating body. Dr. Watt washed his hands in the sink.

"The tube will be inserted through your cervix and into your womb and then we go thwip." He made some such sound of suction.

"I don't need the details."

"I'm only trying to make it all seem routine," he said cheerfully.

"Like buying groceries. Apple goes bad, get another."

"Not quite that coldly." Dr. Watt considered her. "Katrina did say you have an unusual mind."

She nodded dully, fingers hovering over the last button on the blouse before she quickly stripped down to her panties, eager to get it done; the woman gleefully gave her a shot.

"Just a local," Dr. Watt explained.

Her mind tilted, left to right. Right to left. She'd had a local before, when Pablo broke her finger because she wouldn't show him her breast; fourteen percent of a nipple.

"You sure this is a local?" she mumbled.

The woman smiled smugly.

"But Katrina speaks highly of you," Dr. Watt continued. "Said you're an attentive pupil. Lie down, Zelda."

"S'not a local." She resisted the woman's tugs.

"I adore Katrina. We know each other a long time." Dr. Watt picked up a shiny instrument that looked like a sword and Zelda frantically swam into the fog to hold the waves together. Long time? No.

"We go back to the University of Pennsylvania."

She stood, unsure where her feet were.

"Oh yes," he smirked. "We partied a lot."

Zelda grabbed her clothes, staggering to the door. The woman laughed and dragged her back.

"Changed my mind."

"It's a little late for that." Dr. Watt gently gripped her elbow.

Zelda figured the vagina would be the same on anyone else. She kicked and the woman howled onto her knees. Something pulled Zelda's arm from her body, but it was fastened pretty tightly; she whirled, slicing her bitten fingernails across Watt's eyes. His screams faded once she stumbled out of the building, swimming back into her clothes. No one was there to watch.

32

The Black Top scowled through the glass door as if this boring job were Pablo's fault. "It's all paper records that far back."

"That's fine."

The BT yanked up the black reflective visor. He couldn't have been more than twenty-five, uncomfortable about being an asshole, but he had to live up to the uniform. "Not for me. I have to lock down the front door, go up three flights and pull down how many boxes."

Pablo managed an apologetic look. The BT grumbled and, amid beeps and flashing lights, led Pablo inside the musty warehouse.

"Be careful." The BT pointed his Tompkins 340 machine gun at the broken tiles.

"Guess not a lot of care goes into keeping up the building." Pablo followed the BT up the narrow slippery steps to the edge of a dark concrete hallway.

"The name is Dead Past Warehouse. Got the dead part?"

"There has to be something important here."

The BT grudgingly switched on a light. "Shit. Whole floor of computers. Rusted shut. All them cellular phone instruments. You can have your pick if you're willing to fight off the rats. Probably some rats on four. They prefer paper."

The BT was disappointed by Pablo's indifferent reaction to the possibility of fighting six-foot high rodents for his annoying records. "This way, this way." His snapping gloved fingers cracked like rocks being splintered as they turned a dark corner and walked single file up an even narrower staircase.

"What're you looking for anyway?"

"That's a privileged Cousins matter." Pablo paused. "But since you're so cooperative, I can tell you."

"I'm glad someone tells me something so I don't lose my mind."

"Well, Lieutenant…"

"Private."

"Lieutenant someday." Pablo smiled faintly. "I'm trying to make a splash into the Cousins program by looking at the lack of really interesting new restaurants."

"That's making a splash?" Pausing before the thick black door, the BT fumbled for the correct key on the chain.

"You'd be surprised. Somehow I want to combine my science background as a dentist with my love of eating."

"Like food for healthy teeth?"

"Exactly. Clearly you have time to think about things."

The BT snorted and opened the door. Stacks of cartons climbed to the twelve foot ceiling, barely giving them space to prop a huge ladder.

"I gotta go through all of them?" the BT whined.

"Just the letter N, Lieutenant." Pablo winked. "I'm happy to grab a carton myself."

The BT muttered a form of thanks, insisting it'd be worse if Pablo fell and broke his head than if he did, a worthless Black Top in a boring dead-end job. The private climbed the ladder with agitated sighs, disappearing for about five minutes, his loud swearing an audio buoy, before stumbling back down lugging four large boxes. He dug through a cardboard corridor, pulling out a folding table and a chair, which he wearily set up as if this took the last of his strength.

"Can I trust you not to steal anything? Otherwise I gotta watch."

"What if you help?"

The private squinted warily. "I don't know about restaurants or teeth."

"You chew food, don't you?"

They carefully searched the cartons, dumping the last files. The BT wiped his forehead. "All that for nothing."

Pablo muttered, irritated. "You sure about the name?"

Diaz grunted and dug through the leases, architects' plans, building codes and government certifications all over again.

"Maybe it's under something else," the BT suggested. "Maybe all the Jew places are in the same place."

Pablo frowned. "Not back in 2036, anyway."

"You got a year? Shit, why didn't you tell me?" The BT scampered back up the ladder, triumphantly turning two boxes on their side so Pablo could clearly see the date. "I gotta get back to the front door. If you open a special chewing place, remember me. Paterno. Jake. Being a BT ain't any fun if you don't got someone to kill."

"You're top of my list for head chef."

Pablo rolled the marble around the cartons twice for extra luck and opened the first box. More permits for more restaurants. Nikita's Tacos on Sherman Avenue. Genni Ann's Real Chicken on Morris Avenue. About forty more, but not a one regarding the best pastrami in New York, he allowed himself a tired smile.

The second box contained only company names. DeViers. Trumble. Chi-Chi. Kreplach.

Pablo chewed on his lower lip, the name dancing mistily. He opened the Kreplach Inc. folder. Three approved restaurant permits. Phyllis's Soup Palace. Dorsky's Dairy House.

And Needleman's.

All three restaurants had identical personnel requirements. None. He re-read that. None. No people required.

On the last page was another company name, Olark LLC.

Pablo carefully balanced up the ladder, making two trips to the O column and rummaging through three cartons. No Olark, Inc. He clambered back onto the ladder, but 2037 and 2038 were no help. He had just finished 2039 when the BT rapped on the door.

"My shift's ending. Sorry. You gotta go."

"Give me one more second." He fingered the marble and climbed back up another row. It took only five minutes. He was ready when the impatient private led him back downstairs to the front door, signing him out. The BT pressed his hand onto Pablo's chest.

"Do I gotta frisk you?"

"That's not the way a head chef talks to his boss."

The soldier smiled sheepishly and frisked him anyway.

• • • •

BOCCICELLI AND FISHER didn't quite know what to do with Frecklie. They had children. Fisher's daughter attended Harvard State College, renamed in 2077 under the Third Anti-Elitism Act, and Boccicelli had two sons who managed real estate development in the rebuilding of lower Manhattan. These children smiled, laughed, talked. Blinked their blasted eyes.

This child was like a 'bot, except he couldn't make his eyes revolve in opposite directions.

"Wine?" Boccicelli held up a bottle of Jacksonville Chianti.

"He's too young," Fisher whispered before they were reported for corrupting a minor.

"Milk?" Boccicelli tried.

Frecklie shook his head again. His mother wasn't all wrong. The Reg world was populated by morons.

"I have to get back to school soon…"

Boccicelli and Fisher erupted in loud cries about the importance of education, quizzing Frecklie about classes and teachers and interests and future plans.

He just stared, waiting until they'd exhausted themselves, then opened his notebook.

"The store."

"The one downstairs?" Fisher asked, puzzled.

"There were six of them, all different sizes. All selling merchandise."

"Selling's good," Boccicelli perked up.

"We can't sell any."

"Why not?"

The owners immediately assumed Frecklie had deprived them of a profit line. Their P&L was booming, for the little they could keep. But a large P&L recommended them for a stake in the new housing development that would go up just under their feet when this foul stadium was finally torn down.

"Merchandise can't be sold at any war museum. It glorifies evil." He tapped his blank notebook as if it contained the full text of the Remembrance Act 405 of 2074, banning, under penalty of loss of sibling privilege, any profits derived from suffering.

"This isn't a museum."

"It is now since we put up the exhibits, sirs."

They exchanged nasty looks since the exhibits were Frecklie's idea.

"Then what good is a store?" Boccicelli sneered.

"The Forgiveness line. I thought we'd offer t-shirts."

"How can we sell something that glorifies pain or whatever?" Fisher asked, hoping he'd set up a trap.

"This looks ahead, not back. I think."

Boccicelli scowled. "You think?"

"It's a little murky. I only had time for so much research at the Central Library. No one's sure since it's sort of never really been done before."

"Sort of?" Boccicelli proudly seized on the qualifying words.

"Yes sir," Frecklie said, nodding gravely. "After Grandma finished all thirty-two Insights," he waited for them to bow their necks respectfully, "a Fourth Cousin named," Frecklie peered at a blank page in his textbook, "Sam Fuji celebrated Grandma's birthday by unveiling a line of t-shirts with each of the Insights. He also produced plates and cups and some bedding, I think blankets and sheets, and everything went on sale simultaneously. He hadn't told anyone and it wasn't received very well."

Fisher and Boccicelli frowned as one; the Falcons owner asked, "What happened?"

"It lasted only a few hours and the factories were destroyed and Sam Fuji was never seen again."

Fisher visibly trembled. "I've never heard of this."

"Because it was only a few hours, sir. Everything was destroyed, though I've heard, in the DV of course, that some t-shirts are still floating around, thirty-five years later, and that if you're caught with one…" Frecklie shrugged and left the punishment to their imagination, which consumed them for a moment of huddled whispers.

"Then why would we do this?" Boccicelli snapped.

"Because Third Cousin Kenuda thought it would be a good experiment."

"Experiment?" Fisher paled. "Meaning sometimes an experiment doesn't work."

"Yes sir." Frecklie lowered his eyes. "That's why I think we should be careful."

They muttered the obviousness of that.

"If we allow a Reg business to do this, they'll have to market the product according to law. But a DV business is given more flexibility since there's no expectation they'll survive."

The owners waved him on as if they understood what he was talking about.

"I have an option."

Morons, Frecklie smiled unpleasantly as he hurried into High School 44 barely in time for the third period math class. He didn't pay much attention. Thanks to Dale, he was almost a whiz. When the DVs had first been set up, the educational standards were too high; almost no one passed. After the Surrender, The Family had gone the opposite way and simplified the curriculum to make sure that more DVs climbed out. Otherwise it looked as if they were trapped in a permanent cycle of failure. That led to an increase of subtle prejudices when the next generation clearly couldn't keep up.

In 2076, Grandma announced the One Class initiative, which ignored any distinctions between DVs and Regs. One Class, One Country was the slogan. You kept up like everyone else, no excuses for where you lived or your families or your culture or anything that was once thought of an excuse.

Your mind is yours. Take care of it, said Grandma's Nineteenth Insight.

Frecklie rushed through the school day, seeing little in any of the seven classes that would prepare him for his career as a baseball architect. By the time he finished homework and sex with Dale, it was after seven, sending him on a frantic dash to the grocery store; he barely got home before his mother.

Beth walked into the kitchen and sniffed. Something unfamiliar smoked slightly from the oven while seemingly every dish they owned was stacked in the sink. Puffs of white flour spotted her immaculate floor and a reddish ingredient clung to her blue-striped kitchen curtains.

But she had to smile at the flickering candles on the table flanked by the correct place settings. She wearily dropped her heavy bag of sewing to the floor. Frecklie whisked it away and gave her a big kiss on the cheek.

What had he done?

"Smells interesting," she said.

"Greens and sea life casserole," he said proudly.

"And wine?" Beth lifted up the half full glass.

"From Pittsburgh."

"I hear they're making good stuff."

"Yeah. Sit, sit." Frecklie pulled the chair out and she sat, hands clasped. "How was your day?" He refilled her glass.

"The usual. Yours?"

"Productive."

"Yes?"

"School."

"What'd you learn?"

"So much I wouldn't know where to begin."

"Work?"

"Great. Everyone loved the uniforms."

Beth nodded; Puppy had left her a squared note of thanks.

"You're in the Hall of Fame for uniform making. Thank you. They even fit."

"That's helpful."

"You're the expert. Best tailor in the Bronx. Maybe America. Now you have a chance to really show what you can do."

Beth took a long sip and waited.

"Grandma's Forgiveness."

She darkened. "What about it?"

"Well, we want to promote it."

"Who's we?"

"Puppy has nothing to do with this. It's my idea."

She made a doubtful face.

"We want to sell t-shirts at the stadium. I need you to design them."

Beth squeezed the stem of the glass. "You want me to participate in this charade?"

"What does charade mean?"

"I guess Dale isn't doing your English homework too. Farce. Game." She slammed down the glass and turned off the food before they were overcome by the smoke curling around the stove like a tornado. "I won't have anything to do with it. And neither should you."

"I already do."

Beth flushed. "Grandma's selling us out again."

"She's finally saying baseball is good."

"So we don't see what she's doing. It's a distraction. Like her Story, saying we killed refugees who wouldn't have been refugees if the Allahs hadn't thrown them out. We were trying to save those poor people. Now this bullshit about forgiveness. Accept wrongs on all sides. As if they're all equal. They nuke our cities and it's our fault because we fight back? What crap, oh, the world will be better if we turn hate to love. There's going to be another Surrender, Ruben. A worse one, where we'll all live under sharia, tyranny, as slaves, and I won't let you stain the memory of brave men and women…"

"I know all that. I've seen them," he shouted.

"Who?"

"The skeletons. The Miners underneath the stadium. They were trapped and gassed. Children, too. All over the balllpark. I've seen them. I know what the BTs did. So don't tell me I don't know like I'm a damn child."

Beth controlled her trembling and took his hand. "Tell me what you saw."

Frecklie described the ten storage rooms below the stands.

"Who else did you tell?"

"No one." His eyes narrowed. "Neither can you. It'd get the government angry."

She sighed. "Yes it would." Exposing the lies of 10/12. The brave BTs gassing children and slaughtering prisoners. Who knows what other lies would come out about that day? Why'd Hazel want to see all the hiding places?"

Frecklie shrugged. "Who cares? He loves baseball and helped us." He teared up. "Everyone thinks there'll be another season now that Puppy and Dara are going to be role models for Forgiveness. I can really be a baseball architect, Ma. A second season means a third and a fourth and you'll see, Grandma will have to build more parks."

She doesn't have to do anything, you stupid little child.

"Please." Frecklie squeezed her hand in a pleading, needy way he hadn't shown since he was ten. "Design the t-shirts." Like a tender grown-up, he cupped Beth's chin as she turned away.

• • • •

AT LEAST TEN thousand people waited by the podium on a brisk day outside the ruins of Phillies Stadium. Kenuda bored them very quickly by droning about the love behind Grandma's new Thirty-Third Forgiveness Insight and how this wisdom would providing equipment for needy DVs all over the country. When he started reciting exactly how many gloves would be shipped via the finest highways in the world, the barking began.

Soon everyone was woofing it up. Kenuda reddened, thinking he was being booed, but he kept his balance, anchored by his egomania, and introduced Puppy for the inspirational part. Give him this much, Puppy Thought, Kenuda recognized he was dull.

Puppy talked about his baseball career and how it got him out of the DV, even after he hurt his shoulder, because in Grandma's Family, we take care of our own, and then about what it was like to play major league baseball again in this last, thrilling season, and how baseball should no longer suffer for the sins of a few, but should rejoin the family of sports. As should everyone be permitted and encouraged to rejoin The Family.

That's where Kenuda jumped back into the ceremony to formally open Phillies Park. Overnight, DV workers had planted an entire miniature baseball park, about one hundred feet to dead center, with old-style seats, very intimate, probably lifted from a semi-banned book. Two racks of baseball bats stood around home plate, stamped Property of Phillies Park, along with a halved beer barrel filled with balls and a wooden locker brimming with gloves. All new equipment.

Shy kids queued up and Puppy showed them a few basics: a pitcher's motion, a batting stance, fielding a grounder, while the sullen Hazel, who hadn't smiled all day and gave no indication he'd start anytime soon, filmed Kenuda holding up a baseball as if it were a piece of real juicy fruit.

After Philadelphia, Puppy dozed as the 'copter journeyed north, settling behind a clump of trees at the Fenway Garden Society, where they crossed Boylston Street to Yawkey Way. Another large crowd, bigger than Philadelphia, swelled onto Brookline in a semi-circle. Puppy greeted them with a wave of his Yankee cap, earning a few good-natured boos from the sea of bobbing red B caps.

Again, Kenuda jumped onto the stage which overlooked another mini-park, same specifications, as if when they stamped the bats and balls and gloves, they'd somehow stamped an exact replica of what they thought a ballpark should look like.

Better than nothing, Puppy told himself, launching into the same speech which already, inside five hours, had become rote. He was scheduled, somehow between games, to visit Chicago's Wrigley Field, Pittsburgh's Forbes Stadium and Cleveland's Civic Center. Only the sites of the stadiums, he reminded himself.

He finished ad-libbing a crack about the Yankees-Red Sox rivalry when an older woman with tall gray hair shouted, "When do we get the real Fenway back?"

With a big smile, Puppy stepped aside to let Kenuda answer that.

"That's why we built this little park for you," the Commissioner said brightly.

"Ain't Fenway," she snapped.

The crowd muttered and applauded; Puppy realized the semi-circle was around the ruins of Fenway, as if they were protecting it from further damage, a beaten living thing that could rise again, so don't even think about removing another stone or a crumpled seat or burnt light.

"What's important is the notion of forgiving baseball…" Kenuda tried.

"Baseball didn't do anything," a man shouted.

"Which is why we're forgiving you."

"How can you forgive us if we didn't do anything?" someone else called out.

The few Blue Shirts on the edge of the crowd smiled nervously.

"Tell Grandma to rebuild Fenway," a man cried out.

That let loose another chant of "Fenway, Fenway, Fenway."

Kenuda was about to lose his patience when Puppy finally rescued him, grabbing the microphone.

"First we finish refurbishing Yankee Stadium, then Fenway."

The crowd cheered.

"You really think you can beat the Yankees?"

A brief chant of "Fuck New York" startled Kenuda, who backed away, expecting to be trampled. Hazel and Puppy exchanged grins.

"You wish." Puppy waved his Yankee cap to pleasant jeers. "Now let me show the next generation how to play so maybe that can happen someday." He couldn't resist and shouted out, "And that'll be a long time since we got forty-five world championships and you only got nine."

Rousing boos that only someone who loved baseball could understand showered Puppy as he happily conducted the brief clinic, barely making it back in time for the 'copter to take them home.

Kenuda grumbled in the far corner, "That was very rude behavior."

"I thought I was great."

"Not you, Nedick. The crowd. I can see why."

Hazel paused, cleaning his camera as if it were a weapon. "Why what, sir?"

"Why the whole damn sport was banned. You'd never see my football or basketball fans behave like that."

"Aren't these also your baseball fans?"

Kenuda stared at Hazel. "I don't want anything from that crowd in your report."

"Course not, Third Cousin. I'm just here to make you look good."

Elias grumbled out the window at Connecticut.

"And make Puppy look good." Hazel smiled.

That earned a resentful glare.

The 'copter hit some headwinds northeast of the Bronx. Kenuda huffily insisted he had pressing affairs to attend, so they dropped him off onto the roof of the Cousins building, where the wind swept him a few feet off the ground, much to Hazel and Puppy's delight.

"I was rooting for the wind." Hazel snickered as they drifted toward Amazon Stadium.

Puppy didn't disagree. "I thought you guys were buds."

"No one's buds with Elias Kenuda unless they can do something for him." He stored the camera back into his back pack and grabbed the rope as the 'copter let them down to a desolate playground, four blocks away.

Puppy pressed into the stadium through the mass of fans backed up 161st Street. He hurried down the ramp, humming with slow-moving siblings marveling at the glittering white ceilings or entranced like hungry zombies by the new food stands, curry, barbecue, the wondrous smell of fried foods magnetizing long lines. Lots of excuse me, sorry didn't see your foot, please don't spill any more of my beer.

The entire stadium had new seats, top to bottom, all three levels. Even the bleachers. Grass, real green grass. Pale brown infield dirt free of bones and glass. A clean pitcher's mound. Sparkling white paint along the foul lines. Gleaming brocades on the upper decks.

If not for the skulls heads stacked in left center field and only one third of the scoreboard intact, this could've been Amazon Stadium on October 12, 2065.

Puppy burst into the clubhouse like one of Dale's baseball demons were chasing him. The team fell silent as if their eyes were on a string between his padlocked locker and Ty's closed office, which opened with a slow, theatrical squeak.

"Well look who's honored us with his glorious presence," Cobb snarled from his doorway.

Puppy squeezed the lock. "So sorry. I've been busy."

"Well you are famous…"

"Damn straight. I've been killing myself promoting this game so all of you can play. Now open my locker."

"Uniforms and equipment are for players who show up on time."

"Open my fucking locker." He whirled challengingly.

Cobb raged over with clenched fists. "Never talk to me that way again. I don't fucking care how many cameras you suck off, you hear me?"

Mantle dragged the kicking, red-faced Ty into the office. Puppy glowered at Vernon. "Warm me up."

Puppy stomped along the foul lines, darkly waving past the barking fans and into the back of the bullpen. Even the skeletons were gone. An HG fighter jet whooshed overhead, singing the Rolling Stones' *Satisfaction*.

Jackson stared. "What's with you and all that attitude?"

"Famous people can be assholes," he said. "It used to be allowed all the time. Encouraged actually. I'm just tired. Sorry."

"Ain't me you gotta worry about."

Puppy sighed knowingly and spun his cap backwards. "Know how to catch a knuckleball?"

Vernon didn't like the sound of that. "What is it?"

"It's a knuckleball which you don't throw with your knuckles. I need a glove."

"I don't have one except mine."

"If I take yours, then how will you catch?"

Vernon brightened at this little ray of sanity.

"Fine. I won't use a glove which, since I don't have a uniform, makes sense."

The catcher encouraged this continuing logic with a vigorous nod and squatted, holding out his mitt. "How do you throw it?"

The first pitch fluttered over the bullpen fence. Jackson retrieved the ball, ducking under a car full of cackling dancing HG clowns.

"It does lots of crazy things, this pitch," Puppy explained.

"Oh?" Vern rolled his eyes. "Can you control it?"

"I don't know," Puppy admitted.

"Then use your regular pitches."

"I can't," he said between gritted teeth.

"Shoulder?"

Puppy nodded sadly.

"Can you even throw a change-up?"

"I can barely brush my teeth," he said softly.

"Frecklie said there's about thirty-five thousand people here," Vern said helpfully.

Puppy winced.

"But they're probably just here to see how the stadium looks, not to watch you."

He fought back tears of pain, fear. "The stadium looks this way because of me, Vern. It's a lot of pressure. Responsibility. What if I'm not up to it? Then what happens?"

A coquettish HG player in blonde curls and a long pink dress tapped her fingers over center field. "Hello everyone."

The fans yelled back like an ill-tuned orchestra.

"Are you ready?"

More yells.

"I don't hear you." The player's ears grew elephant-sized.

The fans turned it up.

"Then say a big Bronx welcome to Your. New. York. Yankees."

The Yankee logo turned into a magic carpet which whisked the somersaulting HG into the scoreboard. The team raced onto the field. Vern gave Puppy a pleading look.

A pair of spikes landed on Puppy's head. Then he was hit by a glove, uniform pants and a parachuting blouse, followed by socks and underwear landing daintily on his shoulders.

Mick scowled from the bleachers railing. "Ty may be a miserable piece of shit, but he's still our miserable piece of shit manager, so never talk that way to him again."

Puppy nodded, rubbing his head. "Should I apologize?"

"When he stops promising to kill you. Now get dressed."

"He can't throw anymore," Vern offered.

"What do you mean?"

"His arm's shot and he has to throw the knuckleball."

"That true?" Mick demanded.

Puppy nodded, feeling relief in the truth.

"I hate knuckleballs. They make you look like shit."

"He can't control it, either," Vern added.

"And he can't catch it." Puppy nearly stuck out his tongue.

"You both better learn," Mantle threatened. "I was out late getting laid and I ain't chasing line drives all day."

• • • •

ZELDA DIDN'T BOTHER to pretend as if she'd just fallen out of her two-day sick bed. Glazed eyes, snotty tissue stuck in her pocket, epidemic coughs and hurricane-like sneezes. Nah. She bounced into the office with a cheery smile proclaiming to concerned colleagues that this was the greatest day in the history of humanity.

She busied herself in the office, making random notes on a marketing plan based on the battle-tested eenie meenie miney mo analytic school, joining along wih Mooshie's new *A Mound Over Hell* album, blasting the music and her voice on the song *Foul Balls*.

"And keep on fouling 'em off

Until you get me right."

"Hi." Katrina closed the door with grave concern.

"Katrina doll, how are you?" Zelda spun around in her chair.

Boar Face sighed. "This behavior is normal."

"What, darling?" Zelda blinked slowly.

"This reaction," she whispered. "The manic glee."

"Did that happen to you, too, sweetie?" Zelda made a sad face, deeply worried about Katrina's emotional scars.

Katrina nodded. "I felt like I was drunk."

"Yes." Zelda pounded her fist. "Or on some drug. Kind of how I felt when they took out my appendix and the anesthesiologist counted 100, 99, 98…I always wondered what 97 would've been like."

Katrina frowned. "You can take more time off, Zelda. I'll cover for you."

"That is so nice. You've been so good to me, boss."

"We're friends."

"But you went above and beyond. You didn't just make a call. You went to the trouble of a whole plan."

"I didn't do much."

"Come on." Zelda put her elbows on the desk, eyes narrowing. "First there was the warm convo alluding to your previous, you know, condition. That lowered my guard just enough. Then when I was really vulnerable, the offer to help, the vows of friendship."

Katrina reddened. "I meant all that."

"Sure you did. Then offering a casual connection. A friend of a friend of a friend. But Dr. Watt's a bud from U of P. You guys partied it up. Did he get you pregnant? Nah, because you never were."

"You're in serious trouble, Zelda."

"No, you are and sit the fuck down, Boar Face."

Katrina stumbled against the glass wall.

"I didn't go through with it." She waited for the entire gasp to leave Katrina's body. "Oh, I know, you're so disappointed." Her breaths were ragged. "You set me up. Watt wasn't using any surgical procedure, only the mistoprene. Get me loaded first. 100, 99, 98. Now 97. Hands clean. How'd Zelda get a hold of an illegal drug? I said sit the fuck down."

Boar Face meekly obeyed.

"Who knows? There's always a way. You were the kind loving boss. Bet you told more than a few people how you'd taken me under your wing, trying to help. Dr. Watt and the AG nurse, well, they never saw me. Is he even a doctor? How much did you pay Watt? Or was it just in kisses? Baby's gone, Zelda did it herself, murder, Katrina's horrified. And you trusted me. Mr. Saul trusted me. Look at Zelda's erratic record, who can be surprised."

"Now I'm out of the way." Zelda pressed into Katrina's snout. "You take all the credit for my work, as if I never existed. Salmon's a dirty business, ain't it, girl?"

Katrina kept moistening her lips. "What do you want?"

"I'd love to barbecue you, but I'm a nice person. So you'll move me…"

"A promotion…"

"No, no, because then I'd be gaining from deceit. Just reassign me to a new unit where I don't report to you, but to Mr. Saul directly. Sorry, I didn't hear your answer. I'll take the nod for a yes. And maybe someday I'll forget about this. But probably not for a long while, at least until I give birth." Zelda smiled sweetly, patting her stomach. "Now get out of my office before I report you for violating every business ethics violation ever."

She waited a few luxurious moments, feet on the desk, believing that if you could hold your nose, the business world wasn't a complete cesspool.

Skipping out to an early lunch, Zelda stopped at one of those sniveling veggie places she wished would burn to the ground, ordering an AG avocado and tofu sandwich and finishing all of it, only gagging once.

Zelda was still sipping the last of the SC spinach juice, expecting her breasts would turn green eventually, when she walked into Ruby's. Beth stepped through the beige curtain and stopped, really surprised.

"You got anything for a fat pregnant girl who only looks good in blue? I have a big deal event in a couple days."

Beth smiled impishly. "You want something tailored in forty-eight hours?"

"Rush it. Money doesn't matter. I'm betting my old boss will resign soon and I'll get her job."

"Over here." Beth gestured toward a rack. "And I suggest gold. Goes with your eyes."

• • • •

PABLO SPENT THE morning camped in the Cousin's waiting room; after one o'clock, Kenuda finally strolled out of his office, grunting at the dentist.

"I told him you were busy, sir." With an accusing roll of its eyes, the A10 babbled on about everyone thinking their business was the most important to the poor over-worked Commissioner, embarrassing Kenuda, who granted Pablo about forty seconds in the elevator.

"What is it now, Diaz?"

"You need to read this, sir."

"I'm absolutely swamped…"

"It's critical."

"Which is what everyone says."

"Do I look like the sort of person who exaggerates?"

They rode up and down for five minutes as the Third Cousin studied the Olak, Inc. certificate, closing the elevator door on visitors and fellow Cousins. He alternated between frowning and staring suspiciously before agreeing to meet around four, which gave Pablo a couple hours to attend to his patients.

"Susan, where is everyone?" He peered around as if people were hiding amid the HG tooth.

The A27 sadly shook its head.

"They could only wait for so long, Dr. Diaz."

"I've been busy." He tried remembering the last time he'd been here.

"They know that, but their teeth don't."

Pablo arranged some pamphlets on the coffee table, glancing at his watch while cal-culating downtown traffic and rush hour subway and bus schedules for the best way to arrive on time.

"Can you please get some of the patients on the medemerline to apologize and reschedule?"

"But it's not an emergency, Doctor."

"I'm a doctor checking on his patients," he snapped.

"But they went elsewhere so technically they aren't your patients anymore. I'm hap-py to pull up the regulations on the Medical Emergency Line usage, Doctor."

"I think I know them," Pablo growled.

The 'bot's glittering eyes suggested otherwise.

Pablo spent the next hour sterilizing all his equipment, scrubbing the chair and re-hanging pictures; he tossed his white dental gown on the front desk as he left. "I need this washed, please."

"You have a patient tomorrow at eight-thirty, sir," Susan reminded him.

Probably his last one, which was the only thought Pablo gave his moribund dental practice as he suffered through an agonizing extra fifteen minutes on the subway; Kenuda grumpily paced outside Needleman's.

"Apologies, Third Cousin. The local green line was delayed," Pablo explained breathlessly.

Elias winced at the boarded-up warehouses on both sides of the street. "Where am I exactly?"

"Morrisania."

Kenuda didn't like the way the name sounded. He scowled at the deli. "That's it?"

"Yes, sir." Pablo took a step, hoping Kenuda would follow, but the Commissioner held his ground. "We don't need a reservation, Commissioner."

"Oh, I'm sure. But once I go inside, I've acted, and before I act, there are questions."

Pablo glanced through the scuffed window at the three men at their table, eating the same food, moving their arms the same way.

"You found the Olak certificate at the Dead Past Warehouse."

Pablo nodded, suspecting there was going to be a long line of questions.

"Which you went to under the Cousins training umbrella?"

Another nod; this time Kenuda frowned.

"Though you've not been formally accepted into the program."

"I've not formally been rejected, either."

Kenuda darkened. "Are you being smart, son?"

"No, sir."

"A BT was present during your search of records?"

"For most of the time. He had to return to his post."

"Wasn't he supposed to stay with you?"

"I'm not familiar with BT policy and yes, sir, I was being smart then."

Kenuda scowled. "Was he there when you found the Olak certificate?"

Pablo shook his head.

"Did you sign out for it?"

Pablo hesitated, then shook his head again.

"Which means you illegally removed the certificate."

"I unofficially removed it, sir. I'm not aware if that is illegal or simply a gap in process."

Elias wearily accepted that reasoning.

"And the BT searched me," Pablo continued. "He didn't find the document. So I did cooperate in that aspect of the process."

Elias peered. "Was it in a place that a frisking would find?"

"Is that the responsibility of the person being frisked or the responsibility of the Black Top?" Pablo blocked Kenuda from entering Needleman's. "That's not significant, sir."

Pablo explained what was. By 2036, facial 'bots had blended into society until they became nearly impossible to recognize, causing mayhem and mistrust. Winning public office, posing as everything from entertainers to scholars, getting humans to fall in love with them using a potent cocktail of perfect emotional adaptability and sexual skills, the 'bots were hunted down and, in the first wave of panic that society would be taken over, the machines were destroyed.

In 2040, a broad-based committee of concerned scientists, backed by corporations eager for profits, persuaded the government that it was short-sighted to get rid of the 'bots; their faces were removed and their use restored. After the war, the loyalty of 'bots was recognized and they were permitted to have names, rarely acknowledged by humans, and given limited responsible positions; the Little Extended Family was established and strict anti-robot prejudice laws were enacted.

Now Pablo was convinced that was all a sham.

Kenuda waited by the unattended register to be shown to his table.

"Anywhere," Ruffian the waiter shouted gruffly. Pablo led them to his familiar table opposite the counter.

The waiter dropped the menus down and walked away. Pablo was about to call him back so he could launch into the welcome to the glorious world of deli food, but Kenuda impatiently cleared his throat.

"Do I have to eat?" Kenuda sneered at the menu.

"He gets a little touchy if you insult the food." Pablo squinted at the waiter's face, where a slight cut squibbled along the jaw.

"I wouldn't want to offend anyone. If that's the correct pronoun."

Pablo ate a sour tomato. "Olak was part of the robotics program, sir. You saw the certificate."

"I saw that it ended per the edict banning 'bots with faces."

"Except this place."

Kenuda looked around, wishing he were elsewhere.

"It should've been closed down, but it wasn't," Pablo continued. "The other restaurants were shut, which I checked, but not this one."

"Let's say they forgot," Elias said carefully. "The world was tense. Things slipped through the gap."

"Why keep this open and not the others?"

"I just said. It fell through the cracks."

"For sixty years? Look at them." Pablo nodded at the bored waiter and sour-faced old men at the table. "Robots of that era weren't so sophisticated. The details of their physiogomy are astonishing."

"That's why they were outlawed, because they were so lifelike."

"And because they were lifelike, they had limited life spans. Twenty years, tops. You can't make money if you don't have to replace your product."

"Grandma fixed that unpleasant little bit of capitalism," Kenuda said.

"Obviously these are not the original models from 2034."

Elias thought for a moment. "Unless the original models were better than we thought. The democratic government lied egregiously back then."

Pablo nodded for him to continue, but Kenuda threw up his hands.

"Without more research, I don't have anything else to say."

"But you think it's strange."

"I think it might not be any of our business. Certainly not mine without more proof." Kenuda tossed aside the menu and got ready to leave.

"Third Cousin, it's your mandate to investigate irregularities of all kinds. Whether they come under your area or not."

Elias scowled. "Are you telling me my job?"

"Yes, sir."

His eyes blazed. "Investigating without proof is foolish."

"It can be. It's called taking risks. That's why I wanted to join the Cousins program. To be a leader."

"You don't even know if they're really robots."

Pablo fired a pickle, which slammed directly into the waiter's face.

"You just threw one of these cucumbers at an old man," Kenuda shouted.

The customers at the front table turned toward the commotion. Pablo threw sour tomatoes, all of them plopping into the old timers' heads. One of the men flung back a pickle, which sprayed brine onto Kenuda's pants, intensifying his anger.

"Now you threw green vegetables at more senior citizens. What's wrong with you, Diaz?"

The waiter angrily chased Pablo, doused by a canopy of pickles from the yelling men, onto the street, where he caught up with Kenuda.

"Listen to me, Third Cousin. They replaced the robots."

Kenuda whirled. "Who are they?"

"I don't know…"

"But you think these mysterious theys are part of some conspiracy?"

"Damnit, they were robots two days ago. I'm sure of it."

Kenuda stared coldly. "And I'm sure after my report, you won't be in the Cousins program, Doctor, so it no longer matters. Good day and best of luck."

The Commissioner abruptly shook Pablo's hand and disappeared down the subway platform at the end of the block.

Pablo brushed his jacket clean and slumped next to a fire hydrant, baffled.

• • • •

FOUR SHIMMERING DRESSES reclined on their bed, joined by a pile of six shoes, watched by three wigs on heads sitting on the dresser. For a moment, Puppy had to remind himself that he was the only living thing in the room.

"Which one?" Mooshie circled back around the bed; he wasn't sure if she were asking him or the clothes.

"They're all beautiful. Beth does good work."

Mooshie grinned mischievously. "You like her."

He blushed. "Just her work."

"Sure, her work."

"She's a wonderful dressmaker, that's it. Believe me, I'd have to sleep with a gun under the pillow."

"I have," Mooshie said vaguely; she held a blue dress to her neck before the long mirror.

"And are you and Commissioner Kenuda also correct befitting our stations as engaged people?"

Mooshie dismissively tossed aside the dress and held up the black. "He undresses me."

He had visions of Annette rumbling down the Grand Concourse in a tank. "That's not acceptable, Moosh."

"With his eyes, brain dead. I like the black dress and if you don't, say nothing but agree."

"Which wig am I liking?"

"The blonde."

"You on your own about the lipstick?"

Mooshie glared. "Think you're hot shit because of your little pitch?"

"The one which struck out twelve?"

"Fat clumsy people."

Puppy laughed. "Is the great Mooshie Lopez jealous because the humble and low Puppy Nedick fanned the most hitters in major league baseball since 2064?"

"When it was the major leagues and not this crap so get out of my dressing room."

"I have to dress, too."

She pushed him out the door. "You got a bathroom. And I struck out sixteen so match that, cripple arm."

Mooshie waited for Puppy and the Two White Grandpas to head off like three cowboys at a rodeo before she finished dressing. Mooshie Lopez didn't walk into a club with an entourage. Mooshie Lopez walked into a club alone. Especially when she was this nervous.

She huddled in a corner of the local subway, cold eyes warning anyone who might recognize her to stay away. As the train pulled into the Westchester Avenue stop, she draped herself in front of the sliding doors and pulled aside her thick wool coat, posing.

"Dara Dinton tonight, darlings, at the Stanton."

The passengers stirred, surprised.

"Come on down and join me."

Mooshie flipped a handful of tickets into the train, setting off a scramble and, with a whooshing sweep of her coat, rushed down the steps and along Burnside Avenue.

Like a number of the fancy supper clubs, the Stanton hid on a quiet street where, according to zoning regulations, there were no residential buildings; families couldn't be disturbed.

Mooshie remembered the first of the supper clubs back in 2063; Grandma was desperate for distractions. Recreating that frivolous atmosphere with table lamps and big bands and sultry singers and properly suited up guests served by beautiful waiters struck a warm chord, a door opening for a trapped, starving, terrified country. Soon tuxedos were the fashion along with cigarette holders, elegant wave hair styles and glittering jewelry. Mooshie cut a record just of Glenn Miller and Benny Goodman songs. She wouldn't be singing them tonight, she thought grimly, pressing through the crowded backstage with the aloof rudeness all celebrities were inevitably accorded, whether outlawed or not. Talent was still a seductive hypnotic.

"Two minutes, Miss Dinton." A voice rapped on the door.

Mooshie quickly re-applied her bright red lipstick, nudging aside the three dozen red roses in blue vases. She didn't need to read the card.

A murmur spread beyond the small window like a stream gnawing into a river. Mooshie watched Grandma outside the club, waving over siblings on their way home. This was what she did wherever she went. If the event, the movie, the play, the music, was good enough for her, then she certainly had to share it with her darlings. No special screenings or concerts for Grandma. They were all one happy fucking family, Mooshie almost spit down, but there were too many wired-up security guards, some up on the roof; a rifle aimed her way sent Mooshie back into her dressing room.

Grandma hoisted a little boy onto her shoulders and led the crowd inside. Mooshie grabbed her black silk scarf, waited for her intro, the band cueing up, then another couple beats before thrusting out one long meaty leg beyond the satin curtain, curling up her knee and growling huskily.

This'll teach you to bring kids to my gig.

"Let my lovin' fill your glove,

Let my lovin' be your pitch."

In the front row, Puppy, Zelda and Pablo squealed at recognizing the lyrics, while Kenuda beamed alone at a corner table. But she wasn't looking at them.

"Only love lets you keep foulin' 'em off,

'Cause you can't strike out when you feel."

At the back, Grandma lowered the little boy, her mind scampering across the packed room. Mooshie scooted to the other end of the stage as if ducking bullets, spinning around and sweeping her hair back and forth in her trademark head flip.

Here I am, bitch, Mooshie smiled. Surprise.

Mental fingers probed. She sang louder, her voice drowning out her thoughts, up-ended like nuts scattered on a table. Grandma frowned, puzzled.

"Thank you, everyone." Mooshie bowed to the tumultuous applause. "That was one of Mooshie Lopez's great tunes *Keep Foulin' Off*, from 2060. Who here remembers the greatest baseball player of all time?"

Strong applause rippled through the room.

"We got a bunch more of her songs, but I'd like to sing something from a little known singer-songwriter I always admired, Kenny Loggins." Mooshie sat on the stool; Grandma had yet to blink. "Called *I'm Not Hiding*."

Zelda left after the rowdy, hour-long first set which nearly sent the crowd dancing on the tables, mumbling she was too tired to drink.

"Don't you think Zelda's acting strangely lately?" Puppy asked.

"Yeah, but how could you tell?"

"Good point." Leaning forward, Puppy knocked his glass against Pablo's, whispering, "So what about Dara?"

"I'm convinced. This is the third time I've seen her perform. Kenuda took me twice."

"You sneaky bastard."

"Think I'd just roll up like a rug if Puppy barked?"

"That never happened before." The two friends exchanged wistful smiles. "I missed you."

"Missed you, too, though it's hard to really miss you with that billboard."

"Billboards. Plural."

All over America, Grandma smiled beneath FORGIVENESS with Puppy in mid-windup in the foreground, Mooshie singing by his side.

"It's finally happening for you, Pup." Pablo squeezed his forearm. "Kind of amazing."

"Yeah," he answered carefully.

"You pulling a Zelda and Pablo and looking for some reason to doubt it?"

Puppy shrugged. "Ty, Mick, now the Moosh. I'm a poster child. My arm goes, but I learn the knuckler and the batters go down down down…"His hand slowly fell to the table. "Seems it's all too good."

"If it makes you feel better, it won't last." Pablo gave him a hard stare. "Go out on top. However all this happened, it happened. You did it, Pup. You brought baseball back."

He grew embarrassed. "And you, Fifth Cousin?"

"Oh, I think I'll stay a humble dentist for a while longer." Pablo sighed. "I got turned down. The letter came today."

"Why?"

"They don't say. Just 'Your possibility has ceased.'"

"What kind of grammar is that?"

Pablo laughed bitterly and waited for the waiter to leave the drinks. "I pushed the rules. And stop that oh-not-mister-perfect smile." He hesitated, finally explaining about Needleman's, Olak and Kenuda.

Puppy whistled softly. "Weird about Needleman's. I was just there last week."

"No shit, why?"

"Cheng took me to discuss my now famous status."

"Cheng?"

"Albie to me. First Cousin Cheng to you."

"Cheng," Pablo said in grim disbelief. "He knew about the place?"

"They knew him, too."

Pablo's eyes widened knowingly. The lights came down. Puppy draped his right leg over Zelda's chair. "Zeld's putting on the weight, huh? We're going to need a donut intervention soon."

Wearing the sparkling black gown and a two-foot high silver crown, Mooshie traveled over the stage in an aerial seat harness, waving a wand at her loyal subjects, standing and applauding. Even Grandma joined in with a faint smile.

• • • •

WHEN CLARY GOT hungry, she crept out of the woods and into a town, always making sure she stayed near the road saying Nuevo York, only traveling at night. Americans were especially unfriendly at night. A nasty boy with pimples followed her along the grocery store aisles so she couldn't steal anything. Another store turned out to be a bar, where the owner, who also had a gun over the register like all of the Crusaders who must be very scared of Allahs, chased her out; but not before she sipped some warm beer.

She had a few dollars left. The shoes she'd stolen fell apart. What cagar. Her father and mother had beautiful handmade shoes with leather that smelled so good you wanted to eat the toes. But these said good-bye yesterday morning. Suddenly rocks bit her heels and the bottom of the shoes were waving see you Clary, I had enough of this walking. She wrapped a torn piece of shirt around her feet and bought a pair of shoes in Linton Town, making rasping noises and convincing the fat owner that her throat was sore. The owner was like any Crusader and didn't care if she talked as long as she had money.

After buying the pretty green shoes and an ice cream cone, she had only two dollars and coins left. She had a feeling she would need to take a bus or a train; she probably couldn't figure out how to steal a car. So she kept to the woods until her hunger made her dizzy and she had to steal food. Between the polizia and the Crusaders that was hard. She took some cookies in a store by pretending to be sick and moaning "Mama Mama" so the owner would let her run out without checking her pockets. That also worked in a pizzeria. When the waitress asked for money, Clary gagged and managed vomit; the Crusaders preferred no money to a girl poisoned. They were also afraid of polizia.

She was nibbling on a sandwich some Crusader left on top of the garbage when the train hooted noisily, calling her. She threw away the disgusting food and ran down the road, following the train, pulling up carefully by the tracks. Many Crusaders were climbing on, dressed in nice clothes. It would be easy to join them, but she needed a ticket.

Clary squinted at the sign by a clerk's window inside the train station. The words were small and there were many numbers. She poked her head over the counter.

"New York?"

The clerk shrugged. "Roundtrip?"

Clary slid her two dollars and coins under the bottom of the metal frame.

"Roundtrip's $43.20, one way's $23.50, which it'll be?"

The annoyed clerk pushed the money back while an ugly woman behind made impatient noises; Clary wanted to pull out her tongue. She pocketed her money and hurried along the track near two disgusting Crusader men. They stepped aside to let her on; she curtsied and calmly took a seat in the middle of the car. It had lots of heat and felt very good.

She fell asleep, but not for long. A train conductor with a stupid Dia de los Muertos hat poked her shoulder and held out his hand. She shook it and he smiled.

"Ticket, honey."

Clary held up her finger as she searched her pockets. "New York?"

"Fifth stop."

"New York Bronx."

"Fifth stop. Ticket, honey."

She held out the same two dollars and coins, along with an empty candy wrapper. The man sighed since getting money from eleven-year-old girls wasn't a pleasant part of his job.

"One way's $26.75 on the train, but I'll give it to you for the regular $23.50."

Clary mimed that was very nice, but she's happy to give him the two dollars just the same. That didn't please the conductor so she tried acting sick and moaning "Mama, Mama," which caused some alarm among the passengers, but no one gave her more money and the conductor didn't care, holding out his hand again.

"If you're sick, you'll have to get out at the next stop. I'm not cleaning up."

A man with gray hair across the aisle handed the conductor a card. "I'll take care of it."

The conductor shrugged, swiped the card in a little box and left her alone. She watched him go into another car.

"It's okay." The man smiled. "Your ticket's paid. New York Bronx."

Clary curtsied.

She sat with the gray-haired man, who chattered in English for a long time until the forests disappeared and huge ugly buildings jumped up on both sides of the tracks like they were waiting to scare her. The man laughed as she pressed her face against the window, New York Bronx getting bigger and dirtier.

The train went into a dark echoing tunnel and came out slowly onto a track surrounded by lots of trains and lots of people. The gray-haired man pointed out the many trains and the escalators and the posters of happy Crusaders eating cereal and drinking beer, and then all the many stores in what she finally learned was Bronx, Terminal.

Bronx New York, the man made her practice and she felt like a Crusader for the first time, repeating Bronx New York over and over. She showed him the address, hiding the ring, and he led her into a small car.

The nice man was taking her right there. She almost wished she could ride on the trains rumbling overhead, but the car was also warm and he played soft music and she fell asleep, this time for much longer. When she woke, the man had parked the car in an underground garage and was fixing her jacket. She flinched, uneasy. He gestured it was cold outside. She let him zip up her coat but didn't like the way his mouth went wet as he zipped right to her neck.

He took her hand onto the street. It was almost dark and he pointed to a building two blocks away and she understood that was his home. He gestured about eating and she nodded warily. His hand got wet and his lips got wet and she thought of the Allahs with their wet lips and wet hands. He wasn't an Allah but he kept looking down at her as if imagining.

Clary knelt to tie her shoe. She balanced on her hands and kicked back into the man's knee. He yelled and bent over. She kicked his face and he fell. She didn't stop to see if he got up because she was running so fast.

She was proud of finding the right building without any more Crusaders trying to rape her. It was very dark by the time she curled up on the steps, deciding to wait until morning before breaking in. But these Crusaders never slept and someone was always stepping over her; she shoved the name and address at them, but they shook their heads. No one even offered her a blanket.

Someone shook her awake. Clary jumped up, claws out.

The chubby African frowned. "You can't sleep here."

Clary handed her the address and name. The woman looked whiter.

"Who gave this to you?"

Clary studied her carefully. She'd come all this way. She wanted to get it right. Crusaders weren't trustworthy.

"Zelda Jones?"

Zelda nodded and, when Clary just stared doubtfully, she handed over her Lifecard. Clary compared the ID and note a few times; the African grumbled.

"I'm fucking Zelda Jones and I really have to pee so tell me what's going on."

Clary tugged at the woman's coat, but she slapped her hand away. Clary slapped back, sticking out her stomach. The stupido African suddenly understood and slowly unbuttoned her coat. Satisfied, Clary handed Zelda the jewelry box.

"New York Bronx," Clary said.

33

Zelda closed the bathroom door and slipped on the ring, crying as Clary warily searched the apartment, opening doors and closets and drawers. After she had no more tears, Zelda replaced the ring in the box and found the child cradling a plate piled high with AG cold cuts, drinking milk from the bottle.

Zelda made tea and sat across from Clary, whose bandage had fallen off.

"What happened?" She touched her cheek.

"Allahu Akbar," Clary said casually, wrapping bologna around cheese and then ham around both, happily dipping the concoction into mustard.

Zelda sighed and pointed. "English?"

"Espanol." The girl made another breadless sandwich.

"Espanol."

"Si." Clary peered hopefully. "Hablas Espanol?"

Zelda shook her head. "Hablas Ingles?"

Clary shook her head and they continued chewing and sipping. Finally, Zelda couldn't stall anymore and held out the slip of paper. "Dead? No more?"

Zelda collapsed on the couch, miming choking noises, then fell still. Clary nodded, applauding.

"Boat?" Zelda tooted a horn and shuffled around the living room. When the best response was Clary staring dimly, Zelda waved a sheet from the linen closet as a sail. Another dim stare. You couldn't find someone smarter to die around, Diego?

Zelda made salmon sounds, flapping her gills. Clary smiled.

"Pescardo."

That she gets?

"Diego estaba en el barco."

Zelda frowned. Clary emulated the sail-waving. "Diego. Barco."

"Si. Barco, barco."

"Diego murio en la playa." Clary made rowing gestures, dragging a couch pillow along the floor before cradling it. "Muerte. Diego."

Zelda started crying again; the girl coldly ignored her grief, holding out the empty plate, which Zelda refilled with the last of the cold cuts. She returned from the kitchen and tapped her chest. "Zelda."

The girl brightened. "Clary."

"Diego on barco." Zelda made an exaggerated face of wonderment, palms up, then traced a question mark in the air.

The girl raced around the room wildly re-enacting Diego and the barco, popping her mouth with loud explosions, keeling over as if dead and pointing wildly to the sky. Zelda brought out Della's cookies so Clary could, a bit slower, tell the story again. She slumped onto the couch and held up ten fingers twice, tapping her face.

Zelda pointed up. "Airplane?" Clary frowned and Zelda buzzed around, arms extended in wings. Clary countered by rotating her hand upward, whirring.

Whirring? She repeated her 'copter impression; Clary whistled approvingly and finished the milk.

Zelda really wished she had given up alcohol tomorrow. "Allahu Akbar?" She stood on the chair, miming shooting.

Clary shook her head. "Crusaders."

Zelda swallowed, something clicking. "Crusaders?"

The girl angrily babbled in Spanish. All Zelda got was her repeating Crusaders again and again.

Clary fought sleep for a while, eyelids drooping and bulging open in fear before a glance at Zelda comforted her enough to drift off. Zelda covered her with several blankets until sweat beaded on the child's forehead.

She made more tea, carefully pulling out four kitchen knives protruding from Clary's pockets.

• • • •

LIEUTENANT YASAKI WAS deathly pale. He swallowed, unable to respond until Captain Parnassa poked him again.

"She just disappeared, sir."

Tomas pressed his lips together. "That's not a report, soldier."

Parnassa shoved Yasaki.

"Grandma turned south ten feet out of the Stanton's supper club. I, I was on her left."

The Captain added, "I was five feet ahead."

Tomas nodded for Yasaki to continue.

"And she vanished."

"Any sounds?"

"She didn't scream."

That wasn't what Stilton needed, but he couldn't push it. "How much time did it take for Grandma to disappear?"

Yasaki made as if he were counting. "Three seconds, I think."

"You're not sure?" Parnassa growled.

"Three." Yasaki nodded. "Three, sir. I didn't know what to do."

"He reacted quickly, Major," Parnassa defended her charge with a hand on Yasaki's shoulder.

"I'm sure he did." Tomas glanced out of the jeep at the surrounding ten-person detachment. "Keep the shooters on the roofs, 'copter Allie circling, and return 'copter Billie home."

Parnassa saluted. "As if she were still here, sir?"

Tomas nodded, wincing.

"What happened?" Yasaki persisted innocently, earning a painful smack from his Captain.

"Sometimes Grandma likes to just get away, son." Tomas smiled reassuringly.

He waited until the last shooter left before heading onto the four train. The final subway of the night clattered lazily through the dark skyline. Tomas sat in the last car, eyes ahead, mind empty in case she contacted him. But she wouldn't.

Stilton jostled a sleeping drunk out before the subway police arrested him for vagrancy, hurrying along East 205th Street past brooding empty buildings. Protocol AF3E had only been used once, and that'd been way on the other side of the Bronx in a modest walk-up with quiet neighbors. Why Grandma had changed to an abandoned building, he didn't know. He sensed his way up two flights, counting steps.

Tomas stopped at fifty-seven and felt for the door handle. Still locked, thank her painted fingernails. He twisted off the handle and crouched forward, gun drawn, into the bare room which had an extra shroud of darkness. Twenty-three paces at two o'clock bumped against another closed door. Another violent twist inside, then eighteen steps toward twelve o'clock.

He slipped a thin key into the lock and opened the door. A perfect funnel of light streamed onto the A2. He gasped slightly. Except for her real more pronounced wrinkles along the eyes, it was a perfect resemblance. No one would know. Except him.

Tomas fumbled for the switch, unable to look away from the robot. He calmed himself into remembering the code. Lenora 2. Just punch it in. Your job's to protect her.

Or is your job to protect your country? Maybe Cheng was right. Maybe they weren't the same anymore.

• • • •

WATCHING BEHIND THE long glass window, Detective Tad Buca pushed back his brown hat in disgust as the gray-haired man wobbled toward the door, back bent from the exhaustion of proclaiming his innocence.

Buca nudged his partner Layon Y'or, who grumbled in disappointment.

"56 percent," Y'or said.

"Sure?"

"You were watching, too."

Buca rubbed his bloodshot eyes. Three hours of naked young girls and boys in all sorts of poses and all sorts of sex acts in all sorts of outfits. He hated the night shift.

"Still gets him cleansed," Layon said with a faint smile about the man's inappropriate responses to the videos.

Buca grunted. "That's something."

Anytime a complainant or suspect was brought in with anything remotely touching on a child, they got The Kurosawa, epic filmic moments of child pornography. Their reactions were charted on the Perv, officially the Pedophilia Scanning System.

Before they'd been banned, psychiatrists had controlled these tests, but the scandals of using results to generate more patients put them on the streets, where they belonged, Buca felt. Now the Brown Hats, the Detectives, ran the men and women through. To be a cop, a Blue Shirt, Brown Hat, required impeccable morals and judgement. If the people couldn't trust the police, who could they trust?

"Should we send him downtown now?" the more junior Y'or asked hopefully.

Buca considered this for a moment as they returned to their desks in the 34th Precinct squad room. "Keep him around a little longer."

"I can't watch the movies anymore," Y'or pleaded.

The perv protested angrily when he'd been forced into being tested. I was being friendly to a little girl in trouble. I paid for her ticket and she attacks me.

One tough little girl, Buca sneered, giving the guy props for arrogance.

"Why'd he come in?" Layon, only six months into the job, had asked hours ago.

The perv could've let it go, gone on home and popped one of the illicit films in an illicit handviewer and who would've known. But, Buca had explained, he believed he wasn't a pedophile and so, by coming forward, he demonstrated, mostly to himself, his own innocence.

Help the children above all else, said Grandma's Fourth Insight.

Buca waved off the cold pizza floating around the big squad room at five in the morning and rummaged through his desk,

"Where's the morning update?" he asked.

Layon pushed the report over and gobbled down a slice.

Buca poured another cup of coffee. To please his doctor, who said his prostate would be a beach ball if he didn't cut down, he only filled the mug half-way, dousing the bitter brew with powdered creamer. He stirred slowly, glancing at the midnight reports from around the country. Stabbing in Cleveland, suspect at large. Woman, twenty, black curls. New Haven, shooting, teenager, blonde and armed, at large.

374 | GARY MORGENSTEIN

No, it wasn't from tonight, he thought, leaning back at his chipped wooden desk, still stirring and thinking.

"Where's the updates from the previous three days?" he asked Layon, playing with the brim of his brown hat.

"What's up?" His partner handed over the files.

"Something's sticking in my head. The girl the perv described." Buca tapped his cheek.

• • • •

MRS. WASHINGTON SQUEALED with delight at the sparkling gold shoe squeezed around her thick left foot.

"Lovely, dear. Just lovely."

Annette frowned at the way the shoe and foot battled over who'd give up first.

"I see your former husband all over town now on those billboards. Striking man. You must be so proud," the pudgy woman acknowledged the role everyone had in their ex's life, post-marriage, good and bad. "A continuous thread of love, sometimes unstitched, went Grandma's Thirty-First Insight."

"Yeah. He's a big shot." Annette sighed at the expensive shoes she wouldn't sell today.

"And that fiancé of his. Dara Dinkins…"

"Dinton. Dara Dinton."

"That's it. A stunning voice. We heard her at the Cobblers Club last night. She sang a wondrous medley of oldies."

"Was she alone?" Annette reddened.

"There were about two thousand of us." Washington chuckled and returned to her shoes. "You've done wonders as always, darling. I'll take two pairs."

Two. Crap. "No, you won't." Annette yanked off the shoe and Washington yelped. "Sorry, but it just doesn't fit."

"It's only a little snug." Washington held onto the heel.

"Your feet are too big, ma'am, and I will not sell you a shoe that is missized."

"But I like it."

"I'm flattered. But you're still not getting this." Annette gathered up the shoe boxes.

"Doesn't it come in my size?"

"They don't make them that big."

Leaving Washington's apartment, Ramos angrily swung her bag down the fancy streets of Riverdale past stately, impeccably maintained buildings and into the downtown local green stop. Lost that customer, didn't you, she muttered darkly on the bench. Directly across the tracks was a long, long, long advert with Grandma smiling and Puppy with his glove and the Whore singing and the damn FORGIVENESS.

Yeah, forgive the Miners and baseball but I'm not about to forgive you, Puppy.

Annette stomped up the steps over to the northbound side, glancing left and right for any meddling assholes. She drew a mascara moustache on Puppy and Mooshie's faces and hurried back to the street, scowling a teenager off the last seat at the bus stop.

Need more sleep, she mumbled. Annette had waited up for Kenuda until nearly three in the morning when he finally collapsed on the bed, giving no reason to her simple "where the hell have you been" except "on business."

"With who?" she snapped.

He'd grunted that dismissive "go design a shoe with buckles grunt" and turned over. They were in the pre-marriage phase. They should be having dinner every night and telling each other banal stories about their day and snuggling before vidmovies or having wild sex. They hadn't had wild sex or lukewarm sex or even a quickie in twelve days. Leaving open the shower curtain and making extra suds, parading about the apartment, wet hair down to her shoulders, bathrobe flung open, her breasts bouncing off the SC scrambled eggs, begging him to lick the yolk off her nipples, what more could she do?

Kenuda was a virile man with an exceptionally large penis that made her giggle, firing off his cannon twice, three times a night back when they were having wild sex. You just don't dump the gun powder into the gutter. It's gotta go somewhere.

Business. Making that slut famous. Puppy and Dara. Dara and Puppy. America's new darling couple. Star pitcher and star singer. Ooh, would they consider making a vidmovie together, one of those breathless women with bad makeup had asked on *Wake Up My Darlings* this morning. Oh sure, that got Kenuda's attention over breakfast. No grunting I'm tired, Annette, and my gun powder is dry. Oh no, when he watched Dara his head lit up like bulbs had been screwed into his ears.

"Quite a little report," he'd chuckled.

"What time will you be home tonight, dear?" she'd asked.

"Usual."

Usual. Usual. Annette shoved aside the waiting passengers and hailed a cab.

• • • •

OTHER THAN THE faint rumbles of an occasional truck, the only noise in the apartment was the sound of their charcoal pencils scratching across the pad. Zelda would hold up a funny clown face, making Clary smile, then the child would furiously draw her own clown. After a while, Zelda realized that Clary was waiting to imitate whatever she drew.

They'd already drawn the boats; here, the child eagerly took over. One ship with a crescent moon and star flag and the other with a cross. Little children lying around covered in blood. A 'copter with dashes indicating bullets. One larger figure dead.

Zelda hadn't asked for the scene on the playa, but Clary had merrily pressed on, sketching a Diego figure, mouth downcast, charcoal smeared on his torso representing blood. A ring in his hand. Zelda bit her lip. The Clary figure had a big smile. Zelda wasn't sure if that meant Diego died peacefully or whether she'd actually smiled.

The bearded man looking down in all the boat pictures and the beach death scene had a more genuine smile. Wide, warm, with sun rays shooting out of his ears and a crown floating over his head. Zelda wasn't familiar with Allah mythology; maybe this was Mohammad, haunting the child. She pointed at the mysterious figure.

Clary rolled her eyes. "Jesus Christo." Looking around warily, Clary grudgingly letting Zelda hold the silver cross. "Jesus Christo."

"God?" Zelda tried.

"Si, si." Clary chattered on about Catholicism for nearly five minutes, acting out Jesus on the cross and various devastating lightning storms. Zelda smiled politely, disappointing Clary, who shoved the cross deep into her pocket and moodily curled up on the couch.

Gimme a break, kid. I don't speak Spanish and I don't believe in God. Zelda made tea and cookies; eating always brightened the child's mood and soon they were humming together while Zelda drew a house. Clary followed with an exact replica and waited for Zelda's approval.

Shaking her head, Zelda drew a stick figure, pointing at her chest and gesturing for Clary to follow. After a few moments, the girl reluctantly drew herself, abruptly adding a cross on the figure's face. Zelda reached for Clary's pad; the girl reacted with a feral growl.

"Allahu Akbar," Zelda said softly.

Clary glared at the pad.

"Allahu Akbar," Zelda repeated.

The girl cradled the pad onto her knees, but that wasn't enough privacy so she hopped onto the chair. She scribbled furiously, glaring at Zelda. She finally handed over her drawing.

Bearded men with hooked noses and long penises surrounded the Clary figure. The little girl calmly tapped the page.

"Allahu Akbar." She laid on her back and spread her legs, panting, then flipped onto her stomach, wriggling with pathetic moans before rising onto her knees, mouth bobbing.

"Jesus Christo." Clary's mouth trembled, saying quietly, "Donde es Jesus Christo."

Zelda tried hugging her, but Clary ran into the bedroom, slamming the door. No sobs; shortly came the sound of a screeching vidgame. Deep in thought, Zelda carried the pad to the ringing door; she'd already received two get-well-soon flower deliveries from Boar Face. Food would be nice, dear Katrina.

"Hi." Annette brushed past into the living room, where she considered the mess as typical and whirled around to face Zelda. "Look, I know you're not happy to see me."

"That's a deep understatement."

"I tried your office but they said you were sick."

"No chocolate to perk me up?"

"Looks like you're not depriving yourself." Annette sneered at Zelda's drooping belly. "I'll make this brief."

Zelda wrapped her bathrobe tighter. "I hope so."

"I know you hate me for the way I treated Puppy."

"As well as your general warm qualities."

"I'm sorry I'm not your type."

Zelda glowered. "What the hell do you want, Annette? I'm under the weather."

"I need your help."

"From someone who hates you?"

"It's for Puppy. I'm sure if I collapsed and started bleeding, you'd wait an hour to contact the medemerline."

Zelda shrugged.

"His fiancé is screwing my fiancé. Even someone with your morals understands that violates the law. If Puppy knows his fiancé is screwing my fiancé, he is as guilty as his fiancé."

"Dara."

"Yes. Dara the great singer Dinton. She's screwing my fiancé."

"Elias the great Commissioner Kenuda."

Annette gave her the finger. "You don't care about me, fine. I don't care about you, fine. But you care about your little Puppy who you always had a crush on and I'm telling you to tell him to tell Dara Dinton to back off or else."

Zelda stiffened. "Or else what?"

"Well." Annette laughed coldly. "Or else I will tell The Couples what Dara is doing. And then good-bye to America's Sweethearts…"

Growling like a wounded animal, Clary leaped over the couch and rushed at Annette with a kitchen knife. Zelda yanked her away, but one of the girl's kicks found Annette's shin. She groaned and kicked back to cover her retreat.

"What is that thing?"

Clary let loose a torrent of Spanish rage.

"Get out," Zelda screamed.

Annette wagged her finger. "Do it. Or else."

Clary bit Zelda's hand, breaking free for another charge; Zelda caught Clary as she chased the screaming Annette down the hallway.

• • • •

ALBERT CAREFULLY STUDIED the mess of paper clips and pencils on his desk as if they could reveal where Grandma had gone.

"Any ideas?"

Tomas shook his head. Grandma was the only person in America without a Life-card to track.

"What about near Nantucket where she went last time?"

Tomas explained the beach house had already been searched.

"Perhaps she was kidnapped."

"No one gets through my security," Stilton said; Cheng raised an eyebrow. "Grandma did this on her own."

"Yes, she did," Albert said sadly. "Without telling you, her most trusted aide. Or me, who has been with her since the beginning."

Of the Original Eight, only he and Lenora remained. Dell and M'akio died of cancer young; Ellie and Atter, on 10/12; Viktor and Ramon at their homes, the bioregens only able to sustain their wills for so long.

You and I, Lenora. We started this and we'll finish it. One way or the other.

Tomas finally answered, "She has her reasons."

"Everyone always does, Major. The worst creature on the face of this planet has the best logical basis for what they do, from political and religious extremists to schizophrenics hearing voices. The Mufti had tracts of Quran reasoning to justify the murder of innocents and the enslavement of most of the world."

The Major's dark face turned inky with anger. "Are you comparing Grandma to that pig?"

"No." He almost added, not yet. "But then why is she sneaking off to meet his son?"

Tomas had no answer.

"This is not about our loyalty," Albert softened his voice. "That's not in doubt."

The Major nodded wearily and pointed to the Mid-Atlantic coastline on the map.

"She'd have to meet Abdullah nearby. Otherwise it'd be too complicated, even for her."

"Could she have help from someone else?"

Stilton shook his head. "She wouldn't trust anyone but us."

They exchanged ironic nods.

"Any tracking of enemy ships within our waters?" Tomas asked.

Cheng hesitated how much to say. "Our radar's spotty, when we can risk that because it violates the Surrender. Usually the Allahs look away. But Abdullah is as rogue as Grandma."

"So he could've sailed right into an American port without us knowing?"

"Your Collector did, Major." Albert smiled faintly.

"A European, not an Allah. Two Allahs." Tomas said as Cheng frowned. "He's probably traveling with this Captain I met. That'd be too much to hide, no. I think she's gone beyond our waters. No matter what she's thinking, Grandma wouldn't chance letting the Camels inside America."

Albert nodded grimly while Tomas remained focused on the map. Three miles of The Family and then the crescent moon and star. "She'd take a 'copter."

Cheng's eyes narrowed, recalling Lenora leading a wing attack in '60 in the Sinai. "Can she really still fly?" He had trouble walking up the steps some days.

The Major nodded. "Enough." He paused. "The spare one is missing."

"What spare 'copter, Major?"

Tomas hesitated. "In Westchester." He hesitated again. "There's also backups in Albany and Pittsfield, Massachusetts."

"And?" Albert asked impatiently.

"The underground train to Nebraska. The old NORAD headquarters."

Cheng considered the tip of another pencil. "Is there more?" He noted how quickly Tomas shook his head. "Are we in this together, Major?"

"Yes sir."

"No more secrets?"

Stilton nodded glumly. "None. If you make sure I'm involved in every aspect of the search."

Cheng's white teeth flashed. "Of course. We're partners now."

• • • •

ZELDA LOCKED THE windows and the door, but she knew that Clary would find a way out of a vault under Grandma's butt. For distractions she'd left food in every cupboard and every shelf in the fridge; the girl was systematic, like a dog hunting down a bone.

Clary disdainfully waved off Zelda's offer to load more vidgames, demonstrating she'd already figured it out. Good. Just stay put.

Puppy was already at Santo's, talking baseball with two tables pushed together to accommodate his admirers. After a tight hug, he introduced Zelda as a former star second baseman who let artistic dreams ruin a promising baseball career. She spent a couple minutes making up some shit about owning him at bat until the tables settled back, satisfied.

"You look nice," he said, waving Pablo over with a breadstick, followed by another round of hugs and kisses.

Zelda ordered deep fried mozzarella cheese, which earned arched eyebrows. "You don't see me for two weeks and you play the how fat have you gotten game?"

"No," Puppy said gallantly. "We're referring to your voluptuous E sized cups."

Her scowl sent his attention toward a pretty blonde in the corner; he doffed his cap.

"Will you take off your damn Yankee hat?" Zelda growled.

"Okay, evil princess." Puppy laid it lovingly on his lap.

She hailed a waiter. "Can I change my order to a salad? Any fake crap food will do."

Zelda gulped her water as the men watched, worried.

"So. I'm doing pretty well."

"That's obvious," Pablo said wryly.

"I am. Look." She pulled apart her mouth.

380 | GARY MORGENSTEIN

"Job promotion?"

She smacked Puppy. "Would I be this happy if I got a promotion, which I did anyway?"

The boys exchanged another concerned look.

Pablo leaned forward. "Are you in trouble?"

That was a genius sort of question, she realized.

"I know you think I'm porky ass." Zelda glared down their feeble protests. "But this is not all blubber."

"There's nothing wrong with a good appetite…" Puppy began.

"It's not from eating, is it?" Pablo's eyes narrowed. Zelda blinked back tears and shook her head. "Is it mine?"

"Why does everyone ask that?"

"Everyone?"

"Who's everyone?" Puppy persisted.

"She's pregnant," he said with mild disdain.

"Shit," Puppy muttered, sitting up straight. "Oh shit, guys."

"Don't give me that look," Zelda said. "It's a great honor. Maybe I can have another one someday. It hurts and I didn't plan it but I'm going to the Parents once a week and I don't throw up much and I'm kinda relieved and a little happy. Maybe a lot happy."

"We're happy for you, too." Puppy poked the sullen Pablo.

"So it's not mine?" the dentist asked.

"No. I got it tested."

"Diego?" Puppy asked.

She hesitated, nodding.

"Who the hell is Diego?" The name was like fried feces in Pablo's mouth.

She nearly lost it. "How many more questions do you have?"

"Until you give us all the answers."

Zelda jumped up and showed off her belly to the room. "Two months." She curtsied at the approving applause and moved her chair and bread to another table of diners before her friends coaxed her back.

Pablo and Puppy ordered Kansas IPA beers, studying Zelda as if she'd soon fly around the room backwards. She joined them in the silence, figuring the story about Diego, Clary and how Black Tops murdered twenty orphans might be too much for one day.

"You need a partner at the Parents?" Pablo asked softly.

"I have someone. But thanks."

Pablo ordered another round. "I'm still a licensed medical officer. So if you need any help…"

"I'll ask." She squeezed their hands and ordered the mozzarella en carozzo. No one had an appetite.

When Zelda got home, charcoaled sketches of Clary were taped to the walls, on top of the stove, over the bathroom sink and tucked in the couch and chair cushions.

"Buenos noches." Clary burst out of the bedroom, spinning balletically on her toes. "Clary es una persona muy famosa."

Zelda tossed aside her purse.

"Una persona muy famosa," Clary repeated, annoyed.

When Zelda still didn't get it, Clary impatiently dragged her into the bedroom. They watched the vidnews for a few moments. Zelda got up to leave, but Clary yanked her back onto the bed.

"Una momento." She muttered something about loco senorita, then jumped up and down on the bed, applauding. "Clary es una persona muy famosa."

A sketch of Clary, complete with the scarred cross on her cheek, moved along the screen, bordered by HELP US FIND THIS MISSING GIRL. PLEASE CONTACT YOUR LOCAL BLUE SHIRT PRECINCT. THANK YOU.

Zelda rushed into the bathroom and retched. Clary happily sketched another photo.

• • • •

MOOSHIE SQUATTED AT the edge of the dark 167th Street subway platform, then tumbled forward, cushioning herself into a roll several inches from the track. The ground rumbled slightly and, in the tunnel, distant lights of the express spliced the blackness.

You must've landed on your head. Cracked your skull and then the train finished you off. Mooshie crouched, watching the train thunder past, taking the light with it.

She grabbed the edge of the platform to hoist herself back up. A strong hand clutched her forearm. Mooshie gasped.

"You could hurt yourself." Hazel tugged her up; she broke free and stumbled backwards slightly. "That third rail is still alive."

Mooshie shifted her weight from right to left, glancing up and down the tracks to determine which way she'd run.

John laughed at her anxiety and introduced himself. "John Hazel."

Mooshie kept her recognition to herself.

"You do know who I am?"

She jumped vertically back onto the platform. Hazel whistled admiringly.

"Why are you following me?"

"Can't I just hang out here like you do? Quiet. Good place to think." He threw a can at something scurrying nearby.

Mooshie headed toward the steps.

"What, no derisive hair flip, Mooshie?"

She laughed, stopping. "Who?"

"The greatest baseball player ever."

"You got me mixed up, baby."

"Nah." He shook his head.

"I sing her songs. I'm also not Paul McCartney or Goodley Alizi."

"They weren't murdered here, either."

Lopez waited warily as Hazel approached, holding up his hands innocently.

"You didn't much mingle with the fans once you slid downward, Moosh. Okay if I call you that? But when you were the greatest baseball player ever and one of the greatest singers ever, you'd take the subway every day. Your apartment was three blocks away at the Concourse Arms. I used to wait for you every day, in the middle of the boulevard, behind a tree. They hadn't outlawed autographs yet but I was still too shy. I just wanted a glimpse of the great Mooshie heading to the stadium or off to record an album."

He rocked on his artificial leg and began singing, "Blue eyed boy, I'm not your toy. Don't play with my soul 'cause I ain't got one." Hazel puckered his mouth. "*Kicking My Nuts* never took off. Don't get it. The lyrics were so simple and poignant."

"Mister Hazel…"

"John."

"I only sing her songs. I'm Dara Dinton. My mother died on this subway which is why…"

"Your mother died after you, in the chem attack. Along with my whole family," his voice hardened. "Like I said, you didn't die here either. They slipped you some biozine in a bottle of vodka you bought two blocks away. You were already drunk so you didn't notice the seal was broken. You sipped as you walked, not caring anymore about your public persona. They brought you here and tossed your drunk ass under the train. All the crap about killing yourself over guilt for supporting the Miners was bullshit Grandma propaganda to turn an enemy into a tool."

"I don't believe you." Her mind whirled with memories. Falling down, being carried, she did so much of that at the end. The push, the people, the screams.

"Yeah, there were screams, Moosh." He finished her thoughts. "When they found you. Maybe that's what you remember. And that push in the back well, probably they were sloppy carrying you. Had to be ex-BTs. No one active would violate their oath. They paid a few people who were light on their ethics to swear they saw you jump, fall."

Hazel gestured several times. Liars.

She gestured back, jutting out her chin. You too.

John shrugged. "Those are the facts as I know them, Moosh. I don't get why you're surprised. You've come here, what, five, six times since you returned, trying to piece it together. Unless you think you came back to solve this mystery."

Mooshie smiled coldly. "You got a theory about that, too, pretty news guy?"

"I do. You wouldn't believe me. But I have a couple people who might persuade you. Couple people who hate Grandma, too."

"No one hates her like I do," she rasped.

"You'd be surprised."

She listened for footsteps.

"I'm alone." Hazel shrugged.

"And if I refuse this offer."

He sighed wearily. "Why would you, Moosh?"

34

Azhar scratched his freshly shaven face and sniffed at the faint yellow air lingering obstinately around the entrance to the massive building.

"The line's over there," Abdullah said, pointing to about ten people patiently waiting outside a thick door. "Best if we don't loiter like we're strangers."

Mustafa grunted. He disliked everything about this plan since they'd docked hours ago at a secluded spot in the lower half of the strange semi-populated city where people pressed forward grimly with few smiles or even eye contact. Buses and cars crept along reluctantly, sometimes empty. Abruptly, like a mistake, lights blazed out of a skyscraper, receding futilely into wide swatches of dark streets in some weird checkerboard of life and not life.

Death, Azhar rubbed at his unfamiliar bare cheek. A place between Heaven and Hell where millions die and don't know where to go, and those left behind aren't certain how to continue. If he believed in ghosts he would swear he had seen many. But he'd already wasted his share of complaining on being forced to shave.

The Son seemed genuinely fascinated, as if inside a living museum. He'd stopped Azhar's heart a few times already with his recklessness before wandering off to visit the Wall Street area.

"They must satisfy their greed." Abdullah had sneered. "That is what they offer most. Turning dirt into gold."

By craning his head and walking back and forth in front of a large building with the letters NYSE, he'd attracted the stares of black-uniformed soldiers behind thick brick walls, tank turrets peeking out menacingly. Azhar had tugged him away, but a soldier in a reflective black face mask intercepted them.

"Papers." The soldier held out a gloved hand.

While Azhar silently prayed, Abdullah happily produced their forged documents. "This is our first time, my brother and I."

Please be quiet, Azhar pleaded.

"It is so wonderful to see the vibrancy still alive."

The Black Top silently returned the papers and studied Azhar's.

"We have an engagement to the north. Which would be the most convenient path?" The Black Top ignored Abdullah, instead staring at Azhar. "Where are you from?"

Oh Mohammed, I beg you allow me to borrow the Son's tongue for a moment.

"It says there." Azhar smiled respectfully. "Geeohja."

The Black Top grunted.

"So many wonderful accents in our wonderful country." Abdullah bowed slightly. "And what of you, young man? From what part of this great nation do you originate?"

"Woman," the voice lashed out, her head tilting left and right before she returned Azhar's papers, disappointed she had no reason to beat them. Azhar's knees wobbled.

Abdullah had talked about that experience all morning, adding to it with thoughts concerning the bus system while engaging a couple of indifferent passengers about the woes of mass transit back in Geeohja, wretched compared to Manhattan. Boring the middle of the bus, Abdullah went to the rear and asked an older woman with stringy gray hair to point out some of the sights.

Delighted to fill her day with something other than riding the bus, the woman, who introduced herself as Blanche, pleased to meet you Mr. Tekka and Mr. Shymal, described the Greenwich Village as a center of poets and musicians, the Fifth Avenue as a repository of wealthy residences and the Madison Avenue as a hotbed of commerce. Once, she added bitterly. She recalled her youth, which Azhar estimated a hundred years or so ago, and the vitality of the city, especially her succession of female admirers; Azhar was disgusted by the proud perversions.

How did these people ever lead anyone?

Somehow they made it here to the famous Empire State Building. The line moved inside, Abdullah admitting goosebumps at this latest American adventure. Azhar again tugged him to the back of the elevator; he would've had more luck persuading his eldest son to wear a cross. Abdullah continued on and on about the historic building, annoying everyone who hurried away when they got to the 108th floor.

The Son grinned; Azhar nodded respect at his ploy. They wandered, unsure which was north. Mustafa leaned on the icy railing, peering at the twinkling distant lights splayed between black pockets, as if giants had set up immense black curtains. He squinted down onto the tiny figures dotting the streets. Once so many millions and now, so few. That is why we are here, to feel guilt. For what? The terrorists did this. That was not my government, not my religion.

Mustafa sighed. Yes. That is why we are here.

He realized he was alone and panicked, hurrying around the far corner where the Son leaned against the railing, engaged in another conversation with a stranger.

Azhar joined him. The small elderly woman pulled back her shawl and extended her hand, smiling.

"Nice to meet you. I'm Lenora."

Azhar's mouth went dry. He bowed deeply at the waist; Grandma chuckled.

"Perhaps we should keep this casual," she said.

Abdullah clasped his shoulder. "He lost his equilibrium along with his beard."

Grandma's eyes twinkled and Azhar felt as if he were luxuriating in a warm bath.

She winked, her smile slowly fading. "Lovely view, isn't it? Well, it was more beautiful once, but we're working on that. Over there is New Jersey. You've been downtown and there, across the East River, is Brooklyn and Queens. Both have boisterous work forces. New businesses opening daily."

"Manhattan remains behind."

"Yes," Lenora admitted. "But compared to what it was, growing. Sometimes that's the only useful metric."

Abdullah pointed at a cluster of lights. "That is your Bronx?"

"My Bronx." Grandma beamed. "It had always been the, well, there's an old saying, red-haired stepchild." She smiled at their puzzled frowns. "That means neglected. The murderers didn't think it was important enough to attack a poor, less educated community."

They stared at the Bronx as if expecting the lights to join the conversation.

"The trip went well?" she finally asked, edging away from the passing tourists.

"Your sea chart was perfect. Docking codes worked and no one has questioned our papers."

Grandma nodded, pleased.

"But how do you say where we're from? I pronounced it Geeohja and got a few curious looks."

She chuckled again; Azhar felt as if she were scrubbing his scalp with scented shampoo.

"Close enough. We still don't get enough visitors from other states for anyone to distinguish accents. But it's increasing. If you'd gone uptown, north, to 50th Street in the midtown area, you would've seen we're re-opening the famous Radio City Music Hall."

Abdullah did a dainty little kick of both legs. Grandma did her own kicks, putting her arm on his shoulder. Azhar was embarrassed.

"Azhar isn't sure about our dancing." Grandma nudged him.

"He has many virtues," Abdullah said over his protests, "but artistic insights isn't one of them."

"My dear friend Tomas is like that, too. Shall we?" Grandma tucked the shawl back on and slipped her hands through the crook of their arms.

The glow of the restaurant sign, Schulmann's, guided them down a long black street. An old waiter with uncombed white hair warmly greeted Grandma, warily nodding at Azhar and Abdullah as he led them past a few old men by the front door and into a red plastic booth at the rear.

"The usual, Lenora?"

"I'm not sure yet, Nathan. But definitely a Cel-Ray for everyone." She winked knowingly at Abdullah and Azhar, who were peering suspiciously at the bowl of pickles and sour tomatoes on the scuffed black-and-white table.

"You eat them," growled Nathan, shoving the bowl into the center and reluctantly laying the menus down.

"Have I ever brought you bad customers?" Lenora took Nathan's wrist. "Since 2036, right?"

"2035."

"You sure?"

"You ordered a cream soda, pastrami on rye and then I nearly kicked you out because you dumped half a bottle of ketchup on it."

She leaned forward with a girlish grin. "And why didn't you?"

Nathan blushed. "Because you were hot."

"Wasn't I?" Grandma sighed. "We'll order eventually."

"Meaning to leave you alone."

"Please."

Abdullah tentatively bit the end of a pickle, pleasantly surprised. "I'm not familiar with this food."

Mustafa desperately searched the menu for something familiar.

"Nathan won't let you leave without trying the matzo ball soup."

The Son flinched. "Jew food?"

"And very good."

"They're my enemy."

"So am I."

Abdullah smiled slowly. "A lesson contained in a bowl of condiments?"

"Just a meal."

"I don't believe the word 'just' is ever appropriate for you, Grandma."

"I'm having the pastrami." She closed the menu and waved over the impatient Nathan, ordering meat sandwiches and soups all around.

They sat silently for a moment, sipping Cel-Rays.

"I've never made peace before." Abdullah finished his drink with relish.

"Nor have I," she said dryly.

"Our terms were fair the first time. You lost."

"Now both of us are losing." She waited for the Son to nod. "I'll offer you food."

"Not this, I hope."

"You should only be so fortunate. Bio-agra."

"We already have that."

She smiled sweetly. "Is that why your people are starving?"

Abdullah stiffened. "Only where the work is below par."

"It's hard to work when you're dying of malnutrition. Bio-agra techniques," she repeated. "Otherwise you'll never feed the populations. My scientists say the fallout has permanently disfigured the atmosphere flow. Whatever natural foods we grow are a miracle."

"We have scientists, too." Abdullah shrugged, conceding. "And they say the same thing. Fine. All the food we need."

"In stages, of course." She nodded briskly. "The Armistice naval lines must be twenty-five mile territorial waters, the rest, neutral."

"You want us surrendering the seas?"

"We're talking about free trade."

Azhar felt Abdullah tense. "Too soon for that."

"As a goal then."

"Let's keep it vague."

"Within three years."

"Five."

"Four," she said.

"Four and we keep fifteen mile territorial waters."

"Four and twenty miles."

They exchanged nods. The Son rolled a sour tomato. "Anything else?"

Grandma waited for Nathan to serve the three soups. He wouldn't leave until he was satisfied by their response.

"It's good." Azhar beamed.

"Why would you think it wasn't?" The waiter grumbled his way behind the counter.

"Dear, trying eating the matzo ball along with the soup." Grandma demonstrated, leaving Azhar to practice slicing the monstrous ball without spilling the broth. "You allow any non-Muslims to leave. We'll take them in."

Abdullah pulled a face. "There's tens of millions."

"Hopefully more," Grandma said angrily. "The camps were closed, as your father promised, correct?"

"I cannot speak for my father's promises," he said harshly. "But I have no information that any Crusader…Christian executions continued. The Jews, well, they are gone."

Grandma's eyes fluttered around the restaurant. "Then there should be hundreds of millions of Christians in Europe and Africa, as well as South America."

"I don't know." He sighed. "But probably."

Azhar caught Abdullah's hesitation, but remained silent. This was not his place to carve up the world. He had enough trouble with this slippery matzoh ball.

"It'll be thought that as soon as all your people are out, you'll have no compunction about striking," the Son said.

She nodded. "I have some who'd advise that. We both have people who mistrust."

Abdullah nudged aside the untouched soup. "Quotas and small children to begin."

"Children and old people."

"Small quotas."

"How many?"

"I can't answer that."

"I need a sense of some figure."

"You ask something which cuts to the core of our suspicions."

"Yes, losing all those hostages will be unsettling."

Abdullah glared. "You abandoned them, Grandma. You chose surrender."

"Rather than mutual annihilation," she said softly.

"Spare me your piety. I hear enough human interpretations of how Allah wants us to behave."

"And I hear enough of how I'm supposed to behave," she flared, turning toward Azhar. "What do you think, Captain?"

Azhar kept his eyes lowered. "The Jew soup is tasty."

"You know I didn't mean that," she whispered; the feeling of him splashing about in the warm bath resumed.

"I think we should return what isn't ours and regain what is." He glanced at Abdullah, who nodded in sudden respect.

"I believe you just asserted the fundamental principles of war and peace, Azhar," Grandma looked at Abdullah. "An agreement in principle to seek the resettlement of foreign nationals."

The Son wouldn't budge. "That implies you have any of our people. I think you killed the last…"

"Are we going to do this all night?" Grandma snapped.

He glanced at Azhar and shook his head. "The structured return of Christians and reparations for the murder of Muslims."

"A new emigration policy for Christians and review of Muslim repatriation claims. No blame either way."

He nodded slowly. "And?"

"You refer to this as a peace treaty."

"I can't," he snapped. "That strips away our original victory of all its glory. We lost thirty-seven million. They won't be disgraced."

She shrugged. "How about a pan-Atlantic trade agreement. Goods and people."

Abdullah grinned, realizing Grandma had planned that response. "I feel you're picking my pockets, as you might say."

Lenora gestured at the slurping Azhar. "He won't let that happen."

The two leaders laughed wearily at the baffled Captain. Finally Abdullah asked, "Now what?"

Grandma waved over Nathan, who set down the sandwiches, giving a brief guided tour of the differences among corned beef, pastrami and brisket. He proudly added a pile of round fried potatoes.

"Latkes," Nathan said gravely. "Use either the sour cream or apple sauce."

Abdullah bit carefully into the brisket, while Mustafa happily made his way through the corned beef, dumping apple sauce and sour cream onto his potatoes. By the counter, Nathan grumbled satisfaction.

"How long for you to sell in this agreement?" Grandma layered a spoonful of mustard onto her meat.

"I have to get everyone together."

"Who is everyone?"

"Leaders like me."

"That's not good enough. Who are they?"

Abdullah hesitated, before conceding. "Ali Koury in France. Omar Mouluf in Germany. Ibrahim Safar in Palestine. Ismael Shalhoub in Kenya."

Grandma' face tightened. "Two generals, a colonel and a vice-admiral. That's it?"

"All I can freely name."

"But there's more?" Abdullah nodded. "More committed or more you can approach."

"Both." The Son sneered. "We control over two million men in arms along with the Channel fleet."

"The Kaddafy Brigade in Paris alone controls five million and they border Mouluf…"

"The Parisian Army's a shell," he caught himself. "I can't say more, Grandma. Trust only goes so far."

"Screw trust. This is about self-interest."

Abdullah smiled coldly. "Always. These men are with me. Theirs are with me."

"I need proof."

He thought for a moment. "Give me time when I return. I'll send word through the Collector."

"He's compromised. Only use them for misinformation. I'll have a new means of communication shortly. And your father?"

"I'll take care of him."

"Assassination is not a good way to start a peace."

"Perhaps it won't be necessary. But if so." He shrugged carelessly. "And you?"

"No one I can't handle." She chewed the sandwich, murmuring loud approval toward the pleased Nathan. "We can tape the joint spot later tonight."

"Tonight? I haven't prepared anything."

"I think you've spent your life preparing for this, Abdullah."

He smiled faintly. "Can this work, Grandma?"

She pressed a napkin to her lips. "There was a great leader from the past century, Golda Meir, perhaps you heard of her? No? Oh, I'm surprised. Anyway, Meir said that peace will come, she being Israeli, when the Arabs love their children more than they hate us."

The Son's hand trembled slightly with anger. "Another metaphor, Lenora?"

"Yes. For both our people."

• • • •

BETH PRESSED THROUGH the thick crowd swallowing up the entrance to the stadium, but she didn't find Ruben or recognize any of his friends. She could've waited for him to come home, but every night he'd gone straight to Dale's and then back here; there'd been no messages from the school so somehow he was juggling education between work and sex. Beth smiled impishly; Dale's a sweet kid. Ruben needed someone like her, a little more wired so he could learn limits.

She quickly examined herself in the glass door of the Yankee Clubhouse. As best as she could tell against the background of fans buying her Forgiveness t-shirts, this black dress and white blouse worked. Damn hair didn't; she scolded the thin spikes reaching up like stalks.

A husky man smiled admiringly. Beth pulled a face, scanning the long corridor one last time and walking down the lower field boxes to the railing. The Yankees spilled lazily all over the field, hitting and throwing and running and stretching.

Puppy finally acknowledged her silent waves. As he hurried over, about a dozen young men and women poured down the aisle, barking and shouting his name. He happily shook hands, posed for pictures and made small talk in that modest conceited way as the fans drifted away, glazed like they'd spent a minute with St. Peter.

"Hey, how are you?"

She let him kiss her cheek. "Fine. Have you seen my son?"

"No. Is something wrong?"

"Should there be?"

"You look worried."

She frowned. "That's just my face."

"And a beautiful face it is."

Beth rolled her eyes and pulled the white Yankees and blue Cubs banners out of her bag. "I made these for Ruben. I modeled them from that stadium book of yours. Must you look so surprised?"

"Sorry. I'm still getting used to your tender side." Puppy hopped over the railing. "How about we put them up?"

It took them about fifteen minutes to get to the upper deck in left field. Beth frowned, baffled by how tiny the players looked.

"Why would anyone sit up here?"

Puppy clomped awkwardly behind in his spikes. "It has a certain rugged appeal. Folks who sit here and in the bleachers take pride in being far away. Traditions are traditions. Even when forgotten."

"But don't you want to see the game more clearly? Or is that also your tradition?"

He winked at a couple kissing in the next section. Beth sighed as if he were a child and held up the banners. "Where do these go?"

Puppy pointed at the white brocade at the very top of the stadium. She blanched.

"My idiot son was going to climb up there?"

"I don't think we have any ladders."

Puppy held out his hand. Instead, she tossed him her handbag and scampered up the steps, tucking the banners into her waistband. At the top row, Beth jumped with arms outstretched, grabbing onto the brocade and swinging like a chimp to the very corner of the ballpark. She easily climbed to the top and wedged the banners onto the flagpoles, glancing around uneasily as the winds whipped up. She leaned back slightly to see if they were straight, swinging back in the other direction and rejoining the astonished Puppy.

"Have you climbed many stadiums, Ms. Rivera?"

"My first." She slung the handbag back over her shoulder.

"Seriously, Beth. Where'd you learn that?"

"Life's a remarkable teacher."

He stopped her from passing him on the steps. "That's real training."

"I guess it is."

"Were you a gymnast?" Beth nodded slowly. "Or maybe not."

"If you're answering your own questions, I don't think you need me."

Puppy gripped her strong bicep. "Did you learn that at 610 Tremont or 2001 Clay?" Beth reddened, but didn't answer.

"My lesson was on Clay. First and last time my father paid real attention to me. He insisted I go up and down the brick walls on the back of the building." He tightened his grip. "Shouting in that drunk semi-puke voice of his that everyone had to pass the test. Be a spider, he yelled when I kept slipping off. Be a spider, he kicked me a few times in the head…"

"That explains a lot…"

"But I couldn't do it. Even with the grooves onto the bricks from all the kids whose mothers and fathers felt it their DV duty to humiliate their children and remind them why they would have to climb extra hard in life…" Puppy spun Beth around. "…to wash away the Miners in our blood. Which Vet camp did you go to?"

She calmly met his stare. "Lawrenceville. Two weeks. I took it up again after my husband died. Late at night, practicing climbing up and down near my old church."

"You still practice?"

Beth's eyes narrowed. "No. But I still have faith."

"In what?"

"That I can climb any damn building when the time comes."

She smiled vaguely. Puppy suddenly grabbed her shoulders and pressed his mouth onto her lips, but Beth quickly turned. He breathed into her cheek, as cold as the building his father made him climb.

"I have to go." She patted his shoulder. "Tell Ruben I'll kill him if he ever climbs near those flags."

• • • •

BETH DISDAINFULLY SIZED up the squeaky-faced little girls pressed into the couch. Let me hang up your coat, ma'am, who'd like cookies, may we have some tea?

"What're your names again?" she asked.

"I think that's for the Mommy to remember," the woman said sternly.

Zelda squirmed in the chair in the far corner.

"The Mommy gives them names?" Beth asked.

"Goodness gracious, no. They're not pets." The woman looked horrified.

"Amy and Amelie," Zelda said.

"What're your real names?" Beth persisted.

"Ms. Rivera, that's not important."

Amy dismissed Beth as if she were dust, smiling at Zelda. "Where's that lovely man Diego?"

"Yes, Diego. We liked him," Amelie chimed in.

"A thoughtful person," the woman nodded gravely.

Beth started answering, but Zelda waved her off. "He died. That's why he's not here."

The girls glared at Zelda as if she'd murdered Diego along with causing her mother's suicide.

"What kind of accident?" Amy asked in a low, suspicious tone.

"What's it matter?"

"So it's a secret?" Amelie asked.

"No, it's not a secret. He was on a boat. He drowned. Anything else?"

The funeral in Diego's apartment yesterday had been sparsely attended with only immediate family, his mother and two sisters. Afterwards, Zelda had met the oldest one, Maria, at a bench overlooking the Harlem River, where she cautiously showed the letter from Shipmate Sails, the parent corporation, expressing their deepest apologies at the loss of Diego Garcia and Captain Jey Lee in a still unexplained accident. The letter had forwarded a new Lifecard containing payment for Diego's funeral along with two months severance pay.

Zelda rubbed her stomach. "This is Diego's baby."

"I know." Maria's eyes welled. "I helped him pick out the ring. Why don't you wear it?"

She had been tempted. "It's illegal. Mockery of marriage and all that to wear an engagement ring when you've never been formally engaged."

Maria spit into the river. Zelda joined her.

Zelda slowly came back into the room as Beth flared her nostrils in encouragement. They'd rehearsed this all the way over. Zelda took a deep breath.

"That's why I want to be able to name my baby Diego."

"I thought you didn't know the father?"

"I'm sure now."

The woman happily clasped her hands. "Splendid. Oh splendid. This is an enormous step forward as a mother. We just need the DNA tests."

"There are none since he's dead."

The woman quieted Amy and Amelie's singing and dancing around the couch. "You can't name a child after the father unless it's proven the father is the father."

Zelda unbuttoned her blousy top. The woman and the little girls craned their necks as if a vidmovie were beginning.

DIEGO AND MY MOM was evenly stitched in purple letters on her gold undershirt. The woman gasped.

"That's unacceptable."

"Chill down. It's not like it's formal, which would bind the adoptive parents. The name's only for use here. Like Amy and Amelie."

The children cowered behind the couch cushions.

"I've never heard of this before," the woman sputtered.

"You could file a complaint," Beth said.

"I certainly will."

"Though I guess we can ask for a sample of Diego's DNA." Zelda waddled toward the woman. "Only they haven't found the body. We can ask why. I'm going to bet you a few of your stinky cookies that Shipmate Sails, the company who owned the boats, won't like that. I'm going to bet a few of your stinky brownies that some other people, important people, very important people, might not like that either, and they might wonder why you're torturing a pregnant woman whose partner willingly came to a session and then later died. A partner who wanted to marry her." Zelda slipped on the engagement ring. "A woman going by the rules who only wants to remember her lover as she does everything necessary to bring another American child into Grandma's House."

The woman trembled.

"Lizzie," one of the little girls suddenly called out.

"And my real name's Pam," the other one said.

They stuck out their tongues at the sullen woman.

For the rest of the hour, the kids played Zelda's game, imagining little Diego running around knocking over plates and glasses and lamps. Beth was little Diego, taking great relish in shattering a mug and sending the woman into another room.

The woman eventually returned, airily dismissing the girls and insisting the wary Beth also wait outside. Zelda sat on the couch.

How do you feel? The woman gestured.

Fine.

It didn't bother you?

About little Diego? No. My idea.

But it wasn't little Diego.

"I know it's not real. All make believe. I got it. But I'm good at making make believe real."

"You saw your baby then?"

"Yes. I saw him at five. I skipped over the infant part since that grosses me out. The pooping and everything."

"And?"

"And, and…What do you want me to say for your report?"

"This isn't for the report, Zelda. I don't want you slashing open your stomach in a month."

"Women do that?"

The woman sighed. "And Ms. Rivera…"

"Is my friend. She can be surly, but she's my partner here."

"Good. You need friends."

Zelda stared. "Like you?"

"I'm not your friend, Zelda. In seven months I'll never see you again." She folded her hands in her lap. "So tell me how much this all hurts, pretending Diego is running around calling you Mommy."

"More than you can imagine. Isn't that the point? There are no Parents Houses for second time unwed mothers, right?"

The woman nodded grimly.

Zelda and Beth walked within individually bubbled silence to the bus stop. Beth apologetically held up her watch. "I've got to go. Customers."

Zelda led her around the corner by a boarded-up barber shop. "I have another favor."

"This wasn't a favor, so ask away," Beth smiled.

"What demomination are you?"

She wrinkled her pretty face. "Denomination, you mean? Like religion?" Zelda nodded. "Catholic."

"Is that the same as Christianity?"

Beth's eyes narrowed. "Why?"

"I'm just trying to understand."

Beth almost asked why again. "We all worship Jesus, but the rituals and some core beliefs are different. What's this about?"

"I have a friend…"

"Do you?"

"Not me. A little friend." Zelda held her palm down at chest level. "I think she's Catholic. I'd like to understand more."

"I have a book. And yeah," she said as Zelda flinched, "it's sort of illegal to give a book on religion, but not illegal to own it."

"Like Puppy's baseball books."

Beth cleared her throat. "I'm happy to help, Zelda."

"Seems that way."

"Tell me what else you want." Beth cupped Zelda's chin and kissed her tenderly on the lips; Zelda shivered.

• • • •

THE DRIVE UPSTATE took about two hours, most of it stuck in the congestion on the Cross Bronx Expressway. Hazel made idle talk about traffic, the decay of roads, the unreliability of 'bot workers and how many people just liked hiding in their cars away from the interminable vidnews.

Mooshie rarely answered except with an occasional grunt. Hazel took little exception, as if he often talked to himself. Finally he slipped one of her old MDs, a real Mooshie musical disc, into the musplay.

She listened at the smooth texture of her voice dancing off the piano. It was *Dead and Dark*, from *The Dark Depths* album.

"There's many ways to lie down

Even fewer to get up

So don't leave me baby

'Cause dreams can be real," Hazel sang along.

Mooshie clapped sarcastically.

Hazel shot through a small opening in two lanes, up a ramp and onto a wide boulevard heading north.

In a few miles, they zig-zagged along narrow roads until finally squeezing down a dusty street beneath sagging brown trees. The car kicked up gravel, coming to a stop outside Singh's country store. Hazel looked across the seat.

"You ready?"

She bounded inside as if about to repossess the store's contents. Trailing, Hazel pulled a long green candy out of a jar on the counter and, sucking noisily, rang a copper bell in the corner.

An automated door slid open. Derek and Sun Yen gasped audibly; Mooshie leaned against a glass counter filled with hunting knives, staring back.

They look so old, she thought, watching the men approach, shaking their heads.

"Greetings, mi amigos."

Derek suddenly yanked on Mooshie's hair.

"How's this possible?"

She pressed her knee into Singh's groin.

"Still like that move?" he wheezed.

"When there's something to hit."

Derek released her hair and Mooshie lowered her knee.

"How about we go inside?" Hazel suggested.

The reporter sprawled over a chair in the office while Derek sat beside Mooshie on the tattered couch.

Standing in the corner, Sun Yen cocked a shotgun. "Who are you?"

She almost laughed. "Mooshie Lopez, asshole."

"But you're dead."

"I was always tougher than you." She swiveled towards the scowling Singh. "I came back…"

"From where?"

"Heaven, Hell, Grandma's uterus. I ended up on the floor of a baseball historian, Puppy Nedick. He also had two very old white players named Mickey Mantle and Ty Cobb. They came back, too."

"We're following all that in the news," Derek said carefully.

"Then you know I sing as Dara Dinton."

"Let's hear." Easy snickered.

"Buy a ticket. This jerk follows me to the 167th Street subway and says I wasn't killed there. Says he has people who can tell me the truth. I guess you're it. And yeah, ghosts get hungry."

Derek and Sun Yen watched in fascination as she ate a bowl of bread.

"You expect to see the food go around my insides?" Mooshie growled. "So here I am. I don't know how. I only care about proving Grandma killed me."

Singh and Sun Yen's eyes flittered back and forth.

Hazel sighed angrily. "Just tell her."

The men looked away.

"It can't happen unless you're honest."

"About what, mi amigos?" she asked.

"We killed Mooshie Lopez," Derek said softly.

Her fingers dug into the couch. "Now we're even. I don't believe you."

Singh silently ordered Sun Yen to lower the shotgun. "Lopez was a lump in everyone's throats. She had tons of fans who still loved her, despite her drunken babblings. She criticized the government and became a rallying point."

"And we didn't need that," Sun Yen added. "Enough innocents were rounded up and sent north to detention camps in Nova Scotia."

"As long as the great Mooshie Lopez was out there saying there had to be a reason for 10/12, that the war was badly run, we were being betrayed, well, the heat was on both sides. Everyone wanted to hide." Derek gestured around the cozy office. "We had our shot and missed. We had millions. Tens of millions of followers."

"Still do," Sun Yen grumbled.

"Every goddamn ex-military, all the baseball fans who wanted this country back to where you could sing *God Bless America* and not be called a racist. Yeah, we fucked up on 10/12 because we didn't kill Grandma. If we had, then we could've dropped a few tactical nukes and got the Camels' attention and given us time to really re-arm. But we didn't get Grandma and we didn't need Mooshie Lopez pissing into the open wound. No one did."

Sun Yen poked Mooshie in the back with the shotgun. She spun around, bending the weapon over her knee and flinging it into the corner, knocking two pictures off the wall. The men's mouths dropped.

"You bastards. You were my friends. My best fucking friends."

Singh slowly smiled. "It is you."

Mooshie clenched her groin in disdain.

He gently put his hand on her shoulder. Mooshie twisted his arm.

"What the fuck do you pricks want?"

Despite the pain, his smile widened.

"We need you to help finish the job."

• • • •

THE DWARF TOOK pleasure in making them rehearse over and over, especially dabbing the Son's face with powder. Abdullah would blush and the dwarf would shriek about looking like clowns and dab more powder. Finally Grandma sent the dwarf back behind his camera where he made unpleasant noises, dragging the recording process out over hours.

Azhar fell asleep on a cot in the abandoned building a few blocks from the diner. Light peeked through the window and he panicked, running around the grayish floors until he found the Son snoring in a chair in a cramped room.

Grandma burst in with that recyclable energy and served them breakfast. Once they finished, two portions each, she proudly explained that the eggs, called SCs for so-called, were all bio-agra generated. This is how you'll feed your people.

Abdullah had sat before the empty plate with a mild sense of guilt before he made a long speech about the class system in the Caliphates, the rulers and the wealthy and the privileged and the connected. He went on for nearly an hour, Grandma listening politely although Mustafa would've sworn before Allah that she was snoring.

The dwarf or midget, Mustafa could see no difference since he'd never seen either, reappeared, announcing the genius of Ian Schrage had triumphed once again and crowded them into a screening room to show the announcement.

Grandma beamed and even Abdullah seemed pleased; he made a slight suggestion about a camera angle. The little one turned into a moody rock, folding his arms petulantly until Abdullah apologized for his amateurish remark. The tiny person grudgingly finished the screening and wouldn't smile until they applauded.

Was he making the history or were they? Another bafflement of this baffling land. When they finally left the studio, the dwarf disappeared down an alley. Abdullah and Azhar waited for the proper transportation, but Grandma waved down a small black taxi. They crowded into the back seat.

A robot turned around to greet them good morning and Azhar nearly lost his bladder; the Son gripped his wrist in fright. The thing had no face, just eyes and a sort of mouth, but it seemed very cheerful, mentioned its name was Andrew to its friends, and chattered on like a real human all the way through the many secret pathways around traffic only it and it alone knew.

Grandma was very pleased by a robot driving a taxi and explained that in Georgia, where her visitors were from, people still drove cabs. The robot remarked it wasn't the brightest wiring in the socket but that seemed a waste of human skills.

Abdullah muttered inaudibly.

The taxi skipped down a hill and then a ramp, rolling into a subway tunnel. Grandma tried explaining why cars went in a subway tunnel but the robot named Andrew kept interrupting, launching into the history of the Allah attack on Manhattan, the quarantine period and the riots of survivors in '72.

The Son turned brooding, refusing to so much as nod when the tank crew stopped them at the end of the battered tunnel and asked for papers. Grandma, who called herself Lenora Chin, breezily explained her friends were exhausted from sightseeing. The helmeted crew member peered suspiciously at Abdullah before waving them through.

And now here's the Bronx, Andrew announced, zipping up hills and down side streets. At least here there was normalcy, Crusaders walking along, shopping, well-dressed, smiling. Like home. Azhar felt a twinge of sadness, wondering how Jalak was, if she missed him, whether Abdul had scored goals in the last game and if Omar still hated him.

As they passed by a large very green park, Grandma instructed Andrew to bypass the other cars lined up at the main gate and head down a narrow path bordered with artillery and jeeps. Andrew stubbornly swung its metal head back and forth until Grandma handed the robot a wad of purple money, which made its head clang.

From both sides of the lane, two tanks rolled out of nowhere along with a dozen armed black uniformed soldiers, who surrounding the cab with pointed weapons.

"Good morning, my darlings," Grandma said happily. "I think one of you needs to call Major Stilton."

Tomas' mouth twitched as the Allahs entered Grandma's House, through the front door yet. The security detail lowered their guns in shock as they escorted Grandma and the Camels up the public elevator; fortunately it was too early for any school tours.

Grandma sat them all down in her modest sitting room and poured tea.

"You gentlemen already know each other." She made the introductions anyway.

"I didn't bring any of my wife's lamb this time." The Captain smiled.

Tomas grunted.

"Apologies for my dear friend." Her smile contained a warning. "The Major's a little upset about my disappearing."

"As are my people about my vanishing." Abdullah bowed slightly.

Tomas' sneer showed what he thought about those people.

"Grandma, may I have a word?"

"Eventually, my darling. For now, you need to get Abdullah and Azhar back to Iceland. Is that what you eventually decided?"

She spoke to them as if they were friends; Tomas' stomach churned.

The Camel nodded and spoke quickly in Arabic to the Captain, who said little, nodding. He again smiled at Tomas, who edged behind Grandma.

"This is irregular," he whispered.

"Yes, quite."

"Please, Grandma. Please."

She sighed wearily, excusing herself into the adjoining room. Before she closed the door, Tomas gestured to the eight man detail in the living room.

Shoot if they move.

"You're being impolite, Tomas," Grandma said with mock severity.

He stared coldly.

"I'm sorry for the deception about meeting in Cuba. Truly."

"I deserve better."

"Yes you do. And I deserved your faith."

"I have never…"

"Yes, you did. But we have jobs and yours is to accompany them beyond our territorial waters. I can't risk anything happening. Is that very clear?"

He nodded as if his neck ached. "May I first ask what has been decided?"

Grandma's face sagged with exhaustion. "No. Is the spare 'copter in the park fueled? Or did you tell First Cousin Cheng about that one, too?"

35

Zelda dozed on the bus and missed her stop, walking back five blocks along Bruckner Boulevard but never fully waking up; the kiss lingered. She'd smacked her lips together, licked with her tongue, half swizzled a berry drink and still the warmth of Beth's mouth remained. Women and men kissed differently, but this was special.

Still obsessed with her mouth, Zelda barely noticed the two Brown Hats politely waiting by the front door of her building.

"Ms. Jones?" The taller one smiled. "I'm Detective Buca, my partner Detective Y'or. May we have a word?"

"What's this about?" Hands on hips, chin out, the portrait of aggrieved innocence.

They heard it all before, stepping aside from the building entrance until she took the hint. As Zelda unlocked her apartment door, she wished Beth had already given her that Catholic book; she prayed to Jesus Christo anyway, hoping for some first time luck.

The apartment was a smelly mess with plates and glasses scattered high and low, hinting at food turning bad under the couch. The vidnews looped around in a banal report about SC sheep recipes.

"Sorry, I'm, you know." She spread apart her jacket. "Pregnant. Just got back from my Parents meeting. I have a certified slip…"

"That's not necessary, but certainly helpful," Buca replied as his younger partner casually snooped around the living room.

Zelda flung her jacket and purse over Clary's drawings on the couch, then bundled them into the hall closet. "And I have to pee every five minutes. Is it okay if I go to the bathroom?"

"Of course," Buca said with fake warmth.

Zelda said another prayer in made-up Spanish. This worked; Clary was asleep on the bed. As Zelda closed the door, the girl bolted up, instantly alert. Zelda pressed her fingers to her lips.

"Polizia."

Clary nodded grimly. Zelda went to the bathroom, peeing with vigorous singing and returning with a bright expression as if she dumped out a gallon of unwanted waste products.

"Sorry to keep you gentleman, but I see you're making yourself at home." She took a doll from Y'or, gesturing at its siblings on the bookcase. "I collect them. I'd offer you food or drink," she brushed cookie crumbs off the table into her palm, "but my increased allotment is only for me and Diego Junior."

Buca asked if they could sit, like she had a choice. The Detectives took the couch, hats in laps. Y'or opened a notebook while Zelda flopped onto her chair as if without a worry in the world.

"I've never been visited by Brown Hats," she finally said.

"Hopefully it won't be unpleasant," Buca answered. "A recent orphan to America has wandered off. Reports say she's in this neighborhood. Perhaps you've seen the news."

"I don't pay attention to such things."

"Children don't interest you?"

"Just this one." She protectively covered her stomach.

Buca nodded approval, Y'or's pen scratching along the page. "The girl's parents are very worried, obviously."

Zelda shrugged for him to continue. Buca held out a drawing of Clary, the cross disappearing into her scalp while her mouth twisted angrily.

"Why are you smiling, Ms. Jones?"

"She's a funny looking kid."

"All children are precious."

Zelda indicated she shared that belief by lovingly rubbing her stomach again.

"Do you recognize her?"

"No."

"You positive?"

"Yes. I mean, maybe I saw her on the vidnews, but that's it." Zelda caught the quick doubtful look between the Brown Hats.

"As you must be aware, Ms. Jones, anyone with knowledge of a missing child must come forward immediately."

"Okay."

"Failure to do so is a very serious offense."

Zelda tipped her neck forward respectfully.

"There's all manner of reasons why someone would do that. Particular among them is pedophilia."

"Watch it," she snapped.

"I'm not accusing you." He furrowed his forehead. "And that was wrong. Sometimes reciting is insensitive. After twelve years on the job, I should know better. Of course I have absolutely no reason at this moment to suspect you of such a vile crime." Buca bowed stiffly.

Zelda stood unsteadily. "Then why are you here? If you look up my records, as I bet you have, you'll see getting along with children wasn't my strong point as a teacher."

Buca frowned. "Past behavior isn't always the best prognosticator. Regular, non-sociopathic people arc and change."

"Maybe I don't arc as much as others."

"We're trying to help, Ms. Jones," Buca said firmly. "A pregnant woman, a single vulnerable woman who'd suffered the loss of her lover, whose maternal instincts were stirred, it would be understandable."

Buca and Y'or waited patiently.

"I don't know her…"

"We have a witness," Y'or blurted out angrily.

Buca gave his partner a reproachful stare and sighed. "Yes, we do."

Zelda cringed. That bitch.

"If you just bring the girl out, we'll attest to your cooperation. Volunteering goes a long way."

The Brown Hats rose as if the matter were settled.

"Allahu Akbar, Allahu Akbar," Zelda screamed and tripped Y'or as he ran toward the bedroom.

Clary was already on the window ledge. She bounded down the fire escape like a grasshopper, jumping the last four feet onto the sidewalk as the men in the brown clothes shouted above. She sped around the corner and in between stalled traffic, across the street and down an alley.

She could run all day, but where? She crouched by a garbage can, slowly walking onto the crowded streets like she belonged among the Crusaders. Clary squeezed the cross, wound around the money she'd stolen from Zelda on the first night, and slowed down to examine the police drawing tacked to a lamp pole. The picture made her look ugly. She squeezed it into a ball, abruptly thought of another use and shoved the paper into her coat pocket, hurrying toward the train.

Overhead the billboard of Grandma and the Puppy and the Mooshie looked down with a big smile. FORGIVENESS. Clary nodded to herself and got on the ticket line. She didn't see the men in the brown suits but sensed they were nearby. All police were cucarachas, so soon they'd be crawling closer.

The robot subway clerk fluttered its bored metal eyes. "Yeah?"

"Beisbol."

The clerk's eyebrow wiggled a moment, considering her size. "What about school?"

Clary heard commotion around the corner leading to the long corridor. She tapped her chest. "Special."

The A22 made an amused sound. "Half fare. Two stops on the local."

Clary slid her money under the window and the robot slid back change along with a pass.

"School's more important," it warned.

She ducked inside a group of porcos in baseball caps, following them into the packed train. Clary knelt as the idiota police rushed past the moving car. She triumphantly hummed "Grandma Muertas" and joined the crowd pouring outside the huge stadium.

Yankee Stadium, the sign said.

More polizia stood around, tipping their hats in salutes to the fans. Clary lowered her eyes, walking by, but a cucaracha touched her shoulder. Clary was about to kick him in the huevos when he handed her a blue beisbol cap.

Clary curtsied and half-ran to the farthest line. She took the cap on and off several times until she was pleased by the fit over her thick curls.

An ugly Crusader waited at the entrance.

"Ticket?"

She shoved a fistful of money at the boy, who shook his head and pointed to another line to buy the ticket. A couple Americans joined in and soon they were gabbing away and making little sense, as Crusaders often did.

A nice woman with tall hair bent over. "I have an extra ticket, sweetie. My daughter's sick. How about you give me the money directly?"

That set off more babbling, but Clary quickly counted out the money and followed the lady past the ugly boy; she ran through the crowd, ignoring the woman's surprised shouts.

Clary roamed around the ground floor. So many Crusaders and so many of them fat, she marveled, wondering how they could fit into their chairs. She enjoyed running up and down the moving steps a few times, then along the second highest level, but she saw no door marked Puppy. She stopped a couple fat Crusaders and asked for Puppy Beisbol. They pointed down at the field.

Clary bought a hot dog and soda and then skipped on two toes down the moving steps, eating, and toward the green grass. She recognized Puppy from all the pictures in Zelda's house. He was running a few feet back and forth, playing a game and laughing with a puerco old baseball player.

The Crusaders must've been too fat to fight and that's why they lost, she finally decided, pressing toward the railing. A bunch of ugly teenagers blocked the way, barking at Puppy, who wandered over. Clary joined in, howling as she edged closer and kicked the ankles of the remaining fans in front; they moved.

"Puppy Beisbol." She imitated the teens and hopped up and down.

He smiled. He was very handsome for a Crusader. No wonder Zelda loved him.

"I like that nickname. Puppy Baseball." Puppy left with a friendly wave.

"No, no, no." She panicked. "Puppy Beisbol. Zelda. Ayudeme."

He stopped. Clary hopped onto the field and grabbed his arm.

"Polizia."

Clary handed him the drawing.

• • • •

THE CAMELS PEERED down over the ravaged Adirondacks. Were they mapping for an invasion route? Tomas wondered, watching from the back of the 'copter.

"What is there?" Azhar pointed.

"Trees."

"He meant a city," the Mufti spawn jumped in.

"I know what he meant." Tomas looked away. They'd be over water in about fifty minutes. Turn on the cloaking, another hour or so and the Allah boat should be waiting. Surrender was so easy.

"Why are we staying inland?" Abdullah asked.

"Because we're looking for you along the coast."

The Allah smiled. "Grandma is very clever."

"That's why she's Grandma."

Tomas shifted so his back was toward them.

"We ate at an interesting place."

The Major pressed his face against the cold window.

"I wish my wife cooked like that," Azhar said. "The meat was so succulent. Is that artificial, too?"

Tomas shrugged. "Where was it?"

Abdullah waved his finger. "I believe that's a secret."

The Major reddened. "You can tell me."

"If you're supposed to know, then you would." The Camel closed his eyes. "A bumpy ride. This is an older model, no?"

"It works fine."

"No disrespect." Abdullah smirked. "I'm merely making conversation."

"Why? You got what you want."

"So did you."

"Which was?"

The Camel's grainy brown eyes narrowed. "Again, if you're supposed to know, then you would."

This is what it will be like, Tomas thought. They are too pleased. They got what they wanted. Us.

He stared at the Allahs and drifted back to the final deportations. A child, he'd been taken to his grandfather's farm outside Detroit for safety. But the day they sent the last of them away, the stubborn old man had stowed Tomas under a tarp in the bed of the truck and drove back into the city.

His grandfather parked the Dodge at the top of a crowded hill, squeezing among the silent, approving crowd which let out a loud, angry cheer whenever another Allah mosque was hit. After hours of smoke and guns and screams, the Allahs finally surrendered, marching with hands held up, eyes defiant, chanting Allahu Akbar as they were herded into long trucks.

It wasn't the blood Tomas remembered but their expressions. They didn't believe they would lose. Everything was simply a step, sometimes sideways, sometimes backwards, like America used to be. So different from the GI prisoners straggling at the end of the war, hands on their heads. No defiance. Just exhaustion, defeat, almost grim relief.

Through the weary trees of the remaining Adirondacks, Tomas could envision Americans with hands back on their heads, soon surrendering for the last time to these smug Camels. He wanted to kick them out the door and see if they'd bounce.

The Major tapped onto his wrist device. A question mark appeared. He tapped yes. The 'copter tilted slightly to the east.

"Change of direction?" Mustafa asked.

Tomas shrugged. "Weather."

• • • •

THE HUMMING GIRL dangled her feet off the edge of Ty's desk, rolling a ball around her lap. Cobb patted Clary's head and handed her a Carly Caramel Bar. She politely unwrapped the chocolate and saved the foil in her pocket.

"You going to the police station?" Mick asked, Clary perking up.

Puppy shook his head, explaining briefly about the legal system. The arrest of a citizen was kept private. No sensationalism, no gory details, no back and forth with conflicting stories played out in public. Certainly nothing that would give notoriety to a criminal. Or to an accuser. There were no lawyers, either; they'd been long banned under the Anti-Parasite Act. Evidence was decided on the testimony of people who believed in honesty.

There is no honor anywhere in lying, Puppy recited Grandma's Twenty-Fifth Insight.

"That'd be the first time in the world that happened," Cobb said with grunt, reluctantly making a silly face back at Clary; she giggled.

"Where's Zelda then?" Mick asked.

Puppy sighed. "Probably the Bronx Courthouse."

"On the Grand Concourse?"

"You know it?"

Mick shrugged. "I knew people who stayed there."

Puppy sat beside Clary. "Zelda. Polizia."

"Si."

"Why?"

"It's por que," Cobb grumbled.

"You speak Spanish?"

"I had a colored maid from somewhere they mix races. Por que is right. Ask her. Never mind. Little girl, por que?"

Clary's nose wrinkled at the infinite options.

"Just don't say por que." Mantle nudged him. "Por que Zelda."

Clary's eyes watered.

Ty shoved Mickey. "You made her cry."

Puppy led Clary off to the side, where he knelt in a proposal position. "Clary. Por que…How do you say know?"

Ty thought a moment, then brightened. "The maid would say saber."

"Clary, saber polizia Zelda."

The girl pointed at herself, her face twisting into an ugly scowl; she hissed.

"She having a seizure?" Mickey whispered.

Clary stomped around the office, wagging her finger in the air and saying Zelda, then turning around and waving her finger at another imaginary figure. She spit.

"Zelda had an argument with someone," Ty said.

"Who, Clary?"

"Quien," Mick said. They looked at him. "I had Spanish girls in my day."

"Quien, Clary," Puppy asked.

The girl grabbed her hair and pulled it out to make it seem bigger, then puffed out her chest.

"Tetas grandes." Mickey grinned and Clary applauded.

Zelda argued with Mooshie? No, that made no sense.

"Se trataba de perrito beisbol." She jabbed Puppy in the chest. "Puppy beisbol." Clary resumed her pantomime.

Puppy slowly opened his wallet and showed a photo to Clary, who hopped up and down as if electrified. He nodded grimly and kicked off his spikes.

"Go," Ty said softly. "I'll have the fat Chink play left."

• • • •

ANNETTE SMILED DUBIOUSLY from behind the counter of her small boutique Love My Feet in Scarsdale, finishing up with a customer. Puppy nodded for her to continue and walked around examining sleek dress shoes and smart casual wear. Ten percent off today, said a neat handwritten sign on a silver shelf; Annette always believed in the personal touch.

She sent off the happy customer and straightened out a few papers, anxiously waiting for him to leave.

"What's up, Puppy?" She suddenly gasped. "Are you wearing your pointy baseball shoes in my store?"

Puppy lifted his right sneaker, which didn't have a particular calming effect.

"That's dirty."

"Streets and all. Soot. Grime." He picked up a black, buckled shoe. "How much is this?"

"I can discount it."

"Thanks."

He threw the shoe into the tall mirror, showering her with glass. Annette sputtered and ran toward the door, but he flung her onto a chair.

"I'll call the police," she threatened.

"Nice segue. What did you do, Annette?"

"I don't know what you mean." She defiantly plucked glass from her hair.

"Zelda."

Annette's mouth twitched. "So?"

"Zelda."

"I heard you, asshole. That mirror is costing you."

"Why did you bust her?"

Annette pursed her lips. "I didn't do anything wrong."

"You turned her in over the orphan."

"How do you know that?"

"I just do."

"More Puppy paranoid voices dancing in his head…"

He shoved Annette so hard her eyes lolled, bot-like. "Why?" She tried sitting up and he pushed again. "Why?"

"It's all your fault." She slapped him. Blood trickled down his upper lip and he let her up. "I told you to keep Dara from Elias. You didn't. I asked your best buddy and she sent that little demon after me, who tried to stab me. What else was I supposed to do?"

"Nothing."

"That's not how I was raised." She sneered, calmly returning behind the counter. "I see a law is broken and I must report it. That's the law, Puppy. That's what you DVs preach. Every fucking day of our marriage I heard that. Regs lie, DVs don't. Integrity. Well I was integritied."

"Thanks to you Zelda's been arrested." Puppy kicked over a chair.

"That's also going on your bill…"

"Arrested."

"If she did nothing wrong, she has nothing to fear," Annette said archly.

"Do you really think this is about some damn orphan?"

"The vidnews said…"

"They're lying."

An elderly woman stopped in the doorway and Puppy chased her out with a broken piece of glass.

"That was Mrs. Chambliss."

"I don't give a damn if that was Grandma. They're lying, Annette. They wouldn't arrest someone for taking in an orphan."

"It's against the law…"

"Fuck the law." He nearly ground his teeth into the jawline. "You went to the police station."

Annette made a defiant face. "Yes."

"You spoke to Blue Shirts."

"Who else would I talk to there?"

"And then?"

Annette hesitated. "They sent me to the Brown Hats."

"Don't you think that's weird for a missing girl?"

"Obviously you have a greater knowledge of police procedure…"

"They stopped the rescue of ME orphans years ago. But this one still only speaks Spanish."

"Maybe she's stupid."

"Not too stupid to speak an illegal language."

"Maybe there's a program we don't know about." Annette faltered. "She probably stabbed her way free."

"Wouldn't the family post the news and not the cops?"

Annette drummed her fingers, growing angry. "I don't know."

"Isn't that what we always see on the vidnews? My child is missing, please help. Never the cops. Families talking to each other, one on one."

She swallowed deeply, suddenly uncertain. "Maybe this is different."

"Damn straight. "

Annette floundered, ready to lash out as always when she was put on the defensive. "And if it is, how's that my problem?"

"You just bought it, Annette."

She squirmed. "What do you want from me, Puppy?"

• • • •

AZHAR NOTICED THE wind just before Tomas disappeared into the narrow cockpit. More than twenty years at sea had turned his skin into radar. He chalked it up to uneasy exhaustion.

The Son stared out the window like an idiot child, grinning deep in thought. The 'copter turned abruptly to the right.

"Buckle up, please." Tomas popped his head into the cabin.

"What's going on?" Abdullah grew concerned.

"We're setting down until this storm passes."

Tomas avoided Azhar's stare and returned inside the cockpit. The 'copter gained speed, racing over the treetops. Azhar pointed to an artificial clearing half a mile ahead, Abdullah nodding as the 'copter nestled down into a spot.

The doors flung open and the cabin filled with armed black uniformed soldiers. Azhar rose to defend them, but he and the Son were immediately flung to the ground and handcuffed, black hoods draped over their faces as they were dragged down the steps and into the back of a truck or van.

"How dare you." Abdullah twisted away, earning a silencing rifle butt in the ribs.

The sound of 'copter propellers faded as the vehicle bounced on rough roads, leaving just their scared labored breaths and the slight whistling intakes of soldiers guarding them. Azhar nudged Abdullah in the foot to be still. He pressed back.

Crusader traitors, Azhar thought.

The vehicle lurched to a stop after about fifteen bumpy minutes. They were dragged out up a ramp. A door hissed closed, intensifying the sense of darkness, then down a very long corridor before they were tossed into a room, their hoods yanked off and the handcuffs flung into the corner.

Now alone, they weaved slightly and fell onto folding chairs around a small table. Abdullah took deep breaths.

"Are you all right?" Azhar asked.

The Son grunted and rubbed his side. "Where are we?"

Mustafa wished he knew enough to make up an answer. "I think twenty minutes from where we landed. I smelled the ocean."

"You would." Abdullah smiled faintly.

Azhar walked around the room, rapping on the walls and annoying Abdullah.

"What're you doing?"

"Seeing if they're hollow." He squinted at the ceiling. "I assume they're watching."

"Is there anything we could do about it?" His voice contained the slightest reproach.

Azhar considered what they could do about anything including ever getting home, when the door opened slowly and a small Asian man poked his head inside as if he might have the wrong room. He brightened and vigorously shook their hands.

"Apologies, gentlemen. This is so awkward, but sometimes, there's only one way. I'm Albert Cheng, First Cousin, though I suspect you know that. Please, sit, I'll only keep you a little while and then send you on your way."

Mustafa slid a chair in front of the Son; Cheng laughed.

"There's no need to worry."

"One of your Crusaders nearly broke my ribs," Abdullah growled, rising. "We've been kidnapped and abused in complete violation of my agreement with Grandma. Your head of state. But we know what your promises mean."

Cheng seemed genuinely saddened by this outburst. "I'm so sorry to hear all that. We do have mountains of mistrust to climb, don't we? Please." His voice hardened just enough. "Sit."

Abdullah slid the chair around and straddled the back, glaring at Cheng, while Azhar insisted on standing. The Asian Crusader shrugged.

"Until now, how's your trip been?"

They didn't smile. The Cousin arched his eyebrow as if he hadn't expected an answer. "I heard Grandma took you to an interesting little place."

"What do you want?" Abdullah asked coldly.

"Okay. I tried for civility. All I really want is some information. A few more details. I'm Grandma's second in command and it'll be my job to implement this agreement."

"Ask her."

"I did, which is why I suggested you stop by on your way home." Cheng's little eyes froze. "I'm somewhat confused by your allies." He waited for Abdullah to answer, then continued, "Koury's Madr Army in France. Shade under one million, nine hundred thousand soldiers, two hundred tank battalions, fifty air wings."

Abdullah stared hard.

"I have good sources. You're not the only one unhappy under the Caliphate. Important people say the one million, nine hundred thousand should be closer to four hundred thousand. One tank battalion. And air wings? Hard to fly planes when their engines fall off."

"Your information is incorrect," Abdullah said warily.

"Perhaps. As with the Army of the German Caliphate. One point two million on paper. Two hundred thousand in the field. Or the ally in Italy, the Caliphate of the False Messiah. On paper three quarters of a million. Reality, maybe a hundred thousand. No transport support, either. That's endemic throughout the Army of Mohammed."

Bastard, Azhar could hear Abdullah think.

"Try."

Cheng frowned. "Try what?"

"To test us."

The Asian laughed. "I've no interest in testing anything, Your Most Worthy Successor. I'm making sure that when your father moves against you, you can defeat them. Otherwise, it all falls upon us."

"We saw how you handled that." Abdullah sneered.

"Not well," Cheng said blandly. "Which is what we're trying to avoid. The point of peace is not to fight. What is your plan when the announcement goes out and the Mufti labels you a traitor."

"As I told Lenora, that is ours to deal with."

"As I'm telling you, it becomes ours also. If you fail and your Army attacks us, we have no choice but to use nuclear weapons."

Abdullah's jaw tightened. "My father will be eliminated long before."

"You mentioned that," Cheng said dismissively. "What about the Council?"

The Son hesitated. "Them too."

"All eleven?"

"Only those who reject us."

"All eleven, then." Cheng nodded to himself. "And the Holy Warriors?"

"They will fight us."

"To the death."

"Yes," Abdullah conceded.

"Twenty million of them, roughly."

"Closer to thirty," the Son said smugly.

"And you'll have how many men under arms…."

Abdullah kicked aside the chair. "All the armies of the Council. The rot is prevalent. Then what is your concern?"

"That you're fucking us, sir. That you have no solid support. That your head will roll up a Camel's ass and your people will think us desperate and ripe to finish off. Or your head won't be used as a couch cushion because this is a trap."

"Which do you think it is, Mr. Cousin?" Abdullah sneered.

Cheng scowled and left the room. Azhar expected the soldiers to burst in with guns blazing. When one entered, Mustafa lifted up a chair by the leg. The soldier's frown could be felt under his mask as he motioned them down the corridor, dispensing with black hoods or handcuffs.

They walked past soldiers with lifted face visors, expressions disgusted. That was the point, Azhar realized as they settled into the back seat of a car.

The soldiers were supposed to see them.

The 'copter waited in the clearing, but Grandma's Major wasn't there. Azhar wasn't surprised.

36

Annette grimaced slightly in the new green-and-gold open toed shoe as she walked gingerly up the wide wooden staircase in the 38th Police Precinct; a trickle of blood seeped into her heel.

Thank you, Puppy, she made a sound as if swapping out one of her lungs for a cheaper model and hobbled up to the police desk, where a nice looking older Blue Shirt carefully read her papers before returning them.

"How can we help you, Ms. Ramos?"

She indicated her sprightly colored yellow skirt and white, trimmed blouse. "As you can see, I'm a dedicated sibling willing to do what's right."

412 | GARY MORGENSTEIN

"Hopefully, we all are."

"Yes, well, especially you. What would we do without our Blue Shirts?" Annette took in some especially attractive Blue Shirts strolling past.

"We appreciate that."

"So when I saw injustice, I spoke up."

The Blue Shirt wearily nodded for her to continue, wondering when he got his 'bacco break. "Therefore, my question is small. According to the law, I should meet with the defendant…"

"Not a defendant. The person hasn't been charged yet."

"Ah." She lowered her voice. "What should I call her?"

"Zelda Jones. And yes, the law provides the right of the accused to confront the accuser in private."

"Accuser sounds so harsh."

The Blue Shirt squinted. "What else should we call you?"

She felt ashamed. "I guess accuser works. To execute the laws properly, where would I go?"

"The Bronx Courthouse on 161ˢᵗ Street. Know where that is?" She nodded. "But you only have a couple days."

"What happens then?"

He peered at the screen. "Says she's being transferred."

"Where?"

The sergeant frowned. "Doesn't say."

Annette pouted. "Is there a hint?"

The Blue Shirt glanced around uneasily and whispered. "BT facility."

She puckered so deeply a straw couldn't get through. "Is that unusual, sir?"

The Blue Shirt nodded. "In a case like this."

Annette swung her handbag over her right shoulder and limped halfway down the steps. She stopped so abruptly two Blue Shirts bumped into her. I hate you so much, Puppy Nedick. She hobbled back up. The sergeant wasn't thrilled to see her.

"Apologies, apologies." Annette pressed her nipples against the chest-high desk and fiddled with her shoes. "I left a comb at the desk of those kindly Brown Shirts. It was very expensive, made in Mexico. A girl can't let her hair get too wild." She winked at what that might mean. "Are the Detectives in today?"

"You'd have to check with them. They're very squishy about their side and ours. Fifth Floor."

"Of course. Fifth Floor."

Annette limped up the three flights, wishing Puppy a variety of testicular diseases. The two Brown Hats had their feet up on their desks, doodling.

"Good afternoon, sirs."

They tipped their heads without recognizing her. Detectives passed back and forth to get coffee, donuts or answer their squat black phones.

"Annette Ramos. Fiance to Third Cousin Elias Kenuda." Their indifference suggested it didn't matter if she were Grandma's plaything. "The accuser of Zelda Jones."

Buca grunted. He and his partner waited.

"I was just chatting with one of your Blue Shirt colleagues." They nodded vaguely. "At some point I'd like to fully discharge my duties as a member of The Family and allow the accused an opportunity to accuse me back. Not that I've anything to be accused about." The Detectives exchanged bland looks. "Your kind colleague told me she was at the Bronx Courthouse but only for a couple days and since my schedule is crazy, my shoes are very popular and there's a footwear convention coming up in Hartford this weekend, I wondered if there was some way she could be held there until I get back."

"Sorry, ma'am. That's out of our hands," Buca said.

Annette sputtered as if this was in the top five of the most ruinous things ever to hit the human race. "Whose hands is it in then?"

"The government," Y'or said; Harris gave him a sharp glance.

"Aren't you the government, too? I know there used to be balancings and checkings and all those silly useless branches…"

"Why do you want to know, ma'am?" Buca slipped his feet off the desk and studied her more closely.

"I thought as a good sibling I should know these things. You do your duty, accuse and then you like to know what happened next."

"No one does," Buca said slowly.

"Yes. Exactly. Who needs to know? I certainly don't, not with my business thriving. If only I sold men's shoes." She indicated gravely at their scuffed brown Oxfords.

Annette mumbled a few more disjointed thoughts about shoes and hurried out with a cheerful wave to the entire squad room. Buca stared a moment at the door.

"What was that about?"

"I thought it was weird, too," Y'or chimed in.

"Then I must be on the right track," Buca said dryly.

• • • •

SHOVING THROUGH THE crowd nearly knocking the hallway off its concrete blocks, Kenuda slid sideways into the dressing room at the spacious Chandler House Hall. Mooshie barely looked up as she methodically removed the makeup. The Third Cousin leaned against the closed door, exhausted.

"No one's ever heard anything like that."

She glanced smugly into the reflection in the triangular mirror and changed cleaning pads.

414 | GARY MORGENSTEIN

"Three hours," he continued wonderingly.

"That used to be the norm. Back in the day I…" Mooshie caught herself. "Entertainers entertain. Sixty minutes is a stupid length. I'm just getting warmed up at that point."

Elias kissed the top of her mass of red curls, hands stroking her shoulders. She shuddered; he smiled, pleased, and kissed the back of her neck.

"Kenuda." She lit a 'bacco, holding up the nearly empty pack. "I need more."

He paced in a tight circle, energizing his thoughts. "When football season opens next month, I'd like you to sing at one of the stadiums. Perhaps Meadowlands in Jersey. I see it so clearly, an Augmented Reality universe with you at midfield…"

"Football's disgusting."

"Darling, it's number one."

"So am I."

Kenuda laughed with delight, acknowledging Dara's songs had claimed thirty-six percent airtime on the vidrad, a record since Mooshie Lopez died. His name ranked in the top three of Grandma's daily Cousins Thank Yous for the past week. No one had a bottom line like his. Baseball revenue was soaring over a thousand percent. Two new sporting goods factories were opening in Louisville and Milwaukee. There were now baseball day camps planned in twenty-five cities; there were only football camps in twenty-eight.

He'd put in the suggestion to Cheng for one more baseball season. That'd give him time to sell through merchandising, too. The first adverts for baseball jerseys went up tomorrow. Players' numbers, but no names along the top of the shoulder. Just FORGIVENESS.

No wonder baseball evoked such nostalgia. Its quaintness screamed gullibility. Just wait until he reshaped entertainment. Vidrads, vidmovies, vident. New new new ideas.

"That sounds amazing, but I'd like to start a little simpler. Like Yankee Stadium."

He sat on the edge of the dressing table. "You hate baseball, too."

"All sports are stupid. Sorry, I don't mean to trash your world."

"That's why I've expanded into entertainment."

"Seized is more like it."

Elias smacked his lips. "I can certainly arrange for you to sing at the baseball park. What's that ditty they like?"

Mooshie clamped her back teeth. "*Take Me Out to the Ballgame*?'"

"Yes, yes. Why not sing that?"

She turned like a kettle boiling. "I'm supposed to sing an old ditty?"

"Isn't that what you wanted? You sing older songs now…"

Mooshie glared into the mirror, squirming as he touched her shoulder.

"What did I get wrong this time, Dara?"

"You're supposed to be guiding me, Elias."

"I just booked you on a live vidmus concert that went an hour and a half over."

"Are people rioting across the country because some bullshit twiddle my geetar trio got bumped?"

"No, of course not."

"But you want the first time anyone's sung at Yankee Stadium since Mooshie Lopez to be like pulling your pecker? Yawn, buy me some peanuts and cracker jacks." She shook her head at his dim stare. "Those are lyrics from the song."

"That's not my expertise."

"Isn't promotion? Look what you've done for me."

"Yes," he answered carefully, unsure if he was about to be praised or criticized.

"This must be historic. Dara Dinton at an historic moment. The lights come on."

"What lights, darling?"

"The fucking lights at the stadium."

"They have them?" he asked. She flung a brush. "Perhaps we start with a light show? We do that for Grandma's birthday at the Arena in Chicago..."

"Grandma's clit," Mooshie snarled. "They have lights at Yankee Stadium because once upon a time they played night games."

"I know that, Dara," he snapped. "But they stopped evening games because it got families home too late..."

"That's what I want," she screamed.

"Okay, okay..."

"The first time the lights are turned on since 2065, I'm standing at home plate, singing."

Kenuda was relieved that she wasn't going to make one of her demands like the water onstage served at thirty-four degrees or the flowers in the dressing room painted orange. Lights, stadium, simple enough. "I can certainly set that in motion."

"It already is."

"Pardon?"

"In two days the lights go back on and I'm giving a concert." Mooshie let the strap fall off her left shoulder. Kenuda tilted at the bare arm speckled with tiny freckles.

"Isn't that a little soon? There are permits and arrangements..."

"You can handle it, darling," Mooshie said huskily. "Now turn around while I undress."

Kenuda swallowed very deeply.

• • • •

AT EVERY KLICK across the Atlantic, Mustafa expected their Cessna 32 to be blown out of the sky. Neither he nor Abdullah had slept during the ten hours of travel from the Crusader 'copter to a tiny fishing boat, an Islamic 'copter and finally mid-air transfer aboard the Son's private jet, until they landed at a poorly lit airport outside Barcelona. They stumbled on wobbly legs down the portable staircase; Abdullah's bodyguards whisked him into a black sedan.

Abdullah leaned out the open window and took his hand. "I must go alone, my friend. Thank you."

"I will wait for your call."

The Son smiled wearily. A silver mini-sedan rolled to the edge of the landing strip and two beefy men with rifles got out.

"You must go with them," he said sadly. "It's the only way to maintain secrecy."

Azhar tensed. "But my family."

"Their grief will be addressed." Abdullah half coughed, half laughed at Azhar's fear. "Azhar, Azhar, do you think I'm a Crusader? Imagine how delighted your wife and sons will be when you return miraculously alive."

He rolled up the window and the car drove into the night. Azhar just stared, considering running off into the thin forest. But to where? Suddenly he had no home. His home, his family, what would they be told? That he drowned at sea after being killed by Crusaders, like the orphans? Like Clary.

One of the large men climbed behind the wheel while his colleague waited impatiently.

Azhar angrily brushed past into the back seat. A small traveling bag rested on the floor.

"Where am I going?" Azhar asked, not expecting an answer. He rummaged through the bag of toiletries, socks and underwear. He was about to complain, angrily, lividly, whether he was to be a prisoner in socks and undies, when he noticed a leather suitcase under the front seat.

He dumped the clothes onto the seat.

"This is not my size." Mustafa held up a pair of adolescent pants that would be tight on Jalak.

The bodyguards ignored him.

"Nor are these shirts." He flung a pair into the front seat. "I need proper clothes." No, he didn't. If Abdullah had lied about the strength of his allies' armies to Grandma, he could lie to him. No witnesses to the agreement. Or to the shame of being kidnapped. Abdullah could say anything; who would contradict?

He wept for a while, loudly, piercingly; the guards ignored that, too. When he stopped, he noticed the car was heading south on Fuego del Torres.

"Get off at the next exit. I said get off. I am a ward of the Mufti's Son."

Apparently they were killing him tonight, so fulfilling a last wish meant little. The car wound around the narrow hill.

"Next left. Second right. Do as I say," he shouted, smiling at the liberation of imminent death. "Now stop here."

His dark house slept; Mustafa could almost hear Jalak snoring. He carefully folded all the clothes and tossed the suitcase into the front seat.

"Leave that by the door. The clothes will fit my son." The guards hesitated. "Please. My wife will think it is charity."

The driver finally nodded. His colleague gently laid the suitcase on the front step. He returned and they drove back down the hill.

I love you Jalak. I love you Abdul. I love you Omar. Believe nothing they say.

• • • •

THE THIRD GRADE class huddled horrified in the far corner beneath the poster of Grandma, eyes lifted defiantly. BUILD ON LOVE. Zelda went to join them, but the children hurried into another corner, eluding her no matter what angle she took, no matter how many crayons she threw, no matter how many chairs she kicked over.

Shaking her head sadly, the teacher took Zelda's hand and calmly led her into the principal's office. Zelda couldn't remember either's name. Her teacher had the gray hair which all educators had during the war, dyed down to the roots in the short style of the period. You couldn't hide anything in clipped hair. It was 2070. November 18, 2070. She squinted at the calendar in the principal's office, confused because the name on the door was blocked out, like boobies in the vidmovie Pablo had once shown her.

Zelda grew woozy as the pill she'd curled under her tongue slowly disintegrated.

The principal was Mrs. Rogers, of course. She hated Mrs. Rogers. The principal Mrs. Rogers pressed down Zelda's drawing onto the desk as if making an imprint. She asked if that was Zelda's drawing and she'd answered why else would I put my name on it. Mrs. Rogers persisted and asked if Zelda ever put her name on anything belonging to someone else and Zelda had said that was dishonest and DVs don't lie.

Isn't this a lie? The principal sighed. A drawing of dead soldiers wrapped in a flag isn't true. But, Zelda sputtered, soldiers had died. Mrs. Rogers looked very sad, that expression of giving up on you which most people in the DV got at one time or another. Teachers weren't supposed to have that look. They were your friends, sometimes your only friends other than your real friends. They were supposed to protect you and do everything they could to help you learn and make you see truth so you could be honest.

Why? Mrs. Roger asked. Of all the drawings, why this one?

The principal had smiled; Zelda wasn't fooled. She was trying to get something out of her like this kindly prison visitor on the chair in the cell. Not a bad cell, Zelda tried remembering before the pill and the VR and couldn't. Maybe because she was back in 2070 and explaining when things came into her head she just had to draw them. Mrs. Rogers asked what other things came into her head. Zelda said her head was empty. The principal leaned forward and asked if other things like dead soldiers wrapped in a flag came into her head would she draw them or would she maybe think what effect that had on other people when Grandma and the rest of America were fighting so hard.

Don't you want to fight hard, too? Zelda thought of the soldiers in their fake legs and fake arms begging in the DV.

"But didn't you keep drawing whatever you wanted?" The kindly prison visitor asked softly somewhere beyond the Virtual Reality world. "Don't you think you should stop?"

Zelda wanted to yank off the plugs on her eyelids, but her hands were fastened to the chair.

"Look where it's gotten you, dear."

I'm fine, her mouth made the words, but she didn't hear them.

"You've achieved a great deal, Zelda. I don't want to act as if you haven't. You've taught, made a success in business and will bear a child. That is remarkable. How could you do all that if you weren't honest?"

Am honest, her lips were stuck.

"Which makes no sense. Dishonest people don't succeed unless you think the entire system is wrong. Do you think that?"

Yes, Zelda's nose sort of moved near her forehead.

"Certainly not. You're a wonderful person who has overcome a natural inclination fostered by your parents to break the rules. You fought back. You're a champion. Now you have another stumble where someone has put you in a bad spot. If you tell us who, we can help you and the girl. You'll resume your life. This isn't terrible. You've made mistakes before and overcome them."

Now her nose dribbled onto her cheek.

"It's the little girl. You're worried about her. Who wouldn't? That shows what sort of person you are. Taking in a little thing and feeding her. Obviously you transferred the love for your baby to the girl. You must give up your baby and so you decide in your head to adopt the orphan. My oh my, what kind of society wouldn't understand? We'd be upset if you had turned the girl away."

"Diego." Zelda found her tongue hiding behind her teeth.

"Is that who helped you? Is that the father?"

"Yes," she said hoarsely.

"Where is he?"

Zelda tipped over and fell. The kindly prison visitor undid the straps.

"Diego. Where is he?"

"Grandma killed him," Zelda hissed.

• • • •

THE A21 ELECTRICIAN robot sneered at the DVs clinging onto the bottom of the brocades in left field. Frecklie held his breath as an old guy climbed a little too close to the banners.

"They using Rifa 11 lighting?" the 'bot grumbled.

"Whatever you requested," Frecklie answered.

"What I requested was my people installing this."

Frecklie shrugged helplessly. "This was a direct order from Third Cousin Kenuda. You know who he is…"

"All the same to me," growled the 'bot. "Like we're all the same to you."

"A thought like that is against the law."

"So's humans doing work reserved for us." The A21's eyes rotated in two different directions. "My gang is checking their work after." He indicated the bored 'bots sitting in the front row of the upper deck, tossing peanut shells over the railing.

"Whatever you requested." Frecklie smiled politely.

"Stop making litter," the A21 yelled at his gang. "I need to check out the control room."

Frecklie led the 'bot past the stations of battery powered lamps installed every twenty feet. If the lights went, they'd need a path for the crowd to leave. He'd also ordered twenty thousand candles which he'd stored in the toilets throughout the park. He figured it was best not to tell Dale about his backup plan.

Dale stared hard at the A21, wishing she had an acetylene torch.

"He better not touch anything." She watched the 'bot peek behind the large grimy console in the control room.

"He's got to do his job."

"Not if he screws up mine. Hey, tin can."

Frecklie groaned. The glaring A21 poked his head up behind a mass of wires.

"What'd you call me?"

"Sir, of course." Dale blew a curl off her face. "The system is rigged very carefully."

"I got that, girl. If someone sneezed the whole thing'd blow."

"Then don't," she said tartly.

The A21 brushed off dust and flipped open a notebook.

"Is there a problem, sir?" Dale rasped; Frecklie stepped between them.

"You need a master re-routing cable."

Dale considered how much to fake knowing what he was talking about.

"I was planning on that."

The 'bot smirked. "You know what that is?"

"Re-routing juice."

"Good guess. Yeah. Otherwise the damn Bronx goes dark."

"My wiring won't do that," Dale insisted.

"Look here, girl." The A21 gestured toward the wiring system. "If you overload the park, you'll overload the surrounding neighborhood. This re-router makes sure you just blow up the stadium."

The A21 crawled behind the console, muttering and plugging in the re-router, and wriggling back out with a slight cough. He gave Dale a form to sign.

"Which plug is it?" Frecklie asked.

"Don't you mind."

"The black one?"

"Just leave it be. This is her responsibility if anything goes wrong."

Once the 'bot left, Dale sprayed cleaner on the console, glancing at Frecklie out of the corner of her eye. "You have something to share?"

He laughed weakly. "Nope. I have to check the food delivery. The game's a sellout and I don't want to run out of franks."

As Frecklie walked toward the door, Dale sprayed cleaner in his face. "Don't lie to me."

"I'm not," he moaned, eyes burning.

"You don't know shit about science or technology." She twisted his elbow behind his back.

He scooped her leg aside; Dale fell and he landed on top of her.

"Mind your business," he said.

"My lover's life is mine."

"You're quoting Grandma?"

"Yeah, because you're worrying me."

Frecklie relaxed, enabling Dale to leap onto his back and clamp her forearm against his throat. "Tell me."

He choked a no.

"You protecting me like I'm some weak piece of shit you stupid piece of shit?"

Frecklie gagged yes.

"Stop whining, you won't black out for another thirty-five seconds. Tell me. Everything." Dale tightened her grip.

• • • •

BETWEEN THE OBSESSIVE need to drive cars and the round-the-clock delivery of goods on trucks and rails, the sound of engines had replaced crickets as the nation's anthem. Need a bus at four in the morning to get to work? It'd be there. Need a rush order on a pair of shoes? Some van would deliver it somehow. 'Bots and humans, spinning wheels.

Most Americans figured the crushing noise of cars politely lagging along in traffic in the middle of the night was typical. Families should be asleep, children dancing on chocolate clouds, loving parents clutching fingers, tick-tock in the dark. But factories were open

24/7 for a nation cut off from trade with the rest of the world and feeding and clothing and housing and protecting families took precedence over candy cane birdies and your partner's bare flesh.

Screw you, Allahs, you didn't bury us.

Except these caravans weren't confined to the cars on the roads. People waited patiently on long lines at bus stops and train stations. No airports; that was for those who had money to spare. And the siblings trekking across the country had only so much money. For many, only so much savings. For gas and sandwiches and drinks.

And their colors.

There were no first reports because they came at once, like the ground opened. In a way, it had. They met at the rubble of Wrigley Field, Fenway Park, Braves Field, Forbes Stadium, Phillies Field and the Houston Aerodome. And every other stadium razed after 10/12.

No one coordinated this. The news about the night game was announced on Grandma's *Wake Up My Darlings*. There were important announcements where Grandma actually spoke and then there were the announcements where you saw Grandma smiling and her words floated out. Except these didn't even float out of the screen on an HG carpet, they weren't repeated in crawls on the screen, all you saw was the battered front of Yankee Stadium, Puppy striking out a batter, Mick hobbling around the bases and Dara blasting a song. If you rubbed some dirt out of your eye, you might've missed Saturday, August 11 at six-thirty PM. Live on vidsports 2.

Yet somehow everyone in America knew and they all headed toward the Bronx for the first baseball night game in thirty-three years.

Colors everywhere. Factories had started churning out Yankees and Cubs caps and t-shirts with the special FORGIVENESS on the back. But these colors weren't those colors. Those were approved. These were reds and golds and light blues and deep red and light reds and blacks and grays. Caps and t-shirts and full jerseys and banners and sweatshirts and warm-up jackets. How old were some of them? Thirty, forty, fifty years old, hidden in basements and hidden in closets and hidden in holes in the ground. Hidden in a crazy belief that someday a baseball fan could wear his Red Sox and Phillies and Dodgers and Cardinals and Braves and Tigers colors and any team he loved or his parents loved or his grandparents loved.

It didn't matter who you rooted for. They were all baseball fans today.

They drove and hitchhiked and used the last of their spare money for a bus or train ticket, devouring the food in their wake, cleaning out grocery stores of all the goods; some owners closed up shop since they had nothing left to sell anyway, and joined them.

From the northern part of California, Nevada, Minnesota, Texas, Florida, New England, if you'd put the country on a scale, she would've tipped over from the massive population quietly, almost warily making their way to the Bronx. In their expressions you could read, well, what if it's a trap? What if they're really going to finish off all the baseball fans? Not just banning merchandise and memorabilia, not just burning gloves, breaking bats and blowing up stadiums, but gunning everyone down.

But hadn't Grandma preached FORGIVENESS? Didn't they see the billboards of Grandma, Puppy and Dara? So they came. Tens of thousands, hundreds of thousands, more than a few million by the time they poured onto the Cross-Bronx Expressway, traffic stalled for hours, miles, until it couldn't be called traffic anymore.

America had overwhelmed itself in hope on the doorstep of the Bronx.

It'd taken Puppy over an hour through clogged streets and makeshift barbecues to find the cemetery. There was no street movement by wheels anymore. Trying to rush past the shouts of recognition, he'd moved from little bubbles of groups, shaking hands until he realized he'd probably miss the game tomorrow night if he talked to everyone, so he draped his hoodie over his forehead, shrunk his shoulders and hurried, eyes down, hands deep in his pockets, like a fugitive.

He fit in. This part of the borough was more forbidding. He got lost a couple times, backtracking and ducking into alleys as lines of bat-waving fans crept past like a polite, conquering army.

Beth squatted by a small mound. She smiled as he knelt.

"You done praying?" Puppy apologized.

"Some would say you never stop. But aloud, yes. How's it going out there?"

He couldn't answer; it was overwhelming. For a quiet moment, they stared in the forbidden churchyard at the faint moon and the hint of stars; maybe it was real. Beth reached up as if to touch the sky.

"It's like a great cathedral's overhead. One of those wonderful old churches with wonderful arches, golden lights, stained glass, paintings, statues."

"Like when I could imagine what Yankee Stadium once was. Or is that offensive to compare baseball to your God?"

"No. Faith is faith."

They listened to the rumble of the fans walking slowly on the street below.

"You're sure about tomorrow?" Puppy suddenly asked.

"Did you come to talk me out of it?" she scowled.

"Yes."

"We already went through that, Puppy." For three hours last night.

"It's my fault, my responsibility."

Beth draped her arm around his shoulder. "It's your fault you married a crazy person and it's your fault for getting engaged to Dara to make it easier for that crazy person to find someone?"

"I did it for myself."

"It's okay to be a little selfish, Puppy." Beth gently smacked his forehead.

"Good thing psychiatry's banned."

"We don't need it. People can figure things out for themselves. The trick's listening." She smacked him again. "I can handle tomorrow."

He thought of Beth scampering up and down the brocades and smiled wearily. "But I'm insisting on a driver. I'm sure two person missions were taught in vets summer camp."

She ignored him with a meaningful smile. "Just keep Ruben out of this."

Puppy made a tiny space between his forefinger and thumb.

"Because only you know it all."

He shrugged. "Someone has to be the mastermind."

This afternoon, the Brown Hats had interrupted infield practice; Ty chased them down the third base line with a bat. They came back. Himself, Mick and Ty for two grilling hours. Dara was questioned during rehearsal at the vidmus studio. Pablo, who wryly said he had nothing else to do at work. Anyone with a connection to Zelda. Except Beth.

"All Parents records are confidential. Unless it's a capital offense. Another reason I'm perfect for this," she said. Puppy nodded and yawned. "You should rest."

"So should you. I'm just pitching."

Beth doodled in the dirt. "Do you believe in ever-lasting love, Puppy?"

Now Puppy had the opening to say he loved her. He tensed. "I've never been there."

"Not even with Annette?"

He hesitated. "In the beginning. Then the illusion kicked in. Love's a tricky mirror."

"What about Zelda?"

"She's a friend."

"You love her more than you ever could a partner."

He saw Beth's expression, the realization making his stomach sink. "You love her, too. That's why you're doing this."

Beth rested her chin on his shoulder. "Does that hurt you?"

"Because I go to sleep at night imagining kissing your breasts?"

She laughed so loud the dirt on the grave stirred. That didn't make him feel any better. "I didn't think it went quite that far." Beth grew serious. "Yes, I love her. She's very unique."

"Oh yeah."

"Is there something I should know?"

Now it was his turn to make the dirt dance. "This isn't exactly a relationship with a future."

She shrugged sadly. "What is?"

He followed her long look at the grave. "Was he?"

Beth sighed. "It was painful love from the start. He had dreams up his ass and no ladder tall enough to reach them. But he was a good guy. And we had a child." She suddenly squeezed his hand. "I would've liked to have loved you, Puppy. I mean that. It would've simplified so much. Frecklie views you like a father. You have the makings of a good Catholic. You're decent."

"You forgot something. Oh Puppy, kiss my breasts."

She chuckled. "You're obsessed by them."

"Metaphoric."

"If I were a different person I'd let you see them."

"Jesus wouldn't like such talk."

"See. You already have me thinking things I shouldn't."

"That's what friends are about." He hugged Beth. "You better never hurt my Zelda."

She gave him a mock salute.

"Does Zelda love you, too?"

"After tomorrow night, how could she not?" Beth shivered in the brisk wind.

"We should get you home."

Beth patted the lumpy backpack. "Sometimes I nap here."

He cringed. "In a cemetery?"

"It's like being in the waiting room of Heaven."

He didn't buy that, but this would be as close as he'd ever get to spending the night with her. They rolled up, arms around each other, wrapped in two woolen blankets. He prayed to Jesus not to let him get an erection.

"Puppy?" she whispered after a while, waking him.

He sat up in alarm and she gently laid him back down. "Nothing's going wrong tomorrow. Don't worry. But you never know. Most of these people didn't expect to end up here so soon. So if something goes south in a handcart, as my father used to say, I want you adopting Ruben."

He rubbed his bleary eyes. "What?"

Beth kissed his cheek and tucked him in. "You'd do it anyway. I just wanted you to have my blessing."

• • • •

LIEUTENANT ARTITO DIDN'T like being in charge, especially when he'd had no time to prepare. Sure, when Tomas was gone, he was head of the detachment. But Tomas was never gone. In the eighteen years he'd been in Grandma's security platoon, Tomas had always been here wherever she went, whatever the time, whatever the circumstances. Like her sixth toe.

Grandma looked at him impatiently and hurried along the long marble corridor past the fresh flowers on the tables and laughing HG children throwing balls. He still sometimes thought they were real and made a wide arc, catching up to Grandma as they went onto the dark green lawn of the House.

"We weren't scheduled for this, ma'am." He tried blocking her without seeming to.

"Now we are."

"Shouldn't I call Major Stilton?" Tomas had already ignored three pleas, but at least it'd seem like Artito was doing his duty.

"Aren't you capable of handling me?" Grandma smiled faintly.

He stiffened. "Yes, ma'am."

"We'll see about that." She tapped her feet and the 'copter appeared. Grandma hopped in. The baffled platoon looked at Artito for guidance; he snapped orders for them to haul ass up and out.

The 'copter skipped south, Grandma's face pressed against the window in amazement.

"How far back do they go?" She pointed at the streams of cars.

"Northwest to the Poconos, north to Albany, south to Philadelphia, east to Hartford. There's no traffic movement anymore, ma'am. Just cars. People."

"Show me."

Artito grunted at Lt. Onuyomi, who spasmed nervously until he found the raw surveillance footage. Grandma's lips parted slowly in thought.

"How will they watch the game?"

"It'll be on the vidsports, ma'am."

"Are screens on the highways, Lieutenant?"

Artito really hated Tomas at this moment. "I don't believe so."

"Then how will they watch?" She touched his wrist. "That's not an accusation, but a question."

"I guess they can't."

Grandma nodded. "See how much easier it is when you're not afraid? Get Commissioner Kenuda on his tracker."

The platoon exchanged puzzled looks.

"It's that gizmo over there." Grandma pointed to a black keyboard in the corner. "Dial 22, then ask for Third Cousin Kenuda and say it's Grandma."

Three soldiers banged into each other scrambling to fulfill the order.

"Now let's get closer."

Artito nodded carefully and ordered the 'copter to drop a hundred feet. They drifted over the Grand Concourse where tents had been pitched, barbecues grilled, children ran around, between and on top of cars. Everywhere, baseball banners flew.

"I've never seen so many people out," she marveled.

"There were millions for the Surrender, I mean Truce Parade, ma'am."

"Because they had to be. Today, they want to be. Look at them. How happy everyone is. Why is that?"

No one knew the right answer. Grandma laughed her warm, reassuring sound, as if they were being bathed in soapy bubbles. They offered a variety of opinions about this just being spontaneous and fun and an adventure.

426 | GARY MORGENSTEIN

"There's more. Can something spontaneous and powerful be controlled or does that not make it spontaneous anymore?"

No amount of bubbles in their hair could persuade the soldiers to respond.

"Let's set down somewhere."

Artito glanced around in panic; everyone heard the same order, too.

"Ma'am, we can't do that."

"Why not?" They turned down 161st Street.

"Security considerations."

"You think I'll be at risk?"

"Yes."

Grandma shook her head firmly and rapped on the cockpit door. "Land, please."

The Lieutenant grimaced. "There's nowhere to land. Only cars and people. We'll hurt someone, yes," he liked that argument, "we might land on a child or something."

Grandma chuckled and sat back, arms folded. "I have faith in my pilots."

"I should really ask Major Stilton."

Grandma gave him a hard stare. "He's not here. You are, Lieutenant."

Artito scurried into the cockpit.

"I heard." Lt. Jin nodded. "I'll find somewhere." She gestured Artito back into the cabin.

"Okay. We're going down."

Grandma grinned. "Perhaps that's not the best phrase."

Jin circled a while over the carpet of humans before finally landing on the roof of a yellow school bus blocking Gerard Street. The winds startled the crowd. When the 'copter materialized and everyone realized who it was, they let out a great roar.

"It's not steady," Artito shouted into the cockpit as the school bus trembled.

Metal claws from the 'copter dug into the roof.

"Is now," Jin called back.

Grandma pushed the exit button, hopped out of the aircraft onto the roof and, with a quick jump, onto the street.

"Follow her, damnit," Artito snapped.

Grandma pressed forward, anxious soldiers fanning out as another 'copter appeared, just as a reminder; the other two remained stealth and circled 161st Street.

"Where are you from, darling?" Grandma embraced an elderly woman, who explained she was a Cincinnati Reds fan, triggering another explanation about how that was a different red from her neighbor, a St. Louis Cardinals fan.

Soon Grandma was surrounded by fans representing each team, shyly coming forward and showing their clothes and equipment. She received a quick batting lesson, apologizing for cracking a side view mirror on the backswing, tossing balls, effortlessly hoisting children onto her shoulders and slowly making her way toward the stadium.

People parted to let her past, then followed, as if on the train of a long gown, amazed they were here, amazed Grandma was here, amazed she tried fielding a grounder and then chased the ball when it rolled through her legs under the El, where she encountered sheepish workers erecting the stage for the concert behind a long yellow ribbon squaring off the large area.

Grandma decided everyone was going to help and yanked down the ropes. Fans poured through, eagerly hammering and moving stanchions and wires. Someone sang *Take Me Out to the Ballgame*. Soon hundreds, thousands, tens of thousands were singing as they worked, food passing freely. Grandma wielded a hammer, teeth clamped on spare nails; Artito frantically kept her in sight.

Grandma insisted she be taught the words. She picked it up instantly, jumped onto the stage and, waving her hammer as a baton, led the crowd in song.

After a while, Grandma nodded wearily. Artito ordered one of the 'copters to land onto the stage. He held his breath, but it didn't collapse. Half the platoon guarded the perimeter while he led the rest back onto the 'copter. She waved and waved and waved and sang until the 'copter lifted. He only enjoyed a moment of relaxation.

"Go over the stadium," Grandma ordered.

They stealthed and circled the empty park. Grandma's smile faded into a puzzled frown.

How could so much passion and love turn so ugly, she wondered. What did I do so wrong?

The 'copter drifted over center field. She leaned out; the detachment gasped. Lenora grumbled them away, impatient, angry.

October 12, 2065. She heard the sound of gunfire again, felt the bullet crease her head, heard the children screaming, the bombs falling. Americans killing Americans because they cared too much, Lenora realized. Can love be a crime?

Forgiving them isn't enough. I have to forgive myself, too, Grandma thought.

37

Kenuda yanked the phone out of the wall and threw it over Annette's head. She didn't duck since it was the third phone he'd broken. The first two were dramatic, all those weird parts rolling around. Now it was just irritating noise. Snorting at her poise, Elias petulantly kicked a football against the window, grunting triumphantly at the cracked glass.

The 'bot secretary silently replaced the phone and closed the curtains, shooting Kenuda a withering look.

"Get me the damn 'copter company in Allentown," he shouted. "That's in Pennsylvania."

428 | GARY MORGENSTEIN

The A10 turned in disgust. "I know that, sir. Would you like me to recite the names of all the communities in America beginning with the letter A?"

"For now, more coffee. You want more?" he scowled at Annette as if she'd just arrived instead of sitting there for three agonizing hours listening to him fight with every police and military and shipping and aerial and electrical and building and whoever knows who person in the country.

"That would be nice, honey."

Kenuda wrenched the ringing receiver to his ear. Annette gave that phone an hour to live, tops.

"Yes. This is Third Cousin Kenuda. Yes, the same as Commissioner Kenuda. Who's been waiting for the permit to erect the vidscreen on Route 34… Do you understand we don't have twenty-four hours because the game begins in…" He looked helplessly toward Annette, who held up her watch. "In three hours. I didn't have clearance earlier. Now now, wait, wait, Sheriff Baja. Look out your window. What do you see? Past the blasted car wash. All those people. Do you know what will happen if they can't see the game? I'll tell you, damnit. They're going to be angry. I'm going to be angry. Grandma's going to be angry. Not your Grandma, imbecile. The Grandma. That's right. **The** Grandma. Her orders. Good. Get it done now."

He went to yank this phone out of the wall, but the secretary returned, putting down the tray of coffee. "It's the last phone on the floor, sir."

"Kenuda, sweetheart." Annette closed the door behind the grumbling 'bot. "Let me help."

"You?"

She winced. "Yes. Me."

"What could you possibly do, Annette?" Kenuda snarled into his computer screen. "Boston is still not up. And that's at Fenway Park." He paused on Annette's sad expression. "Darling, I wish you could help. There's just chaos."

"So I've been hearing…" Her dress was completely wilted in the steamy room.

"Some temp screens say they can only show the concert, but not the game, too. Why? We have one vid network. It's the same feed. No wonder I'm needed to run both sports and entertainment."

"Maybe they're having problems because you only decided forty-eight hours ago."

"Me?" he yelled.

"Stop yelling. You should've thought of this sooner."

His lips silently counted to three. "That I was able to pull this off is a miracle. Miracle. Booking bands, schedules, rehearsals, the lights, the promotion. Is there anyone in the United States of America who doesn't know about this historic occasion?"

"Mainly been Puppy and Dara on the vidnews," she said sourly.

"Who the hell arranged that? Little flying fairies in the forest? Becoming Second Cousin isn't reward enough."

Annette's eyes widened. "Oh my baby, you're getting promoted?"

"Eventually. What time is it again?"

She twisted her arm so he could read the watch. "We have to leave by five, you said."

"I must go earlier."

"Okay, I don't mind…"

"Annette," he said sternly, "there's a lot of boring backstage crap. The acts, director, oh, Ian Schrage's a pip…"

"He's famous. I can't wait to meet him."

Kenuda looked uncomfortable. "Annette, there's really no place for you there."

"That's where all the real excitement is."

"Stress. Aggravation. Massive egos of weak-minded but gifted people who need a firm hand on their elbow which I can't do if I'm worried about you."

"I'll behave."

"But I've got you a seat for the show and of course, the game, if you like."

"I should be with you…"

"You can't." He frothed slightly at his beeping computer screen. "Be a wonderful and supportive girl and amuse yourself somewhere until then."

• • • •

THE THUMPING ON the door was so persistent it became a beat, blending into the prog-country doo-dad band warming up the crowd out there, somewhere beyond the vodka mist.

"I'm breaking down the door."

How long would that take? Depends if he had an axe. Or bazooka. Yes, a large projectile would work best.

The thumping sounds stopped, replaced by quiet jingling, very secretive to make sure she wouldn't hear. She'd fool them and be waiting with a large projectile herself.

Mooshie was on her hands and knees, searching for vodka when Puppy finally opened the door. He clicked on the light and she dove under the bed, pleading for the dark. He dragged Mooshie out by her ankles. She made no effort to get off her stomach other than gesture for the bottle of Butte's Best Vodka on the table.

Puppy shouted, "What the hell's going on? Your set's in twenty minutes."

"I'm ready. Just relaxing, honey."

He flipped her onto her back and straddled her chest.

"I ain't giving you a blowjob." Mooshie grinned crookedly.

"I don't take blow jobs from drunks."

"Oh, we do have standards." She knocked him aside and stumbled to the table, downing the last of the vodka.

"There are hundreds of thousands of people out there. Maybe a million. The whole country's watching."

"Yes. You and I. Mr. and Ms. America's Favorite Couple. He throws. I sing. Forgiveness. Lights, camera, action. Forgiveness. It's all bullshit, Puppy."

"Maybe to you. Not to them." He jerked his head in the direction of the thunderous applause as the doo-dad band scampered off and the next group, a drum quartet from Philly called Divine Pleasure, pounded their way on.

"I'll be there. Enchanting, brilliant Dara Dinton."

He shook his head. "Spare me your crap."

"Is that any way to talk to someone whose underwear you've cherished for twenty-five years?"

"You can't screw up the concert."

"I will fuck up nothing," she hissed. "Other than my life. For the rest of the world, I live on, Mooshie, Dara, who knows what my next incarnation will be. No, incarnation is when your soul returns in another body. Well, I ain't got a soul. All I got is this."

Cradling the empty bottle, Mooshie slumped sadly in a chair. He knelt, handing her a steaming mug of coffee.

"What happened, Moosh?"

"I'm having trouble understanding why I'm here. Whose side I'm on."

"Mine." He kissed her hand.

"But whose side are you on, Pup?"

"Mine," he admitted. "And that side has brought a night game back to Yankee Stadium…"

"I'm scared, Pup," Mooshie whispered.

"So I see."

"You're scared, too."

"Every day. I don't get it, either, other than we all got second chances. Me, you, Mick, Ty. He hasn't called anyone a nigra or spic in weeks."

They laughed softly.

"What scares you the most?" Puppy asked, almost afraid of the answer.

"That I'll be sent back to wherever I came from before I know why I came." Mooshie blinked back tears. "My friends murdered me, Pup. Derek Singh, Easy Sun Yen. I was an embarrassment. My best friends. The Three Amigos."

Puppy stared, astonished.

"They gave the order. Now I gotta sing a couple songs and walk back into the stadium," her voice dipped harshly, "where I was once hot shit, knowing what they did. All the lies my life was, when the people I trusted the most, loved dearly, thought nothing of killing me. That's what I'm thinking tonight."

Puppy thought carefully for a moment, wiping away her tears. "If it's all bullshit, then what's it matter concocting more bullshit to explain it away."

"You're okay with that?"

"If I can't explain, then there's no confusion. I take the mound at Yankee Stadium, Moosh. My dream. Not a big deal to you..."

"It was always a big deal," she blazed. "I never took it for granted. Lots else. Not that."

"I just thought of something. Maybe you can pitch an inning some game."

She shuddered. "I'm skeeved out this close to the players' entrance and you want me to pitch?"

"You're right. It'd be embarrassing compared to me. I've struck out more than ten batters in eight straight games."

Mooshie staggered up. "And I did it twenty-three straight games."

"Twenty-four. I know old people have bad memories." He kissed her fingers. "You can trust me, Moosh. Totally."

"I know. You're not smart enough to be manipulative." She gulped down the rest of the scalding coffee while he wondered about that compliment. "Now get your ass out of here so the greatest baseball player and the greatest singer in the history of the world can put her makeup back on."

The stage lights were like stepping onto the surface of the Sun. Ian shouted into the earphones to get on; she crushed the plugs with her heels. In the twenty-foot perch directly overhead, Schrage bounced up and down like an ornery child.

The audience stomped their feet. Her band waited, sax, pianist, bass guitar, drums; her old group The Pinholes always knew when she'd start. These folks couldn't be blamed for thinking five minutes of anticipatory noise was enough. She'd know the right moment.

Behind the thick purple curtain, Mooshie tilted her head to catch the faint waves of sound. It could've been building for miles; Kenuda had preened that traffic was stalled for hundreds of miles and he'd rescued everyone with his portable roadside screens. He and that bitch Annette deserved each other.

The sounds congealed, there, she could make it out. One word, two syllables. Out of the darkness, Schrage limped forward, panic on his bleeding face; he'd fallen the last five feet.

"For the love of Grandma's earlobe, will you please get out there?"

Mooshie smiled innocently. "But I was waiting for my director's cue."

Ian nearly swallowed his tongue. Mooshie skipped on stage into the deafening roar of Da-ra, Da-ra.

"Hello America." She flipped her hair from front to back. "What did you say?"

"Dara," they yelled.

"What?" She held out the microphone.

"Dara!"

"What?"

"Dara, Dara, Dara," the chant erupted.

"All right. Now I'm going to feed you."

She exploded through the Mooshie sizzler *Drill My Heart,* followed by the *Dear Drops* ballad and then the number one tune *Boil My Blood Baby.*

"Think you got my temperature

Do you now

When all you got

Is blood that don't boil

I need real loving

Yes I do

When you're up to it

Give me a cue

'Cause until now

You're nothing but a speck."

Mooshie flung the blonde wig into the crowd, which went insane, tearing for a piece. Puppy nearly fainted. Not tonight, Moosh.

Mooshie fluffed up her short black hair and the crowd went nuts again, screaming themselves hoarse. It wasn't until the music quieted that they all became aware of the faint whirring of a 'copter, suddenly hovering above the stage.

Grandma's legs dangled girlishly over the edge, white socks rolling down over her neat purple sneakers. She waved at Mooshie.

"Hi," she paused meaningfully, "Dara. Aren't you going to introduce me?"

Grandma's eyes drilled into Mooshie, frozen as if all her ligaments were sewn together.

"Grandma," Mooshie finally managed.

The crowd roared for a couple minutes before Grandma shooshed them like they were misbehaving before bedtime.

"Are you enjoying yourselves?" She waited for the shouts to die down. "I won't take up much time because we have a baseball game to play." Grandma understood their suddenly silent anxiety. "Which is wonderful and why I'm here."

She wiggled back and forth, trying to find a comfortable place.

"I love you all very much." Grandma brushed off the "we love you too" responses. "That's why I want to apologize. I made a mistake once. I let my anger at what wrongheaded, but sincere Americans believed, to cloud my judgment. Baseball represented an America I didn't understand, an America I never really knew. A strong America. A leader. The leader. Baseball above all else represented that. A time of glory, freedom, a different world where problems could be solved by a game of catch in the backyard. I thought that world was gone. Some ways, it is. But what I destroyed was passion and love and respect for tradition. All the themes The Family represents are captured in baseball. It's part of this country. That with one swing of a bat you can change everything."

Grandma paused. You could hear a pin drop across America. "I destroyed something very special and I'm sorry."

The silence continued because no one knew what to say.

"Thank you, Grandma," Mooshie said quietly and "thank you Grandmas" rippled back into the night, softly, as if the last words before going to sleep.

Lenora smiled faintly.

"You're going to have your baseball back. This isn't the last season. Let's hope there's a hundred more."

The 'copter drifted up and stealthed. Now the crowd murmured, unsure what just happened.

You cunning bitch. You're a genius.

"Didn't you hear what she said?" Mooshie yelled. "This ain't the last baseball season." The crowd started screaming. "There's gonna be baseball all over the country." The shouts got louder. "They're gonna rebuild all the parks. Right? Right? RIGHT?"

Puppy ran onto the stage and hugged Mooshie, joined by Kenuda. America shouted itself hoarse.

• • • •

EMBARRASSED, ZELDA DIDN'T know what to do with the green daisies. Annette took over the domestic situation.

"They put together such a nice layout and don't give you a vase?" Annette briefly re-arranged the lumpy sofa and chair a little further apart, straightening the coffee table and frowning at the wobbly floor lamp. She marched into the kitchen area, ready to issue citations, and rummaged through the nearly empty cupboard before triumphantly brandishing a tall chipped glass which she filled with water.

"I knew there had to be something." Annette balanced the daisies in the glass, muttering about no scissors to cut the stems and spending another minute deciding where the flowers should go. She settled on the end table next to Zelda's narrow, unmade bed. Sighing loudly, she made the bed, fluffed the pillow and sat on the lumpy chair, two girlfriends catching up except for Zelda's desire to cut Annette's throat.

"How are you?" Annette asked brightly. "Not a bad place for a prison. You'll be out of here in no time."

"Is that what you're told?"

"I just assume you'll say where the brat is and be done with it. She's not even yours so why protect her?"

Zelda's mouth curled viciously and Annette continued on in a cheerful tone.

"I've been okay, thanks," she said as if Zelda had done more than glare. "Business is good. All these people in town, well, you'd think that'd help someone like me, but they're not quite my customers. Clomp, clomp. Puppy's pitching tonight. There was a concert by that woman. I couldn't go, too busy."

"You came here, instead."

"That's my right."

"Your right?"

"Well, both our rights. Accuser and accused." Annette's fingers got momentarily confused who was who. "I'm sorry about all this. Grandma asks a lot of us to fulfill our duty. We have to push aside personal feelings. Despite that, I visited. Have you had many guests?"

"I have no family, Annette. No one else is allowed."

"Then it's good I came." She looked around as if the furniture had secretly moved. "Is that a window?"

Zelda turned toward the narrow two-by-two square. "If it could be called that."

"There's a night game at the baseball stadium. Very historic. The first time in ages. I was with my fiance Elias Kenuda, Third Cousin and Commissioner, who put this event together."

Zelda gave her the finger, which only made Annette's smile widen.

"He's a brilliant man. So much to be done. You probably think, oh, a concert, here's the mike, play the piano. Here's a baseball game, throw the ball. Astonishing what goes into it. I did make my contribution to the cause with some advice, he'll get the credit, well, we are a couple and will be getting married in two months once the trial period passes. I bet we can hear the crowd from that window if not actually see something."

Annette pressed her face against the pane. Something about Annette's pitiable expression drew Zelda. Their shoulders touched in the narrow space.

"I hear the fans, don't you?" Annette squinted through the fading sunlight.

"That's my stomach growling," Zelda said.

"Maybe you need to feed the baby." She stared at Zelda's stomach. "Can I pet it?"

Zelda nodded slowly. Annette leaned forward, hand on Zelda's belly, mouth by her ear.

"They're moving you to a BT facility tomorrow."

Zelda stiffened. The Annette she'd always known quickly returned with a boisterous shout out the window.

"Let's go Puppy and all that baseball stuff."

• • • •

DALE LAY FLAT on her back, legs propped against the back wall. Outside the control room, one of her five guards charged with keeping the human race away raised an eyebrow as her skirt fell around her hips, revealing her pink panties. Dale bared her teeth and the girl turned away so quickly her head nearly got stuck backwards.

Once again, Dale blotted out the din from the fans, vendors, flies, grass, clouds. There should've been complete quiet. How can I work with all this noise? Dale pounded the floor. I'm fine, she told herself, sitting up. Everything's going to be fine. She threw back her blonde curls and walked calmly, if a little stiffly, back to her control panel.

Twenty thousand candles flickered from the bleachers to home as the sun slowly set. Down on the field, Dara and a small band entertained, guided by three squat lamps. The teams idly tossed balls in front of the dugouts. The noises, to a person not melting down, were really hums of expectation. Respectful, quiet, unsure what was going to happen since few if any of them had ever seen a sports night game; there were a lot of craning heads looking up at the brocades.

Dale stared at the console. She hated doing anything too quickly because it meant she lost an element of control. Yet she loved spontaneity because it left a part of her behind and she was arrogant enough to know her genius mind had already figured everything out.

She hadn't really figured this out. The scoreboard was different. She understood programming and imagination and creating, glancing at a Dale HG racing past on a carpet resembling an infield. This was boring. She was easily bored. She knew she must really love Frecklie if they'd been together a year and he hadn't bored her yet.

Frecklie waved a flashlight by the Yankees dugout, waiting for the signal back. It was getting really dark now, he gestured. Like she didn't fucking know that. By home plate, Dara shot her a pleading look and launched into another song, her voice like a cow getting it up the ass; Dale shoved in her earplugs.

Shit, she suddenly remembered, crawling under the console and unhooking the rerouter. If you forgot something this important, what else have you forgotten?

Okay. What's the worst that could happen? Dale casually licked a caramel cane. The lights don't go on. That's pretty bad. Or the lights go on and Yankee Stadium blows up. That's even worse. Probably about fifty thousand people here and more outside. That'd be ugly. Dale Danaka, the Butcher of the Bronx.

She smiled. The nearness of catastrophe gave her a sense of calm. Dale cracked her fingers. The stadium was now totally dark, except for the candles and the lamps around home plate. She waved her flashlight, cueing Dara, who began the countdown from ten, the crowd shyly joining in.

At two, Dale hit the switch. Nothing.

She glowered at the console. Work you motherfuckers.

As if God walked in holding one really big candle, the lights turned on, quickly rushing across the upper decks, foul pole to foul pole until Yankee Stadium was ablaze.

The crowd fell into stunned silence, then cheered, turning toward Dale, who bowed, taking full credit, as she should.

Beyond the outfield, the Bronx went dark. Like God blew out His candle.

• • • •

SHE WAITED UNTIL the lights went out before running into the pitch black lobby of the Bronx Courthouse, slipping through the bewildered visitors and guards and past the abandoned security check-in up the steps, two at a time. The floor plans from the library were quite good and she quickly found Room 202, ducking into the doorway as Blue Shirts raced down the steps.

She slid the thin piece of metal into the doorframe and slipped inside so quietly the two shadowed women peering out the window didn't notice.

Two?

Beth pulled off her thin black ski mask. Zelda's surprise lasted a second before she ran into her arms.

"You're rescuing me?"

Beth winked and looked over Zelda's shoulder.

"Who the hell are you?"

"Who am I?" Annette was indignant. "Who are you?"

"It's Annette," Zelda whispered, squeezing Beth's tense back.

"Oh shit."

"What're you whispering about?"

"We have to take her," Beth said with distaste.

Annette laughed weakly. "I'm not going anywhere except to the police. This is an illegal act." She put her hands on her hips, scolding Zelda. "You can't help being a criminal, can you?"

Beth covered the distance to the window in three quick steps and punched Annette in the jaw, who slid against the wall into an unconscious seated position

"I've wanted to do that for so long," Zelda said.

Beth winked again, draping Annette over her shoulders and hurrying out the door. They took the back staircase, ducking into an alcove as more Blue Shirts rushed past. Beth paused by the back door.

"It's going to be noisy."

The clanging alarm finally faded as they ran down East 162nd Street to a parked black van with gold lettering, Basil Hayden's Funeral Home. Wearing a dark workmen's uniform, Mickey hopped out of the driver's seat, kissed Zelda quickly and opened the back door, wonderingly taking Annette.

Two coffins lay in the back. The lid on the smaller one popped open.

"Hola, Zelda!" Clary waved happily.

Zelda burst into tears and hugged the child.

"No time for that," Beth said sternly, helping Mickey lay Annette into the adult coffin. Clary hissed in recognition.

"Try not to suffocate." Beth kissed Zelda on the forehead as she squeezed next to Annette, then joined Mickey in the front seat. "Sure you can drive?"

Mickey shrugged. "Only been a hundred years. Like riding a bike."

By the time they edged onto the emergency lanes, trailing fire trucks and cop cars and repair vehicles, the lights started trickling back in parts. It was hard to say if the fans standing on the car roofs were watching the glow of Yankee Stadium or the stumbling reawakening of the Bronx's electrical grid system. Either way, there was loud music and food and wonderment at the carnival of surprises.

Once past Burnside Avenue, they slowed down at a snake-like checkpoint near 188th Street. A bug-eyed Blue Shirt in need of a nap peered inside as Mick rolled down the window.

"Evening, sir." Mantle smiled. "Big night."

The cop made a face. "I could write a book. You're in the wrong lane."

"We got turned around near the stadium."

"Who hasn't?" The Blue Shirt gratefully rested his elbows on the window. "You have to get back in the civilian lanes."

The cars were backed up for miles on either side.

"We got some stiffs," Mick explained.

Beth handed over the papers from the funeral home authorizing the transportation of two corpses. The Blue Shirt held up the documents, vainly looking for a light to read by. He gave up. "Picked a helluva night."

"Bet they're unhappy, too," Mick quipped.

A faint groan snuck into the front seat. The Blue Shirt frowned.

"What's that?"

"They just died."

The cop rapped his nightstick on the side view mirror and followed them around to the back of the van.

Beth held her breath as Mick opened the door. The Blue Shirt shined his flashlight over the adult and child-sized coffins.

"Mother and daughter," Beth said softly.

The Blue Shirt apologetically tipped his cap. "I got two daughters. One husband." He closed the back door and scribbled on the back of a slip. "Stay in the emergency lane. Anyone gives you grief, show 'em Sergeant Pine said it's okay."

They drove a little quicker, hitting the Major Deegan and finding the lane nearly empty as all the emergency vehicles poured the other way into the city. After a few twists

438 | GARY MORGENSTEIN

and turns along dark country roads, they pulled into a clearing, turning off the engine, killing the lights and waiting.

"Know these people?" Mick jerked his head toward the dark woods.

"No," Beth said quietly. "Mooshie does. It's either this or they keep running. There's nowhere to go."

"This used to be our world," Mantle said.

"It's awfully small if you're a loser."

Mick bristled. "America ain't a bunch of losers."

"We convinced ourselves we were, Mick. That everything we did was wrong. Hateful. That people wanted us dead because of what we did, not because of what they wanted. We were the bad guys by defending ourselves. By the time we realized hey, we're not perfect, but we're not all bad, it was too late."

Mantle brushed away a tear. "You can't lose a country just like that."

She tenderly squeezed his shoulder. "Don't worry. It's still out there."

Four hooded figures brandishing rifles motioned for them to raise their hands as they stepped out. Mick and Beth were quickly frisked. A slight figure circled a match around their faces and nodded approval to his colleagues. He pocketed the spent match.

"In the back." Beth indicated with her head.

Mick unlocked the door while Beth crawled inside and rapped on the coffin lids. Clary popped up, gasping a little, and leaped out as if she had wires under her armpits. Zelda was stuck; Beth tugged her out, then they lifted out the still groggy Annette.

The guards let them lower their hands.

"You disfigured my mouth," Annette yelled at Beth, who handed Zelda and Clary water bottles.

"There's supposed to be only two," said a tall guard, more to his colleagues.

"She was on site and had to be extracted," Beth explained.

"Kidnapped." Annette stepped forward. "I've been kidnapped by these, these criminals. A baseball player yet," she sneered at Mick. "Big surprise. I insist you bring me to the local police station so I can file a full report."

The guards looked at each other, trying to sort out whether Annette was kidding or crazy.

"I will overlook any assault charges." She nodded graciously toward Beth. "I think that's fair under the circumstances."

The tall guard cocked his rifle. "We're only supposed to take two. Her and her. Not her."

"She's a witness," Beth said, voice rising. "We had to take her."

"I understand, ma'am. Now she's our responsibility."

"Excellent," Annette piped up as if she'd just filled a large, expensive shoe order. "If someone has some aspirin please."

Zelda stepped between the guards and Annette. "She comes with us."

"I don't think so," Annette sneered.

"Just shut up for once."

"See the abuse I've received for being nice enough to visit her? I even brought green daisies. Any idea how hard they are to find this time of year?"

Two guards grabbed Annette. Mick and Beth stepped forward, earning rifles in their sides.

"Do you know who she is?" Zelda asked. "Fiance to a Third Cousin."

"That's right, thank you. I have very important connections."

"He's also Commissioner of Sport."

"And entertainment," Annette added. "Soon to be a Second Cousin so get your hands off my expensive blouse."

"You gain nothing by shooting her. She might have value as a hostage."

"What?" Annette bleated.

Shut up, Zelda gestured.

The guards conferred, clearly divided between taking Annette and shooting her. Another spirited debate sent the tall guard forward.

"She comes as a prisoner. Not like you and the girl."

Annette was quickly gagged, blindfolded, handcuffed and dragged towards the black woods. The tall guard gestured impatiently with his rifle. Zelda held up a finger. Mick caught the looks between the two women and took Clary's hand.

"Come on honey, let's see who can run faster." He and Clary raced into the forest, Mick limping noticeably.

Zelda laid her head on Beth's shoulder. "Thank you."

"Thank Puppy. He's the mastermind."

"But you risked your life."

Beth shrugged shyly. "Love and all that."

Zelda seemed a little unsettled. "You love me?"

"Yes."

"Love love?"

"Love love."

"I just got over losing Diego…"

"I understand," Beth said. "It might take time. Unless there's really no basis."

"No, there's a basis."

"You're not just carried away by my heroism?"

The guards muttered for Zelda to hurry.

"A little." She paused, eyes tearing. "We're not exactly looking at a great future."

"That's what Puppy said."

"He has a crush on you."

"I know. Are we going to waste our last moments for a while talking about Puppy's sexual fantasies?"

Zelda leaned forward. "I'd much rather focus on mine."

Their kiss was broken by a rifle wedged between their squirming bodies. Zelda insisted on watching until the van crunched back down the path to return the coffins, which Puppy had ordered for the special Basil Hayden Funeral Home commercial display outside Section 227B which would be seen by more than fifty thousand potential customers.

Zelda and Clary sat in the back of the SUV, feeling Annette's rage through her stuffed mouth and eyes. As they turned onto a narrow path, a large tree loomed ahead. The SUV headed right toward it. Zelda held Clary's arm and yelled a warning, but the guard was oblivious.

Like a zipper, the tree parted in half, swallowing them into a huge, brightly lit cave. Clarry applauded and shouted "Viva America."

38

No one really left.

Nearly two million visitors, the Blue Shirts estimated, were still there. The few citizens who'd run screaming into the streets cursing Allahs and wailing about a new attack had fled home. Some drunks, believing that in forty-two minutes of darkness the world was about to end, were arrested for disorderly behavior. There were several scuffles along the Grand Concourse when people ran into the wrong tents and hugged the wrong partners.

But there was no violence. No fear. No hysteria. People gasped, whispered, wondered, but pretty much just sat there patiently in the dark, passing food and drink and blankets besides the glowing stadium lights and the cheers of the lucky fans inside.

Ellen Paille from Burlington, Vermont, thought the blackout was a brilliant part of the show. Allinor Del Strada of Lynchburg, Virginia, who insisted her grandfather had been buried in a Washington Nationals uniform before cremation, was disappointed that the Bronx lights came back so soon. And Papi Torryes from Amarillo, Texas, wondered if there'd be fireworks for the next game.

"Not a single person was hurt," Grandma said, laying out some freshly baked biscotti on the serving table in her House the next day; she poured Kenuda and Puppy ginger tea. "This is how a Family behaves in a crisis."

They nodded agreeably.

"How many did you eventually strike out, Mr. Nedick?"

He blushed, trying to think of very simple answers that would keep him from blathering like a fool in Grandma's Living Room.

"Thirteen, Grandma."

"That's good."

"Nine straight games of double-digits."

Kenuda patted his knee paternally. "We're proud of our Puppy."

"And I'm proud of both of you." Grandma swirled her spoon. "The blackout was perhaps unnecessary."

Puppy had prepared for this. "Totally my fault."

"No, mine," Kenuda said. "I'm the Commissioner. Everything should've been checked."

Grandma smiled faintly. "The report said a rerouter had been installed."

"And somehow, uninstalled, ma'am." Kenuda didn't back down. "It's a first time. A lot of chaos. But considering the age of the electrical system..."

She held up her hand. "It was a good air raid alert." They joined her in a relieved smile. "I think the rest of the season should be all night games."

Kenuda and Puppy exchanged delighted looks.

"Without blacking out the city."

"You have my word," Elias assured her.

"I'm sure someone will lose the use of a hair dryer somewhere, but..." she airily dismissed that. "There are about two million extra people in and around the Bronx. They don't want to leave. In fact, they're still coming."

"They're called Baseball Buses, Grandma," Kenuda said.

Highways, country roads, you waited at an official bus stop or under a billboard or by a bridge and the bus stopped and took you along. Everyone chipped in for gas, shared food, water, toilet paper. Thousands of buses, flatbed trucks, pick-ups, vans, station wagons, plain ol' cars. Gas stations were closing for lack of fuel. Factories went on hiatus. Makeshift first aid stands and portable potties popped up. Physicians and dentists pitched tents with welcome signs. Grills dotted roads from Colorado to Westchester, serving free food.

Everyone had seen what the game was like. Everyone wanted to experience this. There were no tickets left for the final twenty-one games.

"I'd like to take the Forgiveness campaign one step further," Grandma said. "Puppy, back when, didn't baseball teams honor special groups during a game?"

"Like?"

"First Cousin Cheng had an interesting idea. What if we honored our veterans?"

He and Kenuda exchanged uneasy looks.

"There were Veterans Days around the old national holidays," Puppy said slowly. "Memorial Day, Flag Day, July Fourth..."

"What happened?"

Puppy hesitated.

"If I'm asking, I want an answer," she said, her smile a bit colder.

Once even thinking of such memories was outlawed. "A color guard carried the flag. Veterans would be allowed into the game at a discount price, or free." He swallowed deeply. "We'd sing the *Star Spangled Banner*. Also *God Bless America*."

Grandma grimaced slightly.

"Everyone would salute the flag. Then there'd be a moment of silence for the fallen in the wars." He paused. "All of them, ma'am. Maybe a veteran would throw out the first ball."

"What's that mean?"

"It's ceremonial. They'd go to the mound and toss the ball to the catcher. The pitch didn't count, but it was just a way to start the game."

"What do you think, Commissioner?"

He squirmed visibly. "I appreciate the extraordinary success of the Forgiveness campaign."

"Cut the crap. You're a Third Cousin."

Puppy muffled a smile.

Kenuda cleared his throat. "If I could put together a night game in two days, I can do this. But with all due respect to Cousin Cheng, we must proceed carefully. There has still been a lot of anger since..." He caught himself.

"Since The Story, yes. Forgiveness only goes so far until you really do." Grandma looked through Puppy, who felt as if she were shampooing his brain. "But you don't like this idea at all, do you?"

He avoided Elias's disapproving stare. "No, ma'am."

"Why?"

"I don't want veterans trotted out like pugs in a midnight march."

Grandma's eyes narrowed. "Is that what you think I'd do?"

"Puppy's not saying that..." Kenuda defended him.

"Yes, he is." Grandma leaned forward.

Puppy shook away the water dribbling into his ear. "That's how they've been treated before."

Kenuda paled, but Grandma kept stirring her spoon. "Very true."

"I grew up in the DV. I saw their lives. The bitterness of being forgotten."

"Like your father."

Must be the soap in his eardrums. "Excuse me?"

"Lt. Alvin Nedick, Second Marine Corps. He was wounded in one of the first battles in 2058 when the Allahs attacked Spain." Grandma squinted and a video seemed to hop out of Puppy's forehead; his father, lean, grim, hobbling onto a trooper carrier, handsome despite the grime-streaked face. His father, sober? Alvin half-turned toward Puppy, who pressed in terror against Kenuda; the Commissioner patted his shoulder, but he was also shaken. The vid faded away into a few still moments.

"Mine died, too," Elias said softly. "In Denmark."

"He got the Silver Star," Grandma added quietly. "You shouldn't have thrown it away, Elias."

"I was twelve. And angry."

"You still are. Perhaps this is a bad idea. Look at the two of you. I can imagine…" Grandma sighed and drifted a moment as if circling overhead. Kenuda and Puppy exchanged subdued stares; they couldn't let Grandma down.

• • • •

SWEEP SWEEP SWEEP like Cinderella, Annette muttered, poking at the pile of dust near her tent. No, a cell. Zelda and Clary had a cabin down by whichever direction down was in this stupid place, while she was locked in this black tent. Knock knock guard, I have to piss. Last night she hooted like an owl for fifteen minutes until they let her out; she thought it was fifteen minutes because that's all guesswork since they took her watch and engagement ring and necklace.

Annette glared at the large infants running past. Everywhere, large infants. Singing, racing, dancing, laughing, balls bouncing every which way; Annette ducked under a wayward volleyball so another part of her face wouldn't be ruined.

Lots of large infants but few adults other than the skinny guards who were friendly to everyone except her. Wandering around, retrieving balls, joining in the games. It was like a giant camp or casual prison; she couldn't decide.

Only that she had to escape. When they threw her into that horrid tent, she figured it'd be a matter of time before Kenuda ransomed her. But then it was morning and one of the skinny guards handed her a broom. Was she a prisoner or not? A prisoner had certain rights, they had toilets in their rooms like Zelda had at the Courthouse. They had mirrors so they could see disfiguring bruises.

She was Cinderella, sweep sweep sweep. That's when she realized there would be no ransom. Dara was behind all this to get her out of the way so she could have Elias. Sure sure sure, there'd be the period of mourning, a month, where Kenuda would moan for her loss, but after that, into the arms of that tart. He'd never loved her. Why'd he bother with her then? She had no real money. Sure, she was pretty, but she wasn't good in bed. She had a good body but her thighs were getting gooey. She really wasn't very nice. Or smart. She was surprised Elias didn't dump her a long time ago. Now she was going to be worked to death without even knowing where she'd be buried. Who'd visit her anyway other than Puppy?

Annette sniffled away self-pitying tears and dragged over a green garbage bag. She leaned on the broom and watched the wretched little things chanting around a few other wretched things playing baseball at the base of a hill, shielded by trees. Chanting in different languages, too. Probably all Miners.

There had to be a way out. If they came in they could go out. Annette went up on her toes, looking for a door or window; the bottom of the bag broke. She wanted to cry, but wouldn't give them the satisfaction.

Yankees cap backwards over her thick hair, Clary reluctantly helped Annette shove dead leaves, apple cores and a thick bone, among other delicacies, back into the bag.

"Thank you." Annette tried smiling, but failed.

Clary grunted. "Gracias. Vieja loca."

"Gracias loca means thank you?"

Clary rolled her eyes.

"Can't you speak English?"

The girl grinned impishly. "Depends."

Clary suddenly let out a cry. Blood streamed down her thumb. She viciously kicked the offending plastic fork against a rock.

"Hold still." Annette wrestled with Clary, tearing a strip from her handkerchief and wrapping it around the wound, tightening the bandage a little more than necessary; the child bit her lip, determined not to show pain.

"That hurt?" Annette asked.

Clary stared sullenly at her finger and shook her head.

"I was a nurse once." Annette applied more pressure and Clary groaned. "Nurses training anyway, back when I was looking for a career after Puppy and I broke up."

"Puppy Beisbol." Clary's eyes watered.

"Whatever. I made it through three months but the sight of blood was disgusting. Sit still. The bleeding stopped." She wiped away Clary's tears. "That was my last clean handkerchief."

"Gracias," Clary mumbled.

"You're welcome."

"De nada." The girl sighed impatiently. "De nada. De nada. You are welcome."

Annette smiled grudgingly. "De nada."

• • • •

TOMAS WALKED AROUND the four-foot high plastic mock-up of Yankee Stadium on Grandma's coffee table, shaking his head.

"What if we need to evacuate?"

"Why would we?"

"Because shit goes wrong. Look at the night game."

"There were no problems."

"It was a light show, magic. Veterans Day can't be a show." Tomas stared pleadingly at Grandma, who offered only a shrug. "The emotions are off the charts."

"That's why we're doing this. They need to be controlled and channeled to positive goals."

Tomas wagged his finger at the area bordering River Avenue. "Will this be cleared?"

"There'll be paths to allow the veterans to pass."

"I don't have enough soldiers to provide security."

She sighed. "The BTs will be there."

Stilton about left his boots. "BTs at a ceremony honoring veterans at Yankee Stadium? That's a disaster in waiting. No, I don't like anything about it. There's going to be rogue demonstrations, has to be. And I don't see any way out unless it's vertical. I don't like relying solely on the 'copters. If something happens, you're trapped."

Grandma smiled gently. "There are escape routes."

"Where? Show me." Tomas kicked the table and the stadium tipped over. He didn't help her straighten the model. "And what the hell is John Hazel doing other than building replicas?"

Grandma gently tugged Tomas back into the chair. "He's coordinating with the veterans groups."

"He was in the service for three months."

"Enough to lose a leg," she said sternly. "He's plugged into the Apollo Brigades."

Apollo Brigades were baseball players who signed up for duty after 10/12. Players, amateur and professional, had swarmed into recruiting offices, eager to show they disapproved of the Miners. Tomas had commanded some, all wiped out at Nice. Guilt did not make good soldiers.

"What about the other soldiers? The real veterans?"

"They're invited, but we're only honoring the Apollos. Keeping a simple theme. Again, Cheng's idea."

"I want to see all the names," Stilton insisted. "Every single honoree who'll be on the field. Every single veteran who goes through the gates…"

"Tomas," she cut him off sharply. "Cheng's handling that."

He stared dully. "Your security is my job."

"Not for this."

"I go where you go," he rasped.

"And you go where I need you. It's been more than a week since the Son left. I'm afraid something's happened."

He bristled. "I put him on the plane personally.'

"I'm not blaming you."

"Maybe his friends killed him."

"I would've heard."

He paused. "Maybe he changed his mind."

"Why would he do that? Stop already. I'm tired of arguing. Do as I say."

He stared. "As your head of security?"

Grandma busied herself dusting the armoire, making him wait in agony for an answer he already knew. "No. As my friend."

• • • •

THE WAITER DIDN'T give Pablo a particularly cordial smile as he led him to a table at the rear near an exposed heating pipe, tossing down a menu and shuffling behind the counter. The three old men at the front stared rudely while Pablo slowly bit into a pickle. He held it up in a toast and they looked away, muttering.

It was only ten-thirty, too early for lunch and too late for breakfast; brunch was a concept Pablo always reserved for a relationship. When you had nothing else to fill your day, any time was good for a meal, Pablo thought sadly. His patients had vanished. He didn't know why but suspected getting bumped from the Cousins program played a role. He still had to keep the office open, even if he held a darts tournament in the waiting room; otherwise he'd be placed on the Lazy List and assigned a job.

What positions in Grandma's Family are available for insolent ex-dentists? he could hear Zelda say. Maybe a clown, lean into the whole smile-o-meter thing. How many patients have you wanted to spritz with seltzer? He smiled. Puppy said she was safe. No more info than that. Safe suddenly seemed like a lot.

The waiter stared sullenly. Pablo made him recite the daily specials. It took about five minutes, weighted by a number of questions about matzo brei and the relationship between salami and eggs.

He yawned. "Coffee for now."

He waited until the muttering old man disappeared down the hallway beyond the counter, then rose, stretching like he'd been tied up for a week, and with a loud proclamation informed everyone he needed the bathroom.

Pablo wandered past the kitchen, angling for a better look through the small window on the double doors. The waiter stood motionlessly by a large table as a faceless 'bot in a white apron carved up meats, spraying blood. The waiter dabbed at a stain on his shoulder and ladled out a bunch of pickles into a large serving dish. The 'bot kept chopping.

The waiter went through a side door and, within seconds, another waiter came back in. No stain, no dish.

This new waiter quickly went from food table to table, carrying five dishes at once. Now another waiter returned, shoulder stain intact. The two robots conferred. A pair of eyes caught him.

Pablo ducked into the bathroom, flushing the toilet and loudly running the sink water before returning to his table. One of the waiters ambled over with a pad to take his order.

Pablo was about to order the lox and onions special when a second waiter stood by the table, smiling. Now a third and a fourth and a fifth waiter surrounded him, all holding pencils and pads, all with the same gruff stares.

"I'm not tipping everyone." Pablo lowered his shoulder and tried plowing through, but one of the pencils stabbed him in the neck. As he hit the floor, he noticed the waiters were all wearing gray socks.

39

B uca and Y'or waited for Kenuda to bully the keyboard with his thick fingers; Brown Hats believed justice was patient.

Kenuda glowered at the screen one more time, daring it to disobey. "Bit of a fire drill today. There are about nine million former soldiers that we know of through various pensions, medical care, DV settlements. That we know of. Suddenly many of them want to come to the game. In four days. And I'm in the center of it all."

The detectives shrugged politely, unimpressed as they had to be.

"But I always have time for my colleagues the police," he continued, ready for these annoying little men to leave him alone. "What can the office of the Commissioner of Sport and Entertainment do for you?"

"Nothing," Buca replied, puzzled by the question. "This is personal, Third Cousin." Elias narrowed his eyes warily. "In what way?"

"It concerns your fiancé Annette Ramos."

"What happened?"

"We believe she was abducted during a prison escape on the night of the blackout." Kenuda didn't quite take that in. "I don't understand."

"A prisoner, Zelda Jones, was, we strongly believe, rescued from the Bronx Courthouse. According to the security check-in, Ms. Ramos was visiting Ms. Jones as part of the accused/accuser provision. When the lights were restored, both siblings were gone and blood, tracked to Ms. Ramos, was on the floor of the prisoner's room."

Y'or handed Kenuda the report, which he quickly studied and returned with a shake of the head. "I don't know anything about this. Who would rescue Jones and why would they take Annette?"

Buca straightened the crease on his pants leg. "The former, we're not sure, but suspect it has to do with the missing orphan child. The latter, either your fiance was a witness to this crime or participated in the escape."

Kenuda laughed. "Annette? Unless shoes are involved, that's very unlikely."

The Detectives exchanged a meaningful look. Y'or continued, "When's the last time you saw your fiancé?"

"The day of the night game. She was here in my office."

"Not since then?"

"I've been busy," he said edgily.

Buca cleared his throat. "As an engaged couple, you do live together, correct?"

"Yes, so?"

The Detective raised an eyebrow. "Weren't you concerned when she didn't come home the last two nights?"

"Until we're married, Annette has her own apartment, according to law, so there's space to work out any issues should they arise."

"And are there any?"

Kenuda suddenly darkened. "Are you accusing me of something?"

Buca smiled blandly. "Not at all, sir. We're giving you the courtesy of this information that your fiancé is missing."

"And what're you doing about it?"

"Interviewing everyone who might have information, Third Cousin." Buca and Y'or rose as one and headed toward the door.

"Wait a second." Kenuda came around his desk. "Do you think she's okay?"

Buca shrugged.

Elias was staring blankly at the endless demanding messages from all over the country when a bell tinkled softly and Pablo's face drifted onto the screen. A follow-up to the dismissal of every Cousin candidate was automatically sent to their potential mentor; just because someone failed at achieving candidacy didn't mean they should be dismissed completely. There might be an opportunity for a reach-out on a personal level to guide them to something more suitable. As Grandma's Twentieth Insight said, Being what you can be isn't the same as being what you think you are.

Kenuda was about to file this, but a dancing flower icon kept insisting he had to read the report first. He was too tired to argue with a rose and began skimming, slowing down as he absorbed the details.

Again with that damn diner?

• • • •

HIS BROTHER HAD moved back in right after the Janazah like once their father was dead, he and Mama couldn't take care of themselves. On the first night of the mourning, Omar moved Papa's chair to the corner of the dining room, insisting that was proper according to the Quran.

Mama was too busy crying. She'd cried for a week. She'd cried especially loudly when Papa came already wrapped in the white kafan.

"I must see him again," she'd screamed in the funeral home. The director, who looked like a frog, insisted Papa had been badly burned and they had to wrap him to prevent leakage. All of that sounded disgusting and made Mama yell even more, but Abdul didn't cry. He had to be brave as much as his heart broke. He was afraid to let Mama down.

That was the love and sadness part of his heart. He was afraid to leave Mama alone, but Omar ordered him to resume normal life once the mourning was over. He said that as if Abdul's normal life was bad.

Abdul played a lot of football. In the madrassa, his friends offered their apologies and prayers. But it wasn't like when Khalil's father died last year. Some Crusaders had bombed a school and Khalil's father was one of the police who hunted them down. In the shoot-out, Khalil's father was killed. He was a hero. There were photos of him everywhere, online, in newspapers, on television. Khalil was proud of his father.

There were no photos of Papa. No one mentioned his name. Abdul was convinced he had been murdered on a secret assignment for the Grand Mufti, not when his boat had caught fire.

He'd asked Mama why she believed that Papa, an experienced Captain, wouldn't have escaped. Mama just cried and said he should ask Allah. He had asked Allah that and many other questions like why Omar hadn't died instead, but Allah hadn't answered.

Abdul had no one else to ask.

That night he lay in bed, bouncing his ball from knee to knee. His brother entered, prayed and removed his black robe, sneering at Abdul dressed in a t-shirt and shorts. He disappeared into the bathroom, brushing his teeth like a noisy pig, and flopped onto the bed. He started reading the Quran just to impress Abdul because he didn't turn the page and his eyes kept locked in one place.

"Can I help you?" Omar asked like they were in a store or something.

"No."

"Then stop staring."

"Stop making noises."

Omar angrily turned on his side. "I don't make noises."

Abdul snorted like a pig.

"How dare you accuse me of being unclean."

"You're not unclean. Just your throat."

Omar sat up. "You know nothing."

"I know animal noises."

His brother rolled away and continued pretending to read. After a moment, he said, "What are your plans?"

Abdul hadn't thought beyond bouncing the football. Omar looked at him pityingly. "For life."

"Becoming a football player."

Omar snickered. "You're too short."

"I'm fast. Papa said that's more important."

"What did he know?"

Abdul squeezed the ball. "Everything."

His brother smirked. "Right."

"And he's in Heaven giving me advice now."

Omar shook his head. "No, he's not."

"I hear him."

"Not from there. He didn't go to Heaven."

"Don't say that."

"He liked the Crusaders. He helped the Crusader children."

"He didn't."

"He didn't pray. He wasn't faithful. I had to leave home because he shamed our family."

"No."

"Allah hated him."

"Shut up."

"Allah hates traitors."

Abdul sat up, eyes blazing. "Don't you say that."

"Pay attention," Omar said dismissively, leaning against the pillow. "You're better off that he's dead. At least if you try, you might have a future."

Abdul rolled the ball from knee to knee, then fired an overhead pass which hit Omar in the face. He screamed. Abdul started smothering him with the pillow. There was a lot of blood before his mother pulled him off.

• • • •

DRAWINGS OF FIVE frogs, all very different in the evolutionary process, rested before the children sitting cross-legged on the twinkling grass. The Irish girl with the big green eyes was the only one who spoke English and even that Zelda barely understood. Brogue, was that the phrase?

Zelda squirmed, Diego poking away. She'd barely slept what with Clary using her as a sofa and the other three children in the tiny cabin taking turns snoring. Tired and uncomfortable, but she could somehow sit here for hours; Zelda suddenly missed teaching.

The four boys rolled their eyes, impatient to get away and join their friends in running around rocks and kicking stones, the game of the day.

Zelda pointed at the Irish girl's picture. "Be a frog."

"How?"

"Be what you draw." Wishing she had a crane, Zelda hopped unsteadily; the boys laughed.

The Irish girl rescued her, sticking out her tongue at the boys who, even if they were Swedish/German/Hungarian/Russian who knows what, understood a dare. She hopped and they hopped and soon passing children, leaving their music and dance and language classes, joined in, ribbeting from around the world.

Clary shoved through the circle with a jealous scowl and sat beside Zelda as the class was dismissed to find more wonders in this weird-ass place.

"What's that?" Zelda pointed at a plastic bag under Clary's arm. The girl waited warily until all the children had scattered and unfolded the Yankees t-shirt.

"Bueno," Zelda said.

"Beisbol, si." Clary mimed swinging a bat. "Home run. We go."

Zelda frowned. "We go where?"

"To Puppy Beisbol."

She tenderly squeezed Clary's arm. "No, sweetheart. We don't go to Puppy Beisbol. We stay here. New casa. Amigos, games. Happy."

Happy's a lot easier when you have no choices.

Clary's nostrils flared. "We go to Puppy Beisbol. Yankee Stadium."

Diego kicked and Zelda figured she could only tolerate so much self-indulgence from her children. "Yankee Stadium? No, we don't…"

"Me." She clenched her hands. "Not Zelda. Muchachas go." Clary ran in a dizzying circle mish-mashing different languages of all the muchachas. She finished, surly hands on hips.

Zelda firmly led Clary over to a row of tree stumps which served as a bench.

"Clary and muchachas go?" Clary nodded. "To Puppy Beisbol." Clary nodded again, relieved by Zelda's sudden insight.

"Abuela muerta." Clary hummed the Grandma song.

Zelda gripped her shoulders. "Why are you singing that?"

Clary kept humming, adding a smirk. Zelda shook her to stop, but Clary continued in a melodically defiant sing-song until finally she stopped, as if Zelda were punished enough, and said with finality, "Puppy Beisbol."

Hazel was teaching a class on woodworking by the gentle stream which wound its way around the spidery roads, licking through the massive trees brushing against the gleaming, phosphorous ceiling. Zelda caught his attention and waited near a clump of bushes.

He limped over with a big smile. "Morning. How's it going?"

"Like I've been here for years."

"That's the idea," he said. "Not thinking about the outside world's a nice notion."

Zelda steadily met his stare. "How's Clary doing?"

He chuckled. "Quite a little girl. I think she might run the world someday." They considered Empress Clary for a moment. "And a pretty good athlete. She took out a second baseman with a high slide to his chest yesterday. It was a little dirty."

"She made it all the way from Barcelona. That must have a price."

"So do all these kids. Rapes, beatings, watching their families murdered. About fifteen thousand orphans."

"Just living here."

"Until it changes," he said carefully. "They're not going into Cousins homes anymore. No more brainwashing."

"You rescued them?"

"Sort of," Hazel sighed impatiently. "I can give you more background another time."

"I'm more interested in Clary's Yankees shirt."

"What's the problem?"

"She said you're taking her to a baseball game."

"No." He smiled cautiously.

"Clary doesn't lie."

Hazel thoughtfully tossed aside pebbles. "I think she's a little confused. There are twenty-two languages here, last I checked. Communication can be a problem."

"I've met two teachers who speak Spanish."

"They think they speak Spanish." Hazel rubbed his Gelinium knee. "There's going to be a special game in a few days honoring the veterans. We want these kids who came to America to know our history and what these soldiers sacrificed so there'd be somewhere left in this world where they're wanted. We've found a way to pull down a feed of the game off the vidsport. The kids are getting t-shirts for both the Yankees and Cubs so we can make it a party and have everyone watch. Hot dogs and pizza. You're welcome to join us."

"Will they be singing songs?"

Hazel's eyes narrowed. "Like which ones?"

Zelda hummed the Grandma Muertas song.

Hazel didn't smile.

• • • •

TOMAS COULDN'T CONCENTRATE. Half a bottle of Illinois Blue Bourbon last night hadn't helped. Nor did Cheng insisting he repeat the conversation with Grandma three times, every word, every inflection.

"Damnit, there's nothing else," he exploded. "She wants me gone."

There, he'd finally said it. The bourbon, the anger, lack of sleep, the fear erupted. He turned away, ashamed of his tears. Cheng sat beside him on the narrow couch in his office.

"It's not you, Tomas. This has been a long time coming." Albert hesitated. "I've covered up for her for years."

Tomas frowned. "What're you talking about? Grandma's top of her game."

"You hear the orders, not the deliberation."

"I know how she thinks…"

"Do you really?" That stung Tomas into silence. "She wanted to let Allahs in about three years ago."

Tomas couldn't believe this. "How?"

"Dissidents. We received a report from Morocco about some group, cult, who can keep up with the names, but supposedly, they were unhappy about the Caliphate. Like the Son, but more officially. The Mufti of the Moroccan Caliphate was eager to get rid of them. In the dispatch the Cairo Collector passed along, they were considered dhimmi, infidels, whatever. Grandma swallowed the bait. Can you imagine fifty thousand Allahs back in America under the guise of political dissidents? Oh, she ranted and raved about our roots as an immigrant nation. Finally Laredo and Denise," Cheng referred to a couple Second Cousins, "weighed in and we convinced her they'd be security risks. The children, she kept saying. Where will the Allah children grow up?"

White flecks dotted Cheng's lips. "Where the hell will American children live if the Camels blow us up again?"

Tomas had no recollection of this. Wait. Three years ago. That's when she dropped out of sight the first time.

"She also dabbled in unilateral disarmament," Cheng's voice dropped as if too horrified to even say the words.

"Giving up the nukes?" Tomas was equally sickened.

"Trading some to regain lost territories. She was after parts of South America. Brazil, Venezuela."

"The Allahs would move back the second we dumped our weapons."

The notion of Grandma making a mistake was barely tolerable. Grandma no longer functioning as Grandma was unthinkable. Who'd take over?

Albert acknowledged his hard stare. "Lenora probably wants me gone, too. That could be why she's raising the profile of Kenuda. But you must obey her, Tomas." Cheng exhaled very slowly. "No matter what, you're probably the only one she still trusts, which is good. You can keep me informed."

Spying on Grandma. Equally unthinkable. Yet what choice did he have. Tomas blinked back tears and Cheng rubbed his shoulder.

"She's right to be worried, though. Something's up. Abdullah's allies have changed codes on their army groups."

Tomas frowned. "Maybe they're really gathering strength and expanding the conspiracy."

"Against who? The Mufti? Or us?" Cheng pursed his lips. "We're on full military alert. Yes, I know. That order's only to come from Grandma. But I couldn't take a chance. Our nukes are locked. If they make a move…I'll shit on rubble rather than let those Camels march in." He patted Tomas' knee. "I know what I'm asking."

"I'm not betraying her," Tomas said hoarsely.

"Nor am I, Tomas. We're not the traitors anymore."

• • • •

FRECKLIE BASHED HIS right knee into the tip of the mahogany end table. Exhausted after running up and down a ladder outside the stadium all night, Frecklie wondered if he'd mindlessly walked into the wrong house where bedroom furniture was in the hallway.

He edged his way along the couch in the dark, stubbing his toe on a dining room chair and feeling his way to her door. If his mother was going to re-decorate in the middle of the night, she didn't deserve a knock.

Her room was empty except for a flashlight hanging from the curtain rod.

"Close the door," Beth snapped, kneeling by the closet.

An American flag covered the entire floor like a rug.

"Shit."

That all you have to say, she raised an eyebrow.

Yes. They stared at the flag together for a moment. He counted the stars. Should be forty-eight.

Fifty. Beth's eyes flashed.

Hawaii and Alaska are neutral.

Fifty. She fussed with a stitch, walking sidewise toward him to avoid stepping on the flag. Her eyes shone like when she prayed, Frecklie thought.

Never seen a flag, he gestured.

"I started making this just after your father died." Beth peered into the stripes as if her dead husband were hiding there. "Then I stopped because I couldn't risk getting arrested. Who would've taken care of you?"

"What do we do with it?"

Beth sighed wearily. "It's for the game, Ruben. We're honoring the soldiers. We're honoring our country. Not the Grandma crap. These are real feelings."

Frecklie was startled by her vehemence.

"They'll use this flag when they present the color guard." She paused, thinking. "After that's done, it has to wave somewhere."

"How about by the banners you made?" he asked softly.

"No, we need something more visible. An American flag hasn't flown since the war ended. It has to be special. Like in center field. Yes. Center field." Beth's eyes glittered. "Coordinate that with Dale. I'm sure she'll have an idea."

"She always does." He rolled his eyes.

Beth studied him carefully. "You love her, right?"

"Sure."

"Answers are so easy at your age."

"Only some."

Beth smiled. "You can be a baseball architect now that Grandma's allowing the game to continue."

"We thought they'd start with just a few, but they're rebuilding all the stadiums," he said wonderingly.

"That makes a bigger splash this way. No favoritism for any city." She grunted at Grandma's wisdom. "America's pastime again. Which stadium are you going to design?"

Frecklie hesitated. "Fenway Park. Puppy said he'd give my drawings to Commissioner Kenuda. There's going to be a, a, you know…"

"Process."

"And nothing's guaranteed. There could be people with better ideas."

"I kind of doubt it," she said, laughing. "Show me."

Frecklie went down the hall, tripping over knick-knacks on the floor; he grumbled loudly from his room.

"They're not behind your dresser anymore. I put them back under under your mattress," Beth called out.

Frecklie returned with his portfolio. Beth flipped through the sketches of ivy on the walls, the scoreboard shaped like a glove.

"I love the asymmetrical height of the fences in the outfield," she said after a moment.

"It's not too much?" he asked.

Beth shook her head. "The old Yankee Stadium was like that."

His eyes widened. "How do you know?"

Beth tapped him on the head. "I'm your mother. I know a lot." She paused. "So do you. I'm very proud of you, Ruben.

He blushed and mumbled thanks. Beth nibbled on her lower lip.

"You'll be fine. You'll become a famous baseball architect, marry Dale and have lots of insane children."

Frecklie gave her a long look, flipping up his palms questioningly. Beth shrugged and looked away. He tugged on her shoulder, half-turning her face. She stared very deeply.

"I might decide to relocate, honey."

"What does that mean?"

Beth sighed. "I love someone, too."

"Puppy?" His wide smile faded in disappointment as she shook her head. He continued, almost angrily, "Who then?"

"Someone else then. You don't know her."

"One of your customers?"

"Not really…"

"Dating customers is against the law…"

"Call a Blue Shirt," she snapped back, softening. "Honey, nothing's for sure. I'm just saying maybe I will, maybe I won't."

"Your maybes always mean for certain."

"There's nothing for certain except I love you very much." Beth rubbed his cheek.

"And now you love someone else."

"Yes, I do."

"Does that make you happy?"

"Very much." Beth left out the part about being scared shitless as she hugged him tightly.

40

After the third wrong turn, Zelda slumped onto a rock, searching for her breath in the humid air.

"Are you sure?" she whispered.

"It's a maze, but yeah." Annette squinted. "You okay?"

"Other than four months pregnant, I'm the bahm diggity."

Zelda begged Diego to take a nap as she struggled to keep pace down the shadowy corridors, vines creeping up the walls. The cave was like one of those old vidmovs where dinosaurs and flying creatures lived, she thought.

Two Miners popped out of a dark hallway; Annette grabbed Zelda's hand and burst into tender laughter, two lovers out for a midnight stroll, the kids tucked into bed.

The Miners tipped their rifles as they passed. Annette's face creased, counting and remembering the steps; she dragged Zelda to the left, down a nearly pitch-black path to a cluster of rocks, where they knelt.

Annette pressed her face through a sliver of a hole, gesturing for Zelda to be patient. Finally she moved aside so Zelda could take a look.

The zipper in the cave spread apart and a jeep filled with soldiers rolled inside. The two guards saluted and resumed wandering around in a very bored patrol.

"Every hour," Annette said, pressing her mouth to Zelda's ear.

"How many hours have you studied the pattern?"

Annette held up eight fingers. She hadn't slept, dragging her garbage bag and broom around this stupid cave, following the trash she figured only adults made; these children were too well behaved to toss a candy wrapper.

"Always vehicles?" Zelda asked, watching the Miners slumping on chairs.

Annette shook her head. "Usually just soldiers."

"But you're not positive."

"As much as I could. We can hide there." She pointed to a clump of trees. "The door or whatever it is stays open for forty-two seconds. I counted. We slip behind them and out."

It was a shitty plan, which Annette read in her eyes.

"Got an alternative?"

Zelda shook her head, staring. "Why didn't you go yourself? It's a lot easier with one person."

"I'm afraid," she murmured. "But once we're out, you go your way and I go mine."

Zelda looked at the soldiers again. Will you be at Yankee Stadium, too?

"Okay. I'll get Clary. Wait here."

Annette frowned. "We're going tonight?"

Zelda nodded, remembering Hazel's look with a shudder.

"I didn't pack anything."

Zelda shook her head sadly and, leaving small mounds of pebbles at that archway, leaves by that turn, a footprint there and a torn branch there, cautiously made her way back to the cabin.

Clary slept peacefully, hands in prayer on her side, Yankees cap over her face. Zelda stuffed some of the child's clothes in a plastic bag and shoved it under her blouse next to Diego. Clary's half-eaten plate of greens rested on the communal table; Zelda pocketed the knife and fork.

Zelda gently shook Clary awake. The girl held a sharpened stick.

"We go Puppy Beisbol."

Clary bounded happily off the bed and followed Zelda past the row of sleeping children toward the front door. A little girl with long blonde hair suddenly sat up and said something in a guttural tongue; Zelda froze.

Clary leaned over and whispered, "Balspel."

Her Dutch friend smiled and went back to sleep.

Well-trained, Clary kept quiet as they hurried through the cave. When they arrived at the meeting place, Annette was gone.

Left without them. Or set a trap.

Clary sensed something was wrong. "Hazel?"

Zelda shushed her, frantically trying to read her watch and calculate when the zipper would open.

"Where Hazel?" Clary insisted.

"Will you tell your child to be quiet?" Annette hissed as she climbed out from behind a tree.

"Where were you?"

"Peeing like a dog. Did you bring me extra underwear?"

"She come?" Clary glared.

"Yes, she come. She idea." Annette glared back. "Tell me you at least brought a toothbrush."

"And three changes of shoes." Zelda snorted. "When does the cave open again?"

"In fifteen minutes."

They huddled behind the trees as the guards discussed their latest sexual conquests; Clary paid particular attention. The zipper unraveled slowly and they slunk deeper. Chill, Diego. Please chill.

A Miner wandered in lugging unmarked brown boxes on a dolly. They debated a moment about whose responsibility unloading the cartons were. Finally they decided they'd all share in the work, unslinging the rifles from their shoulders and dragging the dolly onto a path.

Annette nudged Zelda, who grabbed Clary's hand as they hurried toward the six-foot wide opening. Diego stirred and Zelda groaned.

The guards turned, rifles pointing.

"Hey," one of them called.

"Go," Zelda rasped over her shoulder at Annette and walked toward the guards with a bright smile. "Good morning, gentlemen."

Annette clutched Clary's wrist, stepping uncertainly toward the opening.

Thirty seconds left.

"Isn't this a lovely day for a walk?"

The guards cocked their rifles.

"Move away from the opening, ma'am," said one of the guards with shaky courage.

Clary tugged Annette toward Zelda, who glanced back. Twenty seconds; they'd never have another chance.

Zelda stomped on a guard's foot; he howled. With a feral growl, Clary kicked one of the soldiers in the knee and the other in the groin. Annette punched the third guard in the face. The women barely made it through the closing zipper, which muffled the soldiers's shouts.

A thick verdant forest with at least ten different shades of green swallowed them. Annette impatiently led them over the path carpeted with leaves and branches. In a few minutes, they were completely lost, half a mile down a desolate road. There was no chirping or animal sounds, not even a rustling breeze. It was if they were nowhere.

Zelda clung to the edge of a stump.

"We can't stop here," Annette insisted.

"Stop for el bebe," Clary said disgustedly.

Zelda groaned; Diego had morphed into fighting triplets. Clary rubbed her shoulder in between scowls at Annette.

"Any idea where we are?" Zelda asked.

"How should I know? Your friends took us here. I was blindfolded, remember?" Annette gestured helplessly at the thick tree cover.

Zelda squinted up at a glimmer of light. "Even in Grandma's world the sun rises in the east."

"How does that help if we don't know where north is?"

"The Bronx is south."

"Not if we're south of the Bronx. Then we'd go north."

Zelda hated Annette for being right.

Annette broke a few twigs in frustration, finally looking at the squirming Zelda with concern. "You look white."

"Just pale or Caucasian?"

"I can't carry you. Even with the help of devil child. So rest for a couple seconds."

Zelda nodded agreement and unwrapped the napkin, handing Clary her leftovers. The girl shook her head and patted Zelda's stomach.

"For el bebe."

"You muchacha."

"Not el bebe." Clary made a place setting on Zelda's lap and shoveled the veggies into Zelda's mouth.

"You hungry?" Zelda asked Annette between chews.

She grudgingly shook her head. "Puppy always said that about you."

Zelda blinked, convinced she'd dozed and lost a conversation. "Said what?"

"Your humor in the face of shit. I was never good at that."

"That's for sure."

"I can appreciate a joke. Ask my fiancé." Annette wearily leaned against the tree. "If he's still my fiancé."

"You've only been gone a few days."

"Time enough for that whore Dara to move in."

Zelda nudged Clary, who reluctantly offered a tiny piece of bread which Annette wolfed down.

"You and Puppy were perfect for each other," Zelda finally said.

"Now you think that?"

"I always did. I was just jealous. He's still in love with you."

Annette managed to snort and smile at the same time.

"I'm serious. The guy never dates."

"He does that to punish me."

Zelda rolled her eyes. "Like everyone in the world does things just to hurt you?"

Annette slowly shook her head, saying quietly, "No. I do enough to myself." She cried softly for a moment. When she finished blowing her nose on her sleeve, they heard the dry leaves rustling.

Clary helped Zelda stand and they walked quickly, but carefully toward the south, the thick foliage overhead thinning.

The leaves crackled closer, followed by a whisper and the crunching of heavy boots. Clary suddenly hurried past the adults, pointing at the sounds of rumbling and stomping they could almost see. Music, too. Horns, faint cheers.

460 | GARY MORGENSTEIN

A bullet whizzed past, two, then a third thudded into the trees near their heads; Annette screamed. Zelda lifted Clary up, ignoring the sharp pain in her stomach. The girl twisted free and dashed ahead as a bullet skipped at her heel.

Soldiers marched silently down the dusty road in clean, pressed uniforms. Many limped, but the backs and shoulders remained stiff, stoic. Cheering siblings waved small American flags while impromptu bands serenaded the calm, clear faces never looking left or right. The formation disappeared around a bend several miles away.

Cars respectfully edged past, honking salutes. Some makeshift signs read "Finish the Job" and "Forgive Who?" It was a spirit of grim joy.

Clary squirted between the soldiers, waving her baseball cap, Zelda and Annette apologetically following; the two thin Miners watched behind a tree, looking for an opportunity to take a shot. Hazel's orders were shoot to kill.

"Puppy Beisbol." Clary hopped up and down, thrusting out her chest.

A beefy woman in a Detroit Tigers cap behind the wheel of a pick-up truck marked Friedman's Lumber, Kalamazoo, leaned out the window.

"Going to the game, honey?"

"Si. El bebe."

The woman frowned at Zelda's panting expression. She yelled at her pimply-faced son in the back seat of the crowded truck.

Annette and Clary helped Zelda onto the flat bed. Clary gave the two scowling Miners the finger as the truck pulled away. They jostled their rifles and followed along the tree line.

The back of the Ford was crowded with three other women, all wearing Tigers jerseys and hats.

"I'm guessing seven months." A sallow woman pointed at Zelda's stomach.

"Four. I'm just fat."

"Fat's good. More cushioning for the baby," the heavy woman said, smiling at Annette. "What're you naming him?"

"Diego." Annette managed a smile, licking her lips at the half-eaten sandwiches on a plate.

"That's a nice strong name. Are you excited to have a little brother?" The woman asked Clary, who helped herself to some food.

"Clary!" Zelda said sharply.

"No problem." The woman laughed loudly. "You all hungry?"

They devoured the food as the truck rolled past the endless line of soldiers. Clary stood and saluted for a few minutes.

"Lovely sight, ain't it?" The heavy woman smiled. "We're marching all over America. Every scene like this." Her hefty arms flapped at the road, the applause, shouts, music, signs, flags. "Finally getting their due. Respect," her voice hardened. "Making us proud again. Being part of a family's a great thing. But being part of a country's more."

Zelda squirmed, keeping up her polite smile.

"They should've let us finish the job," the woman said loudly, getting appreciative nods from the truck's occupants. "All those boys and girls dying in vain. I lost two uncles. You know the Allahs are planning on finishing their job."

"Allahu Akhbar," Clary growled.

The woman patted her shoulder. "That's right, girl. Wasn't us who started this. We know what they do to our children."

Clary mimed oral sex and the woman flinched, unsure if she were understanding right. The little girl calmly finished her sandwich and reached for another.

Zelda grimaced and re-arranged her legs as the water rolled toward the rear of the truck. Clary laid down her sandwich and lifted up Zelda's skirt to see where the yellow liquid was coming from.

• • • •

THE TRUCK HONKED its way through traffic, the heavy woman shouting, "Pregnant woman having a baby, move aside."

"It's okay, this doesn't mean the baby's hurt." Annette said soothingly. "Your water broke, that's all."

She held Zelda's hand as Clary mopped the liquid with a towel, fascinated. The truck pulled up in front of the emergency room entrance of Ramirez County Hospital, where the heavy woman roared a path, commandeering a wheelchair and leaving them in front of the nurse's station while she pulled aside curtains until she found a doctor.

The receptionist stared. "Lifecard?"

"We lost it," Annette said calmly. "My wife and I were at the the soldiers parade with our little girl." Clary wandered around the waiting room, soaked towel on her shoulder.

"You have no proof?"

Annette shrugged sheepishly.

"Are you giving these folks a hard time?" The hefty woman returned, her voice a club. "They were on their way to honor our soldiers and you're harassing them about a goddamn Lifecard? Damn hospital's free anyway."

"There's paperwork…"

The woman flung her purse onto the counter. "I'm her aunt."

The receptionist inhaled bravely. "Do you have proof?"

"You really want to explore that?" She bared her teeth. The receptionist started processing them.

"Thank you," Zelda said.

The woman waved it off. "Have Diego grow up to be a Tigers fan."

462 | GARY MORGENSTEIN

An orderly took them into a narrow examining room. Another roar from the woman about driving her pickup truck around the emergency room if her niece wasn't helped right away produced a slightly ruffled Dr. Lera.

"What've we got here?" she asked briskly.

"My wife's water broke," Annette said.

"Gush or dribble?" The doctor slipped on the stethoscope.

"Gush."

"Any contractions? And I think Zelda should answer this one." Zelda shook her head, cringing at the cold stethoscope on her stomach. "What color was the liquid?"

"Yellow," Annette answered.

The doctor removed the stethoscope from around her neck. "Heartbeat's normal, thank Grandma's earlobes. Would you mind if I examined your vagina for any fluids escaping?"

Zelda waited for Annette to approve. The doctor smiled and inserted a speculum, nodding, pleased.

"Everything looks all right for now," she said cautiously. "We have two choices. Induce labor or wait twenty-four hours for the contractions to begin."

"We have to get to the baseball game." Zelda tried sitting up.

The doctor laughed. "I don't think you'll make that. But you can watch it here tomorrow. Let's concentrate on the baby."

Annette took Zelda's hand. "We'll wait."

"Yes, wait," Zelda agreed. "The joy of pregnancy isn't something you want to rush."

The doctor raised an eyebrow and left them.

"I can't check in." Zelda lay on her back.

"You already did. I gave a false name."

"Oh that's good."

"Well, you are an escaped criminal."

"Who am I?"

"Dara Dinton."

Zelda laughed until she ached. "Perfect."

"It was the best I could come up with."

Zelda kissed her cheek. "I know. Thank you."

Annette blushed. "De nada."

"Si, si," Clary said brightly.

"Just let me rest and then we'll leave. I've got to warn Puppy."

"I've got to warn Puppy," Annette said mockingly. "Always so noble. Fuck ten guys and get pregnant and you're still a virgin. You can't travel."

"I just need to sleep."

"No." Annette leaned on the edge of the cot. "I can move quicker alone."

Zelda thought a moment before nodding reluctantly, then arched her head at Clary. She cut off Annette's protests. "If the Black Tops were taking me away, what do you think they'll do to her?"

Annette frowned. "The idea's not to have you caught."

"No. The idea is to stop the Miners. And keep our daughter safe." They exchanged wry smiles. "Promise you'll take her."

Annette nodded unenthusiastically. "I have many faults, but I'm not a liar. You damn DVs rubbed off on me."

Zelda struggled to a sitting position and cupped Clary's chin. "You have to go to Puppy Beisbol."

Clary clapped.

"But I can't go with you. El bebe."

"Then Clary stay with el bebe and Zelda."

"No, honey. You go with Annette."

"No," she hissed in horror.

"You have to…"

"No no no," Clary yelled, shaking her head. "Stay with Zelda."

"First help Annette. Help Puppy." Zelda squeezed her tightly. "Go. Before polizia come." The child stiffened in fear. "I love you."

"Te amo de una madre."

The sobbing Clary ran out of the examining room and toward the wide glass exit doors, giving the entire emergency room the finger.

• • • •

IMPROMPTU STORY CENTERS sprouted along the Major Deegan Expressway, snaking down the Grand Concourse. Everyone had a theory about how they started: a soldier stopped to rest, a soldier fainted, a soldier ate some food, a soldier asked where he could poop, kids politely called out a question about the Battle of Copenhagen, Nice, the Kenyan Bloodbath. Or what it was like to have an artificial leg. Arm. Eye. A combination.

Soldiers would climb onto a car, a few hopping DV-style from hood to hood with mischievous grins, and begin answering questions. Modest, they'd call up a colleague when they didn't know the answer; hey, that's artillery, that's for the Navy Seals, I never flew a plane, I'm a Marine, son.

Cars would pull onto the soft shoulders or simply park cock-eyed, funneling lanes and intensifying traffic which barely moved anyway, vehicles scraping each other to allow the marching soldiers to pass. Food would be handed from car to car. Blankets, pillows, sofas were assembled on the spot. Coming to the Bronx for the first night game had been a party, kick down your neighbor's door and barge in with no questions asked.

This was different. These were guests, strange people who had done strange things in your name, like kill human beings to protect your ass, your way of life. Yet they'd failed. Or had they? What if they hadn't fought to the last man on the outskirts of Budapest? What if they'd jumped overboard when the suicide boats roared toward them in the Mediterranean? Maybe the crescent moon and star would be flying over Yankee Stadium.

What defined failure for these men and women? They thought they were doing their duty and got nothing except embarrassment and a generous monthly stipend suggesting a nice place in the country, far away, would work for everyone. We don't have to see you and be reminded of the victory you didn't win and you don't have to see us and be reminded of what ungrateful shits your fellow countrymen are.

So they all came, guilty, awkward, curious to see what the animals did when they were let out of their cages, learning they were just like everyone else, except a little more so. Because they had nothing to be ashamed of. Nothing at all.

Puppy's apartment had been turned into a Story Center/Hotel since there weren't enough rooms for all the GIs. Kenuda had found some obscure statute from the war allowing a Cousin to declare any part of the country as a refugee center, last used for Americans fleeing Los Angeles and Washington.

Now throughout the Bronx, subway stations turned into shelters. Apartment building lobbies, schools, office buildings, idle buses, anywhere that had a floor and a roof were Veterans Homes. Mopping brigades formed to sterilize floors. Groceries and liquor stores ran out.

People overran the Clerk's Office on Burnside Avenue, offering their homes. Soldiers were grabbed on the street, sometimes leading to a brief fistfight, until the vet realized he wasn't being sent away again, but honored.

Nostalgic food appeared, cheeseburgers and tacos and franks on long festive tables set up just about anywhere, in the middle of a street, at a bus stop; Mooshie's old music piped out of makeshift speakers. Siblings danced with soldiers. Soldiers kissed siblings.

It was like they'd won the war. Except for the medals. There were none. Dress uniforms, sure, but not a glitter of gold or silver, a thread of a ribbon. Save your tin, the soldiers had said. Show us something that matters. America finally had.

Unlike most of the Bronx, Puppy had somewhere to go. He and Mooshie left Ty and Mick, hobbling on a bad toe, to serve as hosts for about twenty soldiers. Puppy didn't want to think what the place would look like. For all the anti-privilege sentiment, he was the star player and he was pitching tomorrow night and he needed sleep. It was nearly midnight and he wasn't even close to tired.

"How long did you live here?" Mooshie gave herself a tour of Annette's apartment.

"Thirteen years."

Mooshie admired a painting of ducks attacking a child. "That a LeBeau?"

"Look who you're asking." Puppy searched the liquor cabinet, finding an unopen bottle of Boulder Brandy. He poured them shots.

"Is it hard to be here?"

He shrugged. Over there by the bookcase, Annette had smashed his baseball bat. They'd screwed in that corner where there used to be a divan. She'd thrown many glasses of wine at the dining room table, along with telling him she was pregnant, until the miscarriage decided otherwise. Like any relationship, memories to pick and choose, allowing you to fool yourself into thinking you were always happy or always miserable; gray was not a good color for love.

Mooshie sat cross-legged on the couch, the brandy between her thighs.

"How's the arm?"

"Good enough." He could barely brush his hair anymore.

They listened to the discordant songs rising up from the street. "I should sing for them."

"You'll sing enough tomorrow. What's the play list?"

"Typical Mooshie brilliance."

"Meaning I should mind my own business."

"You're so insightful, my fiancé."

Puppy laid his weary head against the chair, tapping his feet. "Why do you think she's really doing it?"

"Who?"

"What other she or her do we have?"

Mooshie sipped from the bottle. "It's not for us."

"C'mon, Moosh. Where would we be without Grandma?" He waited for Mooshie to answer. "She kept us alive."

"For what?"

"To survive. Twenty-five years. Look how we've rebuilt."

"Again, for what? A society so scared they hide behind false love?"

Someone set up a really noisy sound system right below the window, blasting Griebel's *Spirit Wind.*

"Better than the hate, Moosh. Grandma at least makes us think in the right direction. Hate does nothing."

"Hate settles scores."

"No. Hate's contagious." Puppy took the bottle away and sipped. "Look how the Allahs hate us. What's it got them?"

Mooshie stared hard. "The fucking world."

"For how long? All the great empires collapse."

"Like America's?"

"We were never an empire, Moosh. That was probably our downfall. We acted like we ruled the place, but we were never willing to punish people. To be real assholes. We're too nice to be tyrants. The mirrors of democracy got in the way."

"We got soft, Pup. Bad guys don't respect soft."

"Maybe they respect love." Mooshie snorted derisively. "I'm serious. Maybe once baseball's really back, we can offer to play the Allahs. How's about that for a real World Series."

"You're kidding me."

"Remember the great Allah players Edi Badr, Ali Sadat."

She sneered. "Mediocre."

"Bullshit. Badr hit .400 three straight years. Sadat had a career 1.87 ERA. You never did that."

Her glass shattered against the wall. "I wasn't a traitor."

"People thought you were."

"For speaking up."

"Yeah. For what you believed in. So did they. There were innocent people deported, Moosh. Not everyone was a terrorist."

"If they prayed to Mecca, they believed in sharia, which means world conquest. I was there. None of them fought for America."

"Not true," he said softly. "There was the Prayer Brigade."

"Which turned on us."

"Because the Marines Second Company attacked them at Fort Bragg."

"After their friends took out Washington. They found traitors in the brigade."

"Some. A few. Not all."

Mooshie shook her head pityingly. "We could do this all night."

He conceded with a nod, crawling onto her lap. Mooshie took the bottle over his mild protest.

"You're pitching tomorrow."

She switched off the lights and they listened to the singing on the street. It lasted all night.

• • • •

TOMAS STRETCHED OUT his aching good leg in the back seat of the 'copter. To make the last exchange between the aircraft, he'd slid along the retractable ladder at five thousand feet, not a good place to unwind muscles, dangling somewhere over the Atlantic.

"Any patrols?" He leaned forward into the cockpit.

The young pilot shook his head. "They're either sloppy or so overwhelming we see them miles away. We'll stealth in three klicks."

"You're my last flight. Make it smooth."

Stilton patted the boy's shoulder, nodding at the mute co-pilot and returning to the cabin. Eleven hours and he was edgy. Reviewing the security details for the game didn't help. Artito had whisked them out of a pouch in Cheng's office. Just picking up for Grandma, he'd insisted, bullying the A10 into handing over a copy.

There'd been a top to bottom search of the stadium last night. Old tunnels, passageways, crawl up the butt of every nook in every crevice. Sniff the seats. Two wings of 'copters, overhead and outside the ballpark. Fighters on alert at Mariah Air Base near Montclair. Navy Seals on stand-by at City Island.

Except for the additional phrase "no visible presence of armed military or police personnel to avoid inflammation," Cheng had used every bit of the emergency contingency plan that Tomas had devised and updated for thirty years. How to get Grandma in and out of every situation.

Yet he was worried. He wasn't there, he had no control. Let it go. Cheng's an ass, but Artito knows what he's doing. Their shadow security will work. You trained him. It's only a baseball game. With twenty thousand soldiers who hate Grandma's guts for surrendering. Why should you be worried?

The 'copter tipped southeast and the pilot let him know the stealth procedure was being implemented. A hazy buzzing enveloped the craft. Maybe another hour, he thought, closing his eyes, drifting against his instincts.

He felt the co-pilot walk into the cabin and pause, shifting weight into the back foot.

Tomas dove to the left as the heavy knife plunged into the thick seat. He kicked the pilot's knee out of joint, grabbed a small blade from his hip pocket and slit the attacker's throat. The pilot turned and fired through the mesh of spurting blood; the bullet ricocheted around the cabin.

Stilton winced at the flesh wound on his thigh. Half-hopping into the cockpit, he shattered the pilot's right arm; the 'copter wobbled.

"You're going to land us, son." Tomas held the dripping blade against the pilot's neck.

The young man bit down and convulsed; foam sputtered over his lips. Tomas shoved the body into the other seat and steadied the 'copter, glancing at the board and easing the craft around, west.

He steadied his breath. When's the last time you killed someone?

The fuel gauge flickered warning red. Damn bullet must've hit a line. The board told him he didn't have enough fuel to make it home.

A white Allah patrol boat cruised below. Tomas deliberated, cutting the engines and letting the 'copter glide overhead soundlessly. The boat puttered along obliviously until it was out of sight.

He had enough fuel for about half an hour. He had to get close enough to land.

You couldn't just send me away, Lenora. You had to kill me, too?

He headed towards the curving coastline of Spain. You said you wanted me to find Abdullah. Well here I am.

• • • •

THE DEVIL CHILD saw them first and tugged at Annette's sleeve, muttering in Spanish and gesturing with that mop of hair. The same two Miners from the camp were now standing at the back of the unwieldy line at the bus stop. Annette tightened her grip on Clary's hand and casually led her another few blocks, squirming around the massive crowds who seemed to be swimming in place, punctuated by the blaring of drums now. She had an immense headache.

It was a miracle they made it this far. First there was the fight over the lollies Clary had stolen from the hospital, which she refused to share. Then the little evil thing obstinately standing on the side of the road, insisting on waving to the marching soldiers and shouting "Puppy Beisbol," defying Annette, daring Annette.

She'd scolded, wagged her fingers, threatened.

"No comprende." Satan's Spawn had shrugged innocently.

Should've just left her. She could find Puppy alone. Oh no, how could she call herself a sibling if she broke a promise to a pregnant woman. Sometimes she just really hated life and all those people who made it possible.

"Don't look," Annette warned. Clary growled softly. She'll eat me if she's hungry, Annette decided, frantically looking around, the two Miners getting closer. She nearly pulled Clary off the ground hurrying through the crowd, angrily mumbling apologies.

"Tren." Clary hopped up and down, pointing.

Annette whispered hotly, "Speak English. Spanish is illegal."

"Tren, stupido." She tapped her head and made a loud horn noises; pedestrians smiled at the charming girl with the fat bandage on her cheek.

"Tren. Train. Where?"

Clary clucked disgustedly and dragged Annette into a milling mob shuffling towards the train station a few blocks away. She tried pushing through, but they were jammed. Two New York-bound trains filled up and rumbled away; maybe they moved five feet. The Miners were having better success; their cold murderous eyes were clearly visible.

Clary's mouth curled in a thoughtful sneer. She suddenly ripped off her bandage, shouting, "Jesus Christo, beisbol, hurry, hurry."

People stared uneasily at Clary's scar, stepping aside.

They lost the Miners and made it to the entrance, where Clary turned her face right and left and up and down; as soon as someone frowned or gasped, she darted forward into the gap, Annette ducking and crouching to keep up until they joined the mass of walking talking baseball memorabilia boarding the train.

"Good girl." Annette smiled.

Something hard pressed into her back.

"Now you be a good girl and come with us," the Miner whispered, his comrade jabbing a gun into Clary's spine.

"Let the girl go." Annette didn't know where such brave words came from.

The Miner laughed meanly. Clary glanced over her shoulder, her expression scaring Annette.

"Puppy Beisbol." Clary waved her Yankees cap. "Viva la Yankees."

Nearby fans picked up the chant.

"Viva la Puppy." Clary faced the puzzled Miner, who carefully slipped the gun back into his pocket.

"Viva la Puppy," Annette joined in.

Two tall, thin twins in homemade Yankees jackets lifted Clary off the ground and picked up the chant. A conga line formed, snaking and chanting and barking towards the train ten feet away.

A couple Blue Shirts looked on, laughing.

"Guns, polizia, guns." Clary yelled and pointed at the Miners. "Guns. Shoot Puppy Beisbol."

There was a second or two where everyone froze, trying to understand.

"They're Miners," Annette screamed.

Now the cops rushed forward, the muttering crowd closing around the Miners. They started running before they were smothered by fans.

"Viva Puppy Beisbol." Clary triumphantly brandished her cap as they squeezed onto the train, which slowly chugged away. A voice announced that Monticello would be the next stop.

Annette gave Clary a respectful smile. "Where the hell do you come from?"

"Barcelona." She curtsied and nodded at the conductor trying to collect fares. "Billetes de tren."

Annette frowned. Damn.

Clary reached for a wallet sticking out of the pocket of a sweating man in a Red Sox t-shirt. Annette distracted the guy with a big flirtatious smile.

41

Although it was still four hours to game time, Ty was already stomping in and out of his office grumbling about a bunch of irresponsible lazy players who couldn't get to the stadium on time. He'd made it through the cars and soldiers and marching bands and dancing coloreds and whites, shoving past the dopey-eyed gawkers outside staring at the new Yankee Stadium sign.

Just wait until they re-do Tiger Stadium. Or Ty Cobb Park, as that Kenuda promised. For a licensing fee; Ty had already begun the negotiations with the Big Commish. He gets one lousy salary for managing and playing? And him hitting .331 which was pretty good for someone dead almost 140 years. Endorsements, too, Ty had tossed that onto the table. That lousy funeral home paid shit. Puppy didn't care about the money, just the glory of playing. Mick was happy to be sober.

But he was the Georgia Peach. He was gonna make it back in spades. Another fine expression you couldn't say anymore.

He listened at the door. The lockers had finally stopped creaking, though spikes scuffed impatiently. Someone slapped a hand into their glove. A ball rolled around. Cobb waited another few minutes and re-checked the balance on his Lifecard to make sure no one was cheating him.

"Thanks so much for coming, girls and boys and whoever." Ty sneered, leaning against his door frame in mock surprise. "The Cubs are already out there."

Cobb walked to the middle of the clubhouse and placed his right foot on a stool, hunching forward as if there was a fuse at the base of his spine eager to be lit.

"Tonight's a big deal so everyone says. Ain't that right, Puppy?"

"It's more than a game, skipper." He regretted that cheeky answer.

"More than a game." Cobb smiled blandly. "Just a bunch of people who ain't got nothing better to do."

"I meant the significance…"

"Oh, yes. Our famous pitcher who's won a grand total of fifteen games in his big league career is going to speak on the goddamn significance. Number Seven, want to tell them about significance?"

Mantle rubbed his right big toe. "Like the World Series, Ty?"

"Yeah, that's a good one. Real championships. The World Series. Not the bullshit dreamed up here with the whole country losing its mind because lights go on or some soldiers are getting another medal. Real wins and real losses."

Cobb squinted deeply into Puppy's face; he was afraid to blink.

"But tell us all about tonight's significance, Puppy. Tell us how it'll change what fucking pitches you throw since you can only throw one." He whirled on Jackson. "Or you fat boy. Tell us how the significance will change the way you block the famous pitcher's pitches from rolling to the backstop.

"How about you, girlie?" Cobb spun around, glaring at Shannon. "The significance of tonight gonna change the way you chase the curve ball off the outside corner every fucking time?"

Someone chuckled.

Ty cupped his ear. "What's that I hear? Laughter? You're laughing before a game of such significance?"

The team lowered their eyes.

"That's right, assholes. Tonight you're going to do the same shit you've been doing all season long except better because I ain't gonna be embarrassed on a night of such significance. Anyone not understand?"

Vern slowly raised his hand. "Is this considered a pep talk, skip?"

Ty threw the stool at Jackson, who barely ducked.

"Now on your knees, girls and boys and everything in between, and give thanks to your Lord and Savior, who allowed us to be here tonight." Ty bowed his head. "Thank you Jesus for all we have and all you'll give us. Let us play as hard as we can and kick the butt of the other team. And also thank you for letting us play on a night of such significance that could change the world."

He snorted and clapped his hands for the team to head onto the field. Mick lingered and followed the manager into his office, closing the door.

"What do you want?" Ty made it very clear he was very busy.

Mick slumped in the chair and pulled off his right spike, propping his heel onto the edge of the desk and tossing aside his sock.

"This." He wiggled his big toe.

Ty put on his reading glasses for a closer look, poking at the toe until Mick flinched.

"What the hell am I, skip?"

Cobb fell back into his chair, thoughtfully chewing on a stem of his glasses. He grunted a decision, rolled up his left sleeve and pulled off a thick bandage from his elbow.

"I don't know. But you're the same as me."

• • • •

PUPPY TIPPED HIS cap to the barking crowd, punctuated by a few good-natured "Let's Go Cubs" cries, as he and Vernon sauntered across the outfield toward the bullpen.

"Lots of folks." Jackson took in the vast crowd.

"Another full house."

"Fuller," the catcher said. "More children."

Vern pointed at the neat rectangles of kids who filled the seats in a semi-circle between first and second.

"There's going to be fireworks after, so that always gets kids." Puppy nudged Jackson through the bullpen gate.

"Usually there are families," Vern insisted. "Parents, kids."

"I remember what a family is. My friends had them."

Jackson ignored the attempt at humor. "The late fireworks will be after bedtimes. Parents are supposed to be with children then. Not soldiers."

Puppy pounded his glove. "I think you're reading too much into this."

"Think so?" Vern indicated the right center field bleachers. Sure enough, there were blocks of kids, one row wearing Yankees t-shirts, the next, Cubs, alternating for ten rows; adults sat in each corner of the rectangle. Northwest corner, Yankees t-shirt. Northeast corner, Cubs. Southwest, Yankees. Southeast, Cubs. All in perfect order.

Puppy shielded his eyes against the setting sun competing with the stadium lights. Same configuration in left center. He scanned the grandstands, but they were just too far away to make it out.

"They're there." Vern crept into his thoughts.

"It's a special night of significance." Puppy grinned, a little uneasily. "Which won't be mine if I don't warm up."

Vern squatted, his head twisting around at the stands. Puppy's first pitch bounced off Jackson's mask, getting his attention.

He warmed up for about twenty minutes, tossing easily and opening the distance until he was in his groove.

"Hey." Vern stood as the fastball sailed past. "Save that shit."

"I got at least four more cutters left."

Puppy's eyes wandered again as he waited for Jackson to retrieve the ball. Red, white and blue bunting billowed along the left and right field stands. Dale's monsters in baseball uniforms were flying around the outfield. The Rolling Stones roared *Satisfaction*. From the wonderful food smells, you'd think America was a real agricultural nation again.

He stayed an extra few minutes in the bullpen before rejoining the team in the dugout, where he and Mick watched the groundskeepers sweep the field, night lazily drifting over the Bronx.

"It's a beautiful green, right?" Puppy asked. Mick shrugged. "You're supposed to give me some story about you and two blondes in the lush grass of the Stadium."

"I told them all already." Mantle leaned forward, elbows on knees, frowning.

"Something wrong?"

"Nope."

"Sure?"

Mick looked at him. "How's the arm?"

"The usual shit storm. What's up, Mick?"

"I'm allowed to be serious." Mantle kicked the bat rack and disappeared into the runway.

Everyone's weirded out, Puppy thought, spitting sunflower seeds into his palm. Like you're not? Dancing until dawn. Skipping two vidnews interviews so you can make yourself breakfast in Annette's apartment and pretend to have a full blown conversation followed by a spat. Yeah, that's sane. Or using a spare, illegal key to get into Pablo's place and, not finding him in the clutches of a beautiful boy or girl, trudging downtown to his office, which was locked up. Thanks for abandoning me, pal, Puppy re-started that argument.

Three armed security guards slipped soundlessly into the dugout, stepping past Puppy as if he were invisible. Puppy looked across the field at more members of Artito's detachment taking up positions in the Cubs dugout.

The HGs chased each other back into the scoreboard with demonic cackles. Suddenly the air over second base ruffled and blades whirred. The crowd grew silent. A 'copter drifted toward home plate, touching down near the Yankees' on-deck circle.

Grandma bounded out, waving to the hovering HG Grandma. They pretended to shake hands, bowing. The crowd cheered wildly. The security team converged by the gate to the left of the Yankees dugout and escorted Grandma to her seat, while another squad accompanied Cheng and Kenuda, whose presence generated little response; Dale hadn't thought them important enough for HGs.

Grandma nodded to the crowd and sat down.

"So good to see you all." The Grandma HG hovered politely over the pitcher's mound. "This is an historic occasion, but I'm a guest just like all of you. Now make sure you eat up." Hot dogs, pizza, tacos and popcorn with sweet faces floated into her arms. "One beer only." A foamy cup landed on her shoulder. "And enjoy tonight. I love you all very much."

The Grandma HG whooshed away. Into the delighted din, Mooshie strolled toward home, trailed by a five-person honor guard wearing the uniforms of the Army, Navy, Air Force, Marines and Coast Guard. They presented Beth's flag.

The soldiers stood as one and saluted, while the rest of the crowd anxiously waited to see what Grandma would do. It seemed to take a brief effort, but Grandma finally stood and saluted.

"Hi everyone," Mooshie said. "I'm Dara Dinton."

Roars of greetings.

"As Grandma said, this is a special night of great significance."

Puppy burst into laughter; Ty shot him a dirty look.

"Tonight, we honor the men and women who made it possible for us to sit here and watch a baseball game. "

The stadium shook with shouts. Mooshie's jaw tightened slightly.

"But without Grandma's love, nothing would be possible."

The HG Grandma returned on a flying American flag. FORGIVENESS floated through the air in wispy red, white and blue vapors. The real Grandma smiled admiringly and patted Kenuda's knee appreciatively. The Third Cousin blushed.

"We welcome Grandma back to Yankee Stadium," Mooshie went slightly off script. "We welcome the soldiers back to Yankee Stadium. And now we want to welcome something else back to Yankee Stadium."

The crowd fell still again.

"It's called *The Star Spangled Banner.*" The crowd shifted uneasily. "We outlawed it because folks supposedly took it too seriously." Mooshie stared coldly at Grandma. "But now we're forgiving all that and all those who did."

Grandma grimaced slightly.

"This song is our anthem. This is America's song. First, you gotta take off your caps and hats and place them over your hearts, gang, to remember those who died wearing these uniforms." Mooshie gestured at the honor guard.

Fans craned to see Grandma's reaction. She slowly placed her right hand over her heart. The entire stadium mimicked her.

"Everyone got that?" Mooshie asked. "'Cause it's the respect part. It's the love part. For each other. For what we do for each other."

Mooshie flinched as Grandma's eyes warmed her face like an over-heated washcloth.

"Now we're gonna sing. I don't care how rotten your voice is. You sing or Dara's gonna find you."

A Dara HG in a black witch's outfit whizzed past to loud laughter. Mooshie shook her head, grinning.

"Let's do it."

An HG Honor Guard marched out of the scoreboard and presented arms. In huge red, white and blue letters, the words hung over the infield.

"Oh, say, can you see, by the dawn's early light

What so proudly we hailed at the twilight's last gleaming."

The crowd started finding its footing, buoyed by Grandma's lusty singing.

"Whose broad stripes and bright stars, thro' the perilous fight."

Now a huge American flag filled the entire infield, flanked by marching soldiers.

"O'er the ramparts we watched, were so gallantly streaming

And the rockets red glare, the bombs bursting in air."

Oohs and ahs as HG bombs and rockets exploded.

"Gave proof through the night that our flag was still there,

O say does that star-spangled banner yet wave

O'er the land of the free and the home of the brave."

The HG flag covered the entire infield. Holographic soldiers climbed aboard and saluted the crowd, floating over the stands. The fans stomped and whooped and whistled.

The flag faded and was replaced by FORGIVENESS. The crowd yelled a little louder and Grandma sighed in relief.

Mooshie returned to home plate, waiting for everyone to settle down. "Now we have another wonderful tradition. The throwing out of the first ball. Don't worry, Hsen is still pitching for the Cubs and Puppy for the Yankees." She paused to let the barking subside. "But this ceremonial toss will be from a couple of my..." Dara stopped just in time. "Couple of our all-time favorite players. You remember the Three Amigos?"

The crowd cheered for the HGs of Mooshie, Derek and Sun Yen dancing with baseball bats.

"Well, the greatest player of all time, Mooshie Lopez, is no longer with us."

You're just incorrigible, Puppy shook his head, chuckling.

"But we still have the great third baseman." Sun Yen hobbled to the pitcher's mound. "And the amazing right fielder." Derek joined him. "Easy Sun Yen and Derek Singh."

Grandma, waving a Yankees and Cubs cap in each hand to make sure there was no doubt about her impartiality, came onto the field to make it a threesome.

"Gentlemen." Grandma smiled at the players, who bowed.

"Honored," Sun Yen said.

"Thank you, Grandma," Derek added.

"No, thank you. Now how embarrassing is it going to be when I can't reach home plate?" She held up the baseball.

"It's going to be way worse when we can't." Derek grinned wryly.

None of their tosses made it past forty feet; the crowd cheered anyway. They walked off the field while Mooshie tossed the ball into the air.

"Are you ready?" she shouted.

"Yes."

"What?"

"Yes," the crowd ratcheted it up.

"I can't fucking hear you."

The old ballpark shook.

Mooshie winked at Puppy. "Then let's play ball." She flipped her hair side to side, back and forth, winding up and firing the ball into the second level behind third base.

Play Ball!!! cried an HG umpire.

• • • •

ALL THE TRAINS had stopped at 235th Street. Someone, somehow, had relocated one of the forty-foot vidscreens across the tracks at 234th Street. There weren't enough cops to move it since all of the Bronx's Blue Shirts were on duty within half a mile of Yankee Stadium.

At least they wouldn't get arrested for public defecation, Annette thought, since Clary had threatened to pee on the street unless she found a toilet. Annette jiggled the jiggling child to be still as she searched up and down the jammed block.

"Hurry." Clary squirmed and bent her knees.

"I told you to go on the train."

Clary erupted into angry Spanish and took to squatting every few feet.

Just past what was once a traffic intersection, a thick line poured out of an old ethnic-styled pub, the sort of place Annette's father would call "a place for people with calluses."

Annette pointed hopefully toward the entrance. Clary growled when they didn't move. "El patience," Annette hissed.

A loud gagging noise blasted out of Clary like she was a music speaker. Heads turned and the child clutched her stomach, groaning. Annette yanked Clary, feet scraping listlessly along the ground, through the path of drunks unwilling to house someone else's vomit, and into the bar.

"Bathroom?" Annette shouted over the deafening noise at the bartender, who jerked his head around the corner to the left.

"Puppy Beisbol," Clary shouted at the vidsports screen over the bar where Puppy clenched his fist after striking out a batter.

"You're supposed to be dying," Annette rasped. "Beisbol later, pee now."

Clary made scary noises and darted between bodies. A thick-set man sympathetically shook his head.

"Easier when you could smack them."

"Cooking them would be better," Annette grumbled. The man edged away.

She watched the game a moment. It was already the third inning. When was this disaster supposed to happen? Annette glanced around impatiently, landing on the two Brown Hats squeezing into the bar.

Recognizing the Detectives, Annette frantically crouched behind some beefy guys screaming encouragement at Puppy as Buca and Y'or eased through the crowd, eyes narrowed. Looking for someone.

Relax. There must be other dangerous criminals let loose. Just tell them there's a terrorist attack about to happen and you've done your duty. Have you? It sounded so stupid. Where was the evidence? Look at all those children, she thought as the camera panned over the crowd. They're terrorists too?

She ducked as the Brown Hats scanned the bar. Of course if she's right, she's uh, what did they used to call them, heroes, back when everyone had to be rewarded to behave selflessly. Kenuda would have to marry her. Her shoes would be required buying. She'd probably get her own vidshow about fashion, Annette warmed to the idea, slowly rising.

Clary's head bobbed around the end of the bar. What about her? If they wanted the brat the first time, they'd probably want her more now. So, Annette, so? She's a demon child. Zelda should've kept her.

If she were supposed to be a mother then she wouldn't have miscarried.

The Detectives whispered to each other, moving cautiously towards Clary.

I hate you, Puppy.

Annette grabbed Clary around the waist and charged toward the back door.

"I'm so tired of being chased," Annette yelled as they scrambled down 233rd Street.

• • • •

THAT'S THE TWELFTH STRAIGHT DOUBLE K GAME FOR PUPPY. The scoreboard exhaled a Puppy HG on a horse gunning down Cubbies.

Ty grunted at Puppy as he sat at the far end of the dugout, passing teammates slapping his knee proudly. "Don't get carried away."

Everything was working. The knuckler was dancing, the occasional fastball dipping, the few curves all breaking at the last minute and dropping into the pitcher's mystical black hole. Unable to sit still, he leaned on the top step, peering past Mick swinging a couple bats by the on-deck circle as another contingent of soldiers trotted out to home plate.

"The Army 31ˢᵗ Regiment held out for five days without resupply, enabling their buddies to withdraw safely into Scotland," Mooshie solemnly said. "They were taken prisoner by the Allahs," she was supposed to say Arabs, "for four years."

Mooshie bit her lip. "You can imagine."

The crowd murmured angrily, but a glance toward the box showed a very calm and serene Grandma. Clearly she expected a certain temperature. You don't forgive overnight.

"We salute you." Mooshie tipped her hand to her brow. The men, backs erect, returned the salutes, pausing grudgingly before Grandma.

"Going well, don't you think?" Cheng whispered as the soldiers shuffled down the steps into the Yankees dugout.

Grandma kept her smile. "They hate my guts."

Cheng shrugged. "That'll never change."

Grandma gave him a sharp look.

They went to the top of the fifth, the game scoreless. Puppy had struck out ten of the first twelve batters, but the Cubs' Hsen was nearly matching him, fanning six and allowing only a scratch hit by Ty.

Puppy got the leadoff batter to feebly chase an oh-two knuckler. A Puppy HG in a wizard's robe bewitched a Cubs batter.

In the control room, Dale whooped it up. Puppy doffed his cap in admiration.

The next batter went down on a fastball at the knees which beaded pain on Puppy's upper lip. He walked off the mound, rubbing up the ball. Ty and Mick watched very carefully from their outfield positions. Puppy managed a weak smile and dug back into the mound.

His mind was briefly on the pain, not the pitch, and he threw a wobbly knuckler which forgot to skip. The Cubs shortstop Santiago ripped the ball into right center. Ty and Mick converged, both leaving their feet. The shot sailed over Mick's outstretched glove, but Ty snatched the would-be extra base hit in the tip of the webbing. Together the two old-timers ran gleefully into the dugout.

"Perfect game's still alive," Jackson shouted.

Cobb jabbed the catcher in the ribs with the handle of his bat. "Never say that again. Any of you." To underscore the message, Cobb chased Vern down the runway and ito the clubhouse.

"Is he crazy?" Shannon whispered to Puppy, towel draped around his neck.

"Well yeah. But it's an old baseball superstition. Never jinx a you-know-what by talking about it."

Ty slammed the bat near Puppy's knee. "That means everyone."

An Air Force wing commander was honored in the last of the fifth, HG F-26s gliding over the stands, so lifelike children tried pulling them out of the sky. The Yankees went down in order, Puppy ending the inning by bouncing out to third; Ty screamed at him for not running out the ball.

He almost showed him a clenched groin. Gimme a break, skip.

In the top of the sixth, the first Cub trickled out to short and the next batter swung fitfully at a curve way outside.

THAT'S THIRTEEN, FOLKS. Puppy galloped across the outfield and lassoed a Cubs hitter.

He went to three-and-two on the Cubbies left fielder, who fouled off three straight pitches before swinging an inch over a sinking fastball.

FOURTEEN! The Puppy HG dove toward the real one, who pretended to chase his alter ego around the infield, which didn't amuse Ty.

In the last of the sixth, Vernon smacked a hanging curve into the right field corner, huffing into second with a lead-off double.

Dale concentrated on her console, punching in a gasping Jackson HG wheezing on hands and knees into the base. As always, she made herself laugh. She had to come up with more funny HGs for the Cubs. But they were boring. Well, If anyone could make them unboring, it was her. Dale was so intent thinking of ways to make the Cubs HGs interesting that she didn't hear the three men in orange wigs sneak into the control room.

When Dale looked up, she was clubbed in the head with the butt of a rifle. A Miner dragged her into the corner while his comrades studied the console. They nodded, pleased. It looked just like they planned.

Dmitri grounded out to second, sending Vern to third. The Cubs drew their infield in. Dante tried too hard and popped up to the first baseman, flinging the bat in disgust. Ty broke the discarded bat over his knee.

Ty dug into the left-handed hitter's box and missed a bunt attempt on the first pitch.

"He never misses." Puppy nudged Mickey.

"Who said he was trying?" Mantle grinned.

The Cubs third baseman edged in a foot closer and Cobb whacked a shot past him into left field, Jackson chugging down the line for the first run of the game. Puppy was a little surprised not to see the old white-haired Ty HG skipping around, mocking his opponents. Guess The Perfect One has to miss sometimes.

Shannon flied to left for the third out. Puppy took the mound for the top of the seventh, waiting to begin his warm-ups until Mooshie was done with that inning's salute. The crowd settled in for the new treat.

"I'd like to sing a wonderful old song. It's another song you haven't heard for a while. Not since the last time we all got together, back on October 12, 2065. As you know, it was also outlawed."

She tipped her head toward the tight-lipped Grandma. An HG orchestra floated gracefully out of the scoreboard.

"It's called *God Bless America*," Mooshie said.

God. When's the last time anyone heard that publicly. Privately.

Grandma turned to Cheng, "They only sing this once, right?"

The First Cousin nodded with a vague smile. "That's all that's needed."

"God bless America, land that I love," Mooshie sang.

"Stand beside her, and guide her

Through the night with the light from above."

The orchestra members turned into soldiers.

"From the mountains to the prairies

To the oceans white with foam."

Mooshie faced Grandma.

"God bless America, my home, sweet home."

Mooshie's voice turned hard, savage.

"God bless America, my home, sweet home."

Now the words flew out of the HG soldiers' mouths and the crowd saluted the flag flying over the field. The song ended and, as the cheers faded, a voice echoed.

"We've been lied to."

One of Hazel's kids stood behind the Cubs' dugout, the red-haired girl seen simultaneously on the scoreboard.

"My name is Hanna Duchin," she said with a heavy Dutch accent. "I'm an orphan. I was abandoned by America and raped by the Allahs."

A gasp rippled across the stands. Mooshie stared at the stunned Grandma.

A little boy stood. In Italian, he said, "My name is Francis Mangella. The Allahs killed my parents by scooping out their insides."

Now another girl said in German, "My name is Alycia Stine. I was tortured in an orphanage."

All over the stadium, Hazel's kids talked about the brutality of the Allahs. A contingent of Black Tops rushed toward the control room; so did Frecklie.

The scoreboard filled with vids of the crescent moon and star over Britain's Parliament building, Paris, the Eiffel Tower festooned in Arabic wording. Stumbling lines of unkempt children marched at the point of Holy Warrior bayonets through a swamp. Dead nuns and dead priests. The lush beaches of Hawaii filled with vacationing Allahs, while Islamic soldiers snow-boarded in Alaska. The mushroom cloud floated over Los Angeles. The White House collapsed.

"This is the peace Grandma gave us," the voice said quietly, because there was no need to shout.

On the second level between home and first, Miners ambushed the approaching BT squad with a few quick shots outside the control room. They fired at Frecklie, who barely ducked behind the corner.

"This is the peace she wants to continue," the voice continued.

Grandma and Abdullah, in his white robes, smiled together from the scoreboard. One horrified gasp seized the ballpark.

Puppy saw orange wigged heads fill both bullpens.

"Hello, my darlings. This is the most important talk we'll ever have. You and I and our new friend, Abdullah bin-Nasr. Yes, his father is the Grand Mufti. Yes, our old enemy. Which means you must listen. Because peace isn't enough, my darlings. We sit here, American and Arab, in our secure homes and believe a world which is forever on the verge of a holocaust will last. It can't. Hate doesn't work, even when we have a reason to hate. We had a reason to hate Islam."

"And we, a reason to hate the West," added Abdullah.

Some fans in the bleachers threw food at the scoreboard.

"You oppressed us, but you didn't understand how," the Son continued. "We oppressed you, and justified it. You deported us. We blew up your cities. You blew up ours. We won."

Miners ran to their positions along the foul lines. Faintly, 'copter blades approached.

"Yes they did," Grandma said. "Oh, we could've settled the score by using our nuclear weapons, but that would've meant the end of humanity. There were many who wanted that, who hated so much that destruction seemed sensible. I chose otherwise because we all are one people who have a duty to everyone on this planet to survive until we can figure it all out. Abdullah and I are making a start."

Abdullah fussed with his robes.

"I have taken control of the Caliphate of Europe and expect the Caliphate of Our Ancestors in the Middle East and Africa to follow suit," he said calmly. "Not all my people want to hate. Our religion has been corrupted by the pursuit of power, greed and corruption. Allah teaches us to love."

Abdullah paused, as if he could hear the angry shouts.

"It's difficult for you to believe that. It's difficult for us to believe many things about you, too. But we need to move ahead together. We need to live together. To trust each other. To see each other. Touch each other. Share meals. Laughter. To learn together."

"It will take time." Grandma smiled. "But we must forgive."

"Rabbi aghfir li," Abdullah said in Arabic.

"Rabbi aghfir li," Grandma repeated, the sound of her speaking Arabic shocking. "We need not fear. The love we've shown in rebuilding a new world must be shared. We don't need weapons anymore. Our hearts and our minds are the strongest guns we can ever have. I know this is a lot to ask and a lot to understand. I have faith in all of you. I love you all. May we show the same love to our enemies that we show to each other. Let us build a new Family."

Everyone in the stadium stared at the real Grandma, white-faced, dimly looking at the the video she and Abdullah taped in the secret Manhattan location fade away.

"Is this what we want again?" the voice asked over more grisly scenes of American soldiers bodies washing ashore. "Our survival is at stake. We must take back our freedoms before they're surrendered forever. Finish the job."

In red, white and blue, FINISH THE JOB spurted out of the scoreboard as oranged-wigged Miners poured onto the field, firing at the arriving 'copters. Artito's security team rushed protectively toward Grandma. Miners leaped out of both dugouts and butchered them with a volley.

A 'copter crashed by first base and a second aircraft was blown up by a surface-to-air missile. Puppy dashed around the burning debris, plunging through the rebels toward Grandma.

Ty tossed Puppy a bat; he winged a Miner. Mick brought down another with a blow to the head.

Mooshie reached under her dress for the .38. One shot, two maybe. The bitch was only ten feet away. She aimed, but Puppy was in the way. Damn you, she thought.

Out of the chaos, she saw Hazel rush toward Grandma, raising his pistol. She hesitated and fired two shots; Hazel fell. She jumped over his body, kicking him in the groin.

"C'mon." Puppy grabbed Grandma's arm.

"There's no way out," Kenuda shouted as hysterical fans ran in all directions amid the slaughter.

"Yes there is," Mooshie said grimly. She smashed a bat against the Yankee insignia by the on-deck circle; a door slid open. Ty and Mickey nodded for them to go, turning back to the Miners with bats cocked.

Puppy, Cheng and Kenuda led Grandma down the steps while Mooshie fired a few last covering shots. She smacked a button and the door closed. The tunnel shuddered with an explosion directly above.

They ran through the black underground for about two hundred yards, dirt and concrete falling, then up a steep passage onto River Avenue.

Police cars and fire engines roared through the panicked crowd. Fiery balls illuminated thick clouds of smoke. Blue Shirts pulled Grandma into a squad car.

Her face twisted. "I want it destroyed. Once and for all."

The cop car sped toward a phalanx of 'copters landing on 161st Street on top of scorched vehicles, flaming tents, shrieking people.

Fighter jets lashed the ballpark with rockets, waves of debris crashing onto the burning infield, where Miners fell beneath the withering counter-attack. The upper deck in right field collapsed, burying screaming fans. The dugouts exploded. Concrete blocks tumbled mindlessly onto the street, trapping more screeching people. Guns fired without any targets other than to kill.

Puppy watched Yankee Stadium burn before Kenuda and Mooshie were able to drag him up a ladder into a 'copter. A Miner staggered beneath the blades and fired two shots; a Black Top, perched by the open door, riddled the body with bullets.

They stealthed themselves, but not the carnage.

The Bronx burned, but so did the rest of the country. For the first time since the end of the war, Black Tops patrolled the streets to secure dawn-to-dusk curfews.

It didn't help. Anyone wearing a baseball cap or just plain cap was arrested and beaten; there were reports of siblings simply gunned down. Like 10/12, huge pyres consumed baseball memorabilia. The new sporting goods factories were bulldozed by BTs while siblings trailed, like an infantry following a tank division, ransacking the buildings.

The higher the pyre, the louder the cheers.

Baseball fans fought back. They wouldn't be blamed again. The vidnews screamed non-stop about sleeper Miners cells, touting John Hazel as a ringleader along with Singh and Sun Yen, both in custody. BT attempts to crush the miniature Fenway Park were met with stone-tossing fans, who stunned the guards and stole their weapons. Wrigley Field was another battleground, bodies burning in the newly planted ivy while fans fought BTs with bats. More weapons were stolen.

Kill Allahs signs leaped onto the sides of buildings. Then there were the stunned soldiers, their memories desecrated. They quickly joined the baseball fans, forming small brigades. BTs and soldiers fought house to house in Philadelphia. Reports said parts of Manhattan were infiltrated; a firefight raged at Rockefeller Center.

The vidnews played this up, linking Miners and soldiers and fans in one horrible alliance. Captured GIs were sent to makeshift camps. Pennsylvania Avenue, fenced off as a sacred shrine to Islamic treachery, became a detention center by desperate authorities. Hundreds, thousands of soldiers were rounded up.

That was just the first twenty-four hours.

42

Gunfire crackled outside Azhar's tiny cabin, heavy vehicles rumbling to a halt. Waking from the wary half-sleep, Mustafa slid under the bed and grabbed the thin knife he'd been hiding for whomever came for him first. Mufti's people. Abdullah's people. He wouldn't die alone. The two familiar large bodyguards kicked down the door, flipped over the mattress and shoved him out the door.

They let him keep the knife, a good sign he felt, tossing him into a dark SUV and tearing into the forest ahead of exploding tank shells.

"Where's the Son?" Mustafa retied his shoelace for something to do.

"We don't know." The driver shrugged.

"Then where are we going?"

The bodyguards exchanged vague looks. This was the extent of the plan. In an emergency, get the Captain. Mustafa tipped his head wearily against the seat. A week of waiting. For this?

"What do you think about America?" one of the bodyguards asked after a while, making conversation.

"What happened?"

The bodyguard in the passenger seat shook his head. "You don't know?"

"They took away my mobile device."

"The rebels tried to kill Grandma again."

Azhar swallowed hard. "And?"

The bodyguard passed his cell phone over the seat. A presenter on The Truth news program ranted about the vicious treachery of the Crusaders slandering the Mufti and his son with this false video.

"They wish any pretext to begin another war, so let it be," the old, fat Mufti said calmly, talking from behind his large oak desk. "I love my son and my son loves Allah. These are lies and those who defile our people with their filth will be destroyed. Allahu Akbar."

Mustafa stared hard at the crowds across the Islamic Empire cheering the destruction of the baseball stadium. Angry Crusader soldiers marched, chanting Death to Allahs. Massive Islamic armies ran forward in battle. Crusaders ships sank and their planes blew up. Churches burnt. The last war? Or had this new one already started?

The bodyguard took back the phone.

"Now you know," he said simply.

Fighters roared overhead. The SUV took a wild turn ahead of some popping noises. The back window shattered and Azhar covered his head, kneeling on the floor. They bounced down a rocky ramp toward a small airfield. Something exploded nearby. Azhar prayed, then stopped. Who was listening?

A blue Cessna waited impatiently, guarded by a tank, its turret swiveling menacingly. Three armed guards in white robes angrily gestured for Akhar to hurry up the steps.

Aboard, two more white robed guards shouted to buckle up. The plane began taxiing as the tank fired several shells at an approaching armored truck. Azhar ignored the seat belt warning and simply gripped the edge of the chair as the plane took off and twisted southeast.

What is today, he frantically searched his jumbled mind, not bothering to ask the guards, who were watching the firefight at the airport below. Tuesday. Yesterday I washed my hair. Mondays and Thursdays. Today could be Friday, no no, Tuesday. I've decided it's Tuesday so then it will be Tuesday. There must be something I can control.

Tuesday. Jalak will make Al Kabsa tonight.

• • • •

SHE'D NEVER BE able to hear the word push again. Even five hours later, Zelda still tasted her own sweat dripping down her forehead and over her lips like a waterfall, filling her mouth. Sweat and the pain and the push push push. She should've been a better student at Parents Class. Too busy. Doing what? Everyone's busy today. Zelda pushed the mesh away in her groggy mind and lifted onto her elbows in the empty hallway.

"Hey." Zelda heard her fuzzy voice. "Who stole my room?"

The nurse hurried past, uniform stained with blood. If they hadn't stolen her room, she could look out the window toward the screams.

Grandma's tits, my body aches. Zelda realized her stomach was flat. Flatter. Still fat, but no baby. Where'd he go? She threw up onto the floor. One of the passing nurses shouted for her to be more careful; a resentful orderly mopped up.

She sniffed at the awful smells, recoiling at the moans coming from somewhere. This is a hospital. Moan and puke and scream. Zelda tried sliding off the gurney, but a nurse pressed her back down, tut-tutting and giving her the most wonderful liquid in the history of the world.

"Where's my baby?" Zelda asked hoarsely between sips through a straw. The nurse wiped her face and hurried off. "Where is he?"

They stole my baby, she decided. Along with my room. And my clothes. Zelda stripped off the white nightgown and stumbled forward, holding onto the wall. She made it a few feet before a nurse and orderly firmly laid her back on the gurney.

"We have more important things to deal with, dear," the nurse scolded.

"My baby's missing."

The nurse gave the orderly a meaningful look and they shoved Zelda back into the gown. Off she went on a ride down the hallway. The screams grew louder.

"What's going on?"

"Casualties," the orderly said in a way that suggested that was all the information she was getting. He slid Zelda into a wheelchair, rolling her into a small closet lit by a weak overhead bulb.

"What's this mean?" Her nipples hurt. "I need a pain pill."

"We ain't got any left. Lucky we got bandages after the shit outside," he said harshly, then sighed apologetically. "Be quiet. You know how?"

"No." Zelda shook her head.

The orderly laughed and locked the door. She was trapped. She was going to scream, but her throat hurt, too. She sat there for quite a while, most of the time sleeping. The door opened and the orderly laid a bundle on her lap.

"Know what to do?"

Zelda had no idea what he was talking about.

The orderly pointed to her breast.

Oh.

He rolled his eyes and locked the door.

The bundle shifted slightly; she froze. She thought it was a baby but, to make sure, pulled the blanket from its face. Yes. A baby. It must be her baby. The orderly must've killed the kidnappers and rescued him.

"Diego?" Zelda whispered. The baby, not understanding English just yet, ignored her.

Was it hers? Zelda lifted the infant to the light. Fuck yeah. Looks just like Pablo. The baby scrunched up its face and cried. Panicking, Zelda tore open the gown and shoved her left breast into the baby's face. He greedily sucked on the nipple.

You have any idea how much that hurts? Zelda rocked the baby, breaking the contact of mouth to nipple and quickly restoring the feeding before he began wailing again. This isn't so hard, she kissed Diego's head. Glad one of us knows what he's doing.

Someone yanked on the door. Zelda wrapped the baby, face and all, in the blanket. A shot blew off the lock. A Black Top pointed a rifle in her face.

"Close the door," she screamed. Diego joined her.

"What're you doing in the hospital, ma'am?"

"What the hell do you think I'm doing?"

The Black Top stared sheepishly as Diego regained her nipple. "Boy or girl?"

"Boy. Diego. Junior."

The BT lifted her visor. She was no more than twenty, "Stay out of sight."

The BT closed the broken door, which wobbled slightly open. Zelda gently hugged Diego. Little man, you are the bam diggity. But we gotta get our asses the hell out of here.

• • • •

AN OLD MAN with wisps of gray hair hugging his dark skull was the last to leave, shuffling sadly down the path with an empty pot. Puppy'd counted forty-seven mourners carrying flowers and trays of food and bottles of wine, but he'd only been there over an hour. Maybe he should ask the two BTs in the shadows down the block how many people had showed up to pay respects.

Who you expecting to catch, you pricks? No one's left.

Puppy crossed the street, clenching his groin at the BTs and, after a last deep breath, knocked softly and entered the squat house.

Candles surrounded Frecklie's body lying on the rug. He was dressed in a black suit and white shirt; a crucifix rested in the dimple of a perfectly knotted blue tie. Black shoes gleamed with several coats of polish. Purplish bruises covered the right side of his face. He didn't look peaceful, just agitated. Puppy wanted to spread his lips in a Frecklie half-smile.

"What do you think?" Beth came out of the kitchen, drying her hands on a towel.

"I can't imagine what the question is."

"His tie." Beth gave him a sharp look and adjusted the tie; Puppy expected Frecklie to sit up, gagging.

"Looks fine."

Beth fussed with the crucifix before tucking it back inside the dimple, abruptly lifting up Frecklie's pants leg. "Gray socks are right?"

"Sure."

"Black would've been too much." Beth frowned and disappeared into her son's bedroom, returning with a pair of black socks which she held beside the gray. "Yes. Too much." Beth neatly folded the socks and left them on the coffee table next to a pile of smoked fish. "Eat."

Puppy wiped his tears with the socks and followed her into the kitchen. Beth dried a dish over and over.

"You need help?"

Beth shook her head and laid the plate in the rack, meticulously washing a fork.

"I would've come earlier, but, you know."

"I don't." She mimicked his shrug. He didn't know, either.

Puppy took the fork and dried it. "I can get him a funeral."

"Aren't they illegal? One-stop shopping, pull the body out of the wreckage and burn it on the spot."

Instant cremations were designed to avoid martyrs and too much attention to the dead. Six thousand and forty-eight, he'd been told during a briefing in Kenuda's office about the aftermath. No one had an idea what aftermath meant. He, Mooshie and Kenuda were numb. Baseball was gone forever. Possession of any equipment or memorabilia was a capital offense. Treason. Abort a baby, swing a bat, now equal somehow. He couldn't think ahead to anything. That's why he hadn't come earlier. He was wishing it all away and the smoke of the burning bodies wafting from Yankee Stadium made that impossible.

This was worse than 10/12. That was horrible but, like all tragedies, you could believe there was hope, that lessons would be learned. This was the second chance. There are no real lessons after that.

"Cheng will do me a favor."

Beth laughed listlessly. "I forgot. The famous Puppy, the all-powerful Puppy. Snap your fingers and you can do anything. Can you really do anything, Puppy? Can you bring my son back to life?"

More tears slid down his cheeks. "At least I can get him a proper burial."

"Proper?" Her eyes blazed.

"Not on a goddamn carpet."

"I'm lucky they let me get away with that. He was a suspect."

"What?"

"A suspect. He knew about the weapons stashed in the storage rooms at the stadium."

Puppy didn't think he could feel sicker.

"Ruben thought it was to protect the fans." Beth shouted. "He only told Dale. Bad enough that he's shot saving her life and she watches him die, but once they dragged her downtown… Go on. Go into his room. See what your friends Cheng and Grandma think."

Beth pushed his exhausted body into Frecklie's room. Broken chairs. Ripped mattress. Gaping holes in the walls, the floors. They'd smashed the windows just for fun.

"They did this while he lay in the other room." Beth calmly returned to the kitchen; he followed, grabbing her arm.

"Do you blame me?"

"Is that all you care about?"

"I don't have much left. I loved him, too, Beth."

She stared back through the doorway at Frecklie. "I knew, too, Puppy. Not about any weapons, but I should've suspected Hazel. All the things I wouldn't let my son do and on this, this I look away. But Ruben was so happy. Maybe part of me wanted this to happen. I was one of them, once."

The two BTs stood in the doorway, rifles at a casually ominous angle. "We gotta collect."

Puppy held up his hand. "Just wait. She has until midnight. I have the papers."

The taller BT nodded at the clock. "Two minutes."

Beth knelt by Frecklie, murmuring a prayer and crossing herself. Puppy watched the BTs roll their eyes.

He scooped Frecklie up and headed toward the back door. The BTs blocked his way.

"Sir, please put down the body. It must be cremated."

"Not this one."

"You have the papers. It's a memorial service only."

"I changed my mind."

Their rifles pointed at his chest.

"Do you know who I am? I'm the famous Puppy Nedick. I saved Grandma's life. I'm going to be honored in a couple days at Grandma's House. Now if you want to shoot me and explain what happened, go ahead. You better have a really good story. Otherwise get the hell out of my way."

The BTs nervously fidgeted with their weapons, finally slowly lowering them onto their hips.

"Get the shovel, Beth," Puppy said hoarsely.

In the backyard, Beth dug ferociously, dirt flying into her hair. The BTs exchanged worried looks. The shorter one finally said, "Curfew's starting."

Puppy and Beth wrapped the boy in a clean white sheet and lowered him into the grave, carefully layering the dirt. The BTs stepped forward. Puppy pressed his nose against the BT's visors.

"If this grave is ever disturbed, I will find you."

He poured a handful of dirt into the guard's pocket. The safety went off on the rifles; Beth grabbed the shovel. The shorter BT broke the staring contest with a poke into his comrade's ribs and they angrily stomped around the side of the house.

"Do you want to say a prayer?" Puppy knelt beside Beth.

"It always embarrassed him."

"He won't know."

Beth's nostrils flared. "The point is, he does know. He's with God now. In Heaven. Up there."

"Thanks, I kind of figured out the direction." Puppy smiled weakly.

Beth crossed herself. "Thank you, Puppy." They stood silently staring at the grave. "What will you do?"

"I figure they'll take care of me since I risked my ass to save Grandma."

"You should've let her die," Beth hissed.

"I can't do things like that."

She gave him a long look. "No. I don't think you can."

Puppy smoothed out the dirt on the grave. "At least you have your shop."

Beth looked away.

"Guess not. You're going after Zelda, aren't you?"

She tossed aside a few pebbles.

"Even after this you still don't trust me?" he snapped.

"Remember where you are," she cautioned, sighing. "Yes, I'm going to find her."

"Know where she is?"

"I followed Zelda that night to the camp. I've been there before."

"During your brief summer training." Beth just smiled. "When are you leaving?"

"Well, I have no customers anymore."

Puppy insisted she take his special curfew pass.

"How will you get home?" Beth asked.

"I'm Puppy Beisbol." Puppy searched on hands and knees for a couple twigs, pulling out one of his shoelaces and making an X shape.

"What's this?" Beth frowned.

"A cross."

Managing a wan smile, Beth fixed the twigs into the shape of a cross and planted it into Frecklie's grave. Beth cried for an hour on his shoulder. When he woke up, she was gone.

• • • •

CHENG'S SECRETARY BLINKED its long lashes disdainfully. "I already told you, Third Cousin."

"Thrice, I believe." Kenuda pressed his thick hands on its desk. "This emergency situation falls fully under my area and I insist on being present at any and all meetings. Now where is he?"

The A12 was not intimidated, poking at its computer with two stiff fingers.

"Listen, you impudent little stove…"

The secretary gasped. "That prejudice will be reported."

"I encourage it."

Cheng's inner door opened and Second Cousins Cria and Daniffam walked out glumly. Kenuda brushed past them as if it were his office.

The First Cousin scowled. "What do you want?"

Kenuda slammed the door on the secretary's leg. "An explanation, sir."

"First Cousin, I tried." The A12 managed to press half its face through the door frame.

"Never mind, leave. Well open the blasted door first, Kenuda." Cheng snarled and waited, arms folded. "I'm a trifle busy this morning."

"As I should be."

"Am I stopping you?"

Elias paused. "Yes, you are, First Cousin. There've been several meetings since yesterday…"

"Several." Cheng laughed coldly. "Try a lot more than several. We're in a state of emergency, Kenuda. Perhaps you're aware…."

"I am aware," Kenuda snapped. "This was my stadium. My game. My sport. "

"You're no longer Commissioner of Sport and Entertainment."

Kenuda winced as if Cheng had spit in his face. "Why?"

"Because you fucked up, Kenuda. You took baseball way beyond where it should've gone. Instead of slow steps, your damn ego got in the way."

"Everything was approved," he said stiffly. "Sir."

Cheng rose on his tiptoes. "Are you blaming me?"

Kenuda didn't answer, inflaming Cheng.

"Perhaps you'd like to blame Grandma, too? Perhaps you should blame everyone who trusted your judgment, like the thousands of dead children buried inside that stadium."

Kenuda suddenly felt buried beneath rubble, too.

Cheng sighed disgustedly. "You're a Third Cousin and you bear responsibility for your actions. As I bear responsibility for cleaning up your shit and restoring order. And dealing with the damn Allahs, who've just mobilized their Atlantic Fleet."

"We're at war?"

"We don't know what we're at. Half the blasted country thinks that bullshit video played at your Yankee Stadium was real. The country is ripped apart, Kenuda. Because of goddamn baseball again."

"I can fix everything." He grew flush with manic possibilities.

Cheng looked at Kenuda as if he just crawled out of a hole in the wall. "Why?"

"Because, because I'm a Third Cousin."

"No. Because you don't want to lose your position."

Kenuda steadied himself. "Am I in danger of being asked to leave The Family?"

"That would be Grandma's decision. And she thinks you're shit on a banana. For now, take your wounded feelings and pouting lips and find something useful. Maybe you could assist Cousin Takei with road clearance."

"Fifth Cousin Takei?"

Elias leaned against a pole in the crowded bus, hoping his leaden weight wouldn't rip the shambling vehicle in half. Subways were still haphazard, heavily guarded. Cars crept out of the city, slowed by security checks; no one had any idea how many terrorists were still at large. More buses converged onto Moshulu Parkway. Everywhere, movement without movement. Perched by a comatose traffic light, a giant vidscreen blared about Derek Singh and Easy Sun Yen committing suicide in their jail cells.

Before or after they talked, Kenuda thought sourly. What would they have said, his eyes narrowed. The whole damn stadium had been searched by BTs before the game. Under Cheng's command. Kenuda's eyes narrowed deeper. Convenient.

An elderly woman rocked unsteadily near the back as two teens embraced a few seats away.

"Get up," Kenuda commanded the youngsters, who slid, shamed, into the aisle. Elias steered the old woman into the seat. She smiled with weary gratitude. He glowered at the dazed passengers. "We must not lose our values. Do you all understand?"

The passengers looked away, embarrassed.

Kenuda walked the hour back to his office, brushing past his secretary. He dribbled a basketball for a couple minutes, thinking, before shouting for his A12 to come in.

"Yes, sir?" It blinked wide-eyed.

"Is there a special way to send a message about reassignment?"

The robot hesitated. "Yes, sir. May I ask why?"

"Because I've been reassigned. Or soon will be."

His secretary took on a sad sheen.

"Oh stop it," he snapped. "Prepare a note for me to send. Well go on, I have a life span unlike you."

The secretary leaned over its computer, waiting. "Let it say, I, Elias Kenuda, happily agrees with the decision of First Cousin Albert Cheng to reassign my duties as Third Cousin. Read it back. Never mind," he interrupted. "I'm sure it's fine. Send."

The secretary hesitated.

"Send." Kenuda threw a football against the wall. "Who handles restaurants and food places and that sort of thing where people eat?"

"I don't know, sir."

"Wouldn't that be within your job description to find out?"

The robot typed for a moment. "It was under Fifth Cousin Bitosssanava."

"Isn't he dead?"

"Yes, sir."

"Then it's open. Good. Write, Given the recent tragedy of Fifth Cousin however you spell his name, I am volunteering my extensive experience to handle this area during the national emergency. Why are you not sending that?"

"It's a Fifth Cousin assignment."

He startled the secretary by kissing the top of its head. "Yes. And no one will care. Send. And print out a copy of that and the recent Mentoring report. I don't know what day, I believe I only got one. And will you please stop grinding those damn metal teeth."

Once on the Fifth Floor, he had difficulties with the persistent A8, who couldn't grasp the complexities of a Third Cousin taking over the office of a Fifth Cousin, particularly when the Third Cousin said he was still a Third Cousin.

"Your mentor First Cousin Cheng must approve."

Kenuda pointed out the window, where the smoke continued curling from the smoldering stadium. "We're all busy."

The A8 reflected, eyes rolling in different directions over the suicidal frailty of humans. "I will send the notification, but process the efficacy of the request."

Kenuda followed the A8 into a spacious, expensively furnished office. Elias dully listened to the tutorial on the duties of a Fifth Cousin, pleased he remembered all of them, serve, love, family, dangers of the ego , and settled behind his wide desk, twice the size of his old office. He pursed his lips sadly, then brushed aside all that crap and opened a new messaging account while the A8 watched with polite suspicion.

"I have a few questions." Kenuda indicated the computer.

The A8 held up a small thumb drive. "The files are all here."

"I need some specific answers."

"You must first familiarize yourself with the entire area, Cousin. You should know…"

Kenuda slammed his fist onto the desk. "And you should appreciate the unusual request. I've shed my ego by going backwards. I don't have time for this. Now answer these questions or I'll send my own damn notifications."

The A8 tipped slightly to the left, but remained quiet.

"Good. There's a restaurant called Needleman's on East 188th Street. Is it properly serving the community's needs?"

The A8 blinked twice. "Since 2036."

"How inclined is the personnel?"

"Quite. They've only changed staff once."

Kenuda tensed. "When was the last time?"

"Fifteen days ago."

"Why did the staff change?"

The A8 shook its head. "Codified."

"Cousin Cheng must be careful." Kenuda smiled faintly. "I'm in charge here now."

"Not until I receive the official acknowledgement."

"Which we understand is a formality since by my presence, I'm in temporary oversight. Cousins Code 340-A."

"340-B," the 'bot said testily.

Kenuda tipped his head. "You will be invaluable. Did the restaffing have anything to do with the arrest of Dr. Pablo Diaz?"

The 'bot's eyes drooped in a frown. "The staff was changed before that."

"And how was his case disposed?" Kenuda handed over the Mentoring report. "This supersedes…"

"I understand, sir. Evidence in that case is currently held at the Dead Past Warehouse."

Kenuda broke another Cousins rule and ordered a private car. The bored young BT barely glanced at Kenuda's papers, leading him through the dank corridors and into the stifling elevator of the warehouse.

"How's it out there, sir?"

"Crazy."

"Think it was the Allahs?"

"Pardon?"

"The Allahs posing as Miners. Set us against each other again and then they swoop in for the final invasion." The BT stopped at a door. "Grandma wouldn't sell us out, would she?"

Kenuda assured him such a notion was preposterous. They walked into a chilly, dank room with tall ceilings and exposed pipes running along the chipped, white walls. Cages of carefully packed evidence filled the room. The BT indicated the direction with a quick nod, slowing down suddenly.

Pablo sat on a stool in a cage. Reaching inside, the BT compared the ticket on the request with the yellow evidence tag around Pablo's neck. Kenuda was appalled.

"Open the damn cage."

"All right, all right, I ain't got anything to do with this, sir."

Kenuda pushed aside the BT and knelt by Pablo. "Dr. Diaz?"

Pablo's eyes looked like they'd been bought at a novelty store.

"I been trying to feed him." The BT picked up a plate with an untouched sandwich.

"Release this man."

"It don't say release." The BT held up the consultative form issued by the A8.

"How will you explain him dying of malnutrition?" Kenuda rasped. The BT swallowed nervously. "Now take the damn cuffs off his leg."

The BT resentfully unlocked the chain. "He ain't shit or pissed since he been here, so watch for that."

Kenuda slipped his arm around Pablo's waist. The dentist's knees buckled slightly.

"It's okay, son. It's okay."

43

The area ten square miles around Grandma's House was locked down. Tanks re-directed Puppy and Mooshie through two security checkpoints beneath the circling 'copters they could see and rooftop snipers they couldn't. Fighter jets flew freely and convoys of Army trucks thundered down Moshulu Parkway. No soldiers. All Black Tops. Tens of thousands, darkening the landscape with their sullen visors. America was on war footing.

The crowds were the real problem. When he'd gone over the ceremony with Ian last night over a pitcher of beer at Monroe's, the director slyly mentioned yet another heated argument between Grandma and Cheng, as if there'd been many. He only spoke specifically about this one.

"The mother won't talk to emptiness. Her words, not mine." Ian made a face at the soggy chips. Monroe's was empty; no one dared curfew for a drink. Jimmy diffidently wiped the bar over and over.

"How can we let anyone near her again?"

"Is the point." Schrager held up a stubby finger. "All is well but don't let my children see me?"

"Then all is well?"

Ian gestured for him to lean forward. "I hear there was a clash near Iceland." Puppy frowned. "That's north of here, green eyes. The Allahs have mobilized. Our air force is in the air and yes, we have one. Sneaky little bastards. Least we'll go down humping. Or that could be shit. Also hear Grandma nearly ripped her pubic hair out when she heard we were on alert and made everyone stand down."

"So you're not sure of anything." Puppy couldn't resist a smirk.

"I'm sure I know what you and your pain in the ass fiancé are supposed to say and where the hell is she?"

She never showed for the pre-briefing. Mooshie drifted in and out, glazed like Ty and Mick. Worse, because they at least drank themselves into unconsciousness despite Puppy's assurances they'd all have jobs. Or something. But Mooshie turned vapor-like, slipping into bed, a stone with short breaths, slipping back out and leaving the apartment. She answered no questions, asked no questions, where she went, he didn't know.

At least Mooshie remembered the ceremony. Bright-eyed, up before the dawn, waiting for him to sleepily stumble into the living room.

"You wearing that crap?" She held out a steaming mug of coffee.

He stepped over Ty and Mick's snoring bodies, knotting the tie for his best suit. Blue, Ian had warned. Nothing too somber. Grandma wants to be positive.

"What're you wearing, snowflake?" He playfully tugged at her bathrobe.

"Something hot." She grew abruptly serious. "I don't want to go."

"You got to, Moosh. I'm not comfortable with this hero stuff either."

"But you really are one."

"You got us out of there."

"Because I knew about the tunnels." She laughed bitterly. "We should've met Miners down there."

He gave her a hard stare. "Was that the real plan to kill all of us?"

"No. But it could've worked out that way." She smiled distantly. "I don't like being a fraud."

"Really, Da-ra, Din-ton?"

Mooshie glowered. "I had to do that."

"And now you have to do this. We owe it."

"To who?"

"To the bodies being pulled out of the fucking stadium."

"There's always gonna be bodies pulled out of somewhere."

"Maybe eventually we'll get tired of it."

"You are hopeless."

"Yeah. Otherwise it makes no sense."

"Who said it's supposed to, Puppy? Grandma? God? The voice in your naïve little head?

You're taking this hero crap too seriously. I was a hero to someone my whole life. And here I am trying to figure out what dress to wear to a farce."

They passed the third checkpoint at the entrance to the House, where a trio of BTs triangulated them up a long, winding staircase and into a tiny elevator; Mooshie inspected her hair in the mirror.

"Do I look good, boys?" she asked the guards, who grunted. "I'll take that as a yes, as always."

Mooshie buried her hand into Puppy's and followed the BTs into Grandma's Living Room. A pot of tea and cookies waited on the coffee table.

"Are you nervous?" Puppy whispered.

Mooshie nodded at their script, tucked beneath the saucers. "This is pretty clear." *An honor to be part of our future. We showed we can come together.*

Grandma bustled in with an apologetic smile. The lines in her face had deepened and her voice was thin; she hugged them briefly and with little warmth. *She doesn't want to do this either.*

"Thank you for coming." Grandma stared at Mooshie, who squirmed slightly. "A good thing you didn't kill me. I've still got so much to do."

Puppy and Mooshie exchanged shocked looks. Cheng entered from a side door with a slight, almost sneering bow, and silently took a seat around the table. Grandma poured tea.

"Albert, I was just mentioning how grateful I was that Mooshie didn't kill me."

"I never meant to…" Mooshie's voice faltered.

"I know. But you would've if Puppy weren't in the way. Why do you still hate me, Mooshie? I was a great admirer of yours. Even when you criticized me. But you weren't that important, certainly not important enough to murder. Your friends did. They thought people listened to people like you." Grandma laughed harshly. "Even I didn't realize they were behind your murder until Derek Singh, or was it Easy Sun Yen, admitted it?"

"Singh," Cheng said, grunting.

"Thank you, Albert. Their suicide was a cover, apologies, but how else should we have handled that? With a public trial? Public execution? That only would've upset people. That's the problem with the past. Letting go. Which today is all about." Grandma neatly folded her hands. "Isn't that right, Albert?"

"Going forward," he said with a testy bite.

"Exactly. I want to thank both of you for coming. You're the face of hope. If we let this latest tragedy destroy hope, what do we have? There's been so much confusion the past couple days." She paused to gather her jumbled thoughts, forgetting they were there.

Albert shot them an embarrassed look. "Lenora, save your energy for the speech."

Grandma shook herself back into the room. "The speech, yes. We've bickered a little about that, haven't we, Albert?"

"A little."

"But I won."

"As always," he said sourly.

Grandma pulled aside a purple lace curtain to show waiting children miles deep. "Albert thought the city should be evacuated. That would've entailed enormous security concerns, what with the devils still around. We haven't caught them all, have we, Albert? All those billboards preaching Forgiveness. Oh, we worked so hard, didn't we? And no one listened."

"Now they will," Albert said gruffly.

"Yes." Grandma laid her hand on his shoulder. "Except it's such an odd thing, being the leader. You speak to many people and, after a while, realize that you can't persuade all of them. Some will simply never accept what needs to be done yet fascinatingly, they always have so many different reasons, right, Albert?"

Grandma sighed and refilled their cups, passing around the plate of cookies. "It's much simpler to lie. We've lied about the extent of the peace or rather, the quality of the peace. All of you," she gestured toward the lace curtain as if it were about to take a seat, "now know that it's worse than we admitted. Someone wanted to get that information out. They did a wonderful job, didn't they, Albert? So dramatic. But you covered up nicely. As always, my dear friend."

Grandma insisted Albert take a cookie; he bit warily.

"Now we need another little cover-up, which has actually gone quite well. The video with Abdullah and I. Do you children think it was a fake?"

Puppy and Mooshie exchanged vague looks. He slowly shook his head; Grandma gasped in mock surprise.

"My goodness, dear Puppy. Do you believe I'd jeopardize our Family?"

"No. I think you'd make a deal that would help everyone."

"Isn't that lovely. And Mooshie?"

"I don't know what to think."

"Honesty, please. Honesty."

"Lenora, we don't have time for this," Albert interrupted.

"Yeah, I think's it's real," Mooshie said.

"Good. Isn't that what our society is built upon? Honesty. Yet even I can't be fully honest. Even I have to cut some corners." She inhaled as if needing all the oxygen in the room. "Not anymore. Yes, the video is real. And I'm going to tell the world just that." Grandma tore up her speech. "It was a good try, Albert dear. But I can't let you have your way."

"I think you should reconsider, Lenora," he said very quietly.

"I can't." Her eyes watered. "You were my oldest friend along with Tomas. He's dead. You're a traitor. Those weren't Miners at the stadium. Maybe a few for cover, like Singh and Sun Yen. The rest were all Black Tops. Acting on your orders. I trusted you with my life, Albert."

"Everyone makes at least one big mistake in their life." Cheng pulled a Trayon pistol out of his pocket and calmly fired one shot that blew off Grandma's head, showering them all with blood.

"You shouldn't have done that, Puppy," Cheng clucked his tongue as if Puppy had spiled cookie crumbs. "But Mooshie failed to kill Grandma the first time. Love is touching sometimes."

Mooshie leaped for Albert, who clicked something in the palm of his hand, freezing her with a faint groaning noise.

Puppy stepped back, dazed.

"Excellent, don't you think? She's the highest quality we have." Cheng fluffed Mooshie's hair. "An A2. They'll last forever. We can create millions more with a snap of the fingers, now that we see how well they work. Thank you for helping us stage this trial run, Puppy. Maybe we can't turn out thirteen million just yet, but definitely there'll be enough to finish the job. Speaking of which."

As Albert pointed the pistol, Puppy dove to the floor. The bullet shattered a lamp. He reached for a piece of Grandma's skull and threw what he thought would be the last fastball of his career, hitting Cheng in the forehead; the First Cousin fell over the table.

Puppy scrambled to his feet. Alarms went off. He stroked Mooshie's still warm face and kissed her tenderly on the mouth.

"Oh Moosh." He clenched his groin.

Puppy knelt beside Grandma and squeezed her hand, pressing her fingertips to his lips, then flung his blood-splattered jacket onto the floor and hurried to the elevator. BTs stormed past. Puppy nodded politely, slipping into the elevator. He strolled down the staircase as if off to a gay party and through the white-trimmed double doors, where hundreds of thousands of children lined up waiting for Grandma and her honorees to come onto the patio beneath the huge purple "We Will Survive" banners.

"How's everyone?" Puppy pressed through the kids, who swarmed over him. Shaking hands, he walked with controlled hysteria around the far side of the House, ducking beneath the rose garden. Charged with keeping people out, not in, a diffident BT nodded at Puppy's badge and waved him along.

Sirens wailed. The 178th Street subway station was closed. He walked opposite the spectators, a puzzled murmur sweeping the crowd, and toward the 181th Street station, also closed. BT armored trucks roared past, knocking aside increasingly terrified people and dragging a woman ten feet before she fell off, dead.

Puppy lowered his head and ran down the steps of the station, leaping over the turnstiles and trotting along the tracks. He had no idea where he was going. He passed several shuttered stations before taking an emergency exit off to the left, up the filthy steps and shoving open a rusting manhole cover.

Hysterical crowds screamed and cried. Overhead a vidscreen flashed his face.

ASSASSIN.

"Puppy Beisbol." Clary jumped into his arms and smothered him with kisses.

"Well, you really did it this time, Pup." Annette shook her head.

He was stunned. "What the hell are you doing here?

"Barcelona wanted to see you give your speech."

Cheng's voice boomed "...a treacherous murder by the terrorist Puppy Nedick..."

A couple siblings looked at him in growing recognition. Puppy pressed Clary against his face for cover and they pushed into the pulsating crowd. His face flashed everywhere, his name almost chanted. Puppy. Grandma. Murderer. He stopped Clary from applauding.

Near Fordham Road, Clary scrambled out of his arms like a twitchy dog. She waited until a gray-wigged A24 vendor commiserated with grieving siblings, then snatched three sunglasses off the lower shelf. Clary happily fussed with the oversized glasses, turning every which way to see the world in this new way.

Annette lowered the shades down her nose and gave Puppy a look that said don't even begin to ask about this child.

"We have to get off the streets," Puppy whispered over another deafening wave of anguish as Grandma's face filled the screens. Clary hummed the Grandma Muertas song.

Down the block, three BTs jumped out of a truck and ran toward them, rifles raised.

Puppy pulled Clary onto his back and grabbed Annette's hand.

"We have to hood."

"We're too old."

Three shots missed them, but hit some siblings. More panic as the crowds ran from the BTs.

Puppy hopped on the first car hood, Annette grudgingly throwing away her expensive heels. As they jumped onto the second car, Clary suddenly bounded ahead, squealing with delight. They hooded five cars, before finally losing the shooting BTs on Sherman Avenue.

• • • •

CLARY PUT HER fingers to her lips as they walked into Zelda's living room.

"Quiet. Or polizia." She made soft machine gun noises.

Annette tossed the keys on a chair and wearily gestured to keep the lights off, lighting a couple pine-scented candles. Clary made some sad looking sandwiches, which Puppy greedily ate, while Annette laid out an oversized shirt and baggy pants.

He returned to the living room in Zelda's clothes; Annette stared at the vidnews.

"You never told me about your father."

Puppy slowly turned. Alvin Nedick's face wasn't the drunk, dissipated Alvin Nedick, but a confident, slightly scary man in his thirties with cold eyes.

"…Nedick's father Alvin was a member of the Blue Wigs, a cruel sub-group of Miners responsible for a series of armed robberies," the somber presenter said.

Puppy shook his head. "Can't be."

"Why would they say it?"

"To make me look worse. He was a drunk. A useless fucking drunk." Except when he was a Marine; the thought made him angrier. He knocked the last of the sandwiches onto the floor. Clary swore in Spanish.

"Honey, why don't you play games in the other room?" Annette picked up the food.

Clary frowned. "Puppy's Papa?"

"Si."

"No," he yelled. "Fake Puppy's Papa. Lies."

Annette gave him a warning yank on his sleeve. "Clary, go play. We'll talk about Puppy's Papa later."

Clary saw she could only take this so far and skipped into the bedroom, adjusting her sunglasses. Annette waited until she heard the sound of screeching tires of a vidgame and pulled him onto the couch beside her.

"Tell me one more time you didn't do this."

"I'm not answering that question, Annette. You above all people should know better."

"People do screwy things and have one moment of madness. Maybe this was it." She paused. "I'm just making sure. Please. I need to hear it."

"I didn't kill Grandma."

"I'm glad to hear that." He rolled his eyes. "Since you're not a terrorist, want to tell me what happened?"

He gave her everything, pausing to massage her toes.

"I thought I was in trouble, but this is really the worst thing you've ever gotten yourself into."

He stared at another photo of his father, this time in a blue wig. Puppy found a stash of Omaha cabernet behind pots in the kitchen. He plopped back onto the couch, feet stretched over Annette's knees.

"Thanks for hiding me," he finally said.

"Did you think I'd just abandon you?" she asked angrily. "Shallow selfish Annette?"

He didn't hesitate. "No. So what about your day?"

Annette filled him in. "I'm sure I face some charges."

"For what? Escaping terrorists?" He frowned at the vidnews. "They haven't mentioned Mooshie."

"She wasn't human."

He thought a moment. "No one knew that. Why not throw her in? Or say she was killed. Or a co-assassin."

"I think you have other things to worry about besides robots, Puppy."

They shared a moment of total bewilderment, finishing the bottle.

"You can only hide here for so long until they come looking."

"I know," he said.

"I mean, I can't stay here, either." She smiled at the sounds of the video game. "They'll take the demon child."

Puppy tilted his head, grinning. "You're protecting Clary?"

She reddened. "Get that look off your face. Zelda made me promise. I keep my promises, Puppy. You know how ethical I am. I never cheated on you or lied. You always knew what you had."

"What we had."

"For a while," she said, picking a photograph of them on the roller coaster at Rye Playland off the shelf. "Zelda has a lot of pictures of us."

"We're her friends," he said softly.

Annette nodded and returned with a blanket and pillow; she made up the couch and kissed him on the head.

"Are you going to watch yourself on the news all night?'

"Well yeah."

In a few minutes, Clary marched into the room and sat on the chair, staring disapprovingly. The vidnews reported the uncontrollable mourning sweeping the country with Cheng in the foreground of every report, shouting that the Allahs were now believed behind this assassination and urging all good Americans to come together.

"I'm issuing an immediate amnesty to all baseball fans and soldiers." Cheng sneered into the camera.

Of course you are, Puppy thought.

"Go sleep." Clary pointed at the bedroom door.

"I'm staying out here."

"Annette esposa." Clary made thrusting gestures with her hips.

Puppy blushed. "No esposa. I sleep here. You and Annette in there."

Clary sighed in disappointment. "Donde Grampa Ty and Grampa Mickey?"

He swallowed hard. If Mooshie were a 'bot, so were they. Cheng would come after them, too.

The girls's mouth curled in hatred as a vid of Grandma returned to the screen. "Bravo, Puppy." She made a gun out of his hand. "Muerta, Grandma."

He moved Clary onto the couch, struggling a moment on how to phrase the question. "Why does Clary hate Grandma?"

Clary's eyes welled. "Grandma say Crusaders...say Crusaders matar Allahs." She swung her thick hair around angrily. "But Allahs matar Crusaders. Grandma lie. Mama and Papa..."

Puppy held her tightly, but just for a moment until Clary, embarrassed, wiggled free. She slammed the bedroom door. In a moment, Annette popped her head out.

"What'd you do to her?"

"I lost the war."

He turned up the volume as a breaking news report showed an Allah warship sinking off the coast of Iceland.

• • • •

PUPPY FINISHED THE last of the food for their breakfast, frying up Edison Crackers with a pitiful onion. At least the vidnews only flashed his face every fifteen minutes now. HELP US FIND HIM. Simmering riots in Dallas and ceasefires in the Midwest took priority. He was already old news, Puppy thought grimly.

"Got everything?" he asked, waiting for Annette to clean up the dishes and sweep the floor before they slipped out of the apartment down back alleys and over conjoined roof tops above the deadened Bronx. Annette added a few shortcuts of her own, delighted by his surprise. As they paused around the corner of the stout and stately building, his ex silently gestured for him to adjust the hoodie further over his face.

"Well hello Adam." Annette gave the A31 doorman a quick kiss on the cheeks.

"Ma'am." The 'bot tipped its cap. "We missed you."

"I've been busy building a shoe empire." Annette nudged Clary in front. "This is my niece Clary."

The girl curtsied, eyes widening as the 'bot patted her head.

"Cute." It frowned toward Puppy, calculating. "And you, sir?"

"My brother Pierre." She arched an eyebrow at Puppy, who sunk behind the sunglasses. "It's his first time in the big city."

"Shame you've come under such tragic circumstances."

"Lovely to see you again, Adam," Annette said in a gush. "I'll wait for my fiancé upstairs."

"He's already there," the 'bot called as they hurried across the marble lobby and into the elevator to the twentieth floor.

While Puppy hid in an alcove down the hall, Kenuda hugged Annette, tossing Clary a puzzled look.

"See, I'm not dead at all," Annette said brightly, frantically waving Puppy into the apartment. He slipped off the hoodie and tossed the sunglasses, feeling strangely defiant.

Kenuda stared, shocked.

"Now Elias," Annette started. "We need to explain…"

With a wild cry, Kenuda drove his thick forearm into Puppy's throat and slammed him into the wall.

"Stop it," Annette screamed and jumped on Kenuda's back while Clary chomped into his thigh.

"I didn't do it," Puppy wheezed, feet off the ground.

"Liar," Kenuda snarled.

"He's not lying." Annette clawed at Kenuda's eyes; he flung her against the couch and shook Clary across the room. Kenuda balled his fists and charged Puppy.

"It was Cheng." Puppy coughed. "He killed her."

Kenuda froze. "What?"

On the vidnews, Albert thundered about vengeance against their real enemies to hysterical applause and the chant of "Kill Allahs, Kill Allahs."

"Cheng," Puppy repeated. "He shot Grandma."

Kenuda's face clouded as he stared at Cheng, now invoking the memory of Grandma by telling the wild crowd that their beloved Lenora had finally decided to finish the job before the assassin Puppy and his Allah allies murdered her.

Elias finally settled his internal debate with a brisk nod. "He set you up." His jaw tightened. "He's setting everyone up."

"So do you believe Puppy or do I have to let her go?" Annette held back the growling Clary.

Kenuda nodded, rubbing his thigh.

Puppy filled him in while Annette found more food for Clary, who slowly speared potatoes drenched in catsup, wary eyes never leaving Kenuda. He paced around the couch like an electric train.

"The orders are to shoot you on sight."

"All of us?" Annette asked, frightened.

"Just him. But..." Kenuda gestured helplessly. "Clearly anyone who harbors Puppy..." his voice trailed off; they all stared at Clary.

"I won't put anyone at risk anymore," Puppy stood.

"Sit down, you fool," Kenuda snapped. "I'm already halfway under the wheels." He slowly let out all the air in his body like a tire going flat, beckoning Puppy.

"You two, stay."

Light from the hallway spilled onto Pablo's blank face. Kenuda firmly closed the door, giving Puppy a moment to regain his legs. He sat on the edge of the bed and held Pablo's hand.

"Oh Pablo," he whispered.

Pablo stared at the wall.

"It's Puppy." Puppy kept his eyes on his friend. "What did they do to him?"

"I don't know. He was in BT custody. The damn diner. 'Bots. Waiters, Mooshie. They never shut the program down." Kenuda sighed. "I think he can hear."

"How do you know?"

"I've tried asking him questions. He reacts without saying anything."

Puppy stared deep into Pablo's dark eyes. "Are you in there?"

His right eye blinked twice.

Yes.

"Can you gesture?"

One blink. No.

Tears slid down Pablo's cheeks.

"He's also done that a few times," Kenuda said hoarsely.

"What did they do to you?"

"Come on, man, do you expect him to answer that?"

Puppy gestured. Are you okay.

One blink.

Did they hurt you.

One blink. Two blinks. One blink.

Are you scared.

Two blinks. Puppy stifled a sob and opened his palm to show the marble. Puppy didn't even bother holding back the tears anymore.

"Let him rest." Kenuda took Puppy back into the living room, where he handed out stiff bourbons to the adults and a fizzy cola to Clary. "We've got to get you away, Puppy."

"Both of us," Annette said firmly.

"Certainly not," Kenuda said.

"Absolutely," Puppy agreed.

Annette lashed them with a hard stare. "I'm glad you decided for dumb Annette. But I'm as big a criminal as he is."

"Not quite. I did supposedly kill Grandma," Puppy said dryly.

"I helped you escape."

"We can sweep that aside," Kenuda said.

"Can you protect me anymore, Elias?"

After a pause, he shook his head sadly.

"Maybe you and I could discuss this privately," Puppy said softly.

"Don't you want me?" she asked, hurt.

"I guess I have no choice."

"Well gee, thanks for that."

Puppy and Kenuda exchanged comradely I've-been-there looks. The Commissioner disappeared into his study. Annette glared at Puppy.

"What?" he asked.

"You could act more excited that I'm coming. Like just a little."

Returning, Kenuda cleared his throat with a faint smile, relieved it was Puppy on the end of this Annette barrage, and handed them each a thin envelope. "There's an emergency protocol now. All Cousins receive travel passes to anywhere in the country."

"I just keep running until they catch me?"

"Us," Annette corrected him.

"What good does that do?" Puppy asked Kenuda. "And how does that stop Cheng?"

"Okay Puppy, now you want to kill the First Cousin?" Annette asked, alarmed.

"Someone better," Kenuda said grimly.

"You can."

Kenuda nodded to himself, glancing at F-26 fighters taking off on the vidnews. "There are also other protocols that can be implemented in an emergency. Every First, Second and Third Cousin had a corresponding contact outside the country in case something blew up. They're called Collectors. I believe because they all own antique shops featuring the shattered Judeo-Christian world." He laughed bitterly. "Mine's in London."

"I've always wanted to go to England," Annette said cheerfully.

"Good. Because there's a plane," Kenuda said. Their mouths dropped. "Leaves once a week from Westchester. That's all this says." Elias dropped another packet onto the coffee table.

"A plane. Okay. So I, sorry, we go to London. Then what?"

"You stop World War Four and a nuclear holocaust."

"Well put, Elias. You've totally appealed to Puppy's sense of destiny," Annette said.

Clary made rat-tat-tat sounds at a F-26 shooting down a Holy Drone. The adults pursed their lips. Puppy sat beside the little girl.

"Bang bang. Crusaders matar Allah," he said softly.

"Si. Finalmente." Clary threw up her hands expressively.

"But matar bad. Puppy stop it."

"No, matar Allahs." She bared her teeth.

He shook her shoulders. "Too many die. Puppy's amigos. Clary's amigos. Clary's Mama. Clary's Papa." Her mouth quivered. "No more matar."

Clary was unconvinced, staring sullenly.

Annette sat on the other side. "Puppy and I go."

The girl sighed wearily and started putting on her shoes, muttering darkly.

Annette took away the sneaker. "Honey, we have to go alone."

Clary's eyebrows knitted angrily. "No Clary?"

"Too dangerous. Bang, bang," Puppy said.

"Clary not scared. Clary help."

"You stay here and we'll come back," Annette said.

Clary's eyes flitted between them. Her mother had told her not to worry. Her father had told her not to worry. And where was Zelda and el bebe? She snatched back the sneaker and continued lacing up.

"Clary go." She calmly put on her coat and adjusted her sunglasses. "No matar Allahs." She curtsied. "Clary nice to Allahs."

Annette cupped Clary's face to stop it from shaking no. "We love you." She looked at Puppy. "How do you say we love you in Spanish?"

"You just did." Puppy hugged the tearful Clary. "You stay with Uncle Kenuda."

Clary made a feral sound and stared hungrily at the Third Cousin's shin.

• • • •

ANNETTE COMPLAINED INCESSANTLY as they edged down the Grand Concourse at three in the morning. It was cold. It was windy. Her back hurt from carrying the backpack stuffed with clothes. She had blisters on her feet. The sneakers were ugly.

If so much weren't at stake, she would've welcomed the butt end of a BT's rifle.

"You have your ID right?"

Puppy patted his jacket pocket.

"And the passes?"

"Yes, Annette," he said impatiently, ducking beneath a bent light pole.

"Can I see them?"

"No."

"I think I should hold them."

"I'm not ten years old." They turned left down the hill on 161st Street and walked a block in silence except for Annette's soft obscenities.

"Are you upset about your father?"

"Please."

"I'm just making conversation."

"Quiet would be better in a shoot on sight curfew."

"Were you surprised?"

Puppy flushed. "I told you. It's bullshit. He was a disgusting person. The Miners couldn't be that desperate."

"I never met him."

"Because he was already dead."

"They never showed you the body after they supposedly found him in an alley."

He whirled. "Are you saying he's still alive?"

"I don't know. You didn't know he was a terrorist."

"He wasn't a damn terrorist."

Annette leaned on his shoulder and rubbed her calf. "His brother came to our wedding. Your Uncle Clem."

He resumed walking and she nearly fell.

"We wouldn't let him in." Annette hobbled after him. "Me, Zelda and Pablo. We figured it would upset you too much. He gave us a present."

Puppy waited for her to catch up. "Are you going to tell me it was an orange wig, boom, proof of my father's secret life?"

"No. The present was from Clem. Your father was supposedly already dead." She made an annoyed sound and rubbed her other calf, warning him with a glare not to move again. "It was a toaster. I figured it'd bother you so I gave it to Pablo. I guess he gave it to Zelda because she still has it. That's how you grilled up the last piece of bread today."

He laughed at the nonsense of it all.

"I forgot to tell you," she said.

"You forget nothing."

Annette pressed a tissue against her face from the stench of smoldering bodies. "It stinks."

He didn't care. Puppy took Annette's hand, but she refused to move.

"Where do you think you're going?"

"To say good-bye."

"Just wave." She showed him a cheerful wave. "Good-bye Yankee Stadium. You crushed my dreams and helped wreck my marriage. Now you crushed my heart again. How's that?"

Puppy glowered. "Okay, stay out. I'll be back soon."

Annette considered the piles of debris and weapons shells, a perfect playground for the family of rats crawling towards her. She pulled alongside Puppy by Gate Six.

"I hate you for this."

"I know." He shushed her.

"Someone's still here?"

"Probably not." 'Bots were punctual about work days; no humans were involved in the cleanup.

He guided Annette over a mound of broken concrete and into the ballpark. Large burn marks carpeted the ground. Holes gauged the walls and floors. Like opening day, he thought sadly.

"Are we done now?"

Annette didn't like the way he laughed. She stubbed her toe twice and scratched her elbow breaking a fall on the first level. Puppy was oblivious. He walked around like the lights were on and the crowd was cheering.

Puppy took shallow breaths and dragged her to a narrow clump of infield grass not buried beneath the pavement; the 'bots had started pouring concrete over the field, sealing in the memories. All around, the seats were smashed, the dugouts non-existent except for the shards of the water fountains. The right side of the upper deck was completely blown off and the completely fallen scoreboard smothered both bullpens.

"Why must you torture yourself?" Annette gently touched his arm.

He ignored her, looking around. Frecklie's banners fluttered at the top of the left field stands. She followed his stare.

"No Puppy, forget it."

Annette was sweating and swearing when they finally reached Section 340. She plopped onto a creaky seat and stubbornly folded her arms. He kissed her cheek. "Catch me if I fall."

"That's not funny." She followed him up the aisle. He stopped five rows from the top, then took a running jump, grabbing onto the brocade.

"What the hell are you doing?" Annette shouted several times as he lifted himself high enough to snatch the Cubs and Yankees banners off the flag poles. Puppy dangled for a moment, looking down into the dark Bronx.

Something sizzled and he quickly jumped off. A lone light bulb flickered, somehow set off by his climbing.

"I do not ever want you doing that again," Annette said shakily.

"Ssh. Look. The light."

"Oh, do you want to take a bulb to London, too, assuming we're not shot in a few minutes." Annette stared at his lopsided grin. "What, Puppy, what?"

He threw debris at the lights, admiring his work from several different angles. Annette gave up understanding and obstinately ate their only candy bar. Finally, Puppy led her down to the second level.

"I saw some bodies." Annette panted outside the control room.

"Probably." Puppy shoved aside the rocks from the door. "Can you help me?"

"You mean move those big rocks?"

Puppy fumbled on the floor behind the console, which was still plugged in. He remembered the A21's tutorial. Two different lines, one external, one internal. He searched another couple minutes and found the black circuit breaker. He turned on the switch and the console coughed.

Lights on the upper left field deck flickered and died. Come on, please, come on, he gently rubbed the console. A few more lights stayed on, then spread, popping like gunfire in the silence; Annette watched in amazement.

"How did you make that work, Puppy?"

"I prayed." He grinned.

The lights spelled 4GIVE, surrounded by the broken bulbs.

In the black, moonless night ordered by First Cousin Cheng, Acting Parent of the Family, it was easy to see the lights. Maybe someone went to the bathroom or quieted their child or hushed a barking dog and told a neighbor. Soon the rooftops of the Bronx were filled with silent, awed crowds spilling into the streets. The BTs couldn't kill everyone. Besides, they were watching, too.

At dawn, fighter jets finally demolished Yankee Stadium.

44

The Westchester Airport terminal was black with BT uniforms as if a world of bugs had crawled out of the vents. The BT fingered their IDs.

"Commissioner Kenuda, what brings you here?"

"Government business."

"We're all on government business, sir."

Puppy stiffened, waiting for the roar of three fighter jet formations to pass. "Then you know I can't answer that."

The BT glanced at Annette, slightly wide-eyed at being in an airport for the first time. "And you, ma'am?"

"I'm with my fiancé." She hoisted her engagement ring a defiant inch from the visor. "Papers."

Annette sourly handed over their betrothal agreement which the BT studied, never raising his mask. He handed it back and stared a little longer at Puppy.

He held his breath. Similar physique, just a shade different coloring than Elias. Who'd expect the assassin of Grandma to calmly walk into a BT base?

The Black Top lifted its visor; Annette gasped slightly. The 'bot's pale veiny face surrounded large, blue metallic eyes circling clockwise and counter-clockwise. Silver lips pursed intently, flaring the thin, sharp nose, deliberating for an agonizing few seconds.

The BT returned the papers. "Cargo plane's to the left, Commissioner. Gate 1A."

Annette gave the 'bot a last frightened look as they turned down a corridor.

"It had a face, Puppy," she whispered.

He waited for a squad of BTs to pass with brief salutes. Millions, Cheng had promised. Puppy looked at the swarm of Black Tops and shivered.

An impatient A39 with a thick furry hat scowled as they climbed the steps into the stripped down Mohawk 205, giving their IDs a diffident glance.

"I gotta schedule here. Hurry up. Buckle in."

The faceless 'bot waited until they navigated around four burlap sacks and strapped into raggedy jump seats, then grumbled at his watch and disappeared into the cockpit. The plane bounced down the runway and rose shakily into the air.

"Is it going to be like this all the way?" Annette was pale.

"I hope not."

Neither of them had ever flown. Like obedient children, they sat quietly, desperate to pee, seriously considering vomiting, until the 'bot returned and yanked off its hat, grinning meanly.

"First-timers, huh?"

Annette nodded. "I really have to go to the bathroom."

"Who's stopping you?" He grumpily pushed aside Annette's fumbling fingers and undid the belt; she lurched into the bathroom holding her mouth. The 'bot frowned. "She better clean up."

Puppy smiled over Annette's loud retching. "How long's the flight?"

"Five hours." The 'bot held up its hand. "I been delivering the mail for thirty years. Never had a problem."

Puppy frowned. "Mail?"

"What the hell did you think was in there?" The 'bot's eyes rotated angrily as Annette heaved again. "What kind of supervisor are you?"

"A badly informed one." Puppy managed a weak smile. "So Americans can write to people in Muslim Europe?"

The 'bot looked like its head was about to blow up, aggravated by Annette stumbling back into her seat, head between her legs, moaning.

"Why not? Grandma insisted it be part of the truce. You really don't know nothing, do you?"

Puppy shrugged and rubbed Annette's neck; she suddenly looked up at the 'bot, horrified.

"Who's flying the plane?"

"It's on automatic. Don't worry," it snarled as Annette's forehead touched the cold floor. "Ain't never crashed yet."

They heard the 'bot chuckling in the cockpit over that one for a while. Slowly Annette sat up.

"How are you not sick?" she asked wonderingly.

"The power of being a Third Cousin." Puppy pulled a bag over. "You got a blade?"

"If I did, I would've cut my throat already."

Puppy tugged on the bag, but it was tied too tightly.

"It's private mail, Puppy." With an exasperated sigh, Annette slid a thin finger into the knot and together they yanked open the bag.

"What if it catches us?"

"I guess we learn to parachute."

Puppy draped his jacket over her shivering body and opened a letter addressed to PFC Karen Bishop.

"It's to a soldier," he said. Annette wanly rested her chin on his shoulder, reading along.

"'Dearest Karen, Everyone is fine here. Gramps is recovering from that scare with his heart. Too much chocolate cake I say. Regina's going to farming school up in Waukuh. Hope they're treating you well. Love, Dad.'"

Annette reached into the bag and opened an envelope addressed to Lt. T'hom W'ashington. A photo fell onto her lap. She read softly, "'My T'hom, Jonas had a wonderful birthday. He got a ton of presents. Let me know if the sweater fits. Love 'J'ames.'"

They studied the photo of a little boy with dark curly hair and sad eyes. Puppy pulled out a handful of envelopes. "All to soldiers."

Annette frowned helplessly at the filthy floor and carefully joined him on her hands and knees, tossing aside more envelopes. "We don't have soldiers in ME anymore, do we?"

"Not with guns." He thought a second and ripped open a few more letters, reading quickly. "All these letters are like the soldiers are still on duty. Shit, Annette. Shit. They must be POWs."

"Weren't they all returned after the war?"

"Guess not."

"How much did Grandma forget to tell us, Puppy?"

He was too exhausted to consider that. They fell asleep in each other's arms for a few hours, woken by the clattering of a metal dish dropped at their feet.

"We land in half an hour." The 'bot shuffled back into the cockpit.

They about inhaled the powdered eggs and dry toast, strapping back in as the cargo plane drifted over the brown and green English countryside, decay clearly winning. Wilted crops guarded crumbling farmhouses, sleek trucks and cars indifferently whizzing past on wide, modern highways as if on two disconnected worlds.

The plane skirted a broad billboard where a menacing Allah pointed a sword at a helpless woman, his words lost in the language, though not the meaning.

Annette shuddered and pressed into Puppy.

Ahead lay a long field nestled between brown trees. Landing gear reluctantly groaned and they touched down with several big bounces before taxiing to a halt. The side door opened and the 'bot tossed the bags outside, scrambling down the ladder to hoist four new identical bags back into the hull.

"Whatcha waiting for?" he snapped. "Get out, unless you're coming back with me."

Puppy peered past him at the tree line. "Here?"

"Same as always. They don't like when I stay."

"Who's they?" Annette buttoned her coat.

The 'bot shook its head pityingly and handed them a clipboard. "Hope the flight was in order. I'd appreciate getting a rating. I got a perfect record."

Puppy scrawled a quick note about the comfort of the ride and hopped down, reaching up for Annette.

The 'bot smiled, pleased by Puppy's endorsement. "Train station's a mile down the road that way, I hear. Good luck."

The A39 pulled the ladder up and, inside of a minute, the Mohawk took off. Puppy felt a chill and it wasn't from the wind.

They hurried towards the trees as a battered truck with a crescent moon and star on its panels roared toward the mailbags. Crouching behind a sad tree, they watched a thin Allah cheerfully toss the bags into the back of the truck, singing loudly before jumping back behind the wheel. He playfully drove around in a figure eight as if this were his first time behind a wheel. After a few more wild spins, the Allah drove off.

Walking on the makeshift path, they easily found the main road a quarter of a mile away and followed the sign, Landan, 5.3 km. A tiny yellow car which looked like it belonged in a child's playroom puttered past. Honking arrogantly, a long black vehicle nearly drove it off the road. This was repeated several times, small cars driven by Westerners honked at and, if need be, bumped out of the way by ones driven by Allahs.

They squeezed each other's hands that much tighter and joined the queue winding back out of the train station. Puppy steered Annette toward the passenger line marked by a cross with a red X, guarded by sneering Allahs in black robes.

As the train chugged into the station, Allahs rushed forward, taking all the cars except the last. None of their compartments were remotely crowded. A guard barked a guttural sound supported by waving rifles to hurry the non-Allahs into the rear car.

They could barely turn in the packed car drenched with sweat and stale breath. A conductor, mouth curling at such close contact with Crusaders, snapped his fingers in the doorway and tickets or money were passed down. He didn't worry that anyone would cheat since that was, along with approximately four hundred and fifty-two other infidel infractions, punishable by death.

Annette gave Puppy a weary brave smile and leaned against his arm. He stroked her hair. Several people stirred uneasily.

A ruddy-faced man in a worn suit leaned over, whispering, "Best not, mate. Public affection."

Puppy nudged Annette off. She could barely stand. Puppy gave the man a grateful smile and glanced out the window. Just outside the London city limits, they passed a billboard of a Union Jack smothered by the crescent moon and star. The message was translated.

Allahu Akbar.

More signs flanked the tracks as they rolled into Charing Cross Station, mainly commercials of happy Allahs enjoying wondrous cigarettes or comfy furniture. Loudspeakers in the massive terminal shouted mainly in Arabic with occasional brief, almost taunting breaks in English.

Puppy and Annette walked up and down a pathway of food stores, trying to understand signs.

The ruddy-faced man came up to Puppy's left shoulder. "You look bloody suspicious, mate." He nodded toward the Allah armed patrols. "They'd love an excuse to shoot you. That's good for their morale. Just keep walking."

"We're looking for the subway," Annette said quietly.

"Tube," the man corrected her, smiling faintly. "Where are you going?"

Puppy closed his eyes a moment to remember. "Great Jones Street."

The man's eyes narrowed. "What's the business there?"

"Shopping," Annette said brightly.

He smiled again. "Excellent choice. Take the gray line four stops and get off at Martyrs Lane. Great Jones Street's two blocks south."

"Thank you." Annette stopped the man. "Where's the bathroom?"

"Ladies' toilet is down the corridor," the man said in a loud voice as a three-man patrol passed.

The tube was like the train like the road and, as they realized, like the very streets, Crusaders shouldering aside to allow Allahs to pass. They waited five minutes for giggling teens talking loudly into those strange handheld phones to haughtily allow them onto the subway platform.

Annette squeezed Puppy's shoulder so tightly his arm ached. She nodded, stunned, at a poster of him behind the cross-marked benches. He was exultant in his baseball uniform, eyes skyward; at his feet lay Grandma. No need to translate the Arabic words.

"At least not everyone hates you, honey."

He could only shake his head.

They walked up the tube steps onto Martyrs Lane as the sun started its descent. Carefully keeping as far from the main Allah sidewalk as possible, they strolled casually along the high street boasting colorfully decorated windows touting expensive goods, before turning as instructed along Great Jones Street, where the English stores seemed blighted by comparison.

A sprightly bell tinkled over The Dead Past. Two burqas huddled over a counter, dark eyes narrowing in the slits. The owner, a squat man with wispy gray hair, frowned and flicked his hand, indicating Puppy and Annette should wait outside, returning with an obsequious smile to his customers.

They waited nervously at the edge of the alley in the fading light before walking up and down the street, window shopping.

"Who'd eat that?' Annette whispered at shriveled vegetables tossed in a basket outside a grocery mart, as if the proprietor was angry about selling such crap. A fat man with a funny hat growled in Arabic and they stepped aside. Even the Westerner path was subject to Allah ownership. Everything was subject to Allah ownership, Puppy thought, catching a glimpse of skyscrapers festooned in that squiggly lettering peering out of the darkening clouds.

The burqas passed as if Puppy and Annette were invisible; they casually re-entered the store. The owner wasn't happy to see them.

"Don't you know better?" he snapped. "They could've burnt down my store just for you coming in when an Arab customer's here."

He turned his back. Puppy leaned against the counter while Annette nearly pressed her face against the glass covered jewelry display.

"What do you want?" the man scowled.

"We're friends of Grandma."

The man barely reacted save for a slight twitch of his lower lip. "That's no friend of mine. I've got to close."

"Not yet."

"I said go." The owner polished a silver teapot, wishing he could get rid of Puppy and Annette as easily as the smudge.

"Do you know who he is? Puppy Nedick." Annette laid her elbows on the counter. "Make the happy face, Pup."

"What face?"

"Like the poster. That picture must've been after you struck someone out."

Puppy spread his mouth in a deranged clown smile. The owner stepped back, terrified by the recognition.

"Get out."

"Please. You have to help."

The owner picked up a fireplace poker. "Now."

Annette wrenched the poker out of his hand. "He didn't do it. We got here on the mail plane."

"What plane?" The man sunk deeper into confusion and fear.

"It doesn't matter," Puppy said. "Listen. Albert Cheng killed Grandma."

"Bastard. Always was one. I tried telling her once, but I think Grandma loved him." The man's face colored with anger. "I can't help. I've been cut off."

"Meaning?"

"The Paris and Berlin Collectors are also down. Probably everyone in the whole bloody ME. The Allahs let us operate to keep information going, even if it was distorted. Anyone I knew who could tell me what's happening in your country has vanished. I was planning on slipping away myself."

"You know more than us."

He frowned, perplexed again. "Why are you here? There are safer places to hide. South America. Africa."

"I don't want to hide. I want to contact the Mufti's son and let him know there are people in America who don't want another war."

"Who knows if he's even alive?" The owner made a cautious face and they fell silent until an Allah couple stopped window browsing and moved on. "The Mufti could be dead. Or the Son. There are all sorts of rumors. I do know there was a rebellion near Dublin. Bad battle between the Irish Martyrs Brigade and Holy Warriors."

"We've still got soldiers in the field?"

The man shook his head and spit-polished a smudge on the glass. "Converts. Supposedly. God love the Irish, pretending all these years, just waiting. From what I hear, they gave the Camels a good pasting before vanishing. But the Allahs torched Dublin in retaliation."

"So everyone's fighting everyone?" Annette asked.

"It could be isolated. Or not. Certainly Abdullah and his father. How much…." His voice trailed off. "Their news is piping up about the battle near Iceland, but that's a lot of bollocks. They're using old footage."

"Least that's something," Puppy murmured.

"We can't get to the Allahs anymore."

"But Puppy's a hero here," Annette jumped in.

"I won't be an Allah hero." Puppy snapped.

"You already are."

The owner cleared his throat, waiting until they simmered down. "There is John. He could help."

He scribbled an address on a slip of paper. "This is the only contact info I have for his people. He's in Rome. Or somewhere in Italy, if he's still alive. He and Abdullah recently spoke. I just know, trust me." He held up his hand. "Yes, John could help."

"Why?" Puppy asked.

The owner took a deep breath. "He was the last Pope."

The window-browsing couple bustled in noisily.

"I can only offer ten quid for your filthy heresies. Take it or leave it." The owner brusquely dismissed them, greeting the Allahs with a careful smile. "Masa al-khayr."

Two jeeps overflowing with black-robed soldiers chased the English off the streets, brandishing rifles and shouting. Puppy and Annette ducked down an alley, crouching behind a garbage can.

"Italy was famous for leather goods," Annette said hopefully, making him laugh. They drifted asleep for a moment.

"Hiding?" A long-faced man in a black robe tottered towards them, a whip at his belt.

"No sir," Annette said casually. "We're just getting out of the way."

"Nah." The man grinned fiendishly. "You're hiding. Papers?" He stank of alcohol.

"Left them in the flat," Puppy said firmly. "We'll be heading home now."

"Curfew." He weaved slightly. "No papers, you die. Allah will be pleased."

The whip curled around Annette's shoulders; she fell with a scream. The Allah pulled a long knife from his boot and lunged at Puppy, who punched him in the mouth. The Allah toppled against the garbage can. Puppy wrapped the whip around the man's throat, tightening the leather until the Allah's eyes nearly popped out of their sockets.

Puppy kicked the dead man in the head.

"Shit, Puppy, shit," Annette moaned at the blood oozing out of Puppy's side. He blanched and sat down, watching with dull eyes as Annette ripped apart the corpse's robe, tying it around Puppy's side.

She wrapped her arms around Puppy's waist and dragged his leaden body down the alley. Annette stopped twice to make sure he was still breathing. They staggered down a narrow cobble-stoned street of tightly packed houses. She kicked at doors, crying for help.

A door finally opened slightly.

"Please, help."

The Allah woman frowned at the blood falling outside her neat flower pots. She hesitated, then nodded them inside.

Annette couldn't hold up Puppy anymore and he collapsed to his knees. A wiry old man hopped out of a battered armchair a few feet from a loud vidscreen and shouted at the pretty young woman, who shouted back. She and Annette carried Puppy into the bathroom and laid him on a thin rug. The woman jerked her head for Annette to leave.

"No way."

"Go," the woman said coldly. "Or you both leave."

Annette wanted to smack the woman silly, but Puppy gestured weakly and she reluctantly left. The old man yelled at her.

The woman tore away Puppy's shirt, cleaning and stitching the deep wound.

"You allergic to penicillin?"

Puppy shrugged; she jabbed a needle into his arm.

"Thank you," he whispered.

"I'm a doctor," she said angrily. After washing her hands, the woman fetched a woolen shirt and pants from a bedroom, engaging in another shouting match with the old man and ignoring Annette's anxious question about Puppy's condition. She closed the bathroom door, dressed Puppy and called for Annette. He sat up like a puppet on the stained rug.

"You will go now," the doctor said.

"Is he okay?"

"As good as he can be."

Annette didn't like Puppy's white face. "Can we rest here a little first?"

"No," she said harshly. "Or else they will find you and kill all of us."

The doctor helped them to the door, ignoring the old man's shouts. She tucked a handful of pills into Annette's pocket.

"Give this to him every four hours. And keep the wound clean. Now please leave."

She closed the front door and turned out the lights, room by room.

They hobbled very slowly up a hill through the quiet dark neighborhood.

"How you doing, Pup?" Annette asked as they rested briefly in the doorway of an English hair salon.

His head lolled. "Would like to sleep."

Annette dragged him another few blocks, animal sounds growing nearer. Just around a corner were the remnants of a church, the steeple gone, the stained glass windows shattered, goats and pigs milling in the courtyard.

Annette inhaled bravely and carried Puppy past the noisy beasts and through a door marked with a red X. Stepping around animal shit as best as she could, Annette half-dropped Puppy on a bench in the front row. A statue of Jesus, defiled with red Arabic lettering, looked at them through sightless eyes. Allahu Akbar obscured a large, broken cross.

Annette used her jacket as Puppy's pillow and lay beside him, arm around his shoulder, head against his chest.

"That hurt?"

"Not at all. I could easily pitch five innings." He so wished he had some water.

A pig passed with a haughty snort. Annette snorted back and the pig trotted away.

"Why'd that woman help us?" she finally asked.

"She's a doctor."

Annette considered this. "But she's still our enemy."

"Most people are confused and uncertain, honey. Unfortunately, the certain people rule the world."

She propped up on an elbow. "Are you going to say profound things like that all night?"

"Probably." He returned her smile so she wouldn't worry.

"Is Italy far?"

"A few miles."

"You're lying so I won't worry about the shit we're in."

"Yes."

She rubbed his forehead. "At least we like spaghetti."

"See? All's not lost."

"I never made pasta right."

"Or anything. You're a lousy cook."

"Thanks. Maybe I can buy a cookbook when we get to Rome."

"Good idea," he mumbled.

Annette pulled Clary's silver crucifix out of her pocket. "What's this called again?"

He squinted. "A Christian cross."

"Why?"

"Jesus Christ was killed on a cross. That guy." Wincing, he pointed at the statue. "They nailed his hands and feet."

"Fucking Allahs."

"No, Annette. It was the Romans." He felt so sad at that answer. It would've been much easier to blame the Arabs.

"How come?"

"He talked a lot of shit about people loving each other. We see where that gets you."

"It got us this far." Annette nestled against his chest. "You have to take another pill in four hours."

Father Dempsey woke up at four-fifteen, as always, to shoo the animals out of his church. There were no parishioners and he would be shot if anyone caught him, but he had nothing else to do.

The Father gasped at Puppy and Annette, asleep on the bench, the woman clutching the silver crucifix.

Brave Christians. All I do is chase away beasts. Dempsey knelt and prayed, then covered the couple with a ragged blanket. He drove off a goat gnawing on Annette's shoe.

Overheard, missiles seared the sky.

TO BE CONTINUED...

ABOUT THE AUTHOR

GARY MORGENSTEIN'S OTHER novels are *Jesse's Girl; Loving Rabbi Thalia Klein-man; Take Me Out to the Ballgame* and *The Man Who Wanted to Play Center Field for the New York Yankees.* An accomplished playwright, Morgenstein wrote the critically acclaimed off-Broadway rock musical *The Anthem,* as well as the musical *Mad Mel Saves the World,* and his dramatic works range from *A Tomato Can't Grow in the Bronx* to *Right on Target, Ponzi Man* and *Saving Stan.* Morgenstein, who grew up in the shadow of his beloved Yankee Sta-dium, now lives in Brooklyn with his wife, writer-critic Marcina Zaccaria.

CPSIA information can be obtained
at www.ICGtesting.com
Printed in the USA
FSHW02n1837290518
48801FS